"An utterly unsentimental and elegantly crafted tale from the immensely accomplished Seymour . . . An arresting saga of the world that turns on menace, mistrust, moral ambiguity, and vaulting ambition."

—*Kirkus Reviews* (starred)

"Riveting . . . [Seymour] delivers another masterfully tense tale of throat-grabbing suspense and labyrinthine intrigue. . . . Seymour has come up with another humdinger, a big, gutsy, sprawling, intricately exciting and often deeply sensitive story. It's as rousing and engrossing as . . . his best-ever novel, *Harry's Game*."

—*Buffalo News*

"A qualitative leap for an already well-established author: a tight, taut tale of mounting suspense and emotional drama, reminiscent in places of John le Carré's *The Little Drummer Girl*. . . . Seymour has managed to take the world of the Mafia, so played out in many potboilers, out of the habitual Chicago–Las Vegas context, and bring it back to life in its homeland with a chilling reality that *The Godfather* never aspired to. A thriller in the true sense of the word. Mario Puzo, eat your heart out."

—*Times* (London)

"One of Britain's most authoritative thriller writers."

—*New York Times*

GERALD SEYMOUR

Killing Ground

HarperPaperbacks
A Division of HarperCollins*Publishers*

![HarperPaperbacks logo] **HarperPaperbacks**
A Division of HarperCollins*Publishers*
10 East 53rd Street, New York, NY 10022-5299

This is a work of fiction. The characters, incidents, and
dialogues are products of the author's imagination and are not to
be construed as real. Any resemblance to actual events or
persons, living or dead, is entirely coincidental.

A hardcover edition of this book was published
in Great Britain in 1997 by Bantam Press, a division
of Transworld Publishers Ltd.

A hardcover edition of this book was published
in 1997 by HarperCollinsPublishers.

ISBN 0-06-101196-7

HarperCollins®, ![logo] ®, and HarperPaperbacks™
are trademarks of HarperCollins Publishers, Inc.

First HarperPaperbacks printing: January 1998

Printed in the United States of America

Visit HarperPaperbacks on the World Wide Web at
http://www.harpercollins.com

❖ 10 9 8 7 6 5 4 3 2 1

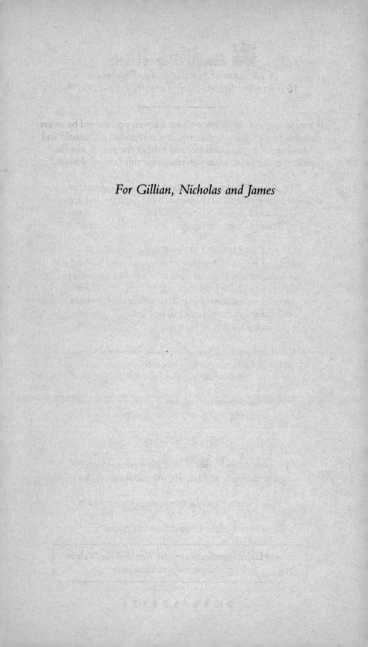

For Gillian, Nicholas and James

The extremely dangerous prospect of a homogenized mode of criminal organization, in which a point is reached where one can no longer distinguish between the methods of the Yakusa, the Chinese Triads and Cosa Nostra, would create a kind of global mafia, and I ask myself how it could possibly be opposed . . .

—Judge Giovanni Falcone

(Judge Falcone, with his wife and three police bodyguards, was murdered on 23 May 1992 at Capaci, northwest Sicily, by La Cosa Nostra.)

Killing Ground

PROLOGUE

MORE WINE WAS POURED.

More salad was offered.

More frequent apologies for the late arrival of the Host were given.

It was a good wine that the Guest drank, and a good salad of sliced tomato and country mushrooms and fennel that the Guest speared with his fork, and good apologies for the unavoidable delay in the arrival of the Host. The suspicion of the Guest that was inherent in his nature, a rock in his life, was lulled. He drank, he reached a thin ribbed hand across the table toward the water bottle. He scooped pasta from the plate in front of him between his dried and narrow lips, then more tomato, and there was a moment when the sauce of the pasta and the juice of the tomato dribbled down from his mouth and onto his chin where the poorly shaved gray stubble caught the sauce and the juice. The Guest wiped hard at his chin with the napkin suspended from the collar of his silk shirt below a scrawny and emaciated throat. He felt at ease.

It was a fine apartment to which the Guest had been invited. The dining table of polished mahogany was in an alcove off the main living area. There was a shined floor of dark wood blocks below him. He had walked to the table from the living area across a thick woven carpet from Iran. He thought the pictures on the walls behind him and in the living area to be of quality and costly but they were too modern for his taste. At the entrance to the alcove, set on a wire pedestal, was a headless statue in stone of a naked woman, maybe Roman or maybe a Greek antiquity and the Guest would not have known the difference, but the shape of the plump lower stomach stirred old thoughts in the mind of the Guest and he leered at the statue that was a meter high and wondered if the missing face of the naked woman would have carried eyes that were inviting or coyly lowered. Opposite him, across the table from him, were two men that he did not know, except that they were the chosen men of his Host. It was hard for the Guest to see the faces of the men because behind them the curtain drapes were pulled back and the faces of the men were shadowed. The Guest could not see the detail of the faces but he could see beyond them the high buildings of the city that were misted from the low cloud that brought a light spitted rain onto the plate windows and that masked the high ground of the mountains of Pellegrino to his right and Castellacio ahead of him and Cuccio to his left. It was a mistake on the part of the Guest to have allowed himself to be sat at a table where he looked into the light, and a double mistake to have agreed to take a chair that put his back to the door of the main living area. And rare for the Guest, in the seventy-third year of his life, to have put aside the suspicion for which he was famed.

The Guest cleaned the last of the pasta sauce of cream with garlic and closely chopped ham with a piece of bread roll. He belched as was his habit when he had enjoyed food. He drank. He belched again as was his habit when he had enjoyed wine. He pushed the plate away. He coughed from deep in his throat and his face colored at the convulsion and the phlegm came from far down in his throat until it settled as spittle on his lips, and he wiped his mouth with the napkin. He was reassured, he could hear the indistinct and soft words of his grandson murmuring from the kitchen beyond the door of the main living area. He was reassured because his grandson was armed as was his driver who would be sitting alert inside the hallway of the apartment and watching the outer door.

One of the men opposite him, the younger man of the pair, perhaps because he had been a waiter in a restaurant or a *pizzeria* before the trust had been granted him, came around the table and expertly cleared away the pasta bowl and the salad plate, and then his companion's bowl and plate and then his own. Done with quiet discretion, while the older man of the pair questioned the Guest on the great events of past times. The questions were asked with respect and probed at the unveiling of years long gone. The Guest warmed to the questions and to the respect with which they were asked. A telephone rang in the living area. Had he ever seen, as a child, Cesare Mori, Mussolini's man on the island? The older man ignored the telephone. Had he ever met, as a teenager, Don Calogero Vizzini who had made the deal with the American invaders on the island? The bell of the telephone was cut. Had he ever known, as a young Man of Honor, Salvo Giuliano, the bandit who had for four years evaded so many thousands of the army and *carabinieri*?

In short, guttural answers the Guest talked of Mori and Don Calo and Giuliano.

The younger man was back in the dining alcove and placed a plate of thin-sliced veal strips in front of the Guest. The Host had rung, a few minutes more, very close, and his most sincere apologies. The Guest's glass was filled, wine not water. The Guest stretched back far in his memory . . .

Yes, once he had seen Mori drive through Agrigento, bad times, with an escort of the bastard Black Shirts, Fascist thugs. His lip curled in disgust . . .

Yes, several times he had been taken by his father to

Villalba and he had stood outside the door of the room where his father had talked with Don Calogero Vizzini and he could tell his listeners that Don Calo was indeed an artist in the control of men. His eyes lit, as if he talked of genius . . .

Yes, twice he had been in the mountains above Montelepre to tell Giuliano what was required from him, but the man was a fool and the man was arrogant and the man outlived his use. He made so small a gesture, but the gesture was of his weathered and nicotine-stained index finger running across the sunken width of his throat . . .

He had known them all. The Guest was of the old world. It was right that he and his memories should be treated with respect. It was usual, in the lifestyle of the Guest, that he should sleep in the afternoon, having concluded his business of the day in the morning. Perhaps because of the wine, perhaps because of the quality of the meal served to him, perhaps because of the flattery shown him when he was requested to dig into that well of memories, the Guest did not feel any sense of resentment that the business of the day would be postponed until the time when he would usually have slept. It was important business. Had it not been important business then the Guest would not have considered traveling with his driver and his grandson across the island from his temporary and loaned home in the hills close to Canicatti. It was important business because it involved the division of interests between himself, the Guest, and the man with whom he sought to make an understanding, the Host. It was important business because it was necessary for the future that hostilities of the past should be put aside.

The Guest gulped at the slices of veal. He did not seem to notice now that the pair of men opposite him merely toyed with their food, only sipped at their wine. He liked to talk of Giuliano, he was happy to find younger men who showed an interest in the former times and were not anxious only about the present, he enjoyed the chance to explain how a man had risen too fast for his own good which was anathema to the Guest who had clawed his way over a period of half a century to control of the southern part of the island. And he was relaxed, and he was shown true respect, and the wine flowed in the tired old veins of his body. He heard the shuffle of feet across the thick carpet.

The Guest broke the flow of his speech.

The Guest turned in his high-backed chair as he sucked from his fork the last of the thin-sliced veal.

The Guest saw his Host.

The smile of helplessness, the shrug from the wide shoulders indicating matters beyond a man's control, the gesture of the thickened hands of obsequious apology. He waved his fork, no need for apology. In truth, he almost regretted that the opportunity was gone to talk further of the bandit, Salvatore Giuliano, and the death of the bandit, the end of the bandit who had gone beyond the time when he was of use, so long ago. He had to tilt his head to follow the movement of his Host who came so quietly from the main living area and into the dining alcove. It was four years since he had last met in person with his Host. He thought the man a little shorter than he had remembered him and there was a paleness in the cheeks and upper lip and chin that a razor had smoothed as if it were a child's face. The smile lit the face. He laid down his fork. He took the hands in his, broad rough hands in his own thin rough hands. Their hands gripped, their fingers clasped, and he felt the raw strength of the hands as if they bonded in friendship. There were some who said, others who knew him, that his Host had cruel eyes, clear blue, but to the Guest those eyes seemed only to show respect. His *consigliere* had told him, before he had left

Canicatti, near Agrigento early that morning, that his Host
had a way of looking at people that struck fear into everybody, a light in his eyes which silenced everybody near him,
and then he had called his *consigliere* an idiot shit, and now he
saw that respect that he believed due to him. The Guest
coughed again, belched again, and yawned, and his Host
broke the grip of their hands and their cheeks brushed in
friendship. They were equals. The Guest assumed that a similar meal would be taken with the family from Catania. They
were equals because they each had control of territory and
resources and men. The time of the single rule of Riina, the
time of the killings and massacres, the time of fear, was over.

The hands of his Host rested on the Guest's bony
shoulders, he could no longer see his face nor against the
light from the window could he see the faces of the men
across the table from him. He did not want to be on the
road to Canicatti after darkness. He wanted the business
done, the understanding sealed between equals. He felt the
hands dig into the bones of his shoulders. The business to
be done was both a matter of the division of interests, and
also the guarantee of consultation between the family of
Catania in the east and the family of Agrigento in the south
and the family of his Host in the north and west. Business
to be done, business to be sealed. The hands of his Host
were off his shoulders. They were close to his ears, first
stretched out so that the joints of the fingers cracked as they
flexed, then clenched together and from the side of his
vision he saw the whiteness of the knuckles as they
clenched. He thought that both the family of Catania and
the family of his Host needed his arsenal of experience. He
thought they required the experience gained from a long
lifetime. He was the day laborer's son who had never lost
the common touch of the land and of poverty. He was
needed. He belched. He was so relaxed. He started to twist

in his chair to face his Host. He did not see the quick movement as his Host made the sign of the cross. He . . .

The fingers and thumbs of the hands of the Host were around the throat of the Guest.

The men across the table from the Guest were rising from their chairs.

Against the ears of the Guest were the cuffs of the Host's jacket, ordinary material.

The Guest saw the coarse skin of the back of the Host's hands. The hands were locked on his throat.

The Guest struggled fiercely. He lashed out with his legs, as if he were attempting to kick himself clear of the hold of the fingers and the weight of the hands and the pressure of the thumbs. The chair on which he had sat lurched backward. He was sliding on his back across the wood block floor of the dining alcove, but always the strength was in the hands around his throat. The croaked cry for help was deep in his chest and stifled while his eyes, staring and bulging, searched for the door of the main living area through which his grandson and his driver should burst with their guns, and they did not come . . . Not to know, in his kicking throes, that a stabbing knife had taken the life of his grandson in the apartment's kitchen, that his driver was gagged and trussed in the hall beside the outer door. Not to know that five men had come with his Host into the apartment . . .

The Guest fought for his life until the will to resist was lost in his old body.

He was on the carpet. He was choking for breath and a little of the pulp from the tomatoes of his salad ran from his lips onto the carpet, and the piss flow came on his upper thigh and into the cloth of his trousers. The face above him, another old face, but flabby and jowled, had the sweat of effort running on it, and there was laughter at the mouth of the face and there was cold light in the eyes of the face. One of the men from across the table held the Guest's sparse hair, the other of the men from across the table sat on his legs, both made it easier for the Host whose hands never loosened their hold and whose thumbs gouged down onto his windpipe.

It helped him not at all that as a child he had seen the Fascist Cesare Mori, that as a teenager he had met Don Calogero Vizzini, that as a young Man of Honor he had carried messages to the bandit Salvatore Giuliano . . . Nothing could help him. He seemed to hear the caution of his *consigliere* in the dawn in the hills above Canicatti . . . He tried to shout that his Host was a shit, cunt, bastard . . . He wished that he could warn the man who was his friend, the head of the family of Catania . . . He knew it could last for ten minutes, the strangulation of a man. He knew it because he had done it. The sweat beads fell down from his Host's face and onto his own, and into his own gasping mouth, and he thought he could taste the salt of the sweat. He did not try to cry for mercy. Those last moments, before consciousness slipped from him, he tried only to maintain his dignity. If he kept his dignity then he would have also the respect . . . the need for respect was so great. He saw the face above him, he heard the cackling of the laughter and the grunted effort. He was slipping . . . It was right that the old man from Canicatti should die at the hand of his equal. That was the mark of the respect in which he was held. He was gone . . .

All the men bent over the still figure on the carpet from Iran laughed and sweated and gasped to soak the air back into their lungs. It was a joke. It was to be laughed at, the way they had fallen on the floor and slid across the wood blocks like kids playing. And to be laughed at too was the way that the old goat's tongue had come half out of his throat, and his eyes half out of their sockets.

The rain beat on the windows of the apartment. The mist shrouded the mountains above Palermo.

The body of a rival was roped in the old way, the way used to throttle a goat, the way of the *incaprettamento*, so that when the stiffness of death gripped the body, it would already be small with the rope tied to the ankles and hooking them up toward the small of the Guest's spine and then reaching up to the back of the Guest's throat. No symbol, just convenience. It was convenient to use the old way because then it would be easier to lift the stiffened body into the boot of a car . . . The body of the Guest would leave the apartment via the service lift from the kitchen to the underground car park beneath the block, and the body of the grandson, and the driver who was tied and bound and gagged and who had the terror in his eyes because he loved life more than respect.

As the lift was called, as the men came from the kitchen to clean the furniture of the borrowed apartment of fingerprints and forensic evidence, and to wipe the vomited tomato dribble from the carpet, and to swab the urine from the marble flooring of the hallway, the Host breathed hard as if the effort required to strangle a man taxed his strength to its limit, and the words came in panted spurts as he repeated what should be done to his Guest's driver. His Guest had been offered, in life and death, respect. The grandson of his Guest was a necessary cadaver, a matter without emotion. The driver of his Guest, strapped and gagged tight, faced a bad death, a bad death for a bad remark made seventeen months before by the driver, a bad remark in a bar about a Man of Honor, a bad remark that had been relayed and was long remembered.

Later, when the two bodies and the live prisoner were taken in a car and a van from the underground car park, the Host massaged the numbness from his hands.

Later, when the two bodies and the live prisoner were carried in the wet dusk from the vehicles to a small launch moored to a quayside west of the city, the Host tapped on a Casio calculator the figures and percentages and profit margins for a deal that would send 87 kilos of refined heroin to the United States of America.

Later, when the two bodies and the live prisoner were weighted with crab pots filled with stones and were slipped into the dark waters of the Golfo di Palermo, the Host satisfied himself that the apartment was cleansed of evidence and let himself out of the main door and locked it behind him.

He disappeared into the night that caught the city, was lost in it from view.

1

"Do we have to have that damn thing on?"

"God, you found a voice. Hey, that's excitement."

"All I'm saying—do we have to have the damn heater thing on?"

"Just when I was going to get wondering whether the Good Lord had done something violent with your tongue, knotted it—yes, I like to have the heater on."

It was the last day of March. They'd left the three-lane highway far behind. They'd turned off the two-lane highway long ago, and a bit after they'd cut through the town of Kingsbridge. When the guy driving had dumped the road map on his lap and told him to start the navigation bit, they'd left the last bit of decent track. The guy driving used the word "lane" for what they were on now, and the map called it "minor road." The lane, the minor road, seemed to him to coil round the fields that were behind the high hedges that had been brutalized the past autumn by cutting equipment and had not yet taken on the spring's foliage. The high hedges and the fields beyond seemed dead to him. They bent round the angles of the fields, they dropped with the flow of the lane into dips and climbed small summits, and when they reached the small summits he could see in the distance the gray blue of the sea and the whitecaps where the wind caught it. It was not raining now. It had rained most of the drive out of London, then started to ease when they were just short of Bristol, then stopped when they were east of Exeter. It was four hours since they had left London, and he was quiet because he was already fretting that the guy driving had made a mess of the equation of distance and speed and time. There was a certain time when he wanted to get there, to the end of this goddam track, and he didn't care to be early and he didn't care to be late.

He asked, sour, "What sort of place is this going to be?"

The man driving looked ahead. "How the hell should I know?"

"I was just asking."

"Listen, man, because I work out of London doesn't mean that I know every corner of the country—and the heater stays on."

There was no rain, and the narrow tarmacadam surface of the lane was dry, but there was wind. The wind that made whitecaps on the gray-blue sea ahead, tossed at the few trees that had survived the winter gales that came hard at the Devon coastline and blustered the flight of the gulls above. If they hadn't had the heater on, if they'd had the window of the Cherokee Jeep down, then he didn't reckon he'd have been cold. His way of sulking, making his protest, was to wipe with his shirtsleeve the condensation of the inside of the door window beside him and on the inside of the windscreen in front of him. He wiped hard, a small release for his stress, but as a way of clearing the condensation it was lousy work and the window beside him and the windscreen ahead of him were left smeared. He heard the guy who was driving hiss annoyance beside him. He bent his head and studied the map and won no help from it. His finger followed the thin red line of the lane across empty space toward the blue-printed mass of the sea and on the map there were names over the sea like Stoke Point and Bigbury Bay and Bolt Tail. He looked down at his watch. Shit. He looked back at the map and the page spread across his knee was harder to see because the evening was closing down, and the width of the Cherokee Jeep filled the lane and the cut dark hedges were high above the windows. Shit. Goddamn it . . .

The brakes went on hard. He was jolted in his belt. It was his way, whenever he was riding as passenger in a vehicle that went to emergency stop, to drop his right hand to his belt, it was the instinct from long ago, but riding as passenger in a lane in the south of Devon in the west of England meant that his belt was empty, carried no holster. And his way also, and his instinct, at the moment of an emergency stop to swivel his head fast, the ponytail of his hair flying, to check the scope behind for fast reverse and the J procedure turn. He grinned, the first time anything of a smile had creased his mouth since they had left London, a rueful twitch of his lips, because he reckoned the guy driving would have seen his right hand drop to his belt and seen the swift glance of his eyes behind. They had come over the summit of a hill, then there had been a hard right turn, then there had been the cattle herd in the lane. The big lights of the Cherokee Jeep speared into the eyes of the lumbering and advancing cows. A small dog, seeming to run on its stomach, came out from under the cattle's hooves and it was leaping, barking, growling at the radiator grille of the Cherokee Jeep. Behind the dog, behind the cattle, down below them, were the lights of the community that was their destination and beyond the lights and stretching away, limitless, was the sea. The breath hissed in his throat. He wondered what time the letter post came round to a place like this, reached the community down at the end of the lane beside the sea—some time that day, but not early, was the best answer he'd been able to get before they'd left London. And he wondered what time a young woman finished teaching the second year—some time in the middle of the afternoon, but she might stay on to check that day's work and to prepare for the next day's classes, and he had to add on to "sometime in the middle of the afternoon" how long it would take a young woman to ride a low power scooter back home along the lanes from the town behind them. It was important, when the letter was delivered, when the young woman came home. He wanted to hit her, meet her, after the letter had been delivered, after she had reached home and read it, but not more than a few minutes after she had read it. It was important, the timing, and it was down to him, the plan . . . He was stressed. He reckoned he could have killed for a cigarette, and in front of him on the glove box was the NO SMOKING sticker which was standard these goddamn days in any Drug Enforcement Administration vehicle, back in the States or overseas. The time to hit her was critically important.

The cattle split in front of the Cherokee Jeep. Either side of the radiator and bonnet and then the side windows, the cattle, a mixed Fresian and Holstein herd, scrambled on the bank below the scalped hedges, slipped, blundered against the vehicle. The driver's-side wing mirror was pressured back. A wet and slobbering tongue squelched against the glass of the window. The Cherokee Jeep shook from the weight of an animal against the body of the vehicle behind him. The lights shone on the face of the man who drove the cattle, unshaven, pinched in the wind, weathered. He could see the agitation of the man as his mouth with the gaps in his teeth flapped in silence, silence because of the noise of the goddamn heater. Beside him, the hand was reaching for the gear stick.

"Where the hell are you going?"

"I'm going to back up."

"How many miles are you going to back up? Stay put."

"He's telling me to back up."

"Then tell him to go eat his own shit."

"You're kind of edgy, aren't you."

The face of the man driving the cattle was close to the windscreen. The mouth still flapped. There were three teeth missing, he reckoned, and he reckoned that there was a denture set back home at the farm for inserting when the day was done and the evening meal was on the kitchen table. He spited himself, turned the Cherokee Jeep's heater higher so that the blast of dry warm air and the roar of the motor drowned the man's protest. The perspiration ran on his forehead and in his groin and down the small of his back but he could not hear the protest of the man driving the cattle. The man was peering at them through the windscreen, squinting through narrow eyes at them.

"Like we're out of the zoo," Axel said.

And he should not have said that, no. Should not have said that because Dwight, the driver, was Afro-American. At Quantico, in an Ethics class, they would have gone ape. A remark such as his last might just have been enough to get a guy busted out of the Training Academy. Axel did not apologize, he seldom made apologies.

The man driving the cattle stared hard at them, at two guys in an American Cherokee Jeep, wrong side drive, peculiar numberplate, one white with a goddam ponytail of hair, one black as a dark night.

"I get the feeling we're noticed," Axel said in bitterness.

Daniel Bent, farmer, sixty-nine years of age, working the land of his father and his grandfather and his great grandfather, who had maintained the development of the twin Fresian and Holstein herds to championship status, cursed Axel Moen and Dwight Smythe. He cursed them richly, obscenities and blasphemies, because he saw the risk of one of his cows falling from the bank between the road and the hedge, plunging under the body of the four-wheel-drive and breaking a leg. He noticed, too fucking right, the bastards and recognized them for Americans, and wondered what was their business late in the day on the lane to the coast.

When the big vehicle, too big for these roads for sure, going at speed and ignoring the 30 mph limit, came past her, Fanny Carthew saw them. Mrs. Carthew, artist of sea views in oils, eighty-one years old, muttered the protest that in the moment afterward gave her a tremor of shame and would have shocked her fellow worshipers at the Baptist Hall in Kingsbridge if they had heard her utter such words. The cause of her protest—she had to heave at the leash on which she walked her venerable Pekinese dog right off the lane and into the nettles of the verge. She knew them to be Americans, the scowling white one with his hair ridiculously pulled back and the colored one who drove. She noticed them and wondered about the business that brought them down the lane that led nowhere.

Because the Jeep was slowing, moving as if with hesitation past the houses, Zachary Jones saw them. Zachary Jones, disabled building worker, fifty-three years old, short of a leg, amputated below the knee from a construction site fall, sat at the window of his cottage. He saw everything that moved in the collection of homes at the end of the lane that was too small to be called a village. With his binoculars he noted every coming and going, every visitor, every stranger. The binoculars' magnification flitted from the face of the white one to the face of the black one, and he thought they were arguing and thought they disputed their directions, and then down to the tail-end registration plate. Zachary Jones had worked the building game in London, knew diplomatic plates, before coming home as an amputee to live with his spinster sister. He wondered what brought Americans from their embassy down to this God-forgotten corner of nowhere.

Mrs. Daphne Farson saw them from behind her lace curtains, then lost them when her view was obscured by the sign in her front garden that advertised bed-and-breakfast accommodation. She knew Americans.

The retired clergyman, the occasional gardener, the crab fisherman, the retired librarian, the District Nurse, everyone who lived in that community at the end of the lane beside the seashore, saw the big Cherokee Jeep edge down over the last of the tarmacadam, pause in the car park for summer visitors, reverse, turn, come back up the lane and stop just short of David and Flora Parsons' bungalow. All of them heard the engine stilled, saw the lights doused.

All eyes on the Cherokee Jeep and all eyes on the front door of David and Flora Parsons' bungalow. The waiting time . . . A small collective shiver of excitement held the community.

"You sure it's right?"

"It's what I was told, a white single story in a crap place," Axel said.

"We got here, so when you going to shift yourself?"

"She's not here."

"You know that? How do you know that?"

"Because her scooter's not parked in the driveway."

"Maybe she put it in the garage."

"Her father's car is in the garage, she leaves the scooter in the driveway, if it matters to you . . ."

"You haven't been within a thousand miles of here before, you've never met this woman before . . . How come you know that sort of detail, or am I getting bullshit?"

"I had it checked."

"You had it checked, down to whether she put a scooter into the garage or left it out in the driveway?"

"Checked." Axel said it sharply, dismissive, like it was obvious that such a detail would be checked. The headquarters in Exeter of the Devon and Cornwall police, through their liaison officer, had provided information on the progress of an airmail letter through the city's sorting service, information on the hours worked by a young woman teacher, information on the nighttime parking of a scooter. He believed in detail. He thought that with detail people more easily stayed alive.

It had been the idea of Axel Moen. It was the operational plan of Axel Moen. What he wanted most, right now, was to smoke a cigarette. He opened the door beside him, felt the cool of the air, the grip of the sharp wind coming up off the pebble beach, heard the rustle of waves on stones. He reached back and grabbed for a windcheater. He stepped down onto the grass beside the road. Ahead of him, behind a low fence and a trimmed hedge was the bungalow and the light was on over the door. He lit the cigarette, Lucky Strike, dragged on it, coughed and spat. He saw the shadowed bungalows and cottages, with their lights in the windows, stretching as a haphazard ribbon away up the lane to the bend round which the young woman would come on her scooter. It was the sort of place he knew. He wondered where the letter would be—in her room and on her bed or on her dressing table, on a stand in the hall, in the kitchen. He wondered whether she would tear the envelope open before she discarded her coat or her anorak, whether she would let it lie while she took herself to the bathroom for a wash or a pee. He heard Dwight Smythe open his door behind him, then slam it shut.

"This young woman, does she know you're coming?"

Axel shook his head.

"You just walking in there, no invite?"

Axel nodded his head, did not turn.

"You feel OK about that?"

Axel shrugged.

He watched the top of the lane, where it emerged from the bend. The woman with the dog stared down the lane at him, and he could make out the man in the window with the small binoculars aimed at him, and he saw the flicker of movement behind the curtains of the house that advertised bed-and-breakfast. It was as it would have been for a stranger driving on a lane on the Door Peninsula, the scrutiny and suspicion. Where the finger of the Door Peninsula cut out into Michigan Bay. And, going north from Egg Harbor and Fish Creek, from Jacksonport and Ephraim, they would have stared at a stranger coming in the dusk and followed him with binoculars and peered from behind curtains. Far in the distance, back beyond the bend in the lane, he heard the engine. It sounded to Axel Moen like the two-stroke power of a brush cutter or a small chainsaw. He dragged a last time on the cigarette and dropped what was left of it down onto the tarmacadam and tramped it with his boot and then kicked the mess of it toward the weeds. He saw the narrow wash of light from up the lane, back beyond the bend.

"You're a mafia man, right? Have to be a specialist in mafia if you're based down in Rome. What's—?"

"Mafia's generic. Don't you work 'organized crime'?"

"You going to play smart-ass? Actually, if you want to know, I am personnel, I am accounts, I am administration. Because of people like me, arrogant shits get to run around and play their games. What's this young woman—?"

"Lima Charlie November, that's LCN, that's La Cosa Nostra. I work La Cosa Nostra, we don't call it 'mafia.' "

"Forgive me for breathing—I apologize. Best of my knowledge La Cosa Nostra, mafia, is Sicily, is Italy, is not quite adjacent to here."

"Why don't you just go wrap yourself round the heater?"

The scooter's light was a small beam, dully illuminating the bank and hedge at the top of the lane, then sweeping lower and catching the woman with the dog, then swerving and reflecting in the lenses of the binoculars in the window, then finding the moving curtain at the bungalow that advertised bed-and-breakfast. He saw the arm of the rider wave twice. The scooter came down the hill and was slowing. The brakes had a squeal to them, like a cat's howl when its tail is trapped. The scooter came to a stop in front of the bungalow where the light shone WEL-COME above the porch. The engine was killed, the light was doused. He had not seen a photograph of her. He knew only the barest of her personal details from the file. No way that he could have had a decent picture of her in his mind, but when she was off the scooter and tugging the shape of the helmet from her head, when she shook her hair free, when she started to push the weight of the scooter into the driveway in front of the garage, when she walked under the light above the porch, she seemed to be smaller, slighter, than he had imagined. She turned a key in the latch, pushed the door open. The hall light flooded over an ordinary young woman, and he heard her call that she was back, an ordinary young woman's voice. The door closed behind her.

Dwight Smythe, above the sound of the heater, called from behind him, "So, when are you going to bust in, no invite?"

Axel walked back toward the Cherokee Jeep.

"So, when are you going to start to shake the ground under her feet?"

Axel swung himself into the passenger seat.

"So, do I go short of answers?"

Axel said quietly, "About a quarter of an hour for her to read a letter? Don't ask me!"

Dwight Smythe arched his eyebrows, spread the palms of his hands wide over the wheel. "Would I dream of asking, would I, what a young woman from down here has to do with DEA business, with organized crime, with La Cosa Nostra in Sicily . . . ?"

The professor had said, "If you take the hip and pelvis of Italy and think about it, and look at the map up there, well, that's the piece that's joined to Europe, and that's the bit that's high class tourism and finance . . ."

When the rookies were not on Crime Simulation or Firearms Procedures or Physical Education or Legal classes or Defensive Tactics, when they were not crowded into the Casino School or the Engineering Research Facility or the Forensic Laboratory, then they sat in on Public Affairs. It was nine years since Dwight Smythe had listened to the professor at the Public Affairs lecture.

"Come on down and you've the thigh of Italy, which is agriculture and industry. Move on lower, and you have the knee joint, Rome—administration, bureaucracy, high life, the corruption of government. You following me? We go south, we have the shin—Naples, Sorrento—and it's going sour. There is a heel—Lecce. There is a foot—Cosenza. There is a toe—Reggio Calabria. The way I like to think of it, maybe that toe is bare inside sandals, or at most the protection is the canvas of a pair of sneakers. Sandals or sneakers, whichever, they're not the best gear for kicking a rock . . ."

At Quantico, out in the Virginia forest off Interstate Route 95, FBI and Marine Corps territory, where the Drug Enforcement Administration recruit program is tolerated as are relations from the wrong side of the tracks, the professor was a legend. Any heat, any cold, the professor lectured

Public Affairs in a three-piece suit of Scottish tweed. The material of his suit had the same roughness as the wild beard splaying from his chin and cheeks. In the lecture room, with his maps and his pointer, he taught the recruits the rudimentaries of the countries that would fill their files, the societies they would interact with, the criminal conspiracies they would confront. And he did it well, which was why he was remembered.

"The government of Italy, for a hundred years, has been stupid enough to kick with an unprotected toe against the rock that is Sicily. My advice, if you've set your mind on kicking rocks with a bare toe, is go and find one that's not granite or flint. Sicily is hard mineral, and the toe gets to be bloodied, bruised. That rock is a meeting point, where Africa comes to Europe, different cultures, different values. The rock, granite or flint, has been shaped by history. Sicily is where the conquerors liked to come. You name him, he's been there—Moors and Normans and Bourbons, and before them the Greeks and the Romans and the Carthaginians and the Vandals. Government in Rome is just seen as another freebooter, the latest, come to cream off more than his share."

The professor used a big lectern that took his weight as he leaned forward on it, and the voice came from deep in the whiskered beard, pebbles churning in a mixer.

"If you've toned your muscles, if you can swing a pickax, if you've journeyed to Sicily, then take a hack at a piece of ground. You may have to go looking awhile first to find ground that's not rock. Find it and hack—chance is you'll dig up an arrowhead or a sword blade or the iron of a spear tip, or maybe a bayonet or a mortar round or a rifle's cartridge case—the weapons of repression and torture. Imagine you live there, when you hold whatever you've dug in your hand. When your history is one of dispossession, expropriation, incarceration, execution, then that sort of colors your personality, sort of shapes an attitude, each new conqueror molded the Sicilian view of life. The lesson dinned by history into the modern generations tells them trust is a luxury to be kept tight round the family, that the greatest virtue is silence, that you wait as long as it takes for the opportunity of revenge, then by God you dish it out. While Europe was civilizing itself a hundred years ago, down there on the rock, close to Africa, they were brigands and bandits. Not our problem, an Italian problem, until . . .

Dwight Smythe remembered him now, like it was yesterday, and the recruits hadn't coughed, or sniggered, or fidgeted, but had sat rapt as if the old academic was telling them the reality of DEA work.

"For protection, the brigands and bandits formed a secret society. Rules, hierarchy, organization, discipline, but relevant only to Italy, running contraband cigarettes, fleecing an extortion racket dry, until—strange, I think, the way the little moments in our existence, the two-cent moments, have their day—until a Turkish gentleman named Musullulu got to share a prison cell in Italy with the Sicilian gangster Pietro Vernengo. They talked for two years. Those two years, in that cell, '78 and '79, it changed the face of society, they put you men in work. The drugs trade, the misery trade began in that cell, two men and their talk . . ."

So clear to Dwight Smythe, the professor's words. Beside him Axel Moen sat quiet and still, eyes closed. Dwight knew the current statistics—a Federal Anti-Narcotics budget of $13.2 billion, of which the DEA took $757 million and said it was inadequate.

"The Turk talked heroin. The Turk could bring unprocessed morphine base into Sicily, via the Balkans. Good morphine base to make good heroin. In 1979, the Italians opened the cell door and Mr. Musullulu went his way, never been seen by a law enforcement agent since, and Signor Vernengo went back to Sicily and told the guys what was on offer. Don't ever think that because they didn't get grades at school the Sicilian peasants are dumb. For killing and conspiracy they are the best and the brightest, for moving money and for spreading the cloy of corruption they are the best and the brightest. They saw the window, they jumped through it. They had more heroin, more morphine base, coming onto that heap of rock than they knew what to do with, and they had the market. The market was the USA, they went international. The money flowed. They had dollar bills up their ears, mouths, nostrils, every orifice they owned. So you've heard of the Colombians and the Yakuza out of Japan and the Chinese Triads, but first on the scene was La Cosa Nostra of Sicily. The people I've just mentioned, the cartels and the Yakuza and the Triads, they're hard people but they've never been fool enough to mix it with the Sicilians. It's difficult to believe, but off that piece of rock stuck out between Europe and Africa come the big boys of organized crime, and what everyone's thrown at them just seems to bounce back. You see, gentlemen, ladies, down there it's a war of survival, as it has been through history, a bad place to be on the losing side, it's a war to the death . . ."

It's what the professor had said at a cold early morning session in the lecture hall at Quantico, with snow flaking against the windows, what Dwight Smythe recalled. He felt a sense of raw anger. The next week, nine years back, the professor had lectured on the marijuana crop out of Mexico, and the week after he had given over the hour session to the coca leaf production of Bolivia and Peru, and the final week of the course had been concerned with opium production in the triangle of Burma and Laos and Thailand. Dwight Smythe felt the raw sense of anger because the professor had seemed only a diversion from the main matter of the induction course. Sitting in the car beside the younger man with the blond ponytail of hair shafted down under the collar of his windcheater, Dwight Smythe knew reality. He was far from the office accounts that he managed on the fifth floor of the embassy, far from the duty rosters and leave charts he so meticulously prepared, far from the filing system he was proud of and the maintenance of the computer systems . . . He was with reality. The anger spat in him as he turned toward Axel Moen.

"What right do you have, what God-given right do you have to play Christ with that kid, to involve her?"

As if he hadn't heard, as if the accusation were not important, Axel Moen, beside him, glanced down at his watch, like it was time to go to work.

"You're a mafia specialist—sorry, forgive me, I apologize, a La Cosa Nostra specialist—and you're not making, what I hear, a good job of winning. Aren't you ever fed to the teeth that you don't ever get to win?"

The chill air with the salt tang came into the cab of the Cherokee Jeep, then the door slammed shut on Dwight Smythe. He watched the hunched shoulders of Axel Moen glide away, no sound against the throb of the heater, toward the little wrought-iron gate and the path leading to the door of the bungalow over which the porch light shone. He watched the shoulders and the resolute stride through the gate and up the path and past the scooter parked in the driveway, and he thought of the preacher of his childhood talking of the Death Angel who came on the unsuspecting with destruction and darkness, and he thought it was wrong to involve an ordinary young woman, just wrong.

Wrong to break, without warning, into a life.

"So sorry to trouble you, I hope it's not inconvenient . . ."

He could smile. When it was necessary, Axel Moen had

a fine wide smile that cut his face. He smiled at the older
man who stood in the lit doorway.

"My name's Axel Moen, I've come down from our
embassy in London, it's to see Miss Charlotte Parsons. I
surely hope it's not inconvenient . . ."

He could charm. When it was asked of him he could
charm sufficient to bring down a barrier. He kept walking.
There had been no gesture for him to enter the bungalow,
no invitation, but he kept walking and David Parsons
stepped aside. The frown was on the man's forehead, confusion.

"You're wondering, Mr. Parsons, at my name. It's
Norwegian. There's a fair few of Norwegian stock where I
come from, that's the northeastern corner of Wisconsin.
They were farmers, they came over around a hundred years
ago. I'd like to see your daughter, please, it's a private matter."

He could deflect. When it was important to him, Axel
Moen knew how to batter aside the doubts and queries and
seem to give an answer where a different question had been
asked. The question would have been, what was his business? But the question was not put. It was a small hall,
recently decorated but not by a professional, and he noted
that the paper pattern did not match where the strips were
joined, and the paint had run on the woodwork. He had a
cold eye. It was a detached observer's eye. The eye of a man
who gave nothing. He saw the small hall table with the telephone on it, and above the table was a framed photograph of
the young woman in academic gown and with a mortarboard worn rakishly. The angle of the mortarboard and the
cheekiness of the grin in the college graduation photograph
rather pleased him, he had hoped to find an independent
spirit. He towered over the man, he dominated him in the
narrow width of the hallway. It was what he had to do and
what he was good at, flashing a smile, breathing charm, and

dominating. He was good, also, at making the fast judgment on the spine of a man, and he judged this one, pullover with the buttons undone and wearing yesterday's clean shirt and frayed carpet slippers, as a coward.

"She's having her tea."

"It won't take too many minutes," Axel said. He was good, as well, at playing the bully. The man backed away from him and shuffled toward the opened door at the end of the hall. There was a television on and a local news bulletin dealing with the day of a small place and a small town and small people. The man had no fight to stand his ground and ask the questions and demand the answers. The man went in through the door, into the kitchen area. Axel had broken into the sanctum of a family, fractured a mealtime, and he felt no guilt. The man muttered to his wife, at the stove, moving pans, that it was an American who had come to see Charley, and the wife had boldness and challenge in her gaze. Axel ignored the man and the man's wife. He stood at the entrance to the kitchen. The young woman was sitting at the table. She had a half slice of bread, margarine smeared on it, in her hand and halfway to her mouth. She quizzed him, a strong firm glance. She wore a full-length denim skirt and a shapeless sweater with the sleeves stretched down over her wrists and no cosmetics and her hair was held up with a band so that it came from the back of her head as a pig's tail. She neither cowered like her father nor challenged like her mother, she met Axel's eye. In front of her, beside the plate with the bread slices and the mug of tea, was a torn-open envelope and beside it were the two sheets of a handwritten letter.

"Miss Charlotte Parsons?"

"Yes."

"I'd be grateful if I could speak to you, a private matter."

"These are my parents."

"It would be easier in private, if you wouldn't mind . . ."

"Who are you?"

"I am Axel Moen, from the American embassy."

"I've no business with your embassy, private or not."

"It would be better, private."

She could have backed off then, but she did not. He pulled his shoulders back, consciously, to fill the kitchen doorway. He held her with his eyes. They talked in the courses about body language and eye to eye contact. The body language was domination and the eye contact was authority. She could have said that it was in front of her parents or not at all . . . She pushed her chair back, scraped it over the vinyl floor of mock terracotta tiles. She stood her full height, then as an afterthought she stuffed the half slice of bread and margarine into her mouth, then she swigged at her mug of tea, then she wiped the sleeve of her sweater across her lips. She was moving from the table.

Axel said, "You received a letter, Miss Parsons, please bring it with you."

She rocked, quick, fast. Her eyes blinked. She swayed, but she did as he asked her because he had the domination and authority. She picked up the letter and the torn-open envelope and she walked past her mother and father, her own person. She went past him as if he did not exist, and her face was set. She led into the living room and snapped on the light in the standard lamp and cleared the morning paper off the sofa, waved for him to sit. She took the chair beside the fire. She held the letter and the envelope tight in her hands. He tried to judge her, to measure whether it was bravado, whether it was an inner toughness.

"Well?"

"You are Charlotte Eunice Parsons, teacher?"

"Yes."

"You are twenty-three years old?"

"How's that of interest to the American embassy?"

"I'm asking the questions, Miss Parsons. Please answer them."

"I am twenty-three years old. Do you need to know that I have a mole on my backside, and an appendix scar?"

"In the summer of 1992 you worked for eleven weeks as a home help and child-minder in Rome for the family of Giuseppe Ruggerio?"

"I don't see the importance—"

"Yes or no?"

"Yes."

"This afternoon you have received a letter from that family inviting you to return?"

"Who the hell are you?"

Out of the hip pocket of his trousers, he took the squashed wallet. He flipped it open, exposed the identification badge in gold-veneer metal of the Drug Enforcement Administration, thumb half covering the title of Special Agent, fingers masking the rampant eagle.

"My name is Axel Moen, DEA, I work out of Rome."

"You've come from Rome?"

"Don't interrupt me, Miss Parsons. I'm sorry, where can I smoke?"

"Sort your answer out. What on earth are you doing here, prying and poking? Come on."

But a small grin was on her face. She marched him back out into the hall, and grabbed a heavy coat off a hook, and then through a darkened dining room. She unlocked the doors, and let him into the garden. The kitchen lights washed half of the patio, but she led him beyond the light and onto the paving slabs outside a garden shed. She turned to face him, looked up at him, and the flash of the match caught her face.

"Prying and poking, so what the hell's your answer?"

"I work out of Rome—you should listen to what I say. I work in liaison with the Italian agencies. I work against the Sicilian-based organization La Cosa Nostra. You were employed by Giuseppe and Angela Ruggerio to look after their son at the time their daughter was born. They have written you to say that two months ago they were 'blessed' with the birth of a second son, Mauro—just listen—and they have asked you to return to them to do the same work as four years ago. They live now in Palermo."

He threw down the cigarette, half smoked. His foot was moving to stamp on it, but she crouched and picked it up and handed it back to him. He stubbed out the cigarette on the ribbed sole of his shoe then placed the dead end in the matchbox.

"They live now in Palermo. How do I know? Giuseppe Ruggerio is sporadically under surveillance. There are not the resources, such is the scale of criminality in Sicily, for the surveillance to be full-time. From time to time he is targeted. Tailed, wire tapped, mail watch, electronic stuff, it's routine. It's a trawl. The letter showed up. Angela Ruggerio posted it. The letter was intercepted, copied, resealed and went back into the postal service. In Rome I was shown the copy. The letter was tracked from Palermo to Milan, international sorting, Milan to London, London down here. We took that trouble to ensure the timing of my journey, so that I should get here after you received the letter, before you responded. This is my idea, Miss Parsons, I have initiated this. I want you to go to Palermo and take up that offer."

She laughed in his face. He didn't think the laugh was affectation.

"Ridiculous . . ."

"Go back to Palermo and work for Giuseppe and Angela Ruggerio."

"I've a job, I'm in full-time work. Before, that was just

a fill-in between school and college. It's just, well, it's idiotic. It's a joke."

"I want you to accept the invitation and travel to Palermo."

Axel lit a second cigarette. The wind was on his face and cutting into the thin material of his windcheater. She was small now, huddled inside the shape of her coat and her arms were clamped across her chest as if to hold in the warmth.

"What do they call you, people who know you?"

"I get called Charley."

"Don't think, Charley, that I would have bothered to haul myself over here if this were not an important investigation, don't think I take kindly to wasted time. We get opportunities, maybe they come convenient, maybe they don't. Maybe we can handle the opportunities ourselves, maybe we need to pull in help from outside. We want you in the home of Giuseppe and Angela Ruggerio."

The bitterness hissed in her voice, and the contempt. "As a spy?"

"The opportunity we have, through you, is one of access."

"They treated me as one of their family."

"Giuseppe Ruggerio is a careful, clever bastard. You should take up that offer and work for Giuseppe and Angela Ruggerio."

"Go to hell. Bugger off and bloody get out of here."

He flicked the cigarette into the middle of the dark grass. He started to turn away.

"Please yourself, I don't beg. You care to live here, you care to spend the rest of your life living here, you care to cross over to the other side of the street when there's something you could do, please yourself. I thought that maybe you had some balls, pity is that I was wrong."

"You are, Mr. Axel bloody Moen, a total shit."

"Big words, but you're short of big action. You want to rot here then that's your problem. Don't talk about this conversation. If you talk about it you might be responsible for hurting people."

A small voice. She wouldn't be able to see his face, see the flicker of satisfaction. She asked, "Why do you need access to Peppino's and Angela's home?"

No sarcasm, and no laugh, and no bullshit, Axel said, "You get on board and you get told, so think on it. And think also on whether, for the rest of your life, you want to remember crossing over the road to avoid responsibility. Good night, Miss Parsons. When you've had a chance to think on it, I'll make the contact again. Don't worry, I can see myself out."

He walked away, back through the darkened dining room, and past the open door to the kitchen, and through the hall. He looked a last time at the photograph of Charley Parsons on the wall above the table with the telephone. He liked the cockiness and cheekiness in her graduation photograph. He let himself out through the front door.

Sometimes he used a driver, most times Mario Ruggerio drove himself. Whether he drove himself, or whether he rode with the driver, he used a mass-produced, factory production line, saloon car. There was nothing flamboyant, nothing ostentatious, in the life of Mario Ruggerio, nothing to draw attention to him. That evening, if a car of the *carabinieri* or the *squadra mobile* or the *polizia stradale* or the *polizia municipale* or the *Guardia di Finanze* or the *Direzione Investigativa Anti-Mafia* had passed the Citroën BX that carried him as passenger, nothing would have seemed remarkable to the police officers of those agencies. He had been released from the Ucciardone prison, down by the city's docks, on 15 June 1960, and he had not been arrested since. He was now aged sixty-two. He was governed by twin obsessions and they were the seeking of power and the avoidance of capture. Without freedom there was no power. To maintain that precious freedom he traveled the city in a series of commonplace vehicles. To any of the police officers of those agencies, the sight of him at the traffic lights or at a pedestrian crossing would have been of an old man, tired by long life, being driven by a son or a nephew . . . but he was, and he knew it so well, to all of the police officers of all of those agencies, the most wanted man in the city, the most hunted man on the island, the most tracked man in the country, the most sought after man on the continent of Europe. He believed himself to have achieved the primary position on what the Ministry of the Interior called the Special Program of the Thirty Most Dangerous Criminals at Large. The police officers of those agencies would have seen, at the traffic lights or a pedestrian crossing, an old man who sat low in the passenger seat, a height of 5 feet 3 inches and a weight of a couple of pounds less than 13 stones, unstyled and short-cropped and gray-flecked hair, a low peasant's forehead, roving and cautious eyes, jowls at his throat and nicotine-stained teeth, broad but bowed shoulders. They would not have known . . . Nor would they have seen the powerful thickset fingers with the nails cut back to the quick because the hands were held down between his knees. They might have seen his eyes, and if the police officers of the agencies had met those eyes, then Mario Ruggerio's head would have ducked in respect to their uniforms and their position, but they would not have seen his hands, clasping and unclasping, stretching and clenching. He moved his fingers and thumbs, worked the joints, because his hands were still bruised and aching from the effort of strangulation, and the rheumatism in his hands was always worse at the end of the wet months of the Sicilian winter.

There was a calmness in his expression as the driver

brought him from their rendezvous point on the south side
of Via Generale di Maria, along the Via Malaspina and across
the Piazza Virgilio, but the expression of calmness was false.
With the obsessions for power and freedom came neurosis.
The neurosis was based on the fear of loss of power and loss
of freedom, and the fear that was always with him was of
betrayal. It was hard for Mario Ruggerio to trust any man,
even the driver who had been with him seven years. The
fear of loss of power and freedom governed the precautions
that he took every day and every night of his life. He had the
keys to sixteen apartments in the city, loaned to him indefi-
nitely by "affiliates" who owed loyalty to him and him alone.
The driver who had been with him for seven years was never
given the address of an apartment block from which to pick
him up, merely a street junction, and never given an address
at which to drop him. When they came, that evening, past
the decayed facade of the Villa Filippina and onto Via
Balsamo, he coughed hard as if to signal for his driver to pull
in to the curb.

He climbed awkwardly, heavily, out of the Citroën , and
the driver passed him a small bag in which a kid might have
kept sports clothes or stored schoolbooks, and then his cap
of gray-check pattern. He stood among the debris on the
pavement, among the filth and the paper wrappings, put on
his cap, and he watched the car drive away. Always he satisfied himself that the car was gone before he moved from the
drop point. The old eyes, bright and alert and clear blue,
raked the road and searched the faces of drivers and checked
the pedestrians. He knew the signs of surveillance . . . When
he was satisfied, only when he was sure, he walked off down
the Via Balsamo and across the wide Via Volturno where the
street market was packing up for the evening, and he disappeared into the labyrinthine alleys of the Capo district of
Palermo.

The most wanted man on the continent, in the country, on the island, in the city, walked alone and carried his own bag in the near darkness and around him radios played and women screamed and men shouted and children cried. He was worth—his own estimate and tapped out each week on his Casio calculator—something in excess of $245,000,000, and his calculator could tell him in the time that it took tired eyes to blink that the value of his worth was in excess of 637,000,000,000 Italian *lire*. The wealth of Mario Ruggerio, walking in the slum district of Capo, was held in government bonds, foreign currencies, blue-chip gilts on the European and New York stock markets, investment in multinational companies and in real-estate.

He pushed open a battered door.

He climbed an ill-lit stairway. He found the key. He let himself into the room.

Only when he had drawn the thick curtains of the room did he switch on the light. The pain in his hands, bruised from strangulation, pinched at his mouth and he winced. He unpacked the small bag, his nightclothes, his shaving bag, his clean shirt and underwear and socks, and the framed photograph of the two children that he loved and the baby.

Carrying the suitcase, Giuseppe Ruggerio, known always to his family as Peppino, was first through the outer door and behind him was *piccolo* Mario heaving the children's bag and then Francesca with her soft toys, and farther behind him was Angela who tried to soothe baby Mauro's crying . . . the end of a four-day break in the San Domenico Palace hotel of Taormina, five-star. Back home in Palermo, and the baby was hungry.

But the hunger of the baby was not high in the thoughts of Giuseppe Ruggerio. He had almost run, in spite of the

weight of the suitcase, the last few steps from the elevator to
the outer door of the apartment, and he had pulled hard on
piccolo Mario's collar to propel the child backward as he had
opened the door.

Inside, snapping on the lights, dumping the suitcase, his
eyes roved over floors and walls—he saw the faint smear
where the marble in the hallway had been wiped. On into
the living area, more lights crashing on, checking the sofa
and chairs where they would have sat, and on into the dining area and over the polished block floor and gazing at the
smooth sheen of the mahogany table where they would have
eaten. Pictures where they should have been, the statue
where it should have been. Turning fast, into the kitchen,
the fluorescent ceiling light hesitating and then shining, and
the kitchen was as it had been left. Everything was as it
should have been. A fast gasp of relief. He refused nothing
that his brother asked of him, nothing . . . It had said on the
radio that morning, on Radio Uno, in the hotel in
Taormina, that the wife of a man from Agrigento had
reported to the *carabinieri* that her husband was missing from
home and her grandson and her husband's driver. The man
from Agrigento with his grandson and his driver would have
come to a meeting point in Palermo, and a *picciotto* of his
brother would have met them there, then traveled in their
car to the apartment in the complex of the Giardino Inglese,
they would not have been able by cellular phone or digital
phone or personal radio to communicate the ultimate destination. His brother was always careful.

"Peppino."

There was the shrill whine of her voice behind him. He
turned. Angela stood in the living room. Angela held the
baby, Mauro, and the face of the baby was red from crying.
Angela, his wife of nine years, pointed down at the thick
woven carpet from Iran.

"What is that?" The whine in her voice was from her accent that was Roman. "That was not here when we left."

Nothing to be seen where the carpet fabric was of magenta wool, but beyond the magenta was pure white, and the white was stained.

She accused, "Who has been here? Who has dirtied our carpet? The carpet cost you seventeen million *lire*. It is destroyed. Who has been here, Peppino?"

He smiled, sweetness and love. "I do not see anything."

She jabbed her finger. "Look, there . . . Did you give the key of our home to someone? Did you let someone use our home? Who? Did you?"

And her voice died. It was as if she had forgotten herself, forgotten her life and her place. As if she had forgotten that she no longer lived in Rome, forgotten she lived now in Palermo. The anger was gone from her face, and her shoulders crumpled. He had hoped so much that the short break, sandwiched between his journeys to Frankfurt and London, would revive her after the difficult birth of baby Mauro. Peppino never cursed his brother, never. She was gone to the kitchen to warm food for baby Mauro. He bent over the carpet, over the stain, and from deep in the weave he lifted clear the dried seed of a tomato.

He went into the kitchen. She would not meet his eyes. Peppino had his hand on her shoulder and he stroked the soft hair on baby Mauro's head.

"When I am in London I will telephone to Charlotte. She will have received it. I will persuade her to come, I promise."

He tapped the numbers on the telephone in the Cherokee Jeep. He waited. He hadn't asked Dwight Smythe for permission to use the telephone, but then he hadn't spoken since he had come out of the bungalow, flopped back into the passenger seat and indicated they could move off. They were out of the lanes, had the speed going. Axel hadn't spoken because there was no requirement for him to talk through an operation with a guy who did accounts and personnel and office management, and if there was no requirement for him to talk, then he seldom did. He heard the phone lifted, the connection made.

"Bill, hi, Axel here. How's Rome? Raining, Jesus. This is not a secure line. I did the contact. She's OK, nothing special. First reaction was to chuck me out, second reaction was to think on it. She's predictable. She wanted to know more, but she's going to have to wait until she's thought harder. I'm going to call in at the local police HQ and work something out that'll help her thinking. I'll call you tomorrow . . . Sorry, come again . . . Hold on, Bill."

He reached forward. He snapped off the heater switch, quietened the cab.

"What were you saying, Bill? Maybe, maybe she could do it, maybe she couldn't, but she's all that's on offer. I'll see you, Bill."

He put the telephone back on the rest. He slouched his legs forward and worked his shoulders lower down on the seat back and closed his eyes.

Dwight said, staring ahead and following the road, "If I'd been her, I'd have thrown you out. You are a cold bastard."

"She called me a total shit. Your problem, her problem, I don't care too much what people call me."

"And you hooked her? Trampled in on her life?"

"Where I come from, northwest Wisconsin, there's good muskie fishing. You know the muskie?"

"We didn't fish round Albuquerque. There would have been trout up in the hills, but it wasn't for black kids in Albuquerque."

"Wear your chip with honor . . . The muskie is a big fine fish, but it's a killer and ugly as sin, it's hard and vicious on its fellows, it terrorizes a reed bank. Most anglers go out after muskie with lures, spoons and plugs. They get muskie, right, but not the daddies. The way for the big killers, the big uglies, is live bait. You get a little wall-eye, could be a small-mouth bass, latch it to a treble hook and sling it out under a float. When the little fish goes ape, when the float starts charging, that tells you that the big killer's close, the big ugly's on the scene. Put simply, the little fish gives you access to a specimen muskie."

Dwight Smythe said hoarsely, "That's rough on the little fish."

"If she goes then we'd try and wind her in when we get the shout, like when the float starts to charge we'd reel in the tackle," Axel said softly.

"You can live with that?"

"I just do a job."

There was a heavy lorry coming toward them, big, high lights, and Axel saw the driver's face and saw the gleam of sweat on Dwight Smythe's forehead, as if it were him that was being asked to travel to Palermo, live the lie, have the treble hook in his backbone.

"She'll go?"

"I should reckon so. Didn't seem to be much to keep her here. Yes, I reckon she'll go. She'll jump when she's pushed. If you don't mind, I'm kind of tired."

$$\frac{\mathbf{2}}{\textbf{\char124}}$$

TRACY WAS FIGHTING VANESSA. Darren was sticking a pencil point into Vaughan's forearm. Lee was drawing with a felt-tip pen over Joshua's writing pad. Dawn was tugging at Nicky's hair. A crash as Ron's chair tipped over backward, a scream from Ron as Ian dived back to his own chair and table . . .

And class 2B was regarded by the headmistress as the best-disciplined and happiest class in the school, and class 2B had been singled out by the Inspectors three weeks before as a model. Tracy kicked Vanessa. Darren gouged the pencil point hard enough for it to draw Vaughan's blood. Lee had destroyed Joshua's careful work. Dawn had a fistful of Nicky's hair. Ian sat innocent as Ron bawled . . .

She could have belted each one of them, and lost her job. She could have smacked Tracy's hand, whacked Darren, twisted Lee's ear, thumped Ian, and that would have been the fast route to an Education Authority Sub-Committee (Disciplinary) Hearing. She imagined in the other classrooms, the other prefabricated blocks that sieved the drafts and leaked the rain, the teachers of classes 1A and 1B and 2A and 3A and 3B, and the headmistress on her rounds, and their surprise that class 2B was audibly and publicly in chaos. It was her second term at the school, her nineteenth week, and the first time that she had lost control of the thirty-eight children. She clapped her hands, and maybe there was rare anger in her voice, and maybe there was total contempt at her face, but the clapping and the anger and the contempt won her short respite. It had been a rotten, desperate night for Charley Parsons. No sleep, no rest. The kids knew her mind was far away. Kids always knew and exploited weakness. Five more minutes on her watch before the bell would go, before a quite bloody day was finished.

She had come in from outside the evening before and heard the front door close quietly after him. She had stood in the hall and heard the big engine of the four-wheel-drive pull away. She had gone back into the kitchen. Her mother, accusing: did she know that her tea was ruined? Her father, furtive: would she have time for the work to be done that night on class preparation?

Her mother: what was that about? Her father: who was he? "I can't tell you, so don't question me."

Her father: hadn't her own parents the right to know? Her mother: shouldn't her own parents be given an explanation when a total stranger barges into the house? "He said that if I talked about him, what he said to me, then I might be responsible for hurting people."

Her mother: didn't she know how offensive she sounded? Her father: had they scrimped and saved and sent her to college merely to learn rudeness? "He's a sort of policeman, a sort of detective. He works for something called the Drug Enforcement Administration."

Drugs? The shock spreading across her mother's face. What had she to do with drugs? The incredulity at her father's mouth and she had seen the shake of his hands. "I have nothing to do with drugs. I just can't talk about it. I have no connection with drugs. I can't tell you."

She had run out of the kitchen and across the hall and into her bedroom. She had flung herself down onto the duvet cover. She had held the bear that had been hers for twenty years. She had heard the worry in her mother's voice and the bluster in her father's voice. She hadn't had her ruined tea, nor had she done her preparatory work for the next day's class with 2B. Later, she had heard her mother's footfall outside her door and a light knocking and she had not replied, and much later she had heard them going to bed beyond the thin partition wall. A tossing and restless and hideous night, with the two images churning her mind. The twin images that denied her sleep were of the warmth and kindness of Giuseppe and Angela Ruggerio, and of the cold certainty of Axel Moen, they confronted her, the love shown her by Giuseppe and Angela Ruggerio, the matter-of-fact hostility of Axel Moen. She should not have given him the time of day, should have shown him the door. She thought she had betrayed the warmth and kindness, the love, of Giuseppe and Angela Ruggerio . . .

Her night had been unhappiness and confusion. Her day had been exhaustion and distraction.

It seemed God given, a moment of mercy, when the bell echoed through the low-set prefabricated walls of the classroom. Perhaps the kids of 2B, the kickers and gougers and scribblers and bullies, felt the crisis and were afraid. They waited for her. Every day, at the end of classes, she swapped jokes and cheerful banter with the six-year-olds, not that day. She swept up the books and notes on her desk. She was first out through the door. It was her decision to go home, to apologize to her mother and father and to make believe that the tall American with the blond ponytail of hair had never walked with her in the garden behind the bungalow, never proposi-tioned her, never talked of necessary "access." Her deci-sion . . . She stopped beside a rubbish bin outside the classroom, reached deliberately into her bag, took out the let-ter of invitation and ripped it to small pieces. She dropped the torn scraps of paper, and the envelope, into the bag. There was a mass of children around her as she walked toward the lean-to shed where her scooter was left for the day.

"Charlotte! Are you all right, Charlotte?"

The shrill voice bleated at her back. She turned. The headmistress faced her.

"All right? Yes, of course, I'm all right, Miss Samway."

"I just wondered . . . Charlotte, there are two men to see you. They're at the gate."

She looked over the running and shouting and charging horde of children going from the playground to the gate that led to the street. She looked between the heads and shoulders of the young mothers with cigarettes at their lips, gum in their mouths, babies on their arms, bulging stomachs in tight jeans, who yapped about the night's TV. So much anger, fueled by the tiredness. She saw two men leaning against an old Sierra car, not the last model but the model before that, and the door which took the weight of their buttocks was a recent addition and not yet sprayed to match the rest of the bodywork that was scraped and rust flecked. They were not like anyone she knew. They wore old denims and T-shirts and one had a leather jacket over his shoulders and one wore a dirtied anorak. The hair of both men was cut short, and the one who was more slightly built had a silver ring piercing his right nostril, and the heavier one waved to her and she could see the tattoo between the wrist and knuckle of his hand.

"I don't know if they're friends of yours, Charlotte, but I don't want people like that hanging round my school."

She went to them. She stood her full height. The headmistress behind her would be watching, and others on the staff, and the mothers would be watching. Little Miss Parsons, stuck up Miss Parsons, entertaining two low-life types who waited on the street for her. Something to talk about in the common room, and as they pushed the prams and led the kids back to the bloody little homes where the telly would blast all through the evening, and reading would involve the figures on scratch cards, and . . . God, she was just so bloody tired.

"Yes? You wanted to see me. I am Charlotte Parsons."

The one with the ring in his right nostril seemed to flick his fist open and in the palm of his hand was a police warrant card, and he said his name was Brent and muttered about "Task Force," and the one with the tattoo showed his card and said his name was Ken and the quiet words were "Drug Squad."

A frail voice. "What do you want?"

Brent said, "It's what you want, Miss Parsons. We were told you were looking for the grand tour."

Ken said, "We were told you needed a run round our patch, so you'd understand better the end of the importation road, that your particular interest was skag and rock."

Brent said, "But, Ken, we shouldn't go too fast for Miss Parsons, 'cos a nice girl like her wouldn't know that skag is heroin, now would she?"

Ken said, "Too right, Brent, and she wouldn't know that rock is crack cocaine. If you'd like to get in the back, Miss Parsons . . . Oh, don't go worrying, we squared it with the caretaker that he'll look after your scooter."

"Who sent you?"

Brent said, "Our inspector sent us."

Ken said, "The American gentleman . . ."

She shook. The trembling was in her arms, her fingers. The heaviness was in her legs, her feet. "And if I say that it's bugger-all to do with me?"

Brent said, "We were told that you might bluster a bit at first . . ."

Ken said, ". . . but after the bluster you'd be good as gold. Miss Parsons, I've been on Drug Squad a bit over four years. Brent's been on Task Force, drug importation team, for six years. All we get near is the creatures at the bottom of the pyramid. What we were told, sort of vague, you've the chance to hurt them right at the sharp end, nothing specific, but hurt the top of the pyramid. Now, if the bluster time's over could you get in, please?"

She did as she was told. She was good as gold, as Axel Moen had said she would be. She took the big step, and ducked down into the back of the old Sierra. Bloody man . . . The car was a fraud, clapped-out exterior but a high performance–tuned engine. Brent drove, and Ken was twisted round in the front seat so that he could talk to her. She thought she was tired, but as the car hammered on the lanes and then the fast road, she came to know the crow's-feet lines and the sack bulges at Ken's eyes. Something of a joke at first, about the tattoo only being a transfer that he could wash off each night, about a limit to the cause of duty, but old Brent had gone the whole hog and had his nostril pierced for the goddamn job. They were not in the style of any policemen that she had met before. She thought a part of the smell came from the discarded polystyrene fast-food plates that were dumped on the floor in the back, under her feet, and the rest of the smell came from the clothes they wore. They smoked hard, and didn't ask whether she minded them smoking. Ken said they weren't interested in cannabis, nor in solvents, nor in amphetamines, nor in the benzodiazapines like Temazepam and the barbiturates like sodium amytal. They worked the world of heroin that was skag, horse, smack, stuff, junk, and the world of crack cocaine that was rock, wash. She listened . . .

They came into the city of Plymouth, where Charley went for best shopping, for a dress for a friend's wedding, for Christmas presents and birthday gifts for her mother and father, and they talked her through the street cost of skag and rock. She listened . . .

They turned out of the city center and went north, climbing the long drag into the big housing estate. The name of the estate was familiar, from the local television, but she had never been there. Nothing urgent in the information they gave her, no passion, but the figures were beyond her comprehension. A worldwide trade in narcotics with a profit margin of 100 billion American dollars. Seizures and disruption of trafficking into UK the last year of £1.45 billion and what was seized and disrupted, on a good day, was one in five shipments and on a bad day was one in ten.

Ken said, "But they're the super glory figures, we don't operate at that level. We work down here in the gutter where the skag and the rock ends up. Down here a kilo of heroin, skag, goes for thirty grand, street price. Crack cocaine, rock, means £7,500 sterling, cheaper because of saturation. Out there in the big world they're talking thousands of kilos, tons—we're little people, we're talking kilos and grams." She listened . . .

Brent said, "You being a teacher, Miss Parsons, you'd be good at arithmetic. Ten grams doesn't give a big long high, ten minutes' worth for an habitual, but it costs, my sums, seventy five quid, and it's addictive, so you get to need a lot of grams, and that means you need a lot of cash, and you steal, fight, burgle, maybe kill, for the cash."

She saw tower blocks of homes, and terraces of homes, and she saw the children, like the ones that she taught, running in dog packs. She thought she saw a poverty and a despair . . . She saw an old man hurrying, limping, heavy on a stick, and his face was frightened and she wondered whether he had £75 sterling in his wallet. She saw an old woman scuttling with a shopping bag toward the dark entrance of a tower block, and she wondered whether the old woman had £75 sterling in her purse, or in the tin under her bed, or folded into her pension book and hidden, and she wondered how many old men and old women needed to be robbed to make a crack cocaine high that lasted ten minutes. She felt sick.

The light was going. Where the streetlights were broken, where the shadows clung, she saw ghost figures gathered. Brent cruised the car. Ken said, "See over there, Miss Parsons? See the tall kid. Most days he's there, he'll do about a hundred grams a week in rocks." Brent said, "He can do you skag as well, maybe some ecstasy. He's not special. He's one in a hundred, going on more. It's got hold of the place. Lift him, there's another ninety-nine." She saw the boy. He wore good Reeboks and Nike leisure wear and the cap on his head was the wrong way round. The contact she saw was short and sweet. Hands moved, money given over by the customer, goods given over to the customer. Brent said, "We're not even holding the line. The price is going down. It goes down when we're awash with it. The job of our young friend is to keep moving the rocks, getting new customers, creating demand. He's good in his marketplace." She listened . . .

Brent said, "I hope you're getting the picture, Miss Parsons. But I wouldn't want you to get the impression that this is C2 or C3 trade only. We could run you down to Plymstock or Roborough, up to Southway and round Goosewell. We can show you it anywhere."

"I want to go home, please."

Ken said, "No can do, sorry. The American gentleman said you should have the grand tour."

The unmarked police car slipped out of the estate. Charley looked a last time for the old people hurrying with their wallets and purses and their fear, for the kid with his Reebok shoes and Nike leisure suit, for the customers.

•   •   •

"Hi, Dwight, how was the vacation by the sea? How'd it go?"

"I'd rate him as cold shit."

His coat was flipped onto the hook of the stand, alongside the coat of the Country Chief.

"You'd better come in, you'd better talk."

He took a plastic cup and filled it with water from the dispenser. He walked across the deserted outer office and through the open door and into the Country Chief's office. It was a lowering dark evening outside, and there was rain in the heavy cloud that settled over the square. He was waved to a seat.

Dwight Smythe shrugged. "I reckon, Ray, I can cope with most sort of men. I failed with that bastard. Is he some sort of zealot? I thought Quantico was supposed to weed that sort. Right, he's rude, I can live with that. Right, he's aggressive, I can handle it. Where we part company, he elbows into a small and unsuspecting life, a young woman's life, and puts together a web to trap her, and does it cold. Me, I'm surplus to requirements, the chauffeur that's no longer needed."

"Did you read his file?"

"No."

"Do you know about him?"

"Not before I picked him up yesterday."

"Happy to make a judgment?"

"My assessment of him, yes, I feel comfortable with it."

"My opinion, Dwight, you're a lucky guy."

"How come, Ray, I'm a lucky guy?"

"A lucky guy, Dwight, because you have personnel and accounts and running this station to keep busy with." The eyes needled on Dwight Smythe. "You have fuck all of nothing to worry about."

"That is not fair."

"And true as hell. You, Dwight, are promotion material. You keep the leave charts regular, you keep wiping your ass, you keep the budget and expenses in blue, you keep your butt clean, you keep us all in surplus paperclips, and you don't have to worry because that is promotion material. It's the road, Dwight, to the big office back home and the pile carpet, but it's not that joker's road."

"That is not fair, Ray, because without administration—"

"I have heard it before, I have practiced it. You are talking with the converted. When did you last carry a sidearm?"

"The way to fight organized crime is through the intellectual deployment of resources, not—"

"I've made that speech, Dwight. You think if I'd preached on body confrontation, nose-to-nose, I'd have climbed the goddamn ladder? Grow up."

"I didn't expect to hear you, Ray, give out that sort of crap."

"Your consolation, what should make you feel good, the like of Axel Moen don't get to climb the goddamn ladder. The ladder's for you and for me. It's you and me that like to collect the plaques for the wall, the photographs of the Director's handshake, the commendations and the bullshit."

"Sorry, I spoke." Dwight Smythe pushed himself up, drank the last of the water. He looked around him. The plaques recorded successful operations, the photographs witnessed the warmth of the Director meeting with a coming man, the commendations were polished print engraved on bronze. "And I don't recognize bullshit, Ray."

"You taking Melanie out tonight, something to eat?"

"Yes, why?"

"My advice, meant kind, call her, tell her to hold an

hour so you can get your face into the computer, take a look at Axel Moen's file."

"For what?"

"Did he tell you his target?"

"He did not."

"Read his file so you get to know what sort of man gets put up against a way big target."

"Maybe in the morning . . ."

"Tonight, Dwight, read it."

It was an instruction. They prided themselves, the Country Chief and the four special agents and the clerical staff working on the fifth floor of the embassy, that they were a close team, that harsh words were rare, instructions came rarer. He walked out of the office. He went to his desk. He called Melanie and he told her he was held up and put her back an hour and asked her to call the curry house on the Edgware Road to hold the reservation for an hour. He checked with the file that was kept locked in the drawer of his desk for the entry code and the password key. He went into the NADDIS computer for the file on the man he called cold shit.

"We've just got the one at the moment. There was another one last month but it died. The other one died about three days before this one came in here," the nurse said. She was a big woman but with a gentle Irish voice. She spoke flatly as if she did not care to feel emotional involvement. "I couldn't tell you how long this one's going to hold on. Myself, I hope it's not too long. You see, she's damaged. She was damaged in the womb, pretty close to conception, she was damaged all the time through the pregnancy, she's damaged now. It's what happens when the mother is an addict. Her mother's nineteen years old, she's into mainlining with heroin, lovely girl, was and still is. The little one is seventeen days old and it's as if she's on heroin, same as Mum, same as if she was using Mum's syringe, Mum's tourniquet. This one's too far gone to be weaned off it, the damage is in the little one's system. That's why I say that I hope it's not too long . . ."

Charley stood by the door. She looked into the room, Children's Unit (Intensive Care). The baby seemed to shiver inside the glass case and the tubes hooked to its nose and mouth waved slowly with the movements. The nurse spoke as if they were alone, as if the mother, the "lovely girl," was not there. The mother sat beside the glass box. She wore a dressing gown, hospital issue. She stared blankly at the quivering baby. When Charley turned away, the nurse smiled at her, and said that it was decent of her to have bothered to come. That was an empty remark because the nurse did not know why Charley had come, did not know of the arrangement made by Brent and a hospital administrator. Charley hurried out. She thought she hated Axel Moen.

Brent and Ken were in the corridor. They led, she followed.

Out into the night air. Across a car park. There was a light over a door.

Brent knocked at the door. Ken rang the bell. They entered the hospital mortuary.

"This one's heroin but it could just as well have been cocaine. On average we get three a year. His father's a retired major in Tavistock, not that it matters who his father was, is," the pathology technician said. He was a young man with an angled nose on which were balanced heavy spectacles. He spoke as if the corpse, the retired major's son, was an item of no particular interest. "When they get started on it, heroin that is, they find the total relaxation from stress, from anxiety, must seem the way out of the problem, but . . . they step up the dosage, the withdrawal symptoms each time are harsher, more frequent. The dependency grows. This one, I heard, he broke into his parents' house and cleaned out his mother's jewelry case, all the heirloom stuff was worth one big fix. He would have been subject to tremors, muscle spasms, sweats. He would have loaded up in panic, but got the dose wrong. He would have been unconscious, then gone into coma. He ended up in here after a breathing failure. Of course, this is just a small city, we don't get that many."

Charley looked down at the corpse. She had never seen a dead body before. It was as if the skin had been waxed pale, and the body hair on the chest and in the armpits and round the penis of the body seemed, to her, like a weed that had been poisoned. There was color in the bruised right arm, but the needle holes were dulled. She thought the body was of a young man of about her age and there seemed to be a peace about his expression. She didn't know, and she didn't ask, whether the people in the mortuary could have given his face the mask of peace, or whether the act of dying made the peace.

In the corridor outside the area where cadavers were stored in refrigerated bays, Ken was smoking a cigarette that was tucked into the palm of his hand, and Brent was unwrapping a boiled sweet.

They drove her back to the school.

They rang the doorbell for the caretaker, who opened up for them.

Charley gunned the engine of her scooter. She sat astride the saddle. She arched her back, pinched her shoulder blades.

"Are you always as subtle as that? Squeezing my emotions. Winding me up, like a damn puppet."

Brent said, "Sorry, love, but it's what we were asked to do."

Ken said, "I don't know, of course, what it was for, sunshine, but it was what the American gentleman wanted."

She pulled the helmet down over her hair. Charley had seen reality, what she read in newspapers and what she watched on television, and she had not cared to know that it was reality in her own bloody backyard. She rode away into the night, and she cursed him and the tears ran on her face and were caught by the wind. On the road, in the lane, a car followed her and lit her back and never closed on her. In her mind was a jumble of images, unproven, of the island of Sicily and the city of Palermo. The lights of the car stayed in her mirror. Palermo . . .

No wind, no rain, no cloud. The island baked in spring sunshine. By early morning, the first warmth of the year suffocated the city. Over that city, which was pressed into a narrow seaboard between the Mediterranean and the mountains, had settled a chemical mist of yellow-hazed pollution from the vehicles jockeying on the Via della Liberta and the Via Marqueda and the Via Francesco Crispi and the Via Vittorio Emanuele and the Via Tukory. Invisible under that mist were the symbols of Low-intensity Warfare, the electronic signals, the microwave boosters, the pulses sent by telephone and radio transmissions, the pictures carried by covert surveillance cameras, the voices distorted by audio intercept bugs. Among the clutter of a modern society's legitimate communications, small fish in the big sea, were the messages, coded and masked, of a contemporary battlefield. Signals, pulses, tones, images, voices of men at war meandered under the foul-tasting mist that clung above the roofs of Palermo.

When she came out of the common room, with the taste of instant coffee in her mouth, to bring in the children from mid-morning break, she saw him sitting in the parked car outside the gate. She thought of the housing estate and the despair and the poverty.

He did not trust the safety of any form of telephone communication.

Mario Ruggerio sat alone in the small room of the apartment on the first floor. The sounds, raucous, of the Capo district came to him through the opened window, through the closed shutters that filtered segments of sunlight into the room. The sunlight lay in shards across the table at which he worked and were reflected from a mirror and onto a side wall so that the brightness and the shadow latticed the picture of the agony of Christ. The crying of the hawkers, the shouting of people in anger and in mirth, the roar of the engines of Vespas and Lambrettas competed with the quiet of Radio Uno. Neither the noise from the alleyway below nor the voice and music close to him disturbed his concentration. Both the outside noise and the radio's voice and music were a necessary part of his security. In the Capo district of hardship and crime and wariness, a surveillance car and a surveillance team would be noticed and a quiet would fall over the alleyway. And if there was the arrest of a *super-latitanti,* a big man on the run, or if there was a swoop and roundup of suspects, then it would be carried on the radio and he would know. The outside noise and the radio's voice and music did not disturb him as he wrote the brief and cryptic messages with a fine-point pen on the sheets of paper used for rolling cigarettes.

Education at school for Mario Ruggerio had lasted from the age of five years to nine years. No schoolmaster, nor schoolmistress, no academic, no lecturer, no professor had taught him the science of electronic communications, but he had no trust in the security of the telephone. There were those he had known who had believed they could talk through the landline system, and they sat now in the stifling heat of the cells at Ucciardone in the city of Palermo. There were others who had believed in the safety of the new analog technology of the mobile telephone, and they rotted now behind the walls of Caltanisetta on the island or at Asinara prison on Sardinia. He had been urged the last year to believe in the total security of the most recent system, the digital network, promised that it could not be intercepted, and those men who had believed and promised now saw the sun and the sky for an hour a day through the net mesh above the exercise yard at Ucciardone or Caltanisetta or Asinara.

He laid the messages written on the cigarette papers across the table. He read them. He lit a small cigar. He coughed and spat phlegm into his handkerchief. He read the messages again and then gathered them into his ashtray. He was satisfied he had memorized the messages. He burned the papers on which they were written. The messages, now held in his memory, dealt with the matters concerning the movement of $8 million from a holding company in the Bahamas to a casino development in Slovenia, the switching of $4 million from a Vienna-based account to a bank in Bratislava, the buying of a block of twenty-two apartments at a Corsican beach resort, the question of the life and death of a man in Catania, the problem of the persistent investigation by a magistrate in the Palazzo di Giustizia. Five messages, now burned, now memorized, would be passed, word of mouth, to five men in five bars over five coffees that morning.

His way was caution and suspicion. With caution and suspicion he maintained what was most precious, his freedom.

Later, when the sun was higher against the closed shutters, when he had smoked a second cigar, when he had listened to the radio news bulletin and heard the report that the

Questura in Agrigento had made no progress in their search
for a missing man and his grandson and his driver, he would
slip in his anonymity onto the streets of the city and into five
bars where his people waited for him. His people were the
"cutout" intermediaries who carried the messages, verbally,
to construction magnates and politicians and the principals of
the Masons or Rotary and bankers, and to the policemen that
he owned, and to the churchmen that he had bought. All of
those who received messages from Mario Ruggerio acted
upon them immediately because he fueled their greed and
fanned their fear . . .

Mario Ruggerio wondered, a fast thought because
there was much in his mind, how were the children and the
baby that he loved, and the thought brought a gentle smile
to his face. The smile was still on his face as he walked down
the alleyway in his gray wool jacket with his check cap worn
forward.

When she came into the playground to halt the football
game and round up the children with their lunchboxes, she
saw him waiting and smoking in his car. She thought of the
old man hurrying to his home on the estate.

From the balcony she watched him go. She held the baby.
Piccolo Mario jumped excitedly on the balcony tiles and
leaned across the pots of geraniums to see his father at the car
below, and Francesca held her hand and cried quietly.

He turned from the car and he waved up at the bungalow, and Angela's answering gesture was a limp flap of her
hand. She did not wait to see him into the car, nor to see him
drive away through the main gates that would have been
opened by the uniformed *portiere*. She left *piccolo* Mario on the
balcony, she carried the baby and led Francesca back into
the living area of the apartment, and past the statue that she

thought disgusting and over the stain she could not remove in the carpet from Iran. She loathed Palermo. To Angela Ruggerio, the city was a prison. In Rome, if they still lived in Rome, she could have gone back to the university, but it was not acceptable in Palermo that a married woman should go alone to a university. In Rome she could have gone to a health gymnasium, but in Palermo it was not permitted that a married woman could go to a gymnasium without a friend for a chaperone and she did not have that friend. In Rome it would have been possible for her to have taken part-time work in a gallery or in a museum, but it was not possible in Palermo that a married woman of her class should go to work . . . She could not, in Palermo, paint the walls of the apartment, wield a roller brush, because, in Palermo, that would imply her husband could not afford to employ an artisan to do the work.

She loathed the city most when he left to go abroad. Then the money for household expenses was left in the drawer beside her bed, because, in Palermo, it was not usual for a married woman to have her own bank account, own credit cards, own resources. In Rome, during the good days in Rome, he would have talked with her the night before a business flight to London or Frankfurt or New York, but not now, because, in Palermo, it was not necessary for a married woman to know the detail of her husband's work.

She slumped down into the depth of the wide sofa. She flicked the pages of a magazine and read nothing . . . The boy shouted. *Piccolo* Mario yelled from the balcony that he had seen his uncle, really, and she must come. She pushed herself up from the sofa. She held the baby tight against her. She went onto the balcony. She looked down, across the car park, past the security gates, onto the pavement. She saw nobody, but *piccolo* Mario shouted that he had seen his uncle, yelled that his uncle had walked past the gates and looked for them and had waved, and she saw nobody that she knew.

How many times did he come, the little old man with the
bowed shoulders and the jowl at his throat and the gray
jacket and the checked cap, and walk past the apartment in
the Giardino Inglese and look up toward the flowers on their
balcony, how often? She knew, of course, all that was said of
piccolo Mario's uncle on the television, all that was written of
Peppino's brother in the *Giornale di Sicilia* . . . She took the
boy from the balcony. It was not right that the boy should
talk of his uncle.

In four days they would be at the villa, they would be by
the sea, where, if it were possible, she would be more lonely
than in the city. She prayed, almost with fervor, that
Charlotte would come.

When she rang the bell for the end of mid-afternoon break
she saw him sitting with a magazine in his car. She thought
of the old woman, in fear, going back to her one bedroom
with the hidden tin of savings that made her vulnerable.

There were only two pictures on the walls of the room in the
barracks at Monreale. There was the picture of his daughter
and there was the photograph of Generale Carlos Alberto
dalla Chiesa. The smiling ten-year-old girl and the militaris-
tic portrait served to heighten Giovanni Crespo's sense of
total isolation.

He dialed the number, he threw the switch that activated the scrambler.

Isolato, isolated, was a cruel word for the captain of *carabinieri*. His daughter was growing up in Bologna. He was
isolated from her, saw her twice a year at best, three days at a
time, and spoke briefly on the telephone each Sunday
evening. That was isolation. But it was the general who had
taught him the true meaning of the word *isolato*. The general, hero of the counter-terrorist campaign against the

Brigate Rosse, prefect of Palermo, had been ridiculed, sneered at, whispered of, isolated and shot to death thirty-eight days after Giovanni Crespo had joined his staff as liaison officer. They were all isolated, all the condemned men, before the gunfire or the bomb. To stay alive, living and breathing and fucking and drinking, he thought it most necessary to recognize isolation.

His call was to an unlisted number in Rome, a quiet side-street office on the Via Sardegna, to the desk of the DEA's Country Chief.

" 'Vanni here. Go secure, Bill."

He was asked to wait out. He heard the clicked interruption on the line. The voice was fainter, with metallic distortion. He was told he could speak.

"Just wanted to know how my friend was, whether my friend had optimism . . ."

He was told the young woman was "OK, nothing special." He was told she was "predictable" and that she had taken time "to think on it."

"You know, Bill, we don't even have a name for this. It is ridiculous, but we don't even have a name. So, we don't have a file, that's good, and we don't have computer space, that's better, but we should have a code name, do you not think?"

Giovanni Crespo, aged 42, captain of *carabinieri,* member of the specialist *Reparto Operativo Speciale* team tasked with securing the arrest of Mario Ruggerio, would never speak a confidence even on a line scrambled with state-of-the-art electronics. On the island he trusted no man. In his life he trusted only one man. He had taken the letter posted by Angela Ruggerio, sister-in-law of Mario Ruggerio, to Rome and to the one man he trusted. The detail of the matter was not shared with his own people, for lack of trust of his own people. He had taken the detail of the matter, the link, to his friend.

He was asked what he thought.

"Helen. Helen of Troy. Bill, when all else failed, in Italian we would say *uccello da richiamo,* I think your word is 'decoy,' yes? The decoy behind the walls. The way through the gate. Codename Helen, for when we talk, Bill. But, Bill, it is to be kept close."

It was authorized in Washington. Herb had authorized it. Yes, he knew Herb. He was told it should be kept closer than a choirboy's sphincter, and the Country Chief's laugh rang in his ear, pealing as if from inside a box of metal.

"Is that dirty talk, Bill? Hey, but, Bill, we keep this close. You call me when you have something, something on Codename: Helen. It's bad here at the moment, so quiet. There is nothing to touch, nothing to feel, nothing to see. When it is quiet then I have the anxiety. You tell him, he gives the Codename Helen a good kicking because I need her here, just tell him."

The one man that he trusted, that Giovanni Crespo would give his life to, was Axel Moen.

"Bill, he is moving, climbing. Did you see that a bad bastard from Agrigento went missing? Old-style, old-school, so conflict was inevitable. It is the *lupara bianca,* the disappearance. Between him and the top place, where he will try to be, is only the Catania man, that's what we hear. If he gets to the top place, our friend, then there is a time of maximum danger, perhaps for many people, when he would seek to prove himself. Bill, I have a big anxiety. The only way for our friend to prove himself is to kill . . ."

When she pushed her scooter out of the lean-to shed and buttoned her anorak and slipped on her helmet, she saw him look up and wipe the windscreen, and she saw him start to maneuver the car. She thought of the young mother, the addict, in Intensive Care.

They were the *ragazzi,* the kids, the boys. Though the magistrate called them, always, the *ragazzi,* three of them were aged over forty, and one was two years off a fiftieth birthday. The fifth, Pasquale, was the only one of the *ragazzi* still clinging to youth. The party, orange juice and a cake, was in the kitchen. The kitchen was for cooking and doubled as the communications room and rest area for them.

In the depths of the apartment, away from the closed door of the kitchen, a telephone rang.

It was as good a party as was possible on orange juice and chocolate cake. No alcohol. No alcohol was allowed on duty, nor for five hours before starting duty. Chocolate cake was permitted, and orange juice. The baby, Pasquale's first, had been born in the small hours of the morning and he had come straight from the hospital to start his duty. And they larked and fooled like kids and boys and there was spilled juice on the floor and broken cake on the table, and the birth of a baby and the pride of a father were celebrated. He had bought the cake himself, and the juice. If he had been a part of them, truly a member of the team, then they would have collected among themselves and bought the cake and the juice. He was too young, too recent, to have been wholly accepted, and his work was under continuous probationer assessment. It could have been that they resented his youth, there were some on the qualification course who said that the reflexes of a younger man were sharper than those of older men . . . He tried to be a part of the team.

The telephone no longer rang.

And those who had three children and four children and two children, and the *maresciallo* who was the oldest and had teenagers, competed with the horror stories of parent-

hood to bludgeon Pasquale. The black execution humor of
his fellows played, mocking, around Pasquale's ears, the tales
of the sleepless nights and the changing of shit-filled diapers
and vomited food and a swallowed ID card and the little
hands that climbed a chair to produce the condom packet
from the bathroom cupboard that was displayed to grand-
parents, and . . .

The laughter died. They heard, all of them, the footfall
beyond the kitchen door.

All faced the door, like *ragazzi,* like kids and boys
caught in a moment of guilt. He seemed with his eyes to
apologize, as if he deeply regretted the intrusion into his
own kitchen, into their communications room and rest
room. They had started the party, opened the orange juice,
cut the cake, because he had told them he was not returning
that evening to the Palazzo di Giustizia, now he shrugged in
his self-effacing way and brushed the graying hair back off
his forehead and muttered that he must return to his bunker
office. He held his briefcase in his hand and his raincoat was
draped on his shoulders.

There was the snap of the *maresciallo's* radio, to alert the
military in the street.

Crumbs were brushed off a Beretta M-12S 9mm pistol,
juice was shaken from the barrel of a Heckler & Koch MP-
5 machine gun. The vests of kevlar plates, proof against
small-arms fire and light shrapnel, were heaved up from the
floor beside the oven by Pasquale, one for each man.

There was the clatter of the weapons being armed.

Left in the kitchen, debris on the table, half drunk
glasses of orange juice, half-eaten slices of chocolate cake.

They went out of the apartment and toward the door.
The woman who lived across the hallway scowled, and the
bodyguards gave her the eye and the finger because she had
twice written to newspapers to complain of the danger in

which she was placed by living in proximity to Dr. Rocco Tardelli. They went fast down two flights of stairs, in front of him, beside him, behind him. He was a small figure, hemmed in between them, skipping to keep pace. They were not his servants, nor his messengers, nor his cooks, they would never be his true friends. They had not volunteered to protect his life, but been given the assignment.

Out on the street the soldiers shrieked their whistles for the traffic to halt at the far junctions. Two of them were out of the main lobby and into the cars and hacking the engines. Guns drawn, the *maresciallo* in front of him, Pasquale behind him, the magistrate was bustled to the open door of his armored Alfa. As if he were pitched inside, as if he were a parcel to be dispatched . . . The sirens blasted. The tires screamed. The Alfa and the chase car hit the first junction and swerved right, scattered the cars and scooters ahead. They were not the servants nor the cooks of Dr. Rocco Tardelli, nor were they his true friends, but each of them in their differing ways felt a fierce loyalty to the small man low on the backseat of the Alfa who struggled through his heavy horn-rimmed spectacles to read a file as the car bucked, braked, accelerated and weaved. The other teams, those assigned to other investigating magistrates, regarded them with pity. They were the escort of the magistrate who worked stubbornly and persistently toward the capture and conviction of Mario Emanuele Ruggerio. They were the *ragazzi* of a walking corpse.

A tremor of a voice from the back of the Alfa. "I understand you are to be congratulated, Pasquale. Is the baby well, is your wife well?"

His mind churning the procedures of "cover and evacuate" and "defensive of life only" shooting patterns and "fight or flight" mode, Pasquale muttered, "Very well, thank you, Dr. Tardelli."

"You will be leaving me?"

"No, Dr. Tardelli."

"Because you now have a baby?"

"Please, Dr. Tardelli, you distract me . . ."

When she pushed the scooter up the drive and parked it in front of the garage doors and took off her helmet and shrugged her hair free, she saw him slowing in his car. She thought of the baby of seventeen days, hooked to tubes, shivering in a glass box.

"Did you read the man's file?"

"I did."

"Did you like what you read?"

"Not particularly, if you need to know."

The Country Chief, Ray, stood at the partition wall that blocked off Dwight Smythe's work area from the open-plan office. He had been a guest observer the whole of the day at a symposium organized by the British Home Office to talk through international cooperation on organized crime—and the day had been crap, the papers read before lunch by a Russian and a Spaniard and the paper read after the buffet by a Brit from the National Criminal Intelligence Service had been shit. The papers had been a recitation of seizure statistics and arrest statistics and asset confiscation statistics, and he'd reckoned them garbage. The papers were garbage because they did not go to the core problem of taking out the men who mattered, the men who made it happen. Complacency was a crime in the Country Chief's Bible, and that day there had been more complacency on show than food on the buffet table. He envied Axel Moen, didn't reckon Axel Moen suffered too many symposiums.

"You want to go work in La Paz, Bolivia?"

"No."

"He did. You want to get yourself into firefights where they need bodybags afterwards?"

"No."

"He did. You want to lift a bad man in Miami, testify to a grand jury, find out then that there's a video of you going into court and that the Cali people, the cartel guys, have the video and have your face?"

"No."

"You want to wear a Smith & Wesson, you want to look over your shoulder, you want to go to Palermo?"

"No, no, no."

He could be affable, the Country Chief, Ray. He could tell a good story at the Christmas party. He could charm the asses off the inspection teams. He could make a sour-minded man smile. He was affable when he cared to be. His voice had a crunch, trodden-down frosted gravel.

"You don't want it, Dwight, so keep your bad-mouthing to yourself."

"What I'm saying—"

"Don't."

"You goddam hear me, Ray. What I'm saying, we are professionals and we are trained and we are paid. The young woman that he's got his hooks into—hear me, because I didn't just take time on the computer for Moen's file, I went into current assessments of La Cosa Nostra, down in Sicily, that's a killing ground—the young woman is an innocent."

The Country Chief, a moment, softened. "Maybe, Dwight, you sell us all short, maybe we're all thinking like you. And maybe we should all clap our hands and sing our hymns and get on our knees and thank our God that He didn't give us the problem. Have you got the budget figures for last month? Trouble is, it's a good plan. Might not, but might just get to work. Bring the budget through, please."

•   •   •

When she looked from the window, she saw him lying back, eyes closed, in his car. She thought of the grief of a retired major and how he would writhe in self-guilt. She thought of the body on the trolley.

Anyone who knew her or worked with her would have described Mavis Finch as a difficult person. Her family was up north, she had no friends in London, there was no one who would have shouted her corner. Those who lived in the same block of two- and one-bedroom maisonettes in a southwest suburb of the capital would have spoken, if asked, of Mavis Finch's complaint flow about the noise of their televisions, about their pets, about their litter, about late visitors. Those who worked with her in the bank in the Fulham Road would have spoken, if asked, of Mavis Finch's carping criticism of balance sheets produced late, of account errors, of extended lunch hours, of days taken for minor illness.

She was unloved and unliked by both neighbors and work colleagues. To the more charitable she was someone to be pitied, to the less charitable she was a vindictive bitch. But the life of this lonely thirty-seven-year-old woman, without a man or a child or a friend or a hobby, was governed by a rule book. The rule book laid down the volume of her neighbors' televisions, what pets could be kept, when their litter should be put out, up to what time visitors were permitted to come banging on doors . . .

It was because of the needle eye of Mavis Finch for the pages of her rule book that Detective Sergeant Harry Compton, SO6, took an early dinner in the hotel fronting onto Portman Square. Her rule book for conduct in the bank on the Fulham Road extended beyond matters of lateness, delays, mistakes, sickness. Regarded by her managers as best kept distant from customers, it had been the previous

June a combination of holidays and pregnancies and sickness that had forced them to detail Mavis Finch to counter work. It was because she had been at the counter, mid-morning, nine months before that DS Compton, Fraud Squad, toyed with a cod mornay in the dining room of a five-star hotel. Probably, Mavis Finch, that long-ago morning, would have been alone among the counter clerks in having read in full the texts of the Drugs Trafficking Act (1984), the Criminal Justice Acts (1988 and 1993) and the Drugs Trafficking Offenses Act (1994). The Acts, taken in totality, made it obligatory for a bank to disclose "suspicious and large transactions." Of course, that mid-morning, Mavis Finch reported the deposit of £28,000 in £50 notes because had she not reported it she would, herself, have been guilty of criminal conduct. She had taken the name, Giles Blake, the address, she had noted what she described in the spidery handwriting of her report as an "impatience" by the customer . . . Compton watched the target, sipped mineral water, listened.

And so typical, Compton thought, that the buggers at NCIS should have taken from June to March to evaluate the bank's disclosure before passing the detail to Fraud Squad. Bloody typical. To Harry Compton, the National Criminal Intelligence Service should more often get its hands out from under its butt.

He had, because time was precious and allocated fiercely to priorities, around five hours of desk time and an evening to decide whether to hold open a file on Giles Blake or whether to scrawl across the existing seven sheets that "no further action" was warranted.

The desk time had produced nothing tangible, no evidence of illegality, but Compton had a nose, nostrils, that sensed an incomplete picture. A nice house in Surrey for Mr. Blake, a nice wife and children for Mr. Blake, bank accounts and stocks and money in building societies for Mr. Blake. Too much that was "nice," and not enough to substantiate it. Compton had gone as a young detective from the Harrow station to Anti-Terrorist Branch, and found the surveillance of Irish "sleepers" in smoky and beer-stinking pubs to be a decent definition of boredom. He had sought and found stimulation, he had transferred to Fraud Squad. He liked to say, if he met up, increasingly rarely, with guys from Harrow or Anti-Terrorist, that SO6 was the steepest learning curve in the Metropolitan Police. He was studying, nights, business management and accountancy, and when he'd those qualifications he'd be going for law. But the old nose still counted.

What had twitched the nose of Harry Compton, stung the nostrils, was the guest that Giles Blake had brought to dinner.

The tables were adjacent. They liked to boast, from top to bottom of SO6, that their surveillance procedures were the best, better than Anti-Terrorist, better than Flying Squad. The ethos was "proximity." They had to blend, they had to risk burning out. It was not sufficient merely to observe, long-range, they needed "proximity" to listen.

He'd heard, once on a course, a hot afternoon, central heating turned too high, head beginning to drop, a lecture line that had hit him. "The accountants are more dangerous than the killers—the killers are small-time scumbags, the accountants threaten a whole society . . ." He had used up the five hours of his allocated desk time, he had started to burrow into his evening's surveillance time, tracked Giles Blake from his London office to Portman Square, to the hotel, to the reception desk, to the bar, to the restaurant. The guest had come to the restaurant, shaken hands, hugged, sat down.

"A good flight?"

"It's every day, every week, not in your papers here, a strike of the airline workers, just two hours—so we were late away. Nothing changes in Palermo."

His nose twitched, his nostrils smarted.

The light came on over the porch. Axel flicked the wiper switch and the windscreen was smeared clear. She came out of the door. The windscreen blurred with the rain. She hurried through the small gate and she was hunched small with her arms tight around her body as if that would keep her dry. At the car she rapped her fingers on the passenger window. He did not hurry himself. He tossed the *Time* magazine copy behind him and onto the backseat and then he pulled out the ashtray and stubbed the cigarette. The rain ran on her hair and her face and she hit the passenger window with her fist. He leaned across and unlocked the door, pushed it open.

She ducked into the car and was wiping the rain off her head and from her face. She turned to him, angry. There was a brightness in her eyes, but her face was wrecked because her mouth was screwed, good anger. It was useful for Axel Moen to see how she handled good anger.

"Thanks, thank you very much."

"What do you thank me for?"

"Thanks for making me stand out there, get bloody wet, while you read your magazine, smoke your cigarette—"

"Care for one?" He held the packet in front of her, Lucky Strike, out of the carton from duty-free at Fiumicino.

"It's a dirty habit . . . thanks for keeping me in the rain while you read and smoke, before you open the door—"

"So you got wet, how's that cause to thank me?"

"Are you stupid?"

"Sometimes, sometimes not."

"It was sarcasm. In thanking you for getting me wet, I was being sarcastic."

"I find it best, Charley, always, so there's not misunderstandings, to say what I mean."

He grinned. Axel grinned because her face had flushed red. He saw the color spreading across her face by the light above him. It was good anger and getting better. She had twisted to confront him. He thought she might have put on lipstick at the start of the day but it had wiped off and not been replaced, and there were no cosmetics round her eyes and they were bloodshot as if it were two nights she hadn't slept well. Her temper was scratched, a nail in wood that the saw blade hits. It was important for him to read her temper.

Forced calm, "All right, what I mean . . . We don't have it now, we used to have a terrier bitch. When the bitch was in season, in heat, then a big Labrador dog used to come and sit at the side gate. He used to sit there by the hour, big bloody stupid eyes. You know what, that dog sitting there, all night, and sort of crying, he got to be just a bore."

"I'm hearing you, Charley."

Enjoying herself. "The town where I went to college, it was an army town, a garrison camp. Soldiers used to sit in their cars, on their bikes, at the gate and watch us, the girls. We called them "lechies," understand, lechers. They didn't have old raincoats, they kept their Y-fronts on, they didn't flash us. They were pretty harmless, but they got to be boring."

"Did they?"

"You here in your car, last night, all night . . . today at school . . . here now . . . it's getting to be a bore. It is causing embarrassment. Danny Bent, he says you could have injured his stock. Fanny Carthew says you damn near ran her dog over. Zach Jones wants to know if we've called the police. Daphie Farson wants to know if you're a pervert."

"Maybe you should go tell them to fuck themselves."

"That is—"

She laughed. He thought she was trying to be shocked and failing, because she was laughing. It was useful for him to see her laugh. When she laughed she was pretty, quite pretty, not especially pretty. She wiped the laugh.

"Where I was taken last night, emotional blackmail, it was pathetic."

"Myself, I'd say it was patronizing."

"Treating me like a juvenile."

"Patronizing, but I doubt it did you harm."

"What do you want of me?"

"Same as I told you first time round. There is an opportunity for you to give me access to the home of Giuseppe and Angela Ruggerio. I need that access."

She stared hard at him. There were shadows on her face that caught the small lines at her eyes and at her mouth. He thought now that he stressed her. It was important to him to see her stressed. He waited on her. It was not for him to lead her.

She hesitated, then blurted, "If I refuse, won't go to Palermo . . . ?"

Axel gazed at the windscreen, at the running water, at the blur of the beach and the jetty and dark outline of the headland. "I lose that opportunity for access. I have one opportunity through you. OK, we thought it out, you get the invitation, you write back and say that you're sorry and can't make it, but that you've a friend. We supply the friend. The friend is the Customs and Excise investigation team, a policewoman, whatever . . . They're too careful over there, wouldn't buy it. You're the one with access, Charley, only you. If you refuse, I don't get the access. Don't think I want someone like you down there, but I haven't another option."

She turned away from him, twisted her back to him.

She jerked the passenger door open. She pushed herself out of the car. She told him that she would think on it one more night, and where she would meet him the next day after school. She asked him if he liked walking. She bent suddenly, peered at him through the door, and it did not seem to matter to her that the rain beat on her head and her shoulders and her spine.

"What would happen to me, if . . . ?"

"It went sour on you? If they were just unhappy about you, they'd fire you, send you home. Charley, I try and say what I mean so there aren't misunderstandings. It's a shit place and they're shit people. If they'd serious cause to suspect you then they'd kill you and go home afterwards and eat their dinner. It wouldn't bother them, Charley, to kill you."

He watched her run toward the light above the porch of the bungalow.

3

Egregio Dottore e gentile Signora.

She sat in the classroom. She took a mouthful of a sandwich from her lunchbox. She sipped at the can of Pepsi. She had brought in with her, in the rucksack that strapped onto the back of her scooter, the sheet of notepaper headed with the address of Gull View Cottage. In the mid-morning break she had gone to the rubbish containers on the far side of the playground and lifted the lids of two of them and tried, hopelessly, to identify which plastic bag had been in the bin outside her classroom. She had not found the plastic bag. It was a fine day, the cloud was broken, and the crocuses in the pots around the prefabricated classroom were already showing with the daffodils, and she thought that the spring season was a time of hope and optimism, and she wondered how the spring season was in Palermo . . . She tried to remember each phrase, sentence, of the letter written to her by Angela Ruggerio and then intercepted and copied and tracked.

> (Sorry, *dottore*, and sorry, *signora*, but that is going to be the limit of my Italian—I remember quite a lot of it, but if you'll excuse me the rest will be in English!!)
>
> Thank you very much for your kind invitation. And my warmest congratulations on the birth of Mauro, and of course I was very pleased to hear that Mario and Francesca were well.

It was so clear to her, the Roman summer of 1992. School finished, exams taken. The miserable response of her father, who had expected too much of her grades. Not good enough for university but sufficient to win her a place at a teachers' training college. It had been her mother who had seen the advertisement in the *Lady* magazine. Her mother had seen the advertisement in the magazine at the hairdresser, copied it and brought it home. An Italian family living in Rome sought a "nanny/mother's help" for the summer months. She and her mother had written the application and enclosed a photograph, and her father had warned that Italians pinched bottoms and were dirty, not to be trusted and thieves, and she and her mother had ignored him as they usually did. The four months of the Roman summer of 1992 had been, quite simply, the happiest months of her life.

> I was very surprised to get your letter, and you will understand that I have had to think about it very hard. Because of the situation today in England I found when I graduated as a teacher (!) that it was really hard to find work. I think I was very lucky, Dad certainly says so, to get this job that I now have.

The Roman summer of 1992 had been magic months for Charley. From the time that she had walked down the aircraft's steps, pushed her trolley through Customs and Immigration, seen Giuseppe and Angela Ruggerio, with Mario holding his father's hand and Angela carrying the baby Francesca, and seen their welcome smiles, she had felt a true liberation for the first time in her life. They had greeted her as if she were a part of them, right from the time that Peppino, as he insisted he should be called, had driven them away from the airport in his sleek BMW, and she had sat in the back with the small boy beside her and the baby girl on her lap, had treated her as a friend already by the time the car had swept into the basement car park of the apartment on the Collina Fleming. She had thought then that her father was ossified in his attitudes and boring, and she thought that her mother was complacent in her outlook and boring, and to be away from them, first time in her life, was true freedom. Most mornings of that June and July Peppino, with the beautiful suit and smile and lotion scent, was gone early to his office in the bank, something to do with the Vatican. And most mornings of those first weeks Charley had taken Mario down to the *piazza* for the private bus to the kindergarten of St. George's School, high on the Via Cassia. And most mornings of that June and July Angela, with beautiful blouses and skirts and coats, was out in the shops of the Via Corso or at her volunteer job in the Keats Museum at the Piazza Espagna. Most mornings, while the *domestica* made the beds and cleaned the bathrooms and put the washing in the machines and did the ironing and tidied the kitchen, Charley had sat on the wide balcony and played with the baby, Francesca, and marveled at the view above the pot flowers, watered each day by the old *portiere,* stretching from the dome of the basilica of St. Peter's across the heart of the city and away to the distant shadows of the mountains. It had been heaven. And more of heaven in the afternoons, the Italian classes in a room off the cool of a courtyard behind the Parliament building, and then the roaming walks through the *centro storico.* When she walked the narrow cobbled streets of the *centro storico* she had never taken a map with her, so that each church and old piazza, each gallery and hidden garden, each tucked-away temple and frieze from antiquity, had seemed a discovery that was personal to her. It had been her freedom.

> I have considered very carefully your offer that I should come to Palermo to help look after Mario and Francesca and baby Mauro. I am happy in my present job, I have ambitions to move to a bigger school when I have gained more direct experience. If I resign my position then I believe it would be quite difficult, at this time, to find another school that would have me in the autumn.

That summer of 1992, for the months of August and September, Charley had gone with Angela Ruggerio and the children to a rented beach villa a kilometer along the coast from Civitavecchia. If he were not away on the bank's business Peppino came to the villa at weekends. Seven weeks of sun oil and sand and ice creams and lazy evening meals and a growing love of Angela and her children. The good clothes from the Via Corso boutiques were left behind. The time for T-shirts and jeans and bikinis, and the fourth day on the beach Charley had taken courage and unhooked the bikini top and felt a desperate blushing shyness at the whiteness and lain on her stomach on the towel while Angela had lain on her back beside her, and never worn the top again and known her own parents would have called her a slut. She had talked of poetry with Angela and known her own mother had never read Keats or Shelley or Wordsworth. She had talked of social sciences, Angela's degree course at the University of Rome that had specialized in local

administration, and known that her own father had
believed the world began and ended with the study of
marine engineering. It was the time of her liberation.
And it had ended . . . It had ended in tears in her small
room at the apartment when she had packed her bag,
ended in tears as she had hugged them all and kissed
them all at the departure gate, ended in tears as she had
walked alone to the aircraft. Magic was not real, was illu-
sory. She had come home from a Roman summer of liberation and freedom to the drab college that trained her
to teach.

> *Basta,* enough of me waffling on. I think you
> are providing me with another fantastic opportu-
> nity to travel—which I certainly cannot afford to
> do on what I am now paid!!—I don't know any-
> thing about Palermo except that it is a city very
> rich in history. I cannot imagine it, cannot see it
> in my mind, and yet already I am excited.

She did not lie often, but it was a lie when she wrote of
her ignorance of the city and its images. She was taken, her
recall, to the images on the television screen of the apartment on Collina Fleming. The killing of judge Giovanni
Falcone had been twelve days before her arrival in Rome,
that summer of 1992, but the killing of Judge Paolo
Borsellino had been forty-five days after her arrival . . . She
sat in the classroom, with her lunchbox and her emptied
can of Pepsi and she remembered the images of the television . . . It was only afterwards, after she had seen the
images, that she had understood the quiet in the capital that
weekend afternoon as she had browsed her way from the
Colosseum to the Partheneum, and the quiet on the bus
that had dropped her by the Ponte Flaminio, and the quiet

on the street as she had walked under the pine trees toward the apartment on Collina Fleming. She had called her greeting in the hall, and not been answered, and she had gone into the little sitting area where they had the portable television. Even the child, Mario, and the baby, Francesca, had been hushed. Peppino grim faced had sat in front of the television and stared at the screen, and the chin of Angela, beside him, quivered. So it was a lie for Charley to write that she had no image of Palermo. The image in bright color was of the front of a block of flats, demolished, and of a car that had held 50 kilos of explosives, disintegrated, and of the faces of Judge Borsellino and five bodyguards, destroyed. That was the image of Palermo, and there were more images for her to recall because the television broadcast, interrupting normal schedules, had then shown the scene of the killing, fifty-seven days earlier, of Judge Falcone and Judge Falcone's wife and Judge Falcone's three bodyguards. The images were of the demolished façade of an apartment block in Palermo and of a cratered highway with broken cars scattered among rubble at Capaci. Peppino and Angela had sat with their silence and Charley had watched, seen and slipped away to her bedroom as if she had feared she had intruded into a world that held no place for her, but it had all been far away from Rome and was not referred to again, far away in Palermo.

> I am happy to take the plunge. I will sort out the matter of a new job when I get back because this is much too good an opportunity for me to miss—I accept your invitation.
> I look forward to hearing your suggestions for my arrival date.
>
> *Distinti saluti,*
> Charley (Charlotte Parsons)

Outside the window the bell clamored the end of the lunch hour. She was twenty-three years old. She heard the screaming excited babble of the children charging back from the playground. Other than when she had gone to Rome four years earlier she had never been outside her country. Her hand trembled. She had agreed to take an opportunity for access. She read the letter back. She would spy on the family that had shown her love and kindness and affection.

"Come on, children. Settle down now. Leave her alone, Dean. Stop it. Writing books out, please. Yes, writing books, Tracy. Darren, don't do that. Has everyone got their writing book?"

She folded the letter. She had been told that if she gave serious cause for suspicion she would be killed and that then her killers would go home to eat their dinner.

To refuse protection in Palermo was to lose the love of life.

Under the yellow haze of car fumes that lay below the surrounding mountains and that was held in place by the light sea breeze, the city was a mosaic of guarded camps. Palermo was a place of armed men, of carefully sited strongpoints, as it had been throughout history. Soldiers with their NATO rifles, huddled inside bullet-proof shelters, held the street corners of the blocks where magistrates and politicians lived. Police bodyguards in armor-reinforced cars, deafened by sirens, escorted those magistrates and politicians from one defended position to another, from home to work, from work to home. Thug-minders watched over the personal security of the men who figured high on the lists of Interpol's and Europol's most-wanted suspects and had Kalashnikov assault rifles secreted in their cars but close

to hand. It was a city of tension and fear, a city where
the industry of protection flourished. The industry offering protection, fortresses and safety was spread thick
across the city. It covered the servants of the state and the
principals of the alternate society, and right on up and
right on down through every stratum of Palermo's society. If the magistrate or the politician was denied protection, was isolated, he was as a floor rag left out on a line
to rot in the sun, he was dead. If the boss of a family
running a district of Palermo ignored the necessary
precautions of survival, then other pigs would come to
snout out the food in his trough. The hotelier running
the four-star *albergo* must pay for protection or face his
guests' cars vandalized, his food contaminated, his business ruined. He sought protection. The bar owner risked
fire if he did not buy protection. A construction magnate
risked the denial of contracts and bankruptcy if he did
not buy protection. The street vendor must buy it or
reckon to have his legs broken, and the street whore on
the Via Principe di Villafranca, and the bag thief on the
Via del Libertà, and the taxi driver on the rank at the
Politeama, and the heroin peddler at the Stazione
Centrale. The seeking of protection was a habit of existence, unremarked and unexceptional . . .

To decline protection in Palermo was to refuse to
live.

His hands were less painful that day. He could hold the
coffee cup with his fingers and not spill the treacle-thick
liquid. He thought that his hands were less painful
because of the warmth of the spring sunshine on them as
he had walked on the Via Marqueda to the bar.

In the bar, where the television played a satellite
channel's transmissions of continuous music promotion

videos, Mario Ruggerio met with a man and talked the strategy of killing.

If he had talked with a man who was close to him, close tied by blood or friendship, he would have said that the matter of killing was abhorrent to him. But there was no man who was sufficiently close to him, not even his youngest brother, in whom he would confide his most prized and inner thoughts. His aloneness, his suspicion of intimacy and sharing, were key attributes that he recognized in his capacity for personal survival. His dislike of the strategy, matter, of killing had little to do with any sense of squeamishness, even less with any hesitation over the morality of taking the life of another of God's creatures. It was to do with security, his freedom.

In the conversation, punctuated by long silences, over the single cup of coffee, down to the dregs of the ground beans and the two sugar spoonfuls, the name of the magistrate was never used.

It was difficult to kill without witnesses. It was hard to kill without leaving traces for the forensic scientists of the *carabinieri* and the *squadra mobile* and the *Direzione Investigativa Anti-Mafia* to analyze for evidence. It was complicated to dispose of a cadaver, even if an oil drum of acid were used or the "heavy overcoat" of liquid concrete on a construction site, or if the body was food for the fishes. All of those who had planned and carried out the killing of Falcone and Borsellino were now in custody, rotting or convicted *in absentia,* and, like wayward children, they had scattered evidence around them. The old way of killing, his father's way, was the *lupara,* which was the short-barreled shotgun with the spread of pellets but that left blood spatters on walls, streets, carpets, rugs and pavements. The Magnum handgun with exploding bullets was the favorite of the wild young *picciotti,* the head-case kids, but that too left evidence, shell cases, fractured bullet fragments, blood running to the street drains and smeared through interiors. He preferred the way of strangulation, but that was so hard now on his hands that had the rheumatic pain in them.

They talked, without using the name of the magistrate, right under the television.

The killing of a man served two purposes for Mario Ruggerio. The killing of a man would send a message to his family and his colleagues, and the killing of a man removed an obstacle that confronted the smooth running of his affairs. The killing of the magistrate, discussed in staccato words under the beat of an electric guitar and the hammer of a drummer, would send a message and would remove an obstacle. It was his belief that La Cosa Nostra should strike only when it was threatened and the magistrate, in the opinion of Mario Ruggerio, now endangered him. The shotgun could not be used, nor the Magnum, nor the Kalashnikov fired from the waist on automatic, because it was not possible to be that close to the magistrate. He did not know the workings of bombs in cars or rubbish bins, nor the methods of a command wire or of an electronic firing pulse, but the man he talked with knew of those workings and methods.

He would have preferred a world of quiet, a world where the interest of the state waned. He wished for a world of coexistence. He could reel off, without consultation of notes, the names of judges and prosecutors and magistrates in the Palazzo di Giustizia who also yearned for such a world of coexistence but in that conversation, in the bar, he did not speak the name of the single magistrate whom he thought now to represent a threat against his precious freedom.

It was agreed that a bomb was the necessary method

of attack. And further agreed that the movements of the magistrate would be more closely observed to find a pattern in his travel. And finally agreed that the matter of killing was a priority.

He slipped away from the bar, an old man in a gray jacket and a check cap on the pavement of the Via Marqueda who attracted no attention, who flexed the muscles of his hand in the Palermo sunshine.

The prisoner had been brought from his shared cell on the third floor of the block. The doctor was the "cut-out." The doctor had asked for the prisoner to be brought to the medical wing for routine examination. The doctor and his own staff had been used three times before by the magistrate. The magistrate would not have reckoned on the chances of the survival of the prisoner if it were known in the corridors and landings of Ucciardone jail that the man, on remand and charged with murder, had requested a meeting. The request for the meeting, a prisoner wishing to talk with Rocco Tardelli, had come in a letter, barely literate, hardly legible, delivered to the Palazzo di Giustizia. He thought the letter, perhaps, had been written by the prisoner's mother. Men died, some quietly through strangulation, some noisily through poisoning, some messily through bludgeon blows, in Ucciardone prison when they sought to collaborate. It was of critical importance, at this moment, that it should not be known among the prison staff that a man had asked to see the magistrate who was known to have dedicated his life to the capture of Mario Ruggerio. When the prison staff who escorted the prisoner to the surgery had been dismissed and the prisoner signed for, he had been taken by two of the magistrate's own security detail, his head covered by a blanket that he should not be recognized by watchers peering from the cell windows high above, across the yard and to the room made available for the magistrate.

Tardelli thought him pathetic.

The cigarette that the prisoner smoked was not half finished and already the man looked longingly at the packet on the table. Tardelli did not smoke but he always carried a nearly full packet in his pocket when he came to Ucciardone. He pushed the packet toward the prisoner and smiled his invitation that the man should help himself again. A new cigarette was lit from an old cigarette and the hands of the prisoner shook.

Tardelli thought him wretched.

They sat in a bare room, on either side of a bare table, they were enclosed by bare walls. There was no window and the light came from a single fluorescent strip on the ceiling around which wafted the spurted smoke from the prisoner's cigarette. Since the message had come from his office at the Palazzo di Giustizia, the report of a letter without signature to request the interview, the message that had interrupted the celebration of orange juice and chocolate cake, Tardelli had spent the major part of two days studying the file of the prisoner. It was his way always to be meticulously prepared before he faced a prisoner.

The prisoner spoke the name of Mario Ruggerio.

He detested personal publicity, he left it to the more ambitious and the more scheming to give media interviews, but it was inevitable that Rocco Tardelli should be known as the magistrate who hunted Mario Ruggerio. Half a dozen times a year he was told that a prisoner had requested, in conditions of secrecy, to meet with him. Half a dozen times a year a prisoner groveled for the freedom of the *pentito* program, for the opportunity to trade information for liberty. Once a year, if he was lucky, Tardelli would hear information that carried forward his investigation, drew him closer to the man he hunted. They came and they squirmed and they crossed the Rubicon. They condemned themselves to death if they were identified, if they were located, when they broke the God-given law of Sicily, the law of *omertà*, which was the code of silence.

The *pentito* Contorno had broken the law of *omertà* and thirty of his relations by blood and by marriage had been butchered in a proxy attempt to halt the information flow he dribbled. There was a saying of the peasants on the island: "A man who is really a man never reveals anything even when he is being stabbed." The *pentito* Buscetta had turned away from the code of silence and thirty-seven of his relations had been murdered. Another saying of the peasants on the island: "A man who is deaf and blind and silent lives a hundred years in peace." The *pentito* Mannoia was now a terrified man, existing on Valium tablets, in crisis. He had heard a woman refer to her *pentito* brother as "a relative of my father." It was an earthquake in their lives when they gave up the silence. Each year one of the prisoners who sat at the bare table in the bare room, hemmed in by the bare walls of the bunker, was useful to the magistrate. Five a year were rubbish wretches.

It was a sparring game for Tardelli and the prisoner.

"Why do you wish to take advantage of the Award Legislation under the conditions of the Special Protection Program?"

The eyes of the prisoner were on the choked ashtray. He stammered, "I have decided to collaborate because La Cosa Nostra is only a gang of cowards and assassins."

He could be cruel. Rocco Tardelli, mild mannered

and round shouldered, could be vicious.

"I believe it more probable that you seek to 'collaborate' because you face the sentence of *ergastolo*. You face the rest of your life in prison, here, in Ucciardone."

"I have rejected La Cosa Nostra."

"Perhaps you have only rejected the sentence of life in Ucciardone."

"I have information . . ."

"What is the information?"

"I have information on the location where Mario Ruggerio lives."

"Where does he live?"

The prisoner snorted, the furtive eyes launched upward toward the magistrate. "When I have the guarantee of the Special Protection . . ."

"Then you go back to your cell, and you consider. You do not seek to bargain with me. Back and consider."

"I can tell you where is Mario Ruggerio."

"When you have told me, then we think on the Protection Program. Then I evaluate and make my recommendation to the Committee. You talk, or you go back to your cell. It is not for you to make conditions."

It was important for the magistrate, Rocco Tardelli, to set the rules from the first interview. A thousand men had been received into the Protection Program. The budget was exhausted, safe houses were filled, *carabiniere* and military barracks bulged with the *pentiti* and their families. Most were useless. Most bartered long sentences of imprisonment for stale information. To a dedicated investigator, as was Rocco Tardelli, it was distasteful to exchange freedom for tired news.

"But I have come to you . . ."

"And told me nothing. Consider your position."

Tardelli stood. The interview was concluded. Most

of those he met, the true leaders of La Cosa Nostra, were men he treated with due respect. It puzzled him, frequently, that such gifted men should require criminality to buttress their yearning for dignity. Because they had lost their dignity, it was hard for him to offer a *pentito* due respect. The prisoner, the blanket again over his head, was escorted back to the medical area. The doctor would call for prison staff to return him to the shared cell on the third floor of the block. The magistrate gathered up his briefcase from the floor, his cigarette packet from the table, his coat from the hook on the door. With his guards, he hurried down the corridor.

The sunshine hit their faces.

"You see, my young friend, Pasquale, maker of babies, I have to make him suffer. He has made the first move, but he will have thought he can control me. I have to show him that he does not. He will have thought he can offer me information, step by step, a little at a time, as he demands further privileges. That is not acceptable. I have to be able to judge that he will tell me everything that he knows. I have to be patient . . ."

They paused at the car, the armored Alfa. The lights were flashed at the gate sentries. The engines roared. The gates swung open. The sidearms and the machine-pistols were cocked.

"Is he a jewel, Pasquale, or is he false gold?"

"Please don't talk to me, not when we are moving, please."

He tucked down into the darkened interior of the car. The young man, Pasquale, was in front of him, the *maresciallo* drove.

He leaned forward, he caught the back of the young man's seat. It was a compulsion for him, to share and to talk. There was no one for him to talk with but the *ragazzi.* He despised himself, but to talk at times was the craving of an addict.

"You know, if I was afraid, if I could not tolerate the fear any longer, I could send a signal. There are routes by which a signal could be sent. Certain people, in the Palace of Poison or in the Questura, even in the barracks of the *carabinieri,* would send a signal, pass a message. I have only to say, in confidence, that a prisoner asked for me. In confidence, I would give that prisoner's name. In confidence, binding such a person to secrecy, I could say that I have rejected the offer of information from that prisoner. It would be a signal that I was now afraid. The message would be passed on, it would be heard. It would be understood that I was no longer a threat. If, in confidence, I sent that signal, then I could again go to a restaurant, go to the cinema, go to the opera at the Politeama, go to the hairdresser . . ."

The young man, Pasquale, sat rigid in front of him.

The magistrate said sadly, "I have to believe that I can live with the fear."

"I hear we cocked your posh grub. You won't find me crying, Harry. Wife was out, so mine last night was sausage, oven chips and beans."

"Didn't do too bad, sir." Harry chuckled. "Managed five courses, two gins for aperitif, bottle of white and red, brandy to wash it down . . ."

"Did we screw you?"

The detective superintendent, it was his show, led the detective sergeant out of the senior partner's office and across the hall and out through the front door, down the steps and across to the pavement where the Transit van was parked. Harry stood back to allow his superior to hand over the cardboard packing case first to the constable at the rear doors. They paused, each of them, wrung their hands, pretty damn heavy the boxes were.

"I was beginning to get the taste for it. Quite a good restaurant, actually, for a hotel."

"Till we horned in. Come on, next load."

They went back into the building on Regent Street, looking straight ahead and ignoring the white-faced junior partners and the secretaries who had little hand-kerchiefs clasped in their hands as if to safeguard them from the Doomsday collapse of their world. It was inevitable, what had happened the previous evening, because of the shortage of manpower in SO6 and the constant juggling of priorities. Listening to Giles Blake's assessment of the immediate future of the gilts market, toying with the cod to make it last because they were slow on their food at the next table and hearing the announcement break into the canned nothing music. "Would Mr. Harry Compton please come to reception to take a telephone call? Mr. Harry Compton to recep-tion, please." Getting a judge out of his club and back to chambers, phoning the wife and pleading excuses, going through the evidence dossier with the judge and asking for a Schedule 1 Production Order under the Police Criminal Evidence Act (1984). Getting the judge's signa-ture on the order, asking him to put nib to paper a sec-ond time for the search warrant, and seeing his reluctance because it was a solicitor that they were going to jump when the office opened in the morning. Maybe that had been worth it, the study of distaste on the good old judge's face, because it was a solicitor, same clan and same tribe. Harry Compton had done the donkey's load of the investigation into the bent bastard whose hands were into clients' savings, the greedy bastard who was excavating trustee funds, the solicitor who had broken trust, but it was the detective superintendent's show and he'd made the call that had hauled the junior man off his expenses dinner. The panic reason was that the senior partner, information received, was going abroad and hadn't given his colleagues a coming-home date. Under a Schedule 1 Production Order and a search warrant the papers and archives were being packed away in cardboard boxes, down to the last sheet and the last file, loaded up and would be driven for close analysis to the SO6 office behind Holborn police station.

Harry Compton was dog-tired, out on his feet. He had finished with the judge at midnight, had the briefing with the team at thirty minutes after midnight, been home and slept three hours, been up and driven to the senior partner's home in Essex for a dawn knock and the clicking of handcuffs. He trudged up the stairs again for the next load of papers.

"Where did we get to?" The detective superintendent stopped on the landing and breathed hard.

"Last night? Sort of nowhere and somewhere. Chummy meets a guy, they have dinner, they talk financials through the evening. It was pretty unexceptional stuff. Anyway, the NCIS material on chummy was kind of vague, not much more than a single report of a medium cash deposit in a bank, £28,000, along with sharp-moving accounts with plenty of action in drops and withdrawals and not a lot to point to where the money comes from and where it's going, but not showing up as obvious illegal. That was the 'nowhere.'"

They were back in the senior partner's office. A small mountain of cardboard boxes remained to be shifted. And there was more to move in the secretary's office, and more from the junior partners' rooms, and then there was the whole of the bloody archive in the basement.

"Get a hernia from this. You're a cussed sod, Harry, always keep the best to last. What was the 'somewhere'?"

The detective sergeant grinned, welcomed the compliment. "Smooth as new paintwork. The guest, wearing his money on his back, Italian, very tasty . . . and he'd flown in from Palermo."

Each of them heaved up a box and headed for the door.

"You wouldn't be telling me, would you, Harry, that every businessman from Palermo is bloody mafia?"

Harry Compton winked. "'Course they are—if it was a grannie aged eighty from Palermo, a kid aged five from Palermo, I'd have 'em locked up for 'organized crime.' It has a sort of ring, doesn't it, Palermo?"

"We can run the name through."

"Don't have the name, had a phone call before I'd even got stuck into the sweets trolley. I'll get the name."

"But you'll work this bloody lot first, too right."

There were forty-seven boxes of papers from the offices, and there would be twenty-nine plastic bin sacks from the archives, and they'd need going through before he could get back to a hotel in Portman Square for a guest's name. It would all be a matter of priorities.

She passed him the letter, but the American made no move to take it. He turned to face her.

"Who else has read this letter?"

She bridled. "Nobody has."

"You are telling me, certain, nobody else has touched this letter."

"Of course they haven't."

She watched. He took a handkerchief from his pocket, shook it, then took the letter from her. The handkerchief protected the letter from the touch of his fingertips.

To Charley, holding the letter in a handkerchief seemed ridiculous. "Why?"

He said bleakly, "So that it doesn't look as if it's been shown round, so that my prints aren't on it."

"Would it be looked at that closely?"

"We do it my way, let's understand that from now."

He was impassive. He talked as if to an annoying child. He swung round, away from her, to read the letter held in the handkerchief. Bugger him. Charley had thought it clever to give him a meeting point on the cliffs. The dusk had been falling when she had ridden her scooter to the car park, empty but for his hire-car, that served the coastal footpath. He had been where she had told him to be. There was a nest of cigarette ends by his feet, enough for him to have been there for hours, from long before she had told him to be there. It was a good place for the big seabirds, and the gulls and shags and guillemots were chorusing and floating in the wind and settling on the rocks below where the sea's charge broke. It was a favorite place, when home just suffocated her, to come to. It was where she came and sat and brooded when the clinging attentions of her mother and father swamped her. It was a place of peace and wildness. She had thought it clever to come to the cliffs, to sit on the bench of coarse wood planks. Here she would be in control. He passed the letter back to her, then pocketed the handkerchief, then flicked a cigarette from the Lucky Strike packet.

"Aren't you going to ask me why I decided—?"

"Not important to me."

"Whether it's excitement or duty, whether it's adventure or obligation—?"

"Doesn't matter to me."

She bit at her lip. She ran her tongue the length of

her lip. She had sought control. The blood was running in her. "Well, sure as hell, it's not your courtesies. You are the rudest man—"

"If that's what you want to think, you should fax it to them in the morning."

She crumpled, and the control that she had sought slipped further. "But . . . but I don't have the fax number."

He said, as if he were tired, as if it were tedious, "The fax number was on their letter."

"But I tore it up, didn't I? I wasn't going, was I? I destroyed the letter, and then I changed my mind."

He should have asked why she had changed her mind. He didn't. He was reaching inside his windcheater and he took out the folded sheet of paper and opened it. From the photocopy of the letter sent to her he wrote the number and the international code on a notepad, tore off the sheet from the pad and handed it to her. There was a growl in his voice. She thought him so bloody cold. "Write it in your own hand on the back of the letter."

She did what she was told. He took the paper from his notebook back and tore it into small pieces. He threw the pieces into the air and they flaked away below them, carried on the wind gusts, down toward the big birds as they settled for the night. Away beyond Bolt Head, off Start Point, she saw the first flash of the lighthouse, the raking beam.

"Is it necessary to be like that, so careful?"

"Yes."

"That's what I have to learn?"

"It's best that you learn, fast, to be careful."

She shivered, the cold caught her. His windcheater had none of the quilted thickness of hers, but the cold did not catch him and he did not shiver. She felt dominated and small. Said with acid deliberateness, "Yes, Mr. Moen. Right, Mr. Moen. Three bloody bags full, Mr. Moen. I'll send the fax in the morning."

"Tell me about yourself."

"Excuse me, shouldn't you be doing the talking? Who, what, you are. Where I'm going. Why?"

He shook his head. "Who, what, I am doesn't concern you."

She snorted in fake derision. "Brilliant."

"It's about being careful."

She felt the cold, the wind on her back, night wind hacking at the strength of her anorak. "Where I'm going and why."

"In good time. About yourself."

She took a big breath. He watched her and his face was shadowed but she did not think that if a flashlight had been shone on his features, or the full beam of the lighthouse on Start Point, that she would have seen any damned encouragement. As if she was being manipulated, as if she was one of the marionettes that were stored in the cupboard behind her desk in 2B's classroom . . .

She blurted, "I'm Charlotte Eunice Parsons, everyone calls me 'Charley.' I'm pretty ordinary—"

"Don't talk yourself short, and don't look for compliments."

"Fat chance . . . I'm an only child. My parents are David and Flora Parsons. Dad was an engineering manager at the naval dockyard at Plymouth, it was his whole life—well, and me—until two years ago, when he was made redundant, the 'peace dividend.' We lived then in Yelverton, which is up on the edge of the moor, north of Plymouth. He didn't think he could afford to stay there, so they upped and moved. He packed in the bowls club and the tennis club, cinemas and shops, he's paranoid about being hard up, broke. He bought the bungalow, he took his place in a gossipy and inquisitive little society, mean minded. God knows why, my mother went along with it. Where they are now, they're boring and sad and empty. Do you think I'm being foul?"

"Doesn't matter what I think."

She gazed out at the sea, at the darkening mass of the water, at the white foam spurts on the rocks, at the distant light rotating from Start Point. She thought she spoke a truth, and that truth was important to Axel Moen.

"I can't afford to live away from home, all I've got went into that silly little bike. If I had a promotion, a better job, when I've more experience, then I could quit and go and live in my own place. Not yet. Their lives are boring, sad, empty, so they're looking for a star, and I fit the role. It's always been like that, but it's worse now. There's days I could scream—don't think I'm proud of being a right bitch—and there's nights I'm ashamed of myself. The trouble with being a star, you learn as a kid how to milk it, you get to play the little madam. Not before, but there are times now that I disgust myself. They wanted me to be quality at tennis, but I was ordinary and Dad couldn't see that. They wanted me top of the form at school, and when I wasn't, it was the teacher's fault, not because I was just another average kid. They wanted me to go to university, and when I didn't get the grades, then Dad said the examiners had made a mistake. What saved me, what sort of opened the window to me, was going to Rome and being with Giuseppe and Angela, they were really lovely, they were wonderful. But you want me to spy on them?"

"I want access, yes."

She peered ahead. He wouldn't have seen it. She

gazed down the depth of the rock face to where a crag hung out as a limp finger. A falcon worried with its killing beak at the feathers under its wing. It was personal to her, the peregrine bird. Sometimes, when she came to this place, she saw it, sometimes she heard the crying call of the female. If it came, she would see it because she could recognize the fast movements of the bird in flight and its rigid profile when it perched on the finger of rock. The bird was her own, nothing to do with him. It flew. She lost sight of the bird.

"I came back from Rome and went to training college. I suppose I was a spoiled little cow from home and a patronizing little cow from Rome. I didn't seem to find it necessary to make friends. All right, let's have it straight. I thought most of the other students were pretty trivial, and they thought I was pretty stuck-up, you know what that means? I didn't have a boyfriend, not one of the students, but there were a few sweaty sessions with one of the lecturers, one of those who always apologizes and cries afterwards and moans about his wife, but he used to give me good marks. Are you married?"

"No."

"Ever been married, Mr. Moen?"

"No."

"Why not?"

"Just stay with the story, Charley."

"Please yourself. I've only once ever done anything worthwhile in my life, what I thought was worth doing. You see, when you know how to milk it's the big temptation to stay on the gravy train—God, that's rotten mixed metaphors. When you can get what you want without trying you get complacent, you stop trying. Big deal, but I went last summer to Brightlingsea, it's a small dock on the east coast, other side of London. There was a protest there against the export of calves to Europe. They were shipping the calves across for fattening up and then slaughter. It's the veal trade. It's revolting. I was there for a month, bawling and hollering and trying to stop the lorries. Yes, I thought that was worthwhile. Are you from a city or from the country?"

"Northeast Wisconsin."

"Is that country?"

"Big country."

"So you wouldn't care about the animals, you'd say that farmers have to live, people have to eat, animals don't feel fear and pain."

"It's not important what I think."

"Christ. What else do you want to know? What color knickers I wear, when my period is? You're a bloody bundle of fun, Mr. Moen."

"I think I've heard enough."

She stood. Her hair was jostled on her face. The wind had risen and now that she no longer talked in his ear she had to shout against the roar of waves battering on rocks.

"Could we murder something, like a drink?"

He murmured, "I don't drink, not alcohol."

"My bloody luck, a bloody temperance nut. Hey, I'll drink, you watch. And while I drink you can tell me whether what I am going to do is worthwhile—or don't you have an opinion on that?"

Charley strode toward the car park. It was her big exit. She pounded up the path from the bench and the cliff face. She was going fast and ahead of him. Her foot, in the black darkness, tripped on a stone. She was falling . . . "Shit." She was stumbling and trying to hold her balance . . . "Bugger." He caught her, held her up, and she shook his hand off her arm and stormed on.

•   •   •

"Yes, Dr. Ruggerio . . . Of course, Dr. Ruggerio, of course I'll tell Charlotte that you rang, I'll tell her exactly what you said . . . It is difficult, Dr. Ruggerio, she has a very good position at the moment, but . . . Yes, Dr. Ruggerio, we're very gratified to know that you and your wife regard Charlotte so highly . . . Yes, she's a lovely young woman . . . We are, as you say, very proud of her . . . I know she's thinking very hard about your offer. She's out at the moment, something connected with school-work . . . Send a fax or telephone to Palermo, yes, I'll see she does that tomorrow . . . You're very kind, Dr. Ruggerio . . . Yes, yes, I'm sure she'd be very happy with you again . . . My wife, yes, I'll pass on your best wishes . . . So good to speak to you. Thank you. Goodnight."

He put down the telephone. David Parsons glanced once, briefly, at the graduation photograph of his Charlotte that hung in the place of honor in the hall. He went into the sitting room. Flora Parsons looked up from her needlework, the cover for a cushion.

"God, you're a coward."

"That's not called for."

"Eating out of his hand and he's soft-soaping you. Crawling to him."

"He sent you his best wishes . . ."

"The letter comes, then the American's here. Half the village wants to know who he is. Where's Charley now? I haven't an idea. Where is she? I'm frightened for her."

"As soon as she's back, I'll speak to her."

"You won't, you're a coward."

It was her bravado, and when she'd finished she had only a few coins left in her purse. Back to the bar, refusing his offer to buy the second round. A pint of Exmoor draft for herself, and a double malt whiskey for herself, and another cup of decaffeinated coffee for Axel Moen with milk in a plastic carton and sugar in a paper sachet.

While she'd drunk the first pint and the first double malt whiskey, while he'd sipped the first coffee, she'd told him about the timbered, low-ceilinged pub. She had given him the history—supposed to be a smugglers' den, and a hundred years earlier it was supposed to have been used as a lodging for a hanging judge in the Monmouth rebellion roundup, supposed to be . . .

He'd looked barely tolerant, just uninterested. He lit another cigarette. "OK, listen, please. What you saw when you had your drive round, pusher's territory, small-time—"

She interrupted. "I wouldn't describe an addicted baby in spasm as 'small-time,' nor would I call an over-dosed corpse 'small-time.' I'd—"

"Be quiet, and listen. What you saw was the symptom of a strategic problem. Too many law-enforcement people spend their time, the resources given them, chasing thieves and muggers and pushers because it looks good and they get to seem busy. But they're attacking the wrong end of the problem. Let me explain. Take a big company, let's talk of a mega-multinational. We'll take Exxon or General Motors or the Ford Motor Company, they're the major three American corporations. The total of their turnover, last set of figures I saw, $330 billion—get that figure in your mind—but the man you see is the salesman from the General Motors or Ford showroom, or if it's Exxon he's the guy who takes your money at the filling station. For the salesman or the guy on the cash till you should read 'thieves and muggers and pushers.' Narco-trafficking, the last set of figures, runs directly alongside those of General Motors and the Ford Motor

Company and Exxon, so we are talking serious money—
You with me?—but organized crime is not only about
narcotics, you can add in the profits from money washing, from arms trading, from illegal-immigrant rackets,
loan sharking and kidnapping and hijacking, from extortion. What the whole thing comes to, worldwide, is figures too big to comprehend, but we try. The figure is $3
million billion. It leaves the top corporations for dead . . .
Hang on in there."

She bolted at the beer. He sat opposite her. The
cigarettes went from his mouth to the ashtray, were
stubbed, were lit, were smoked. He talked quietly and
she clung to his words, as if he'd opened a door to her
that showed a sea without a horizon.

"Hanging, but it's from my fingernails."

She won a quick smile that did not last.

"The salesmen of General Motors and the Ford
Motor Company don't count, nor the guy on the cash till
at an Exxon filling station, they're about as important as
the thieves and muggers and pushers. Where it matters is
head office. Get in the elevator at head office, head on up
past the accountants and lawyers and the marketing people and the public affairs people, keep going up in the
elevator, up past the vice presidents for sales and finance
and internationals and image, research and development,
keep on till it stops or hits the sky. You are, Charley, in
the presence of the chief executive officer. He matters.
What he decides affects folk. He is god. His level is
strategic."

She felt minuscule, a pygmy. The whiskey glass was
empty, just the dregs of the Exmoor draft left.

"There are mafias in Italy, in the United States, in
Japan and Hong Kong, in Colombia and Brazil, in
Russia. Each of those mafias has a chief executive officer,

one man, because there's no space for a gang session in a mafia or in a corporation, who acts pretty much like the chief executive officer of General Motors, the Ford Motor Company or Exxon. He lays down guidelines, he plans for the future, he takes an overview, and if there are major problems, then he gets to roll up his sleeves and go hands-on into detail. I'll hit some differences. The mafia chief executive officer lives out of a hole in the ground, on the run, hasn't a thirty-story tower for staff, hasn't a floor of IBM computer gear. Your corporation guy, take away his support and his computer, he'd fall on his face . . . not his mafia opposite. The mafia chief executive officer lives with a wolf pack. To survive he has to be feared. If he is thought to show weakness, he will be torn to pieces. He stays cunning and he stays ruthless. I'm getting there, Charley, nearly there . . ."

"Fingers are getting a bit tired, nails are starting to crack." She hoped to make him laugh, another bloody failure. She did not believe he had talked this through before, she did not think it was rehearsed. It was not, Charley's opinion, a familiar and patterned story. It made her warm, with the whiskey, to believe she was not carried along a rutted story track.

"There's a commonplace. The mafias in Italy and the United States, Japan and Hong Kong, Colombia and Brazil, in Russia, have a sincere respect for the mafia of Sicily, La Cosa Nostra. La Cosa Nostra, out of Palermo, out of desperate little towns hanging in poverty off the sides of mountains, is the role model of international crime. It's where it started, where it's bred, where it lives well. They call it, in Italy, *la piovra*, that's an octopus. The tentacles spread out all over Europe, into your country, all over the world, into my country. Hack one off and another grows. You have to get to the heart of the thing, kill the heart, and the heart is in those little towns and in Palermo."

She trembled. Her hands were splayed out on the table. She whispered, "What do you want of me?"

"You offer the possibility of access to the chief executive officer of La Cosa Nostra. It's why I came to find you."

4

SHE SAT ALONE ON THE CLIFF, her place.

The headmistress had said, "There were four hundred applicants for your job, eighty applications from inside the county. If we'd realized that there was the faintest possibility you would just walk out on us then you wouldn't have even won an interview, let alone a short-listing. Don't you feel a responsibility to the children? Don't you feel something for your colleagues here who made you so welcome? When you return from this little episode in idiocy, don't think that this job will be waiting for you, and I doubt that any other job in teaching will be opening its arms to you after the report I intend to attach to your record. You've failed me, and your colleagues, and your children . . ."

In the common room, mid-morning break, she had announced her departure, and she had seen the expressions on their faces, orchestrated by the reaction of the head-mistress, change from astonishment to hostility. The sneer of the divorced head-of-year teacher who always looked at her with the ambition of getting his hands into her knick-ers. The angered resentment of the young man who taught 3A and ran the library and took scouts on weekends and whose eyes mooned after her in the common room every day. The rank envy of the teacher of 1A who had three chil-dren of her own and her husband had run and her life was dictated by minders and baby-sitters. Charley had shrugged, she had muttered that her mind was made up. She hadn't said, couldn't see the point in saying, that she thought them all pathetic and limited, small minded and trapped.

From the bench above the cliff she saw the peregrine preen the pure white of its chest feathers, worrying at them.

Axel had said, "You don't only have rights in this world as some gift of God. If you are given rights, you have to take the downside on board. You have to acknowledge obligation and duty. If the citizen has rights, then the citizen also has obligation and duty. You are the citizen, Charley. Bad luck. You cannot always hand over your obligations and duties to other people. Cannot walk away, cannot cross over the road. I don't have to give you syrup thanks for what you're doing, I don't tell you that we're all grateful to you. I'm not thanking you when all that's asked of you is to perform your duties and obligations as a citizen. I hope you didn't want a pretty speech."

They had sat in his hire car up the lane from the lights of the community, and Danny Bent had come by and stopped to peer in through the misted window and had spat onto the ground when he had turned away. Too right, she had wanted a pretty speech. She had wanted to feel proud, flushed and pleasured, and his quiet and cold voice gave her nothing. She had sent the fax. Three days later, the last evening when she had returned from a day at school, the envelope from the travel agent in London had been on the table in the hallway of Gull View Cottage, beside the telephone, under her photograph, and enclosed had been the ticket to Palermo, via Rome. He had said, cool and devoid of emotion, what she should write in a fax to be sent in the morning, why she was stopping two days in Rome, when she would reach Palermo. He had told her, brusque, where accommodation would be reserved for her in Rome, at what time he would meet her. When she had pushed herself out of the hire car and kick-started the scooter, Fanny

Carthew had been watching her. When she had reached home, pushed the scooter up the drive, Zack Jones had spied on her with his binocular lenses. She was turning her back on them, and she knew so little of the man for whom she danced.

Where the sea crashed upon the rocks at the base of the cliffs, a shag bird strutted and held out its wings, drying them in the formation of a blackened cross. It was her place.

Her father had said, "When that Italian telephoned, maybe I should have been a bit firmer with him. Perhaps I should have told him direct, 'She's not coming, there's no question of her traveling to Palermo.' Those sort of people, because they've money, they believe they can buy anything. There's a job down the drain, God knows where you're going to find another one. And what are we supposed to think, your mother and I? But I don't suppose we matter to you. You are treating us like filth, and after all the love we've given you. What are your mother and I supposed to think? You let that American into our house, you skulk out in the garden. You come back from drinking with him, but, of course, your mother and I are not told, and you stink of alcohol. Mr. Bent and Miss Carthew, they both saw you last night, with that American, but we're not told. All we're told is that 'if we talk about it we might be responsible for hurting people.' What sort of an answer is that to two loving, caring parents?"

She had felt then a depth of sadness, and the mood must have been mirrored on her face, because her father had broken his whining attack and her mother had come from the kitchen and put her arm around her daughter. It had been the only time since the American had first come that she could have wept, cried out her heart. Charley had said, head against her mother's chest, looking into the bewilderment of her father's eyes, that she was sorry. She had said that she was sorry, but that she could not tell them more. She had gone away to her room to lay out on her bed the clothes she would pack to take to Palermo. She had not told them that the hostility of the common room had given her raw satisfaction, nor had she told them of the sparse moments of delight when she gained the fast, cracked smile from Axel Moen, nor had she told them of the brutal excitement she felt at the chance to walk away from a life that was trapped on tracks of certainty. She had not told them, "I want out, I want to bloody live." She had gone into her room and laid out on the bed, beside the sausage bag, her best jeans, two denim skirts, her favorite T-shirts, her underwear from Marks and Spencer's, two pairs of trainers and her best evening shoes and a pair of sandals, the severe cotton night-dress that she had been given the last Christmas by her mother, her makeup bag and her washing-bag, two dresses for the evenings, her bear that had been in her bed for twenty years and which still carried the yellow ribbon for the safe return of the Beirut hostages, and the leather framed photograph of her mother and father from their twenty-fifth anniversary, and the airline ticket. She had checked what she had laid out. She had packed the bag.

When she could no longer see the peregrine on its perch, and no longer see the shag bird on the rock washed with the sea, when the darkness had closed over her place, she rode home and back to her small room and her packed bag, and the bungalow was like a place for the dead.

It was raining. The wind drove the rain to run in rivers on the windows. Charley settled in her seat. She didn't screw her face against the glass, she didn't look back, she didn't try to see whether her mother and her father still stood on the Totnes platform and waved. Maybe she was a proper little bitch, and maybe that was why Axel Moen thought he

could work with her. A mile out of Totnes station, as the big
train gathered speed, the world she had known and felt she
was condemned to, was slipping, blurred, away. Behind her
was the suffocation of home, the smallness of her place on
the cliff, the drear routine of the school. She had thought she
lived. The train powered toward Reading. She felt the
adrenaline thrill. At Reading she would take the shuttle bus
to Heathrow airport. She believed, at last, that she was challenged.

From where he sat at his desk, Dwight Smythe could see the
man through the glass of the partition wall and through the
open door. Axel Moen was clearing the desk that had been
given him since he had come to London. He could see him
take each sheet of paper from the drawers, fast read it, then
take the sheet to the office shredder and mince it. Each last
sheet read and shredded, so that when he boarded the plane
he would carry nothing. There were handwritten sheets and
typed sheets, and note jottings, and each one was destroyed.
Dwight's telephone rang. Ray wanting him. Ray had finally
gotten round, taken him four days, to going through the
budget figures.

He walked out of his office and across the open area.
Axel Moen was sat on his desk and turning a file's pages and
seemed not to notice him and he had to maneuver round
him, awkward, and Axel Moen never shifted to make his
way easier. There was a small bag on the floor beside the
desk, and there was an Alitalia airline ticket laid down beside
the file that Axel Moen was reading, hard concentration.

Ray hated figures. He was like a bad housewife when it
came to accounting. He went through the budget figures as
if they might bite him, and scrawled signatures on each
sheet, and didn't seem to know what he was signing. Ray
pushed the budget sheets back.

"That's a good job, thanks. Thanks for taking the weight. Is he about cleared up?"

"Given him his ticket, given him petty cash."

"What time they going?"

Dwight Smythe peered out of the Country Chief's office and across the open area toward Axel Moen, still bent over the last file.

"Oh, they don't travel together, hell, no. He doesn't hold the hand of that poor kid. She goes British Airways, I was instructed to book him with Alitalia. She doesn't get any comfort treatment. You'd have thought . . ."

"You hooked into his file?"

"I did what I was told."

"There was an area blocked off to you."

A bitter, droll response. "There was an area of the file to which I was not admitted. Not suitable for an administrative jerk."

"I hooked in, but my key code doesn't get blocked."

"That is privilege to aim at, that gives my life a goal."

"You have, Dwight, don't mind me saying it, a rare ability to get stuck in my throat so's I want to spit. He was in La Paz, Bolivia."

"I got that far—have you anything else for me, Ray?"

The Country Chief's finger, a moment, jabbed at Dwight Smythe's chest. A lowered voice. "He was in La Paz, Bolivia, that was '89 to '92. Only the best get to go down to Colombia and Peru and Bolivia. Three-year postings for wild guys."

The lip curled. "You talking about cowboys?"

"Don't push. They move into coca-leaf production country, where the *campesinos* grow the goddam stuff. There's remote *estancias* up there, with the small airstrips that the cartels use to ship the coca out for refinement in Cali or Medellín. Back in La Paz life is behind razor wire and walls and with a handgun beside the pillow and checking under the car each morning. Up-country it's serious shit. Our people have CIs out there, our people try to hit the airstrips when the CIs report there's going to be a shipment. We have to fly with the Bolivian military. A Bolivian helicopter pilot might get to earn $800 a month, he's wide open to corruption, but you have to tell him where you're flying, you have to trust him. You can't reckon to fly with your own people every day. You have to trust. You wouldn't know about that, Dwight, living that sort of stress, waiting for betrayal, and pray to your God you never learn. They were up near the Brazil border, hot news from a Confidential Informant, two Huey loads of Bolivian special forces, Axel Moen and another agent. They came in over the strip and there were three light aircraft being loaded—it's what his report in the file says. Understand, when you come in on a Huey you don't go round a couple of sweet circles for recce, you go in and you hit. It was bad, compromised, it was a fuck-up, ambush time. He, your friend Axel Moen, took a high velocity in the stomach, one of the birds was busted, three Bolivians KIA and six more WIA and that was out of twenty-two of the poor bastards."

"I never found war stories that interesting."

"Hang around. The high velocity in the stomach was flesh at the side. They hadn't much choice but to get themselves off the open strip and to the cover of the buildings. It was quite a firefight. When they got to the buildings they met up with the Confidential Informant. Couldn't do much talking with her. She was dead. She'd been gang-banged. She'd had her throat cut. She'd been nailed up, through the hands, to the inside of the door of the building. Are you hearing me? It's a hard world out there, it's better out there when you don't make emotional relationships with a Confidential Informant, it's better when you're a cold bastard."

"Thanks for checking the budget figures, Ray."

Across the open area Axel Moen fed the last sheet of paper into the shredder, and then a photograph. Dwight Smythe had only the most fleeting glimpse of it.

The photograph seemed to show a slight and inoffensive man of middle age, perhaps at a function or a wedding or a reception because there were others in suits around the small man, whose head was ringed in red chinagraph. The target? Shit, and the guy looked nothing and wouldn't have stood out in the photograph if it hadn't been for the red ring around his head. As Dwight Smythe came across the work area, Axel Moen checked that the band holding his hair was secure then picked up and pocketed his airline ticket, and heaved up his small bag.

Axel Moen waved, desultory, at Ray, and was heading for the door.

Dwight Smythe thought that once the intruder had left then he'd spray an air freshener round the office area. He didn't know the world of Confidential Informants and firefights and high-velocity flesh wounds, and hoped to God he never would. And he thought the girl from the small bungalow was an innocent.

He growled, "I'll see you sometime. Have a good flight. I'll see you, maybe—"

"Yes, if I want some expenses signed."

Gone through the door, gone and not closed it behind him.

When the aircraft had lifted, yawed and climbed, as she sat small in her seat and buckled tight, Charley had felt that she crumpled. She had thought then that she was the most minuscule of the marionette puppets locked in the cupboard behind the teacher's desk, not her desk, in class 2B.

As the aircraft cruised, on automatic flat flight, and she

sat numbed in her seat beside the honeymoon couple in their best new British Home Stores outfits, Charley felt numbed. The couple did not seem to notice her, and after she had seen the rampant love bite on the girl's lower throat and the girl was younger than Charley, she did not even consider trying to talk to them. What would they have understood of her acceptance of an invitation that would provide access? Damn-all of nothing . . . She sat far down in her seat, refused the tray of food, turned the pages of the in-flight magazine and retained not a word of the printed text, not a frame of the glossy photographs.

The aircraft lurched in flight, bounced on landing, swayed in flight and bounced again, and Charley thought briefly of the seabirds on the rocks below the cliff at her place, coming to land without faltering on the water-washed rocks. It was behind her. The honeymoon couple, had they bothered to look, but they didn't because they were huddled together in a fear of flying, would have seen at that moment that a stubborn and bloody-minded grimace had caught at her mouth. It was what she had wanted, the chance, what she had chosen, the opportunity. When the aircraft was still, when the music came on, when she had unfastened the waist strap, she strode down the aisle, a small bounce in her step. She was needed, and it had been a long time in her life since she had known the glow of importance, too damn long . . .

Charley walked briskly through the aircraft's door.

"You on secure, 'Vanni?"

"Wait out . . . You there, Bill? OK, I'm on secure."

Bill Hammond, Country Chief of the Drug Enforcement Administration, working out of an office in the Via Sardegna, to the right off the big drag of the Via Veneto, held the telephone tight in a sweaty grip. He was an old hand, heavy experience in the backpack of his career. The walls behind him and beside him had no further space to carry the commendations and the handshake photographs and the team pictures, of which the operations for Polar Cap and Green Ice were the most recent of the blitzkrieg swoops. His desk, on which his shirtsleeved elbows rested, was thick with paperwork, requests from Washington, cross-references with colleagues in London and Frankfurt and Zurich, reports from the Italian end . . . and there was the closed file bearing his handwritten legend, CODENAME HELEN. His fists sweated, always did and always would, when an operation went live.

"How's it going down there?"

"Don't give me Yankee bullshit." A sharp metallic-toned response.

"You got sun down there? May rain up here, always liable to rain when Easter's coming on."

"Don't pee on me."

"Tried to call you last night. Were you out screwing? Your age and you should watch your heart—"

"What's happening, shit on you, Bill."

He took a deep breath, he had the wide smile on his face. "She's coming. She'd have touched down about now."

"Jesu . . ." A hiss distorted by the scrambler system on the telephone. "How did he get her, how did he persuade . . . ?"

"That's my boy, you know my boy. How? I didn't get to ask him."

"Is she stupid, what is she?"

He was laughing. "Go back to your pit, 'Vanni, dream of big hips and big boobs, whatever you spend your time doing, you *carabinieri* bastards. My boy'll call you. Look after yourself, 'Vanni, stay safe. I don't know whether she's stupid, or what . . ." He replaced the telephone. He flicked the switch to disconnect the scrambler.

The Country Chief had worked with Axel Moen for two years and he reckoned, better than any man in the Administration, that he knew him. He did not know the detail of how Axel Moen had manipulated the young woman, Charlotte Parsons, but he had never doubted that face-to-face, body to body, eyeball to eyeball, Axel Moen would bring back to Italy the young woman and her baggage of access.

He would have qualified on his knowledge of the career of Axel Moen.

He would have said that he knew the backgrounder—upbringing, home base, education, work before joining the Administration, the postings of the agent before Rome—but that he was short on the motivation that drove the man.

The Country Chief had the backgrounder on Axel Moen from the headquarters confidential file . . . from his meeting two years back with the Country Chief who had run him in Bolivia . . . from sessions when he was in Washington for the strategy seminars, late at night over whiskey, with the people who had run him in New York and Miami. He could tell the backgrounder.

His man, Axel Moen, was thirty-eight years old. From immigrant Norwegian stock, farm people. Reared by his grandfather and his stepgrandmother on the Door Peninsula of Wisconsin. Complications in the rearing because his father was away with the oil industry and pneumonia had taken his mother. Lonely childhood because his grandfather was divorced before the Second World War and had brought back from Europe a second wife, Sicilian, but the community on the Door Peninsula hadn't held with divorce and hadn't taken in a stranger. Isolated. Went through the University of Wisconsin, finished in Madison with grades not quite decent. Joined the city police, reached detective, applied to join the Administration. Thought to have an "attitude problem" on the induction course at Quantico, given the benefit of the doubt because the DEA was pushing up its numbers and not looking for course failures. Sent to New York, with fluent knowledge of Sicilian dialect, to sit in the darkened rooms with the earphones on and listen to the Pizza Connection wire taps. Sent to Bolivia, good under stress circumstances, good with the locals, poor on a team operation, superficially wounded. Sent back to New York, reported as a "pain" in an office environment. Sent down to Miami, worked well in deep cover, identified by the cartels, shipped out and sharp. Sent to Rome . . . Bill Hammond had been with Axel Moen for two years, run him, knew the backgrounder. Bill Hammond, who did not lie often, would have confessed that he knew sweet fuck-all of the motivation of Axel Moen.

He himself had been a DEA man since the start. Bill Hammond was coming now, and the dates on the year's work planner behind him were the ever-present reminders, toward the day he dreaded most. He was headed for retirement, for the presentation of the carriage clock or the crystal sherry decanter, for the speeches, for the last photo opportunity of the handshake with the Director. Everybody loved a cop, nobody noticed a retired cop. He was headed for minding the grandkids. Over fourteen years of service he had gathered in the detail of the file biographies of, maybe, a couple of hundred agents—men and women he could evaluate and pass a judgment on. But he did not know the source of the drive force governing Axel Moen. OK, right, sure as hell, as his career wound toward that date on the year planner, he wanted to preside over a spectacular arrest operation and he wanted to have the Director on the telephone, personal, and he had given his authorization to the plan that was CODENAME HELEN and he had basked in an anticipation of glory, but . . .

But . . .

But the kid was now off the plane at Fiumicino. But the young woman was now through Immigration. But the kid was in a taxi and headed for central Rome.

But . . .

The kid, the young woman, was now the property of Axel Moen. And it was Bill Hammond who had authorized it, and Bill Hammond had put his goddamn name on the recommendation document that had gone to Washington and onto Herb Rowell's desk. And it was Bill Hammond who had given the big talk and enthused enough for Herb to kick it through the committee that rubber stamped hard point operations. And it was Bill Hammond who had pushed Herb to make the requisition order to the Engineering Research Facility. It was the responsibility of Bill Hammond that the kid, a young woman, was traveling in a taxi toward central Rome. Maybe it would be the glory, maybe it would lie on his conscience . . .

He was old, too old. He was tired, too tired . . . As the bag was dropped down on the floor, his eyes snapped open.

"Good flight, Axel?"

The shrug. "Same as any other."

"She's arrived, Miss Parsons?"

The glint of the eyes, tightening, narrowing. "That, Bill, is a sloppy mistake."

He was in the wrong. He blustered, "For God's sake, Axel, where are we? We are swept, cleaned, hoovered. We can talk—"

"You make a beginner's mistake. You talk a name here, perhaps you get to talk it elsewhere. A beginner's mistake can get to be a habit."

"I'm sorry."

"I don't want to hear it again, that name."

"I apologized . . . 'Vanni, he called her the *uccello da richiamo,* the decoy. We talked about the Trojan Horse. The horse had access. For 'Vanni, she's Codename Helen. Can you live with that?"

Axel, standing loosely, lit a cigarette. "It'll do."

"Where is she?"

"About checking in, I should think. You got my package?"

From the ring of keys on the chain at his belt, he unlocked the bottom drawer of the desk. He took out the padded bag. The bag had come with the cargo on a military flight to 6th Fleet from Engineering Research Facility at Quantico, then had been brought to Rome by a navy courier from Naples.

"Thanks. I'll be getting on."

Axel Moen held the package and seemed to stare at it for a moment, then dropped it into his small bag. He was turning away.

"Hey, Heather rang for you. Seems Defense Attaché's a party on tonight. I said you wouldn't be able to go, I told Heather that."

"Why'd you do that?"

The emphasis steeled his voice. "Because, Axel, I assumed that Miss Codename Helen, described by you as 'ordinary' and 'predictable,' might be stressed up, might need some care before she goes down there. Aren't you taking her to dinner?"

The shaken head. "No."

"Shouldn't you be taking her to dinner?"

Axel said, "It's good for her to be alone. I can't hold her hand, in Palermo I can't nanny her. She's got to learn to be alone."

•   •   •   •

It was as the memory had been, the memory she had guarded as a treasure, in privacy, for the last four years.

In the Piazza Augusto Imperatore, in front of the imperial tomb encased in glass, Charley could have shouted her delight. In the Piazza Popolo, surrounded by the rushing river of cars and vans and motorcycles, Charley could have screamed the news that she had returned.

A heady and excited delight caught at her, as a narcotic would have. It was to her, the solitary young woman walking the old streets and scuffing her toes on the uneven cobbles and skipping over the dog dirt and the refuse, an evening of triumph. Around her were the evening crowds of the beautiful people, beside her were the open shops of clothes and designed furniture, above her were the peeling ochre buildings. Like the renewal of a love affair. Like seeing, after long absence, a man standing and waiting for her, and running headlong to him, sprinting to jump toward him and his arms. It was one evening, it was so precious. She found again, as she had found them in the summer of 1992, the little courtyards off the Via della Dataria and the churches with the high doors off the Corso, the steps above Piazza Espagna where the Arab boys sold rubbish jewelry, the fountain of Bernini in Piazza Navona. She stood by the edifice to Vittorio Emanuele and looked the length of the wide street to the faraway, floodlit Colosseum. It was Charley's heaven . . . For three hours she ran and walked and ambled through the streets of the *centro storico,* and knew happiness again. When she was tired, bruised feet aching, Charley had to kick herself because the impulse was to find the bus stop on the Corso, or the rank of yellow taxis, and head north for the apartment on Collina Fleming. She had thought, many times, that she saw a younger woman walking with Angela Ruggerio and carrying the shopping bags, a younger woman walking with Giuseppe Ruggerio and smiling up at

him as he joked, a younger woman walking with small
Mario Ruggerio and holding his hand and laughing with his
love . . .

She took her dinner in a *ristorante,* a table to herself and
was served by grave-faced waiters a meal of pasta and lamb
with spinach, and she drank all of the gassy water and most
of a liter of wine, and she left a tip that was near to reckless
and felt her self-esteem.

She strolled from the *ristorante* the few yards back to the
hotel in which she had been booked, near to the river, off
the Via della Scrofa, near to the Parliament. Outside the narrow door of the hotel, across the alleyway, a radio blared
from an open workshop and a man in greasy vest and torn
jeans repaired motorcycles. She looked at him, she caught
his eye, she winked at him, as if it were her city. In Italian,
her best, she asked the *portiere* at the reception for coffee in
the morning and a copy of *La Stampa,* and with an impassive
expression he had answered her in English that she would
indeed have coffee and a newspaper, and she'd giggled like a
child.

Her room was tiny and stifling hot. She switched on
the TV, habit, scattered her clothes on the bed and the carpet, habit, went for a shower, habit. She let the lukewarm
water sprinkle on her upturned face and wash away the dirt
of the streets. She toweled herself hard. She would sleep
naked in the sheets. She was alone, she was free, she controlled her destiny, and she bloody well was going to sleep
naked and she looked, her opinion, bloody good naked.
She was standing before the mirror, bloody good and . . .

In the mirror, behind what she thought was her bloody
good nakedness, was the inverted television picture. A body
in a street, a bustle of photographers pressing on the body
and held back by the languid arm of a policeman. The
trousers of the body were down at the ankles, the underpants

were down at the knees, the groin was as naked as her body
and bloodstained, the bare chest of the body was slashed by
torture cuts, the mouth of the body bulged with the penis
and the testicles cut from the groin. She held the towel now
tight against her skin, as if to hide her nakedness from the eye
of the mirror and the eye of the television. The commentary
on the television said that the body was of a Tunisian man, a
pusher of hard drugs, who had tried to trade in the streets
behind the *stazione centrale* of Palermo.

Charley lay in bed. The alcohol had drained from her.
She heard each shout, each siren, each roar of a motorcycle
without an exhaust. Away in the south was the crevice of
what Axel called *la piovra,* the source of the spreading and
writhing tentacles of the octopus. Palermo.

Could an individual change anything? Answer yes or
answer no . . .

Could a single person alter a situation? Answer yes or
answer no . . .

Don't know, don't bloody know.

She put the light out. She lay huddled in her bed and
she held herself as if to protect her nakedness.

The night lay on the city of Palermo. The journalist from
Berlin yawned. Below the apartment windows, muffled
because the glass was reinforced and the shutters were closed
and the drape curtains drawn, only occasional cars passed.
The journalist yawned because he could not see that the
interview granted him, so late, would fit easily into the article commissioned by his editor.

The senator said, "You foreigners, you see La Cosa
Nostra in Sicily as a 'Specter,' you see it as a character in the
fiction of Ian Fleming. It makes me laugh, your ignorance.
The reality is a centaur, half a knight in bright armor and half
a beast. La Cosa Nostra exists because the people want it to

exist. It is in the people's life and souls and bloodstream. Consider. A boy of nineteen years has left school and if he is admitted to the local family, he gets three million a month, security, structure, culture, and he gets a pistol. But the state cannot give him the security of work, can give him only the culture of TV game shows. The state offers legality, which he cannot eat. From La Cosa Nostra he gains, most important, his self-respect. If you are a foreigner, if you follow the image of 'Specter' you will believe that if the principals of La Cosa Nostra are arrested, then the organization is destroyed. You delude yourself, and you do not comprehend the uniqueness of the Sicilian people. As strangers here you will imagine that La Cosa Nostra rules by fear, but intimidation is a minor part of the organization's strength. Don't think of us as an oppressed society, in chains, pleading for liberation. The author, Pitre, wrote, 'Mafia unites the idea of beauty with superiority and valor in the best sense of the word, and something more—audacity but never arrogance,' and there are more who believe him than deny him. To most people, most Sicilians, the government of Rome is the true enemy. You asked me, does the arrest of Riina or Santapaola or Bagarella wound the power of La Cosa Nostra? My answer, there are many who are younger, as charismatic, to take their place. Do I disappoint you? This is not the war with a military solution that you want."

The journalist blinked his eyes, tried to concentrate on what he was told and to write his longhand note.

The Capo district, the old quarter of the narrow streets and decaying buildings that had long ago been the glory of the Moorish city, was quiet. The bars were closed, the motorcycles were parked and chained, the windows were opened to admit the slight breath of the warm air. In his room Mario Ruggerio slept dreamless and a few inches from his limp and outstretched hand, on the floor beside his bed, was a loaded 9mm pistol. He slept in exhaustion after a day of figures and calculations and deals. A dead sleep that was not troubled by any threat, that he knew of, from any quarter, of imminent arrest. Lonely, without his wife, without the few that he loved, with his pistol on the floor and his calculator on the table, Mario Ruggerio snored through the dark hours.

The time of the change of the guards' shift . . . Pasquale hurried, flashing his ID at the soldiers on the street and the sergeant who watched the main entrance of the block.

Pasquale hurried because he was three minutes late for the start of his shift, and it was laid down that he should have been at the apartment a minimum of ten minutes before the shift of eight hours began. He was late for his shift because it had been the first night that his wife and the baby had been home, and he had lain beside her for three hours, awake and unable to sleep, ready to switch off the bleeped alarm the moment it sounded. The baby had been quiet in the cot at the end of the bed. His wife had lain still in the bed, buried in tiredness. He had not woken either his wife or his baby when he had slipped from under the single cotton sheet, dressed, gone on his toes from the bedroom.

The door was opened. He saw the disciplined annoyance on the face of the *maresciallo*. Pasquale muttered about his baby, coming home, asleep now, and when he shrugged his apology he expected a softening of the *maresciallo's* anger, because the older man had children, adored children, would understand. There was a cold, whispered criticism, and he squirmed the whispered response that it would not happen again.

They knew where the polished floorboards of the hallway creaked. They avoided the loose boards. They went silently past the door behind which the magistrate slept.

Sometimes they heard him cry out, and sometimes they heard him tossing, restlessly.

In the seven weeks he had known the magistrate, Pasquale thought the saddest thing he had learned of the life of the man he protected was the going of Rocco Tardelli's wife and the taking of Rocco Tardelli's children. The *maresciallo* had told him. The day after the killing of Borsellino, the month after the murder of Falcone, Patrizia Tardelli shouting, "Sicily is not worth a single drop of an honorable man's blood. Sicily is a place of vipers . . ." She had gone with her three children, as the *maresciallo* had told Pasquale, and the magistrate had not argued with her but had helped to carry their bags from the outer door to the car, and the *ragazzi* had hurried him away from the danger of the exposed pavement and not allowed him even to see the car disappear around the corner of the block. The *maresciallo* had said that afterwards after they had gone, the magistrate had not wept but had gone to work. Pasquale thought it the saddest story he knew.

In the kitchen, among the mess of the heavy vests and the machine pistols, Pasquale filled the kettle in the sink where the magistrate's supper dishes had not yet been cleaned, and made the first coffee of the day. He poured the coffee for the *maresciallo* and himself. Later he would wash the dishes in the sink. They, the *ragazzi,* were not supposed to be the servants of the magistrate, nor his messengers, nor his cooks, nor would they ever be his true friends, but it would have seemed to each of them on the detail to be merciless to sit and watch as the magistrate washed his own dishes, prepared his food alone.

Pasquale asked what was the schedule of the day.

The *maresciallo* shrugged as if it were of no relevance.

"To Ucciardone . . . ?"

Again the shrug, as if it were of no importance whether they went again to the prison.

The forehead of Pasquale wrinkled in puzzlement. It was what had confused him the night before, when he had sat in front of the late-evening television after his wife had gone to their bed and the baby to the new cot. He did not understand.

"The man who tries to be a *pentito,* he was very hard with him. All right, so we are not supposed to hear, to listen, but it is impossible not to hear what is said. 'I can tell you where is Mario Ruggerio.' Nothing happens. It is left. Why? Ruggerio is the biggest catch, Ruggerio is the target of Tardelli, Ruggerio is of international status. Am I very simple?"

"Simple and naïve and with much to learn." There was a weariness in the expression of the *maresciallo.* He held the coffee cup in two hands, as if one hand on the cup might have shaken and spilled the coffee. "There is a saying on the island, 'A man warned is a man saved.' Dr. Tardelli was warned long ago, and he has ignored the warning. But, important, he has not only been warned by La Cosa Nostra, he has been warned also by those who should be his colleagues. He has the quality of honesty, and it is that honesty that humiliates his colleagues. There is no serious effort to attack the enemy, the colleagues stand and watch from safety, and they wait to see Tardelli fall on his arse. How many in the Palace of Justice make certain, Jesu, so certain, that an investigation into La Cosa Nostra never hits their desks? Too many. He is accused of the personality cult, of judicial communism, of denigrating the reputation of Sicily. He is accused by those who have ambition and vanity and envy, but who do not have honesty. Which judge can he trust, which prosecutor, which magistrate, which *carabiniere,* which police officer? Pasquale, can he trust you?"

"That is insane."

"Insane? Really? A judge in Calabria is arrested, mafia collusion. The head of the *squadra mobile* is arrested, mafia association. What is your price, Pasquale, if your wife is threatened or your baby? If a prime minister can be bought, what is the price of a young policeman with a wife and baby? Everywhere is the contamination of the bastards. The former head of International Affairs of the American Justice Department is charged with working for the Colombians. In Germany it is reported that new levels of corruption in public life have been reached. Maybe he trusts us because we ride with him, because we would die with him. He does not trust his colleagues."

"Tell me."

"Each time he offers protection to a *pentito* he has to be certain of the genuineness of the man. He may be dealing with a 'placed' man, he may be sitting opposite a liar. If he diverts resources, the weight of an investigation, in the direction of a 'placed' man or a liar, then he will be weakened. If he is weakened, then he is isolated. If he is isolated, then he is dead. It is necessary for him to go one short step at a time because he walks through a mine field. Heh, what would you prefer, boy? Would you prefer to be directing traffic in Milan?"

The coffee Pasquale drank was cold. He stood. He took off his jacket, and rolled up his sleeves, and ran hot water into the sink and started to wash the magistrate's dishes.

Past two in the morning . . . The night-duty manager reflected his annoyance at being called by the porter from his office and his catnap. He studied the computer screen.

"Difficult to help you, Sergeant. That's nearly a week ago. We've had 827 guests through since that night. All right, the date you want . . . 391 guests in residence. Bear with me. Are you sure this cannot wait till the morning?"

But Harry Compton, after another evening beavering at the solicitor's files and archives, had chosen to visit the hotel in Portman Square on his way home. It was what was called, a bullshit expression, a "window of opportunity." In the morning he would be back at the solicitor's papers, so, definitely, it could not wait.

"Well, of the 391 residents, twenty-one declared Italian passports. Wait again, I'll check the details . . ."

The fingers flitted over the computer's keys.

"You said, 'resident in Palermo.' No, can't help. Of the Italian passport holders that night, none declared residency in Palermo. You're being economical. Could you tell me why Fraud Squad is here at this wretched hour?"

He felt the blow, like a punch. He swore under his breath.

"Are you sure?"

"That's what I said, friend—none lists residence in Palermo, Sicily."

"What about the dinner bill? Table 12 in the restaurant, did one of them sign?"

"No can help. That's a restaurant matter. The restaurant's closed, has been cleared for ninety minutes. Have to come back in the morning."

"Get it open."

"I beg your pardon."

Harry Compton, detective sergeant in SO6, reckoned he loathed the languid little creep across the reception counter. "I said, get it open."

They went into the dim-lit restaurant. A *sous* waiter was found, smoking in the kitchen. The keys were produced. A drawer was opened. The receipts and order bills were taken from the drawer. There had been eighty-three diners on the evening that concerned him. He took the

bundle of receipts and order bills to a table and asked to be
brought a beer . . .

It was near the bottom of the pile, sod's law, the sheet of
paper for table twelve, the printout sheet with the illegible
signature and the digits of the room number of the resident.
He gulped the beer. He strode with the sheet of paper back
to the reception desk and trilled the bell hard for the night-
duty manager.

"Room 338, I want that gentleman's card."

"Are you entitled to that information?"

"I am—and I am also entitled to report to Public Health
that a dirty little creature was smoking in your kitchen."

The bill was printed out for him, with the check-in
card carrying the personal details of the guest who had occupied room 338. It was an afterthought. Should have been
routine, but he was so goddam tired. The night-duty manager was disappearing back to his office.

"Oh, and I require a list of the telephone numbers
called from that room. Yes, now, please."

"Did you go back, where you were before?"

"I did."

"Never worth it, going back. It seems unimportant,
what was once special."

"I walked from the block along past the tennis club and
into Piazza Fleming. It was the way that I used to take small
Mario to the school bus."

"Going back is time wasted, sentimental."

"If you have any other criticisms to make could we do
them in a job lot and get them over with, Mr. Moen? It gets
to be tedious, your criticism."

If Charley annoyed him then, he did not show it. If she
amused him, he did not show it. They were by the foot-
bridge, high on the promenade above the water, across from

the fortress of Sant' Angelo. She had been at the rendezvous
on time and then she had waited. It had been ten minutes
after she had come to the bridge that she had seen him,
coming easily through a traffic flow, stopping then skipping
forward, confident. He'd told her that he had watched her
through those ten minutes and he'd satisfied himself that she
was not followed. He hadn't made a big deal of the fact that,
his opinion, she might have been followed, just said it and
unsettled her. She gazed down into the slow movement of
the green-brown water below.

"Are you going to ask me what I did last night?"

"No."

So, Charley did not tell Axel Moen about walking the
streets of the *centro storico* and dousing herself in nostalgia.
Nor did she tell him of sitting, anarchic and alone, in a *ristorante* and eating till her stomach bulged and drinking the
best portion of a liter of house wine. She did not tell him
that she had showered, walked naked from the bathroom
and seen on the television the picture of a man's body in
Palermo whose balls were in his mouth, and didn't tell that
the night had been a long nightmare.

"What did *you* do last night?"

The dry voice, as if reciting from a catalog. "Went to a
party."

"Could you have taken me?"

"I had someone to go with."

He stood beside her. He held a padded paper bag in his
hand. The labels had been pulled from it. She saw the great
tree logs and the big branches, debris of the winter floods,
now marooned against the piers of the bridge. She looked
up at the fortress of Sant' Angelo. She had been round it,
alone, in the summer of 1992, tramped the narrow corridors
and climbed the worn steps and marveled at the symmetry
of its architects, so many centuries ago, in creating the per-

fect circular shape. It had been then a place of friendship.

"I'm here, you're here, so what happens now?"

"You're on board?"

"Of course I'm bloody on board."

"You don't want to step off?"

She stood her full height. He wasn't looking at her. He was gazing away, distant, toward the dome, misted and gray, of St. Peter's. She took his arm, a fistful of the arm of his windcheater, and she jerked him round to face her.

"For Christ's sake—I came, didn't I?"

He seemed to hesitate, as if he were troubled. Then, he launched. "Terrorism, Charley, is spectacular. Terrorism makes headlines. You know about the bombs in the City of London, you know about Oklahoma City and the World Trade Center, and about hijackings. You know about the charisma of a Che Guevara or a Carlos or an Adams or a Meinhof because the ideology and profile of those people are plastered all over your television. They don't count. For all the resources we throw against them they are minor league. But you, Charley, you don't know the name of an internationally relevant criminal. It's like HIV and cancer. HIV, the terrorist, gets the attention and the resources, while cancer, the crime boss, busies itself with the serious damage, but quietly. With an ideology only of greed, organized crime is the cancer that chews at our society, and it should be taken out at source with a knife. In the ideology of greed there is no mercy if an obstacle—you, Charley—gets in the way . . ."

A small and weak grin. "Is this your effort to scare me?"

"When you're alone, when you're frightened, then you should know what you've gotten into. Down in Sicily, fair to assume, there's a hundred different programs, slants, angles of an operation running. You are one in a hundred. That's your importance. You offer a one-in-a-hundred chance of, maybe, getting up alongside the target. You are Codename Helen, that is the name—"

She snorted and the color ran back into her face. She laughed at him. "Helen? Helen of Troy? Trojan Horse and all that? That is really original—did a genius think up that one?"

"It's what you are, Codename Helen." He flushed.

"What's inside the walls? Who's hiding in Troy?"

"Don't play jokes, Charley, don't. There is a family in the town of Prizzi, that's inland from Palermo. It's a mean little place stuck on the rock. OK, Prizzi is the home of a *contadino's* family. The *contadino* is Rosario and he is now aged eighty-four. His wife is Agata, now aged eighty-three. Rosario and Agata have produced six children. The children are Mario, the eldest, sixty-two . . . Salvatore, sixty, in prison . . . Carmelo, fifty-nine, simple, lives with his parents . . . Cristoforo, would be fifty-seven, dead . . . Maria, fifty-one, married and an alcoholic . . . the youngest, Giuseppe, forty-two, the big gap because old Rosario was called away between 1945 and 1954 to spend time in Ucciardone prison. The name of that family from Prizzi is Ruggerio . . ."

He flicked a cigarette from the Lucky Strike packet. She locked her eyes on the cupola of St. Peter's, as if she thought the mist-shrouded image might strengthen her.

"The family is *mafiosi,* down to the base of its spine, right to the bottom of the root of the weed. But nothing is as it seems. The family has played a long game, which is the style of La Cosa Nostra, to play long and patient. Giuseppe, bright child, was sent by his eldest brother away from Prizzi, out of Sicily, to university in Rome. On to a school of business management in Geneva. To an Italian bank in Buenos Aires. There were connections, favors were called in, work in Rome for one of those discreet little banks handling

Vatican funds. Did he seem to you, Giuseppe, to be the son of a *contadino*? Did he tell you about a peasant family? Did he?"

Charley had no answer. Her teeth ground at her bottom lip.

"I said that the family could play a long game. Only a very few in Palermo, and none in Rome, would know that Giuseppe is the brother of Mario Ruggerio. I don't know how many hundreds of millions of dollars Mario Ruggerio is worth. I know what he needs. Mario Ruggerio needs a banker, a broker, an investment manager, in whom he can place absolute trust. It's all a matter of trust down there. Trust is held in the family. The family has the man to wash, rinse, spin and dry their money. The family is everything. The family meets, the family gathers, and the family does not feel the danger of betrayal. Then, and it's rare, the family makes a mistake. The mistake is a letter written by Angela to a former nanny/child-minder—I have a friend down there and you don't need his name and you don't need his agency, and because it's the way in Sicily he does not share with colleagues what he learns, and he learned of the link between Giuseppe and Mario Ruggerio, and he started to run a sporadic surveillance on pretty little Giuseppe, and the jackpot bonus came up when he intercepted the letter, a mistake. I don't know how often that family meets, no idea. I know that the family will come together, that Mario Ruggerio will need, a deep need because he is Sicilian, to be in the bosom of his family. They all have it, the evil, heartless bastards, a syrup streak of sentimentality for the family. You're there, Charley, you're a part of the family, you're the little mouse that nobody notices, you're at the far end of the room, and watching the kids and keeping them quiet, you're access . . ."

She stared at the cupola of St. Peter's. She thought it a

place of sanctity and safety, and she could remember standing in the great square on a Sunday morning and feeling humbled by the love of the pilgrims for the Holy Father, minuscule on the balcony.

"A man from Agrigento has disappeared. He led one of the three principal families of La Cosa Nostra. It is assumed he is dead. There is a man from Catania, the power in the east of the island. There is Mario Ruggerio. They do not share power in Sicily, they fight for power with the delicacy of rats in a bucket. Mario Ruggerio is one stage away from the overall command of La Cosa Nostra. One step away from taking the title of *capo di tutti capi*. One killing away from becoming the most influential figure in international organized crime. The target of Codename Helen is Mario Ruggerio."

She felt weak, pitiful. "Is it possible, listen to me, Christ, hear me, is it possible for one person, me, to change anything?"

He said, "If I didn't think so, I would not have come for you."

He took her hand. Without asking, and without explanation, he unhooked the fastening of her wristwatch. The watch was gold. It was the most expensive thing that she owned. It had been given to her by her father, three weeks before he had known of his redundancy, for her twenty-first birthday. He dropped the gold watch, as if it were a bauble and worthless, into his trouser pocket. He still held her hand, a strong grip that was without affection. The envelope was laid on top of the stonework above the flowing river. He took from it a bigger watch, a man's watch, the sort of watch that young men wore, a scuba diver's watch. He told her to think of a story as to why she wore such a watch. He slipped it over the narrowness of her fist, onto the narrowness of her wrist. The strap was of cold expanding metal. He showed her, exactly and methodically, which buttons activated the watch's mechanism, and which button activated the panic tone . . . Christ . . . He told her the life of the cadmium battery in the watch. He told her the signals she should send. He told her the range of the signal of the panic tone. He told her that the UHF frequency would be monitored twenty-four hours a day in Palermo. He told her when she should make a test transmission. He let her hand drop.

"When he comes, if he comes, to meet with his family, Mario Ruggerio, you activate the tone. The only other time that you use it is if you believe that your physical safety is endangered. Do you understand?"

"Where will you be?"

"Close enough to respond." She saw the strength in his face, the bold build of his chin, the assurance of his mouth. She reflected that she was placing her life in that strength.

"You promise?"

"I promise. You have a good journey."

She flared, enough of playing the small and pathetic girl. "Wait a minute, Mr. Axel bloody Moen, how often do we meet?"

Casual. "Every so often."

"That's not good enough. Where do we meet?"

"I'll find you."

He walked away. She watched him go over the bridge, toward the fortress of Sant' Angelo. She felt the tight cold metal of the strap on her wrist.

5

HE HAD SAID, back in Devon, that she should travel from Rome to Palermo by train. He had explained, chill and staccato, that the most vulnerable time for an agent was in the sea-change hours of going from overt to covert. If she boarded a plane, he had said, a journey like Rome to Palermo, she would step over the gulf in an hour. Better, he'd said, to spread the transition time. Better to use a dozen hours and have the chance to reflect on the sea change and the gulf that was to be crossed.

Charley had taken the train from the *terminii* in the early evening, pushed her way with a rare aggression through the crowds on the concourse. She had booked the sleeper, a single berth, and not cared what it cost because the Ruggerios would pay for it. She had heaved her bag along the corridor and dumped it inside the little compartment of the snake-length train that was alongside those that would leave later for Vienna and Paris. She had chewed on a ham-and-tomato roll, revolting, and sipped from a bottle of mineral water, warm, and watched from the train as the dusk gathered on isolated farmhouses and avenues of high pines and a long, ruined viaduct from the dawn of history.

She had reflected, as Axel Moen had said she should.

She had considered the distance at which he kept himself. She knew nothing of what lay beneath the exterior of his face, beneath his clothes, nothing of his mind. She had not met before, ever, a person of such sealed privacy. She thought, and it perked her up, that he kept a distance as if he were a little afraid of her. So she wanted to believe that she was important to him, that she was the final piece that made the puzzle complete. It was good to feel that. And, alone in the train, the rumble of the wheels below her, rushing south, the darkness of the night beyond the window, she felt a sense of pride. She had been chosen, she had been challenged, she was wanted. She had lain on the made bed and the glow of excitement had coursed in her. She was needed. She was important . . . She had slept, as if an arrogance and an ignorance had caught her.

She had slept through the shunting of the train onto the ferry at Villa S. Giovanni on the Calabrian coast and the docking of the ferry at Messina, slept a dead and dreamless sleep.

The knocking on the door woke Charley. She had slept in her T-shirt and her knickers. She was decent, but she wrapped the blanket around her as she unlocked the door and took the tray of coffee from the attendant. She closed the door and locked it again. She set the tray down and went to the window and released the blind. Charley saw Sicily.

The journalist from Berlin was awake early. He boasted a tidy mind. He believed it important, at the first sober opportunity, to transfer the essentials of the interview from notebook to laptop memory. He had ordered an early call, before the pace of the city moved, because he had first to dissect the notes he had taken over dinner and two bottles of Marsala wine, and the notes would be a mess and scrawled in confusion. He had dined with the mayor of a small town on the west coast down from Palermo. He had anticipated a ringing cry for action against La Cosa Nostra from a man whose father had been killed because he had denounced an evil. Sitting on his bed in his pajamas, the ache in his head, he had read back his notes.

"Quote Pirandello (paraphrase)—draw the distinction between the seeing and the being, the fiction and the reality—the fiction is police activity, ministers and policemen and magistrates on TV, prisoners paraded in front of cameras, the cry that the mafia is crumbling, FICTION. The mafia is not weakened, stronger than ever, REALITY. No serious commitment by the state against the mafia—think what it is like to be Sicilian, abandoned by central government, not supported, to be alone. No big victory is possible—white sheets on balconies after the killing of Falcone as an expression of public disgust, but the disgust is slipping, collective anger is gone. The thread of the mafia is woven through every institution, every part of life—always the stranger must realize that he does not know who he talks to—being a *mafioso* can mean a man belongs to the upper strata of society, does not mean that he is a crude killer. Nobody, NOBODY, knows the depth of mafia infiltration into public life. For the stranger, NEVER BE UN-GUARDED . . ."

The Country Chief drove Axel Moen to Fiumicino for the first flight of the day going south to Palermo, and parked, and went with his man to check-in.

They walked together toward the center of the concourse; there were a few minutes before the flight would be called. Should have talked in the car, but they hadn't, and it had been time lost, but the traffic had been heavy and the Country Chief had reckoned he needed all of his start-of-the-day concentration to keep himself from shunting with the bastards around him who were weaving and overtaking and braking. The Country Chief shouldn't have left the loose ends to the concourse.

"You OK?"

"I feel fine."

"The archaeology . . . ?"

"It'll do and it'll get better."

"You get a shooter from 'Vanni."

"Yes, 'Vanni says he'll fix me a shooter."

Too old and too tired, and the Country Chief thought he played the part of the fussing mother well. "It's shared with 'Vanni, only him."

"Maybe it has to be shared with a magistrate. That guy, Rocco Tardelli, maybe we share with him. He's a good man."

"He's a friend, useful, but don't . . . You know it hurts me, but you put ten Italian law enforcement people in a room, and you share. If you share, you should trust. Do you know everything about them? Do you know which of them's wife's uncle's cousin is going after a construction contract to build a school and needs a favor from the local boss? So you trust none of them. That bugs me, the lack of trust, it makes for corrosive suspicion, but you cannot take the chance."

"I know that, Bill."

"Because it's her life."

In front of him was the face of Axel Moen, a wall of granite, shielding whatever feelings the damned man had.

"I figured that."

"You know what I want?"

"Keep it quick, Bill."

"I want that bastard, I want Mario Ruggerio nailed, and I want it to be by our efforts. Not a big cooperative, but by our efforts. If it's us that nails him, then I believe, what Headquarters says, we can swing the extradition business. I want him shipped Stateside, I want him put into Supermax. I want him to breathe the sweet air of Colorado. I want him in one of those concrete tombs. I want him to know that for sending over all that filth into our country there's a downside. I want . . ."

"I'll stay close, Bill."

"Look after that kid, damn you, with your life."

Axel shrugged and walked toward Departure.

She was not trained, she was not coached. But she did not think herself stupid.

Charley was dressed. She leaned against the grimed glass of the window and the train lurched slowly along. She was gazing inland. She thought that she did not have to be trained to recognize, in that country, how a corpse could remain hidden and how a fugitive could stay free. On and on, displayed from her window, were the steep and harsh-cut rainwater gullies that were overgrown with coarse grass and scrub that ran from the track up to the hills. She had bought from the English-language bookshop on Via Babuino, the previous day, after he had left her, a guidebook to Sicily. The book had a chapter on the island's history. In the gullies there could have been the corpse of a Moorish invader, of a Bourbon soldier, of a Fascist official, of a Roman policeman, and it would never be found, it would be food for foxes and rats. Among the scrub were dark-set, small caves, and there were the roofless ruins of peasant homes and the crumbled shelters where once a farmer had put his goats or his sheep, and the ruins and the shelters could have been hiding places for fugitives from centuries back to the present moment. Above the gullies and the caves and the ruins, beyond the hills, were the climbing mountains that reached to the clouds. A great emptiness that was broken only rarely by the white scars of winding switchback roads. A ruthless and hard place . . . A body, her body, dumped into a gully, and she would never be found. A fugitive, Mario Ruggerio, hiding in the caves and ruins, and he would never be found.

She murmured, private to herself, as she fingered the

heavy watch on her wrist, "Learning, Charley, learning bloody fast."

She came away from the window. She brushed her teeth. She tidied her sausage bag. She reflected, as Axel Moen had told her to.

They had circled Catania, then come in to land through the early mist. He could see the foothills to the west, but not the summit of Etna, which the cloud held.

He had told her that going back was time wasted, was sentimental.

Palermo, yes, many times, but it was twenty-one years since Axel Moen had been at the Fontanarossa airport of Catania. They were old now and they were living far up the Door Peninsula, up between Ephraim and Sister Bay, and eking out their last days and weeks and months. It was twenty-one years since his grandfather and his step-grandmother had brought him to the airport at Catania. Only the name to remember it by because there were new buildings and a new tower and new acreage of concrete. On Arne Moen's retirement he had brought his wife, Vincen-zina, and his grandson to Catania and Sicily. Didn't matter if he cared not to think on it . . . Most of the emotion juices Axel was ready for, could control. Going through the airport at Catania, the juices worked on him and hurt him. Arne Moen had come to Sicily in 1943, a captain in George Patton's invasion army, and he'd been the idiot who'd drunk too much brandy for his system one night and had fallen in the gutter while swaying back to the commandeered villa at Romagnolo and broken his goddam arm. The army had leapfrogged onto the Italian mainland and left Arne Moen behind to nurse his plaster-cased arm. Taken into AMGOT, given a job with the bureaucracy of the Allied Military Government, and found himself in a minor heaven as a minor god controlling gasoline supplies and transportation between Corleone and the road junction at Piana degli Albanesi. It had provided what his grandfather called an "opportunity." The story of the "opportunity" had been told in self-pity and with moist eyes at the Catania airport at the end of the week's tour, as if it were necessary for a seventeen-year-old to know a truth.

The emotions wounded Axel because the "opportunity" was corruption. He did not care to remember because the "opportunity" was in the black-market siphoning of gasoline and the taking of bribes in return for permission to run lorries down to Palermo. The money from the corruption and the black market and the bribes had gone back to the Door Peninsula and it had paid, dirty money, for his grandson's education at the university in Madison, and had paid for the house and the fields and orchards between Ephraim and Sister Bay. One day, maybe not too long, because Arne Moen was now in his eighty-fifth year, and Vincenzina Moen was in her seventy-eighth year, he would have to decide what to do with a legacy of dirty money . . . After the tour of the battlefields, precious little fighting done, and the visit to the house in Corleone from which the minor god had run his racket, after the cloying visit to Vincenzina's peasant family, after the journey had come to its end, the story of the "opportunity" had been told.

For Axel it was a sharp memory. He had sat between his grandfather and his stepgrandmother in the departure lounge at Catania. His grandfather had sniveled the story of criminality, and his stepgrandmother had stared straight ahead as though she heard nothing and saw nothing and knew nothing. He thought, striding that early morning through the airport, that the telling of the story of corruption had withered his innocence. He had sworn to himself, with the authority of his seventeen years, that he would never again allow innocence to cut him . . . Where he'd sat, between his grandfather and his stepgrandmother twenty-one years before, was now a left-luggage area. What he had learned when his innocence had ended was to trust no man because even a man he loved had a price. Shit . . .

Axel Moen went to the Avis counter for his hire car.

Charley jumped down onto the low platform.

She reached back to drag out her sausage bag.

She was carried forward in the restless rush of passengers surging from the train. Her gaze raked the barrier, and she saw them. She recognized Angela Ruggerio, a little thicker in the hips and a little heavier at the throat and still beautiful, and holding the new baby and holding the hand of Francesca who had been the baby in the happiness summer of 1992, and bending to speak in small Mario's ear and pushing him forward. The boy ran against the flow and came to her, and Charley dropped her bag and held out her arms and let him jump at her and hug her. She held the son of the man who washed and rinsed and spun and dried the money, the nephew of the man who was an evil, heartless bastard. She had arrived, she had gained access. Small Mario fought out of her arms and took the straps of the sausage bag in his hands and scraped it after her along the platform. Charley gave the Judas kiss to Angela Ruggerio and her hands were squeezed. It was a desperate love that she saw in Angela Ruggerio, as if she were a true friend, as if she represented deliverance from misery. She tugged the cheek of Francesca in play and the little girl laughed and thrust her arms round Charley's neck.

"You are very good for time, Charley. I do not think you are a minute late."

She glanced down at her watch, the heavy watch of a

diver, instinct. The minute hand of the watch pointed directly to the button for the panic tone.

"No, it is wonderful, we were exactly on time."

Axel took the *autostrada* route across the heart of the island. He was calm. He cruised in the small Fiat hire car along the dual-carriageway A19 through the central mountains, past the small vineyards that had been hacked from the handkerchiefs of ground available for cultivation among the rocks, past the herds of thin goats and leggy sheep that were watched by men with leathered faces and by restless dogs. He stopped at the old hill city of Enna, long enough to see the crooked lines in yellow and orange and ochre of successive mountain ranges to the north, not long enough for the culture of the buildings, sufficient time for a cup of sharp and hot coffee. On down toward the coast, and he allowed the lorries and cars to race past him, as if he had no ambition to compete with speed. When he reached the coast, could see the blue haze of the sea, he swung west for Terminii Imerese, and he drove toward Palermo. Between the road and the shore were orange groves and lemon orchards, holiday complexes that were shuttered and barred because the season had not yet started . . . A prosecutor had talked of "a power system, an articulation of power, a metaphor of power and a pathology of power . . ." The sun burned the road, the light beat up from the tarmac into his face. Away out on the water were small boats, drifting distant from each other, in which lonely fishermen stood and cast small nets, and he saw old men walking on the gray pebble beaches with long shore fishing rods on their shoulders . . . A judge had talked of "a global, unitary, rigidly regimented and vertical structure governed from the top down by a *cupola* with absolute powers over policy, money, life and death . . ." He felt a calmness because he was not deluded by the peace of the mountains and the peace of the seascape. He drove through Bagheria and Villabate and took the ring road to the south of the city, as if ignoring the close-set tower blocks of Palermo, and then he climbed the switchback road that was signed to Monreale. He was close to his destination.

At the apartment in the Giardino Inglese the morning was spent packing Angela's clothes and the children's bags.

She was told about Mondello and a villa by the sea, the holiday home for the summer. The description of the holiday villa, given by Angela Ruggerio, was curt, and Charley saw already a wan tiredness and distraction about the face and movements of her employer. It was hard for Charley to gauge her mood, but the woman was a changed person: the confidence and humor of four years before were gone, as if the spirit of her were crushed. It was, Charley, thought, as if a wall had been erected. She spent most of that morning in the rooms used by small Mario and Francesca, taking the necessary clothes from drawers and the favored toys from cupboards, but when she had wandered into the principal bedroom and not knocked she had seen Angela at the drawer of a bedside table, taking two pill bottles out, and she had seen a little moment of almost panic because the bottles were noticed, and then Angela had dropped them into a bag. Charley had smiled in embarrassment and said something inane about the number of shirts that small Mario would need, and the little moment had passed.

Charley and small Mario were given the work of taking the bulging bags and cases down in the elevator to the underground parking area. When she came back up and walked into the grandness of the apartment Angela was standing in the center of the living area and was gazing down at a blemish in the beauty of the embroidered carpet and frowning. Then, aware of Charley in the doorway, she replaced the frown by a fixed and tense smile.

The last bags were carried out. The door was locked. In the car park, the bags and cases were pushed into the big trunk of a Mercedes saloon.

Charley sat in the back and held tight to the baby and Francesca cuddled against her as if, so soon, a friendship had been made. They were out of the city, the tower blocks were behind them, they were under the steep might of the Pellegrino mountain, they were passing the first whores of the day waiting in their miniskirts and plunging blouses at the entrances to the picnic sites, when it struck Charley. He had not been mentioned. Dr. Giuseppe Ruggerio had not been spoken of. It was not for her to ask questions. She should not probe, she had been told, and she should not push and she should not display curiosity.

They drove along the slack crescent road that skirted the beach at Mondello. They went through the narrow streets of the old town. They stopped at big iron gates with black painted steel plates to deny a voyeur's inspection of what lay behind them. Angela slapped the horn of the Mercedes. The gates were opened by an old man, who ducked his head in respect and she drove up a hidden drive, past flowers and shrubs, and braked hard in front of the villa.

She had arrived. Codename Helen was in place. She had taken the opportunity of access. She was the horse, she was treachery. Angela, remote and unsmiling, carrying the baby, went ahead and fished the keys from her bag as she walked to the patio of the villa. Small Mario and Francesca ran after their mother. Charley opened the trunk of the Mercedes and started to heave out the family's bags and cases. From by the gate, leaning on a broom, standing among the fallen winter's leaves, the old man, the gardener, watched her . . . She felt small and alone and so cast off.

• • •

"There is no change." The magistrate shrugged as if uninterested. "You tell me what you know, when you have told me then I evaluate, when I have evaluated what you tell me then I decide on a recommendation, when I have decided on a recommendation then the committee will determine if you should be given the privileges of the Special Protection Program . . ."

Pasquale leaned against the door. The Beretta 9mm pistol was against his hip, and the machine gun was draped on a strap and cut into the small of his back.

"I need the guarantee."

The prisoner was hunched over the table and his furtive eyes roamed around the bare walls, and his fingers shook as they guided his cigarette to his mouth. Outside the door, muffled from passage along the concrete-faced corridor, deadened by the distance from the car park, were the shouts and jeers of the men kicking a football, the men who guarded the magistrate and a judge who worked that day at Ucciardone. From the door Pasquale craned to hear the response. The magistrate made the gesture, opened his hands. "If you do not tell me what you know then you will serve a sentence of life imprisonment for murder. It is not for me to offer guarantees."

The prisoner had requested the second interview. Word had again been passed. The prisoner had again been brought by the secret and circuitous route to the bare-walled room. The wretch trembled. Pasquale knew the oath that he would have sworn. In a locked room filled with already sworn Men of Honor, the darkness of night outside to conceal their gathering: "Are you ready to enter La Cosa Nostra? Do you realize there will be no going back? You enter La Cosa Nostra with your own blood and you can leave it only by shedding more of your own blood." Pasquale thought the wretch trembled because he would then have been asked in which hand he would hold a gun, and the trigger finger of that hand would have been pricked with a thorn sufficient to draw blood, and the blood would have been smeared on a paper image of the Virgin Mary at the Annunciation, and the paper would have been lit and it would have been dropped, burning into the palm of the wretch's hand and he would have recited the oath and then condemned himself if he betrayed it—"May my flesh burn like this holy image if I am unfaithful to La Cosa Nostra." The wretch would have sworn it, with blood and with fire, and now he squirmed.

"For Ruggerio, I get the guarantee for Mario Ruggerio . . . ?"

The magistrate's fingers drummed on the table. Pasquale watched him. The shoulders were rounded, the chin was slack, there seemed no evidence of the core strength of the man, but the *maresciallo* had spoken, musing, of his courage and quoted as if it were relevant to this man, too, the saying of the dead Falcone, "The brave man dies only once, the coward dies a thousand times each day." Pasquale listened. If they were close to Mario Ruggerio, if they threatened the freedom of Mario Ruggerio, they were all endangered—not only Rocco Tardelli's life was hazarded, but also the lives of the *ragazzi* who stood in front of Tardelli and beside him and behind him.

"If, through your efforts, Mario Ruggerio were to be arrested, then I would recommend that you be given the privileges of the Special Protection Program."

The silence hung between the bare walls, eddied with the cigarette smoke toward the single fluorescent strip. Because Pasquale knew the oath that the wretch had sworn, the depths of the oath made with fire and blood, he shuddered. The *maresciallo,* sitting behind the wretch, leaned forward to hear better. The magistrate scratched at the head of a pimple on the side of his nose as if it were not a matter of importance to him. There were tears in the prisoner's eyes.

"He is in the Capo district of Palermo . . ."

"Now, today?"

"I heard it a little time ago, Mario Ruggerio is in the Capo district."

"How long is a 'little time ago'?"

"A few months ago, in the Capo district."

The hardening of the accent of the magistrate, leaning forward across the table and allowing the smoke to brush his face. "How many months ago?"

"A year ago."

Pasquale sagged. There was a sardonic and bruised smile on the face of the *maresciallo*. Rocco Tardelli did not imitate them, did not sag and did not smile. He held the prisoner's eyes.

"Where, 'a year ago,' in the Capo district was Mario Ruggerio?"

"He used a bar . . ."

"Where was the bar in the Capo district that was used by Mario Ruggerio?"

"He used a bar in the street between the Via Sant'Agostino and the Piazza Beati Paoli. Several times he used the bar, but once he ate almond cake in the bar and his stomach was disturbed. He said, I was told, it was a shit bar that served shit almond cake."

"That is what you were told?"

"Yes . . ."

The prisoner's head was bowed. An oath was broken, an oath made on blood and fire was fractured. The tears ran brisk on the wretch's cheeks.

The magistrate said, serene, "May I recapitulate what you have said? It is important that we understand the information you pass me. In return for eighteen million *lire* a month, and for your freedom, and for the ending of the legal process against you that is a charge of murder, in return for that you offer me the information that a friend told you that Mario Ruggerio had mild food poisoning in a bar in the Capo district."

The blurted response. "He would only have used a bar in the Capo district if he lived there."

"If he lived there a year ago." So patient. "That is everything?"

The prisoner's head rose. He looked directly into the face of the magistrate. He wiped the tear rivers from his cheeks. "It is enough to kill me."

Later, after the prisoner had been taken with his face hidden by a blanket back across the yard to the medical center, after they had called a halt to the football game in the car park and loaded into the Alfa and the chase car, after they had emerged from the safety of the perimeter fence of the Ucciardone prison, after they had hit the traffic and blasted a way clear with the siren, Rocco Tardelli leaned forward and spoke quietly into the ear of the *maresciallo*. Pasquale drove fast, using brakes and gears and accelerator, and listened.

"It was of importance, or not of importance? I have my own opinion, but I wish for yours. Or is it not fair for me to ask you? I believe him. I believe Mario Ruggerio would indeed inhabit a rat hole like the Capo district. He has no use for luxury, for gold taps, for silken sheets and suits from Armani. He is a *contadino,* and the peasant cannot change. He would be happy there, he would feel reassured there, in safety. But it was a year ago. A summer has gone, an autumn, and a winter, and now I have to deliberate as to whether to use my authority to divert pressed resources to the investigation of information that is stale. We have to pick at crumbs and pluck at straws as if we starved and as if we drowned . . . It is not fair for me to ask you, I must walk my own road."

●　　●　　●

They stood back and they watched.

The swing was good and the pivot was good and the contact was good and the flight was good. The ball flew. Before the ball had landed Giuseppe Ruggerio bent to pick up the plastic tee peg, then he went forward and reached down for the divot, cleanly removed like a dropped hairpiece. Now he glanced up to see the final bouncing of his ball on the sand ground of the fairway, then turned to replace his divot.

They murmured as they watched.

"He's useful, can't take that from him."

"Useful, but, God, he doesn't hide that he knows it . . ."

"Where did you meet up, Giles? Where did your paths cross?"

Giles Blake heaved up his bag. The Italian, his guest, was already striding off down the grassed avenue between the dull winter heather and the broken-down bracken. "I've known Peppino forever . . . You know there's too many generalizations about the old Italian. Get a good one and you've the best you could meet anywhere. He's a dream to know. He's decisive, knows what he wants. Better than that, no cash-flow problem, loaded with investment funds. I had an introduction in Basle, sort of took it from there . . ."

They walked. Their voices were lowered and they held a pace up the fairway that kept them beyond the hearing of the Italian ahead.

"What's he looking for?"

"That about sums it up. I mean, Giles, lunch was bloody good, I'm not averse to a golf round and a decent lunch, but what's the bottom line?"

"He's pretty good company, I'll grant you, but why are we here, Giles?"

Giles Blake could give the sincere smile, do it as well as anyone, and he could laugh quietly. "You're a hell of a suspicious bunch. OK, he has funds. He needs to place monies. He's like any other banker I've ever known. He moves money and he looks for opportunities that will benefit his clients and stockholders. I think some rather seriously wealthy people use him, people who are looking for discretion . . . Hold on, wait a minute, I'm not talking about 'funny' money, I'm talking about 'quiet' money. For Heaven's sake, it's not 'hot' money. Be quite honest, I've always found him good as gold."

"Where do we fit in?" the banker asked.

"What can he offer that interests me?" the investment manager asked.

"What should I pitch for?" the property developer asked.

"How long have I known you chaps? Barrie, fourteen years. Kevin, since '85. Don, we've done business for nine years. I wouldn't think any of you have had much to complain about. Am I going to see you, you know my track record, shortchanged? Am I hell. Cards on the table. Meeting with Giuseppe Ruggerio was the best thing that happened to me. Believe me, I'm really happy to have made this introduction."

In front of them, the Italian had stopped by his ball. The ball would have been at least fifty yards ahead of any of theirs. The banker was no golfer, had no clubs, had come for the walk . . .

Barrie, the banker, asked, "What does he want?"

Kevin, the investment manager, asked, "There's no dirty, nasty bit?"

Don, the property developer, asked, "Where do we go?"

They were, all three of them, trusted and tried friends of Giles Blake. They were friends over the business desk and across the social scene. They met for the rugby at Twickenham, for the cricket at Lords, for the opera at Glyndebourne and they shot together. They put business each other's way, they made money. They were the new élite, tolerant of success, intolerant of obstructions.

"Barrie, what I'm saying is this—what he's looking for is an opportunity to move funds into a good UK house where his cash is going to be rather better managed than where it is now. Kevin, we're talking quite substantial funds—do you really think I'd be involved if it were 'dirty and nasty'? Not damn likely. Don, what I know, you've got a hell of a large white elephant sitting in Manchester, short of the top seven stories, and the backers have pulled the rug on you. We're talking about him having twenty-five available for starters. I would have hoped twenty-five million sterling on a three-way split with commission . . . I'm sure there would be a little mark of gratitude, would go down as well as that Chardonnay at lunch . . . Of course, I vouch for him. Look, you know what Italians are like, Italians are paranoid about the old tax man back in their own yard. They like their money overseas and they like it held quietly. It's the 'no names, no pack-drill' bit. Can't you live with that?"

"There would be commission?"

"Kevin, certainly there would be commission—it's the way they do business. It's no skin off my nose if you're not interested, chaps . . ."

Giles Blake walked away to his own ball. He would push the matter no further. He had done what he was paid to do. He provided discreet introductions for Giuseppe Ruggerio, the overseas player, who constantly searched for new pipelines through which to feed money. He sought out and befriended contacts who would make double damn certain, in return for commission, that the paperwork on "due diligence" would be ignored. He assumed, and he would not have dared to press the point, that he was one of many used as fronts for the washing of money and its ultimate layering into legitimate finance.

He played his stroke. He watched Giuseppe Ruggerio club his own ball toward the distant green. He called quietly to the Italian to come to him.

They stood at the side of the fairway. The banker and the investment manager and the property developer were in deep talk.

Giles Blake said quietly, "They're jumping because they're greedy. Three-way split. They need it, why they're nibbling."

"And quiet people?"

"As the grave, when they've banked their commissions."

"Because if they are not quiet . . ."

The voice died. They walked on up the course toward the green, Giles Blake and Giuseppe Ruggerio ahead of their guests. It was a fine course, used on several occasions a year for championships. Until Blake met the Italian there had been no way, not till hell froze over, that he could have afforded the membership fees. Nor could he have afforded the house a dozen miles away, nor the horses, nor the children's schools. He was owned by the Italian . . .

The threat had been made before the voice died. He thought that Giuseppe Ruggerio understood only too well that the threat did not have to be articulated. He knew of the banker who had unsuccessfully handled the funds of La Cosa Nostra and who had been strangled and then hanged from a rope under a London bridge. He knew of an investment broker in New York who had failed to predict the last great fall in the international markets and who had been found dead on the paving below his balcony. He knew of the import/export man in Toronto who had been found knifed to death off Yongue Street, the hookers' area, with dollar bills stuffed in his mouth. He knew of those who had died after failing La Cosa Nostra because Giuseppe Ruggerio had told him of them.

"A very pleasant day, Giles. I am having a very pleasant day. Before we were joined by your guests we were talking of the opportunity of the antique furniture markets . . ."

Each day the file on Giles Blake had worked lower in the detective sergeant's pending tray. There was a method. Each day the bottom file in the pending tray was retrieved from oblivion, shown the light and placed on the top. Harry Compton, when the Giles Blake file reached the top again, should have given it attention, but the bloody solicitor's paperwork was defeating them. If the paperwork of the bloody solicitor, the bastard, did not give up its secrets then the shit was going to be spinning across the ceiling and they'd be looking, bloody certain, at "harassment," at "wrongful arrest," at "punitive compensation." Over a quick sandwich and tea from a polystyrene cup, he leafed fast through the top file, swore because he had done nothing in the best part of a week, then scribbled a note.

TO: Alfred Rogers, Drugs Liaison Officer, British Embassy,
Via XX Settembre, Rome, Italy.
FROM: SO6, D/S H. Compton.

Alf, Sorry to interrupt the rest module in which you have, no doubt, settled easily, and hope this does not disturb your necessary siesta. Meanwhile, some of us are paid to work, not scratch their blackheads, you jammy bugger!!

If your Italian colleagues have learned how to operate the computer *(if!!)*, get them to P check

Bruno Fiori, Apartment 5, Via della Liberazione 197, Milan. Confession, don't know what I am looking for—was it ever different? He stayed last week at the Excelsior Hotel, Portman Square, London W1. See attached copy of hotel reg. form for passport details etc. In haste. All in chains here and hacking at the coal face. I imagine it's tough, too, in Rome.

In envy, Harry.

He brushed crumbs from his shirt, wiped the tea from his chin, handed the scrawl and the photocopy to Miss Frobisher, requested transmission to Rome, then stumbled back to the rooms in which the solicitor's documents and archives were piled.

The last time they had met had been a year before, and they had argued.

There was no love between Mario Ruggerio and the man from Catania.

It had taken a week of bickering by emissaries from the two for the meeting to be arranged. It had been decided after a week of sour discussion that the meeting should take place in a no-man's-land in the Madonie mountains. Off a dry, rutted farm track between Petralia and Gangi, in a remote farm building, they met to talk of the future. They were two scorpions, as if in a ring, watching each other.

No love, no trust existed between these two. Each had sent men the day before to sit on the high ground above the farm building, and to look down over the ripening fields and over the flocks of grazing sheep and the herds of browsing goats, to check the security arrangements. Neither Mario Ruggerio nor the man from Catania feared intervention by the *carabinieri* nor by the *squadra mobile,* but they feared the trap and the trick that might be sprung by the other. The man from Catania had come first, driven in a Mercedes and with a following car of minders. Mario Ruggerio had deemed it right that the other should come first and then wait . . . He had made his statement, he had come with two BMW cars filled with his own men but had driven himself in an old Autobianchi, a poor man's car, a peasant's wheels.

Outside the building the two groups of armed men stood apart. All would have known that if it came to war between the two families then they must make, and fast, the decision as to whether to stand and fight in loyalty or to attempt to switch sides. If it were war it would be to the death. It was said—and the minders who stood apart from each other would have heard it—that a thousand men in the defeated factions had died when Riina had killed his way to supreme power. There was no tolerance for a loser . . . Some carried machine pistols, some were armed with automatic assault rifles, some slipped their hands nervously inside bulging jackets as if for reassurance. There was no room inside the organization for shared control.

They talked, the two scorpions maneuvering in the ring for advantage, across a bare board table. Ruggerio spoke of his view of the future, and the view was of increased international dealing in the world of legitimate finance. The man from Catania gave his opinion, and his opinion was that the organization draw in the reach of its tentacles and make a concentration of effort on the island. They talked in fast bursts of dialect-accented words, and they smoked through the long silences.

In the silences were soft smiles. In the silences they smiled compliments and felicitations to each other, and both sought to decide whether it would be necessary, in order to achieve supremacy, to fight. In the matter of body language, of assessing strength, Mario Ruggerio was an artist. It was his quality, through his cold and clear blue and darting eyes, to recognize weakness. In the ring, it was not the time for the scorpion to strike. He thought that the chin of the man from Catania displayed weakness.

Outside the farm building, Mario Ruggerio watched the three cars head away for the long drive back to Catania. His own men watched him for a sign. Franco saw it, and Tano and Carmine. They saw Mario Ruggerio watch the dust clouds billow on the track from the wheels of the cars, and they saw him spit into the mud, and they knew that a man had refused to take second place and that a man was condemned.

The tourists came by bus up the hairpin road from the city to the cathedral of Monreale. They brought to the *duomo* voices that bayed excitement in the languages of French and German and Japanese and English. They came with their blinkered eyes and closed minds to the cathedral and monastery for Benedictine monks built nine centuries before by the Norman king William the Good, and they clucked their pleasure as they stood at his sarcophagus and gazed up at the gold of his mosaics and walked through his cloisters, and marveled at the site he had chosen with such care above Palermo. When they returned to their buses to drive on and away from Monreale, the French tourists and the Germans and the Japanese and the English and the Americans knew only of the past, had learned nothing of the present. No guide had told them of the ownership by La Cosa Nostra of the water they had sipped, of the *ristorante* they had eaten in, of the souvenir trade in religious relics they had boosted. No guide had told them of the priests who had offered hiding places to men of La Cosa Nostra on the run, or of the priests who had perjured themselves in court in offering alibi evidence, or of the priests who had permitted the *super-latitanti* to use their mobile telephones, or of the priests who said that La Cosa Nostra killed far fewer of God's children than the modern abortionists. No guide had told them of the new *carabinieri* barracks in the town that were the base of the *Reparto Operativo Speciale*, nor shown them the plaque on the wall of the barracks of the *polizia muncipale* in the memory of d'Aleo killed by *mafiosi* and of the plaque in the principal piazza in memory of Vice-Questore Basile killed by *mafiosi*. The tourists surfeited on history and did not know and did not care to know of present times.

He had the top floor of a widow's house.

She was a tall and elegant woman and wore the traditional black of mourning, but she told Axel Moen that it was six years since her husband, the surveyor, had died. She led him around the apartment—a bedroom, a living room, a kitchen and a bathroom—and in each room her fingers seemed to brush the surfaces for imaginary dust. He used his actual name with her, and he showed her the doctored passport that had come from the Resources section back in Washington along with the wristwatch, and he told her that he was a lecturer at the university in Madison and that his subject matter was archaeology. She was polite, but she had no interest in digging through the past. The widow, his view, was a fine woman with education and dignity, but she had no complaint when he paid her three months' rental in advance with dollar bills. He thought they might, the dollar bills, go to Switzerland or they might go to a tin under her bed, but sure as hell they would not go onto a tax return form. She treated the payment as if it were a necessary moment of vulgarity and continued the tour of the apartment. She showed him how the shower worked, told him when the water pressure would be high, she took him to a small balcony that looked out over the town and the valley beyond and then to the mountains and it would be his responsibility to water the potted plants. She gave him the keys of the outer door to the street and of the inner door to the apartment. Perhaps because he wore jeans and an old check shirt, perhaps because he wore his hair long in a pony-tail, she remarked coolly that she expected a "guest" in her home to be quiet in the evenings, that she should not be disturbed, as she was a light sleeper. She was Signora Nasello. She closed the apartment door behind her. She left him.

He had sat alone in the chair by the open doors to the balcony, alone with his thoughts, before 'Vanni Crespo came.

They hugged. Their lips brushed the other's cheeks.

They were as kids, as blood brothers.

"It's good?"

"Looks fine."

"Not easy to find, a place in Monreale . . ."

"You did well."

He was short of friends. Friendship did not come welcome to Axel Moen. Friendship was giving . . .

"You are the spirit of generosity, Mr. Moen."

Not many others, in Italian law enforcement or in the DEA's place on Via Sardegna, cared to goad Axel Moen. Not many others cared to tease or taunt him.

He had learned from his childhood to exist without friends. After the death of his mother, when his father had gone abroad, at the age of eight he had gone to live for five catastrophic months with his mother's parents. They were from the south end of the state, close to Stoughton. They were big in the Lutheran church and ran a hardware store and had forgotten how to win the love of an abandoned child. Five months of screaming confrontation, and beatings, and Axel had been sent on the bus, like preserved cod going to market, like a bale of dried tobacco leaf going to the factory, away up north to his father's father and the "foreign Jezebel." There had been no friends at the small farm between Ephraim and Sister Bay. In the tight-bound Norwegian community, his grandfather and his grandfather's second wife were shunned. He was a child living as an outcast. He had learned to live without a friend on the bus taking him to and from the school in Sturgeon Bay, and without a friend to make the long journey with down to Green Bay to see the Packers play. Vincenzina, from faraway Sicily, dark and Catholic, treated as a medieval witch and a danger and a threat, existed alone, and taught the young Axel how to ignore isolation. He had learned, alone, to sail a boat and fish and walk with the dog as his company. And Vincenzina had never mastered fully the English language and they had talked an Italian of the Sicilian dialect at home in the farmhouse. They had been, forced to be, their own people. Axel had little trust in friendship.

'Vanni took a Beretta pistol from his waist, and two filled magazines of 9mm bullets from his trouser pocket. He passed them to Axel.

"It's good. I'm an archaeologist. I'm digging for antiquities. I teach at the University of Wisconsin, Madison, I'm over for the summer semester. You'd better believe it."

Axel grinned, and 'Vanni was laughing with him.

Axel had known Giovanni Crespo for a full two years. The first trip with Bill Hammond down to Palermo, called "frontline acclimatization," they had been assigned the tall and angular-faced *carabiniere* captain as a guide. Bill had said, and believed it, that any Italian policeman should be treated as a security risk. Two days of whispering between the two Americans until the last night, when the big trip was winding down, and they had gone to 'Vanni's flat and 'Vanni and

Bill had drunk themselves half insensible on Jack Daniel's and Axel had sipped coffee. 'Vanni had been the first Italian Axel had met who said the sociologists and the apologists talked shit about La Cosa Nostra, that the bastards were simple criminals. He had known 'Vanni was worth the trust because it had been 'Vanni who had held the pistol at Riina's head. Salvatore Riina, *capo di tutti capi,* blocked off in a south Palermo street, and shitting himself and wetting himself, and lying in the gutter with 'Vanni's pistol at his temple as the handcuffs went on his wrists and the blanket went over his head. If a man held a pistol at Salvatore Riina's head, at the squat killer's temple, then Axel had a man who did not compromise. 'Vanni drank, 'Vanni screwed a prosecutor from Trapani and usually in the back of a car, 'Vanni talked too much and didn't know how to protect his back. They were different species, and their friendship was total.

"She's here?"

"She's here, and she's Codename Helen."

"That was mine, I thought of that one."

Between the knuckles of his fingers Axel caught a pinch of 'Vanni's cheek. "She said, 'That is really original—did a genius think up that one?' That's what she said."

Axel told 'Vanni the detail of the watch with the UHF panic tone, and he told him about the range of the pulse signal.

'Vanni had the maps, large scale, of Mondello on the coast, and of the high points of Monte Gallo and Monte Castellacio and Monte Cuccio, and of Monreale. They marked, bold ink crosses, the high points on which the microwave boosters would be placed.

"What have you told her?"

"When she should use the signal—only at the time of a contact with Mario Ruggerio or at a time of risk to her personal safety."

"She accepts that?"

"I think so."

"Think? Jesu, Axel, does she understand what she does, where she goes, with whom?"

"I told her."

'Vanni said, soft, "Is she capable of doing what is asked of her?"

"What I told her, 'Don't think I want someone like you down there, but I don't have the option.' And I told her that if she gave cause for serious suspicion then she would be killed, and I told her that after they'd killed her they'd go eat their dinner."

There was astonishment on 'Vanni's face, "And she is just 'ordinary,' your word?"

"She is ordinary and predictable."

"Don't you have a feeling for what you have pushed her toward—do you not have any goddamn feeling?"

Axel said quietly, "It's her strength that she is ordinary. And what was lucky for me, she was bored. She saw her life stretched out, the tapestry of her life was insignificance and underachievement and waste. She yearns to be recognized, she wants excitement . . ."

"Don't you go fucking her, she might go to sleep."

They were in each other's arms. Together, crying in laughter. Holding each other and laughing in hysteria.

'Vanni said, and the laughter dribbled at his mouth, "You are a cold bastard, Axel Moen, and you are a cruel bastard. How close did you say you would be?"

"I said that I would be close enough to respond."

"But that's shit, you know you cannot be, not all of the time."

"It's best for her to believe that, all the time, I am close enough to respond."

As if the laughter had served as a bonding, as if now

there was no time for more laughter, they talked together into the night. They worked the detail of the exact locations of the microwave boosters, and where the receivers should be, and what were the codes that Codename Helen might use. They talked of the response team that must be made available, and with whom the information could be shared. Later, 'Vanni would slip out of the apartment and then return with boxed fresh-cooked pizzas. They talked in urgency, into the night, as if a life was suspended from their fingers.

She stood back. *Piccolo* Mario was frantically working open the bolts and locks of the door. Angela was in front of the mirror and she touched her hair and then flicked with her nails to remove something unseen from the shoulders of her blouse. Francesca ran from her bedroom. Charley stood at the back of the hall.

He was a little grayer at the temples. He was, perhaps, a few pounds heavier in weight. He was as she remembered him.

He carried bags and flowers and gift-wrapped parcels. The wide smile on his face as he pecked a kiss at Angela's cheek and swung small Mario high in the air and crouched to cuddle Francesca.

He came forward, across the hall, and he beamed pleasure at the sight of her. She held out her hand, shyly, and he took it and then lifted it and kissed it, and she blushed.

"So wonderful that you could come, Charley. You are very welcome in our small home."

She stammered, "It's lovely to be here . . . thank you."

The man who washed money, whose brother was one killing away from becoming the most influential figure in international organized crime, let her hand drop. She was there, she had been told, because the family had made a "mistake." Angela and small Mario and Francesca, as if according to a ritual on his return and she remembered the ritual, were opening their presents, discarding to the floor the ribbons and the bright paper.

"And you have been in Rome, Charley?"

"Yes."

"Why did you go to Rome?"

She blurted, "For nostalgia . . . because I had been so happy there . . . because it was the best time of my life. It was an opportunity." She felt confident because she thought she had lied well.

A brooch of diamonds for Angela, an electronic game for small Mario, a soft toy for Francesca . . .

"I missed the direct flight, had to change in Milan—delay, of course—fog, of course. You should not have stayed up for me, not until so late."

Charley instinctively glanced down at her watch. The watch was heavy on her wrist. She glanced at the watch and the button on her watch. She slipped away. She should not intrude. She went to her room. In her bed Charley pressed the watch against her breast and felt the hardness of it, and she wondered where he was, where Axel Moen waited.

6

▼

He had been up early.

He had seen Signora Nasello, through a ground-floor door, in her kitchen and wearing a bright dressing gown, as if in the privacy of her home she did not need to clothe herself in widow's black. In a bar he had taken a coffee and a pastry, and he had gone to the meeting place.

He had not shaved. He was dressed in old jeans and an old shirt, and his hair was gathered back into an elastic band.

Axel waited at the meeting place and gripped a plastic bag close against his thigh, and the Beretta pistol was under his shirt and held by the waist of his trousers. He was off the main street that led down to the piazza and the cathedral. He was high in the town and close to the rock face of the dominating mountain. He stood beside the stall of a man who sold vegetables and while he waited the housewives came and bartered for beans and artichokes and lemons and oranges and potatoes and shrugged and made to walk away and turned back to give the man their money and to take the bags in return. The van came from behind him. It was poor procedure on Axel's part that he did not see the approach of the van. He was jolted by 'Vanni Crespo's sharp whistle. It was a builder's van, the sort that would be used by an artisan working alone, small and dirty and rust flaked. The door was opened for him, and he slid inside and his feet had to find space between a plastic bucket and paint pots, and he needed to duck to avoid the stepladder that jutted from the back of the van out between the front seats. He held the bag on his lap.

"You like it?"

"Taxed, I assume?" Axel grinned.

"Taxed, even insured. Did you sleep well?"

"I slept all right."

"Did you dream?"

"No."

"You didn't dream of her, of Codename Helen, not of her?"

Axel shook his shoulders. "You play CIs, you use them, and when you have finished with them then you pack them off back where they came from, end of story."

"And you did not dream of Ruggerio?"

"No." Axel, quite hard, punched his fist into the side of the Italian's chest. "Hey, big boy, ugly boy, this woman from Trapani, does she have to go with you in the back of this heap?"

"She has, I thank the Virgin, her own car."

They lapsed to quiet. They had come to a four-lane road below the town. He felt the keen thrill of pleasure, like he was dosed on ephedrine, like it was when the adrenaline coursed. The adult life of Axel Moen was divided, sharply, between the good times and the bad times. There were no gray-shade compromises.

The university at Madison was bad times, no friends and no tolerance of student life and finding what he rated as juvenile kids, and working alone to get the grades that were necessary. The city police department was good times, interesting from the start and better when he'd made detective status and gone to the surveillance team. A Drug Enforcement Administration investigation in Madison that used him as liaison and included him on a covert stakeout, that was good times. Taking the jump, quitting Madison and going to the DEA, joining the recruits at Quantico and being told he had an attitude problem and struggling to stay with the flow, that was bad times.

No warning, 'Vanni swung the wheel. They were checked at the gate by the smart-uniformed *carabiniere* trooper. They were passed inside, went under the raised barrier. They were a pair of workmen going on a small contract into the main *carabiniere* barracks on the island. He turned to 'Vanni, nodded his approval. Of course, the comings and goings at the main barracks on the island could be watched . . . They parked away from the main fleet of shining squad cars, near the memorial to the guys shot down in the line of duty. And still they could be watched, and 'Vanni gave Axel a bucket to carry and took the stepladder for himself, and they headed for a side door. He liked 'Vanni because he thought the guy trusted no bastard.

The first assignment with the DEA had been bad times. New York City, and the file had said that he was fluent in the Sicilian dialect, and the Pizza Connection case was going to trial, and there were the hours of wire taps to be listened to and noted, and he had sat week after week, month after month, in a small, darkened room with the earphones on his head and the tapes turning and the light blazing at his notepad . . .

When 'Vanni had fingered in the entry code and they were inside a corridor, they dumped the bucket and the stepladder.

La Paz, Bolivia, that had been good times, working with a small team, running his own CIs, riding in the local Huey birds, getting used to wearing the flak vest and to carrying the weight of an M16. The big shootout, the end of the day, hadn't changed La Paz, Bolivia, from rating as good times. Nor being shipped out on a walking wounded ticket.

They went down a corridor and past the open section

of an operations area with consoles and radios. Past a rest room where men sat in chairs and wore casual clothes and the firearms and the vests and the balaclavas were heaped on a table with the coffee cups and the used plates, and 'Vanni told Axel they were the Response Squad of the *Reparto Operativo Speciale*. 'Vanni said, if the panic tone went for real, that they'd be the guys who'd go running. He'd called in a favor, been allocated the team, dragged in a big debt, refused to explain.

Back to New York, three more years, and that had been bad times. They'd said in DEA and FBI and the prosecutors' offices that the American mainland end of La Cosa Nostra was finished. Tommaso Buscetta, turncoat, *pentito,* had blown them away to the federal penitentiary at Marion, Illinois. All over. The Bureau said, on the record, assholes that they were, that the "mafia myth of invincibility" was torpedoed. A prosecutor said, for quoting, "The Sicilian mafia's drug connection has been dismantled." The resources were being drained from the Organized Crime Drug Enforcement Task Force. Three years of scrapping with FBI over investigation priorities and pushing reports from desk to desk, three years of hearing that the Sicilians were a back number by comparison with the Colombians, and wondering then why the streets of Chicago and Philadelphia and Atlanta and Los Angeles and New York and Washington, a short walk from Headquarters, were stacked high with goddamn heroin. Bad times, until the posting to Rome . . .

Up a flight of stairs, down another corridor, through a door that could be opened only with an entry code, into 'Vanni's office. Axel looked around him.

"If this is home, Christ . . ."

He thought it was a monk's cell. A bare room, with bare walls except for the photograph of a general in best uniform and a smiling portrait of a little girl, with a bare, plastic-topped table and a hard chair, with a bare bed and blankets folded neatly on top of the single pillow.

Axel took from the plastic bag the second of the receivers he had brought to Sicily. The box was a little longer and a little thicker but the same depth as a hardback book. He extended the aerial. He showed 'Vanni the on/off switch. He wrote on a sheet of paper the UHF frequency that was programed into the wristwatch worn by Codename Helen.

'Vanni said, "I am only backup to take the signal. She is your responsibility."

"I understand that."

"You can take the signal in Mondello, if you sit there, which is not sensible. You can take the signal in Monreale, which is better but you are a long way from her. On the road, in Palermo, you are beyond contact."

"I understand that, too."

"In the operations area the frequency will be monitored, through the twenty-four hours, but I cannot tell them the detail of the importance of the signal, I can only lecture them on the priority. At the bottom line, it is your responsibility, Axel."

Axel said, "I told her to make a test transmission this afternoon."

"This afternoon. That is idiot. It's not in place."

"So, shift yourself."

"You think I have nothing else?"

The quiet smile played on Axel's face. "You held the pistol to Salvatore Riina's head—what I think, you'd give your right ball to hold that pistol at Mario Ruggerio's head."

'Vanni reached for the telephone. He dialed, he spoke, he swore, he explained, he gave his rank, he ordered, he laid down the telephone and looked straight into Axel's eyes.

Distant and quiet, 'Vanni said, "It will be, for her, like a
bell calling from the darkness . . ."

She half woke when Francesca crawled under the sheet of
her bed. A moment before she knew where she was.
Charley woke fully when *piccolo* Mario dragged her bear
from her arms. She looked at her watch, she laughed and she
tugged back the bear from the boy. God, the time . . . She
heard a radio playing and the squeals of the children, excited,
drove the sleep from her. She went, dazed, to the bathroom.
Washed, teeth brushed, she wandered to the kitchen.

The note was on the table.

> Charley, you were like an angel in peace.
> Giuseppe has gone to his office. I am shopping for
> lunch. Mauro is sleeping, feed him when he wakes.
> We meet later, Angela.

The whole of her life was a lie. She thought the lie
worked well because she had been given, with the children,
the run of the villa for the morning. She was accepted, she
had gained access . . . She walked out onto the terrace.
There was a freshness in the morning air and she hugged her
arms across her chest and the tiles were cold under her bare
feet. She could see, through the gaps between the shrubs and
the trees of the garden, over the high wall that ringed the
villa. Beyond the wall were rooftops of other villas and
beyond them was the bay. Where was he? Did he watch her?
Was he close by? She saw only the glass shards set in the wall
and the roofs and the distant blue expanse of the sea.

The children followed her into the kitchen. She pulled
open the fridge for coffee and juice and a day-old croissant.

Charley thought the villa, its construction, was magnificent, but it was for the summer. Large rooms with high ceil-

ings and floors of tile or marble. Big windows that could open out onto the patios. There was not the furniture to go with the magnificence, nor yet the weather. Angela had explained, seemed to apologize for, the functional furniture that was so mean compared to the fittings of the apartment in Palermo. Angela had said, head dropped, "I had the place aired, of course, the week before we came, but it is built for the sunshine, not the rain and damp of the winter. You have to excuse us for the wetness. I can barely live with the furniture. You see, Charley, we pay a man a hundred thousand a month and he is supposed to watch the security of the villa. Twice this last winter we were thieved from, we were broken into. You would not leave anything of value here through the winter, the thieving is so bad . . ." She washed the cup and the glass and the plate and the knife. She wandered.

She was alone. She walked barefoot on a paved path. She bent to take the scent of the first of the spring's roses. So quiet around her. The cotton of her nightdress was pressed against her by a light wind. She crouched and took in her fingers the fragile petals of a crimson geranium. She went by a small fountain that spluttered water and she held out her hand and let the cascade run cold on her palm. The watch weighed on her wrist. She tried to believe, as if it were her anthem, that it were possible for one person, Charlotte Eunice Parsons, to change something . . . had to believe it. If she did not believe that she could change something then she should have stayed at home, ridden her scooter to school each morning and ridden it back to the bungalow each evening. Should have bloody stayed, if she could not change something. She came round a screen where honeysuckle sprawled over a trellis frame.

He watched her.

Christ, the bloody "lechie" eyed her.

The man who opened the gate, who swept the leaves, who watered the pots of flowers, gazed at Charlie. She felt the thin cloth of her nightdress against her nakedness. She had thought she was alone . . . An old face, lined by the sun and weathered by the sea's salt, and he stared at her and leaned his weight on his broom. She heard the cry of the baby. The old man with the old face and the old hands watched her. She ran on the coarse stones of the path back toward the villa and the crying baby, and it was seven hours until she would make her test transmission.

Where was he? Did he watch her? Was he close by?

They worked with a drill that was powered by a portable petrol-driven generator to pierce the rock so that the stanchions could be buried securely and be proof against the winds on the higher point of Monte Gallo. When the stanchions were secured, the antennae of the microwave radio link were bolted to them, along with the booster that would enable the pulse of a panic tone to be carried across five kilometers to the higher point of Monte Castellacio.

Only when the sun over the city has climbed high, to its zenith, does the fierce light and warmth reach the cobbled alleys and broken pavings of the Capo district. Most of the day the district is a place of shadows and suspicion. It was the old Moorish slave quarter, and it is where the history of the men of the modern La Cosa Nostra is rooted. In the gray and run-down heart of the Capo district is the Piazza Beati Paoli where, it is said, was the beginning . . . There is a church in the piazza, there is a small hemmed-in open space, enclosed by high buildings with damp-scarred and crumbling walls and the night's bedding is draped from balconies. It is said by the historians who rejoice in the nobility of the anarchic Sicilian character that the piazza was the safe house of the Beati Paoli, the secret association formed more than 800 years ago. The men of the secret society claimed the right to protect the poor against the foreign rulers of the island. Their motto was "Voice of the People, Voice of God." Their meeting place was in the caves and tunnels under the present piazza. By day they practiced normality, worshiped in public. By night they roamed the black alleys, cloaked in heavy coats under which they carried rosaries and knives, and punished and murdered by ritual. From the men of the secret society of the Beati Paoli was born a word, the word was "mafia." Some say the word comes from the old Italian *maffia,* which describes a man of madness, audacity, power and arrogance. Some say the word was the old French *maufer,* which denotes the God of Evil. Some say the word was the old Arabic *mihfal,* which is an assembly of many people. The children of each succeeding generation have been taught the mythology of the secret society, and its fight against the persecution of the unfortunate, and its punishment of the oppressor, and its justification for murder. What began eight centuries ago had spread now from the gray piazza, flowed and eddied into the city, across the island, over the sea, but it began in the Capo district of Palermo.

"The Capo district, I see. You wish, Dr. Tardelli, to cordon off the Capo district . . . Wait, Dr. Tardelli, you have already spoken. Throw a surveillance cordon around the Capo district because—forgive me if I recapitulate—because you have been told by a source that must remain anonymous, that may not be shared with us, because you have information that a year ago an almond cake upset the bowels of Mario Ruggerio. An interesting proposition, Dr. Tardelli."

The grim smile played at the face of the oldest of the Palermo prosecutors. He shrugged, his fingers were outstretched in the gesture of ridicule, his throat burrowed down into his shoulders.

"I request the resources of a surveillance team."

"Now, I, of course, Dr. Tardelli, am not able to devote my life to the investigation of one man." The voice of the magistrate quavered in sarcasm. A tall man, ascetic, his fingers clinging to an unlit cigarette, he rolled his eyes around the table, before bringing them to bear on Rocco Tardelli. "My desk is piled with many investigations, all of which require my attention. I, too, need resources. But on the basis of information that is as old as was, no doubt, the almond cake—No, Dr. Tardelli, I do not seek to make a joke of this—you wish for a special surveillance of the Capo district. There are, my recollection, at least fourteen entrances into that area. Should we have surveillance cameras for each of them? To do a job at all correctly you must have eight men at any one time on surveillance duty. Mathematics, I regret, is not my strength, but with the duty shifts that would take away twenty-four men from other duties. Then, I make a further addition, and I ask whether the eight men on surveillance duty must have the support of backup. A further addition, those who watch however many cameras we install. A year ago, on the word of your informant, an almond cake made a problem for Mario Ruggerio, and we are asked to divert an army . . ."

"I ask for what can be spared."

"Please, Dr. Tardelli, your indulgence . . . I work in a more simple field, I attempt investigations into the extortion of payments from the public utility companies. To you, Dr. Tardelli, I have no doubt that would seem to be valueless work, it is as if I hunt for many cats and not just one tiger. The tiger, of course, may by now be toothless and maimed and harmless, but that is another matter. I assure you, the cats have claws and teeth and kill." The prosecutor was younger than Rocco Tardelli, was in his first year in Palermo, had traveled from Naples, and would have seen his appointment as a step on a career ladder. He would not be long on the island of Sicily. "You put in place the valuable resource of a trained surveillance unit, a resource that each week, for my investigations, I beg for, but do you even know what he looks like, the elusive Mario Ruggerio? How—am I being stupid—how can a surveillance team operate, how can video cameras be monitored, if the only photograph of Mario Ruggerio is twenty years old? I do not wish to be difficult . . ."

"The photograph found when his brother was arrested, taken at his sister's wedding in 1976, has now been computer enhanced. We have aged Mario Ruggerio."

"You must not misunderstand me, Dr. Tardelli. I, I can assure you, am not amongst them, but there are some, a few, who would be less than generous to you. Some, and I am not amongst them, would see an unfavorable motivation in your request for these valued resources. They would look, some would look, toward a desire on your part for promoted status. Not me, no . . ." Older than Tardelli, less gray in the visage because he did not live behind shuttered windows and drawn curtains, heavier in the stomach because he ate in the restaurants of the city, the magistrate had long ago sent a signal that had been transmitted, mouth to mouth, and received. He carried out his work, with punctilious care, but always those arrested, charged, convicted, imprisoned, were from a losing faction. ". . . Myself, I believe Ruggerio to be irrelevant, but his capture would play well on television, it would make the headlines in newspapers. The man who claimed credit for that capture would be fêted, by the ignorant, as a national hero. Would the finger beckon, would Rome summon him? Would he sit at the right hand of the Minister? Would he go to Washington to lecture the FBI and DEA, and to Cologne to meet the BKA, to Scotland Yard to take wine? Would he leave us all behind him to go about our daily work in danger, here in Palermo? Some might say that—"

"When you arrest a man of the stature of Mario Ruggerio then you dislocate the organization—it is proven."

They were his colleagues and they mocked him. They might as well have laughed in his face, they might as well have spat upon him. It was what he lived with.

He looked around the table. He raked his eyes over them. He was accused, behind his back, in conversations in quiet corridors, of "careerism" and of chasing "handcuffs for headlines." In his mind was that description of the dead Falcone, "a lonely fighter whose army had proved to consist of traitors." Some of them, he thought, were crushed by the coward's desire to return to normality. But . . . but he should have been more tolerant of cowards. Not every man could make such a sacrifice, pigheaded in righteous duty, as he had done. Not every man could see his wife walk out and take the children, and then go from the silence of a lifeless apartment, in the armored car, to the bunker office. There had been no contribution at the weekly meeting from the representatives of the *squadra mobile* and the *Resparto Operativo Speciale* and the *Direzione Investigativa Anti-Mafia,* as if those men stood aside while the prosecutors and magistrates carped and cut at each other.

Tardelli began to gather together the papers in front of him. There was a hangdog sadness in his face and his shoulders were bowed as if under the weight of disappointment. He spoke with the diffidence that was his own. "Thank you for hearing me, gentlemen. Thank you for your courtesy and consideration. Thank you for pointing out to me the folly of my ambition and the idiocy of my request . . ."

He stood. He placed his papers in his briefcase. It had been the same for Falcone and for Borsellino, and for

Cesare Terranova and "Ninni" Cassara, and for Giancomo Montalto and for Chinnici and for Scopellitti, all ridiculed, all isolated, all dead. He had been to the funerals of each of them.

"I will call, in one hour, a news conference. I will tell the world that I have a lead, a slight lead, for the hiding place of the *super-latitanti,* Mario Ruggerio. I will say that my colleagues in the Palazzo di Giustizia, and I will name them, do not consider this a matter important enough for the allocation of resources. I will say—"

The bluster beat around him.

"That would be disloyal . . ."

"Unfair . . ."

"We merely pointed to the difficulties . . ."

"Of course there are resources . . ."

When he was out in the corridor, when the door behind him was closed on the hatred, when his *ragazzi* gathered around him with their guns as they did even on the upper floor and questioned him with their glances, the magistrate showed no triumph. Falcone had written, "One usually dies because one is alone, because one does not have the right alliances, because one is not given support," and Falcone, with his wife and his *ragazzi,* was dead.

Walking briskly, he said to the *maresciallo,* "I have been given nine men of the *squadra mobile* for the surveillance of the Capo district, three shifts of three, and no additional cameras. I have to hope. I have nine men for ten days. If they find nothing, then I am isolated. We should, my friend, be very careful."

They sweated in the cold wind that hit them. They were at 890 meters above sea level. The wind buffeted them and rocked the stanchion arms. They struggled to hold the antennae as the bolts were tightened. The clear line of sight was established from Monte Castellacio, across the Palermo-to-Torretta road, to the greater height of Monte Cuccio.

In a new block, overlooking the moles against which the big ferries from Livorno and Naples and Genoa docked, Peppino had his office. It was lavishly furnished, modern and expensive-Italian. He sat in the wide room with the picture window that faced out over the harbor. The office was a home from home for him, necessary that it should be of the greatest comfort because Peppino spent fifteen hours out of the twenty-four hours of the day there, six days a week, hugging the telephone between his ear and his shoulder, feeding the fax machine, flicking between the channels on the screen that gave him the market indices in New York and Frankfurt and London and Tokyo. He did not take a siesta in the afternoon as did every other businessman in the city's Rotary or in the Lodge he attended, the third Thursday in the month. He avoided the luxury of a siesta because, single-handed, he managed and moved and placed, each year, in excess of four billion American dollars on behalf of his elder brother.

It was the way of the organization and, in particular, the way of his elder brother that matters of finance should be kept inside the family. It was why he had been brought back to Palermo from Rome. He lived a life consumed by the need to "clean" money. He was the trusted laundryman for Mario Ruggerio. He was a master at his work, the consolidation and placement, the immersion, the layering, the heavy soaping, the repatriation and integration, the spin dry. What Angela did in the utility room off the kitchen, Peppino did in his office in the new block on Via Francesco Crispi. Angela washed and cleaned a dozen shirts a week, a dozen sets of socks, half a dozen sets of underwear. Peppino washed and cleaned in excess of four billion American dollars a year. The office was his home. He could cook and eat in his office. He could shower and change in his office. He could take his secretary, when the businessmen of the Rotary and the Lodge were at siesta, to the stark black couch by the picture window.

If the office were his home, if the scale of his work increasingly kept him from the apartment in the Giardino Inglese and the villa at Mondello, Jesu, it was necessary for him to take his secretary to the couch. What his brother said, Mario said, a wife should never be embarrassed . . . Would Angela have cared? If the condoms had spilled out of his pocket, fallen at her feet, would Angela have noticed? Not since she had come to Palermo. Angela would not be embarrassed by any indiscretion of his secretary because the young woman's father was sick with a carcinoma and the treatment was expensive, and Peppino paid for the principal consultant in the field of that necessary treatment. The rows with Angela came more often now. They lived in physical promixity and in psychological separation. She could have everything that she wanted except divorce, divorce was unthinkable . . . So good in Rome, so different. They maintained an appearance. His brother had said that appearance was important.

His feet, shoes discarded, rested on the glass top of his desk, his leather chair was tilted far back. He talked through the final details of a leisure complex in Orlando with the bank in New York and the construction company's operations manager in Miami. Two phones going, and the talk "in clear" because the money coming down from New York was cleaned . . .

And just as he washed money for his brother, so Mario Ruggerio had immersed and soaped and spun dry the younger Peppino. Sent by his brother away from Prizzi, dismissed from his mother, sent abroad, dismissed from his past, sent into the world of legitimate finance, dismissed from his family. The businessmen that he knew in Rotary and the Lodge, the trustees of the Politeama who sought his advice on financial planning, the charitable orphanage in Bagheria and the priests at the *duomo* in Palermo who sought his help did not know of the connection of his birth, were unaware of the identity of his elder brother. Perhaps, maybe, a few policemen knew. There was a magistrate who knew. One interrogation, one summons to come to the offices of the *Servizio Centrale Operativo* in the EUR suburb, one journey out of Rome. The magistrate who knew had been a pitiful little man, obsequious in his questions, up from Palermo. He had attacked. Was he to be blamed for the accident of his birth? Should he carry his blood as a cross? Because of his brother, he had left home, left the island—what more could he do to break the association? Was he obliged, because of blood and birth, to wear the hair-shirt of a penitent? Was he to be persecuted? He had thought the magistrate, Rocco Tardelli, an insignificant man who had cringed at the attack. He had not been interrogated again in Rome, and not since he had come back with Angela and the children to Palermo. It had been important, in that one session with the magistrates at the offices of SCO, to dominate and kill the investigation of his affairs. He knew the way they worked, submerged with paper, starved of resources, scratching for information that would take them forward. He imagined that the transcripts of the interview, no information gained and nothing moved forward, was now consigned to a file shut away in a basement, was buried beneath a mountain of other sterile interrogations, was forgotten. If it were not forgotten, then he would have been investigated again following his return to Palermo. He felt safe, but that was no reason to drop, ever, his guard. He kept his guard high, as his brother demanded.

The deal was concluded. The papers would go to the

lawyers for fine analysis, then the bank in New York would move the money, then the operations manager would move on site. Peppino said when he would next be in New York . . . dinner . . . yes, dinner, and he thanked them.

Peppino looked up at the clock on the wall, cursed. Angela was never punctual, and they were to be at the opera. As a trustee it was necessary for him to be at a first night of the Politeama's spring program.

He called to the outer room, to his secretary. She should telephone Angela. She should remind Angela at what time she should drive into the city, what time she should be in the Piazza Castelnuovo. A wry smile, cool, on his face. No excuse for Angela not to come, because he gave her everything, the brooch of diamonds that she would wear that evening, and he had given her the little English mouse to watch the children.

Charley carried the baby, easily, as if it were her own. She came off the patio as Angela was putting down the telephone.

Charley said, "Please, Angela, I would like to go for a walk later."

"Where?"

Down to the Saracen tower beside the harbor. "Just into the town."

"Why?"

To press the panic-pulse button for a test transmission. "Because I haven't been in the town. It would be nice to walk by the sea."

"When?"

Told to send the transmission in an hour and ten minutes. "I thought it would be nice in a hour or so."

"Can't you go now?"

The time was fixed by Axel Moen. "It's too hot now. I think it would be nicer in an hour."

"Some other time. I have to go with Peppino to the opera. I have to leave in less than two hours. Another time."

They would be waiting for the signal to be sent in an hour and ten minutes, waiting with their earphones, twisting the receiver's dials to the UHF frequency. "I'll be here when you go out."

"Charley, the children, and Mauro, they have to be fed, they have to be bathed, they have to be put to bed."

"I can do all that, don't you worry. I'll take *piccolo* Mario and Francesca and baby Mauro with me. They'll like to walk when it's not so hot. You don't have to worry about them, it's what I've come for, to help you."

Charley tried to smile away the unhappiness of Angela Ruggerio. She did not know the cause of the sadness. She was not the woman Charley had known in Rome, the woman who laughed and talked and lay on the beach without the top to her bikini. She did not recognize the new woman.

"Perhaps . . ."

"You should have a rest. Lie down. Don't think about the children, that's for me, that's why I'm here." Here to send panic-pulse transmissions, here to spy, here to break open a family's life and to smash the parts . . .

They were beyond the height to which the shepherds brought the flocks and herds. From Monte Cuccio they could see, direct line of sight, to Monte Castellacio and on to Monte Gallo, and when they turned away from the swaying antennae and looked down the scree slope, and on past the track's limit where the Jeep had been left, there was the ridge line of yellow-gray rock that lay above Monreale. One more set of antennae, on that ridge, and they would have made the boosted microwave link from Mondello to the aerial on the roof of the *carabinieri* barracks.

'Vanni Crespo asked gulping air, panting, "It's good?"

The technician pouted. "If a signal is transmitted, on the frequency you have given me, from Mondello, then it will be received in Monreale."

He scrambled down the scree slope, slipping and falling, and when he was on his feet, 'Vanni ran for the Jeep.

Anxiety furrowed the wide forehead of Mario Ruggerio. His fingers tapped restlessly at the keys of the Casio calculator.

The figures, the *lire* totals, were worse than they had been a year ago.

Losses, that column, stood at forty billion a month, the calculation for income was down 17 percent on the previous year and these were the balance sheet figures that were held in his mind. His estimate of outgoings was up by 21 percent. Each time he played the figures onto the calculator's screen the answer came the same, and unwelcome.

He sat at his table in the drab room on the first floor of the house in the Capo district. The figures were estimates, given him by an accountant from Palermo.

He wrote occasional words with figures beside the words that he ringed. He had written "decline in public works expenditure": the new government in Rome no longer poured money into the Sicilian infrastructure for roads and dams and the administration offices for the island. He had written "legal fees," and the estimate was that four thousand Men of Honor, from the members of the *cupola* to the *sotto capi* and the *consiglieri* and the *capodecini* and right down to the level of the *picciotti,* were in custody and must receive the best legal representation—if they did not receive the best, and if their families were not supported then there was the chance of men taking the foul option of joining the bastard *pentiti*. He had written "asset seizure," and the figure for the previous twelve months stood, in his careful hand, at 3,600 billion for the state's sequestration of property and bonds and accounts, and the calculator, purring through fast additions and multiplications and divisions and subtractions, told him that "asset seizure" was already up in the first months of the year by 28 percent. He had written "narcotics," and there the figure was down because the habits of addicts had changed to the more recent creation of chemically based tablets, and the organization did not have control of the supply of such products as the LSD and amphetamine range. He had written "cooperation," the payment each year to politicians and policemen and magistrates and the revenue investigators, and the figure alongside the word was five hundred billion. He thought the words and the figures were the result of three years of drift. The drift had begun with the capture of Salvatore Riina, and had continued while others had scratched eyes and killed in their attempts to succeed him as *capo di tutti capi*. When he had control, full control of the organization, then the drift would be halted.

He lit his cigar, and coughed, and he held the flame of his lighter against the sheet of paper on which he had written the words and the figures. He coughed again, deeper in his throat, and tried to lift the phlegm.

Axel saw her.

He sat on the warm concrete of the pier and he looked across the curve of the bay toward the dun tower that was, he guessed, four hundred meters from him.

He saw her, and in his mind she was Codename Helen. She had no other identification. He stripped her, as he gazed across the bay at her, of personality and of humanity. She was the Confidential Informant that he used.

Axel sat with his legs casually dangling over the edge of the pier and the water lapped below his feet. Around him were small fishing boats and men working at the repair of their nets and at the tuning of boats' engines. He ignored their solemn faces, walnut colored from salt spray and the sun's strength. He watched her.

The small boy ran ahead of her the moment they were across the road and she released his hand. A small girl clutched the side of the pram that Codename Helen pushed. There was a bright awning on the pram to shelter a baby from the brilliance of the late-afternoon light. It was so normal. It was what Axel might have seen beside any bay on the island, on any esplanade above the gold of any beach. A hired help, a nanny and a childminder, pushed a pram and escorted two small children. He had good eyesight, no need of spectacles, and he could see her face as a whitened blur. He had reckoned that binoculars could draw attention to himself; without binoculars he could not see the detail of her face, did not know whether she was calm or whether she was stressed.

On Axel's lap, shielded by his body from the fishermen who moved behind him on the pier from boat to boat, covered by his windcheater, was the equipment designated as CSS 900. The crystal-controlled two-channel receiver, the best and most sensitive that Headquarters could supply, had been stripped of its microphone capability and would receive only a tone pulse. In the canal of his right ear, buried from sight, was an induction earpiece, no cable necessary. The equipment, and the earpiece, were activated only when a tone pulse was transmitted. Protruding from under the windcheater, protected from view by his body, was the fully entended aerial of the receiver. He waited.

He thought that he saw her head drop and for a moment the whiteness of her face was gone, and he thought that she checked her watch and he wondered whether she had synchronized with the radio during the day, as he had done, as she should have. His eyes roved over the shoreline, sweeping inland from the tower that had been built by the Moors centuries before as a defensive position and across the piazza where the kids were gathered with their motorbikes and their coke tins and up over the roofs toward the final line of villas set against the raw gray stone of the cliff. Later he would go, on another day, to see the villa. She was at an ice-cream counter, and he saw her hand a cone to the small boy and another to the little girl. She did not take an ice cream for herself.

It was Axel Moen's life. His life was made of waiting for covert transmissions from Confidential Informants. There was, to him, sitting with his feet above the vivid colors of the water that was polluted by oil and above the floating plastic bags and fish carcasses, nothing that was particular or special about the CI given the title of Codename Helen. His life and his work . . . Shit. He had no feelings for her that he could summon, was not concerned as to whether she was calm or whether she was stressed. Couldn't help himself, but his head jerked.

The pulse tone rang in his ear. So clear, three short blasts, so sharp. It cavorted through his head. There was little static, and the pulse tone was repeated. It beat within the confines of his skull bone. It came again, a final time, three short blasts.

The static was gone, the silence returned.

He thought she looked around her. He thought she looked for a sign. He saw her turning slowly and looking at the road and at the pavement and up into the town and out across the sea. It was good that she should be alone and good that she should know she was alone. He pushed down the aerial, lost it under the cover of his windcheater.

Axel stood. When he was standing he could see her better. She was going away, alone, with the children and with the pram. She stopped to cross the road, and when there was a gap in the traffic she hurried. He did not see her on the far side of the road because a lorry blocked his view of her.

He walked away.

'Vanni handed the second headset back to the technician. He leaned against the technician's chair as if a weakness sagged through his body. The grit and dust of the scree slope on Monte Cuccio was on his hands and on his face, and on the knees and seat of his jeans and on the chest and back of his shirt. He breathed deeply . . .

The signal had come so clearly, and he had said that it would be for her like a bell ringing from the darkness, like the light of a candle in the black of night. It might just offer success . . . He wondered where she was, their Codename Helen, whether she shivered in fear, whether she felt the chill of isolation . . . He wrote on a piece of paper the number of his mobile telephone and he told the technician, smacking his fist into the palm of his hand for emphasis, that he must be called every time that the frequency was used, night or day. The number was clipped to the banked equipment in front of the technician.

"You have that? Any hour—whether it is the triple pulse, short and repeated three times, whether it is the long pulse, repeated four times—at any hour, if that signal comes . . ."

The technician, laconic, shrugged. "Why not?"

His fists gripped the technician's shoulders, his fingers gouged at the technician's flesh. "Don't piss on me. The early duty and the late duty and the night duty, whatever *cornuto* sits here, he calls me. If I am not obeyed, I will crack the bones in your spine."

"You will be called."

He loosed his hands. He shook. He had heard a bell ringing in the darkness. He felt the weakness because he believed, for the first time, that the plan might work. Not since they had turned Baldassare di Maggio, not since di Maggio had told them where to look for Salvatore Riina, not for three years had a source been in place so close to the heart of the organization. They would kill her. If they found her they would kill her.

One piece of paper . . . One telephone number scribbled on one piece of paper . . .

The party spilled noisily through the offices. Of all the boxes taken out of the solicitor's premises, and all the plastic bags, one piece of paper had done the business, one telephone number on the back of a commercial property conveyancing draft had launched the party. The solictor would have been checking a subordinate's work on the draft, and a telephone call would have come through, and he would have been given a number, and he would have jotted it on the back of the nearest sheet of paper. Trouble was, for the solicitor, the number was that of a small and discreet Zurich bank. Further trouble was, for the solicitor, that Swiss banks weren't what they had been. Cold feet in Cuckoo-clock-land, and the small and discreet Zurich bank had not been prepared to fight the recent Swiss legislation contained in Article 305 ll of the penal code which made its directors liable to prosecution if they shielded illegal funds. With the solicitor's name and account number on the top page of the evidence file, and the reckoning of what was stashed there of his clients' cash, the party had started.

Six-packs of beer from the off license, and three bottles of wine, and a bottle of Scotch which was the detective superintendent's fast track to getting pissed up, and music from a transistor. They didn't come often, the good ones.

Harry was called.

Harry Compton was called out of the party area and into the administration office. Miss Frobisher, and the place fell apart when she took her five weeks of leave, didn't drink and didn't approve, but she'd stayed put to answer the telephones. She would have read the secure transmission, and she scowled as she handed it to Harry.

TO: Det. Sgt. H. Compton, SO6, London.
FROM: Alf Rogers, DLO, Rome.

Harry, Regards. Assuming they could find it, some nasty soul has been pulling your insignificant pecker. No trace in Milan on available records of BRUNO FIORI. The address provided in Via della Liberazione does not exist. That section of the street was pulled down six years ago for the construction of a municipal swimming pool. Details on hotel reg. were totally fictitious. Back to your tin/gonics. We, here, are involved in important work and don't need to be diverted from the necessary with duff info.

Luv, Alf.

Harry took the single sheet of paper to his desk, locked it away, went back to the party. The detective superintendent was into his joke repertoire and had an audience, and Harry didn't think he'd take it kindly if his punch line was interrupted. It would wait till the morning, till they crawled in with their headaches. He had a nose, that was his bloody trouble, and the nose was smelling something rotten, but it would be better talked about in the morning.

7

"HOW LONG?"

"I don't know."

"If you don't know how long it would take then, Harry, leave it to the locals."

Maybe it would have been better the night before, perhaps it would have been better to have crashed the boss when he was in his joke session. Water under the bridge, because Harry Compton had let that moment go.

"I don't want to do that."

"Did I hear right? 'Want?' Don't 'want' me, young man."

The morning after, and the SO6 office was a dead ground. Miss Frobisher, of course, had been in early, before seven, and she'd removed all the plastic cups and emptied the ashtrays and wiped the bottle stains off the desks, but the place still stank, and their heads ached. He thought the detective superintendent's head hurt worse than most because the boss man's mood was foul.

"What I'm trying to say—"

"Rein in, young man. What you are 'trying to say' is that you want two days down in the country. Well, we'd all like that, wouldn't we?"

"It should be followed up."

"The locals can follow it up."

Harry stood in the detective superintendent's office. The boss was hunched over his desk and he had a second coffee mug in front of him and the heartburn pills that squeezed off a little tinfoil platter. He held in his hand the message received the last evening from Alf Rogers, and the hotel registration sheet, and the printout from the night manager of telephone calls made from the room occupied by Bruno Fiori, alias for Christ only knew. He was on a short fuse that was getting shorter. His wife, Fliss, had bitched at the time he'd come in. Hadn't he remembered that they were supposed to be going out shopping for the new living room suite? Wasn't there a telephone he could have used? He'd an accountancy exam, first part, coming up, and wouldn't he have been better at his books, after late-night shopping then lurching in smelling foul from drink? Why'd he forgotten to put the cat out? The cat had been shut in the kitchen and crapped on the floor. God.

"The locals down there are useless, they're parking-ticket merchants."

"You've got nothing, nothing, that warrants me kissing you good-bye for two days."

"It's worth doing."

"How many files on your desk?"

"That's the bloody point, isn't it?"

"What's tickling up your arse, Harry?"

"It's trivia, that's what's on my desk. It's nothing stuff. It's corrupt little men, high street dwarfs, fiddling pensions, fiddling savings."

"Those pensioners, those savers, they just happen, young man, to pay fucking taxes. Those taxes are your wages. Don't you get on a high-and-mighty horse and forget where your bread comes from."

For a moment Harry closed his eyes. He squeezed the lids tight shut. He took a big breath.

"Can I walk in again? Can we start again?"

The coffee dribbled from the sides of the detective superintendent's mouth. "Please yourself, and keep it short."

"What I'm saying is this. We have a trace that is just routine on this tosser, Giles Blake, bank disclosure on a cash deposit. We run the check on his accounts. Nothing special, no alarms, except that it's not clear where the wealth comes from. Ninety-nine times out of a hundred, we'd say that's as far as it runs, file it and drop it. But, you authorize an evening's surveillance, and Mr. bloody Blake takes an Italian to dinner, and they talk about nothing that is illegal. File it and drop it. But the Italian says he's come from Palermo. But the Italian has given the hotel a false name, a false address. We don't know who he is. But his telephone records indicate that from his room he called a travel agent for his flight back to Milan and the nonexistent address, to a limousine company for a ride to the airport using the fictional name. But there was one more call from his room. He rang a Devon number. He rang a number listed as belonging to David Parsons. That's where I want to go, to see Mr. David Parsons."

"Why can't the locals—?"

"Christ, don't you understand?"

"Steady, young man."

"Don't you understand. I repeat myself, what we do is trivia. Trivia are good for the statistics. We lift enough second-rate people on second-rate scams and you get to make commander, and I get to make inspector, and we get pissed together, and we are achieving damn-all. But, don't worry, it's easy and it gets fast results, and aren't we bloody clever?"

He was on the edge. Over the edge was insubordination, was a bollocking, was a mark on his file. Maybe it was last night's drink, perhaps it was the tiredness, could have been the row with Fliss. It didn't seem to matter to Harry Compton that he was on the edge.

"Then, onto your plate falls something that might just

be interesting. Can't quantify it, can't put bloody time and motion to it, can't put a balance sheet on it. Might spend a week or two weeks or a month, and might get nothing. No, it's not for the locals, it's our shout and I want to go to Devon."

The boss man hesitated. It was always that way with the boss, because the man was a bully. If the boss's shin were kicked, if he had pain, then he usually crumpled, what Harry had learned. "I don't know . . ."

"If you're trying to send a message then the message is being heard. Looks to me that you're saying that Fraud Squad can chase greedy little bastards with their fingers in the pensions accounts and the savings accounts, but we're not smart enough for the international scene. I hear you. The big-time is too complex for SO6, like we're not fit enough to run on dry sand where it gets to hurt. I hear you."

"For two days, when you've got your in-tray down to half empty, not before," the Detective Superintendent said, sour. "And get the fuck out of here."

Four days gone, and the excitement had drained. Four days gone in a numbed routine of getting up, getting the kids dressed, getting the kids their breakfast, getting small Mario to school, getting Francesca to kindergarten, getting baby Mauro changed. Charley was four days into the routine and was bored. She sat at the iron-legged table on the patio and she wrote her first postcards.

It was four days since she had gone down to the town and stood by the Saracen tower and pressed the button on her wristwatch, and looked around and tried so desperately to see him and failed. That had been the last moment of excitement. For God's sake, she hadn't come to Sicily to walk the kids to school and kindergarten, to deal with a baby's stinking backside, to skivvy for Angela Ruggerio.

She'd come, spit it out, sunshine, she'd come to gain the access that would lead to the capture of Mario Ruggerio. Who? What for? Why? A postcard for her mother and father, and another for her uncle, and another for the 2B class. All the week Peppino had been in Palermo, not come to Mondello, and Angela said that her husband had too much work in the city to be able to come back to them in the evenings. Now that was just plain ridiculous because it was twenty minutes' drive in that big bloody fast car from central Palermo to Mondello.

On the postcards Charley didn't say that she was bored out of her mind. Having a wonderful time—weather brilliant—soon be warm enough to swim, Love, Charley. The same for her parents and for her uncle and for the 2B class.

She had come because she had decided she was trapped at home, netted at work. But nothing bloody well happened here either, except that she fussed round the kids and changed the baby and swept the bloody floors. God. Come on, speak the bloody truth: Charley Parsons had come to Sicily because Axel Moen had told her to. She wrote the addresses on the cards, a fast and clumsy hand. Damn Axel Moen. What did he mean to her? Meant nothing, and she threw the pen down onto the tabletop. God, and just once he could have said something decent, could have given her something that was praise, something that was bloody compassion.

She had come with the excitement holding her. Like when she had gone to the home of the lecturer at college, the first time, and known his wife was away, and worn the sheer blouse and no bra, and drunk his wine, and stripped for him in front of the open fire, and climbed on him as they did in the films. That had been excitement, till the dull fart had cried. Like when she had walked to the caravan at the edge of the campsite at Brightlingsea, where the long-term activists lived who each day tried to break the police cordons and halt the trucks carrying the animals to the continental abbatoirs, gone to the caravan where Packy slept, with the cap in her hip pocket, walked to his caravan because the other girls said he'd a prick bigger than a horse's. That had been excitement, till the stupid bugger had spurted before he'd even got over her. Hey, sunshine, excitement's for books. The villa was a mortuary, it was the death of excitement.

It was the third day that *piccolo* Mario and Francesca had been to school and kindergarten, and Charley thought they were like a pit-prop to their mother. She seemed to weaken when they were gone from her sight. Charley, too damn right, she'd tried. Tried to make conversation, tried to earn some laughter back—a lost bloody cause. Some mornings Angela went into Palermo, some mornings she stayed in her room. Some afternoons Angela walked with the children, some afternoons she went, remote, to a sunbed at the bottom of the garden. Charley tried, Charley failed, to get through to her. Charley giggled, Charley remembered the face of the mistress at school who taught sixth-form history and who'd come to hammer the Civil War into them the morning after the miserable cow's husband had moved out to set up home with a nineteen-year-old boy, same school. God, that was bloody cruel, but it was the face of Angela Ruggerio, struggling to keep the appearance, and tortured . . . Charley would try, and fail, and try again. As though she were haunted, as though . . .

The gardener watched her. Whenever Charley was outside the gardener was always close, with the hose for the plants, with the broom for the paths, with the fork for the weeds, always near to her, where he could see her. One day, bloody certain, one day she'd put a towel on the grass and lie on it, and give the "lechie" something to look at. One day . . .

"Charley. Do you know what is the time, Charley?"

She turned. She looked toward the open patio doors.

"It's all right, Angela, I've not forgotten the time, about ten minutes, then I'm off for them."

Angela Ruggerio stood in the doorway. It made Charley miserable to see her, to see her drawn face, to see her attempt to smile, to see the woman pretend. There was no love, Charley reckoned, and there had been love in Rome. But not her problem.

"I was just doing some postcards, friends and family . . ."

Angela repeated the word, rolled it. "Family? You have a family, Charley?"

"Not really, but there's my parents and there's my mother's brother, lives up in the north of England. We hardly see him . . . I'm afraid we're not like Italians in England, family doesn't matter that much. But—"

The bitterness snapped in Angela's voice, as when a mask slips. "Find a Sicilian, and you find a family."

She must never pry, Axel had said, never push. "I suppose so."

"When you were with us in Rome, you did not know that Peppino was Sicilian?"

"No."

"With a Sicilian there is always a family, the family is everything . . ."

She was gone. Angela went as quietly as she had come.

Charley finished the addresses on the postcards. She had come into the villa to find Angela, to ask when the post office closed and whether she would have time to buy stamps. She moved, barefoot across the marble of the living area and the tiles of the hallway at the back. She moved without sound. Angela lay full-length on the bed. Charley saw her through the open door. Angela lay on her stomach on the bed and her body convulsed in weeping. She knew of the family. The family was Rosario and Agata in Prizzi, and Mario who was hunted and Salvatore who was in prison, and Carmelo who was simple, and Cristoforo who was dead and Maria who drank, and Giuseppe who washed the money. She knew of the family because Axel had told her. Charley watched the woman weep and sob. She felt humbled.

She left the villa, the prison, and walked with the baby in the pram into the town to collect small Mario and Francesca.

"You'd like a coffee?"

"Yes, I'd like that, *espresso*, thanks."

"Three coffees, *espresso*, please."

The policeman bobbed his head in acknowledgment. He was an old tired man, in a uniform that bulged over his stomach. He looked to be the sort of fixture in the upper corridor of the Palazzo di Giustizia that they had in the same upper corridors at Headquarters. He wore a pistol in a holster that slapped his thigh, but his job was of little more importance than bringing coffee for guests.

The magistrate gestured that 'Vanni should go first through the outer door. Axel followed. There were minders on the outer door and minders on the inner door. Both the doors were steel-plated. There had been razor-wire coils on the walls around the compound in La Paz. They had lived in Bolivia, and worked, with a pistol at the waist, with constant apprehension. They had been careful in their movements, avoided nighttime car journeys. The screen around the magistrate, Dr. Rocco Tardelli, even on the top floor of the Palazzo di Giustizia, jolted Axel and he tried to imagine what it would be like to live a half life under guard. It was over the top, above anything he had seen on the previous trips down to Palermo. The inner door, steel-plated, was closed behind them, his view of the harsh and suspicious-faced guards was lost. He blinked in the low light of the room. Behind the drawn blinds there would have been shatterproof and bulletproof glass . . . A shit of a way to live.

The man was small and so bowed and while he tried to play at the necessary courtesies his eyes flickered in a constant and moving wariness. Axel knew the phrase the "walking dead." He could laugh about the "walking dead" in Rome, make gas-chamber humor of it, but not here, not where the reality confronted him. His Country Chief rated Dr. Rocco Tardelli, took him to lunch when he was in Rome. Headquarters rated Dr. Rocco Tardelli, flew him to the Andrews USAF Base once a year on a military transport and had him talk to the Strategy teams, poor bastard. The Country Chief said, and Headquarters said, that Dr. Rocco Tardelli was a jewel—but not precious enough to share with . . . The poor bastard seemed, to Axel, a caged creature.

A knock at the door. The coffee tray was set down on the desk, and the machine pistol of the young guard swung on its strap and clattered against the desktop. Shit, the goddamn thing was armed, and the magistrate seemed to wince.

"Careful, Pasquale, please."

They were alone.

The soft voice. "So the DEA has come to Palermo. May I be so impertinent as to ask what mission brings you here?"

Axel said, "We have an operation going, the target is Ruggerio."

"Then you are one of so many. What is the scope of the operation?"

Axel said, "We hope to mark him. If we mark him, then we send for the cavalry."

Said dry, with a gentle smile, "Of course you would expect that we have plans for the arrest of Ruggerio. What is the range of the operation from which the DEA believes it will taste success when we eat failure?"

"This is what you'd call a courtesy call. We have a small range of facilities organized by our friend. 'Vanni is looking after our interest." Axel shifted awkwardly in his chair. "I'd rather not be specific."

The smile widened, warmth flowed and there was a brightness in the magistrate's eyes. "Do not be embarrassed—I am the same as you. I trust very few people. You would not expect me to tell you of the locations of the physical surveillance and the bugs and the cameras, where we watch for Ruggerio . . . You would not expect me to tell you what information I have from the *pentiti*. But it is a sad game to play when there is no trust."

"It's not personal."

"Why should it be. So, we are engaged in competition. You wish to achieve what we cannot. You wish to show the Italian people that the power of the United States of America is so great that they can succeed where we fail." The smile was long gone, his eyes fixed on Axel. "If you succeed where we fail, then I assume you would seek the extradition of Ruggerio, and fly him back in chains to your courts as you did with Badalamenti."

"We have charges to lay against Ruggerio. It would be a message because we'd lock him up till he was dead."

"There are many here who would appreciate such a situation, and the poison whispers would pass in these corridors that Tardelli, the seeker after glory, was humiliated. You have put an agent into Palermo?"

What he'd heard, more prosecutions were blocked by the jealousies, the ambitions, the envy, of colleagues than by the efforts of La Cosa Nostra. The man yearned for a rope to be thrown him. Axel looked away. "I'd rather not."

"My assumption, Signor Moen, you have put an agent

of small importance into Palermo. I do not wish to insult you, but if it were an agent of big importance then Bill himself would have come, but only you have traveled . . . Do you know of Tom Tripodi?"

Axel scratched in his memory. "Yes, didn't meet him, gone before I joined, I heard of him. Why?"

"He was here in the summer of 1979, not too long ago for lessons to be remembered. He was the star agent from Washington, and he worked with *vice questore* Boris Giuliano. He posed as a buyer of narcotics, he found himself an introduction to Badalamenti, who was then *capo di tutti capi*. For those who made the plans in Washington it would have seemed so simple. An agent in place to achieve what the Italians could not. So sad that there was disappointment, that Badalamenti did not bite. It ended with Tripodi running for his life, taken to the docks by Boris Giuliano, with escort cars, with a helicopter overhead. We paid a heavy price, maybe because of Tripodi and maybe not, on the twenty-first of July of that year. Some days, a few days, after Tripodi ran from Palermo, *Vice questore* Giuliano went to his usual bar for his usual coffee early in the morning, and he did not have the chance to reach for his gun. But, of course, Signor Moen, the danger to your agent and to those who work with you, and to yourself, will have been carefully evaluated in Washington . . ."

There was steel in the magistrate's eyes, there had been the rasp of sarcasm in his voice.

Axel said brusquely, "We have made an evaluation."

"I am very frank with you, Signor Moen, I do not have an agent in place. I do not have an agent close to Mario Ruggerio, nor do I try to put an agent in proximity to that man. I would not wish it to lie on my conscience, the danger to an agent. Unless your agent is scum, a creature of the gutter, whose life is held to be of small importance . . ."

Axel stood. "Thank you for your time. Bill wanted to

be remembered to you. It was only a courtesy."

The magistrate was already at the papers on his desk as they closed the door on the inner office. God, and he wanted to be out of the goddamn place, like it was a place where he could suffocate on foul air.

The guards watched them go, and drew casually on their cigarettes and stopped the card game. Axel led, pounding down the corridor, past the policeman who had been instructed to bring them coffee. Didn't wait for the elevator, but skipped down the wide stairs.

Out into the fresh air, the goddam building behind him. He turned his back on the great gray-white building, Fascist architecture and a crap symbol of the state's power. He strode between the high pillars that were built to impress, through the parked and armor-reinforced cars that offered status.

"What I cannot comprehend—"

"What you cannot comprehend, Axel, is how small brother Giuseppe is not a priority to Tardelli's investigations. I tell you, he works alone. He does not trust a staff. He works from early in the morning till too late in the night. He pushes paper until he is exhausted, because he does not trust . . . A long time ago he talked with little brother Giuseppe, in Rome, and was satisfied with what he was told. Think, how many meters of paper have crossed his desk since then? His mind is governed by priorities, and what he dismissed four, five years ago is low with priority. Of course he should target the family, every root of the family, but his mind is cluttered, his mind is tired, he has lost track of the distant root of the family. Do you complain that I don't help him? We are not the wonderful DEA, Axel, where colleagues are trusted, where work is shared. We are just pathetic Italians, yes? We are just food for your prejudices, yes?

He did not look back to see the troops on the flat roof

with their machine guns, he did not glance sideways to see the troops patroling the outer fence, he went by the troops at the gate ignoring them as they pushed the antibomb mirror on the pole under a car. 'Vanni had to run to keep up with him, and Axel pitched himself into the traffic flow, and the protest blasts of the horns beat in his ears. On the far side of the street, Axel swung round and he gripped 'Vanni's shirtfront.

"Why did he do that, why did he piss on me?"

'Vanni was laughing. "He goes to all the funerals. Maybe he is too busy to go to your funeral or the Codename Helen's funeral. Maybe he was telling you to be careful because he does not have a hole in his diary."

He thought of her, standing beside the Saracen tower, looking for him, alone, not finding him.

Carrying the small bag, with a raincoat sagging from between the straps, Mario Ruggerio walked out of the Capo district.

He came from behind the Palazzo di Giustizia. There was no expression on his face as he went past the building site backing onto the building where new offices were under construction for the sprouting kingdom of the magistrates and prosecutors. An old man with a small bag and a check cap on his head and a gray tweed jacket on his peasant's shoulders drew no interest from the soldiers of the *bersagliere* regiment on the roof, on the gates, beside the fence, on the pavement corners. In front of the Palazzo a policeman strutted importantly into the traffic flow and blew an imperious whistle blast, stopped the cars and vans and allowed the old man and others to cross safely over the Via Goethe.

He walked a full 750 meters along the Via Constantino Lascaris and the Via Giudita, and he did not turn his head to see the approach of sirens behind him. He walked until the breath was short in his lungs, until the tiredness was in his legs. The figures from the Casio calculator played in his mind, absorbed him. His concentration on the figures was broken only when he rested and faced a shop window, when he turned to watch the pavement behind him and the pavement across the street, when he checked to see if a car dawdled slowly after him. Near to the junction of the Via Giudita and the Via Giuglielmo il Buono, tucked away behind an apartment block, was the garage.

At the entrance to the garage, by the high gates that were topped with wire, he turned again and checked again.

The cousin of the owner of the garage had shared a cell in Ucciardone, four years before, with Salvatore Ruggerio. The cousin had received the protection of Salvatore Ruggerio. Four years later, in return for that protection, a debt was called in.

The garage was a good place to meet. He went between the cars parked out in the forecourt and into the building that was alive with the music from a radio and the hiss of the welding burner and the clatter of spanners and the clamor of the panel-beating mallets. He carried his bag into a back office and the owner of the garage looked up, saw him and immediately cleared the papers from his desk and dusted the chair, as if an emperor had come. He was asked if he wished for coffee or for juice, and he shook his head. He sat on the cleaned chair, and waited.

It was a good place for a meeting with Peppino. It was where Peppino had, for the last year, brought his car for servicing. He lit a cigar. He assumed that Peppino, though he denied it, was under sporadic surveillance.

When Peppino came, they embraced.

"You are well?"

"Fine."

"A good journey?"

"London was for me, for us, very good."

They talked the business. Peppino told his brother, close detail, down to each contractor's percentage, of the deal for the leisure complex at Orlando in Florida. Peppino spoke of the money that would be moved from Vienna to the account of Giles Blake in London and then invested with a merchant banker and a broker and a building contractor who needed the funds to complete seven stories of a Manchester office block. He said what arrangements were made for the visit of the Colombian from Medellín who managed onward shipments into Europe. And there were the Russians he would meet the week after in Zagreb.

And Mario thought his brother spoke well. Only rarely did he interrupt. What was the commission for the clients of Giles Blake? Where would the meeting be with the Colombian? What percentage, down to a quarter of a point, would the Russians pay? He loved the younger man, so different from himself, and every phase of the differential had been planned by him, as though he had made and fashioned each stage of Peppino's life. He could smell the talc on Peppino's body, and the lotion on his face. The suit was the best, the shirt was the best, the tie was the best and the shoes of his brother. The irony was not lost on Mario Ruggerio. Wealth and success clung to Peppino. Their parents lived in the old terraced house in Prizzi with Carmelo. Salvatore rotted in a cell in the prison at Asinara. Cristoforo was dead. Maria was cut off from them because the alcohol made her dangerous. His own wife, Michela, and his own children, Salvo and Domenica, were in Prizzi, where she looked after her mother. Only Peppino lived the good life.

Nothing was written, everything was in their heads. He told Peppino of what the accountant had said, recited the figures of declining income and increasing outgoings.

"You should not listen to him. If you were a small man,

if you were concerned only with investments and product on the island, then this would be perhaps important. Your portfolio is international. You are better without him."

"There are some who say that I do not interest myself enough in the opportunities given by Sicily."

"I think in Catania they say that, where there is a small man—as the man in Agrigento was a small man . . ."

It was, for Giuseppe Ruggerio, the confirmation of a death sentence. "It is possible for a small man, as from Catania, to obstruct progress. If a tree falls in the wind and blocks a road, it is necessary to bring the saw, and to cut the tree, and to burn it."

"Burn it with fire."

They laughed, the chuckle of Peppino merging with the growled snigger of Mario Ruggerio. They laughed as the sentence of death was confirmed.

And the smile stayed on the old and lined face. "And how is my little angel?"

"*Piccolo* Mario, the same as his uncle, a rascal."

"Francesca and the baby?"

"Wonderful."

"I hope very much soon to see them. I have their photograph. I carry their photograph. I do not carry a photograph of your aunt, nor of Salvo and Domenica, but I have with me the picture of Francesca and the *birichino*. The day you went to London, I was near to the Giardino Inglese, I saw the rascal. I have few enough pleasures. And Angela, how is your wife, how is the Roman lady?"

"She survives."

He noted the coolness of the response. He shook his head. "Not good, Peppino. Sometimes there is a problem if the wife of someone like yourself is not happy, sometimes there is an unnecessary problem."

Peppino said, "In Rome we had a girl to help Angela

with the children, an English girl. Angela became fond of her. I have brought her back, to the villa in Mondello, to make Angela happier."

The eyebrows of the old man lifted sharply, questioning. "That is sensible?"

"She is just a girl from the country. A simple girl, but she is company for Angela."

"You are sure of her?"

"I think so."

"You should be certain. If she has the freedom of your home, there should not be doubt."

When Mario Ruggerio left, he walked from the garage to the corner of Via Giuglielmo il Buono and Via Normanini. He had the time to go into the *tabaccaio* and buy three packets of his cigars, and then the time, while he waited on the corner, to think of the small man from Catania, a tree that blocked the road and should be cut and burned, and more time to think of the family that he loved and the rascal boy who was named in respect of him. The Citroën BX came to the corner. The driver leaned across to push open the passenger door. He was driven away. A dentist had moved from Palermo to Turin and the apartment on Via Crociferi that was now vacated would be the safe house, for a week, used by Mario Ruggerio. At least he would sleep there, be free of the shit noise of the Capo district.

He could not sleep. He stood at the window. Behind him was the bed and the sound of his wife's rhythmic snoring— he had not told her. In front of him were the lights of Catania, and out at sea were the lights of the approaching car ferry from Reggio. He could not talk about such matters with his wife. Never in thirty-two years of marriage had he talked of such matters, so she did not know of his fear and she slept, and snored. Alone, unshared, was the fear. Because of the fear, the loaded pistol was on the table beside his bed and the assault rifle was on the rug under the bed. Because of the fear, his son had come from his own home and now slept in the adjoining room. The fear had held him since he had come away from the meeting in the Madonie mountains with Mario Ruggerio. Other than his son, he did not know now in whom he could place his faith. It would come to war, war to the death, between his family and the family of Mario Ruggerio, and each man of his family, in his home and his bed, would now be making the decision as to which side he would fight on. He knew the way of Mario Ruggerio. It was the way that Mario Ruggerio had climbed. From among his own family of men there would be one who was targeted by the bastards of Mario Ruggerio, targeted and twisted and turned and bent to compliance.

One of his own family of men would lead him to death, and he did not know which one. The fear, in the night, ate at him.

"I don't want Pietro Aglieri, I don't want Provenzano nor Salvatore Minore, I don't want Mariano Troia. You see them, you light a cigarette for them, and you offer them gum, but you don't show out."

A weak and nervous ripple of laughter played in his office. Rocco Tardelli believed that each man on a surveillance team should be in at the briefing. He reeled off the names of the *super-latitanti* and grinned humbly. They would have thought him an idiot. They stood in front of his desk, seven and not nine of them because one was on holiday and one claimed illness. He turned over the photograph on his desk, showed it to them.

"I want him. I want Mario Ruggerio. Aglieri, Provenzano, Minore, Troia are men of yesterday, gone, spent. Ruggerio is the man of tomorrow. There are insufficient of you. We have no more cameras than before. We do not know where to put audio devices. The photograph is twenty years old, but it has been through the computer. I do not know now if Ruggerio has a mustache, I do not know whether he routinely wears spectacles, I do not know whether he has dyed his hair. You are going into the Capo district, which is the most criminally aware sector of Palermo, I believe, more so than Brancaccio or Ciaculli. The prospect of your maintaining a cover for ten days is minimal, and you know that better than I. The information I have is that Ruggerio took an almond cake in the bar in the street between the Via Sant'Agostino and the Piazza Beati Paoli which caused him to shit, but that was a year ago."

The men of the *squadra mobile* surveillance team laughed at the magistrate, which was the intention of Rocco Tardelli. The surveillance teams, whether from the ROS or the DIA or the *Guardia di Finanze* or the *squadra mobile,* were in his opinion the cream. They looked so awful, quite beyond salvation—they were like street thieves and like beggars and like pimps for whores and like narcotics pushers. They looked like the filth of the city. But, his *maresciallo* knew them all, and had sworn on the loyalty of each of them. He wanted them to laugh at him. He needed them to reckon that what was asked of them was idiot's work. Others would have lectured them, others would have minimized the problems. Rocco Tardelli challenged them.

"And, of course, you should know that you are not alone in hunting Ruggerio. Every agency has a plan for his capture. You know, even a foreigner has come to me, as a matter of courtesy, to inform me that he is on the ground and hunting *il bruto.* You are considered to have the least chance, you are at the bottom of the priority heap, you are assigned to an obsessional and neurotic and vain investigator. You are given to me."

They gazed at him. The time of laughter was over.

He said quietly, "If he is there,—if,—I know you will find him. Thank you."

Peppino had come home the night before, late.

When she made breakfast for Francesca and small Mario, while she heated the milk for baby Mauro's bottle, Charley had heard the sounds of the lovemaking from the main bedroom of the villa. Tried to concentrate on what measure of cereal for the children, and what temperature the milk should be heated to, and she had heard the groaned whisper of the bed. It was eight months since she had had sex, been screwed by the creep in the caravan who'd come over her stomach before he was even inside her . . . She turned the radio up loud. On the radio was the news of a train strike and a rail strike and an airline strike, and a man had been shot in Misilmeri, and there was a demonstration of pensioners in Rome, and an excavator digging a drain's trench in Sciacca had uncovered the buried bones of four men, and the treasurer of the Milan city administration had been arrested for taking the *bustarella,* and . . . Christ, it was better listening to the sex. All through the breakfast of the children, all the time that she chewed on an apple and peeled an orange for herself, all through feeding the baby, Charley heard the whisper of the bed.

When she was ready to take the children to school and kindergarten, when she had laid the baby Mauro in the pram, and taken the housekeeping purse from the drawer and Angela's shopping list from the table, there was the sound of the shower running. She didn't call out. It had sounded like good sex, like the sex the bloody girls at college had bragged of, like the sex Charley hadn't known with the bloody lecturer and the bloody man in his caravan, like the sex she never heard from her mother's bedroom. She went

down into Mondello and she saw Francesca into the kindergarten class and she kissed small Mario at the school gate and
saw him run inside.

She walked in the street behind the piazza, where the
bars were open behind scrubbed and sluiced pavements,
where the *trattorias* and *pizzerias* were being prepared for the
day with swept floors and laundered tablecloths. She bought
salad things from a stall, and cheese and milk and olive oil
from the *alimentari,* and some fresh sliced ham. She ticked
each item on Angela's list.

Every morning, when she took the children to school
and kindergarten, and shopped, she looked for him, and
never saw him.

That morning she did not linger in the town. Her shopping was completed. She pushed the pram with the sleeping
baby back up the hill, past where the workmen were repair-
ing the sewerage pipes, past the leaping and barking guard
dogs, back to the villa. She whistled sharply at the gate, like
she was in charge, and she had learned that the bloody
"lechie," the miserable toad, the gardener, came running
when she whistled and opened the locked gate for her. She
didn't thank him, ignored him and walked past him. She left
the baby, sleeping in the pram, on the patio that was shaded
from the rising sun. In the kitchen she put the salad things
and the cheese and milk and ham into the refrigerator and
the olive oil into the cupboard. She wanted her book.

She almost crashed into him.

The door to her bedroom was open. Peppino stood in
the corridor beside the open door.

He said that he had come to look for her. He wore a
loose toweled dressing gown. The hair was thick on his legs
and on his chest, and he had not shaved. He said that he had
not realized she had already gone with the children and with
the shopping list. Well, she hadn't wanted to disturb him.

had she? Wouldn't want to muscle in on a good fuck, would she? He said that he wanted her to buy flowers, fresh-cut flowers. Very good, sex and flowers to buy off Angela's misery, no problem in tramping down to the town again and buying flowers. He was sleek headed from the shower, and the talc dust was a frost on his chest hair. She thought it amused him, using her as a messenger, a fetcher and carrier. She wondered if Angela, back in the bedroom, smiled or cried, whether a fuck changed her life, whether flowers would lift her spirits.

She took the purse from the kitchen drawer. Back down the path between the flower beds, back past the gardener, back through the gates, and she slammed them behind her and the lock clicked into place. Back past the fury of the guard dogs, and past the workmen who leered at her and stripped her from the sewerage trench. Back to the piazza . . .

Right, Giuseppe Ruggerio, right. Expensive flowers. At the stall she took from the housekeeping purse a note for 50,000 *lire*. Not enough. She took a note for 100,000. She gave the 100,000 *lire* note to the man. What would the *signorina* like? She shrugged, she would like what she could have for £40 sterling, and he should choose. She took the wrapped bunch, chrysanthemums and carnations, and crooked them on her elbow. She was walking away.

"Go down to the sea front."

The voice was behind her.

"Don't look round, don't acknowledge."

The voice, quiet, belted her.

Charley obeyed. She didn't turn to see Axel. She fixed her eyes ahead of her, took a line between the Saracen tower and the fishermen's pier. She assumed he followed her. The American accent had been sharp, curt. She walked through the piazza. She waited for the traffic and crossed the road.

She stood beside an old man who sat on a stool on the pavement, and in front of him was a box of fresh fish with ice around them and he held up an ancient black umbrella to shadow his fish.

"Keep walking, slowly, and never turn."

Charley walked. The sea was blue-green, the boats in the sea rolled at their moorings.

She thought he was very close, near enough to touch her. The voice behind her was a murmur.

"How does it go?"

"Nothing goes."

"What does that mean?"

"Nothing happens."

Said cold, "If it happens, anything happens, it'll be quick, sudden. Is there any sign of suspicion?"

"No." She looked ahead, out over the sea and the boats, and she tried to show him her defiance. "I'm a part of the family, it's just a damned miserable family, it's—"

"Don't whine . . . and don't ever relax. Don't go complacent."

"Aren't you going to tell me?"

"Tell you what?"

"The test? Did your gadget work?"

"It was OK."

She flared, she spat from the side of her mouth, but the discipline held and she did not turn to face him. "Just OK? Brilliant. I've been wetting myself. If you didn't know, it's my link. My road to the outside. It's like a morgue in there. I feel so much better to know that your gadget works OK. Not magnificent, not incredible, not wonderful."

"It was OK. Remember, because it's important, don't be casual. Keep walking."

"When'll I see you again?"

"Don't know."

"You bastard, do you know what it's like, living the lie?"

"Keep walking."

She was able to smell him, and she heard the light tread of his footfall behind her. She walked on with the flowers. The tears welled in her eyes. Why, when she cried out for praise, did he have to be so damned cruel to her?

She could no longer smell him, no longer hear him. She wondered whether he cared enough to stand and watch her go. She smeared the tears out of her eyes. She carried the flowers back to the villa. Bloody hell. In less than an hour and a half she would be going again into the town to collect the children. Peppino was dressed. Peppino thanked her and smiled gratitude. He told her that she was very welcome in their home, and that they so much appreciated her kindness to the children, and she had not had a day off, and she should go tomorrow on the bus to Palermo, and he winked and took a wad of notes from his pocket and peeled off some for her and told her of a shop on the Via della Liberta where the girls went for their clothes, young girls' clothes. He was sweetness to her, and he took the flowers into the bedroom to Angela. Charley went for her book.

Her book, on the table beside the bed, alongside the photograph of her parents, had been moved.

She felt the cold running over her.

Only slightly moved, but she could picture where it had been, a little over the edge of the table.

She could tell nothing from the clothes hanging in her wardrobe. She could not recall exactly where her sausage bag had been on top of the wardrobe.

She thought that her bras had been on top of her pants in the middle drawer of the chest, and now they were underneath.

Charley stood in her room and she breathed hard.

•　　•　　•

"Is that all you said?"

"I said the test transmission had been OK, I told her that she was not to relax. Because nothing has happened she should not be complacent."

"That's all?"

"There wasn't anything else to say."

The archaeologist was hunched down on the stone slab and his back was against the square fashioned rock that was the base of the cloister column. He sketched rapidly, and to reinforce the detail of his work he used a tape to measure height and width and diameter. It was natural, when an expert came to the *duomo* and studied the history of the construction of the cathedral, that a busy-minded and prying bystander should come to talk with him, question him, disturb him. So natural that none of the tourists or the priests or the guides took note of the archaeologist and the bystander. There was a bag by the feet of the archaeologist, and from the bag a chrome aerial was extended to its full length, but the aerial was wedged between the spine of the archaeologist and the base rock of the column and was hidden from the echoing flow in the cloisters of the tourists and the priests and the guides.

'Vanni said, "You make it hard for her, very hard."

Axel did not look up from his sketch pad. "She has to find her own strength."

"You gave her no comfort."

"That's crap."

"Did I tell you the story about dalla Chiesa?"

"General dalla Chiesa is dead."

'Vanni grinned. "I don't wish to be impertinent to my friend, to the eminent *archeologo*, and I think you are most sensible to pursue the cover, give it authenticity. I think it is right you are not 'complacent'—but an *archeologo* takes lessons from the past, and General dalla Chiesa is of the past and offers lessons."

"It is difficult to study detail when one is subject to the boring interruption of a stranger, don't you think?"

'Vanni said, conversational, "There was a story that the general told of when he was a young *carabiniere* officer in Sicily, some years before he achieved the fame of destroying the *Brigate Rosse*. He had a telephone call from a captain under his command who was responsible for the town of Palma di Montechiaro which is near to Agrigento. The captain told dalla Chiesa that he was under threat in the town from the local *capo*. He went to the town, he met the captain. He took the captain's arm, held his arm, and walked with him up the street of Palma di Montechiaro, and back again. They walked slowly so that everyone in the town could see that he held the captain's arm. They stopped outside the home of the *capo*. They stood in silence outside that house until it was quite clear, no misunderstanding, that the captain was not alone. Do you still listen to me, my friend the *archeologo?*"

Axel did not look up from his sketch pad and his calculations. "I listen to you."

"Years later, General dalla Chiesa came to Palermo to take the post at the Prefettura. He found himself mocked, sneered at, obstructed and alone. Each initiative he tried to make against La Cosa Nostra was blocked by the corruption of the government. In desperation he telephoned for a meeting with the American consul in the city. I drove him there, to see Ralph Jones. I sat in on the meeting. The general begged of Jones that the government of the United States should intervene with Rome, 'do something at the highest level.' At the finish of the meeting, the general told Jones the story of Palma di Montechiaro, and he said, 'All I ask is for somebody to take my arm and to walk with me.' I drove him back to the Prefettura. At the end of the day he dismissed me. His wife came to take him home. He was killed, with his wife, that night in Via Carini. He was killed because he was alone, because nobody had taken his arm and walked with him."

"What do you want of me?"

'Vanni's voice was close and hoarse. "Should you not take her arm, Codename Helen's arm, and walk with her when she is alone, and give her comfort?"

"I can't give her the strength. She must find it for herself."

The bystander walked away from the archaeologist, left him to his research.

"No."

"I'm sorry, Mr. Parsons, but I have to be quite clear about this. My question was, did you have a telephone call a week ago from Bruno Fiori?"

"Same answer, no."

They sat across the fireplace from Harry Compton. He thought they were scared half out of their minds.

"And you don't know an Italian who uses the name of Bruno Fiori?"

"No."

"Would you care to look at this, Mr. Parsons?"

He was deep in his chair in the small front living room, and reaching into his briefcase, and he passed to the man the printout list of the telephone calls. The woman sat close to her husband and her eyes were down and staring at the card he had given them. His card had that effect on people. METROPOLITAN POLICE FRAUD DEPARTMENT, HARRY COMPTON, DETECTIVE SERGEANT, FINANCIAL INVESTIGATOR frightened the shit out of them. The man glanced at the list of calls made from the hotel room, two London numbers and his own number.

The man glowered back defiantly, like he was trying to show that he wasn't scared half out of his mind. "Yes, that's my number."

The woman said, eyes never leaving the card, "It was Dr. Ruggerio who called."

The man's glance flashed at his wife, then, "We were telephoned by Dr. Giuseppe Ruggerio. And may I ask what business that is of yours?"

"Better that I ask the questions. Why did this Giuseppe Ruggerio telephone you?"

"I'm not going to be interrogated, without explanation, in my own home."

"Please, Mr. Parsons, just get on with it."

He wrote a fast shorthand note. He heard the name of Charlotte, an only daughter.

He could see from his chair out through the open door of the living room and into the hall. He could see the photograph of the young woman in her graduation gown and her mortarboard at a cheeky angle. He heard the story of a summer job in 1992. And a letter had come, and the invitation for a return to minding children. The information came in a slow and prompted drip. Charlotte had given up her job and was now in Sicily. The wife had gone to the kitchen and come back with an address, and Harry wrote it on his pad and underlined the words GIARDINO INGLESE.

The father said, "Dr. Ruggerio telephoned but Charlotte was . . . she was out. I spoke to him, he just said how much they wanted her. I was against it, her going. She's thrown up a good job. God knows what she's going to do when she gets back. Jobs aren't on trees."

The mother said, "They're a lovely family. He's such a gentleman, Dr. Ruggerio, very successful, banking or something. David thinks that life is all work, and what's work done for him? Chucked out without thanks, redundant. I said that she would only be young once. They treat her like one of the family. If she hadn't gone she'd have been old before her time, like us."

He closed his notebook, slipped it into his pocket. He stood. He was asked again why he had an interest in Dr. Giuseppe Ruggerio, and he smiled coolly and thanked them for their hospitality, not even a bloody cup of tea. He went out into the hall. He looked at the photograph of the young woman and made a remark that she was a grand-looking girl. He took his coat from the hook. The man opened the door for him. He could hear the sea beating on a shingle away in the evening darkness. A woman was across the lane, clinging to a dog's leash and staring at him as he stood under the porch light. He saw a man hunched in a lit window across the lane and peering at him through small binoculars. Behind a board advertising bed-and-breakfast (VACANCIES), a curtain fell back to its place. God, what a dreary and supicious little backwater. He started down the path to the gate.

The hiss of the woman. "Aren't you going to tell him?"

The man's whisper. "It's not his business."

"You should tell him."

"No."

"You should tell him about the American . . ."

Harry Compton stopped, turned. "What should I know? What American?"

To: Alfred Rogers, DLO, British Embassy, Via XX Settembre, Rome.
From: D/S Harry Compton, SO6.

Please get your leg off the beautiful women and ditch the bottle you will inevitably be busting open. Do me SOONEST a P check on Dr. GIUSEPPE RUGGERIO, Apt 9, Giardino Inglese 43, Palermo, Sicily. Ruggerio believed to be in finance, banking? Interests me because he uses alias of BRUNO FIORI. Don't break a blood vessel at the chance of actually doing something useful. Come up with the goods and I'll stand you a half-pint at the Ferret and Ferkin on your next extended (!) leave.

Bestest, Harry.

He had the scent, the smell was in his nostrils. He gave the sheet of paper to Miss Frobisher for transmission to the DLO, jammy sod, in Rome. Bloody good job, that one, soft old number. His detective superintendent was out of the building. It would have to keep, what he had to share, but there was a good bounce in his step. The day that the invitation to travel down to Palermo had reached Charlotte Parsons there had pitched up on her doorstep an American from the embassy, from the Drug Enforcement Administration. "He said that if I talked about him, what he said to me, then I might be responsible for hurting people." He'd bloody well find out, too right, what Americans were doing running round foreign territory to scoop up compliant and untrained agents. Charlotte Parsons's father had said that his daughter was "pressured" to travel. The boss would like it. Harry's boss had been skewered and minced and chewed by the FBI the last summer at the Europol fraud conference in Lyon. He'd come back bruised from France, worked over for suggesting that international crime was a figment of American imagination. He'd said, loud, at a seminar that international crime was a fantasyland, and been told for all to listen that he was talking rubbish and that the Brits were just part-time players. Harry had heard it from the inspector who'd traveled as the detective superintendent's bag carrier. If the Americans had taken an English girl, "pressured" her, dragged her in, then his boss would not mind hearing of it, too right.

$$\underset{\blacktriangledown}{\overset{8}{\text{─}}}$$

IN TWO YEARS, not more than three years, he would have sufficient money to buy the *pizzeria*.

Each time that he was paid, in American bills, he sent them by post to his son. He had enough money already to buy a *pizzeria* in Palermo, nearly enough money to buy a *pizzeria* in Milan or Turin. But to buy a *pizzeria* in Hanover, near to the railway station, was more costly. His son and his daughter-in-law and his grandchildren lived in Hanover. They were, and he thought it was quite shameful to his own dignity, a part of the immigrant underclass in Germany. His son worked at night in the kitchen of a *trattoria* in Hanover, his daughter-in-law went to the *trattoria* in the mornings to clean it and to lay the tables. When there was sufficient money his son would use it to buy a *pizzeria,* and he would go to Hanover with his wife and with his daughter and he would live the last of his days there. The *pizzeria* in Hanover was the limit of his dream, and he and his wife and his daughter and his daughter-in-law would take it in turn to sit behind the cash desk. In return for the money, a thousand American dollars a month, he supplied information. The money came to him each month whether the information he supplied was important or whether it was insignificant. The money was a certainty, just as it was a certainty that he could not cease to provide the information. Trapped, corrupted, he stood one morning each month in the park in front of the Palazzo Reale and he watched the mothers with their children and their babies and waited for the contact to be made. He did not know the name of the man who came to him, nor did he know to whom the information was delivered. One morning every month he reported on what he had seen and heard, nothing written down, and then he walked from the park and along the Via Papireto and he would stop at the post office and buy the stamps for Germany. He would send the money. At the Palazzo di Giustizia he would show his identity card, walk past the soldiers, climb the wide steps, go to the rest room and open his locker and change into his uniform, and then he would go to the armory and draw his firearm and the holster, and then he would take the elevator to the upper corridor where he saw and he heard, and he would bring the small cups of *espresso* coffee to the magistrates and prosecutors. One morning each month his dream of buying the *pizzeria* in Hanover came closer.

A man stood beside him, and asked with courtesy whether he had a match for a cigarette, and they talked, as men talked who stood in a park and watched the mothers with their children and their babies.

The policeman said, ". . . He spoke in Italian, but the accent was American. 'Yes, I'd like that, *espresso*, thanks.' He was not Italo-American because he had a fair skin and gold hair. I recognized the one who brought him, that was Giovanni Crespo who is of the ROS in the Monreale barracks. He was not an American journalist because Tardelli never sees journalists, and when I brought the coffee I was not permitted by Tardelli's guards to take the tray inside myself. The tray was carried inside by Tardelli's man. I remember last year, in the winter, when an American came and I was not permitted to take the coffee inside, and then I heard the guards say that the American was the Country Chief of the DEA from Rome. The American was with

Tardelli for fifteen or twenty minutes. What I can tell you of Giovanni Crespo, he is with the squad of the ROS that searches for the *super-latitanti*. The American wore casual clothes, not the clothes that are worn for a meeting with a person of the position of Tardelli, jeans and an open shirt, it surprised me, and he did not carry a briefcase but a small bag. I cannot be certain, I think there was a firearm in his waist but under his shirt. I estimate that he weighed near to 80 kilos, a height of perhaps 1.80 or 1.85 meters. He wore his hair long, like a hippy, and his hair was taken at the back with an elastic band, fair hair. I wondered how it was possible that such a man could be brought to meet Tardelli . . . I know also that Tardelli has met with a team from the *squadra mobile,* they were dressed very roughly, so it is a surveillance team. Again, I was not permitted to take in the coffee. The story on the corridor, but it is only gossip, is that Tardelli had the big argument with the prosecutors and magistrates, I don't know . . ."

An envelope was passed. The policeman talked of the information scraps he had gained in a month of the work of other magistrates and other prosecutors.

He went on his way to the post, and dreamed of the *pizzeria* near to the railway station in Hanover, then to the Palazzo di Giustizia.

Her mother would have said that she should not have taken the money, and her father would have said that it would have seemed ungrateful to refuse the money. The purse in her handbag bulged with the roll of notes. Her mother would have said that it was simple human nature, like it or not, for people to look in the drawers of a guest, and her father would have said that she had probably forgotten where she had laid down her book and whether her pants had been on top or below her bras.

Charley had the money, and she wore the handbag draped from her shoulder across her chest. She didn't know.

She could not know, and all through the night she had tossed and twisted it in her mind, whether the movement of her book and her clothes was the mark of suspicion against her, or was in innocence, or was her bloody imagination. The taxi driver in Mondello had quoted her 20,000, sod that. She had come on the bus along the road that was shadowed by the height of Monte Pellegrino, on the road that skirted the La Favorita park where the whores were already gathered, on the road that cut through the high-rise blocks. Where the Via della Libertà merged into the Piazza Crispi, Charley had pushed her way to the bus door.

Better to think it was her bloody imagination. But, he had said, the damned faceless man creeping behind her, "Don't ever relax, Don't go complacent." She felt a freedom, as if the garden gate of the villa, when it had slammed shut behind her, had been a jail's gate. She walked along the Via della Libertà. They were beautiful shops, they were better than any of the shops in Plymouth or Exeter. The temperature was near to the seventies, and the women around her had fur coats hoisted loose on their shoulders, and the men wore their best *loden* coats. It was so bloody hot, and she was in a blouse and jeans with a light cardigan tied to the strap of her handbag, bloody peacocks around her. The women had their jewelery on, rings and bracelets and necklaces, as if they were out for an anniversary dinner and not merely promenading, and Charley only wore the thin little chain of poor gold that her uncle had sent down to her for her eighteenth birthday . . . And bugger Axel Moen who was a cold bastard . . . She had bounce in her stride, she had control. There was no street like the Via della Libertà in Plymouth or Exeter. Three lanes of traffic running in each direction and a wide center area with benches under the shade of trees. To Charley Parsons it was a little piece of joy. She heard the shouting. She looked across the traffic lanes and the center area, and she saw a street leading away in which there were no vehicles parked, and a soldier was gesturing with his rifle, and playing dumb innocent was a squat little man with a pickup truck loaded with builder's gear. She watched the yelling soldier and the obstinate little man trade insults. She murmured, "Go on, old boy, give the pompous bastard stick," just as they had given stick to the bloody policemen in their battle gear at the harbor in Brightlingsea. She had been free then, on the picket line and trying to block the lorries carrying the animals to Europe. She could have clapped because the squat little man had won the day, and the soldier stood, threatening, over him with the rifle, had gained the right to park his pickup and to unload his sacks of concrete mix. She grinned, she moved on. Her mother would have said that she had insufficient respect for authority, her father would have said she was a damned little anarchist . . . She held tight to her bag because Angela had told her she should.

Not the Via Siracusa, the next street off the Via della Libertà from the Via Siracusa. She couldn't think when, if ever, she had had as much cash, as thick a roll of notes, in her purse. She saw the sign of the boutique, where Peppino had said it would be. She was flushed, a little thrilled. God, that amount of money to spend on herself. What would the cold bastard have said? She stopped outside the boutique, in front of the window of clothed model figures. She looked around her. As with a child's guilt, she looked for Axel Moen. Did not see him. Nor did Charley see the young man who sat astride a motorcycle, up the street from her.

The prices on the model figures were just incredible, out of this bloody world, but she had the money in her purse. Best foot forward, ma'am. She pushed open the door of the shop. Go hack it, Charley. She did not see the young man astride the motorcycle, the engine idling, slide down the smoked black visor of his crash helmet.

Soft music played. The lighting was clever. She was of importance. God, eat your heart out, British Home Stores in Exeter, Marks and bloody Spencer in Plymouth. She tried four blouses, her mind played the calculations of translating from *lire* to sterling. Christ, Charley . . . Big breath, deep breath. She chose a blouse of royal blue, and the touch of it on her fingers was so soft. She tried three skirts, short minis, and they'd be better when she'd done time on the beach and burned the whiteness off her knees and thighs. She chose a skirt in bottle green. She paid, stripped the notes off the roll. She took the bag they gave her. Bugger where the money had come from. Bugger that Giuseppe Ruggerio washed money. She had enough in her purse to go on to find a throat scarf and maybe a good pair of dark glasses. She came out of the shop, and she did not see the haughty smiles of the sales staff, as if they thought her an *ingenua*. She stood on the pavement, savoring the moment. Her mother would have said that it was criminal to spend that much on clothes, her father would have said they were the clothes of a spoiled child. She did not see the young man, head hidden in the crash helmet, nudge his motorcycle forward.

It was a few yards from the open space of the pavement of the Via della Libertà . . .

Meandering past a shoe shop . . .

Heard nothing and seen nothing, and the blow belted her.

As if her chest was torn apart, as if the strap of her hand-bag cut into her back and her breast.

She clung to the strap. Trying to scream, and spinning, and there was the roar of the motorcycle against her, and the black shape of the crash helmet was above her.

Falling, and the boot came into her face. The boot came from below a scarlet-painted fuel tank, and on the tank was an eagle's head. The boot savaged her. She held the handbag strap and she was dragged on the pavement. Kicked again, and letting loose of the strap and covering her face.

On the pavement and the foul filth of the motorcycle exhaust blasting at her, choking. The gloved hand came down, crude, bulged fingers, and caught at the necklace that was the present of her uncle, and ripped at it, and it broke and it was coiled in the gutter beside her.

Charley lay on the pavement and under her body was the shopping bag. She sobbed into the dirt of the pavement.

The motorcycle was gone.

A man walked past her, and looked away. She sobbed and she swore. Two women, queens in their finery, quickened their step and hurried by her. She wept and she cursed. Kids were going by her, fast little trainer shoes scurrying. After them were high heels and shoes of worked leather. In pain, she wept. In anger, she cursed. The pain was in her chest and her face and her elbows and her knees. The anger was for all of them, the fucking bastards, who hurried by. She pushed herself to her knees, Christ and it hurt because her knees were red-raw from being dragged, and she could see right down to the Via della Libertà and across she could see a soldier on the far corner with his rifle held in alertness and he didn't come to help her. As if she carried a yellow flag, bloody leprosy, bloody HIV, was quarantined, they went by her, the fucking bastards. She was on her feet, she staggered, she lurched toward a man and she saw the horror on his face, and he pushed her away. She fell. She was on the pavement.

"Are you all right?"

" 'Course I'm not bloody—"

She looked up at him.

He was bent down and close to her. "You are a tourist, yes? English, German?"

"English."

He was young, maybe a couple of years older than herself. Concern was on his face, and sincerity, sympathy.

"Nobody helped me, nobody tried to stop him."

"People are afraid here, afraid to be involved."

"Bloody bastard cowards."

"Afraid to interfere. It is different to England, I apologize."

Such kindness. He was tall. He had a fine angled face, strong bones in the cheeks. He pushed the falling hair back from his forehead.

"I haven't broken anything. I just feel so angry. I want to get him, kick him. There was a soldier across the road, a bloody great gun, didn't move."

So soothing. "He could not help you. It might have been a diversion. In Palermo anything is possible. You are a foreigner, you would not understand. Can I help you? Take my hand. The soldier would have been disciplined. If he had left his place and come to you, it could have been a diversion, it could have been an attack on the home that he guards. It is Palermo."

He took her hand. He had long and delicate fingers. She felt them close on her hand. He lifted her up. The anger had gone. She wanted to be held and she wanted to cry. He picked up her bag from the shop.

"It happens every day in Palermo. They target tourists."

"I'm not a tourist, I've come here for a job. It was my first day in Palermo. The job's in Mondello. I'm sorry that I swore. I am Charley Parsons."

He grinned, embarrassed. "But that is a man's name."

A smile cracked her face. "Charlotte, but I am Charley to everyone."

"I am Benedetto Rizzo, but I am called Benny. You are sure there is no bad injury?"

"I am not going to hospital. Damn, shit, fuck. Sorry, and thank you."

"I was in London for a year, people were very kind to me. I worked in the McDonald's near Paddington railway station. I apologize that this is your first experience of Palermo."

Charley said, "Trouble is, I feel like a fool. I was warned to be careful, I was bloody miles away. I just feel humiliated. I was warned, and I forgot. Excuse me, you said that in Palermo people are afraid to be involved, afraid to interfere, but you were not afraid."

"It is our city, our problem. You should not dissociate yourself from responsibility from a problem. If nobody does anything, then the problem will never be solved, it's what I believe."

She looked into his face. "Small people can change something, is that what you think?"

"Of course."

He crouched. His hand, the long fingers, were in the gutter and the filth, and he lifted up the broken chain of poor gold. He seemed to Charley to recognize its value to her. He lifted it with care and he placed it in her hand.

"I'm sorry, I am a teacher, I . . ."

"I was a teacher in England."

"Then you will know—I have to be back. I have my class, at the elementary school behind the Piazza Castelnuovo." He grinned. "Maybe if I am not back, there will be a riot of the children, maybe the police will have to come with gas."

Her face was puffing from the bruises, her elbows were scraped, the knees under the tears in her jeans were oozing blood.

Charley grimaced. "I can't go to a bar, not looking like this. I am really grateful for what you did for me, for your kindness. When I am repaired, can I buy you a drink? Please let me."

He wrote for her his address and a telephone number, gave it to her.

"But, you are all right, Charley?"

"I'm fine, Benny. It's just my bloody dignity that's damaged."

Aching throughout her body, Charley limped with her shopping bag toward the bus stop. Only when she stood at the bus stop did she realize that the bloody bastard hadn't gone for her watch, that the watch was on her wrist.

Axel watched the bus come.

He saw her, in pain, drag herself up onto the bus.

As the bus drove away, the bus for Mondello, her face was in the window for a moment in his vision. She was white-faced except for the vivid bruising where the boot had caught her, and she seemed to him to be in shock.

He was on the pavement, a few feet from the bus, close enough to see the markings on her face.

Axel had seen it all. He had seen her, Codename Helen, come out of the boutique, carrying her bag, alive with pleasure, and he had seen the motorcycle accelerate down the side street toward her, and then weave through a gap in the parked cars and come onto the pavement. He had seen each detail of the attack, the snatch of the bag, her being dragged behind the motorcycle, the motorcycle stopping on the pavement and the boot going into her face, and the gloved fist going for her throat, and the motorcycle accelerating away down the pavement before it cut between the cars and out onto the side street.

He had not tried to intervene.

He would have intervened if it had been life threatening. If he had intervened, if it had been life threatening, if he had used his firearm, if the police had been called, then his cover was broken.

He had recognized the situation from the moment the motorcycle had moved on her. It was a bag snatch, it was the life of Palermo. It was not worth the breaking of his cover. From his viewpoint across the side street he had satisfied himself that the situation was, by the terms on which he operated, harmless. The young Palermitan had come to her and helped her, and he had seen her weep and then curse and then soften as she was dosed in his sympathy, and at the end he had seen the small and rueful grimace on her face. She had not needed him.

And Axel did not need the smart talk of Dwight Smythe who pushed paper in the London embassy, nor of Bill Hammond in a safe billet on the Via Sardegna up the road from the Rome embassy, nor of 'Vanni, nor of a magistrate who had probed and warned of responsibilities. Didn't need them whining their consciences at him . . .

He had been to Mondello each morning. Each morning he had seen her come from the villa with the children. He had tracked her, unseen, each morning. Surveillance tactics were the skill area of Axel Moen, always behind, always on the far side of the street or the piazza or the alleyway. Each morning he followed her, Codename Helen, stayed back from her. He did not need any hand-wringing bastards to tell him of his responsibility. There had been a girl crucified on the back of a door, and he had used the pliers and a claw hammer from the tool kit of the Huey's pilot to get the nails from the palms of her hands. He did not need to be told about his responsibilities.

He walked away. He wore a cap so that the long fall of his hair was tucked up inside it. He had sunglasses on. The windcheater was not one she had seen him use.

She could have panicked, could have pressed the pulse tone button that was the alarm on her wristwatch. She'd done well. She had shown good sense. He thought the best of her and it did not cross his mind that she had simply forgotten that she wore the wristwatch with the panic alarm. He went to a shop and brought some sketch pencils with soft lead and buried them in the bag with his sketch pads and his tape measure and the CSS 900 receiver. He was heading for his car. By the late morning he would be back and protecting his cover at the cloister aisle of the *duomo* in Monreale. He used people, and he goddamn well knew it, used them and squeezed them and dropped them.

There was a parking ticket on his car, pinned under the wiper on the windshield. He glanced at it. He tore the ticket into small pieces and dropped them into a street drain. It would be several weeks before the office where the duplicate tickets were lodged stirred themselves to trace the registration back to the hire company at Catania's airport, and by then Axel Moen would be back in the Via Sardegna office. It could not last more than a month, his reckoning, she could not survive the lie for more than a month. The Confidential Informant designated Codename Helen would, in several weeks, have been used and squeezed and dropped.

It had been a shit shift, but the next shift would be worse. The shift from six in the morning until two in the afternoon was difficult, but at least the street stalls were up in the Capo district, and it was possible for Giancarlo to walk between the stalls and to finger a lemon or a pear or turn over an apple and to look at faces, and to drift on. The shift from two in the afternoon until ten in the evening was worse shit because the stalls had done their trade for the day and were packing and emptying the alleyways, and it was harder in the after-noons and the evenings to hold cover. He had not yet been assigned to the shift from ten in the evening until six in the morning, and that would be the worst shit duty, and Jesu alone would know how to hold cover in the bastard place when the alleyways were darkened, when people hurried, when the *bambini* roamed over the cobbles on their scooters. Maybe, Jesu would tell him, when he had the shift through the night . . .

A man brushed against his shoulder.

"Anything?"

A sardonic smile. Giancarlo coughed on his cigarette. He spoke from the side of his mouth. "That has to be a joke. Perhaps, a better joke. Yesterday I took home three lemons, a pear, a quarter kilo of cheese and an artichoke. Today I take home one lemon, three apples, and a cauliflower." He held up the plastic bag. "My wife said last night that I intruded on her lifestyle. You would think you would be thanked for doing the shopping."

"But you don't bring home *il bruto?*"

"The photograph is twenty years old. He could walk past me."

"We need the *buona fortuna.*"

"I think, more than luck, I need to have a taste for lemons."

A sharp smile between them. They were chosen, this team from the *squadra mobile,* for the quality of their patience. The patience bred an attitude to their work. They could go each day to a street, to an apartment that was used for observation, they could sit in a car and in a closed van, do the shift for a week or for a month and watch the same view and look for the same face. They did not fret and they were not bored, and that was the training bred into them.

Giancarlo left the Capo district. The sun was now on

his face, and the smells of the dog shit and the rotting food bags and the old drains were out of his nose. There had to be patience. The guys of the DIA had watched a shop for eight weeks before Bagarella was spotted, and the ROS team of the *carabinieri* had watched a street for eleven weeks before Riina was seen. He went for his bus.

He was an anonymous figure riding the bus home. He bought the clothes for work in such a place as the Capo district from a charity shop. He was forty-seven years old, had served eighteen years in the *squadra mobile,* had volunteered four years back for work with the team specializing in the *sorveglianza.* They had moved home then. In the apartment block where they had lived before it had been known on the landings that he was a police officer. They had moved on when he had taken the surveillance work. It was the cross that his wife carried, in the new apartment, that he seemed to their neighbors to be another of the city's *disoccupati.* Better that he should appear as one of the city's unemployed or as a casual tradesman . . . He promised his wife that there would be one more year and then they would move again. It was hard for his wife, difficult for her. She had to tolerate his shabby old handed-down clothes. She had to exist alongside the pistol in the holster and the radio carried in a harness against his skin that were permanent to him when he was on assignment. She had to tolerate the fruit, the vegetables and always the lemons that he bought to hold his cover and dumped on her.

Even on the bus, he watched faces. But the photograph that Giancarlo tried to match to the faces was twenty years old. Faces riding with him, faces on the pavement, faces in cars.

Another day's work finished. There were some operations when Giancarlo, and the guys in the team with him, would feel the chance of a success strike was good, and there were others . . .

Small Mario ran back into the house and shouted for his mother to come.

Francesca stood rooted to the patio, clutching her toy.

The gardener eyed her as he methodically closed the gates behind her.

She struggled up the the drive and then up the path between the flower beds, and then onto the patio. Charley grimaced when Angela came through the open doors. She saw the collapse of Angela's mouth and chin, as if in shock. Angela had come to her, hurrying, and took Charley in her arms. Charley wept. The tears streamed. Charley hung in Angela's arms, as if she were held by a friend. The tears were wet on the shoulder of Angela's silk blouse, staining it, and she tried to make an apology, and Angela would not have it, and held her. It was a moment of bonding. The tears flowed down Charley's cheeks. Small Mario had taken the cue from his mother and clutched at her waist, as if that were his own gesture of comfort love, and Francesca held herself tight against Charley's legs and cried with her. They went together inside the villa. Charley felt as though, now, she was protected by Angela and small Mario and Francesca. She was taken through the hall and as they passed the full-length mirror they saw the pavement dirt in the confusion of her hair and the bruising on her face and the grazing on her elbows and the ripped material at the knees of her jeans. She was sat on a chair in the kitchen. When Angela loosed her, to put on the kettle to get hot water, to find the medical box and the cotton wool, the children still held her. Charley tried to blink away the tears. She wore the wristwatch. She spied against their love.

"You were robbed?"

Trying to be brave. "Afraid so."

"You are hurt, badly hurt?"

"Don't think so. I didn't go to the hospital, didn't seem necessary."

"The physician will come—robbed of your bag?"

Angela gathered the medical box, the plasters, the ointments, the cotton wool pad on the table and she waited for the kettle to boil.

"When I came out of the shop, which Peppino had recommended—I still have what I bought, they're lovely—I just didn't see him come. He must have been watching me. As I started to walk, he came from behind me."

"It's a foul place."

"I had the strap of the bag across me, when he pulled the bag I was dragged . . ."

"It's a place of the jungle, home for animals. What have you lost?"

"Nothing that's life-threatening. A diary, that's a nuisance. A credit card, boring. Makeup, thank God, I'd spent most of what Peppino gave me. He got nothing."

The water from the kettle was poured into a bowl. Angela, so gentle, began to clean the wounds.

"He stopped the bike. He kicked my face. That was when I let the bag go. He didn't have to, he had my bag. He leaned down and he snatched at the necklace. It broke."

She took the necklace, broken, from her pocket. She put it on the table. It seemed to her so cheap, so trivial, and the necklace of Angela was heavy gold and dancing in front of her eyes as Angela bent across her to dab the soaked hot cotton wool on her face.

"For what happened, I feel ashamed. Did anyone help you?"

"Most didn't, one did. He was very kind, a teacher."

"I am so sorry, Charley. I will call Peppino. It is a foul

place, Charley, because the society is bred on violence, a city that makes fear. I feel so great a responsibility."

"Please, please don't," Charley said.

The whisper of desperation. "You won't go back to England, because of this, you won't—?"

"No."

Angela kissed Charley. The children held her. She would not go home because she was a spy. She thought the watch on her wrist was a talisman of treachery. She was under the control of the cold bastard Axel Moen, who had not been close by, who had not protected her. It was not the filth of the gutter in her hair that dirtied her but the watch on her wrist. The kiss was love, and the children held her in love.

The baby was crying when Pasquale came home, and Pasquale was dead on his feet. A bad night broken by the alarm at four, little sleep before the alarm because the baby then had been crying. And he couldn't tell whether the tiredness on his wife's face was because of the baby's crying or because of her anxiety for his work. Her mother was in the kitchen and trying to quieten the baby, and failing. He didn't want to talk in front of her mother, so he went to the bedroom, and he lay on the bed staring at the ceiling light. He didn't want to tell his wife, in front of her mother, that he had received snapped criticism from the *maresciallo*. "If you are tired, you are useless, if you are a zombie, you endanger us all. Don't think you are the only one that has fathered a baby that cries in the night." He should pull himself together, remember that he was a part of a team. The *maresciallo* had said that he had the promise from Tardelli, the magistrate was working at home that afternoon. They could manage, once, without Pasquale. If Pasquale were again found yawning, blinking tiredness, then he would be off the team, the *maresciallo* had said. He had gone home, feeling shame, and he lay on the bed and could not sleep.

His wife came into the bedroom and she carried a glass of juice for him.

"Is there no overtime? You are early."

"I was sent home."

"What had you done?"

"I was told I was too tired. I was told I was not effective. I was told I endangered the team."

He could not tell whether it was the exhaustion or anxiety that made the lines at her mouth and the bulging bags under her eyes. He did not know whether the end of her prettiness was marked by the birth of the baby or by his joining the team that protected a "walking corpse."

"They will get rid of you?"

"I don't know."

"If they got rid of you . . . ?"

"Then I could patrol outside the Questura, I could stop the traffic for schoolchildren, I could be on the pavement and watch the sirens go by."

"What do you want?"

"I want to be with him and stand beside him."

The magistrate had been in the living room of the apartment when the *maresciallo* had spat the criticism at Pasquale. The living room was his office. The desk where he worked at his computer screen was on the far side of the room from the reinforced plate glass of the windows. The room was always in gloom because the shutters were across the window and the curtains were drawn. When he had left, been sent home, he had passed the door to the living room and seen the magistrate hunched over his computer with the mess of files on the desk and opened on a chair and on the carpet around the desk. He had felt humility toward the magistrate because all the team knew that the phone call had been made at dawn to the magistrate's wife in Udine and the telephone had not been picked up by Patrizia Tardelli, nor by the children, but by a man. All the team had heard the poor bastard stammer to a man whose name he did not know, in his wife's house at dawn. A bad time of the day to learn, for sure, that a marriage had foundered, that his wife was fucked by a stranger.

"And me? Do you want to stand beside me? And do you want to stand beside our baby?"

"That is stupid talk."

"So I am stupid. Each day that you go out, when I am left, I have to consider whether, again, I will see you."

"He asks of you each day, and he asks of the baby. Each day he remembers you."

"Each day, Pasquale, I am so frightened."

"He asks after you, as if he blamed himself for your situation." Pasquale pushed himself up on the bed. He spoke in bitterness. "What would you have us do? Would you have us walk away from him, abandon him?"

"Is he so stubborn?"

"He has the fear, we all have the fear. He jokes of the fear, he has learned to live with it. As I try to, as you have to. Stubborn? Will he surrender to the fear? He is stubborn and he will not give in to the fear."

"Is the danger very great?"

He looked away from her. His shoulders dropped back to the bed. He gazed up at the ceiling light. She sat beside him and she held his hand. He thought that she struggled to reconcile their fear with her own fear.

"You have the right to know. We are not supposed to talk of it, not even in the home, but you have the right. He could compromise, he could exist, he could move paper across his desk, he could ride through the city in safety, and we could go in safety with him. The *maresciallo* says that a man such as Tardelli faces real danger only when he has become a threat to those people."

"Please."

"I should not tell you. There is a prisoner in the Ucciardone who seeks the privilege of the *pentito* program, and he has given information about Ruggerio, the target of Tardelli. The information is not good but if it is acted upon, it could threaten Ruggerio."

"I listen."

"An American came from Rome, an agent of the DEA, to see Tardelli. If he sees Tardelli, then it is connected with Ruggerio, so the threat increases."

"Tell me."

"There is a third factor, the *maresciallo* says. It is a time of great danger to Tardelli. Ruggerio seeks to be the *capo di tutti capi*, he looks for absolute control. There is a rival in Agrigento, disappeared. There is a family in Catania, but they will be destroyed. When, the *maresciallo* says, the control of Ruggerio is absolute, then he will demonstrate his new power with a strike against the heart of the state. It could be the life of Tardelli because that is the man who most threatens him . . . You wanted to know."

"I asked . . ."

"Are you better for knowing?"

She loosed Pasquale's hand. She left him in the dim-lit room. He slept with his mind dulled to dreams. Later he would wake. Later he would find her sleeping beside him, and the baby asleep in the cot at the foot of the bed. Later he would shower and dress and strap onto his chest the pistol holster. Later, he would go into the kitchen to make himself coffee to clear away the sleep taste from his mouth and he would find the small bunch of flowers on the table and he would read the note his wife had written. "Please give them to him, and thank him for asking

after me each day and after our baby. God keep you."
Later, Pasquale would go to work.

The boy was seated in a chair.

His arms were tied tight behind his back and the rope
chafed against his skin. The boy's ankles were strapped to the
legs of the chair. The gag filled his mouth. He did not
understand . . . He was of the Brancaccio district. He came
from the high blocks of crumbling apartments. He had never
been employed, nor had his father ever been in work. He
thieved to keep his family, stole the bags of the tourists.

He did not understand . . . He paid the *pizzo* each
month to the Men of Honor in Brancaccio. He never failed
to give them the percentage from what he took out of
tourists' handbags.

He did not understand . . . He had been told that one
day, perhaps, he would be invited to join the ranks of the *picciotti,* that a final decision would be made when he had completed tasks set for him by the Men of Honor in Brancaccio.

He did not understand . . . A task had been set for him.
He had taken the handbag. He had brought the handbag to
the address given him. A pistol had been pressed against his
neck, he had been strapped to the chair. The handbag was
now in front of him on a bare wooden table.

He did not understand . . . The money from the handbag was in a neat pile. Two men were looking carefully at the
diary from the handbag. Their hands, which held the diary,
passed it between them, were protected by transparent plastic gloves. They examined the diary with minute care.

The boy was condemned. They had not hooded him
and they had not blindfolded him. He had seen their faces.
He could not know whether they would strangle him or
knife him or shoot him, whether they would put him in
acid or in concrete or whether they would dump him,

under cover of darkness, in an alley. They did not seem to notice that the piss ran hot on his thigh and he shivered without control. He did not understand . . .

As a child, he had been told by his father, Rosario, an old saying of Sicily. "The man who plays alone always wins."

Any detail relevant to his personal security was passed to Mario Ruggerio. He alone would decide the importance of information. The message came by word of mouth to the apartment off the Via Crociferi. In conditions of secrecy the magistrate, Tardelli, had met Capitano Giovanni Crespo of the *carabiniere* ROS, and the *capitano* had brought with him an unnamed American. Alone in the apartment, in the kitchen, he heated up his favorite meal of *trippa* that he would take with a sauce of boiled tomato. A woman had come to the apartment the day before he had moved in, and cleaned it and filled the refrigerator with sufficient small and simple-to-prepare meals that would last him for a week. He would be gone after a week, and then the apartment would again be scrubbed clean. He could search in the far recesses of a huge memory. The recesses of his memory were compartmentalized so the name of Giovanni Crespo, of the *carabiniere* ROS, was not obscured by the bank of information held on financial movements and cash investments and future strategy and opponents and affiliates. He could sweep aside his thoughts on the plans of an explosives expert, and on the matter of a handbag thief, and of a meeting with a Colombian who was skilled in the movement of refined cocaine to Europe, and of discussions with the new men from Russia.

He remembered the name of Giovanni Crespo, and there had been a photograph, which was blurred, of a white and tensed face, published in the *Giornale di Sicilia,* beside the blanket-covered head of Riina as the big man was driven away after his arrest from the *carabinieri* barracks. The memory was dismissed. He considered what he had been told of an American, poorly dressed, unnamed, perhaps armed, admitted to the inner office of Tardelli. In his mind he turned over the information, analyzed it, pondered it. If the Americans mounted an operation in Palermo, if an agent came to visit Tardelli, then he believed that only he could be the principal target.

The water in the saucepan boiled around the *trippa*. The sauce made from boiled tomatoes bubbled in a second saucepan. He took a bottle of Perroni beer from the refrigerator. He was ready to eat. There were times that he yearned for the cooking of Michela, and to be surrounded by his family, and to sit the little boy, his nephew, who was a rascal and who was named after him, on his knee . . . So much to think of . . . He took the *trippa* from the saucepan and spooned the sauce of tomato over it. He poured his beer. He seemed to imagine that his wife, Michela, put the plate on the table in front of him. It was a compartment in his life. All his life was in sealed compartments, and that was his strength. He allowed three men, Carmine and Franco and Tano, to be close to him. It was what he had learned in his climb to power. There should always be three, because two men could agree, in secrecy, on conspiracy, never three. The three men competed with each other, in insecurity, for his favor. Carmine would look to the matter of the *carabiniere* officer, Giovanni Crespo, and the association with the American. Franco had already been given responsibility for the security of the meeting with the Colombian. Tano liaised with the expert in explosives. He divided them, and he ruled them. He must be strong.

There was an old saying in Sicily that his father, Rosario, had told him. "A man who makes himself a sheep will be eaten by the wolf."

•   •   •

The physician, elderly and elegant and expensively considerate, had examined Charley with soft and cool fingers, probed at her grazes and bruises, and told her with a distant smile on his lined face that her injuries, though painful, were superficial. He had congratulated her on the good fortune that her experience had not led to serious hurt. Charley thought of what it would have been like in England, waiting in Casualty or at the general practitioner's clinic. Bloody hideous it would have been. But she had been calmed by the physician. She lay on her bed.

He knocked. Peppino was smiling sympathy at her from the door.

"You are better now?"

"I feel a bit of a fraud."

"Angela tells me that you were very brave."

"Just wish I'd been able to scratch his eyes out or kick him in the bloody balls. Sorry, I mean leave him something to remember me by."

Peppino chuckled with her. "It would have been nice. I am so sorry that I could not come at once. Have you reported this matter to the police?"

"I just couldn't face it."

"Of course. It happens all day and every day in Palermo. The beauty of our city, its heritage, is despoiled by such crime, and the police can do little. If you report to the police, then you invade the world of their bureaucracy. Believe me, they are not fast."

"But, for the insurance, shouldn't I have a chit from the police?"

He sat on the end of the bed, friendly, kind but not familiar.

"What exactly did you lose?"

"There was my purse. I'd spent most of what you gave me . . . You'd like to see?"

She swung off the bed. She took the blouse and the miniskirt from the bag. She held them in turn in front of her. She thought it was what she should do, what would be expected of her, what was expected of a spy. He nodded his approval.

"When there is a special occasion, please, you will decorate it. What was in your bag?"

"Not much. My purse and thirty or forty thousand, my lipstick and the powder compact and the eye stuff, some keys. There was my Visa card, but I can get that canceled, and there was my diary with phone numbers and addresses."

"You see, Charley, these scum are only interested in cash, probably for drugs, and they are very impertinent. Many times, after they have taken the money they will dump the bag in a rubbish collector very close to the Questura. It is possible, I cannot say probable, that your bag will be found. And I would not wish you to be concerned about your card. Allow me to take care of it. Angela said there was a necklace."

"He tried to snatch it, broke it. Just of sentimental importance, a present from my uncle."

She pointed to the thin chain that had luster. The chain was on the table beside the book that she thought had been moved.

And across the room was the chest, containing her underwear that she thought had been taken out of the middle drawer and replaced. Maybe it was her imagination. Maybe it was a vicious lie of Axel bloody Moen. Maybe. She was the spy in their home.

A frown, questioning, was on his forehead. "You see, Charley, how greatly Angela depends on you. It is not easy for her here. It is a different culture from her life in Rome. It is impossible for her, in Sicilian society, to recreate the freedom of Rome. To her, your companionship is so important.

Why I say that, very frankly, we hope you will not wish immediately to return to England."

"I didn't consider it—and God help the next low-life who tries anything."

He asked her to describe the handbag. He told her that he knew a man in the Questura and he would go directly to see the man and himself report the theft of the bag. For a moment his hand rested on the cleaned wound on her knee.

"All of us, Charley, we admire your courage."

The detective superintendent winked across the table at Harry Compton, like it was going to amuse him. He cradled the telephone between his cheek and his shoulder to free his hands to light a cigarette.

". . . I quite appreciate you're a busy guy, Ray. When you've a moment . . . I know how busy you DEA people keep yourselves. Won't take more than a moment, just something that's come up, needs clarification. I'll fit in with you. Down here at SO6 we're not that stretched, not like you are. Keep for a couple of days? I should think so . . . Oh, yes, the Bramshill conference would be excellent. I'll see you there. Very good of you, Ray, to get me on board your schedule. I appreciate that. See you then, Ray . . ."

9

"... I TURN TO THE ISSUE of organized and international crime. The international scene is developing with increasing pace and we cannot afford to get left behind. Borders are coming down, trade is expanding, financial markets and services are becoming integrated. In short, we are no longer an island protected by the sea from unwelcome influences . . ."

So, you got the message, sir, and about time. The Country Chief eased back in his chair. It was a chore of his work that he should attend the set-piece speeches of the Commissioner of the Metropolitan Police. But he'd get a good lunch, and over lunch he'd have the opportunity to bend the ear of people who were useful to him, and he was out of London, and in spring the gardens at Bramshill College which hosted senior men's courses were rather fine.

"... We should be in no doubt that organized crime will exploit every opportunity, technological advance or weakness in order to expand. Organized crime, with its international links and quasicorporate structures, is responsible for flooding the streets with dangerous drugs, undermining financial systems, and by the sheer financial muscle it has available, it is a real threat to the integrity and effectiveness of the rule of law and is becoming ever more complex and sophisticated . . ."

Good to have you on board, sir. The Country Chief looked out of the window, at the view of the daffodils and crocuses in flowered islands in the lawns, and around the lecture room. The guy from the National Criminal Intelligence Service was listening, and impassive. That was the guy who had told Ray, a year back, that there was no Sicilian La Cosa Nostra problem in little old UK. About time they grew up and joined the real world.

". . . There is the question of the role, where appropriate, of the Security Service, and the future involvement of the Security Service in matters which have historically been the responsibility of the police. There is great strength in exploiting fully the experience, methods, powers and potential of different agencies in tackling common problems. The challenge is how to take advantage of diversity without creating confusion . . ."

Heh, come to Washington, sir. Come and see the "confusion" when the FBI and the CIA and the DEA and the ATF and the Revenue and the Customs get their noses onto the same scent. Come and see the catfight when the agencies get to hunt the same target. He knew the guy from MI5, a languid dick of a guy, sitting a row behind the NCIS man. Always looking for new territory. Take my advice, sir, keep the bastards at arm's length.

". . . Time is not on our side. I do not think our current structures allow us to punch at our full weight and the *status quo* will not serve us well in the next century. Our European and indeed world partners will run out of patience if we do not evolve a one-stop-shop approach to their involvement with us. I hope we will develop an appropriate mechanism to do justice to this formidable challenge. Thank you, ladies and gentlemen."

Spoken like a man, sir, because patience was certainly wearing thin. Put bluntly, and Ray liked to speak his mind, he thought he found in little old theme-park UK a quite stunning complacency. He could have pointed to specialized police units that were starved of resources, to the Customs and Excise investigators who were driven by the culture of statistics, to the financial institutions in the city who blandly ignored the matter of dirty money. He applauded politely.

Time for coffee.

He was in the queue and talking banalities with a man from Drugs Squad.

"Morning, Ray."

The man from SO6 was beside him.

"You were looking for a word. How you doing?"

"Coffee's usually pretty revolting. Let's walk and talk."

The Country Chief, good ears, caught the snap in the voice of the detective superintendent.

"You go without, please yourself, I'm taking coffee."

So he stayed in the queue, made his point, had his cup filled, balanced it on the saucer and walked to the door. The detective superintendent was ahead of him. They went across the wide hallway and out onto the driveway where the chauffeurs waited with their bullshit cars. He liked to say that DEA had a "blue collar" mentality, and chauffeur-driven black cars didn't fit the work ethic he believed in. They walked on the lawns and skirted the daffodil clumps and the crocus carpets.

"Nice time of year. So what can I do for you?"

The detective superintendent was smiling, but malevolent. "Just something that crossed my desk. You have an agent called Axel Moen on your staff—"

"Wrong."

"I beg your pardon?" The smile had shifted, the face had hardened.

"Put in one-syllables," the Country Chief spoke slowly as if to an idiot child, emphasizing while his mind racheted, "I do not have anyone of that name on my staff. Does that settle your problem?"

"An agent with DEA accreditation named Axel Moen."

"We have around twenty-five hundred special agents, can't know all of them."

He never lied. He could divert, interrupt, head off, but he would not lie. He knew, from his deputy who had been to Lyon, that quite the most memorable twenty minutes of the Europol conference had been when Garcia, FBI out of Moscow, had put down the Brit from SO6. The man's throat was tightening, and the veins were up on his forehead.

"Did you know that a special agent, Axel Moen, traveled down to Devon a bit more than two weeks ago?"

"Maybe I did."

"Where's he out of?"

"Is that your business?"

"Don't fuck me around."

"If it's your business, he's out of Rome."

"Working with your facilities?"

"Maybe."

"With your knowledge?"

"Maybe. I'd kind of like to catch the next lecture." The Country Chief threw the dregs from his cup down onto the grass. The lawns around them, between the islands of daffodils and the carpets of crocuses, had just been given their first cut. The dew damp flecked his shoes. "What's your concern?"

"He went to the home of a young girl, a school-teacher."

"Did he?"

"She had received an invitation to go and work for a Sicilian family."

"Had she?"

"Her parents say that your man, Axel Moen, 'pressured' her into accepting that invitation."

"Do they?"

"The man who has offered her employment has just

traveled to the UK under false documentation."

"Has he?"

"You want it, you'll get it. We reckon you are running some sort of antimafia job. We reckon you have trawled round for someone to do the sharp end for you, and you've got your sticky fingers on some poor girl."

"Do you?"

"You have taken it upon yourselves, you arrogant bloody people, to pressurize and then send a small-town girl to Palermo for some bloody operation you've dreamed up. Who've you cleared it with?"

"Among your crowd, I don't have to."

"You are running some naïve youngster, filled with crap no doubt, down in Palermo. So help me, I'll see you—"

"Should have listened to what your fat cat said. Your world partners will run out of patience. Maybe they already have."

He remembered what Dwight Smythe had said. The words rang in his mind. "He elbows into a small and unsuspecting life, a young woman's life, and puts together a web to trap her, and did it cold." He remembered what he himself had said: "And maybe we should all clap our hands and sing our hymns and get on our knees and thank our God that He didn't give us the problem." He looked into the flushed anger of the Englishman's face.

"Have you thought through the consequences? Do you take responsibility for the consequences?"

"It's something you shouldn't get your noses into."

"That's shit, that's not an answer."

"It's the answer you're getting, so back off."

The Country Chief walked away. He went back into the hall and gave his cup and saucer to a waitress.

He didn't have the heart for the session from the Italian attaché on preventative measures being taken by the Banco d'Italia concerning disclosure, nor for lunch, nor for the afternoon session when they would be "entertained" by the police colonel from St. Petersburg. He felt bad, and he wanted to get the hell out. He felt bad because he had said himself that it was a good plan, a plan that might just work. He had justified, himself, the use of a pressured innocent. He took his coat from the cloakroom. The poor goddamn kid . . .

She had stayed in the villa the day before, fussed over by Angela, lain in the sun while the gardener worked around her, but she had argued that morning with Angela. Yes, she was quite fit enough to take small Mario to school and Francesca to kindergarten. Yes, she was quite able to do the day's shopping. Yes, she would be able to walk the children to school and kindergarten, and do the shopping, before the threatened rain came.

Shouldn't make a bloody drama out of a bloody crisis.

She walked the children, with the baby in the pram, down from the villa and into Mondello. All her childhood, the star who was the center of attention, she had learned to milk a crisis. Perhaps it had been her going to Rome for the summer of 1992, perhaps it had been leaving home and living lonely at college, but the thought of draining sympathy from others now disgusted her. She could reflect, viciously, that her father had whined drama out of the redundancy crisis, made a growth industry from it. Her mother complained drama out of the cash-flow crisis. God, it was why she had gone away. She thought, cruelly, that her parents fed off drama, drank off crisis.

Shut up, Charley, close it down. What was drama to Axel Moen, what was his definition of crisis? And where was he? Wrap it, Charley, forget it . . .

She dropped small Mario at the school gate, bent down so that the child could kiss her. He ran, as he did each morning, through the playground to his friends and was engulfed by them. He was a happy and sweet little boy. If the plan worked, Axel's plan, then the drama would hit the child, the crisis would come with the arrest of the child's father and the child's uncle. She wondered who would play with the child at school the morning after the arrest of his father and his uncle, and the thought hurt deep. So considerate of those children, lying little bitch that she was, Charley acknowledged the growing strength each day of the sun, and she adjusted the parasol over the pram to keep baby Mauro in shade and she had Francesca walk in the shadow of her body. The forecast on Radio Uno had claimed there would be rain later, then promised clear weather for the rest of the week. In a couple of days it would be warm enough to lie on the beach and go into the sea, and get some of the bloody sun onto the white of her legs and onto her arms and shoulders, and onto the bruises and scabs. Put it on the list, Charley, sun lotion. The children would like it, going to the beach. She left Francesca at the kindergarten.

Through the shopping list. Tomatoes, cucumber, salami, nonfat milk, potatoes and oranges, apples . . . She ticked each item on her list. There was a *farmacia* on the road below the piazza, near to the Saracen tower.

She wondered if the habit of coming each morning with the children and the baby to the piazza and the shops and the school and the kindergarten meant she was now recognized. The old man who sat on his chair under the black umbrella that protected the ice blocks around his fish, he nodded gravely to her, and she flashed him her smile. Angela only bought fish on Friday mornings, and then from a shop. Charley promised herself, if Angela were out for lunch one day, if Charley had the responsibility to make a hot meal for the children, then she'd buy fish from the old man with the black umbrella. She was on her way to the *far-*

macia for the sun lotion when she saw the photograph.

On the newspaper stall, on the front page of the *Giornale di Sicilia,* in color, was the photograph.

The photograph leapt at Charley, caught at her throat. She stood numbed in front of the newspaper stall.

In color, in the photograph . . .

An old woman with thick legs held in bulging stockings wore the widow's clothes of black. She sat on a small household chair and her arms were held out and her head was raised as if she screamed anguish. Behind her was a priest, behind the priest was a crowd of watching men and women and children, behind the crowd were the tall and wide symmetrical lines of the close-set windows and narrow balconies. In front of her was the motorcycle that tilted on its stand. In front of the motorcycle with the red fuel tank and the eagle's head was the body. In the foreground of the photograph, in color, was the head of the body. Blood was spread on the ground from the mouth and throat of the head of the body.

She rocked on her feet. The eyes of the woman behind the counter of the newspaper stall glinted at her.

It was a young head. She had not seen the bloodied head before. The head had been hidden from her by the helmet with the dark visor. A young and thin-faced head that was topped with a wild mat of close curled hair was clear in the photograph. Charley knew the motorcycle. When the boot had lashed her, when she had loosed the strap to her handbag, when the glove had groped for her necklace, her face had looked up at the motorcycle.

Her words, Charley had said to Giuseppe Ruggerio, "Just wish I'd been able to scratch his eyes out or kick him in the bloody balls."

Her words, said to show that she was the big brave kid, "I mean to leave him something to remember me by."

She turned away. She thought that if she stayed to look

at the photograph, in color, she would vomit on the street in front of the newspaper stall. It was the motorcycle she remembered, definite. Charley walked past the old man who sold the fish from under his black umbrella. She pushed the pram to the pier where the fishermen worked on their nets and at their boats. She stared out over the water. Such peace. As if it were a place for poets, a place for lovers. Scattered cloud shadows of turquoise on rippled water. Christ, she understood. The power of life and the power of death was around her. Axel had told her of the power. No poets around her, no lovers. Men were around her who would kill a boy, cut his throat, leave him with his motorcycle outside the block where his mother lived, and go to eat their dinner.

She murmured, "Don't worry, Axel Moen, I am learning. I am learning that there is no love, no kindness. Satisfied, you cold bastard? I am learning to be a lying bitch. I am learning to survive. That boy had, Axel Moen, quite a decent young face and probably where he came from there was no bloody chance of work or opportunity, what I've had. So he's dead, and I am learning. I am learning that any bloody sentiment is just a luxury for tossers. My promise, I have forgotten the kindness of Angela Ruggerio and the love of small Mario and Francesca, I will stitch them up, do my best. It's what you wanted, right? You wanted me to learn to be a lying bitch. Satisfied?"

She pushed the pram to the *farmacia* and she bought the sun lotion for the beach. She pushed the pram to a bar where there was a telephone and she rang Benedetto Rizzo and told him when she had next had a free day, and she didn't speak of love and kindness. Charley doubted that, until the day she died, she would forget the photograph in color. While the first drops of rain fell, she pushed the pram back up the hill to the villa.

•　•　•

As snails and slugs come out after rain has fallen and leave tacky and shining tracks on concrete paths that merge and cross and meander, so too moved the surveillance teams.

The man from Catania was first followed by a taxi driver as he went in search of a declaration of loyalty from his brothers. When the man from Catania journeyed on across his territory to gain the same declaration from his wife's brothers, he was watched by three *picciotti* on motorcycles. The driver of a bread delivery van shadowed the man from Catania as he drove the big Mercedes, weighed down by the reinforced windows and by the armor plating inserted in the doors in his cousin's repair yard, reported on a meeting with his *consigliere*. A student from the medical school of the university watched the home of a *capodecino* in the Ognina district of the city to which the man from Catania came. All of them, the taxi driver and the *picciotti* and the driver of the bread delivery van and the student, were paid by the man from Catania. All of them betrayed him and reported his movements to Tano who belonged to Mario Ruggerio.

Slugs and snails, after rain has fallen, move from their cover, leave the slime of their tracks, ignore the hazard of poison pellets, crawl forward to kill the plants that have no defense.

Slugs, on their bellies, on the move . . . A woman who cleaned the living quarters in the *carabinieri* barracks at Monreale had met with Carmine before her slow and labored walk to work. Her husband's first cousin's son, from Gangi in the Madonie mountains, was held awaiting trial in the Ucciardone jail . . . Her security clearance to clean the living quarters of the barracks had not picked up the blood association, but the vetting had not been strict as her work did not give her access to sensitive areas of the building. On her knees she scrubbed a floor. Two pairs of feet were in front of her, waiting for her to move her bucket of soaped water. When she looked up she saw the uniformed *carabiniere* officer and his colleague who was dressed in the clothes of a building artisan. With reluctance, she pulled the bucket to the side of the corridor. They passed her by, as if they did not notice her. She knew the names of all of those officers whose rooms she was not given access to, and the door of the room of Giovanni Crespo was locked to her. When she reached the end of the corridor, where the doors opened out onto the car park behind the barracks, she could see the small builder's van, washed in the driving rain, with the ladder tied to the roof frame and with the stepladder jutting up between the seats. The cleaning woman had a poor memory. In pencil, on a scrap of paper, she wrote the registration number of the van. Without the help of a good lawyer, her husband's cousin's son would spend the next eight years of his young life in the Ucciardone jail.

Snails, crawling in their slime, on the move . . . The leader of the surveillance team of the *squadra mobile* had read the reports of each of the teams working the Capo district, pitifully brief reports. He took those reports to the apartment of the magistrate. Three days gone, seven days remaining, nothing seen that related to Mario Ruggerio. The magistrate smiled his thanks, seemed to expect nothing else, as if he realized that only ten days of surveillance with only three teams of men, only three men to a team, made the task impossible. What surprised the leader of the surveillance team, there was a brightness in the gloom of the room that the magistrate had made his workplace. The brightness was from flowers. He knew, everyone knew, that the magistrate's wife had gone north with the children, but the flowers were a woman's choice. The flowers were on the magistrate's desk, right beside the computer. He told the magistrate that his men were the best, that they were all committed, but that the time and resources given them were inadequate. When he left the magistrate, he went through to the kitchen where the bodyguards smoked and played cards and endlessly read the newspapers' sport pages and drank coffee, he asked after his friend, the *maresciallo*. But his friend was away on a course. There was nothing more to keep him in the apartment. He left the guards and the lonely and isolated man. He hurried through the splattering rain to the Capo district and his own shift. It would be a bastard, wandering through the labyrinth of alleys in the rain.

It was three years since Peppino Ruggerio had needed to drive to Castellammare del Golfo. Then to eat a meal with his brother and to meet with a foreigner, today to take lunch with his brother and to meet with a foreigner. It was the Spanish language that Mario had needed three years before, and again today . . . There was a direct route from Palermo to Castellammare del Golfo, on the *autostrada* to Trapani, and there was the country way. His choice, today, was to use the remote road, narrow and winding, that went south of Monte Cuccio and north of Monte Saraceno.

The clouds had gathered from early morning, darkening and spreading from the west. The rain had hit the car as he approached Montelepre. Not until he had driven his big car out through the villa's high gates had he made the snap decision to go to Montelepre on his way to Castellammare del Golfo. He came as a pilgrim to Montelepre, the town hanging as if on crampons from the rock face. He came today to Montelepre to see the birthplace and the living place of Salvatore Giuliano. It was right that he should come to Montelepre as a pilgrim and consider and learn the lessons of the life of the bandit, and of the death. Nothing changed in Sicily. The lessons remained, as apposite now to

Peppino and his brother as they had been nearly half a century before to Salvatore Giuliano. He came in humility, as a pilgrim, that he might better learn the lessons.

Peppino parked his car outside the Pizzeria Giuliano at the top of the town, where the roofs were merged with the cold rain cloud. He looked around him. He was huddled under the drop of his raincoat, which he had draped over his head and his shoulders. The rain bounced from the cobbles and spattered his shoes and the legs of his suit trousers.

There was no money in the town, no opportunity, no work. The rainwater gushed down the steep alleys around the Chiesa Madre and the terraced homes faced with cracked ochre plaster seemed to crumble before his eyes. A lesson: there had been money in the town when Salvatore Giuliano, the bandit, had lived here, but with his death it was gone. A lesson: Salvatore Giuliano had been hunted by many thousands of *carabinieri* and troops from the regular army, and it was said he was responsible for the killing of more than four hundred men, and he had been destroyed when his usefulness had expired. He did not know where in the town Giuliano had lived, did not know in which piazza Giuliano had organized the firing squads that executed men for "disrespect of the poor." A lesson: Giuliano had been the master tactician, the expert in the art of guerrilla warfare, and he had been an angel to the poor of the town, and he had been the handsome idol of the young women, and nothing could have saved him. A lesson: far from home, abandoned by those who claimed to be his friends, in Castelvetrano to the south, the cheek of Giuliano had been kissed by the Judas-man Gaspare Pisciotta. A lesson: a man who had been a king was shot to death as a dog in a gutter. Peppino stood in the high streets of Montelepre and the rain ran in his shoes and wet his socks and soaked the trouser legs at his ankles. It was important to him to learn the lessons.

Power ended when usefulness expired. A man climbed fast, reached beyond himself, and fell fast. Trust was a kiss and a kiss was followed by a bullet. He felt the better for it, felt as though the lessons learned by a pilgrim made him wise and more cautious.

Old men hurried past him, sheltering under black umbrellas, and they would have clapped when Salvatore Giuliano had stood in the piazza, and they would have spat when the news had come of his death like a dog in a gutter. A girl watched him. She had a young plain face, she was fat at the ankles, she wore a cotton dress and had no coat against the rain. She stood outside an *alimentari* and held a plastic shopping bag. Her father would have told her, and her grandfather, of the fate of the man who climbed too fast, ended his usefulness, and was betrayed. Her mother would have told her, and her grandmother, of the beauty of the face of Salvatore Giuliano. He wondered if the girl dreamed of the bandit. When the rains were finished, when the evenings were hot, did she go to the cool grass under the olive trees, did she look for him? For her, did Salvatore Giuliano live, a fantasy between her thighs? Did she worship him, conjure him to her, an imagination in the hair of her belly, when she was alone in the darkness? He laughed, in grimness, in privacy, as he looked at the young woman's face. Ridiculous. OK for the Americans, OK for the Presley freaks . . . Another lesson: after the Judas kiss and the death like a dog in the gutter, perhaps there was no memory of him other than the fantasy and imagination of a girl with fat ankles. He walked back to his car. There was a last lesson to be found by the pilgrim in Montelepre: Gaspare Pisciotta, the trusted deputy of Giuliano, had betrayed him, had died in the medical room of the Ucciardone jail in shrieking agony, poisoned by strychnine. It was important to learn the lessons of what had gone before.

He drove down the switchback road out of Montelepre, away from the rain-drenched homes and the legend of Salvatore Giuliano.

He went through Partinico, and on through Alcamo, where there had been the first refinery for Turkish poppy paste, and his brother's share of the wealth from the refinery in Alcamo had been the beginning of the cash cascade that had paid for an education at the university in Rome and the school of business management in Switzerland. Alcamo stank of sulfur fumes, said to have been released by the fractures caused by a minor earthquake. Money held in the cash deposit markets in New York and London, good and long-term and steady-earning money, had come from the refinery in Alcamo.

He drove down toward the sea.

He would not have dared to ask his brother whether he ever hesitated to consider the lessons to be learned from the life and death of Salvatore Giuliano. Would not have asked Mario whether he had climbed too fast, whether his usefulness could expire, whether he feared the Judas kiss, whether he believed that death would come in the way that a dog was shot in the gutter. He had the same fear of his brother that infected all men who met Mario Ruggerio.

He took the road that bypassed the old town and the harbor.

Each time he was in his brother's company, Peppino guarded himself. He was held at the same distance as Carmine and Franco and Tano, and the other heads of families, and the affiliates. When his brother smiled or praised, then Peppino was the same as every other man and felt the warm flow of relief. When his brother glanced at him in savagery, then Peppino felt the same terror as every other man. He could not quantify the personality of his brother, could not determine the chemistry that made him, and every other man, flush with relief at a smile and cringe in fear at a criticism. His brother had control over him, over every other man. Peppino knew that he could never walk away from his brother.

He parked in a lay-by above the town. Below the crash barrier and the wilderness of wild yellow flowers was the sharp crescent of the harbor from which once, in the good times, the fishing fleet had sailed for the tuna grounds, but the tuna had been fished to near-extinction. In better times, the same boats had left the same quayside and gone to sea at night without lights and collected the floating bundles of Turkish opium paste dropped by merchant ships, but there were no longer refineries on the island. The small town, shrouded in rain mist from Peppino's vantage point, with its good times and better times, was solid in the heritage of the organization his brother would control. It was said that in a single decade, from 1900 to 1910, one hundred thousand immigrants had sailed from that small harbor to the promised land of America and made the bedrock of the associations that Mario now collaborated with. It was said of Castellammare del Golfo in the 1940s that four out of every five adult males had been in jail. It was said in the 1950s, in the first great war between the families, that one of every three male adults had committed murder. Nothing was said of Castellammare del Golfo today, it was a town from which history had passed on. Peppino waited . . . Often he looked in the mirror in front of him, and he checked the side mirrors, and he saw no indication of surveillance.

Franco drove the car that came alongside.

In the backseat and sitting low down, uncertain and insecure, was the Colombian who had made the long journey.

Tano was in a second car, with more men.

Franco made the gesture for Peppino to follow. He

eased his car forward, nudged down the steep road after their brake lights. Franco and Tano would know the same thrill when praised by his brother, and the same hopeless fear when caught in the savage glance of his brother.

Close to the Norman castle, at the heart of the harbor's crescent, facing onto the small blue-painted boats that no longer fished for tuna, was a *ristorante*. On the door of the *ristorante* was the sign CHIUSO.

They went quickly from the cars, the rain beating on them, into the *ristorante,* and Peppino saw the way that the Colombian's eyes flickered around him in nervousness. Carmine met them, and they walked straight through the empty interior, past the empty tables, to a back room. Peppino saw, dumped on the floor, the open box that housed the countermeasures receiver. The back room would have been swept the night before, and again that morning. Everywhere that Mario Ruggerio did business was cleaned first to his satisfaction.

His brother rose from the laid table. His brother smiled with kindness and friendship and held out his hand to the Colombian and he gestured for the Colombian to sit and, himself, eased the chair back.

Peppino sat opposite Mario and the Colombian, from where he could lean forward and translate the Sicilian dialect into Spanish and the Spanish into the language Mario understood.

Because the Colombian, Vasquez, merely toyed with his food, Mario Ruggerio ate all that was in front of him. Tano never left the back room, Franco brought the food from the kitchen. Because the Colombian snatched at morsels, Mario ate slowly. Because the Colombian gulped the Marsala wine, Mario drank only water. His demeanor was of respect, offering the warmth of hospitality, but he dominated. Peppino watched and admired. The Colombian, Vasquez, had come to Sicily, made the long journey because the expertise of Mario Ruggerio was needed. Peppino felt a certain pride for his brother who had never traveled outside the island. The questions he translated, spoken by Mario in a tone of unmistakable gentleness, were the snake's questions.

"From your journey, you are not too tired?"

The Colombian had flown from Bogotá to Caracas, from Caracas to São Paolo, from São Paolo to Lisbon, from Lisbon to Vienna, from Vienna to Milan. He had driven from Milan to Genoa. He had sailed on the ferry from Genoa to Palermo.

"Is there such a great problem when you travel?"

There were many problems.

"What is the reason for the problems?"

The Americans were the problems.

"In what way are there problems from the Americans?"

Because the DEA were in Colombia.

So mildly, as if he was an old man who was confused, as if the Americans were not a problem that concerned him in Sicily, Mario Ruggerio shook his head in surprise.

"And I hear that there is crop destruction paid for by the Americans, is that so?"

The Americans were paying to have the fields of coca sprayed from the air.

"And I hear, also, that Gilberto Rodriguez Orejuela has been arrested, is that true?"

He had been arrested.

"And his brother, Miguel Rodriguez Orejuela, arrested?"

Both the brothers were under arrest.

"And Henry Loaiza Ceballos?"

He, too, had been arrested.

"And the treasurer of the cartel?"

He had surrendered.

"Were they careless? How is it possible for so many principals to be arrested?"

They had been arrested because they had used telephones, and the DEA had brought in interception technology.

A sad smile of sincere sympathy seemed to spread on Mario Ruggerio's face. He made a gesture with his hands that implied he himself would never have been careless and used a telephone. Peppino translated. He recognized the domination his brother achieved by making the Colombian confess to the weakness of his organization.

"You are disrupted?"

Business continued, with difficulty.

"What weight can you provide?"

They could provide five tons.

"Refined?"

It would be five tons refined.

"Where is delivery?"

The delivery would be on the European mainland.

"The price, what is the price?"

The price was $6,000 a kilo.

He had taken, as he had asked the question, as Peppino had translated the question and the answer, his Casio calculator from his pocket. His finger, for a brief moment, hovered over the "on" switch. He listened to Peppino's translated answer. He was laughing. He put the calculator back in his pocket. His rough hand was on the Colombian's arm, squeezing it as he chuckled.

"I hope you have a good journey home. Before you go home I hope you will find someone else to do business with, and I hope you enjoyed our humble hospitality. There was a dear friend in Agrigento with whom you might have made a deal, but he has disappeared. There is another dear friend in Catania, but I hear he has lost the stomach for such trading. Of course, if you have a vest to deflect the bullets, if you have a tank to travel in, you could go to Moscow. You know that if you do business with me, then it is honest business. There are others in many countries who would like what you have on offer, but you would have to be confident that you would not be cheated. If you do business with me then there is no possibility of deception." What was the price he could offer?

The Casio calculator was back on the table. The screen lit. Mario's thick fingers were off the Colombian's arm and tapping the keys.

"Four thousand per kilo. Do you take it or do you leave it?"

The figure was acceptable.

"Four thousand per kilo, delivery over six months, through Rotterdam and Hamburg docks. You can do that?"

That, too, was acceptable.

"I pay on delivery. You understand that I cannot pay for what is not delivered past Customs at Hamburg and Rotterdam?"

That was understood.

"How do you wish to be paid? I can send you heroin, refined or unrefined, for distribution in the North American market. I can make available aircraft, 707s, a Lear executive, whatever, that you can sell on. I can pay through cash transfers, or in stocks or government bonds, whichever currency. How do you wish it?"

The Colombian, Vasquez, wished it in cash, invested and cleaned in Europe.

"For cash, invested and managed in Europe by ourselves in proxy for you, we charge commission of 10 percent of profits. Do you wish to use our facilities?"

The offer was accepted.

Peppino did not need the calculator. His mind made the calculations. For five tons of cocaine, refined and delivered through the docks at Hamburg and Rotterdam, the Colombians would be paid the sum of $20 million. Five tons of cocaine would be sold on to the dealers and pushers and peddlers for a minimum of $45 million. When the dealers and pushers and peddlers released it on the streets of London and Frankfurt and Barcelona and Paris it would be worth $70 million. Initial profit, for minimum risk, was $25 million and the little bastard, the Colombian, would have known that the old man beside him was perhaps the one individual boss in Europe in whose word he could place trust. Plus $20 million dollars for investment, a profit margin of perhaps 8 percent a year for total safety. A further income of $0.16 million . . . There had been no raised voices, no vulgar bartering. It had been, Peppino thought, a demonstration of mastery and control. The deal was closed with a handshake, the Colombian's small-boned fist wrapped tight in Mario Ruggerio's broad fingers. The number of a post-office box on the island of Grand Cayman was given for further communication.

The Colombian was led away.

Mario lit his cigar and coughed. Peppino made the equation. His brother's deal would make a profit of $25 million, plus the commission on the investment, and his brother had no requirement for the money. There was no luxury that he sought, no means to spend the money. The money was the symbol of power. As if to tease Peppino, because Peppino wore a good suit and a good shirt and a good tie, his brother spat phlegm onto the floor and laughed.

Then, like it was an afterthought, something that could so easily have slipped his mind, Mario bent toward the floor and lifted a supermarket shopping bag from beside his feet, put it on the table, pushed it toward Peppino and tipped a handbag from it. Each stitch of the handbag had been sliced, each panel of the handbag had been cut open. With the handbag were a purse and keys and cosmetics and a credit card and a diary, and tied to the strap was a thin cardigan.

"She is what you called her, a simple girl, but it is necessary always to be careful."

Peppino took the *autostrada* back to Palermo. When he saw the road sign for Montelepre he slowed and he looked up toward the mountains. He could not see the town that was built against a rock fall because the rain cloud was too low. What always astonished him about his elder brother was his capacity to merge the broad frame of strategy with the minutiae of close detail, the strategy of a deal with a profit margin of $25 million along with investment commission, and the detail of a hired help's handbag. He had gone that morning to Montelepre, stood in the rain and walked on the cramped streets, to search for lessons. He accelerated when he was past the turning. His brother had learned all the lessons that could be taught.

The journalist from Berlin had to run to keep alongside her, and her small floral print umbrella covered only her head and shoulders. The rain ran on his head and his neck. To the journalist it was quite ludicrous that he should have to conduct what he regarded as an important interview on the street and in the rain with the woman who claimed to have founded the first of Palermo's groups for antimafia education. He had waited a week for the interview. Three times it had been postponed. She was a finely built middle-aged woman, dressed well, and she constantly covered with a slipping scarf the jewelry at her throat. While she talked, while she gave him his interview, she was incessantly yelling into a mobile telephone. The journalist from Berlin was a respected correspondent of his newspaper, he was a veteran of the Russian invasion of Chechenia and of the Gulf War and of Beirut. Palermo defeated him. He could not see the mafia, could not touch it, could not feel it. The woman he had waited to interview did not help him to see, touch, feel. A passing car's tires carved through a rain lake and drenched his trousers.

". . . I founded the antimafia group in this city at the time of Falcone's *maxi-processo* in 1986. I believed the trial of four hundred mafia men would make a turning point. I was a systems manager with Fiat in the north, but I gave up my job, very well paid, to return to Palermo. I have big support in some of the most hard suburbs of deprivation, I am particularly well known in Brancaccio. My car, my Audi, I can leave it in Brancaccio and it will not be destroyed . . . I accept that the mafia offers more to young people than the state offers, but it is possible to go forward through education, through the school environment . . . I have to accept also that progress is very slow, and the culture of the mafia is very strong, but a sense of duty drives me to continue . . . I can take you to Brancaccio next week, and you may sit with me while I meet mothers of young boys who may be exposed to the contamination of the mafia, that would be most interesting for you . . . I beg your pardon? Do the criminals regard us as a threat to their way of life? Of course we are a threat to them, through the policy of education and group meetings . . . If I am a threat why am I not silenced? I think you are impertinent, I think you are not truly interested . . ."

Charley sat on the patio.

The rain of the day had gone, its legacy fresher and keener air. The light came low and settled as a creeping bloodred rug on the water of the bay. It should have been a vision for her to marvel at, it should have been a place where she sat and enjoyed a vista of magnificence, but she was alone and she could not find beauty in the sun's fall across the crescent bay. She had given the children their meal, they were in their rooms. Later she would read to them. Angela had taken the baby to the main bedroom. Most of the day Angela had been in the bedroom. Perhaps company enough for her was the sleeping baby and the pill bottles. The joy of the Roman summer had been in the company of Angela Ruggerio, and the woman was now withdrawn, as if overwhelmed. One reference only, fleeting, to the great bloody god of family, and nothing to follow it. Sitting in the fresher and keener air, turning the reality in her mind and twisting it, Axel Moen's concept of a visit to the villa by Mario Ruggerio seemed to her to be laughable. She murmured, "Sold a bum steer, Charley, sold shop-soiled goods." Her fingers rested on the button of the wristwatch. Would he hear her? Would he be running? Such a small action, to press the fast code onto the button. The sun far out and bloodred on the bay was losing strength. So bloody alone . . .

The car came.

The gates were opened.

The car came forward. The gates were slammed shut, a jail's gates closing.

The car came up the drive and stopped.

Peppino was home. He was half across the patio when he saw her alone and in the shadow. He stopped, he turned, and the smile spread on his face.

"Charley, on your own—you are better?"

On her own so that she could better think of reality and cure herself of the danger of complacency, and better live the lie. "Been a long day, just sitting quietly."

"Where is Angela?"

The villa was in darkness. Angela was in her room and maybe she was weeping, and maybe she was at the pills. "Having a little rest."

"I have some good news for you."

Good news might be that there was a ticket for a flight, that she was being sent home, that she was returning to a room in a bungalow, to a classroom in a school. "What's that?"

As if he played with her, as if he mocked her. He laid his briefcase on the patio table. He went to the doors and switched on the patio light. The light on the patio made the night fall around her. He opened the briefcase. Smiling such sweetness.

"I told you there was a small possibility that your hand-bag might be dumped. We are very lucky. It was left near the Questura. Damaged, but containing your possessions."

So close to her, his waist and his groin beside her head and her shoulders. He took her handbag and her cardigan from the briefcase, and each panel of the bag had been cut, and he said that the thief must have searched for a hidden compartment and something more valuable, and he put the handbag on the table. He gave her the keys and the lipstick and the powder box, and the credit card, and the diary, and he said that thieves were interested only in cash, and he gave her the purse, empty.

Peppino said, "I am really so sorry, Charley, for your experience."

She blurted, "He's dead. The boy who robbed me, he's dead."

His eyes narrowed. She saw the tension in his body. "How can you know that?"

Axel Moen would have kicked her. Axel Moen would have slapped her. For a moment she had played the clever bitch. She had come out into the shadows of the patio, into the keener and fresher air, to clear her mind, and bloody waded in with two feet. She hesitated. "I'm being silly. There was a photograph in the paper. A boy was dead in the street in Brancaccio."

Soothing. "But you did not see his face, you said he wore a helmet."

Retreating. "I thought I recognized the bike . . ."

"They are scum, Charley. They live on drugs to give them the courage to rob young girls and old women. They steal many bags in a day to feed their revolting habit. Perhaps, before he had stolen from you, or afterwards, he thieved from a young girl or an old woman whose father or sons had influence. They lead a very dangerous life. You know, Charley, once there were some young boys, not aged more than sixteen years, and they stole the bag of a woman who was married to a *mafioso*. This criminal identified the boys and had them strangled and had their bodies left in a well. You are a caring person, but you should not concern yourself with the life or death of such scum."

"Maybe I was wrong about the motorcycle. I am very grateful to you for taking so much trouble."

His stomach and his groin rested against her shoulder. Always the smile on his face. He took another handbag of soft leather from his briefcase and laid it in front of her.

"But you have no handbag. I took the liberty, Charley, to replace your handbag. Please, open it. You see, I remember also that your necklace was broken. I cannot replace its sentimental importance to you, but I do my poor best."

Angela stood in the doorway, and her hair was disheveled from sleep and the blouse hung loose from the waist of her skirt and she was barefoot. Angela watched.

Inside the handbag was a thin jewelry box. Charley opened the box. The necklace of gold shimmered. She took the necklace in her fingers, felt the weight of the gold links As she lifted it and draped it at her throat, Peppino, so gentle, took it and fastened it, cold against her skin.

Angela turned away.

"Thank you," Charley said. "You are very kind to me."

Peppino asked her to excuse him. He said that he was away early in the morning, that he must pack his bag.

She sat under the patio light, alone, and gazed out over the darkness. God, she wanted so much to be loved and to be held . . .

TO: D/S Harry Compton, SO6.
FROM: Alf Rogers, DLO, Rome.

GIUSEPPE RUGGERIO, Apt 9, Giardino Inglese 43, Palermo, interesting because the heroes of the *carabinieri* do not have files on him, Guardia di Finanze likewise, BUT a lady from SCO no doubt fancies my body. RUGGERIO is a financial fixer, listed by SCO as living at Via Vincenzo Tiberio, Rome. No criminal history. (Unsurprised that locals have lost him—workload, long lunches and inadequate resources to track movement, cannot cope.) BUT, BUT if we talk about same joker, he is younger brother of MARIO RUGGERIO (Grade A mafia fugitive). Because I am over-worked, underpaid, reliant only on my considerable charm, difficult for me to learn more. DEA/FBI (Rome), underemployed and overpaid, have big dollar resources hence greater access than me—do I check with them for more GIUSEPPE RUGGERIO information?

Two pints, please, in Ferret and Firkin.

Luv, Alf.

Harry Compton stood over Miss Frobisher as she typed the reply for transmission to Rome. She oozed her disapproval, as if in the days of her youth, the days of carrier pigeons, certain standards prevailed in communications.

And he didn't care what she thought and ignored her curled upper lip because the excitement ran with him.

> TO: Alfred Rogers, DLO, British Embassy,
> Via XX Settembre, Rome.
> FROM: D/S Harry Compton, SO6.

> Two half pints coming your way. We are concerned about use of your body with lady from SCO—could lead to Post-coital Stress Disorder and her requirement for counseling. Do not, repeat NOT, share our interest in GIUSEPPE RUGGERIO with Yankee cousins, nor with locals.
>
> Bestest, Harry.

10

▼

"DO I REALLY NEED TO KNOW THIS?"

The grievance, the story of the "pressurization" of a young girl from south Devon, was climbing the ladder. From Detective Sergeant Harry Compton to his detective superintendent. From the detective superintendent to the commander of SO6. From the commander to the assistant commissioner (Specialist Operations). At each step of the ladder the grievance was elaborated.

"I rather think, Fred, that you do—and I'd like to hear the views of colleagues."

Around the polished table, bright in spring light thrown through the plate-glass windows, in a room on the sixth floor of the New Scotland Yard building, were the commanders who headed what they believed to be the élite specialized teams of the Metropolitan Police. Comfortable in their chairs, at the end of their monthly meeting, were the men who ran Anti-Terrorist Branch, International and Organized Crime, the Flying Squad, Special Branch, Royal and Diplomatic Protection and SO6.

The assistant commissioner moved behind them, refilling the coffee cups from a jug. "Right, shoot then."

"Am I peeing in a gale? None of you knew that the DEA, our American friends, were recruiting in this country?"

Gestures and shrugs and shaken heads from Anti-

Terrorist Branch and Special Branch and from Royal and Diplomatic Protection, hardly likely to have been blown past their desks. The Flying Squad man said that he rarely dealt with Americans, when he did it was FBI and, snigger, then when he was short of a good meal on expenses. International and Organized Crime denied flatly that he had joint operations with DEA currently in place.

"Get to the point, please."

"Of course, Fred. I am not a happy man, I regard this situation as intolerable. American agencies are based in this country on the very clear understanding that they operate through us, and that means they do not have the right to run independent operations. What we know, no thanks to them, is that a DEA operative flew here from Rome in pursuit of a letter sent from Palermo to a Miss Charlotte Parsons, teacher and first job, aged twenty-three, just a naïve youngster. The letter the DEA tracked was an invitation to Miss Parsons that she should go to work for a Palermo family as a childminder and nanny. The DEA wanted that girl in that household, they worked her over, they put quite intolerable pressure on her. A member of my team has established, at stiletto point, from Devon and Cornwall, that the locals behaved like cowboy bullies at the DEA's request, took the girl on a tour of druggie housing estates, to a morgue to gawp at an overdose victim, to a hospital to visit a narcotic-addicted baby. That is disgusting abuse of influence."

"I've not heard anything that I want to know."

"It is our belief that Miss Parsons is now exposed to real hazard. Whether you want to know it or not, sir, you'll hear it. Sorry, but this gets up my nose. Not any old family, no, but a quality, tasty, mafia family. Miss Parsons has been kicked by the DEA's boot into the

Ruggerio family. She has gone to work for the younger brother of Mario Ruggerio."

The commander paused for effect. Not that Royal and Diplomatic Protection, paring his nails, knew who the hell Mario Ruggerio was, nor Anti-Terrorist Branch who was swirling the coffee dregs in his cup, nor Special Branch. Flying Squad was gazing at the ceiling, frowning, trying to gather in a memory of that name. He gestured to International and Organized Crime.

"Yes, I know the name. It's in most of that interminable stuff the Italians chuck at us. Mario Ruggerio is coming through, fast-track, to fill the vacuum created when the Italians finally put a bit of their act together and lifted Riina and Bagarella. Same mold as Liggio or Badalamenti or Riina, a peasant who's made the big-time."

"And a killer?"

The commander of the International and Organized Crime unit grimaced. "That's integral to his job description. Riina had a hundred and fifty killings down to him, forty done himself, mostly manual strangulation. Goes without saying."

"Kills without hesitation, kills what threatens?"

"Reasonable assumption."

The assistant commissioner rapped his silver pencil on the table, hard. "Where are we going?"

"When challenged their Country Chief gave us a right put-down. I'll tell you where we're going. The DEA, the Americans, have inserted this innocent young woman, untrained and with zero experience of under-cover, into a prime and vicious mafia family. Stands to reason, the Americans see her as an access source. Christ, down there the Italians cannot even protect their own judges and magistrates who're ring fenced with hardware—what sort of protection are they going to be able to give this young woman? Nil."

The lips of the assistant commissioner pursed. "Do I not hear a little of injured pride? Wasn't there a word of a little spat in Lyon last year, the Europol conference, rather a public put-down of one of your people? I would hope, most sincerely, that we are not edging into vendetta country."

"I resent that."

The assistant commissioner smiled, icily. "And we are, I believe, supposed to be on the same side, wouldn't you agree?"

"There are potential consequences. Because of the possible consequences, I felt it my duty to raise this matter. A naïve and pressurized young woman has been inserted into an area of hazard. Take the bad side. She's blown out. Our little Miss Parsons, of south Devon, schoolteacher, ends in a ditch with her throat cut and her body showing all the marks of sadistic torture. Italian media with their cameras crawling all over her body, our papers and TV picking it up. Going to try and wash our hands of responsibility, are we? Going to say, are we, that she was put in this position of real danger from right under our bloody noses, and we did nothing? A lamb to the slaughter, and we did nothing. Would you, gentlemen, sit on your backsides if it were your daughter? 'Course you bloody wouldn't, you'd raise the bloody roof."

"What do you want?"

The commander of SO6 said, "Try me on what I don't want—I don't want bloody Americans running riot in this country on recruitment trawls, short of consideration of consequences."

"I said, what do you want?"

"I want Charlotte Parsons extricated. You postured that we were on the same side. The same side is co-operation. They didn't cooperate. I want the Americans sent a message. I want Charlotte Parsons brought home."

"Shit in the fan," from Special Branch.

"Would kind of knock down bridges," from Royal and Diplomatic Protection.

"Poor friends the Americans if peeved. They'd not enjoy interference," from Flying Squad.

"I rely on their help, be reluctant to see them offended," from Anti-Terrorist Branch.

"I'm taking SO6's position, we'd be hung on lamp-posts if it went sour, if she came back in a box," from International and Organized Crime.

"I want her brought home, before harm comes to her."

Silence fell. The assistant commissioner stared out of the window. Where the buck should stop was in front of him, in front of the neatly piled papers on which his silver pencil beat a slight tattoo. The commander of SO6 watched him. The commander was going no higher, but the assistant commissioner was five years the younger and would have his eyes on the top job and the knighthood. Squirming, wasn't he? Working over the tangent lines of consequences. Wriggling, wasn't he? The commander of SO6 felt himself in good shape because the responsibility for consequences was now shared with his superior and with his colleagues . . . But the bastard, true to form, judged.

"Before we confront the DEA, I want more information on Mario Ruggerio."

"Like what he has for breakfast, what color are his socks?"

"Steady, my friend—detail on Mario Ruggerio. There's

a slot in my diary same time next week, just the two of us. I'm sure it'll keep for a week. Don't want to run before we can walk. And, so that I can better evaluate, I want to know more about this girl."

"Hello—wasn't any trouble finding it."

She had lied again, but then the lying was a habit. Good at lying, Charley had told Angela that it was important for her to go again to Palermo. So reasonable a lie, so fluent. "It's the same as if you've been a driver in an accident, Angela, then you have to get back behind the wheel as quickly as possible. It's really kind of you to offer, but I need to be alone, just as I was alone then. I don't want anyone with me. I want to walk the streets, get it out of my system. Tell you what, Angela, I'm now taking that lovely bag that Peppino bought, I'm going to buy one of those stomach things that tourists have. I don't know what time I'll be back . . . I have to do this for myself, I have to put it behind me."

The gardener had let her out of the gates, the bloody "lechie," and she had almost run down the street from the villa in impatience to get clear of the place. Peppino was long gone, driven away while she was still asleep. She had already taken the children to school and kindergarten. The baby was sleeping. When she'd talked to Angela, lied, she'd thought that Angela was close to spitting out the great confidences. Little Charley, she could be a vicious little bitch, she hadn't wanted to hang around and hear the confidences, nor the weeping. Stick to the pills, Angela, keep popping them. She had run to get the bloody miserable place behind her . . .

"You are well, recovered?"

"Do I look awful?"

"The bruise has gone, the scratches are good." H

was so damn solemn. "You do not look awful."

"Aren't you going to invite me in?"

She grinned, she felt mischief. He was so damn solemn, and so damn shy. He stepped aside with courtesy.

"It is a big mess, I am sorry."

"No problem."

She was early. Because she had lied well and run fast down to the seashore in Mondello she had caught the bus before the one she had planned to take into Palermo. She wore her tight jeans that hugged her waist and contoured her stomach and thighs, and the T-shirt with the wide cut at the neck that left her shoulders bare. She stepped through the door. She had taken time, unusual for her, with her lipstick and with her eyes, and she wondered now, as Benny let her into his apartment, if Angela would have registered that she had been careful with her cosmetics, might have known she lied. Perhaps it was a mistake to have been careful with the lipstick and with her eyes, and maybe Axel bloody Moen would have slagged her off for it. The apartment was a single big room of an old building. A small cooker in a dark corner beside a washbasin that was filled with dirty plates and mugs, a wardrobe and a chest, a single bed not made and with the pajamas lying dumped on it, a table covered with papers and a hard chair and an easy chair that was covered with clothes. There were posters on the walls.

"I was going to clean it, but you are early." Said as an apology, without criticism.

"It's lovely. It's what I don't have . . ."

It was what she yearned for, her own place and her own space. A place, space, where she was not a lodger in her mother's home, not a paid guest in Angela Ruggerio's villa.

She was a lying little bitch and a bullying little bitch.

She had invited herself into his life. She went to the basin
and ran the water till it was hot. She didn't ask him if he
wanted his plates and his mugs cleaned, she did it. She
ignored him and he hovered behind her. The poster on
the wall above the basin was of a pool of blood on a street
and the single slogan, BASTA!. When she had finished at
the washbasin she went to the bed and stripped back the
sheets and saw the indentation where his body had been,
and she made the bed neatly and folded hospital corners
as her mother had taught her. She put his pajamas under
the pillows. It was a narrow bed, a priest's bed, and she
wondered if it whispered when his body moved on it, a
chaste bed. The poster, fastened with Sellotape to the
wall above the bed, was of white doves rising. She didn't
look at him, it was her game with him, and at the chair
she started to fold the clothes and to take a suit back to
the wardrobe. In the bottom of the wardrobe she found
dirty shirts and socks and underpants; she assumed he
went back to his mother every week with a bag of washing. She turned. Beside the door was a poster on the wall
showing, black and white, the long snaking column of a
funeral and mourners. Her hands were on her hips,
Charley grinned. It was her cheek.

"Another Sicilian boy who needs a woman to look
after him. Christ, how did you survive in London?"

She had embarrassed him. "Where I lived, there were
men and there were women. I used to bring back the left-
over chips at the time we closed the McDonald's—they
would have been thrown away. I fed the women, the
women did my washing and they cleaned my room."

"Grieves me to hear there's a male chauvinist piggery
alive and well in London."

He did not understand. He stood awkwardly. What
she liked about him, he seemed so bloody vulnerable.

"So, that was me saying thanks, saying you were brilliant. Thanks for being brilliant when everyone else looked the other way. Now, I've been really conscientious, I've read the guidebook. I want to see the *duomo,* the Quattro Canti on the Marqueda, the old market in the Vucciria. I want to get to the Palazzo Reale for the Cappella Palatina. I reckon we can do the Palazzo Sclafani as well before lunch. Big lunch, a good bottle, then if we've the stamina—"

"I am sorry . . ."

"What for?"

"You did not give me a telephone number for you. I could not telephone you." He hung his head. "I do not have the time to walk in Palermo."

Charley blinked. Trying to be casual, trying not to show that she had looked forward to the day, the escape, ever since she'd rung him. "So you got your room cleaned up and you don't have to do the guide bit, lucky old you. I suppose that makes us quits."

He fidgeted. "I have the day off from the school. It was my intention to escort you around Palermo. I have the school, and I have another life. For the work of my second life I have to deliver, urgently, some things."

"I'll come."

"I think, Charley, you would find it very boring."

As if he sought to dismiss her. Shit. She could turn round and she could walk out of the door. As if he told her that she intruded.

"Try me. What's the second life? I've nowhere else to go. I mean, the *duomo* has been there best part of a thousand years, expect it'll keep another week. Where have you got to go?"

"I have to go to San Giuseppe Jato, and then to Corleone . . ."

"Heard of Corleone. Interesting, yes? Never heard of the other one. Is that countryside?"

"It is into the country." He seemed to hesitate, as if undecided. She gazed back into his quiet almond-colored eyes. Come on, Benny, don't play the bloody tosser. She could not tell him about the claustrophobia she had fled from for a day. "I am a teacher, but I have also other work. I have to see people in San Giuseppe Jato and in Corleone, and I think you would not find it interesting."

"Then I'll sit in the car."

"My other work is for the Anti-Mafia Coordination Group of Palermo—how can that be of interest to you? Can we not fix another day?"

Her chin jutted. Axel bloody Moen would have told her to run, not to bother to close the door, run and keep running. The watch was on her wrist. His fingers, twisting, were fine and gentle, a pianist's. She should never relax. His face was of narrow angles, but without threat. She understood the posters on the walls of the room. She challenged him.

"I think that might be of more interest than the *duomo*. I think I might learn more about Sicily than from the Quattro Canti and the Cappella Palatina, yes?"

As a response he went to the door and unhooked his anorak. He looked around him, as if his room had been invaded, as if he had been boxed and bullied, as if he were too polite to complain, from the basin with the cleaned plates and mugs, to the chair from which the clothes had been taken, to the bed that had been made. He led her outside and onto the wide landing above the old staircase. He turned two keys in the heavy mortice locks.

"Safer than Fort Knox."

So polite. "I'm sorry, I don't understand."

"Just something you say, forget it, something silly.

Benny, why do you work against the mafia?"

He started to walk to the staircase. He said, matter-of-fact, "Because the mafia killed my father. When he was driving me home from the school, they shot him."

Pasquale had run along three blocks from where the bus had stopped, and run into the building, and not waited for the elevator, and run up three flights of stairs, and leaned panting against the wall while he waited for the apartment door to be opened. He was three minutes late. He had not overslept, he was late because his car had not started, battery gone, and the man on the floor below who had the jump leads was not at home, and . . . He was let inside. Jesu, and they were waiting for him, and they wore their vests and they carried their guns. The magistrate, Tardelli, sat in a chair in the hall with his coat on and his briefcase between his feet, and he looked up at Pasquale and there seemed to be sympathy on his face. The one who drove the chase car scowled and looked at his watch pointedly. The one who rode passenger in the chase car stared at the ceiling as if he did not wish to have a dog in this fight. The one who sat in the back of the chase car stared at him hard and without pity.

The *maresciallo* said, "We would have gone without you, but it is against regulations to go when we do not have the full complement. Dr. Tardelli has been obliged to wait for you."

Panting hard. "Car didn't start—battery gone—my apologies, *dottore*—one minute, please, one minute . . ."

He felt sick. He felt like dirt. He stumbled away to the spare bedroom, still decorated and furnished for two of the children taken by their mother back to the north. Beside the wardrobe, empty, was the reinforced-steel gun box, full. Fumbling for the key that opened the gun box, and knowing the angered presence of the *maresciallo* behind him. Jesu, the wrong key. Finding the correct key. Taking out the Heckler & Koch, dropping a magazine that clattered on the wood floor. Blessings to Mary the Virgin that he had refilled the magazine the previous evening because it was routine that magazines must be emptied at the end of each shift or the mechanism might jam, groveling thanks to Mary the Virgin that he had refilled the magazine. Snatching the Beretta 9mm with the shoulder holster from his numbered hook, and more magazines for the Beretta, and a box of bullet shells for the Beretta because he had not filled those magazines. Crouching down and searching in the heap for the bulk of his vest. He stood. He had to peel off his coat, sling the harness of the holster for the Beretta. He had to heave the vest over his head, heavy onto his shoulders. He had to throw on his coat again. The box of bullet shells for the Beretta into the coat pocket, and the emptied magazines. He slapped one magazine into the machine pistol, and the eyes of the *maresciallo* were fixed on him, and, thank Jesu he remembered to check that the safety was on. He breathed hard. For a moment he stood. Blessings to Mary the Virgin. He came back into the hall and they all stared at him, and there was no movement to the front door, still business to be completed inside, and the expression of the magistrate was sympathy and the shrug which said the matter was beyond his intervention.

The *maresciallo* beckoned with his finger, an instruction to follow. Pasquale went after him into the kitchen. The *maresciallo* pointed with his finger. The flowers his wife had bought, the bright flowers he had taken to the magistrate's apartment, were dumped in the trash can under the sink. Alive, still with color, thrown away.

"You are, Pasquale, pretend to be, a close protection

guard. You are not the servant of Dr. Tardelli, nor are you his friend. Whether you have sympathy for him or a dislike of him, you do your job, and you take your money, and you go home. What you do not do is snivel sentiment. I will not have on my team any man who, remotely, becomes emotionally involved. I come back from three days away and I find that little presents, little gifts of flowers, have been given. Your job is to protect Dr. Tardelli, not to make a friendship. He is a target, a principal target, and the best way to protect him is to remain aloof from him as a personality. We do not travel each day with a friend, but with a *paccetto*. To you he should be just a parcel that is taken from here and delivered safely to a destination. You should not try to wrap ribbons around a parcel. You are on assessment, on probation, and I remember everything. If you are ready may we, please, leave?"

Pasquale stumbled out into the hall. He had told his wife how much the magistrate, poor lonely man, had appreciated her flowers. There was the clatter of the guns being armed, the static and distorted chatter of the radios. They took the *paccetto* down to the street, to the cars.

"Do you want to wait in the car, or do you want to come in?"

"I think I'd like to walk around the town—I mean, it's sort of famous, isn't it?"

Benny said, somber, "You should not walk alone around the town. Afterwards, if you want, I can show you the town. For now you should come inside with me or you should wait in the car."

Charley said, sullen, "If I should not walk around the town without an escort, then I will come with you."

She snapped her body out of the tiny AutoBianchi car. She stretched and felt the sunlight. Of course she had heard of Corleone—she had seen the first film at college with Marlon Brando starring, and she had seen *Godfather III* on video with Al Pacino starring. They were parked near the *carabinieri* barracks. Pretty bloody ordinary it looked to her, Corleone. They had come into the town on a wide open road from San Giuseppe Jato where Benny had left her in the car while he collected a photocopier from a small house. He hadn't talked much as he had driven through the countryside between San Giuseppe Jato and Corleone. Axel Moen would have kicked her backside because she had bullied her way into Benedetto's day. It had been spare and empty talk on the road after they had left the confined tight streets of San Giuseppe Jato. They had talked of the horses that grazed the grasslands in the expanses between rock outcrops, and of the wildflowers of yellow and burgundy, and of the handkerchief-sized plots of vines growing where a vestige of cultivation could be scratched in soil above the stone, and there had been hawks climbing above the outcrops of rock which she recognized as the kestrels and buzzards of home. Benny didn't know what the horses were used for, didn't know what the flowers were called, didn't know what was the sort of grapes grown here, didn't know about the hawks. She had been talking, nothing talk, about the hawks on the cliffs at home, when he had told her abruptly, almost with rudeness, to be quiet, and he had slowed, and then she had noticed the military roadblock, and they had been waved through, boring . . . If Sicily was a battleground, if it were the place of Axel bloody Moen's war, then she had only a single military roadblock to tell her of it. They had driven into Corleone on a broad street and past a street market that seemed to sell everything from clothes and furniture to vegetables and meat. No

troops and no police, nothing that was familiar from
television of war on the streets of Belfast. The sun was
on her back and she walked after Benny as he carried the
photocopier.

So she had annoyed him by pressing her presence. So
he could bloody well put up with her. Doggedly, she followed.

They went by a school and there was a clamor of
kids' voices from inside. There was an emblem on the
wall of the school, not large and not ostentatious, of
doves flying. She read AI MARTIRI DELLA VIOLENZA—
hardly a monument to war, not much of a mark for a
battleground. He went through the open door of
a house. Quite sharply, he gestured for her to sit on a
hard chair in the hallway, and he left her there as he went
through to an inner room. She heard the excitement of
women's voices, and two women came into her view and
were hugging Benny and thanking him and he carried
the photocopier into the room where she could not see
him. Their voices clattered in her ears. She thought she
was excluded—bugger that. She stood, she walked to the
door. They were bent over the old photocopier and
Benny was on his knees and plugging it to a socket.
Their voices died. She was excluded because she was a
stranger. There were the same posters on the walls that
she had seen in his Palermo room. Benny flushed. He
told the women that the Signorina Parsons was English,
that he had met her when she was attacked in the street,
that he had promised to show her the antiquities of
Palermo, but the photocopier had to be delivered.

"So she is a tourist in Corleone?"

"So she comes to see the wickedness of Corleone,
and perhaps to send a postcard?"

Charley rode the sneers. She turned away, defiant,

and took her seat again. She heard their laughter from the room.

Perhaps they teased Benny, for bringing a tourist. He was distant when he came out of the inner room and each of the women made a show of kissing him on the cheek, and she thought their politeness to her was a charade. Did he screw them? Did he screw anyone on that narrow little priest's bed? Did Axel Moen fuck anyone on any bed? She smiled, lied her simplicity with a smile.

Out in the street, innocent and simple, "What do they do?"

"They have a newsletter to issue, but the photocopier is broken. They produce a newsletter for the Anti-Mafia Coordination Group of Corleone."

"Is it a big circulation?"

He matched her innocence and simplicity, but there was no lie. "Very small, very few people, which is why we have such humble resources, a room and two women and a photocopier. In Corleone is the culture of the mafia, but you would not know that. It is the heartbeat of the mafia—from Corleone to Palermo, from Palermo across the island, from the island to the mainland, from the mainland to Europe and over the ocean to America. It is why we speak of the octopus, with many tentacles, but the heartbeat of the beast is here. The *sindaco* speaks against the mafia, the priest denounces the mafia from the church, but that is politics and religion, and they change nothing."

"When will something change?"

He smiled, innocent and simple. "I will know that something has changed when we need two, three photocopiers."

"Tell me about Corleone. Show it to me."

He looked at her. His eyes that squinted against the

sun were grave as if he feared that she mocked him. "Forgive me—so that you can buy postcards and boast to your friends at home that you were in Corleone?"

"Please, walk me through the town?"

"Why?"

Axel bloody Moen would have kicked her arse, would have said that she lurched on the edge of disclosure, would have snarled that she was at the cliff face of complacency. "It's just, what I've seen, a street and a market and a school and blocks of apartments and a barracks. I can't realize what you are fighting against."

"I think you would be bored."

"I want to understand."

They walked to the piazza. Old men watched them from under the bars' awnings and youths sat astride their motorcycles and eyed them from under the shade of palm trees. The sun beat on Charley's arms and on her shoulders.

"It is the town of Navarra and then of Liggio and then of Riina and then of Provenzano. Now it is the town of Ruggerio. To you, the stranger, it will appear like any other town. It is unique in Sicily because here no businessman pays the *pizzo*. Literally that is the small bird's beak that pecks for a little food but on the island the *pizzo* is the extortion of money for 'protection.' In the 1940s, after the liberation from Fascism, a good statistic for you to carry home to your friends, there were more murders here per head of population than in any town or city in the world."

Charley said quietly, "You don't have to talk me short, Benny, like I'm only a tourist."

At the start of the old town, where the streets darkened and narrowed and climbed to the left and fell to the right, Benny bought her a coffee and a warm roll with ham and goat's cheese. His voice was a murmur. "I will tell you one story, and perhaps from the one story you will understand. It is not the story of Navarra who was the doctor here and the parents of a twelve-year-old boy brought the hysterical child to him and told the doctor that the child had seen the killing of a man, and Navarra injected the child with a 'sedative' that killed him, and then apologized for his mistake. It is not the story of Navarra. It is not the story of Liggio who was a cattle thief before he developed the heroin trade of the mafia. And not the story of Riina who ordered the killing of the bravest of the judges and drank champagne in celebration. Not the story of Provenzano who is called the *trattore* here, the tractor, because of the brutality of his killings. It is not the story of Ruggerio. Come."

She gulped the last of the roll. She wiped the crumbs from the front of her T-shirt. She followed him out onto the street.

"You will hear, anywhere in Sicily, the stories of Navarra and Liggio and Riina and Provenzano, maybe you can hear the story of Ruggerio. You will not be told the story of Placido Rizzotto, but that is the story that will help you to understand."

They walked down a narrow street, on cobbled stones. The balconies with wrought-iron railings pushed out from the walls above them, seeming to make a tunnel. Watched by an old man, watched by children who stopped their football game, watched by a woman who paused to rest from the weight of her shopping bags. No sun on the narrow street.

"First he had been in the army, then he was with the partisans. Then he came back to Corleone where his father was at a low level with the mafia. Placido Rizzotto returned here with opened eyes from the mainland. He became a trade-union organizer. The mafia detested the trade unions because they mobilized the *contadini*, worked against the mafia's domination of the poor. To the Church he was a communist. To the police he was a political agitator. Perhaps the mafia and the Church and the police were distracted, but Rizzotto was elected as mayor of Corleone. Do I bore you, Charley?"

They stopped. They were near to the church, a huge edifice at the front, and a bell tolled, and black-dressed women hurried for the door but swiveled their heads as they went that they might better watch them. Ahead of them was a bank. A fat-bellied guard leaned against the door of the bank and his finger rested loosely in his sagging belt that took the weight of his holster, and he watched them.

"Ten o'clock at night, a summer night. A friend calls for Placido Rizzotto at his father's home, invites him to come for a walk. All the men in the town are walking in the Via Bentivegna and the Piazza Garibaldi. He was betrayed by his friend. He strolled along the street, and one moment his friend was with him and the next moment his friend was gone . . . All of the men walking that evening on the Via Bentivegna and the Piazza Garibaldi saw Liggio approach Rizzotto, saw the gun put into Rizzotto's back. All of the men, all of those who had voted for him and who had cheered his speeches, watched him led away as if he were a dog led to a ditch to be killed. Are you bored, Charley?"

The ravine was in front of them. Water tumbled from above them and fell, and the flow was broken by dark stones that had been smoothed over the centuries. Above the ravine was a fortress of decayed yellow stone built on the flat top of a straight-sided rock mass, dominating. They were alone now with the ravine and the fortress, and the watchers were behind them.

"The people went home. They emptied the streets and they locked their doors and they went to their beds. They had surrendered. And Rizzotto did not even threaten the mafia, or the Church, or the police, to all of them he was merely a nuisance. It was in 1948. Two years later his body was recovered by the fire brigade from here. His father could identify him from the clothes, and from his hair that had not been eaten by the rats. A man who had seen Rizzotto taken away said, 'He was our hero and we let him go. All we had to do, every one of us, was to pick up a single stone from the street, and we could have overwhelmed the man with the gun. We did not pick up a stone, we went home.' It was in 1948 and the culture of fear is the same today. Does my story bore you, Charley, or do you better understand?"

Her father had been three years old when Placido Rizzotto had been pitched, dead, into the ravine below. Her mother had been one year old. She had walked along the same street as the man with the pistol in his back, walked on the same pavements the watchers had stood on, walked past the same doors through which they had hurried and which they then locked, walked past the same windows in which the lights had been extinguished. Charley Parsons, twenty-three years old, stared down into the ravine below the mountain rock on which the ruin of the fortress stood, and she thought the smell of a rotted corpse was in her nose, and she believed that at last she knew the scent of evil. Christ, yes, she understood.

"Where does Ruggerio come from?"

"From near here."

"Can I see where he comes from?"

"For what reason?"

She lied, so easily. "What you said, Ruggerio is the present. Right, I'm just a bloody tourist imposing on your day. It's what tourists do, go and visit a birthplace. If you don't want to . . ."

"It's not difficult."

Each afternoon, after the quarry had closed, after the drivers of the big dumper lorries had gone and the stone-crushers had been silenced, they blasted for the next day's supply of broken rock.

The quarry was cut into the mountain across the river from San Giuseppe Jato and San Cipirello. It was where the expert tested all the explosive devices he designed.

In open ground, clear of the rock face where the dynamite charges were set, the expert and Tano had carefully parked the two cars. The car the expert had driven was an old Fiat Mirafiori. The car that Tano had driven, level with it but separated by ten meters of space, was a Mercedes, low on its wheels from the weight of the armor plate lodged in the doors. The distance between the cars had been measured with a tape, because the expert had said that in matters involving explosives detail was important.

The two explosions were finely synchronized. At the moment that the dynamite in the quarry face was detonated, the final digit of a six-figure number was pressed by Tano on his mobile telephone and the connection was made to the telephone pager set into the bomb on the backseat of the Mirafiori.

In San Giuseppe Jato and in San Cipirello, the people would have heard the explosion, what they always heard at that hour, and a reverberating echo would have masked the second explosion.

The great dust cloud from the quarry face had barely settled when the expert and Tano went forward. The Mirafiori had disintegrated, beyond recognition. The Mercedes was what interested them. The two parts of the Mercedes, and it had been sliced precisely in half, burned fiercely.

They laughed, the expert and Tano, they were bent at the waist and shouting their laughter at the quarry face from which the last of the fractured rock fell.

By the morning, before the quarry opened for work, the parts of the Fiat Mirafiori and the halves of the Mercedes would be buried under waste stone away to the side of the quarry.

"Do you have a camera?"

She started, she had been alone with her thoughts. "A camera? Why is it important?"

Snapping, and she thought now he was frightened. "Charley, I asked, do you have a camera?"

"No."

It had been brilliant country. Bigger hills than those on Dartmoor that she knew, greener than Dartmoor, but the same wilderness. They had stopped once, when she had told him to stop. She had stood beside the car, leaned against the warmth of the body of the car and gazed across a field of wildflowers to the shepherd with his flock and his dog. Something of the Bible of a child, pastoral and safe, and she had heard the symphony of the chime of bells from the sheep, and the shepherd had sung. She thought it would have been an old song, handed down from his family, a song of love. The shepherd never saw them as he sang. Benny had stood beside her, close to her. Her sort of place . . . And the town was above them, and now the nervousness played in his face.

"I don't have a camera. Why?"

"Where we go, you should not use a camera—doesn't matter."

On a winding road Benny drove toward Prizzi. He parked in a lay-by. The town stretched away from them and above them, a mosaic of yellow and ochre tiled roofs so dense that the streets were hidden.

Benny looked around him, locked the AutoBianchi. He took her arm, fingers on her elbow. He hurried her.

They were on a climbing street. The window of a *macellaio* took her eye, the thin strange cuts of meat, unfamiliar to her, and her arm was pulled.

There would not have been room for cars to pass in the road. Two terraced lines of three-story homes, wooden doors set under low arches, balconies fronting shuttered windows, plaster and paint in yellow and orange and primrose. He walked fast and she skipped to keep up with him.

"You don't stop, you don't stare." His lips barely moved as he spoke and his voice hissed as if fear caught him. "The sixth house beyond the black-painted drainpipe. You have it? Don't turn your head. That is the house, the balconies one above the other, of the parents of Mario Ruggerio. It is where they live, with the brother of Mario Ruggerio, who is simple. You see it?"

He walked and he looked straight ahead. Charley saw a cat, low on its stomach, run from them.

Nothing moved in the street, but the cat. The sunlight fell on the house that had been identified for her. The door to the house was open and she heard, fleeting, a radio playing. She smelled, fleeting, the cooking of vegetables. Was that it? Was that the bloody lot? No Mercedes, no gold taps, no 9-inch cigars, no rottweilers, no Harrods curtains, bloody hell . . . She defied him.

Charley stopped in front of the open door and she twisted her head to look inside, and her arm was jerked half out of the socket at the shoulder. Only the sound of the radio and the smell of the cooking. When she was three doors past the house, he loosed her hand.

"Was that quite necessary?"

"Where do you think you are? Do you think you are at Stratford-upon-Avon? Do you think the Japanese come here in buses? Are you stupid?"

"You don't have to be rude."

"I am rude because you are stupid."

He was breathing hard. His lips twitched in nervousness. He walked fast. They came to the end of the road, where more roads, identical and mean and close, veered away into shadow. Christ, where were the people? Where were the kids?

"I am sorry, Benny, I am sorry if I am stupid. Spell it out, start with the camera."

His feet, a stamped stride, clattered on the cobbles. "You see nothing here, but you are watched. There would be, of course, a police camera on the street, but that is not important. Because you do not see anybody it does not mean you are not watched. Behind doors, behind blinds, behind shutters, behind curtains are people who watch. It is the home of the family of Mario Ruggerio, and Mario Ruggerio is responsible for the deaths of many people. Such a man does not leave his family vulnerable to the vendetta of revenge. Because you do not see something it does not mean that it does not exist. If you had a camera, and took a picture of the house, it is likely that we would be followed, and the number of my car would be taken. I do not want, because you are stupid, to have those people match the number of my car with my name. To a man like Mario

Ruggerio the family is the most important feature of his life, only with his family does he relax. We should not stay here."

"Where is the wife of Ruggerio?"

"Two streets from here. Why do you ask, why are there so many questions?"

"Just me, I suppose. Always talked too much."

"It would not be sensible for strangers to walk from the street of Ruggerio's parents direct to the street of Ruggerio's wife."

"I was only asking . . ."

He was walking back toward the car. Charley followed.

"In the story you told me, Placido Rizzotto was killed because he was a nuisance. Was your father a nuisance?"

"Not a threat, only a nuisance, which is enough."

"With the work you do, Benny, are you a nuisance?"

"How can I know? You know when you see the gun."

"Benny, damn you, stand still. Benny, what is your dream?"

He stood, and for a moment his eyes were closed. Charley took his hand. She waited on him. He said, soft, "I see him standing, and his head is hung in shame, and the handcuffs are on his wrists, and he stands alone without the backing of his thugs and his guns and his acid barrels and his drugs. He is an old man and he is alone. Around him are the children from Sicily and Italy, from all of Europe and from America. The children make a ring around him with their joined hands and they dance in a circle around him, and they laugh at him and they reject him and they jeer at him. My dream is when the children dance around him and have no fear of him."

He took his hand from hers.

Peppino had the dollars. They had the bank.

He had not met Russians before, and he thought them quite disgusting.

Peppino had the dollars on deposit in Vienna. They owned the bank in St. Petersburg.

His first meeting with Russians was in a hotel room near the railway station in Zagreb. The two Russians wore big gold rings on their fingers, as a whore would, and bracelets of gold at their wrists. Their suits, both of them, were from Armani, which had brought the only dry smile to Peppino's face. The one smile, because he did not think were people to laugh at, and the cut of the Armani suits did not disguise the muscle power of their shoulders and arms and stomachs and thighs. He assumed they carried firearms, and assumed also that a single blow from the gold-ringed fist of either of them would disfigure him for the rest of his life.

The deal that his brother envisaged was for $50 million to go from deposit in Vienna to their bank in St. Petersburg, and on then into investment in the oil-production industry of Kazakhstan. They owned, they boasted in guttural English, the Minister for Petroleum Extraction and Marketing in Alma Ata. His brother said that the Russians were not to be ignored, that alliances must be forged, that every effort must be made to find routes of cooperation. The cooperation would come through the investment in Kazakhstan, and in return Peppino was instructed to offer facilities to the Russians for the cleaning of their money. For himself, Peppino had only a view of money. His brother had the view of strategy. The strategy of his brother was for cast-iron agreements between La Cosa Nostra and these Russian thugs. His brother said that within five years these crude and vulgar people would have control of the biggest opium-growing area in the world and the biggest arms factories in the world, and their power could not be ignored.

They frightened Peppino.

And he was nervous also because they seemed to have no care for their personal security. It was Zagreb, and the Croatian capital was a place for scams and for racketeers, but the city offered easy access to the FBI and to the DEA. He had doubted their hotel room had been swept. He had come into the room and he had immediately turned the TV satellite rubbish up loud and he had sat himself beside the TV's loudspeaker, and they had to strain to hear him against the blast of game-show sound. Himself, he was against dealing with these people, but he would never contradict his brother.

He glanced at his watch, gestured with his hands. He apologized. He must leave for his flight out. Nothing written down, and nothing signed. He must take them on trust. He gave them a fax number in Luxembourg, and told them slowly, as if he was with imbeciles, what coded messages would be recognized. He offered them his hand, and his hand was crushed by each of them.

He stood.

One Russian said, "When you see Mario Ruggerio you should pass to him our good wishes that are sent in respect."

The second Russian said, "Mario Ruggerio is a man we learn from, we acknowledge his experience of life."

Rubbing his hand, Peppino charged away down the hotel corridor. They had spoken in deference of his brother, as if they held his brother to be a great man. What did it say, their respect, of his brother? He hurried across the foyer of the hotel and out into the street for the doorman to call him a taxi. He had thought them coarse, crude, brutal, and they were the men who offered him their admiration of his brother. He lay back in the taxi. He believed he was the messenger boy of his elder brother, coarse and crude and brutal, who owned him.

The telephone was ringing. Charley had been back an hour. The telephone was shrill. Charley was with the children in the bathroom, soaping them and trying to laugh with them. God, where was Angela to answer the phone? Charley was splashing water and making a game with the children and their shrieks did not drown the bell of the telephone. Angela had the second telephone beside her bed—the bloody pills. Charley wiped her hands on the towel. She hurried into the hall, past the closed door of Angela's bedroom.

"*Pronto.*"

"It's David Parsons. Could I speak to my daughter, Charlotte, please?"

"It's me, hello, Dad."

"Are you all right, Charley?"

"How did you get the number?"

"Directory inquiries—are you all right?"

"Didn't you get my card?"

"Just one card. We were worried."

"No cause for worry, I am very well and having a wonderful time."

"Your mother wanted me to call, you know what your mother is for worrying. Charley, there was a policeman came, from London, he wanted to know about the American. We—"

Charley snapped, "Don't talk about it."

She had heard the click on the telephone, and the sound of Angela's breathing.

". . . wanted to know—"

"You are not to call me here again. It is very inconvenient for me to take a telephone call. I am fine, and very happy. I'll try and send more postcards. I'm a big girl, Dad, if you'd forgotten, so don't call me again. Love to Mum, and to you, Dad."

She heard the breathing.

"Charley, we only wanted you to know——"

She put the phone down. Her fingers rested on the watch on her wrist, and she felt herself to be a cruel and vicious bitch. She could picture it in her mind, her father holding the telephone and hearing the purring of the dial tone, and then going into the little living room and away from the telephone on the table below the photograph of her at graduation, and then her father would have to tell her mother that their daughter had brushed him off, as a vicious and cruel little bitch would have, put him down . . . She was Axel bloody Moen's creature. She thought that, one day, she might tell her father of the dream, might tell her father of Benny's dream of dancing children and of an old man in handcuffs who suffered the humiliation of the children's contempt, one day . . .

Angela stood, sleep-devastated, pill-damaged, at the bedroom door.

"Sorry if it woke you, Angela," Charley said, and the cheerfulness was a lie. "It was my dad, I've been a bit naughty with the postcards, he was just checking I was all right."

She went back into the bathroom and took the big towels from the hook. If it were their father in the handcuffs, and their uncle, would small Mario and Francesca be dancing with the dream children? She started to rub them dry.

•   •   •

"It took me time to recognize him—it was the guy who picked her off the street when she was mugged."

"So, she wanted to thank him—why the blow-out?"

"She was with him all day."

"So, she's lonely, and maybe it's her free day—maybe."

"I could kick her arse, hard, with my boot. 'Vanni, she only goes to San Giuseppe Jato, and that's a poison place. Then she goes to Corleone, and that's a bad place. Where in Corleone? She only goes to the Anti-Mafia Coordination Group, meets up with those low-life dead-beats."

"They are brave people, Axel, committed people."

"Who achieve nothing, might as well jerk off. You know where she went after that, and you could see it on the guy's face, like he was shitting himself, she went to Prizzi."

"So it's a pretty town, it's interesting."

"It's a crap place, Prizzi—there's no scenery that's good, no architecture, no history. She wasn't looking for anything good. For Christ's sake, 'Vanni, she only goes marching off down the little shit street where the big guy's parents are. Can you believe it, she walked down the street where Rosario and Agata Ruggerio live? I mean, is that clever?"

"She's got balls."

"She's got a hole in the head where her brain fell out."

"And you don't trust her?"

"To box clever? Not on this show, no, I do not."

"But, Axel, you have to trust her. That's your problem isn't it, that's the shit on your shoe? She's all you've got. The criticism is irrelevant. And you had an interesting day?"

"A great day, what I really wanted, hiking round San Giuseppe Jato and Corleone and Prizzi."

"But you were there, the chaperone."

"It's my job to be there. She was endangering herself—she could have compromised me. That is not goddamn funny."

Back in Corleone, back where he had come with his grandfather and his stepgrandmother when he was a teenager. Back where his grandfather had found the "opportunity" and taken the bribes and handed out the gas coupons. He had been dragged by them past the street where his grandfather had pointed out the wartime AMGOT office. He had tracked Charley past the street to which he had been taken as a teenager to meet his stepgrandmother's family, and he had sweated that he might be remembered. Ridiculous to believe that he might be remembered, the features of his face recalled, but the sweat had run on his spine.

"Who is the man?"

"He dropped her off in the town. First goddamn sense she'd shown, she didn't march him up to the villa. She was going nowhere but home. I went back to his place, asked around."

"Then you came running to me, like you're booked for a coronary."

"He's Benedetto Rizzo, late twenties, built like a streak of piss—he's nothing. You know, she stood in the middle of goddamn Prizzi after they'd walked the Ruggerio street, and she held his hand and she looked into his face, like she was hot for him."

"Perhaps you're short of a woman, Axel."

"I don't need shit from you."

But Axel Moen had always been short of a woman. There had been women at the university, just casual . . .

There had been a good woman when he was on the police in Madison, working in real estate in Stoughton, and he'd brought her flowers and wrapped chocolates, and she'd been of old Norwegian stock, and she'd made Arne Moen laugh when Axel took her up to the Door Peninsula, and it had finished the night he told her he was accepted by DEA, and going to Quantico because she said she wouldn't follow him . . . There had been a good woman, Margaret, from a publishing house on East 53rd, when he had his head buried in New York with the earphones for the wire taps, and it had taken time but he'd persuaded her to come to the weekend cabins up-state, and they'd done the long hikes and they'd loved, and it was over when he told her he was posted down to La Paz, Bolivia . . . There had been a good woman in La Paz, out of order to mess with a Confidential Informant, a sweet soul and a dedicated mind and with guts, and it was ended when he found her crucified on the back of the door at the airstrip for the *estancia* . . . There had been a good woman, Margaret again, when he had returned to New York with the bullet hole souvenir in his stomach flesh, and she liked to run her finger down the scar when they went back to the weekend cabins, but there hadn't been the love as before, and it had been trashed for all time when he'd said he was posted to Rome . . . There was a good woman in Italy, Heather, out of the Defense Attaché's office in the main building, and she was wiser than the rest and kept him at arm's length, just convenience for both of them, and they went to the parties together, kept the matchmakers at a distance by showing up at the barbecues and the functions, were seen together when they mutually needed a partner, no loving and nothing to finish . . . And there was a good woman, Charlotte Eunice Parsons . . .

"So she makes a mistake, walks down a street, isn't sensible. Maybe she knows that, maybe she won't do it again. She's lonely, she holds a man's hand to whom she has reason to be grateful. You know what I believe?"

"What?"

'Vanni laughed quietly, and whispered, "I think you are jealous of the 'streak of piss,' I think you are jealous of him."

"You are pathetic."

Axel walked out on the best friend he had in Sicily, out of the cinema.

A cinema, dark and showing an unpublicized French-language film, empty, was a useful place to meet.

He took a side entrance out. It was a basic precaution, the sort of care that came naturally to him.

He was not aware that, at the front of the cinema, a man watched the builder's van that was parked half on the street and half on the pavement.

TO: Alfred Rogers, DLO, British Embassy,
Via XX Settembre, Rome.
FROM: D/S Harry Compton, SO6.

Action stations this end, going to a war footing. Big politics being played . . . To impress top brass we urgently require updater on MARIO RUGGERIO, inclusive of bullshit you so expert in. My last still applies. The Pepsi/peanut-butter brigade are not, repeat NOT, Need To Know. Hope this does not interfere with your leisure schedule. Think of Queen and Country as you sacrifice your obese body.

Bestest, Harry.

11

MISS FROBISHER HANDED the brief message to the detective sergeant.

> TO: D/S Harry Compton, SO6.
> FROM: Immigration Desk (EU entrants),
> Terminal Two, Heathrow Airport.
>
> BRUNO FIORI (Your ref: 179/HC/18.4.96) arrived ex Zagreb, 18.35 Monday. Regret not delayed as requested.
> Barnes, Dawn, Supervising Officer.

He read it five times, then telephoned the Supervising Officer—Barnes, Dawn. She had one of those chill efficient voices. Yes, Italian passport holder "Bruno Fiori" had come off last night's Zagreb flight. Yes, he had been passed through the European Union passengers' desk. Yes, there had been a request from SO6 logged, that Italian passport holder "Bruno Fiori" should be delayed—had the detective sergeant any idea of how many EU passport holders journeyed through Heathrow at that time of an evening? Yes, he had been positively identified, but the logged request for delay had only triggered with the immigration officer, a new probationer, after the passport had been returned. Yes, that officer had shut down his desk and gone through to Customs, Green Channel and Red Channel, but had failed to find Italian

passport holder "Bruno Fiori" . . . "There's no requirement for that sort of talk, Mr. Compton. We do our best.
If you don't like our best, then I suggest you refer the
matter to the Home Office and request additional funding for Immigration (Heathrow). And a good day to you,
too." So that was a brilliant bloody start to Tuesday
morning. Giuseppe Ruggerio back in UK, and the hope
had been that if he returned he would be held first on a
passport technicality, and then done over by Customs as
a "random" check and held long enough for the tail to
be scrambled. The brilliant bloody start to a Tuesday
morning was a quality foul-up. He hammered down the
corridor to his detective superintendent.

He explained.

"Shit."

He showed the communication.

"Bloody hell."

"So what do I do?" Harry Compton could play
dumb insolent as well as the next. He stood in front of
the boss man, with his hands folded across his groin, and
the look of innocence on his face. He knew the track
that the investigation had taken, that it had gone up the
ladder to the commander, from the commander to the
assistant commissioner (Special Operations). He knew
the spat with the Americans had reached the stratosphere
level.

"It's out of my hands."

"What's best then—that I bin it?"

"Don't smart-talk me."

"I rather need to know what I should do. We can put
a full surveillance on Blake for a start, go for a full search
warrant for Mr. Blake. We can shake him up."

"I'm not permitted to scratch my bloody nose on
this one without authorization, not before we've heard

from Rome, then I have to have you back down in Devon and a fat lot—"

"What I'm asking, do I do something or do I go back to sifting minimal scams on the good old pensioners' savings?"

Harry Compton thought the biro in the hands of his boss man might just break, big fingers twisting it in frustration. "You're a clever little chap, Harry. Put yourself where I am, ringfenced by the God Almighties, make a suggestion that's half sensible."

"Fair assumption that Fiori, Ruggerio, will go back to his good friend. I'd stake it out, and I'd sweep his paperwork—and I'd belt Alf Rogers hard, so's it hurt, and keep belting him till he delivers."

"So get on with it, and don't embarrass me. You embarrass me and you'll be back helping old ladies across the road."

He went back to his office. He phoned the car pool and the Stores section and told them what he wanted. He scrawled the message, and he was whistling because he felt good, and handed it to Miss Frobisher for transmission.

TO: Alf Rogers, DLO, British Embassy,
Via XX Settembre, Rome.
FROM: Harry Compton, SO6.

Relevant word in my last was "urgently." Stop squeezing your blackheads and do some WORK. Soonest, we must have updated biog. on MARIO RUGGERIO with assessment of links to brother GIUSEPPE. I grovel because I need ACTION. I would have thought you have a small window of opportunity for research between getting out of your pit, paying off your

women, and the opening of the many bars you maintain in profit. PLEASE . . .
Bestest, Harry.

P.S. Don't know where this one's going, but it's tasty.

.

"Would you like to come, Angela?" No, Angela did not want to come because she had a headache and needed to stay in her room.

"Can I leave Mauro?" Yes, Angela would look after Mauro in her room because the baby was asleep.

And Charley was to be certain that small Mario and Francesca did not get cold—God, and it was 70 degrees out there, and Charley had swum off the beach at Bigbury and at Thurlestone and Outer Hope when it was bloody freezing, when her legs and body and arms were goosed. She thought it would do small Mario good, be a useful lesson to the little blighter, to be in the water and struggling because he could not swim. Small Mario was already getting to be, Charley's opinion, revolting and Sicilian, already standing in front of the mirror to check his hair, already posturing at her as if she were merely the hired help. She'd seen it that week, the difference in the child. She might just make certain that he went right under and took the seawater into his nose. It wasn't the child's fault, just the culture of the place . . . "I'll make sure they don't get cold."

So many times each day Charley had to pinch herself, gouge the nails of her fingers into herself, because then she could keep the reality with the fantasy, marry the mundane of life in the villa with the lie that was tight on her wrist. She had the towels and the swimsuits for the children in a beach bag, and in the beach bag were her own underclothes because she had already changed into her bikini, and her sun-lotion tube. She had the bright, colored water rings for the kids, and Francesca had found a toy sailing boat from last summer and small Mario had his football.

Angela's call—they would be all right? "They'll be all right, Angela. Hope your headache gets better . . ."

The gardener opened the gate for them. She didn't think he knew much about swimming. The gardener stank. She didn't think he knew much about washing. She'd get round to it one day, her bikini on the sunbed, and she'd loose the top, she'd give the old "lechie" a sight to keep the bastard awake at night. They went down the hill, and Francesca held her hand and skipped along and small Mario bounced the football like a basketball player. She wondered where he was, where Axel Moen was. Always with her, the dulled routine of minding the children and the exciting sensation of the lie. Twice she looked behind her, tried to be casual, but she didn't see him, didn't see his face nor the hanging ponytail of his hair. It would have been good to be on the beach with him, clear of the kids, on a towel on the sand with him, and in the water with him . . . They went through the piazza and the teenagers were gathered there, boys and girls, with their scooters and motorcycles, and they went past the shops that were opening again for the afternoon, scraping up the shutters, expanding the awnings. She told small Mario, sharply, that he must not bounce the ball as they crossed the road near the newspaper kiosk and close to the Saracen tower. It might have been wonderful, she thought, going through Mondello to the beach if it hadn't been for the bloody watch she wore on her wrist. And with the watch, as if to hammer her, like a replaying tape, was her voice snapping at her father, and her voice taunting the young man, Benny. It might have been perfect, going in the warm sunshine toward the gold of the beach and the blue of the sea, except that she lived the lie. The fingernails dug at the palm of her hand to kill the lie.

Across the road, they walked alongside the beach, hugging the shade of the spread pines. The tide was out and the sand was golden clean. The junk litter would come later, with the crowds, the next month and the month after when all Palermo descended on Mondello. The beach was brilliant to her, like the beaches of Thurlestone and Bigbury before the tourists came. Charley led the way down onto the sand and she kicked off her sneakers and hopped at the sudden heat on the soles of her feet, and the children laughed with her. Small Mario booted his football ahead and they ran after it, whooping and noisy, all the way to the tideline that changed the sand from pale gold to the luster of ochre. Charley was first to the football, never could kick a ball, and it skewed off to the right and careered toward a couple on a towel, and the couple were kissing, the boy under the girl. Lucky cow. She went to the ball, and the couple didn't notice her, cared not to look at her, and she picked the ball up and took it away, as if she were a prim and proper little miss. There were four boys with a transistor radio some yards behind her, and they whistled once, and Charley turned and gave them a single finger, and they jeered once. There was another couple, away toward the new town and the pier, reading magazines.

She put the bag down on the tideline.

The sea ran out into the crescent bay in front of her. Far ahead were the small boats, far beyond the small boats was a car ferry coming toward the docks at Palermo that were hidden by the scree slopes of Monte Pellegrino. From the bag she took a sheet of plastic and laid it flat on the sand, and then she laid two towels on the plastic. The sun beat on her, the strength of the sun on the sand and the water dazzled her. She wrapped her towel, the big towel, around Francesca and undressed the little girl and helped her, full of giggles, into the swimsuit, and to do the same for small Mario she had to pull faces and make a game and beat the shyness of the child. She folded their clothes and put them carefully in the bag. Francesca was puffing her breath into the plastic water-ring and small Mario dribbled the soccer ball around the towels. Charley pulled off her blouse and unbuttoned her skirt, and she did not look round to see if the boys with the transistor ogled her. The sun's force caught at the whiteness of her skin. It would have been perfect if it had not been for the lie. Francesca was pulling her hand, wanted to go to the water. Small Mario was tugging her hand, wanted to play football with her.

"A minute, darling, wait a minute. Mario, you can only learn to swim in the water, you can't learn on the beach with a soccer ball. OK, please yourself. Play soccer, don't learn to swim."

The lie hit her. The lie was the destruction of the world of the little boy who wanted to play soccer, and the lie would be agony to the little girl who wanted to learn to swim. She took the watch from her wrist, slipped it in the bag. The watch was supposed to be waterproof. The watch was the lie.

"You play soccer, Mario. You don't want to learn to swim, then that's fine."

There was the white ring on her wrist. It was as if she'd shed the lie. She walked with Francesca toward the sea. It was wonderful. She arched her back. The sun's warmth was on her shoulders and her stomach and her thighs. It was perfect.

He had been the day before, and the day before that, to see his *consigliere*. It was a good assumption that he would go again that day. Tano waited. It was a good assumption that the man from Catania would come again that afternoon, as the crisis isolated him, to try to confirm the support of his *consigliere*. The home of the *consigliere* was a large house, in half a hectare of ground that was enclosed by a wall topped with broken glass set in concrete, and in a private cul-de-sac. Tano watched. Where he waited and watched he could not see the *consigliere's* home—he was on the public road, away from the turning into the cul-de-sac—but he could see with an uninterrupted view the parked car that had been taken the night before from a street in Acireale to the north, near the church of San Pietro e Paolo. If the man from Catania came in his Mercedes then he must drive past the parked car. Tano held the mobile telephone.

Tano was a careful man. He had been able to travel back across the Atlantic twelve years before because he was careful. When the net closed on his friends, colleagues, family, when the FBI sprang the trap in New Jersey, his name had not figured in the files collected around the Pizza Connection investigation. When the *squadra mobile* had mounted for the bastard Falcone the big arrest operation of the year after his return to the island, four hundred men, again his name was not included. It was natural, when it came to his offering his loyalty to one man, that he should have chosen Mario Ruggerio. Mario Ruggerio was the most careful man he had worked with. With the care came Tano's loyalty.

He believed himself to be the favorite of Mario Ruggerio, and he had begun to feel in the last months that he might, one day, succeed Mario Ruggerio—not this year, not next year, not for many years, but one day . . . He thought he was the favorite because Mario Ruggerio had entrusted to him the preparation of the bomb, the planning for the bomb and the detonation of the bomb. When this bomb was exploded he would prepare and plan and detonate the second bomb, and his position as the favorite would be confirmed, not Carmine who had the brains of a wood plank, not Franco who he thought was stupid. His future was linked inexorably with the future of Mario Ruggerio. They climbed together, him a step lower on the ladder, but it was together. He could not bear to imagine failure, slipping on the step of the ladder. Could not bear to consider the iced fury of Mario Ruggerio. But he could imagine, consider, the praise of Mario Ruggerio, the quiet half-spoken praise that brought the thrilled flush through him. Tano would do anything, *alcuna cosa,* to win the praise of Mario Ruggerio, and think nothing of what he had done. Tano had lost no sleep, not a minute of rest in his bed, after he had slit the throat from ear to ear, drawn the sharpened knife through the windpipe, of a street thief.

He saw the Mercedes.

His fist tightened its hold on his mobile telephone, his finger hovered over the button of the final digit of the number built into the telephone pager. The telephone pager was integral to the bomb of dynamite packed inside a wall of ball bearings.

He had held the scrawny legs of the man from Agrigento while Mario Ruggerio had grunted and perspired through the process of strangulation. They climbed the ladder together, and higher. He pressed the button of the final digit . . . The flash of light. The hammer crash of the explosion. The Mercedes picked up and tossed across the road, the impact collapsing the wall that the body of the Mercedes hit. The blue-gray of smoke, the flicker of the fire . . . They were at the top of the ladder.

He saw, in his mind, the pleased smile of Mario Ruggerio, and he seemed to feel the hand of Mario Ruggerio cudgel his shoulder in praise. He was the favorite . . .

The fire ripped through the body of the Mercedes.
Tano walked away.

The journalist from Berlin settled in his seat as the aircraft
banked over the sea and then straightened on its course.
Looking left from his window seat he could see the urban
sprawl of Catania, and looking right he could see the
coastline and the mountains of the toe and foot and ankle
of the mainland. He reached down and took his laptop
from the bag beneath his feet. He was an unhappy flier and
felt more comfortable when he worked during a flight, his
attention distracted from the syndromes of vertigo and
claustrophobia, and it was easy to work with the laptop in
the business class compartment that his contract guaran-
teed him. He was not a vain man, but it was part and
parcel of his trade that the cover of the laptop should be
festooned with the adhesive stickers of airlines he had
flown with and cities from which he had reported. The
laptop boasted of visits to Beirut and Dhahran and Hanoi
and Belfast and Grozny and Sarajevo and Kabul. He
started, two fingers, to type, and he was going well and his
mind was diverted from the warm air turbulence until the
passenger beside him spoke.

"I see you are a journalist, a journalist from Germany,
and you have been in Sicily to write about the *malvagita* of
our society—did you find that wickedness? It is a strange
time for you to be leaving, it is peculiar that you should
choose this day to leave. Myself, I am a physician, I work
with children, I do not see any foreign journalists, they do
not come to my surgery. I presume you have been meeting
with our illustrious politicians and with our social workers
and with magistrates. Are you confused? I met once with a
British engineer working on a sewerage project here. The
engineer said that he believed the evil in our society to be a

product of imagination, a subject of discussion in the same way that the British are obsessed with discussion of the future of the weather. He told me also that in his part of Britain there was a great inland sea in which there was said to live a huge monster, a creature from prehistory, which was elusive whenever scientific examination was made of the inland sea. But the engineer said that many people desired to believe in the existence of the monster even if there was no proof that it lived. I remember, it was the monster of Loch Ness. The engineer said it did not exist in reality, and he said, his opinion, that La Cosa Nostra was similar, something that is in our imagination. If you are leaving Sicily today then you must surely follow the belief of the British engineer. I said to him, but of course he did not have the time, that he should come with me to the rotten apartment towers of Brancaccio in Palermo, where I work. He should see the children without hope who live under the heel of La Cosa Nostra, who eat when La Cosa Nostra says they should eat, whose parents work when La Cosa Nostra says they should work. And I said that he should go to Rome and Milan and taste the corruption in government and commerce that is brought by La Cosa Nostra. And he should go, I told him, to Frankfurt and London and New York and walk among the addicts of Grade A drugs and think further about La Cosa Nostra. But he said that I made a fantasy, that I saw a monster like the one in the inland sea. You leave now? It was on the car radio just before I reached the airport, a killing in Catania, a bomb. I am surprised that you are leaving at a time when there is proof of wickedness. I am sorry that I interrupt you from your important thoughts. Excuse me, forgive me . . ."

The pulse tone traveled from the antennae on Monte Gallo to the antennae on Monte Castellacio to the antennae on

Monte Cuccio and on to the antennae that waited for the UHF signal. It traveled clear, sharp.

His mind was a wreckage of scrambled thoughts because, Christ, it was actually happening . . .

He had come out of the cloister and gone to a stall and bought a carton of juice and taken it to one of the solid seats on the wide and shaded balcony garden at the back of the *duomo,* where the wisteria hung in flower from high walls, where the vista reached down the valley to Palermo and the sea.

The pulse tone, carried from the CSS 900 crystal-controlled two-channel receiver and into the cordless induction earpiece, beat in Axel's skull. His hand shook, tightened on the carton, spilled the juice from the plastic straw onto his shirt and his trousers. The pulse tone hammered its coded rhythm in the confines of the bone of his skull.

It was what they taught at the camp in Laurel, Maryland. "Christ, it is actually happening." They taught the guys of the Secret Service, the bullet-catcher guys, that they'd freeze, that they'd lose the power of action because, Christ, it was actually happening. When the headcase had gotten himself up close to the president, gotten his shots off, there was the photograph of one of the Secret Service guys with his arms splayed out and holding his hardware up to the skies, useless and rooted. The guy would have gone through every training simulation that could be thrown up by the Secret Service firearms instructors at the camp in Laurel, and the refreshers, and what he'd done, when the moment came, was shout, "Christ, it's actually happening."

For a moment Axel was useless and rooted.

It was the Immediate Alert code, played a second and then a third time. Shit. He was scuffling with his hands down in the bag at his feet, and the carton was on the ground and spreading juice on his trainers. He had the mobile telephone and he was belting through the numbers. He switched the goddam thing off, couldn't concentrate on the numbers. Axel needed 'Vanni Crespo. Axel needed 'Vanni Crespo because he could receive a pulse tone on the CSS 900 receiver, but didn't carry with him the electronics for location of the signal. Shit. The goddamn number was engaged, was whining engaged.

Christ, it was actually happening, and he was behaving like a goddamn fool, like he'd freaked. He sat still. He cleared the failed call from his telephone. 'Vanni had the backup. They would be calling 'Vanni from the communications area, why the goddamn number was engaged, they would be identifying the origin location of the pulse tone, and 'Vanni would call him and he must wait to be called. Shit. He had panicked and he felt sour with himself. He waited. He wondered where she was, how she was, and it was goddamn hard to wait to be called.

He snatched the paper with the coordinates from the technician. The technician said that he'd not heard the initial signal firsthand, been out of the operations area and refilling the coffee machine, but the light on the equipment had alerted him. The technician apologized for the time it had taken him to replay the tape recording of the pulse tone and then to check with the code system, but the code system was in the floor safe, and the technician had had to recall the correct combination for the lock . . . 'Vanni snatched the paper from the technician and was running for the door and the corridor.

The technician shouted after him, "But it's confusing—please, listen to me. Three Immediate Alert signals, then a pause, two minutes, then Stand Down, then two Immediate Alert—"

'Vanni ran. 'Vanni didn't stop to listen.

The technician stood in the door to the operations area.

He shouted a last time, "Pause one minute, then Stand-by code, and again Immediate Alert. I don't understand."

'Vanni had run faster, fourteen years younger, the length of the Via Carini toward the knot of sightseers and firemen and policemen, toward the bullet-spattered cars of the general and the general's wife, of the single *ragazzo* who had guarded him. Of course, then, as he had run the dark, sunless length of the Via Carini he had known he was too late to intervene, to do anything, to be other than helpless. It was a scar on the soul of 'Vanni Crespo that he had stood, panting and helpless, beside the cars and the blood pools, too late to intervene. He did not even know what she looked like, the Codename Helen, tall, thin, fair, short, fat, dark, did not know. As he ran the length of the corridor, slower than he had run the length of the Via Carini, he prayed to his God, soundless, that he would not again be too late to intervene.

He burst, a fool stammering, into the rest room. The men of the Response Squad stared at him through the smoke haze, looked up at him from their magazines and their card games.

"Now, hurry, you bastards. Immediate Alert. We have—God, I hope we have—Ruggerio. We have a location for Mario Ruggerio. Mondello. Please move. It's Ruggerio."

There was the gathering of the weapons. There was the stampede out of the ready room. There was the thunder of boots in the corridor. There was the roar of the cars' engines.

'Vanni, in the backseat of the second car, three more behind him, yelled into his telephone, "Don't tell me what I should have done, I have priorities. I have to respond to the signal. The priority is to move. You are at the *duomo*? The piazza in front of the *duomo*, by the camera shop. Two minutes and I am there, a green Alfetta. If you are not there I don't wait."

The convoy of cars swerved through the gates of the

Monreale barracks. Two boys up the road, astride motorcycles, were held back by a uniformed *carabiniere* soldier. They were not interested, there was no builder's van in the convoy. The scream of the tires hung in the afternoon air.

Not necessary, but the excitement raced in 'Vanni, forty-two years old and like a child with the anticipation of a favored present. "It's an open line, Dr. Tardelli, not secure. Our mutual interest, we have a location . . . You should clear your desk for the rest of the afternoon because I hope to bring our friend as a guest to you. Please make yourself available."

The American was running, reaching the camera shop. The second car slowed, and behind it the rest of the convoy hit their brakes. 'Vanni had the door open and he caught at Axel's arm and pulled him inside, and Axel's jerked body tangled with the cable lead that linked 'Vanni's headset to the communications console beside the driver's knee.

"Still transmitting, confused but transmitting from Mondello. I have these hooligans, and I also have a helicopter coming . . ."

'Vanni hugged Axel.

Of the *squadra mobile* surveillance team working the Capo district, it was the turn of Giancarlo to report in person to the investigating magistrate, Dr. Rocco Tardelli. He was not even asked to sit down. He stood in the room at the Palazzo di Giustizia, and held tight in his hand was the plastic bag of vegetables he had bought along with three lemons. He explained that, in the previous twenty-four hours, the three shifts had seen nothing of Mario Ruggerio, and the man seemed hardly to hear him.

"I regret very much that as yet, *Dottore,* we have no trace, but there is still time, and we have to hope that tomorrow, or the day after, is different."

He had expected a head sunk in disappointment, and an exhortation to greater vigilance, but the magistrate merely shrugged. Giancarlo believed it possible that he had interrupted the preparations for the celebration of a birthday because one of the *ragazzi* was at the table beside the draped curtains and was cleaning glasses and another of the *ragazzi*, while Giancarlo spoke, carried in two bottles of champagne.

He believed, with his talk of failure, he intruded.

The helicopter came over her.

It came in from the sea, a thunder of noise, and Charley caught at Francesca and lifted her from the water and held her close. She could see, very clearly, the figure in the open hatch door of the helicopter, the face covered by a mask with eye slits, the legs dangling, the machine gun that covered her. She held the child as if to protect her and she did not realize that the plastic water-ring drifted away from her, driven by the rotor blades of the helicopter. She followed the curved flight of the helicopter that was painted in a livery of midnight blue with the big white lettering, CARABINIERE, across the cabin and broken by the opened hatch, she watched the helicopter go stationary, hovering, like one of the big hawks on the cliffs near her home. She looked for the prey of the helicopter.

Oh, Christ. God, no . . .

Through the water, across the wet sand, across to the tideline and to the towels laid on the plastic sheet. Small Mario stood alone and the sand was whipped around him. The helicopter edged on, was above the esplanade and the deep foliage of the pine trees that wavered as if a gale hit them. She carried Francesca, she tried to run through the water and was stumbling and pitching. The helicopter was facing her, a predator. The water splashed around her, and once she fell and the water was in her mouth and nose and Francesca was crying out loud. She ran toward small Mario. There was a loudspeaker shouting at them but she could not hear the words above the helicopter engine. She saw the couple who kissed, the boys who had the transistor, the couple who read magazines, and they all stood and they all, as if commanded, had their hands on their heads. She did not have her watch and she did not know how long she had been with Francesca in the water, how long she had left small Mario with his football on the sand. She burst from the water. Her feet gripped the wet sand and gave her speed. She could see the men who waited in the shadow of the trees.

Beyond small Mario and the couples and the boys with the transistor that still shouted music, under the trees were men and women still as statues and children clutching them and weeping, and men in black overalls and balaclavas holding stubbed guns. She saw Axel Moen . . .

She reached small Mario. He held her wristwatch limply in his hands. The boy gazed, frightened, at the helicopter, at the men with the guns.

Charley took the watch, took it gently, from small Mario's hands. From the shadows under the pine trees, from among the men with guns, Axel Moen gazed at her.

Said quietly, as if she were back in the classroom of 2B and not wanting to drive a child to silence, "What did you do with my watch?"

Said distant and quavering, "Poppa is in England. Poppa said it was one hour behind Sicily in England. I tried to make the time where Poppa is."

"You should have asked me. I would have made it the time where Poppa is."

"I tried the buttons, I could not make it work to Poppa's time."

She put Francesca down. Charley said to the boy, "We

have to go home. Please, Mario, fold up the towels."

She faced Axel Moen. She made small gestures. She reeled from the humiliation. She held the watch, she placed it on her wrist and snapped the clasp shut. She was too far from him to see the expression on his face, and the face was in shadow, but she thought that she saw his mind. She pointed to small Mario as he knelt and dutifully folded the towels. She had failed Axel Moen and the men with guns and the men who flew the helicopter. She crossed her hands, uncrossed them, crossed them again, it was over, it was finished. She took the big towel and started to rub dry the body of Francesca, and in her bikini she was shivering. She saw Axel Moen speak to a man beside him, and the man spoke into a radio. Charley wrapped the big towel around Francesca and dressed her under the towel. The helicopter came overhead, flew out above the sea, then turned toward Monte Pellegrino and Palermo. When it was gone, when she could hear the boys' transistor again, when she had put the towel around her own body and was wriggling out of her bikini, she looked again toward the pine trees beyond the beach. They were no longer there. She shed the bikini top and the bikini bottom. She could not see the men with the guns and the balaclavas. She dragged on her pants and buttoned her skirt, and the towel fell from her as she lifted on her blouse. She could not see Axel Moen. The sun of the late afternoon caught at the skin of her arms and her shoulders, at the whiteness of her breasts . . . Hey, Charley, enough of the damn crawl. Hey, Charley, he was out there, and he was waiting, and he came running.

"Come on, Mario, time for home, time for tea. Come on."

"What was it for, the helicopter?"

Charley said, "They have to do exercises, have to do practice and training. It keeps them busy. It's something to tell your mother, that you saw the *carabinieri* on a training exercise. You won't learn to swim, you know, not by playing soccer."

Hey, Charley, that's power. He came running.

He put down the telephone. He sat for a moment very still.

In the room with him were Pasquale and the driver of the chase car and the one who rode in the chase car with the machine gun on his lap, and they had all been caught with the infection of his excitement. He sat for a moment with his head buried in his hands.

They knew. He did not have to tell them.

He said, "You know, when Riina was caught, when he had been brought to the barracks, when he realized that he was not in the hands of his enemies but only of the state, he wanted to be told who was in charge. It was at that moment important to him to know that he spoke to the senior man, important to his dignity. Santapaolo, when he was held, he congratulated the arresting officer that he would be on TV that night, as if he would be famous for a day. Leoluca Bagarella, when he was trapped, was said to be in a condition of shock, as if punched on the end of the nose and stunned. I wanted to know how he would be, Mario Ruggerio. For an hour I have sat here and I have allowed myself the fantasy of considering how he would be when I walked into the interrogation room to confront him. It was my hour of vanity. Pasquale, I do not think we require the glasses, and I do not think we will be drinking champagne—would you, please, take them out because they remind me of one hour of vanity. It is hard not to believe that we snatch at stars . . . Right, I have work, you should leave me."

Pasquale carried the unused glasses through the armor-plated door of the magistrate's office, and the driver of the chase car followed him with the two bottles of champagne.

He had not told his wife about the flowers, their rejection, but he would tell her of the bottles that were not opened and the glasses that were not dirtied. He felt an idiot because there was moist dew at his eyes. Perhaps the driver of the chase car saw the damp gleam in his eyes.

"What do we do with the champagne?" Pasquale asked briskly.

"Keep it for the funeral," the driver of the chase car said, impassive.

"What funeral?"

"His, yours, ours." There was a growled laugh from the driver of the chase car. The other men of the team were around the table in the corridor. They mocked Pasquale, as if he were an idiot for their sport.

"What sort of shit is that?"

Coolly, the driver of the chase car said, "Don't you know anything? Don't you listen to the radio? Don't you have ears? Worry less about flowers and listen more. Once, in Palermo, there was a jeweler who sold fine stones and necklaces and watches from Switzerland and he had a great fear of thieves so he protected the window of his shop with armor-plated glass. One night a car drove slowly past the shop front and half a magazine from a Kalashnikov assault rifle was fired at the window. High-velocity rounds. And the window was broken, but the car did not stop, nothing was taken. A few days later, from the same Kalashnikov, the same make of bullets, a *mafioso* who rode in his car that was fitted with armor-plated glass was shot dead. The attack on the jeweler's shop was merely to test whether the bullets of a Kalashnikov could pierce reinforced glass."

Pasquale stood holding the tray and the glasses chimed as his hands trembled. He was the object of their sport.

"If you listened to the radio. The *capo* in Catania was

killed this afternoon by a bomb in a car that had been parked
in a street and was detonated as he drove past. He was a rival
for the supreme position sought by Ruggerio, but he was
already isolated. That is what Tardelli says. Why a bomb?
Why a huge explosion? Why something so public? Because
that is not the way of La Cosa Nostra. Why was he not shot,
or strangled, or disappeared with the *lupara bianca* into acid
or into the bay or into concrete? Why a jeweler's shop?"

Pasquale shook. He thought of his wife and of his baby
and of the man behind the armor-plated door who was
alone with his work. They were watching him from the
table, amused.

"Maybe, Pasquale, because you have his ear, because
you bring him flowers, you should tell him to go back to his
wife in Udine. Maybe you should request him to use his
authority to have every parked car on every road in Palermo
towed away. Maybe you should arrange, very quickly, for the
arrest of Ruggerio. Maybe you should resign."

"You talk shit."

They were all laughing as Pasquale stumbled away down
the corridor carrying the tray of clean glasses.

"What did you expect?"

"That she wouldn't be so goddam naïve."

The argument started back at the barracks. They hadn't
fought in front of the ROS men, had held back their frustration at the failure until they were clear of the squad and alone.
And the attitude of the men had been so predictable to 'Vanni
Crespo. Into the cars on the beachfront at Mondello, balaclavas pulled off, weapons made safe, another day and another
fuckup, and their talk in the car had been of soccer and the
size of the breasts of the new PA to the *colonello*, and then
about the next issue of boots to be given them. Another day
and another fuckup and nothing changed.

"She's an amateur."

"Of course she's an amateur. Picked up on the cheap, fast little run in and out that doesn't cost the great DEA much. I know she's an amateur and cheap because the great DEA left it to you to run her, and you, Axel Moen, are insignificant."

"Not so goddamn precious yourself. You were so naïve. The signal was a mess—Immediate Alert, Stand Down, Stand-by, Immediate Alert. Didn't you think?"

"I thought that she was an amateur. I thought she was in panic. She is not the wonderful Axel Moen, hero of the great DEA. She is a girl, she is untrained. It was reasonable to assume she'd be in panic. For the sake of Christ, Axel, think where you've put her, and what you've told her, and the job you've given her. That would make panic."

They were in a corridor. The argument had been whisper-hissed as the business of the corridor went on around them. 'Vanni took the American's shoulders in his fists and caught the material of the windcheater, and shook his shoulders.

"You make a good argument, 'Vanni, but it's flawed— she wouldn't begin to know how to panic."

But Axel Moen had let his head fall against 'Vanni's chest, and they hugged. They held each other and let the anger slip.

Axel broke the hold. "I'll see you around, someplace."

"Take some food. Yes, stay close."

'Vanni called for an escort to take Axel Moen to the gate. He watched him go away down the corridor, carrying the bag with the two-channel receiver and the notes and drawings of the cloister columns of the *duomo,* watched him until he was gone through the door at the far end of the corridor. He could get away with it once, calling out the squad and not filing a report, in triplicate, on white and yellow and blue flimsies, only the once. He went, heavy-footed, to his room. Ridiculous, he was a senior officer, he had been in the force for twenty years and two months, and a single failed call-out was like a wound to him. He had been one of the chosen few who had hunted, first, and closed down, second, the terrorists of the *Brigate Rosse*, the scum kids of the middle-class affluents who claimed to kill for the proletariat. He had been especially chosen as the liaison officer to Carlos Alberto dalla Chiesa. He had been nine years in the wilderness of Genoa, murders, drugs, kidnapping. He had been five years now with the *Reparto Operativo Speciale*. And he had held his pistol against the neck of Riina. How many stakeouts, how many charges in a screaming car with the firearms oil in his nose, how many surveillance operations? He thought himself a cretin because this time, among so many, the failure had wounded him. In his room he lay on his bed. It was the habit that he kept to, twenty minutes each afternoon of catnapping. He lay on his bed with a cigarette lit and with the whiskey glass on his stomach. When he had smoked the cigarette and drunk the whiskey, he would set the alarm for twenty minutes ahead and sleep. Later, in the early evening, he would make the telephone call to his daughter in Genoa and talk about her school that he had never visited and her friends that he did not know. In the late evening, with the mobile phone in his pocket and the pistol in his waist, he would drive to Trapani and bounce the arse off the woman in the back of her car. But the call would mean little and the sex would mean less because he was wounded.

He spiraled the smoke up toward the bland shade of his light, he gulped the whiskey. They came more often, now, the doubts. They came to him most afternoons when he lay on his bed with his cigarette and his whiskey, with the alarm set for twenty minutes of sleep. No doubts of ultimate victory when he had tracked the *Brigate Rosse* cells, no doubts when he had stood with controlled emotion in the congregation at the funeral of dalla Chiesa, none when he had investigated murders and trafficking and kidnapping in Genoa, and none when he had pressed the pistol down against the flesh of Riina. The doubts now were with him most afternoons. Unshared, unspoken, he doubted in ultimate victory, as if he beat against a wall and the wall did not break the force of his blows. The arm was cut, the arm grew again. The heart was knifed, the heart healed. If that was his life, fighting and not winning, then what was the point of his life?

'Vanni stubbed out his cigarette and drained his glass. He swung onto his stomach and pressed his face down into his pillow. He could not cut the sight of her. She was on the beach. She was light against the darkness of the sea. She was white skinned as the towel slipped. She was naïve and innocent, she was alone. She was being used as a weapon in a war without the prospect of ultimate victory. Mother of Christ. She was the wound that hurt him.

He was still awake when the alarm bleeped through the bare room.

It was raining hard.

There should have been backup, there should have been support.

No support and no backup, and so Harry Compton was dependent on a short truncheon and a pair of image-intensifier binoculars and a suction microphone linked to a tape recorder. It had been the best that Stores could supply him with, which was pitiful. About the only thing going for Harry Compton was the rain, tipping down, which meant it was unlikely that the man's wife was going to come walking round the garden with the dogs. Small mercy, because there were enough things steepling against him. With the image-intensifier binoculars he had been able to identify the heat-sensitive exterior floodlights, and the location of the bloody things meant that he had to crawl through the depths of the bloody shrubs, wet earth sliming on his stomach and thorny pyracantha clinging to the material of his overalls. He was up against the wall of the house, but couldn't bloody move, because if he moved he would be into the arc of the heat-sensitive kit. He was wet. His hands ran rainwater. With wet hands, and he couldn't use gloves because they would deny him the sure touch of his fingers, the suction microphone had become smeared and wouldn't bloody stick on the window glass. He'd had to hold the microphone in position against the glass, and stand up to do it, like a damn prune in a cereal bowl. Music on in the room, bloody pop music, and he could not filter the music from the voices of Giles Blake and Giuseppe Ruggerio. Now, that was just incredible, these two men talking after-dinner business and with kids' music turned up strong. Blake's own house. Of course, they hadn't talked confidential in the hotel restaurant, but if they had music to drown them now, sure as hell they talked serious business, and he could not hear a bloody word. He was wet, he was cold, he was bloody miserable, and sometime soon the bloody dogs would want putting out. He was an hour's drive from home, and at home there would be a darkened bedroom and the wife's back, cold.

There was the jewel moment. Harry Compton, wet and miserable, could have bloody well jumped and cheered. The CD, Oasis, had played out.

". . . working hard at getting their different acts together. I think they'll be all right."

"You know of Roberto Calvi?"

"Yes, of course."

"They want the business?"

"Of course, and they want the commission."

"If they want the business, the commission, then they should know of Roberto Calvi. They should be told that Roberto Calvi deceived people, that he was strangled slowly."

"Do we have to have more of the same? Kids'll think I'm on monkey glands."

"Remind them to be careful. Please, something else . . ."

And something else was Elton bloody John. Harry Compton would hear nothing else for forty-five minutes, maybe an hour. Within an hour, damn certain, rain or no rain, the bloody dogs would be put out into the garden. He dropped on his hands and knees from the window of the house, the nice bloody pad that went with soaping and rinsing and drying mafia money, across the flagstone path. Onto his stomach and the crawl into the landscaper's shrub bed, and caught immediately by the thorny pyracantha. His wife had planted one of the bloody things beside her little greenhouse, and he might just, next Sunday, dig the damn thing out or plaster it with weedkiller. What he'd seen of Giles Blake, and of Mrs. Giles Blake when she'd been clearing up the kitchen, luxury bloody fittings, they wouldn't do the garden because they paid for maintenance, and that was good because there was no way he could avoid smearing a trail across the earth and the mulch of the shrub bed. He went fast. He reckoned he had enough for a disclosure warrant from a judge, for a telephone-intercept order from the home office, maybe enough for a dawn knock and handcuffs. The name of Roberto Calvi was the diamond. Rotten investments for bad people, bad people's money down the drain, strangled and left hanging from Blackfriars Bridge where the world and the world's dog could see what happened to a joker who lost bad people's money.

As he went over the wall, dropped down into the lane, Harry Compton heard the voice of the woman calling out the dogs. He loathed the sort of people who lived in that sort of house behind that sort of wall. He himself had earned a maximum of £27,380 (inclusive of overtime) the last year. The sort of people he loathed, through scams and greed and criminality, would have clawed in a minimum of £273,800 (part-time working) the last year. He had the big thrill, like best sex, when he did the dawn call on the bastards, when he had the handcuffs open. And it would be good, best, to have the Sicilian bastard in the interview room. He reached his car.

He peeled off his overalls, kicked out of his boots. One nagging thought—what was the role of the young woman, "pressurized" by the DEA, gone as a childminder to Sicily? Where did she fit? He cut it. The young woman was altitude politics. He fed in the world of mud-smeared overalls, filth-scraped boots.

He drove home.

▼

"IT DOESN'T MATTER WHAT IT SAYS." The detective superintendent swung his chair so that he faced the window. Harry Compton held the audio cassette in his hand, then made the gesture and dropped it on the desk, onto his unread report. "I had a hell of a drenching. I crawled through the garden."

"What do you want, a medal? We are not playing at Scouts."

Harry Compton had come to work bubbling in a froth of personal satisfaction. Had left the kit, smeared in dried mud, outside the locked door of Stores section. Up to his desk in the open-plan area, first one in apart from Miss Frobisher, and she too must have realized that a jackpot had been won because he had the success gleam in his eye, and she had put the kettle on and made him a mug of her own particular coffee which was not the muck out of the vending machine in the corridor. He had listened to the tape, twice. Gone through the last Oasis track, the clean conversation, the start of the first Elton John track. He had typed his report, transcribed the tape, underlined in red the references to Roberto Calvi and then sat on his hands while the office filled and waited for his detective superintendent to get to work.

"What I am trying to say, Roberto Calvi is not a name that trips off the tongues of every pair of businesspeople sitting down for a little chat on how to make a good buck."

"You don't cop on quick, do you?"

The detective superintendent was searching his drawer and coming up with his cigarette packet. About two days in every five, it was said, the detective superintendent tried to pack in his smoking, and the intention usually lasted about an hour or up to the first of the morning's crises. But two days out of five he could be foul tempered and sarcastic with it.

"I used to think, Harry, you were quite bright, a clever little sod. Right now I reckon you're dumb. Hear me, and I'll do it slowly. This is politics. We stumbled into something, we pushed it a bit, took it to the bosses, and they've claimed it as their own. That is politics. The politics are between us, way above me, and the Drug Enforcement Administration, way above their London man. It's good politics for us to have a stick to belt the DEA with because that's the route to trading. We make a noise, a high-level noise, we promise to make their life difficult. And to shut us up we get something in return—could be equipment, could be priority on an investigation in their backyard, could be computer access or something from their phonetap capability, anything—that is politics. Politics are on the high ground, you and I are in the gutter. Don't make bloody faces, Harry, don't bloody sulk. While you were doing the gardening down in Surrey last night and hunting medals, the commander had the AC (SO) beating his ears for half an hour. Up above the clouds they see this as good politics and your suggestion would screw those politics, ditch the chance of trading for something in return. We play 'civilized.' Your suggestion, lift this Ruggerio man, would blow apart the DEA's insertion of that young woman—what's her bloody name?"

"Miss Charlotte Eunice Parsons. Sorry you'd forgotten."

"Can't help being clever, can you? That young
woman's insertion into a mafia family is now politics."

Harry Compton flared. "She was pressured."

"She's between a rock and a hard place. She's for bartering for political advantage. She's about as irrelevant as
an individual as bloody Giles Blake and bloody Ruggerio."

The cigarette smoke hung between them. The noise
of the traffic below wafted through the window. He was
flattened. Harry Compton reached forward and picked
off the desk his report and his audiocassette.

"I'm sorry, Harry." The detective superintendent had
his head down. "I was the one who flew it high, got the
kite into the wind, and fucked up. You've done well, and
no thanks to me. If I authorized, here, now, what you
want, quite reasonably, I'd be dead in the water. Don't
think I feel good."

"I doubt you do."

"Give that bugger in Rome, idle sod, another belt,
then get yourself down to Devon like I told you."

"Thank you."

"I want to bury those arrogant bastards, poaching
from our patch, so get me a profile on Miss Charlotte
Eunice Parsons . . . and don't make waves that splash me."

"Charley? Where are you, Charley?"

She lay on the sunbed. The warmth played on her
body. She lay on her back and she splayed out her legs so
that the sun's heat was on her thighs. Her eyes were
closed, but she could hear the scrape of the brush used by
the "lechie" on a path farther down the garden. Each
time that the motion of the brush was silenced she

assumed that he gazed at her. She had looked in the dictionary that morning, after coming back from the school and the kindergarten, to find the word. The word was *libertino*. That was too good a word, in translation, for a lecher, foul old bastard with his peering eyes . . .

The watch was on her wrist. The watch would not leave her wrist, not when she was in the bath or the shower, not when she was in the sea. The white ring on her wrist, under the watch, would not be touched by the sun. But the rest of her body, too damn right, that would get the sun . . .

She had rung Benny that morning from a pay phone in a bar facing onto the piazza, after she had dropped the children at school and kindergarten, and heard his voice that was distant and unsure, and gushed her thanks for the day in the countryside, and resurrected the invitation for him to guide her around the *duomo* and the Quattro Canti and the Cappella Palatina and the Palazzo Sclafani. She'd bullied him and told him when she could next be in Palermo. She wanted the sun to have been on her, on all of her body except for her wrist, when she went into Palermo to see Benny. God, he wasn't much, didn't have much other than a dream, was all that was on offer.

She hadn't thought, not when she had sat on the cliff with Axel Moen, not when she had stood beside the river with Axel Moen in Rome, not on the train, not in Mondello, not in the villa, that the waiting would be so bloody hard. And it was worse now, the waiting, because she had seen the helicopter and the men with the guns, seen the response of Axel Moen to the pressing of the panic button. So bloody hard to wait. She opened her eyes, blinked at the brightness. The gardener was some fifteen paces from her and used the brush with a desultory and bored motion, and he looked away when she caught his glance. She rolled over onto her stomach. She twisted her hands over her back and unfastened the straps of the bikini top. She had never thought the waiting would be so bloody hard, maybe it would all be waiting, maybe it would never happen, maybe it was just the illusion of Axel Moen. God, it was eating at her, the waiting.

"Here, Angela. I'm here."

She pushed herself up and the bikini top fell away. Her elbows took her weight. She could not see the gardener, but away behind the bushes there was the scrape of his brush. Angela came from the patio. She saw Angela's face, distracted, and there was a tautness. Angela had seen her.

The lips pursed, the frown dug deeper. "I don't think, Charley, that is suitable."

Bloody hell, but Charley grinned. "You used to."

Snapped. "That was Civitaveccia, that was not Palermo. Please make yourself decent."

Did she want to talk about it? Was now the time to press it? Would there be tears? The lie came first. Each day she thought that Angela was more distanced from her. It was not in the interest of the lie to flush out the feelings of Angela Ruggerio, poor bitch. Charley acted the lie, the chastened girl, and slipped her arms through the straps of the bikini and wriggled to fasten the clasp. Angela held a small piece of paper in her fingers, and her purse, and the fingers moved restless and wretched. It was all going to come, one day. Whether the lie was served or not, the confidences would gush and the tears would follow. Charley sat up.

She said cheerfully, "Expect you're right."

"I have a list for the shops."

"Right, I'll do it when I get the children."

"For now, Charley."

It was hell's hot out there. It was all right in the heat lying nine-tenths stripped, but it was bloody hot to be traipsing back down the hill, and in two hours she would be going to get the children. But she lived the lie.

"No problem."

Charley stood. Gently she took the list for the shopping from Angela's fidgeting fingers. A long list, a list for a meal for guests, not for a meal around the table in the kitchen where they ate when Peppino was away. She scanned it— oils, sauces, vegetables for a salad and vegetables for cooking and meat, mineral water, wine, cheese and fruit.

As if Angela pleaded with her. "You don't tell Peppino that I forgot, you don't tell him . . ."

"Of course not." She tried to smile comfort.

"Am I pathetic to you?"

"Don't be daft." She didn't want the tears, didn't want the confidences. "So how many are coming?"

"It is tomorrow the birthday of Peppino's father. It is the eighty-fourth birthday tomorrow of Peppino's father. Peppino's father and his mother. Did I tell you that Peppino's father and mother lived near to Palermo?" Her voice was brittle, slashing. "They are peasants, they are ignorant, they are not educated, but Peppino would want them fed well, and I forgot."

"Peppino, he won't be here—"

"Back this evening, hurrying back from wherever." A sneer flickered the muscles at her mouth. "Back because it is the birthday of his father, which I forgot."

Charley interrupted briskly, "So the children, yes? You and Peppino, yes? His parents? Me?"

"Of course, you live with us, of course you are there."

Charley smiled. "That's for four, six, and me which makes seven. I'll go and get changed."

She took the list and the purse. She headed for the patio.

"For eight—it is possible that someone else comes," Angela said, from behind Charley. "But I do not think I would be told."

Charley stopped. She didn't turn. She thought that if she turned, Angela Ruggerio might see the brightness in her eyes. Charley said, "Eight, fine, I'll buy for eight. I'll just chuck on a skirt and a T-shirt."

Every time before he had ridden in the lead car, and sometimes he was given the keys to drive the lead car. But the *maresciallo* had promised that he was watched, as a probationer, and from their keen watching they would have seen his tiredness. Pasquale had been told to drive the chase car. He could not blame the tiredness on the baby, or on the soft and rhythmic snoring of his wife beside him, the tiredness was from the nightmare that had stayed with him through the night.

The route chosen by the *maresciallo* for the journey between the Palazzo di Giustizia and the Ucciardone jail took them around the sharp bends of the Piazza San Francesca di Paoli, onto Via Mariano Stabile, from Mariano Stabile a sharp left for Via Roma and then Piazza Sturzo, then straight on before the final right turn into Via della Croci, which would run them the last stretch to the gates of the Ucciardone. The route of every journey in the city was decided first by the *maresciallo,* who poured over the street maps each morning, who badgered Tardelli for his day's program and the timing of the program. The routes chosen by the *maresciallo* were not communicated to a central switchboard for fear of betrayal or interception. Now, one thing for Pasquale to drive the lead car, another thing for him to take the chase car and have his speed and cornering and acceleration and braking determined by the car in front. He was stressed. He did not have the traffic opening ahead of him in response to the blue lamp and the siren wail, he had rear brake lights and the winking indicator to guide him, and his horizon was the back of Tardelli's head, and the sun was in his eyes.

Because they had teased and mocked him, he had slept falteringly with the nightmare.

Every street they went down, every piazza they crossed, was parked up. Cars and vans and motorcycles were at the side of every street and piazza, half on the tar-macadam and half on the pavings. "Why a bomb? Why a huge explosion? Why a jeweler's shop?" All through the night, twisting and tossing in his bed beside his sleeping wife, near his sleeping baby, the nightmare had been of parked cars and parked vans and parked motorcycles. They could wait for a day or a week or a month, and they would know the inevitability that the lead car and the chase car must travel between the Palazzo di Giustizia and the Ucciardone jail, they could wait and watch a particular route and know the options for the journey were limited, and they could hold the detonator switch. And after the nightmare, after he had showered and shaved, after he had sat at the table in the kitchen while his wife fed their baby, he had seen on the television the picture of an armor-reinforced Mercedes, burned out and on its side, a death cage.

The sun was in his eyes, the tiredness was in his mind. It was the skill of a driver of a chase car that he should always anticipate the speed and cornering and acceleration and braking of the lead car. Pasquale did not see, in front of the lead car, the woman push her baby buggy out from the pavement and into the road. The junction of Via Carini and Via Archimede, parked cars and vans and motorcycles. The brake lights of the lead car blazed. At Pasquale's horizon, the head of Tardelli jerked forward. The man beside him swore, let loose his machine gun, flung his hands forward to brace himself. Pasquale stamped the brakes. Pasquale swerved as the tail of the lead car seemed to leap back at him. The sun was brilliant in his eyes.

The woman with the baby buggy was back on the pavement, arms up and shouting. The lead car was surging away. Pasquale had locked the wheels, was skidding. The siren screamed above him. He hit the lamppost. He was in shock and dazed. The woman was thrusting the baby buggy toward him, stationary against the lamppost, yelling in hysteria. The crowd was looming around him, hostile and aggressive. He threw the reverse. He clattered into something, didn't bother to look behind him. He pulled forward and nudged the crowd aside, and a man spat at his windscreen. He accelerated. Ahead was the open road. He could not see the light on the roof of the lead car, he could not hear the siren of the lead car.

Pasquale, in his tiredness, with the sun in his eyes, could have wept.

The man beside him spoke with a patronizing calmness into the radio.

"No, no, no, no ambush, no emergency, no panic. Yes, that's the problem, the idiot can't drive. The engine sounds like shit, a lamppost, we'll get there. If I have to rope the idiot up and make him pull it, we'll get there. Over, out."

He tried to go faster but the bumper bar was loosened and scraping the road. When they reached the gates of Ucciardone, as the gates were opened by the police, Pasquale could see two of the crew of the lead car and they were clapping him home, cheering their applause, laughing at him.

"I have to know more."

Desperation. "I don't know more."

"Then we do not do business."

Pleading, "I told you what I knew, everything."

"It is a disappointment to me, which means there will be a disappointment for you."

Sniveling. "Everything I knew I told you, and you promised . . ."

The magistrate scratched the scalp under his thick gray hair, and then he swung his spectacles from his face and took the arms of the spectacles, where they would fit over his ears, into his mouth. He chewed the plastic. It was his tactic. The tactic was to permit the silence to cling in the interview room. The prisoner was a criminal killer, but Tardelli, in truth, felt some slight sympathy for the wretch. The wretch had crossed over, had tried to cooperate, but with inadequate information. The next day was the tenth day, and without information of substance he would not be justified in requesting an extension of the surveillance operation. The wretch tried to barter other names, other crimes, but they were not of interest to the magistrate.

"You have to tell me more about Mario Ruggerio and the Capo district."

"I was told he used the bar. I was told he had the stomach pain. That is all."

"Not enough. Where did he stay?"

"I don't know."

"The bar is sold, new owner. The old owner, conveniently, has died. I have no one to ask but you. How often did he go?"

"I don't know."

"What did he wear?"

"I don't know."

"Who was he with?"

"I don't know."

The magistrate laid his spectacles carefully back on the table. The door opened quietly and closed quietly. He shut the file that he had studied and lifted his briefcase from the floor and placed the file in it. The youngest of his *ragazzi*, Pasquale, stood by the door. There were many approaches, differing tactics, that he employed when questioning Men of Honor. He could be stern or gentle, contemptuous or respectful. He could make them believe they were integral to an investigation or that they were irrelevant rubbish. He clicked the catch on his briefcase.

He said, uninterested, "You see, my friend, when you are taken back to your cell you will have completed the program of subterfuge visits to this room. Your mother, a good and devout woman I am certain, requested that I see you, and I obliged her. Not again because I am a busy man. Let me explain to you the consequences of your lack of detailed knowledge about Mario Ruggerio and your failure to gain protection status. There will be someone, I assure you, on the landing of your cell who will know that three times you have been taken to the medical unit. There will also, I assure you, be someone in a different block, who from a high window will have seen me arrive here three times. Someone will have seen your movements, and someone will have seen my movements. You have to hope those people do not meet, do not talk, do not compare what each has seen. But there is much talk in a place such as this, many meetings. I see that you will have a visit from your wife this afternoon, later. I suggest you talk to your wife, to the mother of your children, and tell her of our meetings, because I believe she might have the possibility of persuading you to remember more. Try hard to remember."

The prisoner was taken out.

The magistrate said, "The problem, Pasquale, is that I must deal each day with such a man. It is possible to be desensitized, to be dragged down, to lie with them in filth. You think I am vicious, Pasquale? He won't get the protection status, but after a few days for him to consider the depths of his memory, of his knowledge, I will transfer him to somewhere on the mainland where he is safer. When you lie in filth you become dirtied."

He came home from the early shift. He dumped the two plastic bags on the kitchen table. His wife ironed a skirt.

Through the kitchen's open window came the noise of the tower block, music and shouting and the crying of children and the smell of drains. One more year . . . Perhaps a small apartment by the sea on the east of the island, near Messina or Taormina or Riposto, where La Cosa Nostra was less formidable, perhaps a bungalow with two bedrooms and a pension from the state.

She hated what he did, and she did not look up from the ironing board.

Giancarlo poured himself a glass of juice. He drank the lemon juice that she had made. He took the bags from the table and carried them to the cupboard. There were four cardboard boxes on the floor of the cupboard, one for potatoes, one for fruit, one for green vegetables and one for lemons. Another kilo of potatoes, another kilo of apples and a kilo of oranges, another cauliflower and a half kilo of spinach, and three more lemons. He looked down at the boxes, all close to being filled.

She hung the skirt on a wire hanger. She took a blouse from the washing basket.

He closed the door of the cupboard.

"It is finished. From tomorrow you do your own shopping."

Giancarlo took his pistol from the shoulder holster under his lightweight jacket, and cleared it and took out the magazine. She went on with the ironing. He went to their bedroom to rest. After tomorrow there would be no more lemons for the cardboard box in the kitchen cupboard, and no more potatoes nor green vegetables nor fruit. He had been too long in the job of surveillance to feel a sense of failure.

Franco drove. It was an old Fiat 127, a model that was no longer in production. The bodywork was rusted, but the engine beneath a layer of oil and grime left for casual police inspection, was finely tuned and capable of reaching a speed of 170 kilometers per hour. It was the right car to bring a humble and elderly priest from a country village to a home in mourning. Nothing was left to chance, everything had been prepared with care, the movement of the humble and elderly priest was the responsibility of Franco. Franco, with a day's stubble on his face and wearing a poorly fitting coat and a tie that was not quite straight against the collar of a shirt that was a centimeter too tight, drove slowly because Mario Ruggerio did not like to be thrown around in a fast car. The radio set in the dash between the knees of Franco and the priest did not play the music and talk of the RAI stations but was tuned to the extremity of the VHF band to receive warnings of military roadblocks from the two cars that traveled ahead and warnings from the car behind of any possible suspicion of a police tail.

The sun was down now over the mountains to the west. The lights of Catania merged with the dusk.

The responsibility of moving Mario Ruggerio to the home, in mourning, of the man from Catania brought rare pride to Franco. There would be police, not in uniform, on the pavement outside the apartment block. There would be hastily rigged cameras, positioned by men dressed in the overalls of the telephone company or the electricity company, covering the front and the rear of the apartment block. The number of the Fiat 127 and its paint coloring would be noted, of course, but by the morning the car would have been resprayed and the registration plates would have been changed. A humble and elderly priest, from the country, would not be harassed by the police, not questioned and/or body searched, in the aftermath of death. The pride of Franco came from his belief that the responsibility given him provided an indication, clear as mountain water, that he was now the favorite of Mario Ruggerio—not Carmine, who was an arrogant idiot, not Tano who was a toad and blown out with self-importance. He believed that more responsibility would be given him until he stood at the right shoulder of Mario Ruggerio, undisputed as the *consigliere* to Mario Ruggerio. The radio stayed silent. No military roadblocks on the approach to the apartment block and no tail. The bastards would be relying on the surveillance teams on the street and the remote cameras. He drove along the street, and when he started to change down through his gears he nudged Mario Ruggerio, respectfully, and pointed to the ashtray. The humble and elderly priest stubbed out a cigarillo, coughed hard, spat into a handkerchief. He pulled up smoothly in front of the main entrance to the apartment block, where the street lights were brightest. When he was out of the car, when he would be seen by the surveillance men and by the cameras, Franco seemed to examine a scrap of paper, as if directions had been written on it, as if he were a stranger to the city, as if he merely brought a humble and elderly priest from a village in the country.

Two young men stood in the shadow near to the door, and there would have been two more across the street, and two more down the street, and they would have cameras. The priest walked with the help of a hospital stick, one that had a reinforcing clamp for the upper arm, and Franco walked with him as if ready to take his other arm should the priest stumble. The priest murmured a greeting, perhaps a blessing, to the policemen as he passed them, and they ignored him. The priest walked hesitantly over the marble floor of the hallway to the block as if such luxury were not a part of his life in the village. They took the elevator. The face of Mario Ruggerio was impassive. Franco could not read his thoughts. The man was magnificent. The man had such authority. Small, old, and such presence. The empire of the man extended across the width of the island, the length of Europe, the ocean, and Franco was his favorite. It was typical of the magnificence of the man that he came to the front door of the apartment and rang the bell for admittance to the home of a slaughtered rival.

The door was opened.

Franco carried a pistol strapped to his shin. He felt a winnowing of fear.

The apartment was crowded with the supporters of the dead rival and the family. A moment's gesture, Mario Ruggerio's hand on Franco's arm, a grip that was steel-hard, the order that he should stay back, and he was passed the hospital stick. Mario Ruggerio, murderer, now *capo di tutti capi* because a rival had been removed, went forward and the supporters and rivals backed off and made an aisle for him. Franco saw that none dared catch his eye, none had the courage or the stupidity to denounce him. Franco followed, into the living room, and he waited by the door as Mario Ruggerio approached the widow, black-clothed, sitting, eyes reddened. The widow rose to greet him. He took the widow's hands and held them in his own, he spoke the words of sincere sympathy. He brought respect. He declined the offer of alcohol from the son of the dead man, a juice would be most welcome. He gave dignity. Gravely, Mario Ruggerio, watched by Franco, thanked the son of the dead man for the juice. His presence was accepted because he brought respect, gave dignity, to a dead man. Franco understood. The power of Mario Ruggerio, dressed as a humble and elderly priest, over La Cosa Nostra was absolute.

For more than an hour Mario Ruggerio talked with the widow and the widow's son and the widow's family. When he left, he hobbled on his hospital stick past the policemen on surveillance duty, past the cameras.

With two cars in front and one behind, Franco, who was swollen with pride, drove him back to Palermo through the night's darkness.

She looked the prisoner straight in the eye, and when he dropped his head, she reached forward and lifted his chin so that he must look at her.

She was the daughter of the *capo* of the Kalsa district of the city. Her brothers followed in the footsteps of her father.

Across the table, in a low voice so that she would not be heard by the guards and by the other prisoners and their families, she spat at him her message.

"I will tell my children, not your children, my children, that they no longer have a father. I will tell them that they should forget their father. To me, to my children, you are dead. You listened to your mother, always to your mother, so now your mother can wipe your arse for you, but not me and not my children. If I am offered protection, then I will refuse it. What you intend will bring shame on you and on me and on your children. It now disgusts me that I lay with you and made children for you. You swore the same oath as my father, the same oath as my brothers, and you betray the oath. I tell you your future, from the time that I leave here, from the time that I meet with my father and my brothers. Wherever they put you, look to see if anyone is behind you when you stand on steep steps. When you approach any group, consider which man carries the knife, when you lie at night and hear a footstep, consider whether the rope is brought for your throat. When you eat then consider whether the poison is in your food. That is your future. Not my future, not the future of my children, who have no father. To me, to them, you do not exist, never existed."

She let his chin fall. The tears flowed on his cheeks. With poise, without looking back, she walked to the door.

"What I am saying, Bill—you secure at your end?"

"Secure. Go."

"I'm saying there is regular shit stirring at this end."

"Am I dumb, Ray? What's your end to do with it?"

"This show, Codename Helen, the baggage your guy came for."

"That's our problem."

"My problem, too. I got mugged by one of the local

people here. Quote, 'Taken it upon yourselves, you arrogant bloody people, to pressurize and then send a small-town girl to Palermo for some bloody operation you've dreamed up. Who've you cleared it with?, end quote. Bill, that's why it's my problem.'

"Where's that going to lead?"

"Why I'm sweating on it, don't know. I've been in this city, Bill, three years. In three years you get to know the way people work. Here they work devious. The old lion is losing his sight, got flea scrapes, yellow teeth, but he still thinks he hunts with the best of the pride. I'm accused of getting hold of his tail and twisting it. He's angry, and he's quiet, which means he's thinking devious."

"You're way ahead of me, Ray."

"I thought you should know, they may try to fuck us about."

"Aren't we all going in the same direction?"

"Wouldn't that be nice? What I'm getting to, it would raise a powerful shit-smell if anything happened, unpleasant, to Codename Helen, to your bit of baggage, like I might be run out of town, like it would go all the way to the top floor. I'll stay close. Goodnight, Bill. I just have a bad feeling."

He put down the telephone. He switched off the scrambler, then dialed again. He told his wife that he was about through for the evening, and he gave her the name and address of the restaurant in the Fulham Road where he'd meet her. He was clearing his desk when he realized that Dwight Smythe was still at his desk outside, and it was always necessary, when the secure scrambler was used, to speak that bit louder.

"Did you hear that, Dwight?"

"Sorry, but it would have been difficult not to."

"What are you thinking?"

"Same as I told you first time, same as you ignored. The plan was crazy. When a crazy plan gets disseminated, goes to the top, when the big guys have to guarantee a crazy plan, they run for cover. You're out on your own, Ray, but I expect you thought of that."

She lay on her bed and she turned the pages of her book.

"If that's everything, Angela, I'll get on with the children's baths," Charley had said. "I think you've done wonders."

"Thank you for your help," Angela had said.

And Charley had gone into the living room where Peppino, home an hour before and jacket off and whiskey in his hand and tie loosened, sat and where the children played with the presents that had been brought them. There was a battery-powered car that *piccolo* Mario raced across the tiled floor, and a doll that Francesca had stripped and then dressed again. For Angela there was a silk headscarf, and for Charley there was a box of lace handkerchiefs. She had left Angela in the kitchen with the pasta ready to go into a saucepan and the sauce already mixed, the meat thin-sliced and in the refrigerator, the vegetables washed, the fruit in a bowl and the cheese on the wood block. The wine was chilled and the mineral water. Beyond Peppino and the children, in the dining alcove, the table had been laid by Charley for eight people.

"Come on, Mario and Francesca, bath time, come on," Charley had said.

"So soon, so early?" Peppino had asked.

Charley had glanced down at the watch on her wrist. "Think I'd better be getting on because then I'll need a shower and time to change. I thought I'd wear what you—"

And Peppino had said, so casual, "I don't think you need to be with us, Charley. I understand Angela told you that it is my father's birthday—family talk, Sicilian talk. I think that for you it would be very tedious, very boring for you."

"Don't worry about me, I'll just sit—"

And Peppino had said, "My father and mother are from the country here, Charley. I think it would be difficult for you to understand their dialect. They would not be at ease with a stranger—not a stranger to us but to them—so it is better that you do not sit with us tonight. Angela will put the children to bed."

"Of course, Peppino. I quite understand . . ."

Into the dining alcove, to the table, and Charley had stripped a laid place and removed a chair. Seven places left, and seven chairs. She had gone into the kitchen and told Angela, without comment, that Peppino thought she would be bored by dinner with his parents. She had watched Angela, and seen the woman's face stiffen, and she had wondered whether Angela would stride from the kitchen and into the living room and make an issue of Charley at dinner. Angela had nodded, as if she did not have the will to fight. She had bathed the children, dressed them in their best clothes and brought them back to Peppino. She had made herself a sandwich in the kitchen. She had gone to her room.

She tried to read. She lay on her bed, dressed, and she turned the pages and learned nothing from them. She listened. A car came. She heard the murmur of voices and the happy shouting of the children. She heard footsteps in the corridor, beyond her door, which she had left an inch ajar. She heard the sounds of the kitchen.

She tried to read . . .

For Christ's sake, Charley . . .

She turned the page back because she was absorbing nothing of what she read.

For Christ's sake, Charley, it is just a job of work.

She put the book on the table beside her bed.

For Christ's sake, Charley, the job of work is playing the lie.

She pushed herself up off the bed. She straightened her hair.

It was what she had come for, traveled for, it was why she had left the bungalow and the class of 2B. She took a big breath. She put a smile on her face. She walked out of her room and she went first toward the kitchen and she saw the dirtied plates of the pasta and meat courses, and there was another plate beside the cooker that had a saucepan lid put on it as if to keep the plate warm. She went along the corridor toward the voices in the dining alcove beyond the living room. She came into the living room and the smile was fixed hard on her face. Only the children bubbled laughter at the table and played with the car and the doll, but the talking died. The chair at the head of the table was empty. She kicked away the quaver in her voice, spoke boldly.

Charley asked Angela if she could help by putting the children to bed.

Angela and Peppino sat opposite each other, then the children, then the two old people. There was a smear of annoyance on Peppino's face, and the expression of Angela was pain. At the end of the table, either side of the empty place and the empty chair, were the parents of Peppino. The old man wore a poor-fitting suit, but good cloth, and his collar and tie drooped from a thin neck. The old woman wore black, with white sparse hair gathered in a bun. Charley had seen their house, she had walked past the open door of their house, she had heard the radio

playing in their house and smelled the cooking in their
house.

Peppino said, "That will not be necessary, Angela
will see the children to bed. Thank you for the offer.
Goodnight, Charley."

He did not introduce her. The eyes of the old man
were on her, bright in his aged and lined face. The old
woman looked at her, disapproving, then started again to
peel the skin from an apple.

Charley smiled. "Right, I just wondered. It will be
good to get an early night."

She went back to her room. She again left the door
an inch ajar. She sat on the bed. Her fingers rested on the
face of her wristwatch. She wondered where he was,
whether Axel Moen listened. Plain to her that she was
not welcome and there was the empty chair and there
was the food kept warm on the plate. The rhythm of the
codes played in her mind. Where was he? Did he listen?
Her finger edged toward the button on the watch on her
wrist.

She made the signal. She paused. She made the signal
again. Where was he? Would he have heard it? She
pressed the button, the same rhythm.

The excitement ran in her. It was her power . . .

She went to the bathroom, washed and peed, and
back in her room she undressed. The pulse tone she had
sent, three times, was her power . . .

For a moment she held the bear close to her, as if the
bear should share the excitement that was hers because of
the power. She switched off the bedside light. She lay in the
darkness. Trying to stay awake, hearing sounds in the
kitchen, hearing the flushing of the lavatory, hearing
the children going with Angela to their rooms, hearing the
indistinct murmur of the voices. Trying to stay awake, and

drifting, with the finger resting on the button of her wristwatch, and drifting further, as if the excitement exhausted her. When she drifted, she dreamed. When she came through from each dream, sporadic, she jerked herself awake and killed each dream and looked at the fluorescent face of her watch. Ten o'clock coming, and eleven, and midnight, and the dreams were harder to kill, and she drifted faster, further.

She dreamed of the young man in the newspaper photograph with the throat cut and the blood spread, and of the story that Benny had told, and of the helicopter.

She dreamed of the shadow in the doorway, and of her door closing.

She dreamed of the hovering helicopter and the men in balaclavas, and of the soft-shoe shuffle in the corridor, and of Axel Moen standing under the trees beyond the beach sand . . . Charlie slept.

"What time is it?"

"It's thirty minutes on from when you last asked."

"What the hell's she at?"

"You want me to go to the door, wake the house, request to speak to her, then ask her?"

"She sent the Stand-by."

"She sent the Stand-by. She has not sent Immediate Alert, nor has she sent Stand Down."

"It is seven hours since she sent Stand-by."

"Correct, Axel, because it is now three o'clock, which is half an hour after we last had this discussion."

"Don't understand it."

"What I understand, Axel, I am quite pleased that I did not call out the heroes of the *carabinieri*. Overtime, the need for a report, I am very pleased."

"I'll kick her butt."

"She will be very bruised. You said that half an hour ago, and an hour ago."

"But, it is just goddamn unprofessional."

"Exactly, Axel, because she is not a professional."

They sat in the car. The last of the discos had long closed, the piazza bars had shut, the kids on the motorcycles and the scooters had roared away into the night. Mondello was emptied. The street where they were parked, off the piazza and a block from the shoreline, was deserted. Axel took a Lucky Strike from the packet and swore under his breath and passed the packet to 'Vanni and 'Vanni took the last cigarette from the packet. The match flashed in the interior of the car.

"That sort of settles it, doesn't it? I mean, I'm not goddamn sitting here without cigarettes."

Axel crushed the empty packet. He dropped it on the floor beside 'Vanni's finished packet and beside the squashed wrapping of the pizzas they'd eaten. They smoked. They eked out their cigarettes until their fingers burned. They dropped their cigarettes through the open windows.

"What do you think?"

"I think, Axel, that we go to bed. You are angry?"

"I'll kick the butt off her."

"I think—you know what I think? I think, and you will not love me." 'Vannie grinned wide. "I think you care, and I think you are very frightened for her."

"I'll kick her so's my foot hurts."

There was only the night-duty officer as company for Harry Compton.

In a mood of stubborn anger he had telephoned Rome, and been told by Alf Rogers that the report was coming, but late that night, and he said that he would wait on.

There was a phrase the commander liked to use, something about the primary work of SO6 being "putting faces to illegality," a phrase recited to visiting politicians and bureaucrats. In front of the detective sergeant, on his desk, was the source of that stubborn anger. A camera at Heathrow had put a face to illegality. Italian passport holder Bruno Fiori, seven hours earlier, had passed through Terminal Two, Heathrow. The photograph, taken by a camera on a high wall bracket, showed him presenting the Italian passport at the emigration desk, and the order that the holder of that passport should not be delayed, not be quizzed, not be made aware of any investigation, had been most specific. The bastard had gone through, without let or hindrance, to his flight. The photograph showed a smoothly handsome man, well dressed, relaxed, and the bastard should have been in the interrogation rooms or in a cell.

A bell rang. The bell was piping and sharp. The night-duty officer was pushing up from his chair, but Harry Compton waved him down and back to his newspaper. He hurried through to Miss Frobisher's office, abandoned and left pristine for the morning.

The message churned from the printer. He read . . .

TO: Harry Compton, SO6.
FROM: Alfred Rogers, DLO, British Embassy,
Via XX Settembre, Rome.
SUBJECT: MARIO RUGGERIO.

DOB: 19/8/1934.
POB: Prizzi, western Sicily.
PARENTS: Rosario b. 1912 (still living) and
    Agata b. 1913 (still living). Their other chil-
    dren—Salvatore b. 1936 (imprisoned),

Carmelo b. 1937 (mentally subnormal),
Cristoforo b. 1939 (murdered 1981), Maria
b. 1945, Giuseppe b. 1954 (see below).

FAMILY: Married Michela Bianchini (from
LCN Trapani family) 1975. Salvatore (s) b.
1980, Domenica (d) b. 1982. Living now in
Prizzi.

DESCRIPTION: Height 1.61 meters. Weight
(est.) 83 kilos. Blue eyes. No surgical scars
known of. Believed of heavy and powerful
build (no photograph for 20+ years, no positive sighting in that period). Not known
whether dark brown hair now grayed or
dyed, also nk whether wears spectacles routinely.

He carried the sheets of paper back to his desk.

"Like a mug of coffee, squire? Just making one for
myself." The night-duty officer was folding away his
newspaper.

"No, thank you."

BIOGRAPHY: Formal education, elementary
school, Prizzi, 1939–43. Traveled with his
father—contraband lorry driver. 1951—convicted of attempted murder, Court of Assizes,
Palermo (victim alleged to have denied him
"sufficient respect"). In Ucciardone prison
alleged to have strangled two fellow prisoners, no witnesses, no evidence. Released
1960, having become sworn Man of Honor.
Not arrested since. Charged *in absentia* with
murder, narco trafficking, much else.
Believed FBI/DEA have sufficient evidence

for indictment in USA. An ally of Corleonesi
(Riina, Provenzano, etc.), but thought to
have maintained independence. In power
struggle (post-Corleonesi arrests) indications
that RUGGERIO is responsible for disappearance of Agrigento *capo* and most recent
murder of Catania *capo*.

"You all right, squire? Sure you won't have a coffee?
There's a sandwich here, missus always makes enough for
a bloody tea party."

"No, thank you."

"Just asking. Only you look like someone's grabbed
your goolies and given them a god-almighty twist. Didn't
mean to interrupt . . ."

ASSESSMENT: Extraordinarily secretive, reputation of taking extreme care of his personal security, no successful wire taps, no
documentation found. Has also tightened
overall security of "families" in LCN under
his control, introduced cellular system,
hence no recent information provided
against him by the *pentito* (super-grass) program. Seen by Italian authorities as ruthless
killer.

SCO report: "Ignorant but he has intuition and
intelligence, his actions are most hard to predict."

Squadra mobile report: "Violent, aggressive, vindictive, with above-average shrewdness and
determination."

DIA report: "He has power over life and death,
an incredible personal presence, and a streak

of violent sadism, BUT (my emphasis, AR)
he is reduced to a miserable condition
because he cannot move openly, cannot live
with his family openly. He is submerged in
the terror of assassination, exists in an atmo-
sphere of tension and fear, hence violent
paranoia."

Magistrate Rocco Tardelli (investigating
Ruggerio) in a recent report to Min. of
Justice: "[Ruggerio] is a supreme strategist,
believes future of LCN is in international
dealings, acting as broker for cartels, Triads,
Yakuza, Russian mafia. His reputation goes
ahead of him, he is seen as combining experience with shrewdness. If he achieves domination of LCN, he will seek to direct the
enormous power of that organization beyond
Italian frontiers."

At a time when the effort of the Italian
state against LCN is losing impetus, it would
seem that Ruggerio has taken control.

(See attached for GIUSEPPE RUGGERIO.)
Alfred Rogers, DLO, Rome.

He had thought once that the young woman, in the
graduation photograph on the wall above the telephone,
was not his concern. He felt a keen sense of shame. He
locked the report in the wall safe.

"I think I'll push off then, I'm about wrapped up."

"Best place, squire, in bed with the missus. They
don't thank you here for playing all conscientious. Don't
mind me asking—you seen a ghost or something? Sorry,
sorry, just my little joke . . ."

13

"YOU WILL BE LATE, CHARLEY. Can that not wait?" Angela shouted from the kitchen door.

She was hurrying along the back path, past the gas tank and the rubbish bins, to the washing-line. Her bras and knickers and T-shirts and jeans dripped in her hands. The washing-line was behind the villa. Beyond the washing-line was the rear wall to the property. Recessed into the wall was a strong wooden door with a padlock fastening it shut. The wall was too high for her to see over, but above the wall was the coarse scree and rock-sheer slope of the cliff.

"Won't be a second, Angela—won't be a minute."

She grabbed a fistful of pegs from the plastic bag hanging from the washing-line.

She was pegging the clothes to the line. She saw the bastard. Hey, "lechie," *libertino,* getting a thrill from watching bras and knickers hung out? Want to get your dirty hands on them? He stood beside the barrow and when she challenged him with her gaze, he started to scratch with his broom at the path to the door in the wall. He bent. The old hand, weathered and bony and dirty, reached down to the ground beside the path and he picked something up, and threw it into the barrow. She saw it. She saw the crushed end of a cigarillo on the top of the leaves in the barrow. The line of clothes was complete. She stopped, she considered, then she ran back to the villa.

Angela had the children ready on the front patio, and

the pram with baby Mauro, and the shopping list for the day.

"Don't bother to wash up last night's dishes, Angela, I'll do that when I'm back. And it's all right for me to get a bit of culture into the system this afternoon? I'll see you. Come on, kids."

When she'd woken, Peppino was already up and sitting in the living room with work papers. When she'd gone into the kitchen to get the kids breakfast and to warm the milk for the baby, the sink had been filled with the dirtied dishes topped by saucepans and Angela had been making coffee. Not possible for her to examine the padded seat of the chair at the end of the dining table, not possible for her to check the number of plates used, nor the number of knives and forks. She thought herself pretty damn clever to have offered to wash the dishes. Right, pretty damn clever that she had noticed the "lechie" pick up a cigarillo end at the back of the villa near the door in the wall. He smoked cigarettes, foul Italian ones, and Angela didn't smoke cigarillos and Peppino didn't smoke cigarillos, and the old man from last night would hardly have been sent out through the kitchen and past the gas tank and the rubbish bins for a sharp puff. And there was the jumbled memory of her dream.

Not pretty damn clever that she had slept . . . shit . . . had failed to stay awake.

Her mind was compartments. One compartment was walking down the hill and easing the pram around the dog dirt and the street rubbish and the road holes, taking the children to school and kindergarten, having the purse and the shopping list. A separate compartment was the lie and the watch on her wrist, and dirty plates in a sink, and a chair, and a cigarillo end . . . She dropped small Mario at school and walked Francesca to the kindergarten door. She was in the piazza, a hand resting casually on the pram's handle, and there was the blast of a horn. She was studying the shopping list. She swung round. Peppino waved to her and then powered away in his big car. She waved back. If she were pretty damn clever, clever enough to arouse suspicion, then would it be Peppino who strangled her, knifed her, beat her and then took his dinner? She bought the milk and fresh bread rolls. She was going to the fruit stall.

"Keep walking, down to the sea, don't turn."

A cold and harsh voice. God, and the bloody voice was without bloody mercy. She stiffened her back, like she was trying to show defiance, but she did as she was told and she walked down to the main road, waited for the lights, never turned, pushed the pram across the road. She leaned against the rail. The baby was waking and she rocked the pram gently.

"If you can't cope with it, then you should say so, and you should quit."

"That is bloody unfair."

The growled voice, the sharp accent, rasped behind her. "If you can't handle it then go. Go home."

She stared out over the water. The small fleet of fishing boats was putting out to sea, riding the swell. The wind freshened on her face. "I'm doing what I can."

"You want the list? Item, you give your communications to a goddamn child to play with. He plays, we scramble. We had a helicopter up, we had a full team out—you fouled up."

"It won't happen again."

"Won't happen if you quit. Item, you send Stand-by last night. I am sitting with company, holed up in a car till half after three this morning. I have a heavy team on Ready till half after three. Did you forget to send Stand Down?"

"I am doing my best."

"If your best isn't better, then you should go home."

"I am sorry."

"Goddamn should be. Why didn't you send the Stand Down?"

She heaved the breath into her lungs. The wind whipped her hair. She said, small voice, "I thought he might come. It was a little family party for Giuseppe's father's birthday. I wasn't included. I was told it would be 'tedious' for me. I tried to stay awake in my room, I tried. I went to sleep."

"That is pathetic."

"I did my damn best . . ."

"Did he come?"

"Does he smoke cigarillos?"

"How the hell should I know?"

"Then I don't know if he came."

"Think about going home if you can't do the job."

She turned. She broke the rule he had made. She faced Axel Moen. She saw the coldness in the eyes of Axel Moen, and the contempt lined at the mouth of Axel Moen, and the anger cut in the frown of Axel Moen. She wanted to touch him, and she wanted him to hold her . . . She turned away from him. There would be a storm because the wind was rising.

He said, hacking the words, "If you can't handle it, then you should walk out."

She was watching the fishing fleet, diminishing, riding the wave crests. She went to buy the fresh fruit.

Back at the villa, Charley found that Angela had finished washing the plates and cutlery from the previous night, and they had been put away in the cupboards, and the upholstered chair in the dining room had been brushed with the other chairs and she could not see whether it had been sat on.

"The conclusion?"

Giancarlo stood with the others of the team, all of

them except for those who had done the last night shift. It was not routine for the *squadra mobile* surveillance unit to meet with an investigating magistrate who tasked them at the beginning of an operation and at the end of an operation, but it was the requirement of this small and sad man. The small and sad man sat on his desk, his legs a little too short for his feet to reach the floor, and his arms were hunched across his chest. Giancarlo thought, a ridiculous thought and inappropriate, that the magistrate had in his eyes the dull tiredness of death, that the dimmed room had the gloom of a *cella dei condannati a morte*. They had nothing to say and nothing to report, but he had insisted on seeing them.

There was no conclusion. No sighting of Ruggerio, no trace of Ruggerio. But it had been three teams of only three men, and a labyrinth such as the Capo would swallow a hundred men. It had been a gesture, but the gesture was a token.

"Thank you for your endeavor." The endeavor was to walk and to stand and to look at faces and to try to match the faces of old men to a photograph. The photograph was twenty years old. Some computer enhancements of photographs were good, some were useless. They might have seen him, might have stood beside him. "Thank you for your commitment."

"For nothing . . ." The leader of the unit gazed, embarrassed, at the floor.

And Giancarlo held the present behind his buttocks. That moment he wondered how often there was laughter in this room. Like a mortuary, this room, like a place of black weeds and hushed voices. A place for a man who was condemned . . . Did the poor bastard, small and sad, condemned it was said, ever get to laugh? The men on the door outside, condemned with him it was said, they didn't seem fun creatures who would make the poor bastard laugh. Giancarlo was the oldest on the team, the most experienced, the one who gave no respect to any man, and he had been chosen to offer the gift to the small and sad man, to make him laugh.

"As an appreciation of working for you, *Dottore* . . ."

Giancarlo handed the parcel, wrapped in shiny paper and bound with gift tape, to the magistrate. They watched as his nervous fingers unbound the tape and unwrapped the paper.

Lemons cascaded on the desk, lemons bounced, lemons fell to the floor, lemons rolled on the carpet.

He understood. A quick smile slipped to his mouth. He knew their work, knew the difficulty of going into the Capo district day after day and finding a process that enabled them to blend with the crowds in the alleyways. He slipped off the desk and came to Giancarlo and pecked a kiss on each of the man's cheeks, and Giancarlo thought it was the kiss of a condemned man.

When it was the time for exercise, when the bells clamored and the keys scraped in the doors' locks, the prisoner stayed on the bunk bed.

The men with whom he shared the cell went on their way for exercise in the yard below. A *carceriere* saw him sitting hunched on the lower bunk and asked the prisoner why he was not going to exercise and was told that he had a head cold.

When the landing of the block was quiet, as it would be for thirty minutes, the prisoner stood. It surprised him that his hands did not shake as he unbuckled his belt. Holding his belt, he scrambled up onto the upper bunk. He could see now, through the squat window, through the bars, the panorama of Palermo. The window of the cell was open. A hard wind came on his face. Through the bars he could see the mountains above Palermo. In the mountains was the home of his mother, in the city was the home of his wife and his children. As he hooked the buckle of his belt around a bar at the window he heard only the howl of the wind.

His wife had told him that he was dead. The magistrate had told him he would die by the push, or by the knife thrust, or by poison.

He pulled the belt hard and tested that it was held strong by the bar.

Suicidio was a crime against the oath he had taken many years before. When a man took his own life he lost his dignity and his respect, and that was a crime against the oath.

The prisoner wound the end of the belt around his throat and knotted it. There was not an adequate drop from the top bunk bed, nor was the belt long enough, for him to break his neck when he slid his weight clear. He would strangle himself to death.

He had nothing more to tell the magistrate, nothing more to tell of Mario Ruggerio.

He mouthed a prayer, and he tried to find in his mind the faces of his children.

He was suspended, kicking, choking, writhing, and below the cell window men walked the monotonous circles of exercise.

"So this is home?"

"This is Cinisi and it is my home."

"Quite a nice-looking little place, a lot of character," Charley said brightly. She looked up the main street, the Corso Vittorio Emanuele. At the end of the street was a granite mountain face, and above the rim of the mountain there was a clear azure sky in which cloud puffs raced in the wind. Against the gray rock face, dominating the street below, was the church that had been built with sharp and angular lines.

"My father, before they killed him, called Cinisi a *mafiopoli*," Benny said. He held the door of his car open for her. She thought it a nice-looking place and the character was in the smart terraces of houses that flanked the main street. The windows of most of the houses were masked with shutters, but there were potted plants on the balconies and the paint was fresh on the houses' walls, white and ochre, and the main street was swept clean in front of the houses. Set in the paving between the houses and the street were flowering cherry trees, and under the trees was a scattering of pink blossom.

"I can't see anything, Benny, can't feel it. Maybe I could not see much in Corleone, maybe I could feel something in Prizzi, but not here. There doesn't seem to be anything to touch."

"Look to the mountain," Benny said.

Charley wore her best skirt, which she had bought with Peppino's money, and her best blouse. She stood with the sun and the wind on her thighs and shins. The force of the wind tunneled down the main street. She stood boldly with her feet a little apart, as if to brace herself. There was scrub on the lower slope of the mountain, where the fall was less severe, but higher on the rock wall nothing grew. The mountain was a harsh presence above the main street.

"It's a mountain, it's rock, it's useless."

He touched her arm, a small gesture as if to direct her attention, and there was a softness in his voice. "You are wrong, Charley. Of course you are wrong, because you do not live here, you do not know. They own the mountain, they own the rock, they own the quarries. Did you not come on the plane to Palermo?"

"Came by train," Charley said. Axel Moen had told her that the vulnerable time for an agent was the sea change between overt and covert, the journey from safety to danger, told her it was good to take time on the journey to reflect on the sea change. Charley lied. "I thought it was wonderful to come by train, sort of romantic, on a train through the night and crossing a continent."

"Because they own the mountain and the rock and the quarries, they wanted the airport for Palermo built here. The runways are two kilometers from here. There is too much wind and the mountain is too close, but that was not important because they owned the mountain, the rock, the quarry. Cinisi was a place of farms and vines and olive trees, but they turned the *contadini* off their land, and the stone made the base for the runways, the stone could be a base for the concrete, and they came to own the airport. They own everything that you see, Charley, every person."

They were outside a smart house. There were recently fitted hardwood surrounds to the windows and a heavy hardwood door with a polished brass knocker.

"Is your mother inside?"

"Yes."

She said with mischief, "And waiting for your washing?"

"Yes."

"Can she wait a little longer for your washing?"

"Of course—what do you want?"

"I want to see where they killed your father, where you were in the car when they killed him."

Perhaps she had startled him. His lips narrowed and his eyes glinted and his cheeks were taut. He walked away from her. She followed him. Benny went past small groups of old men who stood in the sun and let the wind grab at their jackets and they did not meet his eyes and he did not look at them. A woman with shopping stopped as he came close to her and then in ostentation she turned her back on him to stare into the window of an *alimentari*. As he went by them, three boys who gossiped and sat astride their scooters revved their engines so that the black exhaust fumes carpeted his face. Charley followed. He stopped, as if challenging her, pointed to a *gelateria*, every sort of ice cream, every flavor, and she shook her head. At the top of the Corso Vittorio Emanuele was the piazza of Cinisi. A priest came from the church and saw Benny and looked away and hurried on, his robe driven by the wind against the width of his hips. There were more men in the piazza, more boys idle and squatting on their motorcycles. She was making him live the moment again, and she wondered if he hated her.

He talked her through the chronology of a death, as if he were a tourist guide in the *duomo* or at the Quattro Canti or at the Palazzo Sclafani. He pointed to the street beside the church.

"It was done there. I had been late at the school for instruction in the violin. My father had collected me on his way back from Terrasini, he came for me because it was raining, and they would have known which afternoon I stayed at the school for music, and they would have known that if it were raining he would collect me. It was not important to them that I was in the car, that I was ten years old. That afternoon it was convenient for them to kill my father . . ."

There was a bar on the corner of the piazza. The wind gusted the wrapping of a cigarette packet past the closed door to the bar. It had been seventeen, eighteen years before—of course, there was nothing to see. A narrow street leading into a pretty piazza under the shadow of the church of San Silvestro, a killing zone.

"What had he done? What had your father done?" She knew that she would take him to bed, that day or that night.

"He told the *contadini* that they should not give up their land. He said that they would be robbed if they agreed to sell their land. He said that they were farmers and they should continue to harvest the olives and the oranges and to grow maize. He said that if they sold their land and the airport was built they would never work again because the jobs made by the airport would go to people from Palermo, who were not *contadini*. He said to the people that the success of the airport would be a triumph for the *mafiosi,* and a disaster for the *contadini*. He was only a shopkeeper, but he was an honest man, his honesty was respected. There was a time when people began to listen to him. My father called a meeting of all the people in the town and the peasants who had the olives and the oranges and the maize. The meeting was to be here, where we stand. My father was going to tell the people that they should oppose the building of the airport. The meeting was for that evening."

"So they killed him, to silence him." She would lie with him on a bed, that day or that night.

"Because he obstructed them, and because he made fun of them. The night before, I had heard my father in the bedroom practice the speech he would make. He had many jokes to tell about them. The family in Cinisi at that time, destroyed now, replaced, was the family of Badalamenti. He spoke of the 'Corso Badalamenti' where they lived and of the leader of the family as 'Geronimo Badalamenti.' He had jokes to tell about the wealth that would come from the airport when they had stolen the land from the *contadini,* about the Badalamenti family eating from silver plates and taking baths with hot water from gold taps. He was a threat to them because he would laugh at them, and have the people laugh with him."

"What happened? Tell me what happened?" On a bed she would take the clothes from his body, that day or that night.

"How is it important to you? Why do you wish to know?"

"Please, tell me."

The sneer was at his face, and the wind caught at the fineness of his hair. "You are a nanny for a rich family. You take your money for minding small children, for doing the work of their mother. Why—"

"See, touch, feel, so that I can understand."

"Am I an amusement to you?"

"No, I promise. Help me to understand." She would take the clothes from his body and kneel over his body and kiss his body, that day or that night.

"A car crossed the piazza and it stopped in front of my father's car. He did not recognize the people in the car because he shouted at them. Did they not know where they were going? It was late in the afternoon, the light was going because of the rain. Already in the piazza the preparations had been made, there was the sound equipment for my father, there was a place for him to speak from. He shouted at the people in the car because he thought he would be late for the meeting. There was another car that came behind us, it drove into us. I saw one man only. The man had a small machine gun and he came from the front toward us and he threw a small cigar from his mouth and he raised his machine gun. There were more men, with guns, but I did not see them because my father pushed me down in the seat. He tried to protect me. If he had been alone, I think he would have attempted to run, but I was with him and he would not have left me. There were eighteen shots fired, thirteen of the shots hit my father. The priest who came, who was there first, before the *carabinieri* and the ambulance, the priest said that it was a *miracolo* that the child was not hit. I think credit was given to the killers of my father because I was not hit. I can remember still the weight of his body on me, and I can remember still the warmth of his blood on me. Someone brought my mother.

She came, and the body of my father was lifted off me. My mother took me home."

"It happened here?"

"Where you stand is where the car stopped to block my father. Do you wish to learn more?"

"So that I may understand . . ." She would kiss his body and put his hands on her body and find his love, that day or that night.

"Two days later there was the funeral for my father. Where we stand now I walked then with my mother and the whole length of the Corso and the width of the piazza was lined with the people of Cinisi, and the church was filled. There were eight thousand people then living in Cinisi and around the town, and three thousand came to my father's funeral, and the priest denounced the barbarity of the *mafiosi*. It was a fraud, it meant nothing. It was a spectacle, like a traveling theater on a festival day. The airport was built on the land stolen from the *contadini*. The people who had filled the church, stood on the Corso and in the piazza, were bent to the will of the Badalamenti family. There was a short investigation but the *carabinieri* told my mother that guilt could not be proved. They own the town, they own the airport, they own the lives of everybody here."

"Why, Benny, do they not kill you?"

His head hung. She thought she had slashed at his pride. He looked away from her and he murmured in bitterness, "When opposition is ineffective, they do not notice it. When opposition is only an irritation, they ignore it. When opposition is threatening, they kill it. Do you seek to humiliate me because I am alive, because my father is dead?"

"Let's get your washing home," Charley said.

They walked back down the Corso Vittorio Emanuele. She took his hand and led him, set the pace for him. It was useful for her to be able to touch warm blood and feel the weight of a father's body and to see the shock in a child's face . . .

She should think about going home, Axel Moen had said. She should think about going home if she could not do the job, Axel Moen had said . . . He did not speak, they reached the car, he lifted a filled pillowcase from the floor at the back of the car. The gale, funneled down the main street, beat on them. He rang the bell at the door.

She was introduced.

She played the part of the innocent.

She was offered juice and a slice of rich cake.

She was the nanny to a rich family from Palermo, and she was ignorant.

She talked, innocent and ignorant, with Benny's mother. The mother had darting sparrow's movements and bright cobra's eyes. Charley thought the woman must have quite extraordinary courage. She had trained, since her loss, as an accountant. She could live anywhere on the island, work anywhere in Sicily or on the mainland, but she had chosen to stay. She wore a bright scarlet skirt and a grass-green blouse, as if it would have been a defeat to take to widow's black. The courage of the woman, Charley thought, would come from facing each day the people of the town who had stood aside when her man was butchered, and from facing each day the people who had filled the church and lined the Corso for her man's burial. Charley ate her cake and drank her juice, sucked in the strength of the woman. The courage of the woman was in walking, each day, up the Corso past the home of the people who had ordered her man's killing, and seeing their families in the bars, and standing with them in the shops, and knowing that they slept well at night.

If she were not to quit, go home, walk away, she needed that courage.

She waited for the woman to clear away the glasses and the plates. She waited for the woman to take the pillowcase to the washing machine in the kitchen.

Charley reached for Benny's hand. The hand was limp. She controlled him. She led him to the staircase of cleaned and polished wood. She heard the churning motion of the washing machine. The door to the bathroom was open. The door to the principal bedroom, the woman's room, was open. She led Benny through the door that had been shut, into his room. It was cool in the room because the shutters were closed and the sunlight came in zebra lines, filtered, onto the single bed, onto the skin rug on the floor, onto the picture above the bed. The picture was from a newspaper. A car was isolated in an empty street. The body of a man was beside the car. A woman stood near to the car and held a small child against her. Giving space to the body and the woman and the child was a crowd of onlookers. Charley fed from the photograph, as she had eaten the cake and drunk the juice. She must draw strength from the woman and the child.

She took the jacket from his shoulders and he made no move to help her.

She kneeled and slipped the shoes from his feet, and the socks.

She took the tie from his throat and the shirt from his chest and loosed the trousers at his waist. She stripped the man bare and she saw the tremble of his knees and the smooth flatness of his stomach, and she saw the heave of his chest below the hair mat. She thought he pleaded to her. She heard, from below, the rattle of the plates being rinsed and the clatter of the glasses.

He lay on the bed. She squatted over him. She kissed the mouth and the throat and the chest and the stomach of Benny, drank the juice of his sweat. She made lines with the nails of her fingers on his skin and tangled his hairs. Only when the moaning was in his throat, as the wind moaned in the cables outside the shuttered window, did he reach for her. He tore at the buttons of the blouse and at the clasp of her bra and at the waist of her skirt. She had control of him. She put the rubber over him, as she had known she would.

Charley rode the man.

Not the lecturer from college on the carpet, not the guy from the picket line in the caravan, not the schoolteacher who had lifted her, bruised, bleeding, scarred, from the pavement.

Charley held his head and her fingers, frantic, searched for the ponytail of blond hair that was held tight with an elastic band. Charley pounded her fingers into the pale face with the day of stubble beard on it. Charley pulled the arms around her, muscled and powerful. He drove at her, hard in her, as if he were trying to buck her from him.

She murmured the name of the man . . .

"Axel . . . fuck me . . . Axel . . ."

He came, he was sagging, he was spent.

She crawled off him. He tried to kiss her, to hug her, to hold her, but she pushed him back and down onto the bed. She took the rubber off him. She walked, cruel and vicious bitch, from the bedroom to the bathroom and she flushed the rubber down the lavatory. She sat on the seat. She wondered where he was and whether he had watched her. Her fingers rested on the nakedness of her arm, on the coldness of the watch on her wrist. She came back into the room. He lay on the bed and his arm was across his face so that he should not see her.

Charley started to dress.

"Who killed your father?"

"My father is mine. He is not your business."

She was dressing fast, snatching at the crumpled heap of

clothes. "Is it good to be so ineffective that one is unnoticed? Who killed him?"

"When a man from Catania is to be killed they bring in an assassin from Trapani, when a man from Agrigento is to be killed they find a man in Palermo." He hissed the explanation. "It is an exchange of favors, a barter of services. When a man from Cinisi is to be killed—"

"They bring a killer from Prizzi? Is it good to be only an irritation and ignored?"

"What is it to you?" His arm was off his face. He pushed himself up on the bed. She thought he had a fear of her.

"I'll take the bus back," Charley said. "I'll go on the bus because your mother won't have had time to dry your washing and iron it. You're safe from Mario Ruggerio, Benny, because he won't even have noticed you."

Carmine brought the minister to the apartment.

The apartment was at Cefalu and the business of the minister was at Milazzo, which was nearly 150 kilometers to the east. Carmine had been given, by Mario Ruggerio, responsibility for bringing the politician from the oil refinery at Milazzo to the holiday apartment at Cefalu. It was a serious and important responsibility. The minister was now in charge of the budget for Industry, but Mario Ruggerio had told Carmine that the minister was a rising star and eyed Finance. A half year before the minister had sent a signal, in a speech in Florence he had spoken of the glory of a united Italy and the duty of all Italians to support their fellow citizens of Sicily. Mario Ruggerio had read the code of the signal: government funds should continue, as before, to cascade onto the island, and the supply of government money, trillions of *lire,* were the lifeblood of La Cosa Nostra. A month before, the minister had sent a second signal; on a late-night television program broadcast by a private channel, he had warned of the excesses of the judiciary in Palermo in their use of *pentiti* as trial witnesses. Two signals, two coded messages that the minister was ready to do business with Mario Ruggerio. A contact through an intermediary at a Masonic meeting in Rome, and now Carmine had the responsibility of bringing the minister in secrecy from Milazzo to Cefalu. Not simple, not for an arrogant shit like Tano, not for a fool who had air in his brain like Franco, to bring a minister from Milazzo to Cefalu. The responsibility was entrusted to Carmine because he had the intelligence to arrange the security necessary for the meeting. The minister had toured the oil refinery with his guides and his guards, had worn the hard hat, had walked alongside the kilometers of pipelines, had stood in the control areas with the technical directors and his guards, and had pleaded a headache from the fumes of the refinery. The minister had taken refuge in his hotel room. The guards of the minister of Industry, not a prime target, were relaxed. They had been called, at Carmine's direction, to the end of the hotel corridor for refreshment. In the few moments when the distraction of the guards was total, the minister had been brought from his room, through the door on which the NON DISTURBARE sign hung, and out onto the fire escape.

Carmine drove the car from Milazzo to Cefalu. He had given the minister a flat cap to wear, and the minister had a scarf half across his mouth. The beauty of Carmine's plan, the guards in the hotel would never admit to loss of control of their subject, they would never confess that the minister had been given an opportunity to leave his hotel room unseen.

He took the car into the parking area under the apartment block. He parked beside the Citroën BX, the only other car there. The tourists, they would be Germans, had not yet come to Cefalu to scorch themselves on the beach and to wander in the Piazza del Duomo.

The minister, at the base of the concrete steps, hesitated, but Carmine smiled reassurance. The stupid bastard was already hooked, the stupid bastard had nowhere to go but up the concrete steps. He led. They climbed. The minister panted. Three raps at the door of the second-floor apartment.

The door was opened. The damp of the winter had been at the wood of the door, warped it, and it whined as it was opened.

The small body of Mario Ruggerio was framed in the door, and his head ducked as if in respect to the minister's rank, and the smile on his face was of gratitude that a man of such importance had made such the journey to visit him. He wore baggy trousers that were hoisted with a peasant's braces to the fullness of his stomach, and the old gray jacket that was his favorite, and he took the minister's hands and held them in welcome. And the old worn face of the peasant brushed a kiss to each side of the minister's cheeks. He gestured with his hand, humbly, that the minister should come into the apartment.

Carmine was not a party to the meeting. He closed the door.

Carmine waited.

He assumed that by the next morning a bank draft for, perhaps, a million American dollars would have been transferred to an account in Vienna or in Panama or to the Caymans or to Gibraltar. Mario Ruggerio said, always said, that there was a price for every man, and perhaps the price for a minister of the state was a million American dollars. And Mario Ruggerio would know because he had already found out the price for judges and for policemen and for a cardinal and for . . . It was the power of Mario Ruggerio, Carmine was under the protection of that power, that he could own those at the very heart of the state. There was so much that could be bought with a million American dollars,—the blocking of investigations, the opening of contract opportunities, recommendations and introductions abroad. He stood outside the door and basked in the glory of the power of Mario Ruggerio. One day, at some time, when Mario Ruggerio tired of the glory of power, stepped aside, then it would be Carmine who replaced him . . .

An hour later Carmine led the minister back down the concrete steps. Three hours later, when refreshments were again offered to the guards, the minister climbed the fire escape of the hotel in Milazzo. Four hours later, the minister appeared at his door and called to his guards that the headache from the oil refinery fumes was gone.

The telephone rang.

It shrilled through the darkened apartment. In the kitchen the *ragazzi* of the magistrate had their own telephone and their radio. They pretended an indifference each time the telephone rang, talked louder among themselves, took a greater interest in their card game. They pretended they did not listen, after the telephone call, for the quiet scrape of Tardelli's feet coming from his room to the kitchen. Pasquale felt the new mood of the protection team. The joke, sad, sick, had been against him, but he recognized now that the joke affected all of them. He had been the sole target of the joke—"Why a jeweler's shop?"—but it claimed them all. Less talk, raucous, of the last two days of overtime and screwing women and holidays. More talk, somber, of the last two days of greater speed in the cars, less predictable routes, more weapons training. Each time the telephone rang they waited for the scrape of Tardelli's feet coming from his room to the kitchen, stiffened, pretended, listened. Pasquale suffered each night the dream of a parked car or a parked van or a parked motorcycle exploding in fire as they passed, and he knew the bomb would be reinforced with ball bearings and detonated via the link between a mobile phone and a telephone pager. He knew it, they all knew it, because the *maresciallo* had told them what he had heard from Forensics. He knew, they all knew, and the *maresciallo* did not need to tell them, that there was no protection against the bomb in the parked car or van or on the pannier of a motorcycle. They waited, they listened, as they did each time the telephone rang in the apartment.

He came, scraping his feet, to the kitchen door. There was a grayness to the color of his cheeks, his fingers moved fidgeting in a clasp across his stomach. With his eyes he apologized.

"I have to go out."

The *maresciallo* said breezily, "Of course, *Dottore*—the Palazzo, the Palace of Poison?"

"There is a church beside the prison . . ."

"On the Piazza Ucciardone, *Dottore* . . . ? When would you like to go?"

"Please, I would like to go now."

"Then we go, now—no problem."

"He took his life. The man I played a game with, made fear for, to help his memory, he hanged himself in his cell."

He was gone, shuffling through the hallway for his coat. The *maresciallo* rapped out a route to the Piazza Ucciardone, a route past the close-packed parked cars and vans and motorcycles with panniers. They lifted their vests off the floor, they took the machine guns from the table and the draining board beside the sink and the work surface beside the cooker. The radio carried the message, staccato, to the troops in the street below the apartment. They took him out. They hurried him down the staircase, with the two drivers stampeding ahead so that the engines of the cars

would have been started before he hit the pavement. They
ran across the pavement, into the last light of the afternoon,
and the gale scorched grit into their faces. Pasquale was front
passenger in the chase car, and the *maresciallo* was behind
him. Sirens on. Lights on. At the end of the street, as the soldier held up the traffic, they swerved onto the main road and
past the lines of parked cars and vans and motorcycles. They
went faster than usual, as if it were necessary now always for
them to go faster than the time taken by a man to react and
press the last digit on a mobile telephone linked to a pager.

"Pasquale. What are you, Pasquale?"

The voice of the *maresciallo* whispered in his ear. His
eyes were on the traffic ahead, and on the line of parked cars,
vans, motorcycles they hurtled past. He held the machine
gun hard against his chest.

"What are you, Pasquale?"

"I don't understand."

"You want me to tell you what you are, Pasquale? You
are a stupid and pathetic cretin. You do not have a magazine
loaded."

His hands were rigid on the stock and trigger guard of
the machine gun. He looked down. He had not loaded a
magazine, thirty-two rounds, into it. He bent and laid the
machine gun on the floor between his feet. He took his pistol from the shoulder harness. The cars swerved, screamed,
cornered.

The journalist from Berlin was settled comfortably in his
chair. The embassy was a little piece of home for him. There
was a strong beer from the Rhineland on the table beside
him. To be back in Rome again was to have returned to
Europe, to have left that Arab world of half-truths, coded
statements and conceit. He had telephoned his editor for
more checks to be sent him and they would arrive in the

morning at the American Express. He had won a few more days . . . As a veteran of so many wars, he was reluctant to make the last leg home and have it said in the office, by younger ankle-snapping colleagues, that he had failed. In truth, so far his journey in search of the mafia was a failure, but he believed that a few more days in Rome, distanced from this war that he could not sense or smell, would supply him with the copy for his article. There was a counselor at the embassy who liaised for the *Bundeskriminalamt* with the Italian agencies. He wrote a sharp shorthand note of what he was told.

". . . We had the opinion, five, six years ago that the collapse of the Christian Democrat machine, and those of the communists and socialists, would remove from the mafia the protection they had enjoyed for forty years. We thought then that for Italy a new era of clean politics was coming. We were wrong. There was the businessman's government that followed. Far from attacking the mafia this government took a most dangerous line. Antimafia magistrates in Palermo were denounced as self-seekers and opportunists, the *pentiti* program was condemned for making bad law. There was a small window of opportunity to strike against the mafia after the killing of Falcone and Borsellino, when the public, in outrage, demonstrated against criminality, but the opportunity was not grasped. I believe it now lost. What I hear, it is increasingly difficult to persuade prosecutors and magistrates to travel to Sicily, there is ongoing and debilitating rivalry between the many agencies, there is incompetence and inefficiency. The Italians forever plead with us to make greater efforts against a common enemy, but—hear me—look at the construction of the businessman's government. There was a Fascist appointed to the Interior Ministry, there are men with proven criminal associations introduced to the peripheries of power. Would we wish for such people to have cooperation given them? Should they be granted access to BKA files? Only because the Sicilian mafia pushes drugs and dirty money into Germany, do we have an interest in the matter of organized crime in Italy. The British, the Americans, the French, we are all the same. We are obliged to be interested as long as the Italians demonstrate their unwillingness to tackle their own problem. But, Sicily is a sewer of morality, and our interest achieves nothing. Do I disappoint you?"

There were two women in the church, in black, kneeling, several rows of seats ahead of him.

He had taken a place near the back of the church on Piazza Ucciardone, and at the far end of the seats from the aisle.

He kneeled. He could hear the traffic outside and he could hear the beat of the wind against the upper windows of the church. In his mind, in silence, his knees cold on the floor tiles, he prayed for the soul of the man who had hanged himself . . .

It was what he had chosen. It was the fifteenth year since he had chosen to come with his wife and children to Palermo, brought by ambition and the belief of career advancement. It was the fourth year since he had chosen to stay in Palermo, in the comfort of his obsession, after his wife had left with the children. Huddled on his knees, he prayed for the spirit of a wretch. To come to church, to pray, he must have an armed guard at the door to the priest's room, he must have a *maresciallo* sitting with a machine gun three rows behind him, he must have a young guard with a sullen and chastised face standing at the door of the church with a pistol in his hand, he must have two armed guards on the outer steps of the church. There was no more ambition. The ambition was dried out, a cloth left on the line in the sun.

The ambition had been overwhelmed by the assassination of his character, by the drip of the poison, by the scheming stabs at his back in the Palazzo di Giustizia. He was left only with the obsession of duty . . . for what? The obsession hanged a man by the throat until his windpipe was crushed . . . for what? The obsession brought the risk of death, high probability, to five wonderful men who were his *ragazzi* . . . for what? The obsession brought him closer, each day, to the flower-covered coffin that would be filled with what they could find of his body . . . for what?

The priest watched him. The priest was often in the prison across the piazza. The priest knew him. The priest did not come to him and offer comfort.

If he sent the message, if he cut the obsession from his mind, then on offer would be a bank account abroad and a position of respect in Udine and the return to his family and the last years of his life lived in safety. To send the message would be so easy. Within a few hours a message would reach the small man, the elderly man, whose photograph had been aged twenty years by a computer . . .

He pushed himself up from his knees. He faced the altar and he made the sign of the cross. He turned. The magistrate, Rocco Tardelli, saw the face of the youngest of the *ragazzi*. To reject the obsession would be to betray Pasquale who had come with his wife's flowers and who had crashed the chase car and who had forgotten a magazine for his machine gun, to betray all of them who rode with him, gave their lives to him. Each day the weight, the burden, he thought, was heavier. Back to his office where the obsession ruled him, back to the files and the computer screen, back to the aged photograph.

He laughed out loud.

His laughter cracked the quiet of the church, and the women who prayed turned and glowered at the source of the noise, and the priest by the altar scowled hostility at him. He laughed because he remembered the long-haired American who had introduced into Palermo "an agent of small importance." There was a manic peal to his laughter. If "an agent of small importance" should lead to Ruggerio, succeed where his obsession failed . . . He bowed his head.

"It is a difficult life, *maresciallo,* for us all. I apologize for my unseemly behavior."

They closed around him as he walked out of the church and hurried him the few paces to his armor-plated car.

". . . It's Bill Hammond . . . Yes, Rome . . . Not too bad. Hey, Lou, when did you get to Personnel? That's a good number, yes? . . . Lou, this is not official, I'm looking for guidance. No names, OK? . . . Something we're doing down here, I can't talk detail, it might, might, get unstuck. One of my people, he's put a heck of a time into it. If it gets unstuck I'd want some candy for him. What you got going, foreign placement? . . . What sort of guy? . . . No, not a high-flier, not like you, Lou. He's a field man, not a computer guy, one of those people that scratch in the dirt. The sort who's going nowhere but that we wouldn't want to lose, you with me? If it gets unstuck I wouldn't want a bear with a thorn in its ass round my patch, and I'd want to see him right . . . Lagos? Is that all you got, Lagos in Nigeria? . . . Yes, we could dress Lagos up. Yes, I could make it sound like San Diego. Be kind to me, Lou, don't fill the Lagos slot till you've heard back from me. It's just that too many people have gotten involved, and they're sort of squeamish people . . . Yes, we could have lunch when I'm next over, that would be good . . ."

It was dusk when Harry Compton drove down the lane. He saw the light, bright in the porch of the bungalow, but it was not his intention to visit David and Flora Parsons. He stopped halfway down the hill at the outer gate to the farm-yard. They had nothing they would willingly offer him about their daughter that he did not already know. The obvious way was rarely the best way. When a child was missing it was from the neighbors that detectives learned whether the disappearance was "domestic" or a genuine abduction. When a company had gone crooked it was the competitors who most often dished the serious filth.

He ignored the dog snapping at the back of his trouser legs.

He rapped on the back door of the farmhouse.

Daniel Bent, aged sixty-nine, farmer . . . "What's she done? If you've come from London there's something she's done. Don't expect you to tell me. You want to know what I think of her? Write this down. She's a stuck-up little bitch. When she came here with her parents, they're all right but just feeble, you could see from the first day that she didn't think we were good enough. Doesn't say anything, of course not, but it's in her feckin' manner. She's superior. Look at her, butter wouldn't melt in her, but under the skin she's a right little superior madam, and hard as feckin' nails. That's not what you expected to hear, is it?"

He went on down the lane.

He rang the bell of a pretty cottage where the honey-suckle rambler was greening.

Fanny Carthew, aged eighty-one, artist . . . "I don't like to speak ill of people, particularly young people, but it would be difficult for me to speak well of her. You'll think I'm rather old-fashioned. You sometimes find the unpleasant trait of pushiness in that class of girl. You see, she's manipulative. She looks for self-advancement through people she can manipulate. It's not my business as to what trouble she's in, why a policeman has come all the way from London, but I doubt you'd want lies from me . . . She seeks to control people. If she perceives someone to be useful to her, then she is their friend, if she decides they are no longer useful to her then they are ignored. Quite a few of us offered a little hand of friendship when she came four years ago, but we've now been outgrown, we don't matter. 'Determined' would be the nice description, but I'd prefer to call her ruthless. Well, I've said it. Two years ago my daughter came down with her boy, Gavin, a very quiet boy and academic. The Parsons girl took him onto the cliffs and then she persuaded him to climb down, sort of taunted him. Well, it was all right for her, she knows the place, but my daughter lives in Hampstead, very few cliffs. He managed to get back up the cliffs, but he was quite traumatized, quite affected. Normally he wouldn't have done anything so idiotic, but she'd taunted him. What I mean, there's a rather soft exterior but underneath there is something quite distastefully tough."

He knocked.

The shouted response told him the door was not locked, he should come on inside.

Zachary Jones, aged fifty-three, disabled . . . "Can't stand her. She'll look at you, all sweetness, but the eyes are the giveaway, she's reckoning your importance to her. If you don't measure up, then you're ditched. I thought she might be company for me. I'm not much, but I've good stories to tell, I can get a giggle out of people. She used to come here, drink a beer and smoke a fag, and her pompous goddamn father would have burst blood vessels if he'd known—Even used my toothpaste to clean her breath. Hasn't the time of day for me now. So she's in trouble or you wouldn't be here. Bloody good. No tears from me. I'll not deny it, she's a pretty little face—what she's short of is a pretty little mind. It's like she's trying to capture people all the time, capture and milk them and when they're dry she walks away. I'd not trust her as far as I could throw her."

The light from the porch of the bungalow shone across half the lane.

There was a fresh spit in the air, and the sea crashed in the dusk on the shingle. He went in shadow past the creaking VACANCIES sign.

Daphne Farson (Mrs.), aged forty-seven, bed-and-breakfast . . . "You stay out in the kitchen, Bert, this is none of your business . . . My Bert thinks the sun shines out of Miss Parsons's bum, he'll hear nothing against her, but he's stupid. I thought I liked her once. I gave her work the first summer she was here, helping with the beds and cleaning up in the season. It was good pocket money for a schoolgirl. Doesn't speak to me now, like I'm beneath her, because she's been to college and had an education. I haven't an education, but I know kids. She went to college but she didn't have any friends, no one ever came to see her in the holidays. My nephew's been to college, Bert's brother's boy, his home's like a damn dormitory in the holidays. She can't make friends because she's so bloody, excuse the French, superior. Tell you what I think, I think she sets herself targets, and if you can't help her reach the targets, then you don't exist. She's a very hard young woman. If you weren't strong with her, then she'd destroy you . . . Bert, put the kettle on, and there's cake in the tin."

He saw a clergyman and an odd-job gardener and a crab fisherman and the district nurse and a retired librarian.

He built a picture of Charlotte Eunice Parsons.

He had not heard a good word said of her. Some had hacked her with a meat cleaver and some had stabbed her with a stiletto.

He sat in his car halfway up the lane. With his pencil torch he leafed through the pages of his notebook. Harry Compton was not a psychologist, nor was he an expert in the science of personality, but he thought he knew her better for what he had been told. He wrote in his notebook, and she was in his mind.

> CONCLUSION: A very strong-willed and
> focused young woman. DEA most fortunate to
> have unearthed her. The danger, she will push
> to the end, she will hazard herself to reach her
> target (whatever that may be). She will not
> have the necessary background to assess fully
> the hazard of a covert operation(?) in Sicily.
> Because of her quite obvious determination to
> succeed, I fear for her safety.

14

SHE RANG THE BELL.

She hadn't telephoned ahead, hadn't called to be
certain he would be in his apartment. Charley kept her
finger on the button. She could hear the shrill baying of
the bell behind the door. There was no response, no
shout from Benny that he was coming, no slither of
footsteps from behind the door. She had her finger a
long time on the bell and she swore under her breath.

When the door beside Benny's scraped open, bolts
drawn back and locks turned, she took her finger from
the bell button. The couple coming through the door
beside Benny's were elderly and dressed for Sunday. The
man wore a suit and the woman wore black with a dark
gray headscarf over her hair. They eyed her, they seemed
to indicate to her that it was not appropriate to make so
great a noise on a Sunday morning, then looked away. It
was Palermo. They did not ask if they could be of help,
they did not tell her if they knew where Benny was. It
was Palermo, and they minded their own affairs, did not
involve themselves. The man in his suit performed the
ritual of locking the door behind him, two keys. Not
easy to gauge their wealth. His suit was poor and his
watch looked ordinary and his shirt was well washed.
Her dress and coat were tired and the scarf on her hair
was frayed at the hems and her brooch was very simple.
It was Palermo, they made a fortress of their home,

guarded their possessions, however meager, and they hurried to commune with their God and carried their Bibles and their prayer books. Her finger was off the bell's button, the couple were going slow and unsure, down the formal staircase, and again Charley cursed. She cursed Benny for not being there when she came for him. She had not considered that he might not be there, and waiting.

A Sunday morning . . . Peppino going with Angela and the children to Mass, not to the church nearest the villa in Mondello, but to their regular church beside the Giardino Inglese. She had begged a lift, she had said that she would wander in Palermo and made a joke that Sunday morning was the safest morning to be alone on the streets. She had left them, as they had mingled outside their church with the *professionistici* and the wives in their finery and the children in their smart best. Now she cursed Benny Rizzo because he was not in his apartment, not available to her. Perhaps he had gone to his mother, perhaps he had gone to deliver a photocopier, perhaps he had gone to a talk-shop meeting. She felt raw annoyance, and she stamped her way down the staircase and out into the sunshine. She could not see him, and she wondered if he was there, and if Axel Moen watched her.

Sunday morning . . . She walked aimlessly. She was on the pavement of the Via del Libertà. The heat was rising. The sun was bright. The street was taped off as the long-distance runners prepared for their race. They were slapping their bodies, or jogging nervously at the thought of pain, and some were checking that they had brought the silver foil to wrap around themselves after the exhaustion and dehydration of the run. The pavements were her own. A few responded to the tolling church bells and hurried past her. She went by shuttered restaurants and darkened shops, past the strident monuments of cavalier men posturing on rampant horses, past the deserted market of the Borgo Vecchio with the empty, skeletal frames of the stalls. She had no map with her, she did not know where she was going. She passed the shadowed alleyways that led into an old quarter, and the modern blocks of the new buildings on the harbor front, and she saw the towering hulks of the waiting car ferries. She was so alone. She had not considered that Benny would not be there, waiting, available. She stared at the prison, the ochre walls in which weeds grew, the guards with the rifles on the walkway above the wall, at the high, small windows from which underpants and socks hung to dry, at the patroling military truck in which the soldiers carried rifles, where Peppino would be taken and where Angela would go with small Mario and Francesca and the baby at visiting times. She had needed him, needed Benny, and she despised him.

Sunday morning . . . Charley walked without purpose. She went by cats that glowered at her then ripped at the rubbish bags, past packs of dogs that slunk from her. She lingered outside the Teatro Massimo where the walls were boarded against the vandals and the weather, where pigeon dirt and vehicle fumes had stained the walls in equal measure. She stood under the trees beside the derelict building and she looked at the horses that were harnessed to the *carrozzi,* and she thought of the picket line of decent people at Brightlingsea and of how they would have responded to the dismal horses hooked to the empty tourist carriages. There was a lovely roan-and-white horse with its head down in passive acceptance. She was at the Quattro Canti. It was where Benny should have brought her. Shit, it wasn't much. Shit, all the fuss in the guidebook. Shit, the statues were grimed, fume-polluted, crumbling. So alone, so miserable, so lost . . . She swore again because he was not with her, was not available.

She was on Via Mariano Stabile. The church was a red-stone building. She heard the singing of the hymn, familiar. She did not go to church at home, nor did her father and nor did her mother. The red of the church was so out of place in the gray and ochre of Palermo. She did not go to church at home because there she was never alone and miserable and lost. She crossed the street to the church. She stood outside the opened iron gates. It was so bloody unfair that she was alone and miserable and lost.

The words were faint, feeble. A reedy chorus.

Then sings my soul, my savior come to me,
How great Thou art, how great Thou art.

She was drawn to the door. She walked into the gray light of the church, broken only where the sun was against the many-colored glass of the window. The door slammed shut behind her and faces turned to notice her, then looked away. She stood at the back. She saw the plaques remembering the long-dead. The organ rose in a crescendo, not matched by the scattered voices.

Then I shall bow in humble adoration, and then
*   proclaim,*
My God, how great Thou art . . .
Then sings my soul, my savior come to me,
How great Thou art, how great Thou art.

It was the end of the service. A woman came and

spoke to her, in piping English. Was she new to Palermo? Had she mistaken the time of Sunday worship? She was most welcome whether or not she could sing, but could she sing? Would she like coffee? Charley hoped so much to be wanted, loved, and she said she would like coffee. She went with other ladies, dressed as they would be for church in Exeter or Plymouth or Kingsbridge, up into the living room of the clergyman's apartment beside the church. She wanted so much to please and to be welcomed . . . She was told that they were the remnants of a great English society that had been based in Palermo, they were the nannies who had married Sicilians and stayed, they were the artists who had fallen for the light over the mountains and on the sea and stayed, they had come to teach the English language and stayed . . . She was a toy plaything, exciting because she was new. She fled. They wanted her name and her telephone number and her address. She could not lie to them. They wanted to know whether she would sing with the choir, whether she would come to the barn-dance evening, whether she could help with the flowers. If she stayed she would lie. She left them bewildered, confused, she fled out into the bright sun of the street.

Alone, miserable, lost, she went to the bus stop on the Via del Libertà that would take her back to the villa at Mondello, and she cursed Benny for not being available.

In the car, beside her husband, Angela had withdrawn into the web of her mind.

She wore a fine dress of respectful green, chosen by her husband, and a coat of fox pelts, chosen by her husband. She wore discreet jewelry at her throat and round her wrists and on her fingers, chosen by her husband. Her husband liked the coat of fox pelts and she wore it as if it were a badge of submission. The air conditioner blew cool air over her. Her face was hidden from him by the dark glasses, chosen by her husband, that protected her eyes from the sun's glare that glittered up from the road. The children were in the back of the car, and the baby was corraled in the special seat and they were quiet, subdued, as if they caught her mood. In the web of her mind were cascading thoughts . . .

She loathed Sicily. After Mass they had been to an apartment along the Via della Libertà, near their own apartment in the Giardino Inglese, and they had drunk aperitifs of Cinzano and nibbled at canapés, and her husband had murmured that their host was useful as a contact in business, and deference was shown her by the other wives . . . She had magnificence around her, status, ever more lavish presents brought from abroad . . . She loathed the half-truths of the people and the double-talk of their coded whispers. She was a prisoner . . . She had asked, quietly, if they could go to their own apartment in the Giuardino Inglese, just to visit, not important, to collect clothes and more toys, and her husband had dismissed the suggestion. She had wondered if his woman was there . . . She could not leave him. Her upbringing, her schooling, her rearing all served to prevent her leaving her husband. Her upbringing was the influence of her father, Catholic conservative and working in the diplomatic section of the Vatican. Her schooling was the work of nuns. Her rearing was the effort of her mother to whom divorce was unthinkable and separation was disaster and marriage was for the extent of life. No court in Sicily would give her custody of the children if she left . . . If her husband recognized her unhappiness, driving the fast route to Mondello, if he cared for her unhappiness, he gave no sign to her. Only once had the mask cracked on his face, the morning he had been called down to the EUR to meet with the magistrate and the investigators of the *Servizio Centrale Operativo*, only that one morning had the bastard man crumpled—and he had come back, and he had laughed off the ignorance of the magistrate, and the matter was never talked of again. She did not know the detail of his involvement, she was the Sicilian wife kept quiet and beautiful under the weight of presents. She believed now that her husband's involvement was total, and she could not leave. The wife of Leoluca Bagarella had tried to leave, and it was said that she was dead, it was said in the *Giornale di Sicilia* that her way out was to have taken her life . . . He stroked her hand, a small and unimportant gesture to him, as if he patted the paw of a prized pedigree dog, and he smiled in his confidence . . . Angela detested her husband. If it were not for the brother, the stumbling fat little snail of a man, then her husband would be nothing more than another criminal on the streets of the island she loathed. It made her sick, physically sick, when the rough hands of the brother touched the smooth skin of her *piccolo* Mario, when he slipped through a back door early in the morning or late in the night and touched her son and played on the floor with her son . . .

Angela smiled at her husband, and he could not see her eyes.

The tail was on 'Vanni Crespo.

Before, the tail had been successful only sporadically, but Carmine had directed more men, more *picciotti*, to the tail.

The tail could now report each day on the pattern of the life of 'Vanni Crespo. They knew the clothes he would wear, casual or formal or the builder's overalls. They knew the cars he would use, the Alfetta, the Fiat 127, the builder's van. By trial, by error, Carmine had dictated what resources were necessary to cover the movements of 'Vanni Crespo. Each end of the main road leading from the *carabinieri* barracks at Monreale was watched that Sunday morning by a car and by two youths on motorcycles.

The previous evening, it had been reported to Carmine, 'Vanni Crespo had driven the builder's van to meet with a woman in a lay-by on the road between Trapani and Erice, and the previous afternoon he had used the Fiat 127 and called on the home of a colleague living in Altofonte, and the previous morning he had been in the Alfetta to the barracks at Bagheria.

Carmine had learned the patience of Mario Ruggerio. Each time he met with the men who drove the cars and the *picciotti* with the motorcycles, he repeated the description—weight near to 80 kilos, height near to 185 centimeters, fair skin, gold hair—of the American man taken to see the magistrate, Tardelli.

Two cars, three motorcycles, changing position as they went, followed the Fiat 127 from the barracks at Monreale down the fast road, Route 186, toward Palermo.

"I said to him, 'It is a sad game to play when there is no trust,' I said that to him."

"He told you that it was not personal."

"I suggested to him that he had put 'an agent of small importance' close to Mario Ruggerio."

"Which he did not care to confirm."

"I remarked to him that I would not wish it to lie on my conscience, the danger to that agent, unless the life of the agent was held to be of no importance."

"He did not debate semantics with you," 'Vanni said. "May I tell you, *Dottore,* what he asked me when we came out of your place in the Palazzo? He asked why you pissed on him. I said you were anxious that you might not have a free hole in your diary for his funeral and for his agent's funeral. They're earnest people, the Americans, he found it difficult to register the humor of what I said."

" 'Vanni, please, I need help."

They were alone in the sunless room of the apartment. Out in the kitchen a radio played, and there were the distant voices of his *ragazzi.* He had apologized sincerely for interfering with the Sunday plans of the *carabiniere* officer, but that was the day in the week when he conducted his business within the confinement of the office in his apartment. He did not go to Mass on Sundays, did not take the bread and the wine of Communion, did not think it right to go to a church with his guards and their guns. He would go to church only for funerals and for occasional moments of stressed reflection when he could judge that a church would be emptied, but not on Sunday mornings. His wife would be in church for the Mass in Udine with his children, and he could tell himself that he did not care what man now stood and sat and kneeled beside his wife.

"How may I help, *Dottore?*"

"I grasp at straws. Mario Ruggerio has taken, with blood, the supreme position."

"I read the digests from Intelligence."

"Each new man, when he takes the supreme position, must demonstrate to the families that he has strength."

"I know the history."

"To demonstrate that strength he must attack the state, show that he has no fear of the state. It is now, 'Vanni, a time of extreme danger." The *carabiniere* officer, without asking permission, had lit a cigarette, and the smoke from the cigarette watered his eyes. "It is possible that I am the target, possible, that will demonstrate the strength, but there are many others." The *carabiniere* officer was shifting in his seat, awkward, dragging at his cigarette. "I take you into areas of confidence, 'Vanni, as I hope you will take me into your confidence. This morning I go to the chief prosecutor, by whom I will be criticized and taunted, with great politeness, concerning my efforts to capture Mario Ruggerio. I had a wretch who wished for the status of *pentito*. On the limited information he provided I was given meager resources for a surveillance of the Capo district, a failure. I urged the wretch to give me more information, played on the psychology of his fear, and he hanged himself, a failure. I have spoken in the last hours with the DIA and with the *squadra mobile* and they have nothing for me, more failure. All around me is the murmur of sneering laughter."

"What do you want of me?"

"You run an agent of small importance, you collaborate with the American, you thought last week that the agent was close. We had champagne iced, and we waited . . . It was a blow to my stomach. Please, give me hope, more than a floating straw, 'Vanni, share with me the detail of your agent."

"You embarrass me, *Dottore,* but the gift is not mine to give."

The *carabiniere* officer jackknifed to his feet. The magistrate saw the turmoil that he had made, and the reached for the source of the pain in his back. He found the hardness of the knife's handle, and the wetness. When his knees gave, when he could no longer see the swarthy and heavy-set youth, when the telephone swung beyond his reach, when the screaming burst from grotesquely blurred mouths around him, Giancarlo realized, puzzled, that he could no longer remember the questions that control had asked of him.

The pain was a spasm through his body.

A square had been made.

The bar was at the center of the square. The north of the square was the Via Giacomo Cusmano, the south was the Via Principe di Villafranca, the west was the Via Dante, and the east was the gardens of the Villa Trabia.

A hundred men with guns, with flak vests, quartered the square. They were from the DIA, and there were two sections of the ROS, and there was the standby team of the *Guardia di Finanze*, and there were men from the *squadra mobile*. The cordon around the square was given to the military, Jeeps at street corners, soldiers with NATO rifles. They did not know what the man, Giancarlo's target, looked like, they did not know how he was dressed, they did not know in which direction he had gone, they did not know whether he walked or whether he went by car.

The bar was emptied but for the owner and the matriarch who guarded her cash till.

The body was on the floor. In the back of the body was a short-bladed, double-edged knife. The owner of the bar, facing a wall, his wrists handcuffed in the small of his back, had seen nothing. Perhaps the customers had seen something? The matriarch had seen nothing. The customers were all strangers to her and she knew none of them.

A car brought the wife of Giancarlo to the bar, and a young priest had run from the church on Via Terrasanta. The photographers from the newspapers and the cameramen from the RAI crowded the pavement.

The *maresciallo* elbowed a way through for the magistrate and Pasquale bullocked him into the bar, into the crush that circled the body. There were some who had come from family gatherings and wore their suits, some had come from the tennis courts, some from their seats in the soccer stadium, some from their sleep. Beside their shoes and sneakers and sandals was the body and the blood. The magistrate saw the face, bleak, of 'Vanni Crespo, and pushed toward him.

"It was shit luck," 'Vanni Crespo said. "We were so close . . ."

The tail had watched the car of 'Vanni Crespo, the *carabiniere* Alfetta car, from the barracks at Monreale to the bar on Via Sammartino. The tail was locked on 'Vanni Crespo.

"He brought me lemons, 'Vanni. I had fish for my meal on Friday. They are not supposed to do my shopping, my boys, but they prefer to do it than to take me to the market, so they break the rule, they bought fresh mullet for me. He had brought me lemons and made a joke of it. I had one of his lemons with my mullet. He was the best of men."

"It was shit luck," 'Vanni growled. "He was on the bus with his wife. He saw Ruggerio. He got off the bus. He ran through the traffic. That's the decision. You wait and you lose the target. You run and you alert the target. You've ten seconds, five seconds, to make the decision, and you live by it and you die by it."

"The lemon was most sharp in the taste."

"He would have shown out when he ran. Ruggerio would have had a back marker. He had to go to the bar for communication. The back marker would have followed him. You need the luck and all you get is the shit."

"There are six more of his lemons in my kitchen . . . Do you believe in luck, 'Vanni?"

He saw the tears well at the eyes of the magistrate. He took out his handkerchief. He did not care who saw him. In the crowd in the bar, he wiped the running tears from the magistrate's face. "I believe in nothing."

"Do you believe your agent of small importance will be lucky?"

He remembered her, as he had seen her, the last look back from the side of the road before he had dropped down into the car. The last look, across the pavement, and between the trees, and across the sand, and she had stood against the brightness of the sea, and the sun had caught the white of her body skin as her towel had slipped. In the bar, with the corpse, with the soft whimpering of the widow, with the crowd, with the smell of cigarettes and cold coffee, he remembered her.

"I am sorry, *Dottore,* I cannot share with you because it is not my gift."

He drove a way through the crowd in the bar, pushed through the crowd on the pavement and the street. A good man had had ten seconds, five seconds, to make a decision and the result of the decision was a mistake, and the result of a mistake was to lie dead on the dirty floor of a bar that was lit by flashlights. He went to his car, walked leaden in the dusk light.

• • •

The tail followed the Alfetta driven by 'Vanni Crespo. The tail was delayed by the military cordon around the square of streets after the Alfetta had been waved through, but it was of no consequence. The tail was linked by radio to a second car and to motorcyclists who waited outside the cordon. As if a chain held the tail to the Alfetta car . . .

When he had heard the explosion of the car horns, and then heard the insults shouted, Mario Ruggerio had paused in front of a shop window. He had appeared to study the contents of the shop window. An old practice, one that his father would have known, was to use a shop window as a mirror. He had seen a man come at desperate speed through the traffic lanes, and then reach the pavement and stop. The man, stopped, had stared up the street toward him. If the man had had a radio he would already have used it, if the man had had a mobile telephone he would not have run through the traffic lanes, if the man had carried a firearm he would not have stopped. In the reflections of the window he had seen the *picciotto*, a good boy, behind the man. He had known he was recognized and he had known the man panicked. He had realized it was a chance recognition and not a part of a comprehensive surveillance. He had made a small gesture, a single movement of his index finger, a cutting motion. He had walked away. He had turned the corner . . .

It was two hours later. Mario Ruggerio sat in the darkened room on the first floor in the Capo district. His feet ached, his lungs heaved, the ashtray was filled with the stubbed ends of his cigarillos. The two *picciotti* who had been ahead of him on the Via Sammartino had made a brutal pace for him, up to the Piazza Lolli, one pocketing the cap he had been wearing, across the Via Vito la Mancia, one taking his jacket and folding it on his arm so that the material could not be seen, past the Mercato delle Pulci, hurrying him along as if he were an old uncle out with two impatient nephews. He had slipped away from them behind the *duomo*. Even when he gasped for breath, when exhaustion bled him and he swayed on his feet, he would not have considered allowing the *picciotti* to take him to his safe house. The sweat ran on his face and on his back and on his stomach. He smoked. He held the photograph of the child he loved.

Charley sat on the patio.

The sun had gone down and only a feeble layer of light fell on the seascape ahead of her. The family had gone down to the town. She had lost the loneliness that had hurt her in Palermo. She felt, sitting in the comfortable chair on the patio, a supreme confidence. The villa was her place. The family would be walking on the esplanade, under the trees, patroling like the caged bears she had seen in zoos, where they would be seen . . . It was the time of waiting. She was in control, she felt her power. The power was the watch on her wrist. She sat with her legs apart, and the cool of the evening air made feather strokes on her thighs. She was at the center of the world of Axel Moen and the people who directed Axel Moen. She had power over Giuseppe Ruggerio and over the brother. She watched the last of the sunlight flee the smooth surface of the sea. Because of her control and her power it would be her story that would be told, the story of Codename Helen.

In the gray light, on the patio, an arrogance tripped in Charley's mind.

•　　•　　•

The tail was locked on 'Vanni Crespo. Three bars in Monreale. The tail watched him drink alone in a bar near the *duomo,* in a second bar near the empty market stands, in a third bar high in the old town. The tail watched and followed where 'Vanni Crespo led.

Through the window of the *pizzeria* he saw 'Vanni. 'Vanni was going slowly, confused. He was lit by a street lamp and his face was flushed, and his hair hung on his forehead in careless strands, and he lurched to a stop beside the window and was struggling to find the cigarette packet in his pocket. Axel turned away. There was nowhere in the *pizzeria* for him to hide. He turned away and hoped that his face was not seen, but he heard the whip of the door opening and then the slam of it shutting and he heard the shuffle of the feet and then the scrape of the chair opposite him.

'Vanni sat in front of Axel, and he swayed on the chair before his elbows thudded down on the table.

"I find the American hero . . ."

"You pissed up or something?"

"I find the American hero who comes to Sicily to achieve what we cannot."

"You're drunk."

"We Italians are pathetic, we cannot wipe our own arses, but the American hero comes to do it for us."

"Go fuck yourself."

"You know what happened today, because we had shit luck, what happened . . . ?"

"We don't break procedure," Axel hissed across the table.

Two young men, carrying their crash helmets, were at the counter of the *pizzeria* and asking for the list of sauces.

The hand in which Axel held his fork was gripped in 'Vanni's fists. "We had surveillance people in the Capo, that's a shit place, to target the bastard. The surveillance was called off, nothing seen . . . One of the team, on a bus, sees the bastard. Off duty, no communications. We are pathetic Italians, we do not have the money to give out, sweets and chocolates, mobile telephones. Not carrying his personal radio, off duty, no sidearm. He tries to use the telephone in a bar. The bastard would have had a guy behind him, back marker. The message was incomplete, that's the shit luck. No profile and no description, no clothes, before he was stabbed to death. The bastard's gone. It's cold."

At the bar the boys with the crash helmets studied the list of pizza sauces.

"Get the hell out of here."

"He was in our hand. We snatched. We lost him. Isn't that shit luck?"

"Go and sleep with your woman."

"I drink, I don't weep. The man was dead on the floor with the crap and the cigarettes and the spit and his blood. Tardelli came down, he wept, he doesn't drink. He asked me—"

"Get some water down you, some aspirin, get to your bed."

"He's isolated, he's got the stink of failure. He has nothing, nothing to hope for. He begged . . ."

The boys with the crash helmets had seen nothing on the list of sauces that they wanted. They pushed their way out of the door, into the street.

"What did he beg?"

"Offer him something to hold to. I said it was not my gift to give. His mind is blocked, too much work, too tired, he cannot see the obvious, not followed the line of the family, as we have. He wanted me to share with him the detail of your agent."

"Bullshit."

"Your agent of small importance. He wanted the crumbs off your table. 'All I want is someone to hold my arm and walk with me.' But that's the usual sort of shit talk in Palermo when a man is isolated, that's not the talk to impress an American hero."

"I don't share."

"With Italians? Of course not. I tell you, Axel, what I saw. I saw a body on the floor, I saw the blood, I saw the fucking crowd of people. I saw her, I saw Codename Helen, I saw her body and her blood. I drink, I don't weep. Enjoy your meal."

The fists released Axel's hand that held the fork. The table rocked as 'Vanni levered himself to his feet. Axel watched him go . . . He did not see her on the floor of the bar, but she was clear in his mind and she was hanging from the nails on the back of the door of the hut at the *estancia* airstrip . . . He pushed the plate away from him. He lit a cigarette and he dropped the match on the plate, into the pizza sauce.

The tail learned the name of the woman who owned the house, and late into the night the tail watched the light burn in the upper room.

"What are my options, Ray? What do I chew on?"

The voice boomed back, metallic, from the speaker. Dwight Smythe leaned over the Country Chief's desk and twisted the volume dial. The Country Chief was scribbling headlines.

"Could you wait out, Herb? Could you let me have a minute?"

"Have two—I fancy it's better we get this right, now."

It had been a bad bloody Monday for Ray. He had been called, two hours' notice, to New Scotland Yard for late-morning coffee with biscuits and a hard-going session. He had sat with Dwight, he had been faced by the commander (SO6) and the assistant commissioner (SO) and the detective superintendent who was a cat with cream, and there'd been a young guy there who'd not spoken. He'd had a heavy time and they'd done their work on Mario Ruggerio (worse than the worst) and they'd a profile on Charlotte Parsons (Codename Helen). He'd broken, he'd said he needed to talk to Headquarters, and back at the embassy he'd sat on his hands waiting for Herb to show up in his office from the beltway drag into Washington. It had to be Herb he spoke to, because it was Herb who had authorized the operation.

"Got it together . . . I'm not happy, Herb. I feel I'm pushing in over Bill's space."

"Forget Bill, he'll do as he's damn well told. I get the feeling this isn't a time for standing on ceremony. Hell, I've fourteen situations going in Colombia, I've eight in Peru. I've situations running in Bangkok, Moscow, Jamaica. I'm not getting an ulcer for one situation in Sicily. I want the options."

Again Ray paused. What they hated, the big men in Washington who'd made it to the floor with the pile carpets and the drinks cabinets and access to God, was getting bounced for a decision early on a Monday morning. It was a time when his own career could go down the drain, and his hopes of ever getting his feet on that carpet and his hands on the cabinet keys, but he reckoned there wasn't room for evasion. He plunged.

"At high-grade level, the British have *Angst*. They say, and I quote, 'It is intolerable that a young woman should have been pressurized by the DEA, entrapped, and then persuaded to travel to Sicily as the central part of an American-sponsored antimafia operation,' end quote. That's, my opinion, not the core of their hand-wringing. What's right up their nose, quote, 'All DEA activities inside the UK are governed by procedures of liaison and we were not informed, prior to your invei-gling Miss Parsons, of your intention to recruit her,' end quote. And most important, they have the shits on this one. They see her dead, they see the *paparazzi* crawling over her, they see an almighty inquest on what an untrained innocent was doing there in a role central to an investigation, they see the blame hammering on their door . . ."

"I asked, what are the options?"

"Two, Herb. You can tell them to go jump, tell them they are small guys running small shows and sug-gest they stick to softball in the park."

"We do good business with the Brits. My second option?"

"You can withdraw your sanction, Herb, close it down, you can pull her out. You can wind it up."

"Ray, we've known each other a long time, too goddamn long. I am not interested in the sensitivities of Bill Hammond. The plan isn't Bill's anyway. The plan belongs to that guy Axel Moen, and I do not care whether I massage his ego or whether I kick him. Which side of the fence are you falling? I want it straight."

He glanced up at the loudspeaker on the wall, beside the Green Ice operation photograph. Herb, front row, smiling, was always the bastard who turned up late and took the credit, and hacked off early to avoid the blame. Dwight Smythe, opposite him, made the quick gesture, a finger across the throat. He spoke into the microphone, he felt dirty.

"What I want to say, Herb, I don't give a fuck for the susceptibilities of the British. They'll complain for a week, and after a week they'll be good as gold and looking for a candy handout. Myself, I'd ignore them."

"I hear you. Right, thanks, I'll call Bill Hammond and tell him."

"Sorry, Herb, I'm not through. This kid is on a limb, this kid has no covert training. She's been given the glamor treatment. She should never have been asked to go. I can take newspaper flak, I can handle an inquiry if she ends up dead. But I don't think I'd want that at my door. It's a precious thing, my self-respect. But, of course, Herb, if it goes sour, then it's on your desk that it lands because you authorized it."

He thought he had rolled a hand grenade across a pile carpet and the grenade might just bounce against the imitation antique of a drinks cabinet and it might just come to rest against a desk on a high floor of Headquarters. He winked, grim, at Dwight Smythe.

The voice boomed, "Kill it."

"I think that's a good decision, Herb."

There was rain falling on the garden of the square that the embassy faced onto. The square was a goddamn morgue, and the daffodils were flattened by the rainfall, and the crocus blooms were crushed. Dwight Smythe drove, and held his peace. Ray reflected. He had bled his conscience over the telephone link. Maybe he was too old and too tired, too fucked-up, for the job. Maybe he had gone too soft for the work. If the work mattered, sure as Christ it mattered, then maybe it was worth haul-

ing any kid, any innocent, off the street, then maybe
pressure was justified, if the work mattered . . . Axel
Moen had been in his office, Axel Moen had treated
Dwight Smythe like he was just the hired hand, Axel
Moen hadn't gone hiding behind conscience, Axel
Moen was a cold bastard, Axel Moen would believe the
work mattered . . . They crossed central London and
Dwight Smythe parked up outside the main doors of
New Scotland Yard and threw the keys in an arc to a
constable . . . Maybe he should feel comfortable because
his back was protected, and Herb's back was safe, and the
men waiting for them upstairs in the building could feel
good because their backs were covered, and maybe he'd
be offered a drink because all the big guys were protected and safe and covered, and in this fucking awful
world that was what mattered. If it had been for the kid,
the innocent, if it had been for protecting and saving and
covering the kid, then he could have felt good, but it
wasn't . . . They came out of the elevator and stamped
along the corridor behind the constable escorting them.
It was a bad bloody Monday.

"I talked with Washington. Washington says we
abort."

The AC (SO) said, "Not next week, not next month.
We'll send our own man."

The commander (SO6) said, "The operation will be
terminated immediately. For verification, you understand."

The detective superintendent said, "We'd like to be
certain there's a degree of urgency. So we know you
haven't welshed."

He was introduced to Harry Compton, who hadn't
spoken, who had the thick file. He said that since it was a
DEA operation into which there was now British input,
gagged on "intrusion," he would send his administrative

officer, Dwight Smythe, to accompany Compton, gagged on "hold his hand."

The AC (SO) said, "Very satisfactory, good cooperation."

The commander (SO6) asked, "Not too early for a drop of the hard stuff, eh, Ray, and you, Mr. Smythe? Ice, water?"

"Are you into this story, Mr. Compton? Scotch, yes, stiff."

"I am."

"You've evaluated Charlotte Parsons, this innocent?"

He had intended to sneer, never could do it well, was a poor hand at sarcasm.

"Yes, I have. Your people chose well. I'd rate her as brilliant. Stubborn, tough. That's why I fear for her safety. What I've heard and learned, she is the type who will cling in there. And, sir, when you have a very strong personality placed in such position as she is, I would also fear for the safety of those around her."

"Would you now? A hell of a shame she's coming home, don't you think, gentlemen? A shame we all needed to get our snouts in the trough . . ."

15

AROUND HIM WERE THE SMELLS. He was blindfolded. He could see nothing, not even strips of faint light at the bottom of the cloth over his eyes nor at the top. The cloth had been wound tight round his head at least three times and on top of the cloth was a broad, sticky tape. He did not know how many hours, how many days and nights, he had been there.

The smells cloyed at Benny's nose, they hung in his nostrils. They were the smells of the animals and of his own body. The smells were of the excreta and the urine and the filthy hair coats of animals, and of the shit in his trousers and the piss that was raw-warm on his legs, and the sweat at his armpits and his groin that came from the fear.

His arms had been wrenched behind him when they had dragged him from the vehicle and brought him to the byre. Any movement that he tried to make carried fierce pain because his arms had been looped round a post of coarse wood and his wrists had been lashed tight, and if he tried to move, the sockets of his shoulders seemed about to break. He did not know how many hours he had been there, but he believed that when he next heard men's voices they would have come to kill him. He did not want to hear them come, hear a car reach the barn, hear the voices, because then they would have come to kill him. But, in his fear, Benny strained for the slightest sound. There were the heavy clumsy movements of the animals in the byre, jostling each other, and there was the grunting of their breathing, and there was the heavy chewing as they ate. Sometimes they touched him, great creatures that seemed in the black-ness of his imagination to tower over him, but it was always with gentleness. Sometimes they nuzzled at his face, hot breath, and sometimes they licked the hands that were lashed tight behind the post, slobbering tongues. Because he waited for the car to come, and the voices, he heard every movement of the animals around him. He did not know how many hours it was since the muscles of his stomach had broken and he had messed in his trousers, but the slime was now cold. It was more recently that the piss had burst from his bladder, and his thighs were still wet. It was because of the girl.

The animals heard the car before Benny did. The animals bellowed, great voices booming in the byre. He heard the car. It was because of the girl, and he hated the girl for what she had made him do. The car pulled to a stop and he heard the tires on loose stones. He would, if it had not been for the girl, in the afternoon of tomorrow or yesterday—he had lost track of time—have driven after school to Corleone and collected the photocopier and driven it back to San Giuseppe Jato, and would have known that he was involved and caring and playing a part, but the girl had destroyed him. The girl had made him tell the story of his father, and his father had not car-ried a photocopier back from Corleone to San Giuseppe Jato, his father had fought them, and the girl had made him tell his father's story. He heard a padlock unfastened. It had been the fault of the girl. The hysteria rose in him and he tried to push himself farther back against the post. It was his father who had the blame. He heard the door scrape open. He heard a coughed spit and the smack of a hand on the body of an animal and the sounds of the stampede of the feet of the beasts as if a way was cleared to him. Benny wanted to shout, to plead with them, tell them that it was the fault of the girl, that the blame was with his father. He had no voice.

His hands were pulled back from the post and the pain riveted in his shoulders. He felt at his wrist the sharp nick of a knife blade, then the twine that had bound him to the post was loosened. He was pulled upright. They laughed. Three separate shouts of laughter, growled and shrill and quiet, and he stood and they would have seen the stain on the front of his trousers and the damp weight in the seat of his trousers. He was led, stumbling, over the fodder floor of the byre.

There was sun on his face, on his cheeks, below the blindfold. He heard birdsong. His feet caught on the stones. Without warning, the hair of his head was caught and his skull was pushed down, but his scalp caught against a metal edge. He was forced low into the trunk of a vehicle, and there was the slam of the top closing on him. He was crushed, fetal, the way he had lain as a child in his parents' bed, between his mother and his father. The vehicle bumped away and his body was pierced by what he thought was a jack, but it might have been a heavy wrench-spanner. They were taking him away to kill him. The petrol stank in his nose, and the fumes of the exhaust. They would not hear him when he shouted that it was the fault of the girl, that his father should be blamed. He hated the girl. He rejected his father. He was so frightened. He could go into the drum of acid, he could go into the concrete, he could go into the dark depths of the gully where the crows did not feed and where Placido Rizzotto had been thrown. No one knew where to search for him. He had not told his mother that he was going to Prizzi, nor his friends in Palermo, nor the man who owned the photocopier in San Giuseppe Jato, nor the women who wrote the newsletter in Corleone. The vehicle was on tarmacadam and speeding. He wept, and the tears clogged his eyes beneath the cloth blindfold. On his side, squirming in the trunk of the car, choking on the fumes, he screamed for their mercy, but he could not be heard. He wondered if they all shouted for mercy before they went into the drum of acid or the concrete or the gully, if they all rejected their fathers and their girls. The vehicle stopped sharply, and the piss was running warm on his thighs again.

The air was on his face. There were the sounds of other cars and of a motorcycle speeding past, and a dog barked and radios played.

"Please . . . forgive me . . . please . . ." He heard the croak of his own voice.

He was pulled from the trunk of the vehicle. The piss dribbled hot on his legs. Hands gripped his arms. He was led down a slight slope and his feet were on old cobbles. He could not break free, could not run, he was broken. The arms jerked him back and stopped him. The tape was dragged from the cloth. The cloth was unwound from his face.

ASSASSINO.

The word was in paint on the door. The door was beside a black drainpipe. In front of the door was a plastic bucket of steaming water, and an old brush with stiff bristles floated among the suds of the water. He took the brush from the water and he started to scrub at the word he had written in paint. The dog that had taken the spray can came and sniffed at him and snarled. Children came and shrieked laughter and held their noses because he stank. As if the house behind the door was empty, there was no sound from inside, no radio, no movement. The girl had destroyed him. He scrubbed at the painted word until his fingers ached and his arms ached and his shoulders ached, until he had removed the trace of his protest. The girl had made him tell the story of his father. He scrubbed until the door was clean, as if the word had never been written. He was broken.

He straightened. The last of the water had been used, the bucket was empty. He placed the brush in the bucket and put the bucket on the step of the door. The road was in shadow and deserted. The children had gone, and the dog, and the men who had brought him. On the cobbles behind him was his wallet, pegged down with a stone. There was no trace of the word, as there was no trace of his life. He walked away. His car was where he had left it.

Later he would return to his apartment in Palermo, and before he had stripped his clothes and washed his body he would tear the posters from the walls.

"I should apologize, yes? I should ask you to forgive me?"

Charley held the plastic tub of washed, wet clothes. Angela pegged the clothes methodically to the line. It was inevitable. The only surprise to Charley, it had been so long coming. Angela did not look at her and she spoke in a flattened monotone.

"When I told Peppino that I wanted you here, I thought if you came it would be different. I thought it would be the same as it was in Rome. But this is not Rome, it is Palermo. Palermo is not our home, as was Rome. Do I make a confusion for you? You are not an idiot, Charley, you can recognize that we have changed. Why have we changed? Palermo is the true home of Peppino, Palermo is the place for the peasants, it is the place of the family. I knew nothing, in Rome, of the truth of Peppino, I lived my own life and I was happy, and you came and you were a part of that happiness. Do you look around, Charley, and do you wonder what is now different?"

Charley passed the children's clothes and the pegs. She stayed silent, she could offer no comfort. To offer comfort was to endanger herself.

"We were comfortable in Rome, we had a wonderful

apartment, we had the good life. You saw it and you went away. Four years later you come back—what do you find? We are a new generation of Sicilians, we live like the princes of the Bourbons, the caliphs of the Moors, the nobility of the Normans. An apartment that is a palace, a villa, money so that it ceases to have meaning, jewels, cars from the latest production, always the goddamn presents. Do you ask, Charley, alone in your room, where it comes from? Do you ask how it is that Peppino, a businessman in Rome and ordinary, is now in Sicily a businessman of the superstratum? I would ask, if I were you. But you see, Charley, in Sicily there is the web of the *famiglia*—I have every material possession I could want, perhaps I seem ungrateful, and I have the family of Peppino . . ."

The voice drove on, breaking off when a garment slipped from the line because a peg did not hold it. She lived the lie, she had the watch on her wrist, she had the access and she waited for the opportunity. She kept her silence.

". . . Do you know, Charley, that while you were in the city on Sunday, when Peppino and I and the children were at Mass, that men came into our home, my home, and they swept it with electronic devices to see that we were not listened to, to see that the police had not placed listening devices in our home, my home? Every second Sunday they come. Why? Have you heard Peppino talk here about confidential business? Never. It is not for industrial sabotage, it is for police microphones. Peppino must be certain that conversations concerning the *famiglia* are not listened to. Put it together, Charley, the wealth and the family, the affluence and the family. Where does the wealth come from? From the family . . ."

In front of Charley was the strong wooden gate set in the high fence. Beside Charley was the path from which the gardener had picked up the crushed tip of a cigarillo. She held Peppino's shirts and the damp ran on her arms. She played her part, the innocent home-help, played the lie.

". . . He is a grotesque sham. My Peppino is a creature created by his family. He fulfills a need for the family. What would he be if the need did not exist? A criminal? An extortionist? A killer? Do I upset you, Charley? There are enough of those in the family, they have no need for more. They need the sham that is *rispettabilità*, you understand me, Charley? They have the wealth, the family, but they need the sham of respectability. I am a part of the sham, I am from the pedigree of the Vatican, I give respectability. He is a criminal, my husband and my children's father, as his family. Why I am so alone, Charley, so isolated here, so devastated here, why I need you, Charley. He is controlled by his brother, has the criminal guilt of his brother . . ."

Her voice died, as if in sudden submission. For a moment she looked behind Charley, then at the pegs and washing on the line. Charley thought, like she's trapped, like she has no escape. Charley turned. The gardener pushed the wheelbarrow, on the path round the villa, toward them. She passed Angela the last of Peppino's shirts.

Back in the kitchen the baby was crying. The confessional was finished. Angela, in her kitchen, made the baby's feed, brittle, sharp movements.

Harry Compton and Dwight Smythe met at Heathrow. Each had made his own way west out of the capital, each would have said that there was no requirement to share transport. They met at check-in. If there was mutual respect, they hid it. The detective sergeant of SO6 and the office administrator from the DEA were brusque in their greetings, showed a minimum of courtesy. Harry Compton would have said that he, alone, was perfectly capable of extracting Miss Charlotte Parsons. Dwight Smythe would have said that he, alone, was perfectly capable of aborting Axel Moen. They went through departure, showed no sign of being colleagues who traveled together, they went their separate ways in duty-free and the Briton bought Scotch and the American bought Jack Daniel's. They sat on the bench and read newspapers. Each was an intrusion into the world of the other. They were called for takeoff.

Cautiously, Pasquale knocked at the door. The call came. He carried the mug of hot coffee into the room, and he went to the magistrate's desk and put the coffee mug down beside the computer's screen.

"Thank you, that is very kind. Very considerate of you. How goes it, Pasquale?"

He grimaced. "This morning the *maresciallo* wrote his assessment of me."

"He read it back to you?"

"That is the regulation, I am entitled to know." He had come to work at five and then the bedroom door of the magistrate had been open, and the door of the living room had been closed and the light had shone under that door. He saw the wan tiredness on the face of the magistrate.

"It is good coffee. Thank you. What did he write of you? If you do not wish to . . ."

Pasquale said, "That I was unsuitable, that I was inefficient, that my enthusiasm did not compensate for my mistakes, that I tried to make a friend of you, that I crashed a car, that I was late for duty, that I had forgotten to load a magazine—"

"You are very young, you have a baby, you have a wife, you have a life in front of you. Is it for the best?"

He said simply, "It's what I want to do. But the *maresciallo* says I endanger you and my colleagues by my incompetence."

"Do you wish my intervention?"

"I would be ashamed if, through your intervention, I held my job."

"So each of us, Pasquale, each of us has a bad day."

Such sadness on the magistrate's face, and no attempt to hide it. He bled for the man. He could not ask the magistrate to intervene for him, could not call that card. More than anything in his police career he wished to succeed in this work. To turn his back on the magistrate, Rocco Tardelli, to return to the uniform, would be humiliation. He hesitated. He was a humble policeman, without rank and without seniority, and he wanted to say something that was of comfort to this older and troubled man. He did not know what he could say. He hesitated, then started for the door.

"Pasquale, please—sometimes it needs a younger mind, sometimes it needs the freshness. I have no lead, I have nothing, I have to begin again. Please. Where does Ruggerio go? What must Ruggerio have?"

He blurted, "A dentist?"

"How many dentists in Palermo? How many more dentists in Catania and Agrigento and Messina and Trapani? Has he dentures? Does he need a dentist? I cannot have every dentist on the island watched for the one day a year when he is visited by Mario Ruggerio."

"An optician?"

"I do not know that he wears spectacles and, again, if he does, how many opticians on the island are available to Mario Ruggerio? Help me, with a young mind."

Pasquale furrowed his forehead, considered. "You have investigated the family?"

"I ask for a young mind, not the obvious. The family is the beginning, the middle, the end. We have a camera at his father's house. I should not tell you. And I should not tell you, we have a camera and we have audio close to the house of his wife. His brother, a brute, in prison in Asinara—you do me great damage if you repeat what I say—we have audio in his cell. His other brother is handicapped and we forget him. His sister, we forget her, alcoholism. Please, my boy, give us credit for the obvious."

The apology was on his lips . . . He stared, amazed. A shock wave seemed to Pasquale to flow across the magistrate's face. Tardelli jerked out of his chair, slipped, was on the carpet. Pasquale was rooted. He crawled on his hands and knees to the bedroom wardrobe that was so strange in a living and working area. He dragged it open. Files cascaded on him. Closed files and opened files, files held with tape and files bound with string. Pasquale watched. He groped among the files, scanned the titles of the files, pulled more files from the wardrobe. He whistled an aria as the heap of files grew. Papers scattered and he swept them clear, and they were buried by more files. He found one. He ripped the tape from it. No longer whistling, he now cooed like a dove. The papers fluttered from his hands. He shouted, a noise of exaltation. He held two sheets of paper.

"There was a brother, Pasquale, I interviewed him myself. Four years ago, in Rome, I interviewed him. A banker. So plausible, the link with the criminality of the family cut. I accepted it. No surveillance, no telephone intercept. I buried the memory. The memory was lost under blankets of information, new strata of information, further leaves of information. My mind lost him. I am ashamed . . . It is the place to look, isn't it, Pasquale, where you have forgotten to look, where there is no connection?"

He stood. His face, to Pasquale, was ripped by a sort of manic happiness.

He hugged Pasquale.

At the desk he snatched for the telephone. He dialed. He waited and the aria climbed to a peak.

"Gianni? Tardelli, the 'walking corpse' of Palermo. Gianni, four years ago, in EUR, I met with Giuseppe Ruggerio. Yes, no connection. What of him now? Gianni, call me."

There were two and a quarter hours between the arrival of the London flight and the departure of the Palermo flight. There was no ceremony. They sat in Bill Hammond's car, Dwight Smythe in the front with the Country Chief and Harry Compton in the back. Bill Hammond had brought coffee from a kiosk.

"It's a sad damned day . . ."

"What we're saying in London, Mr. Hammond, it should never have gone this far," Harry Compton said, sparring. "We are also saying that if there had been correct consultation at the start, then there would never have been this difficulty. I don't think anyone's enjoying it."

"As you eloquently put it, Bill, it is a 'sad damned day' because the plan was irresponsible from the kickoff," Dwight Smythe said, sullen. "We are left with dog shit on our shoes."

It was a new world for Harry Compton. He had never before been overseas for SO6. All pretty structured back in London. A good pattern of seniority to lean against back in London. He sat in the car and held the coffee, had a single sip and thought it gritty. Perhaps, he had thought, when the two of them were together on the flight, beside each other, they could defrost the chill of the inter-organization spat, and they hadn't. They'd worn their badges, different armies, in cold hostility. Perhaps, he had thought, they'd be given the good treatment when they landed at Rome, and given a good meal and a good briefing and a dose of civilization, and he was uncomfortable in a car out on the edge of a bloody parking area.

"Did I hear you right? Dog shit?"

"That's what I said," Dwight Smythe intoned.

"And you, what did you call it? A 'difficulty'?"

"That's our opinion," Harry Compton said.

"I wasn't happy, I had cold feet. Hear me through—the plan was brilliant. It's the sort of plan that comes along off the rainbow, and it just stands a chance. It stands a chance because Axel Moen is one hell of a fine operator. He's not you, Smythe, not you, Compton, not a blow-in, not a smart-ass who comes in on the big bird and thinks he knows the fucking game. Axel Moen is top of the tree. What does he get for being top of the tree? He gets a posting to a shit place like Lagos, and a bastard like me dresses Lagos up as a good slot."

Harry Compton said, "I don't think obscenities help. Our priority is to get Charlotte Parsons . . ."

"Where'd they dig you up from? A creche? A nursery? Training school? You don't ever name names. She's a code, she's Codename Helen. You don't throw names in Sicily. You work in Sicily, you have to be big, not a fucking ant. It's a sad damned day when people like you—and you, Smythe—get to interfere."

"Has your agent been told that we are bringing Codename Helen home?"

A bitter smile crossed the Country Chief's face. "You are a funny man, Compton, you make me laugh. You think I'm doing the crap work for you. I messaged him to meet you. You tell him his plan was shit and made a 'difficulty.' Tell him yourself."

He thought he was followed, but he was unsure of it. He thought he was followed as he left the *duomo* in Monreale. As

Axel walked away from the cloister he saw, on the other side of the street, a man of middle age and wire-thin build take off his cap and slip it into the hip pocket of his trousers, and a hundred meters farther on, at the edge of the piazza, the man wore another cap of a different color and a different material. A hundred meters farther on, by the stalls that sold fish and meat, vegetables and fruit and flowers, the man had gazed into a shop window, studying women's clothes, and Axel had passed by him, and he had not seen him again. He could not be certain that he was followed. Maybe the man, forty-something, with the wire-thin build, had bought a new cap and was dissatisfied with it and put his old cap back on, and maybe he looked at women's underwear because that gave him a jerk-off thrill or because his wife's birthday was coming up, or maybe he followed the procedures of foot surveillance. Axel breathed hard. In La Paz he had been followed, once, and he had hit the numbers of his mobile and called out the cavalry and two streets later he had walked on a wide pavement that was suddenly crawling with his own guys and with the Bolivian task force people, and the tail had flaked away. He had no cavalry in Monreale. His training was in surveillance, not in countermeasure tactics. He breathed hard, deep. He assumed, if he was indeed followed, that they would use the technique of the "floating box." There would be men ahead of him, men behind him, men on the same side of the street and men on the opposite side of the street. But it was early in the afternoon, and the siesta hours had not started, and the pavements were full. If he ran, suddenly tried to break out of the box, then he told them, put it up in neon lights, that he knew he was followed. His mind ratcheted, going fast, considering how he should act . . . His problem, on the busy streets, he could not identify the operators or the command operator of the floating box. He walked faster and slower, he lingered in front of shops and in

front of stalls, he passed a *tabaccaio*, then turned sharply to
retrace his steps and went inside and bought a throwaway
lighter, and he could not confirm that he was the center-
piece of a floating box, nor confirm that his strained imagination merely goaded him. He walked on. He did not know.
He made a long loop, and he came back to the garden terrace at the back of the *duomo*. He sat on a bench. From the
terrace, among the flowers climbing on walls and under the
wide shade of the trees, he could look down onto Palermo
and the sea, where she had been. Axel did not know if he
was watched . . .

"It is the thirteenth."

"No, the ninth."

"I do not wish to dispute with you, Mama, but it is the
thirteenth."

"You told me, it was fifteen years ago, that it was the
ninth, it is what a mother remembers."

"Mama, I promise you, it is the thirteenth."

His father said, growl of the peasant's *dialetto*, "Last year
you said it was the eleventh, the year before it was the four-
teenth, the year before that it was—"

"Papa, I assure you, you are mistaken."

"No, Mario, it is you that are mistaken. Each year you
make a different number and argue with your mother."

At the start of the viaduct, where it climbed on columns
of concrete to cross the river valley and carry the *autostrada*,
No. 186, from Monreale by the high route over the mountains to Partinico, the car was parked on the hard shoulder.
Each year they made the argument because each year Mario
Ruggerio forgot the number he had given in 1981. The
problem, for Mario Ruggerio, he did not know in which
column of concrete was the body of his brother.

Franco was at the wheel of the parked car and had his

head down in a newspaper. Franco would not dare to snigger at the ritual dispute over which column of concrete carried the body of Cristoforo. There was a second car parked farther back, and a third car stopped at the far end of the viaduct, near the sixtieth column or the sixty-first.

His mother held the lavish bunch of flowers. He could not tell his mother that he hazarded his security each year when he came to the viaduct and then argued over which column of concrete held Cristoforo's body. He could not lash his mother with his tongue because his mother had no fear of him. He could not tell his mother that he did not know in which column of concrete . . . His father always sided with his mother, as if his father wished to cut him to size. Did they want him to blow up the viaduct, drop it, then dynamite each column of concrete, then break each column with pneumatic drills? Did they need to know so badly in which column was his brother, Cristoforo?

"I think you are correct, Mama. It is the ninth."

His mother bobbed her head, satisfied. He loved two people in the world. He loved his small nephew who was named after him, and he loved his mother, loved them more than his own wife and his own children. And he could not spend the day standing in public view on the viaduct and arguing. His father would not let the matter go. His father had three reasons, he accepted, to be in a foul temper.

"You were wrong then, Mario? You accept that you were wrong?"

"Yes, Papa. I was wrong."

"Cristoforo is in the ninth column?"

"The ninth, Papa."

The first reason for the foul temper of his father. A young man, the son of a nuisance enemy, had daubed paint on the door of his father's house. The young man could not be adequately punished because the door of the house in

Prizzi was covered by an unmanned police camera. If the young man disappeared or was found adequately punished then the *carabinieri* and the *squadra mobile* would be swarming through the home of Rosario and Agata Ruggerio and stressing them. The matter was dealt with, the camera would show the act, and the camera would show the contrition. The film from the camera was taken, a poor secret, each fourth night for examination. His father had wanted, personally, to slit the throat of the young man.

The second reason for the temper. The pilgrimage to the viaduct had been delayed for twenty-four hours, missing the exact anniversary of the entombment in concrete, because it had been necessary for Mario Ruggerio to review his security after the close call in the Via Sammartino, and that he would not discuss with his father. His father no longer understood, at eighty-four years of age, his son's life.

The third reason for the temper. It had been a long journey for his parents. He could not guarantee that they were not under surveillance. A bus to Caltanisetta, from the crowded market in Caltanisetta to the rail station, escorted by Carmine. The slow train to Palermo. Picked up by himself and Franco at the *Stazione Centrale* in Palermo and driven to the viaduct.

He walked back to the start of the viaduct. He counted. He strode toward his parents and the parked car. It was beneath his dignity to rush. He came to the ninth column of concrete. His brother had worked for the Corleonesi of Riina. His brother had been killed by the men of Inzerillo, and Inzerillo was dead from armor-piercing bullets, tested on a jewelry-shop window, in his car. The men who had acted on the orders of Inzerillo were in the bay, once the food for crabs. He had been told the same month, by the Corleonesi of Riina, that they had heard his brother was buried in wet concrete during the construction of the viaduct. The Corleonesi had killed Inzerillo. Mario Ruggerio, with his own hands, with rests to regain his strength, had strangled the four men who had taken Inzerillo's orders. He had only the word of the Corleonesi that Cristoforo's body was in one of the viaduct's columns of concrete. In truth, the cadaver of Cristoforo could be any-where . . . It would distress his mother, whom he loved, should he raise a doubt about the ultimate resting place of her favorite son.

"Here, Mama, the ninth column . . ."

He looked over the edge of the parapet, leaned forward so that he could see the great weatherstained column of con-crete. He had thought, and never said so to his father and mother, that his brother had been an idiot to have associated with the Corleonesi of Riina.

His father grumbled, "But there are two columns, one for each side. Is it the ninth column on the left, or the ninth column on the right?"

"On the right, Papa, the ninth column on the right."

His mother held the flowers over the parapet. They had cost 50,000 *lire* at the stall beside the entrance to the *Stazione Centrale*. He held his mother's arm. She crossed herself. She let the flowers slip from her hand, and they fell far down past the column of concrete and broke apart, scattered, when they hit the rocks of the riverbank.

He still held his mother's arm, to propel her back to the car where Franco waited. His father trailed behind, refusing to be hurried. The ritual was done. He opened the door for his mother and Franco had the engine running. He helped his father into the car after his mother. It would be bad for the dignity of Mario Ruggerio to scurry but he went fast to the front passenger door of the car. They powered away. He turned to his mother. It was a question that would not have been appropriate while they mourned the dead Cristoforo.

"Have you had notification of when Salvatore is brought to Ucciardone for the court? When does he come? I would wish you to take a personal message from me to Salvatore . . ."

"'Gianni, I would not have called you if it were not important . . . It is not good enough, my friend, please . . . Please do not just tell me that he no longer lives on the Collina Fleming. Where does he live? Another place in Rome, in Milan, in Frankfurt or Zurich, where? I think, 'Gianni, I have not much time, how could you understand because you are not in Palermo? I know, I know, we said there was no connection . . . I know, I know, he attacked because he was persecuted without cause for the blood relationship. I am blundering in darkness, 'Gianni, I look for any light however faint. Please, where now is Giuseppe Ruggerio?"

Axel sat in his room.

He heard the widow, the Signora Nasello, moving on the floor below, and he heard her television. The smell of her cooking came into his room.

Axel sat on the bed in his room.

It was a long time since he had felt true fear, but the memory stayed clean. It was back to his fifteenth year, when he had been with his grandfather out on the water of Eagle Harbor, out from Ephraim and toward the distant shape of Chambers Island, and the storm had come fast out of the mist. Gone after the muskie with his grandfather, trolling big spoons from an open boat. The landmass of the Peninsula State Park, and the lighthouse on the Eagle Bluff, had disappeared, so quick. No sight of land, the white wave caps above gray, cold water . . . The boat pitching, the bilges filled, the spray coming into the boat, the engine failing. He had felt, in his fifteenth year, a true fear then. His grandfather had spent thirty minutes, seemed an eternity, working at the outboard with the cowling off, and had regained the power. Cold, soaked, frightened, his grandfather had brought him back to the jetty at Ephraim, and not remarked on it . . . He had not felt fear in La Paz, not when they had hit the fire-fight on the *estancia* airstrip. He had not felt fear when he had been called in by the big guys in Washington and told, seri-ous and heavy, that a video of him arriving at the grand jury hearing to testify had been picked up in a house search down in Colombia's city of Cali . . .

Axel sat on the bed in his room and, with a handker-chief, he wiped each moving part of his dismantled pistol.

He felt the fear because he was alone. The guys in La Paz, the guys in New York, the guys at Headquarters and the guys on the Via Sardegna would have, he reckoned, bet money that Axel Moen didn't know true fear—they would have bet their shirts and their salaries. The bastards didn't know . . . Couldn't call 'Vanni, he had bad-mouthed 'Vanni. Couldn't call 'Vanni to tell him that he understood the story of the general who wanted the comfort of having his arm held because he had pissed all over that story. Couldn't call 'Vanni to tell him that he might be under surveillance, and might not, couldn't, tell him that he had shit fear because a middle-aged man on the far side of the street had changed caps and then stood in a window and eyed ladies' clothes. He was too goddam proud to be laughed at, as 'Vanni would have laughed at him. The fear held him . . .

When he had reassembled the pistol he cleared the magazines and let the bullet shells lie on the coverlet of the bed, and then he began carefully to reload the magazines.

She would have understood. If she had been beside him, sitting with him on the bed, he could have told her. He could have said, slow, to her, that he apologized for the bullshit he had given her about being strong. He could have said that it was the tactic to use smart talk to toughen her, and he could have held her hand and talked to her of his fear. He could have kissed her forehead and her eyes and talked about his fear and his loneliness. She'd know the agony of fear. She would be in the villa, and maybe sitting on her bed, and maybe her fingers ran on the face of the watch against the skin of her wrist. The world seemed to him, to Axel, to close around him, as the darkness had closed on him when he had come back from the terrace behind the *duomo*, when he had made all the clever moves that the instructors predicted would be used by a target under surveillance in a floating box, when he had failed to confirm the tail . . . He saw her face. She was in the garden behind the bungalow, and on the cliff near to her home. She was by the river in Rome. She was on the pavement in Palermo and bleeding. She was on the beach and dressing. He saw the frightened bravery on her face. He wanted to be sick. He felt, never before, that he despised himself. She should not have been asked . . . She might be on the patio in the darkness or in her room, alone. She might be with the family, living the lie. She would have the fear, as he had the fear. He shivered.

He reloaded the pistol with the filled magazine, and he pocketed the other magazines. The guys would be at the airport. He could not be at the airport as he had been instructed, because, maybe, he had a tail on him. He thought he knew why they came.

'Is this the way you normally do business?"

"Don't bad-mouth me."

"Your man said we'd be met."

"I heard it, like you heard it."

"Well, where's the welcoming delegation. Where is he?"

"I don't know."

And Dwight Smythe, again, looked around him. It had been the last flight of the evening into Punta Raisi airport from Rome. The passengers had gone, gone with their baggage. Policemen watched them, and check-in girls, and porters. They stood in the middle of the arrivals hall. Harry Compton wouldn't have admitted it, not willingly, wild horses to drag it from him, but he was frightened. Because he was actually frightened, he sneered at the American.

Dwight Smythe, honest, said, "It's kind of threatening, isn't it? It's just an airport, it's just like any other goddamn airport, but you feel sort of sick in the gut. I mean, it's a place you've heard about, read about, seen on the TV, and you're here and your greeter doesn't show and you're kind of scared . . . When I was at Quantico, where we train, years back, there was a professor who talked to us, Public Affairs, he said, 'Down there it's a war of survival, as it has been through history, a bad place to be on the losing side, it's a war to the death.' I just push paper, don't aim to get onto the battleground, it's why I'm scared."

"Thanks."

"One more thing, but it's worth saying. You gave your evaluation of that kid—'brilliant, stubborn, tough'—but that doesn't justify what was asked of her. This war's going nowhere, it can't be won. Sending her was a gesture, and that's not right, gestures are lousy. You scared?"

He hesitated. He nodded.

Harry Compton was frightened because he had spent six hours the previous evening, gone on until the street outside the SO6 office was quiet, in their library. He had gutted what they had in their library, the files that were headlined MAFIA/SICILY, and then he had driven over to New Scotland Yard and kicked the doziness out of the night-duty man in

Organized Crime (International) and read more. He had taken in the statistics of product, volume, profit of La Cosa Nostra—and the figures of homicide, bombings, extortion cases—and the photographs of the Most Wanted—and the assessments and intelligence digests.

The night-duty man must have warmed to him, had seemed pleased to talk, to break the boredom of the empty hours. The night-duty man had coughed through a life story. Northern Ireland as liaison with the local force for AntiTerrorist, a stress-created breakdown and shipped out to a desk job, handling informers, the twilight people in the Provo ranks who were turned, had built the stress running "players" with a future of torture, and then a bullet in the skull had bred the breakdown. "They get dependent on you, you're not supposed to but you get involved with them, you put them in place and you use them and you manipulate them, they lead bloody boring lives and they're there for one moment in time that matters, you've put them there for that one moment, if they can't handle the one moment of something that's important then they're dead."

He thought he was sharp, he hoped to make the grade through night study for the business management degree, and he had realized when he had finished with the files that he was going into water where he would be out of his depth . . . Christ, miserable Miss Mavis inquisitive Finch, counter clerk in the bank on the Fulham Road who had filed the disclosure report on the cash deposit of Giles bloody Blake, had pitched him in . . . He'd gone back home to Fliss, some god-awful hour, and she'd sulked and said it was her mother's anniversary he'd be missing . . .

Dwight Smythe grinned. "Maybe we get to share a room tonight, maybe we leave the light on . . ."

The American tried again on the mobile telephone. It was the fourth time since they had landed that he had tapped the numbers for Axel Moen's telephone, the fourth time the call had not been answered.

"So what's to do?"

Dwight Smythe flashed his teeth. "Ride into town, get that big room with the bright light, and wait. You got anything else to suggest?"

They took a taxi into Palermo.

The journalist from Berlin waved his bank note for 20,000 *lire* at the steward. He thought the bar of La Stampa Estera to be the most dismal drinking hole that he knew, a heavy and darkened room and company to match. But they should know, the journalists who worked the Rome beat, the reality of the strength of La Cosa Nostra. He bought his second round of drinks, and none of those he entertained had complained and demanded the right to buy. They drank what he bought, and he believed they mocked him. He was not proud of himself for coming to such a place and seeking the input of fellow trade hacks, but his story was littered, so far, with cavities and loose ends. He needed their assessments. Was the corruption in central government so widespread? Was there indeed a third tier of bankers and politicians, generals and secret servicemen, who protected the principals of the organization? Was a victory in Sicily possible? What was the lifestyle of the *capo di tutti capi* and how did he evade arrest? They mocked him, and they drank the Scotch he bought and the beers.

A magazine writer from Rotterdam said, "Never go down there, a played-out story. Go to Sicily, and all you end with is confusion. What my people are interested in is the Tower at Pisa, after the last earthquake, whether it's going to fall on a busload of our tourists."

A freelance writer from Lisbon said, "I can't get a word in the paper about Sicily. Haven't been down there for nine months. It's expensive. Anyway the food in Palermo is revolting. Nothing changes. It is the most tedious story in Europe. Now the Brazilian who is playing for Juventus, the striker, that is a page lead . . ."

An agency lady from Paris said, "The mafia? The mafia make my people go to sleep. If I want anything in the paper, and I have to want it because I am paid by the line, then I write about fashion and I write about the new gearbox in the Ferrari."

A super-stringer on retainer to a London daily said, "Nobody is interested, nobody cares, Sicily might be another planet. It is where they make an art form of deception, an industry of misinformation. Do you think they will use your story? I doubt it, I think you chase ghosts."

An Italian woman under contract to nine evening newspapers in Japan said, "There is no interest because the mafia story is not about real people. The judges, the policemen, the criminals, they are the characters of a cartoon strip. People we can understand, people we can believe in, they do not exist in Sicily . . ."

The telephone rang. They listened. When the telephone was on secure, and the voice strength was diminished, then the magistrate always shouted. It was past midnight, it was quiet in the kitchen. In deference to the magistrate's request they did not play the radio in the kitchen late at night. If they played the radio late at night then the cow from the next apartment, with the common wall, would come in the morning and rail against the magistrate that she could not sleep. It was as if the *ragazzi* believed their man had sufficient problems without adding the cow's complaints. They listened.

". . . I do not believe it, 'Gianni . . . How is that possible? Why was I not told? We all have a workload, 'Gianni, we

are all buried under a workload . . . Yes, I have it, I have written it. Of course, I am grateful . . . I told you, I look for any
light, I do not know where I will find the light . . ."

There was a time of silence and then they heard the
shuffle of his feet.

He came to the kitchen door. He wore his slippers and
a robe over his pajamas. There was a gray tiredness in his
face, and his hair hung clumsily on his forehead. The *maresciallo* snapped his fingers at Pasquale.

Pasquale asked, *"Dottore,* would you like juice, or coffee,
or tea?"

The shaken head. Pasquale wondered if the magistrate
had taken a pill. He had gone to his bedroom a good hour
before. He could have taken a pill, he could have been deep
in sleep. There were four of them round the table with their
newspapers and their cards and the filled ashtray.

"Nothing, thank you. *Maresciallo,* please, I ask a favor of
you. It is only a request because what I ask is outside the
remit of your duties. What I ask is forbidden, you would be
within your rights to tell me that what I ask is not possible."

Pasquale watched the face of the *maresciallo,* and the face
was impassive and gave no answer. They were not permitted
to shop for the magistrate, and they did. They were not permitted to cook for him, nor to clean the apartment.

"It is always the family, correct? I follow the family of
Ruggerio and always it leads me into darkness. There has
been a member of his family that I have missed—my own
fault, I cannot justify my error: his youngest brother. The
error is with me because, four years ago, I interviewed this
brother in Rome. The youngest brother is Giuseppe
Ruggerio, a businessman, he attacked me with what I
believed to be justification. Was it his fault that his eldest
brother was a *mafioso?* What more could he do than leave
Sicily, make his own life away from the island? Was I not

guilty of persecution? I believed him, erased him from my memory. I can make excuses. I can justify why I let the trail slip from me. But, the reality, I am humiliated. Now, I am told—I grovel because it was my error—the youngest brother is in Palermo. I have his address. I want confirmation that he is here. I ask you, *maresciallo,* to go and confirm for me that Giuseppe Ruggerio now lives in Palermo. It is always the family. Please . . ."

It was forbidden that the *ragazzi* should shop, cook, clean for the man they protected. A more serious offense, to take active part in an investigation. Grim faced, the *maresciallo* reached out and took a scrap of paper from the magistrate. Pasquale saw an address written in pencil on the scrap of paper. They faced the same danger as the man. Because they rode with him and walked with him they were as exposed to risk as he was. Pasquale understood why the *maresciallo* took the scrap of paper and lifted his coat from the draining board, and checked his pistol and went out of the kitchen. They walked with death, together.

THE GREAT WOODEN HORSE FIGURE was being towed by
men in modern dress into a farmyard, and the men carried
firearms and were swarthy-faced, hard-weather faced, and
from the pockets of their trousers and their jackets and their
anoraks spilled American dollar bills, and there were dollar
bills in the mud and ignored, and they started to search the
interior of the wooden horse figure, clambered into the
hatch door in the horse figure's belly, and she was far to
the back of the interior, and the torches of the men found
her, and she screamed, and he heard the sirens . . .

The first sirens of the day had woken Harry Compton.

He'd slept rotten. Not the fault of the bed in the hotel
room that he'd tossed half the night. He'd tossed, he'd put
the light back on in the small hours and he'd tried to win
some sleep by reading the file he had accumulated on
Charlotte Parsons, Codename Helen, and he'd dreamed.

He thought he might have slept a little over three hours.
He had thrust himself out of the bed and walked over the
scattered bedclothes, and gone to the window and pushed
back the shutters. He had seen the two cars powering along
the street with the lights on the roofs and the sirens blasting.
He'd seen the guns, he'd seen the guards, he had seen the
slumped figure in the back of the lead car.

They'd met for breakfast.

At home, Fliss left him alone for breakfast. If she sat
with him they argued. He took his breakfast alone in the
kitchen at home, a snatched apple and a piece of toasted

bread smeared with honey and coffee. The American didn't seem to want to talk, which suited Harry Compton. The American had eggs and sausage and bacon cooked to extinction. They'd talk after breakfast, that seemed to be the deal. It was the American's problem that they hadn't been met, for the American to sort out, and for the American to argue that the mission of Codename Helen was dead in the water, aborted . . . There were mostly tourists in the breakfast room. There were couples from Britain and Germany and they wore bright clothes that were ridiculous for their age and their eyes were on their food and their guidebooks. Breakfast would be inclusive, so they were eating big, like the American, and they were gutting the guidebooks so that they would seem intelligent each time they were dumped off the bus and marched to the next antiquity. He was contemptuous of tourists because his mortgage was £67,000, monthly repayments hovering at £350 a month, and if the baby came then they would need a bigger place, bigger mortgage, bigger monthly drain. Most summers he went with Fliss for two weeks to her aunt's cottage in the Lakes, and most summers after a week there he was yearning to get back to SO6 work. Harry Compton had told his wife that he'd be gone forty-eight hours, that he wouldn't be getting to see anything . . . He chewed on the bread roll, not fresh that morning, and the coffee was cold . . .

The man came from behind him.

The hand of the man brushed across the table and bounced the small basket that contained the bread rolls.

He had his back to the entrance of the breakfast room, hadn't seen the man come.

The hand was tanned and it had fair hairs growing on it. The hand scooped up Dwight Smythe's room key from beside the basket of bread rolls.

He was half out of his chair, the protest was in his throat, and he saw the American's face, impassive except that the big lips moved nervously.

"Leave it, Harry," the American growled, water on shingle. Dwight Smythe, no fuss, laid down his fork and rested his hand loose on Harry Compton's arm.

He subsided back onto his chair. The man walked on, slipped the key to Dwight Smythe's room into his trouser pocket. The man was dressed casually, a check shirt and jeans, and he carried a plastic bag that was weighted, and the top of a sketch pad protruded from the top of the bag. The man wore a long ponytail of fair hair, held close to his neck by a red plastic band. He was, to Harry Compton, like a dropout, like a druggie. The man went to the end of the breakfast room and he was looking around him as if for a friend, as if to find someone he was due to meet. The man turned, the man had failed to find his friend, and he came back past them. Harry Compton saw the man's face. He saw drawn lines, as if the man were scarred with anxiety. He saw the man's waist and the bulge below where the shirt was tucked into the trouser belt. The man was gone past him.

"I think we'll have fresh coffee," Dwight Smythe said, and his tongue brushed on his lips. "This coffee's cold shit."

Dwight Smythe called the girl, and it was ten minutes before the coffee came, and while they waited for the coffee the American ate two rolls of bread with jam on them, and he didn't talk . . . He was a detective sergeant, head-hunted for an élite unit, he was supposed to have the qualities of a policeman and an accountant and a lawyer, and he reckoned that he knew nothing . . . They drank most of the second pot of coffee, and Dwight Smythe wiped the crumbs off his face . . . He wasn't firearms-trained, he had never carried a weapon more lethal than his truncheon, he knew nothing . . .

They went out of the breakfast room and crossed the hotel lobby. The British tourists were loading noisily into their bus, and the Germans were crowding round their courier. They walked up the wide staircase, and then down the corridor. There was only a chambermaid in the corridor with her trolley of clean sheets, clean towels, soaps and shampoos. Harry Compton realized that he had glanced her over, as if a chambermaid could be a threat. The NON DISTURBARE sign was on Dwight Smythe's door. He thought there would be a fight, but the fight was the American's problem. The chambermaid was in a room down the corridor. The American knocked lightly on his own door. The accent, American, was a murmur—the door was not fastened.

The man sat on Dwight Smythe's unmade bed. On the crumpled pillow was an ashtray. The man smoked his second cigarette, looked up as they came in, his hand had been over the bulge in his waist and now dropped away. The strain was stamped on the man's face. It was the American's problem, the American's job to do the dirty talk.

"Hi, Axel, good to see you."

"Sorry, for last night."

"Not a problem. Axel, this is Harry Compton, out of London, a detective in the—"

Axel jerked across the bed and his body upset the ashtray and spilled the cigarette debris over the pillow, and he reached for the TV control and flicked buttons until he found loud rock, and he raised the volume.

Dwight Smythe said, soft, "We were sent together, there's been high-grade crap between London and Washington."

The cigarette went to the mouth, the hand snaked forward. The murmur stayed with the voice as if, Harry Compton thought, the shit had been kicked out of him.

"I'm Axel Moen, happy to meet you, Harry. Sorry I didn't make the airport."

"Didn't matter, we had a good ride in," Harry Compton said awkwardly. Not his problem, it was for the American to dish the shit.

"Axel, I'm not carrying good news," Dwight Smythe blurted, "I'm sorry, I'm only the goddamn messenger."

"What's the message?"

"Let me say this. When we met in London, when we traveled, we may not have hit it. I might have sparked you. Maybe I thought you arrogant, maybe you thought me fourth grade. That's past, gone."

"Spit it."

Dwight Smythe scratched at the short curled hair of his scalp, like he was buying time. "It's not easy, not for me and not for Harry . . . Up on high, Washington and London— Axel, they've killed it."

Harry Compton waited for the fight back, waited for the anger to jut the chin, waited for the tirade about big men being short of balls.

"They're aborting. They've gone cold. They're frightened. They want your Codename Helen shipped out. They want her home."

He saw Axel Moen's shoulders drop, as if the tension drained.

"They want her removed, immediately, from the field of danger. It's why I'm here, why Harry's here."

He saw the light flicker back in Axel Moen's eyes, like a lamp hit them where before there had been darkness.

Axel Moen said, conversational, "That's good thinking it's right thinking, it's what I was getting to think myself You see, not certain, but I think I am followed."

He saw the slight smile break on Axel Moen's mouth like ice was fractured.

Axel Moen said, "They'd be too good for you to know it. It's what I think, that I am followed. I think they have a tail on me. Don't have the moment how, where, they made the link. It's why I didn't come to the airport to meet you. It's why I didn't plug in the phone when you were calling. If they can put the tail they can put the bug. If there is a tail then I have to believe they are here, outside, and waiting on me. When you think you have a tail then you get sort of neurotic, because it can't be confirmed and it can't be denied. You know what I do each morning? I go out where she is, I watch her, I see her take the kids to school. I'm not close up, you understand. I'm two hundred meters away, three hundred, but I see her. I see her take the kids to school and I see her do the shopping. Sometimes, when she comes into the city, I follow her, I see where she goes and who she meets. I'm there, I'm a goddamn shadow . . . You see, she's alone, it's like she's in a pit with them . . . I didn't go last night, and I didn't go this morning. Maybe they've seen me near her, maybe I'm providing a pattern for them. Maybe, if I'm there each day, I give them a chance to see the pattern . . . I'm cut off from her, I can't watch her, I can't protect her."

He saw the shrug of Axel Moen, like a dream had died. The music played loud.

Harry Compton said, boorish, "My instructions are to terminate this operation, to bring her home immediately."

The cigarette was stubbed into the ashtray. The man had taken a pad from his pocket and he wrote briskly on it. Harry Compton waited. He had thought the man would fight and the man had crumpled. He had recognized the stress of Axel Moen and he saw now only a spent relief. The single sheet of paper was torn from the pad and passed to him. Axel Moen lifted the bedside telephone and dialed. He read the message again. He understood. He took the telephone from Axel Moen. He shivered, as if he crossed a chasm.

"Hello, hello . . . I am afraid that I do not speak Italian . . . I do apologize for the intrusion . . . I am the chaplain to the Anglican church on Via Mariano Stabile, just out from England for a few weeks. Miss Charlotte Parsons came to our service last Sunday . . . Oh, she's out at the moment, is she? Please, could you pass a message to her? I wanted her to know that we have an escorted tour this afternoon of the cathedral, with a guide. She seemed so interested in church history in Palermo. Three o'clock we are meeting outside the cathedral. We would be so delighted to see her if her duties permit it. Thank you so much . . ."

When the *maresciallo* had returned to the apartment he had not disturbed the magistrate. He allowed the poor bastard to sleep. He had crossed the hall of the apartment, walking on his toes, and he had heard the dull snoring of the magistrate. His report on the residence in the Giardino Inglese would wait. He should have gone off duty, should have gone home to catnap for a few hours. He stayed on. He sat quiet in the kitchen, nursing the cold coffee, when the day shift arrived. They were all quiet men when they came, the driver of the chase car, the passenger for the chase car, Pasquale, all subdued.

They were making the breakfast, heating the bread rolls when the alarm bleeped in the bedroom. It was good that he had slept, the poor bastard, and the *marescialllo* wondered if he had taken another pill. He had not yet shaved when he came to the kitchen door. He was a figure of wreckage.

"I spoke, as you requested, with the *portiere,* who declined to be cooperative. I made a call. My friend on night duty at the Questura gave me what I needed . . . The *portiere* had a conviction at the assizes in Caltanisetta, many years back but a conviction for theft. If it were known that the *portiere* of such a building had a conviction then he would lose his job . . . now, he was cooperative. Giuseppe Ruggerio is a banker, he is a man of ostentatious wealth. He has the apartment, and he has a villa for the summer on the coast. His family—his wife and his children, a foreign girl who helps the *signora* with the children—are at the villa. The villa is at Mondello. Sometimes Giuseppe Ruggerio is at the villa, sometimes at the Giardino Inglese. At the moment he is in Mondello, I have the address of the villa. *Dottore,* I have to tell you that I was not kind to the *portiere.* He made the wise decision to be more cooperative. Three weeks ago, perhaps a little longer, Giuseppe Ruggerio took his family away for a weekend and men used the apartment. He knows that because there was a rubbish bag left out for him to clear, and he saw that there were many cigarettes in the rubbish, and the waste from food and bottles, but the *portiere* was sensible, he saw none of the men. It is the classic indication, *Dottore,* as you will know better than I, of the use of the apartment as a *covo.* That is all I have to report." The *maresciallo* shrugged, as if it were nothing that he reported, and he saw the frail smile break on the magistrate's mouth, like there was light, small and faint light.

The magistrate shuffled away, scraping his slippers on the floor of the hallway. At the table they ate the bread rolls and drank the coffee, and read the newspapers. He kept his secret, but the eyes of Pasquale were never off him. He heard the voice of the magistrate, from the office, across the hall-way, into the kitchen.

The *maresciallo* chewed on his bread . . . Was the captain, 'Vanni Crespo, available to take a call?

He drank the coffee . . . When was it expected that the captain, 'Vanni Crespo, would return?

He glanced over the headlines of the newspaper . . .

Would the captain, 'Vanni Crespo, meet with Dr. Rocco Tardelli at five o'clock that afternoon at the *posto di polizia* at Mondello?

All the time that he ate, drank, read, he kept his secret and avoided the eyes of the young man, Pasquale. His name was called. He heard the reedy voice of the magistrate. He was a dour and hard man, he was not popular with those who worked for him and nor did he seek popularity. He surrounded himself, picked the team, with men of a similar black-humored resignation. They were unique in the service, they were aloof from the other teams of *ragazzi,* they guarded the magistrate who was the "walking corpse." He could make an error of selection and when he knew his error then it was rectified. He heard his name called and with a studied slowness he finished his mouthful and drank another gulp of the coffee and folded his newspaper. He went to the office in the living room, and he closed the door after him. He loved the man, he loved Rocco Tardelli as if they were family, he loved the poor bastard who sat at his desk in old pajamas and a frayed dressing gown. He thought he had brought the glimmer of light to the magistrate.

"You called, *Dottore?*" Said in complaint.

"I have asked 'Vanni Crespo of the ROS to meet me this afternoon in Mondello. I want to see it for myself, the villa of Giuseppe Ruggerio."

"To go to Mondello is to take an unnecessary risk."

"I have to go, please, I have to see. I believe I have missed an opportunity, I believe the opportunity was there for me, I believe I have no one to blame but myself."

"Then we go to Mondello," the *maresciallo* said without kindness. "We take the unnecessary risk."

It was not in his way to show kindness to the man he loved.

"Thank you."

"You have to a[dmit there's something] between us."

"That's not the point," Jane insisted. "Neither of us is suited for a relationship."

"I'm going to play dumb for a second so you can tell me why we're not suited for one another," Holden replied.

"There's no way I could ever bring you home to my family."

"Last time I checked I was a pretty good catch."

"It's nothing to do with you. It's the way my family would perceive you."

"I'm confused. You're saying it's not me, it's your family?"

"Sort of."

"Oh, good. For a second I thought you were throwing up imaginary obstacles," he said. "Listen, just admit that you and I shared something pretty incredible. And I'll leave it at that."

"You'll drop it?"

"Sure," he lied. "Just admit that I rocked your world and we'll go back to being simply partners without benefits."

"Okay, Holden. You were pretty amazing and quite possibly the best guy I've ever slept with. Is that enough?"

"Yeah, it'll do. Now tell me again why we shouldn't be partners with benefits?"

"You're impossible."

Dear Reader,

Go big or go home—that was the prevailing mantra that kept running through my head with the final chapter in this exciting series of books. The stakes are the highest they've ever been, the characters rich with life and the situation without easy answers. Of course, it makes for good reading, but it makes for really hard writing! This book didn't come together easily, but it was worth the trouble, as I think this story is one of the best (which is hard for me to say because all my books are like my babies).

I hope you enjoy *The Agent's Surrender* with its twists and turns and ultimate conclusion. If you're just coming to this story, you might want to check out *The Sniper,* which is Nathan's story, and *Moving Target,* which is Jake's story. Both are a great complement to Jane and Holden's story.

Hearing from readers is a special joy. Please feel free to drop me a line via email through my website at www.kimberlyvanmeter.com or through snail mail at Kimberly Van Meter, P.O. Box 2210, Oakdale, CA 95361.

All the best,

Kimberly

THE AGENT'S SURRENDER

Kimberly Van Meter

HARLEQUIN® ROMANTIC SUSPENSE

Recycling programs
for this product may
not exist in your area.

ISBN-13: 978-0-373-27891-6

THE AGENT'S SURRENDER

Copyright © 2014 by Kimberly Sheetz

Printed in U.S.A.

™ www.Harlequin.com

Other titles by this author available in ebook format.

KIMBERLY VAN METER

wrote her first book at sixteen and finally achieved publication in December 2006. She writes for the Harlequin Superromance and Harlequin Romantic Suspense lines. She and her husband of seventeen years have three children, three cats and always a houseful of friends, family and fun.

With all my love and admiration...

To my editor, Johanna Raisanen...you've taken my words and made them shine. I'm so lucky to have you on my side. From *The Call* to now, we're a great team, and I am so grateful for your wisdom, your guidance and your talent! Here's to many more collaborative books in our future.

Chapter 1

"They can't do this." Holden Archangelo, CIA special skills officer, held his temper by the thinnest margin as his superior, Reed Harris, chief of staff, military affairs, looked up at Holden's sudden appearance in his office. Holden gripped the door frame with Jane Fallon hot on his heels. "There's been a mistake," he said, ignoring Jane's rigid, unwelcome presence.

"Your personal feelings are clouding your judgment," Jane cut in, her lithe and muscular frame nearly as stiff as her inability to see Holden's side. "If the accused were anyone other than your twin brother, would you have the same objections?"

He ignored her point. "Miko's innocent."

"He was proved guilty," Jane countered. "And he

will be treated as any person found guilty of treason."
She looked to Reed for affirmation.

"We all can sympathize with your position,
Holden," Reed said, leaning back in his chair with
a heavy sigh.

Holden swallowed. Yes, the entire department
knew Miko was Holden's twin brother, which was
why the case had been given to Jane and not Holden.

He kept his gaze trained on their superior, effectively trying to ignore Jane's presence, which was
near impossible. Pissed as hell would've been too
mild of a phrase for the impotent rage choking him.
He could admit Jane was a solid investigator, but he
believed her final determination had been personal.
Very personal. "Permission to remove Agent Fallon
from the case for someone less biased."

Jane sputtered, and he could feel the force of her
glare even though he kept his stare focused on Chief
Harris. "Sir, I take offense to his accusation," she
said. "My service record is impeccable, and I've given
this office no reason to question my skills or my ability to separate my personal feelings from a case."

Chief Harris grunted in agreement, giving Holden
a sour look that warned him to tread carefully. "Don't
let your mouth overload your ass, son. Agent Fallon
is more than qualified to handle this case. Permission
denied. What's this about anyway?" He pushed the
paperwork on his desk and tapped it with his stubbed
finger. "Nothing is in this file that we all didn't already know was coming."

Jane had concluded that Miko had been guilty of

killing several people—including his own boss at the U.S. Department of Informational Development, or I.D. for short—and then committing suicide when the situation got too hot.

From the minute Holden had been told that Miko had killed himself at his own bar, something hadn't passed the sniff test. No way would Miko have committed suicide. Not in a million years. Honor was something the Archangelo boys held sacred, and there was nothing honorable about taking a coward's way out. "He didn't do it," he said between gritted teeth.

Jane shook her head, irritated. "Why are we having this conversation? I have eyewitness testimony that your brother ate a bullet. Harsh, yes, but sometimes the truth doesn't pull punches."

Holden had talked to Nathan Isaacs briefly about Miko's death and, though Nathan had been there when Miko died, this was not an open-and-shut case. As difficult as it was for Holden to accept that Miko had pulled the trigger, he could not believe the story ended there. "Something was missed. No one knew my brother like I did, and I'm telling you, something isn't right," he finished hotly.

"I'm sure the family members of most suicide victims share similar conviction, but I assure you, nothing was missed," Jane retorted, almost bored. "The truth is it doesn't matter how you feel about the matter, your brother did, indeed, kill himself and you're going to have to find a way to deal with that knowledge. It's time to face facts and move on. Miko Archangelo was found guilty of his crimes and, as per the regulations, will be stripped of all military honors effective immediately. Frankly, I find your outrage a little confusing. The report was finished a month ago."

"Yeah, and someone made sure that I'm just now seeing it," he shot back, leaving no doubt he believed it was Jane's doing. "Funny how that happened. If I'd known about your findings, I would've found a way to put a stop to your little celebration ceremony."

Jane colored but held her ground and looked to their superior to end the controversy once and for all. "Sir?"

Reed considered a moment and then said, "Son, I know you're hurting. You and your brother shared a close bond. But there comes a time when you have to accept the facts as they are given. Miko made a grave error in judgment and got in over his head. It's that simple. It hurts, I know, but we're not in the business of sugarcoating the truth."

Holden spied the tiniest lift of Jane's mouth and burned at the thought she might get the upper hand in this. Not because of their shared history—but because Miko's honor depended on Holden succeeding.

"I have new evidence," he blurted, taking a risk when he didn't have all his ducks lined up just yet. Jane frowned and opened her mouth to speak, but Holden wouldn't give her the chance to shoot him down. "Sir, I know I've got a dog in this fight, but that's all the more reason to let me at least see this through, whatever that end might be. Let me chase down this one lead, and if nothing comes of it, I'll let it go."

"This is ridiculous," Jane protested, shooting Holden a dark look. "The case is closed. What's next? Reopening every closed case when a family member squawks at the outcome? This sets the potential for a very dangerous precedent."

"If your investigation is solid, Jane, you have nothing to worry about," Holden returned. He couldn't give a rat's ass if Jane Fallon came out looking like a junior officer with her first real case. All he cared about was clearing Miko's name.

"And what's this new piece of evidence and why didn't you present it when Jane was conducting her investigation?" Reed asked. The older man watched him intently. "Did you purposefully withhold information in an attempt to protect your brother?"

"No sir. This information came to me only recently."

"What information is that?" Jane crossed her arms.

"It's my lead," he said coldly. "I'll chase it down. I wouldn't want your bias to color your judgment."

"My bias? What about yours?"

"If my brother is truly guilty, I'll close the book and let it be. I know he's not, though. If you had known my brother, you'd know he couldn't have done the things you say he did."

"And would you say your brother wasn't capable of gunning down innocent people? Because he absolutely did that," she countered. "That's irrefutable."

Holden swallowed. True, and that piece of the puzzle didn't make sense. All kinds of bad stuff had been happening under the auspices of I.D., which had subsequently been shut down, but Holden had a feeling the rot went even deeper than they'd uncovered. And somehow Miko had been at the heart of it.

"So spit it out," she pressed, her green eyes narrowing as she awaited his answer. "What's this new compelling evidence that miraculously appeared at the eleventh hour?"

He glanced at Reed. "I'd prefer to share that information in private."

His boss shook his head. "Jane is the investigating officer. Technically, any information you have should be shared with her, too." Reed's stare bounced from one officer to the other. "I really have no reservations with Jane as an investigator, nor do I feel she was biased. She followed the evidence and arrived at the conclusion that we all did." He drew himself up and effectively put an end to the conversation, saying, "I'm sorry, son, but this case is closed. You're going to have to make peace with it."

"My brother was a highly decorated marine." Holden's throat was tight. "To strip him of his medals… They were all he had left."

"He should've thought of that before he committed treason," Jane said, nodding to Reed with smug approval. "Sorry to have bothered you, sir."

Finished, she turned and left Holden standing in Reed's office, his anger smoldering so hot he didn't trust himself not to blow his entire career with one expletive. He reined in his anger enough to ask, "Sir, is that your final decision on the subject?"

"It is."

Holden accepted his superior's answer with a stiff nod and exited the office, but instead of going straight to his desk, he grabbed his coat and headed out. He needed air. Or else he was going to do something as foolish as throttle Jane Fallon.

From her desk, Jane watched Holden stomp out of the building. She released a pent-up breath. What possible evidence could Holden have that she hadn't uncovered in her investigation? She was known for her sharp eye and attention to detail. It wasn't possible she'd missed something. Right?

She returned to Reed's office, and her boss offered a brief, knowing smile. "He planted a seed, didn't he?"

"I didn't miss anything," she protested, but Reed was right; Holden had definitely planted a seed of doubt, and it was already germinating like a weed in her mind. "What do you think he was he talking about?"

"Does it matter?" Reed countered, and she supposed he was right. It didn't matter. The case was closed. "You have to understand that Holden is grieving the loss of his brother on several different levels. He'll survive this, and it will all become an unpleasant memory best left in the past."

She didn't think so. She'd known Holden for a year. They'd both transferred at the same time to the CIA, military affairs department, and ever since their brief, ill-fated and definitely secret affair, they'd been at odds with one another. However, if pressed, Jane would have to admit Holden was as thorough an officer as she—which meant if Holden thought he had new evidence, he likely did. "Maybe I ought to look into the case, make sure there aren't any loose ends."

Reed arched his brow. "You want to reopen it?" he asked.

"No," she said quickly. The last thing she wanted to do was reopen the case that had finally given her a measure of approval from her father, but if there was even the slightest chance she'd missed something, she couldn't let it go. "But I don't want Holden questioning my skills. I have no doubt that my investigation will hold up."

"Then why do you care what he thinks?"

"I don't." *I care what others will think if Holden starts spreading his theory around.* If word reached her father that she'd potentially buggered up the high-profile case…. She shuddered to think of how heavy his disappointment would be. "I just like to be thorough," she finished.

Reed sighed, as if knowing the exercise was pointless and a waste of manpower, but he shrugged and said, "Fine. I'll reopen the case for one week. But here's the catch," he added. "Holden is going to work with you."

"With all due respect, I don't think that's wise," she said, her heart skipping a beat. "He doesn't have a clear head. He's too emotional about this. Holden is a wild card that will only impede my progress."

"Potentially true, but Holden is a good officer—as good as you—and I have a feeling if he doesn't get the opportunity to chase this down, he's going to do something rash. I don't want to lose a good officer over this."

Work with Holden? She'd rather chew nails. "Sir, I can appreciate your concern but—"

"Decision is made. You and Holden have a week to get this cleared up. Try not to kill each other in the process."

And what if they did worse than kill each other? Jane's mouth dropped open in dismay, hating the idea of working side by side with Holden. From the minute they'd met, sparks had flown—the kind that made for incredible, earth-shattering sex but only made things messy everywhere else except the bedroom. She found him arrogant, harsh, cocky and too good-looking to be trusted. Anyone with eyes like his ought to be quarantined as a matter of national security. He was bad news. He reacted emotionally instead of rationally, and he didn't care how his actions affected other people. Such as when he wanted to come clean about their relationship and she wanted to keep it quiet. She had known her father would never approve, and she had told Holden this, which somehow had prompted him to have a conversation with her father, The Major. And that had gone down exactly as she'd imagined—not well. She'd ended her relationship with Holden and he had been adversarial with her ever since. Now whenever they were together, her armpits immediately started to sweat, which was why she'd switched to clinical-strength deodorant. He set her teeth on edge.

He also hogged the office exercise equipment. Of course, he would be the only other person who arose at a ridiculously early hour to get in a good workout before the day started. It was hard enough to forget his near-perfect body without having to exercise beside him each morning, but she was not about to purchase a gym membership when she had a free gym readily available to her.

And now she was supposed to work with him like they were buddies in a Sandra Bullock film? No way. Again, she'd rather eat nails. Rusty ones, at that.

She returned to her desk and glowered at her screensaver—flying blue stars streaking in wild patterns across her monitor. The pattern bothered her and she jiggled her mouse to make it stop.

"Why don't you just change your screensaver?"

Jane swiveled to stare at her officemate, Special Skills Officer Ursula Benza. "Because sometimes you have to assert your dominance over your OCD tendencies," she quipped before exhaling a short breath of annoyance at her situation. She frowned. "What do you know about Holden finding new evidence regarding his brother?" Ursula's blank look answered Jane's question. "Okay, so he didn't share," she surmised, not surprised. Holden was a locked box when he chose to be. "No idea what it could be?"

"Does anyone know what goes through that handsome head of his?" Ursula asked, smiling when Jane grimaced. "You're the only woman within a ten-mile radius who seems to be immune to his freakishly hot body, which begs the question about a certain lady's sexual orientation."

Jane shot Ursula a dark look. "Don't even go there. Maybe the reason I don't find him attractive is because he has the personality of a wet shoe." When it was obvious personality didn't matter to Ursula when presented with a hot male body, she added, "It would be inappropriate and weird to date a coworker." It was a good thing she wasn't overtly religious because the lie that just tripped from her mouth was entirely too convincing. Holden was her Achilles' heel and she was determined to root out that weakness.

"Hmm…who said anything about dating?"

Jane wrinkled her nose and Ursula grinned. Ugh. Knowing that her colleague harbored less than office-friendly fantasies about Holden made Jane twitch with discomfort. Okay, so it was complicated.

"So." Ursula tapped a finger on her desk. "What's this about more evidence about his brother's case?"

"I don't know. Holden wouldn't share, but Chief Harris put us both on the case just to be sure every stone has been checked and double-checked."

"Ouch. That's not going to go over very well with Daddy, is it?" Ursula guessed accurately, but Jane didn't want to think about it.

"My dad will understand this is just a formality. Nothing is going to change. Miko was guilty and that's what Holden will have to come to realize. Brother or not, Miko killed several people in cold blood and then offed himself. Sad but true."

"Brutal. Kind of makes you wonder why, though, right?"

"No." Jane disagreed sharply. "It's not my job to wonder about the motivations of criminals, and if this was anyone but Holden's twin brother, we wouldn't be having this conversation. Once again, his personal feelings are getting in the way."

"Can you blame the guy? I mean…family, you know? What if it was one of your brothers?"

"My brothers wouldn't shame their family by doing something like Miko did, so I can't imagine how I would feel. In my family, there are no shades of gray."

"Girl, you have a heart of stone." Ursula tsked with an arched brow. "Someday that quality is going to bite you in the ass."

"Not likely. However, I can definitely see Holden reaping terrible consequences if he keeps poking at the hornet's nest."

"So what are you going to do?"

The only thing she could do. "Put an end to this waste of time and prove once and for all that Miko Archangelo was a traitor to his country so we can all move on."

Case closed. Again.

Chapter 2

Holden was nursing a beer when he heard a knock at his front door. It was nearing eight o'clock in the evening. He grabbed his cell and checked his security camera feed, surprised and irritated when he saw Jane standing outside. "What the hell does she want? To gloat?" he muttered, pocketing his cell and going to the door, beer still in hand. He cracked the door and fixed her with a baleful stare that he hoped sent home the message she was the last person he wanted darkening his doorstep. "What do you want?" he asked, moving straight past the pleasantries to the point.

"Aren't you going to invite me in?" she asked. When he shook his head, her mouth firmed, but she didn't press the issue. Instead, she said, "Reed has agreed to reopen the case."

He straightened, surprised and immediately suspicious. "Why?"

She shrugged. "What does it matter? The case has been briefly reopened, and in the meantime, all disciplinary actions are pending the conclusion. However, there's a catch."

"Isn't there always?" he countered with a narrowed stare. "What is it?"

"Reed put me and you both on the case."

"Screw that."

"Exactly how I felt, but he's not going to change his mind."

"He will once he realizes that you and me working together is the worst idea since hydroponics."

"*Hydroponics?* You mean the world's first successful attempt at creating a sustainable way to grow food in a world with diminishing land resources? *That* hydroponics?"

"Yeah, exactly. Anything grown without dirt isn't natural. It's Frankenfood. So yeah, bad idea."

"Weird analogy aside, Reed has made up his mind, so we're working together on your fool's errand. Don't think for a second I believe you're operating on anything other than emotions and ignoring the facts—as usual. Frankly, I find your behavior an embarrassment to the department."

"Don't hold back. Let it all out, Agent Fallon," he said wryly, tipping his beer back and swallowing. "And since we're sharing, I should go on record as saying I think you're operating from a place of ego and fear because you're afraid you truly did miss something and you can't bear the thought of looking sloppy."

She lifted her chin with a cold grin. "Holden always has all the answers, doesn't he?"

"Most times. Particularly when the question isn't all that hard to figure out. Face it, Fallon. I've had you figured out from the day we met, and if you weren't so afraid of Daddy's disapproval, we could've been a helluva team."

"You're the one suffering from an inflated ego," she said, eyes flashing. "And I would appreciate it if you would stick to the case. Leave the personal crap out of this—that is, if you can manage."

"Cold as ice, as usual." His gaze darkened as he tipped his beer back again. "Tell me, Fallon, were you born this cold or did you work at it?"

She smiled. "I guess that's none of your business as it doesn't relate to the case. If you can't handle being a professional, I'll just let the chief know your interest in the case has died and we'll all happily close the book on this wild-goose chase."

He straightened, shaking his head. "You're a piece of work."

"As much as I would love to continue this conversation, I have a life and need to get back to it. I just came by to let you know you got your wish."

"Well, thank you for your consideration," he said with open sarcasm; he knew the real reason she'd dropped by was to get the slip of evidence he held to his chest. Good luck with that—he'd made it up. "Have a good evening, Agent Fallon."

She glared, standing rigid, looking as if she'd just sucked a lemon, but she forced a smile. "See you tomorrow. Be prepared to work. I want to get this over with. Some of us have real work to do and don't have time to chase fairy tales."

He chuckled. "Nice try, but I don't bait that easily. Good night, Fallon." He shut the door before she could retort. Work with Fallon? Nope. That woman was the original ice queen. And to think at one time he'd thought he was falling in love with her. What a joke. Besides, he worked alone. Fallon could do whatever she pleased as long as she stayed out of his way.

That'd gone about as well as she'd expected. But a girl could hope, right? Of course, she hadn't expected him to welcome her into his home with open arms and offer her a beer, but she hadn't quite expected him to be so rude. Well, yes she had. They weren't buddies, and she preferred it that way.

She walked with strong, purposeful strides to her car, suppressing a shiver at the bitter cold of a Washington, D.C., winter, and pushed the reality of working with Holden as far from her mind as possible. She was a strong investigator. Holden couldn't have anything in his hot little hand that would change the outcome of her investigation. And that was exactly what she'd tell her father in about fifteen minutes, when she was expected for dinner with her brothers.

There was a chance her father, retired Major General Gregory Fallon, hadn't heard of this recent development, but then her father still had scarily deep connections, and a reverberation of this sort was bound to ripple some water under the boats. However, if he didn't mention it, she'd keep the information to herself.

She walked into her father's house and followed the sound of voices to the living room, where her father and two brothers, Ian and Walker, sat enjoying a beer and talking shop. For a brief moment, a familiar envy arced across her heart for their easily defined relationships. Simply put, The Major was openly proud of his marine sons for their varied accomplishments, but when it came to his marine daughter, he always found cause to criticize. What would it be like to sit and enjoy a beer with her dad like her brothers did? The Major frowned upon women drinking—he said they lacked the constitution to handle their liquor. Yeah, her dad was unapologetically sexist and there was nothing she could do about it, least of all change him. Time to run the gauntlet. "Hey, Dad," she said, announcing herself as she entered the room.

"There she is, only a little bit late this time," The Major said with a wink at Ian, who laughed at her expense.

"Work kept me late," she said, hating the defensiveness of her tone. "Reed threw me a big case," she added, though she immediately wished she hadn't.

"Oh?" her older brother, Walker, said, intrigued. "Anything as good as that Archangelo case?"

Her dad grunted. "Those Archangelo boys, waste of good military training… Twisted branches never grow into strong oaks," he said, repeating the same bit of advice he'd shoved down her throat when he'd found out about her and Holden.

"Yes, Dad, I'm well aware of your feelings about Holden," she said, mildly irritated that she found herself defending the man. "But Holden is nothing like his brother—he's a good investigator with a solid record."

The Major shook his head. "The man has no respect for authority, which points to a weak character. Add in the fact that Miko was Holden's twin…mark my words, he'll show his true colors sooner or later."

Why was she wasting time defending Holden when she knew there was no winning this argument with her father? Total waste of energy. She'd long ago learned to pick her battles, and this situation was no different.

"So what's the big case?" Walker asked.

"I don't have details yet," she hedged. "I will know more in a few days." Her father narrowed a speculative gaze at her, as if he were reading her mind and discovering her secrets, and she suffered an uncomfortable moment. "When I can divulge details I will," she clarified. Anytime she tried to act as their equal, they managed to shoot her down with the equivalent of an indulgent pat on the head. Well, that was how her brothers handled it. Her father? He just got that look on his face that said, "Girl, you'll never be as good as your brothers because you're a woman and incapable of critical thinking" and she ended up doing and saying something that invariably started an argument. So tonight, she was determined to steer clear of any potential land mines. Yet…she'd just lobbed a big one in her own path. Self-destructive much? "I probably shouldn't have mentioned it."

The Major grunted and returned to his sons. "Walker, tell us about the latest detail in Afghanistan."

"Dad, you know I'm not supposed to talk about that—it's classified," he said, winking at their father. The Major laughed as if they were sharing a big private joke, and Jane hated she couldn't just enjoy an evening with her family like normal folks. Her thoughts wandered to Holden, and she pushed them back. She didn't want to think of him. Not now. She was already surrounded by big, tall, muscular numbskulls with too much testosterone. She certainly didn't need to muddy her brain with one more.

"Dad, how was the summit?" she asked, trying to steer the conversation. "Anything worth reporting?"

"Bunch of politicians jockeying to be top dog," he said. "Nothing new. Food was adequate for the situation, but I was more than happy to be home where a man can get a decent steak."

Adequate. Top chefs catered the military summit each year. It was mildly gratifying to know her father was difficult to please on all fronts. "Well, maybe you shouldn't be eating so much steak at your age," she countered. "Your cholesterol is probably through the roof."

"My cholesterol is fine," her dad said. Then his brow arched in a knowing fashion, and Jane's stomach flopped. He knew and he'd simply been waiting for a convenient segue. Damn the man's connections. He probably had a line to God so he knew when to pack an umbrella. "Let's get back on topic. Jane, an interesting conversation floated my way concerning the investigation you closed on that Archangelo man."

"Yes? Such as?" she asked, feigning polite interest when she really wanted to forgo eating and split this dinner invitation. She grabbed a handful of pretzels and tossed one back. "Anything good?"

"Talk is that his brother is asking questions."

"Well, that's not surprising. It was his brother after all," she answered, trying not to choke on the pretzel. "What's the big deal?"

"The big deal is the whole I.D. debacle was an embarrassment to this country and everyone is ready to put it to bed. You did a decent job closing that investigation to everyone's satisfaction. Perhaps you could persuade your peer to let sleeping dogs lie," The Major suggested, but his tone told her it was anything but. She hated when her dad pulled rank. "I.D. was a toxic extension of the government that ended up with gangrene. Many good people went down on that ship. No one wants to dredge it up again."

"I told him that," she said, biting her tongue too late. She looked to her brothers for help, but they were watching her as keenly as their father was. Damn boys. They stuck together, no matter what. Well, cat's out of the bag. No sense dancing around. She tossed back the last pretzel and said, "He's never going to stop asking questions. He doesn't believe Miko was guilty."

"The guy was caught red-handed," Ian said with a snort. "He couldn't have been more guilty than if he'd filmed himself doing it and mailed the evidence to the authorities."

"It's an open-and-shut case," Walker agreed. "I wish all my cases were that easy."

She bristled. "It wasn't that easy. The I.D. corruption went deep. There's always the potential we didn't root out all of the rot. I assure you, it wasn't an easy investigation by any means."

"Of course, Janey," Walker soothed in a patronizing way that made her want to sucker punch him in the kidneys. "It was a nice feather in your cap, for sure."

"Thanks, Walker," she gritted, her temperature rising. "Listen, I don't know if Holden has anything of value, but he says he has some new evidence."

Ian raised an eyebrow. "Like what?"

"I don't know," she admitted, hating that she'd blabbed at all. But no sense in hanging on to a half story. "Reed has temporarily reopened the case with Holden and me investigating."

Her dad scowled. "That's some special kind of bullshit. What possible evidence could this Holden character have that would warrant reopening the case?"

"I don't know, Dad," she answered truthfully. If only Holden hadn't been such a jerk and shared what he knew, she could've had solid answers, but now it seemed as if she were on the outside looking in on her own case. "I'm sure it's nothing truly substantial, but Reed thinks this will give Holden closure."

"Whole lot of hand-holding if you ask me." Her dad groused and her brothers nodded. "If I was in charge, none of that would be going on."

"Yes, Dad," she said dutifully, though she wanted to roll her eyes. Her dad had little faith that anyone could do their jobs as well as he could. Well, you didn't rise up the marine ranks by sitting back and letting the tide carry you. Her dad had the chops to back up his claims, but he wasn't the least bit gracious about it, which put him on the outs with almost everyone beneath him. "Anyway, I'm starved. When's dinner? I have an early day tomorrow and I still need to go over the case files."

"It should be ready now." Her dad motioned for everyone to follow him to the dining room. He nodded with brisk approval at Claudine, the live-in maid and cook, and then seated himself at the head of the table like a king surveying his subjects, which Jane thought was an apt analogy.

"Smells great, Claudine," she murmured, ready to dig in and get the hell out.

"How are you, Miss Jane?" Claudine asked, placing the gravy boat nearest to her father because he practically drank the stuff with a straw. Her father was waging a war against time, determined to prove he was damn near invincible, no matter that he was nearing seventy.

"Good, and yourself?"

"Can't complain." The older woman smiled. "When are you going to meet a nice young man?"

"No time for that," she said briskly, shaking her head as she scooped a spoonful of mashed potatoes. Why didn't anyone ever ask why Walker or Ian hadn't settled down? Because men were allowed to be footloose and fancy-free, she answered herself in a sour tone. "I'm married to my job," she said, thinking briefly of the time she and Holden had spent together. If things had been different…maybe…but they weren't, so what was the point in wallowing in the past?

Her father nodded and said, "There's more to life than getting married, Claudine. Don't be putting foolish thoughts into the girl's head. She's *finally* doing all right. Time to focus on the priorities."

Somehow having her father echo the same sentiment sent a stone tumbling into the pit of her stomach when it should've made her grin from ear to ear. She was constantly yearning for a smidgeon of her father's approval, yet sometimes the smidge just tasted hollow.

Hell, she must be tired. This whole situation with Holden and the case had put her off-kilter. Tomorrow she'd find out what the hell kind of evidence Holden thought he had and then she'd start putting this baby to bed. For good.

Chapter 3

Per usual, Holden awoke at 4:30 a.m., and after pounding back an organic whey protein shake, dressed, grabbed his workout bag and headed for the office.

Being in the top level of the CIA had its perks, one of them being the executive exercise facility, which Holden took full advantage of. After a career in the military, he didn't relish the idea of going soft at a desk job, so he worked out just as hard as he ever did. And also, per usual, Jane was there, too.

It was always a small punch to the gut whenever he saw Jane dressed like a civilian in her workout clothes. It reminded him too vividly how that lithe, muscular body had fit so well against his, and it was in those raw, primal moments that his guard slipped, if only for a heartbeat. And then he remembered how she'd thrown his feelings in his face and walked out on him and the wall went back up.

"Would it kill you to exercise at a different time?" he asked as she joined him, stuffing her bag in the locker and grabbing a towel. "Or is this some twisted scheme to spend more time with me?"

"Don't flatter yourself."

He didn't know why he'd assumed she'd cut out on her morning workout after getting the news that the case had been reopened, but obviously it hadn't stopped her. Seeing her there put him instantly on edge.

She headed directly to the treadmill and punched in her usual workout, a punishing ten-mile run in fifty-five minutes. Holden, deciding to bypass his lifting routine, stepped onto the treadmill beside her. He punched in ten miles and kicked up the pace.

After they'd started running, Holden asked, "So why'd Reed change his mind? You have something to do with that?"

"What does it matter?"

"It matters to me."

She cut him a short look. "I don't like my work to look sloppy. I realized that if you think you have hard evidence, chances were you did, and I didn't want to run the risk that someone else might question my skills as an investigator. I figured chasing down the lead was a minimally small risk when I feel confident the end result will remain the same."

"Why are you so willing to believe the worst of my brother?"

"I didn't know your brother, so I have no opinion of him. I followed the evidence. Your brother's death was the catalyst to the entire I.D. network becoming a pile of rubble. That much is easy enough to document. Your brother was implicated in the killings of several high-ranking officials internationally, as well as domestically, and his suicide—"

"*Alleged* suicide," he interrupted with a growl, and she shrugged, keeping an easy but brisk pace without breaking a sweat. She was in remarkable shape. One would have to be blind not to notice—and Holden was not blind. Not to mention he had first-hand knowledge of every curve and valley carved into that hot body. "And Nathan Isaacs, his good friend and fellow sniper for I.D., had also been accused of committing unsanctioned hits, and he wasn't stripped of his medals."

"Nathan didn't know he was carrying out someone else's agenda. Miko did. That much was said in his suicide note."

"We don't even know the note was written by Miko because it was printed out and not handwritten. For all we know, my brother was set up by someone higher up the chain."

"How high are we talking?" she asked, a faint note of mockery in her tone. "C'mon, Holden, Occam's razor. Sometimes the most obvious explanation is the right one."

"And sometimes what may seem like the obvious answer is in actuality what someone wants you to believe."

"Well, you got your wish. We're going to chase down your lead and see where it takes us. Just don't blame me when we end up in the same place we started."

He knew it was possible Jane was right, but his gut said otherwise. He couldn't explain the twin bond to someone who'd never experienced it. But he could chase down a lead like a bloodhound, and that was what he was going to do. He supposed he owed Reed a note of gratitude for opening the door so he could walk through instead of having to scale windows in the dead of night. Sneaking around wasn't his favorite game.

"So what's your story, Fallon?" he asked, curious as to what went on behind those jade eyes.

She shot him an irritated look. "Are you going to gab all morning or let me run in peace? You'll have plenty opportunity to flap your jaws later."

"I forgot that your workout takes all your concentration," he said, knowing the subtle jab would ruffle her feathers. From what he knew of Jane, she didn't take shortcuts and didn't do girl push-ups. In fact, she worked harder than most men. She was a marine through and through. As expected, she cast him a dark look and punched in a higher pace as if to prove a point. He chuckled and did the same. They were running side by side, like a cheetah and a gazelle, except they were evenly matched in skill and strength. Sweat began to drip down his temple and soak his T-shirt. A quick look at Jane revealed high points of color pinching her cheeks as she kept up the pace. At this rate, their hearts would explode, and she was so damn stubborn she'd never quit before him. He didn't want to show weakness, but running had never been his strong suit. Her legs pumped, strong and fierce, as she kept her gaze trained forward, and he had to wonder where she went in her head to withstand such a grueling workout. Running was a mental activity as much as it was physical and Jane was in the zone. He envied her detachment, her ability to compartmentalize the pain of her burning legs and lungs as she pushed herself beyond most people's capability. Maybe that was how she had been able to just cut him loose and walk away without looking back. *Don't start that crap again,* a sharp voice in his head warned when he went too deep into the whys of their breakup. *Ancient history—keep it there.*

Just when he thought he might collapse, the ten-mile marker dinged and the slowdown began, not a moment too soon. Another five seconds and he might've embarrassed himself. His legs were rubber, but he wasn't about to let Jane see that, particularly when she looked ready to go another five miles. The only indication she'd labored was the ruddy color in her cheeks and the quick rise and fall of her chest as she wiped away the sweat. She ended the run and popped off the treadmill, calling over her shoulder before she headed for the showers, "Be ready to share this game-changing lead, Archangelo. Time is wasting."

* * *

Jane stood for a full two minutes under the hot spray, groaning silently at the dull ache in her quads and calves from the grueling run. Why'd she have to push it so hard? What did she need to prove to Holden? It wasn't just Holden—it was to everyone. There was no grace for her. Being the only girl in a military family dominated by men, she'd had no choice but to meet or exceed all expectations. Hell, she'd been doing boy-style push-ups since she was three. She loved her brothers to death, but they were jarhead carbon copies of their dad, and because she was the exact opposite of her father, it must mean she was her mother's mini me. She stifled another groan. Why couldn't she have been born a male, too? Life would've been so much simpler. No having to constantly prove her worth or justify her existence. No having to defend the fact that she'd been born bearing a striking resemblance to their mother.

The mother who'd left them all behind.

Sometimes she bore her mother's abandonment as a scarlet letter simply because she had the misfortune to share the same gender.

Jane indulged in a moment of quiet as the water soothed her throbbing muscles and calmed her ragged spirit. Why was she going on this stupid waste of time with Holden? Why didn't she just stand her ground and discard Holden's theory? There was no basis of fact, only Holden's insistence that something was amiss, and that wasn't enough to reopen a case like Miko's. Why? The question pelted her as surely as the water jets, but there was no relief answer in sight. Jane groaned, hating the self-doubt niggling at her brain, cutting chunks out of her confidence. Maybe she should've gone to Holden when she had first started the investigation. Perhaps if she'd done that, they wouldn't be questioning anything now, putting a stain on her reputation. But then, as now, she didn't trust herself around Holden for too long; he did something to her insides. Too much time around Holden and she started to question too many things, and she couldn't have that. He put a wrinkle in her life that stubbornly refused to iron out, no matter how hard she pressed. And that just wouldn't work in the overall scheme of things. *Enough of this morose, angst crap.* She pushed away from the spray and grabbed the soap. *It's not as if things are going to change.*

She'd have to put some ointment on her calves tonight, she realized, twisting her foot in a circular motion and grimacing at the immediate protests in her muscles. That was what she got for trying to show off.

But Holden could handle the challenge, she realized with grudging respect. Most people would've quit the minute she upped the pace. A secret part of her was glad he hadn't. She couldn't respect a man who couldn't keep up with her. Did she want Holden's respect? Why should that play into the equation? Jane had to admit, something about Holden made her want to look twice in his direction. She'd seen plenty of hard bodies during her military career—so much so it was more surprising to see a soft physique— but Holden's body was carved from granite, all hard planes and razor sinews of strength that made her itch to touch them. Just admitting that to herself sent shameful heat scuttling to her cheeks, and she actually heard her father's voice in her head ranting about "female hormones" and the pursuant "unstable" nature of all women.

Get a grip, Fallon. Stay focused on the big picture. Protect your reputation in the department and find a way to show Holden he's wrong about his brother.

She shut off the water and wrapped her towel around her with a grim smile. Sounded like a solid plan. *Now get to it.*

Chapter 4

Fifteen minutes later both Holden and Jane were alone in the conference room ready to work. Despite the fact she'd just run a grueling distance and had just hopped out of the shower, Jane looked impeccable, dressed in a tailored suit and her short, dark hair blown dry and styled. Holden, however, could still feel water dripping down his back from the quick towel off and subsequent dash to the office. Suddenly, he felt disheveled. He shifted in discomfort at the pull of his shirt beneath his suit jacket and took a seat opposite Jane.

She got right to it. "Okay, Holden, here's your chance. What's this new evidence you're talking about?"

Time to come clean. "I lied." He watched as a

storm immediately sprang to life in her eyes. He held his hands up in a conciliatory gesture, hoping to ward off the lightning before she incinerated him where he stood. "I knew that if I said I just had a gut feeling, there's no way anyone would've taken me seriously."

"You lied?" Her voice registered cold disbelief as she stiffened. Jane skewered him with her gaze, saying in a low whisper, "I knew it."

"Let me explain," he started, but she wasn't interested in his reasons, not that he blamed her. Anyway, he didn't really care about her opinion of him.

"This only further proves my point," she said, waving off his attempt. "You are definitely not thinking clearly if you are willing to jeopardize your entire career for a disgraced brother who'd made his own bed." She rose abruptly. "I'm telling Reed. This farce of an investigation is finished."

"Wait," he said, compelling her to stop. "Reed has agreed to let us investigate, to dig a little deeper. What will it hurt to flip over a few more stones?"

"What will it hurt? *My credibility.* I know it seems crazy to think of someone aside from yourself, but I have a personal interest in seeing this case closed. This was my case and I investigated it to its successful conclusion. Just because you don't like the outcome doesn't mean you get to change the ending of the story. With your military background, I'm surprised you would sink this low."

Maybe he should've made something up. But a small voice inside his head had urged him to be truthful. He'd thought maybe if he could convince Jane he was right, she'd be a powerful ally. But now he was thinking that voice was insane and had definitely steered him wrong. Holden recalled another time he'd listened to that little voice and it'd blown up in his face—the time he'd told Jane he loved her and wanted to build a life with her. She couldn't dump him fast enough. Yeah, when was he going to learn to tell that voice to shut the hell up?

Time for damage control before things went sidewise fast. "I shouldn't have lied, but look at it from my point of view. I can't explain to you a twin bond because frankly, I don't understand it myself. But my brother and I knew each other like we knew ourselves. My brother was involved in something bigger than what we've seen. We've only scratched the surface of what's really going on. I know this as strongly as I know that I can't stand peas." He shrugged. "It's an ingrained knowledge. We have a week to figure out what really happened. If you truly believe my brother is guilty, how will giving me that one week to chase down any leads hurt your case? If I'm wrong, I'm wrong. Nothing changes. But if I'm right—and I believe I am—there's so much more at stake than my brother's honor."

"Such as?"

"If someone else was pulling the strings, then the real threat is still out there. And it's our job to find it and neutralize it."

Jane frowned. "I did my job, and now you want to come along and tear it apart just to soothe an emotional wound? I'm sorry, but I can't do that."

"What if it was one of your brothers?" he asked.

She shook her head. "It wouldn't be. My brothers would never do anything so rogue. You and I both know that I.D. was on the fringe. Your brother was attracted to that department because of who he was. He was an adrenaline junkie who craved excitement and glory. And I.D. gave it to him. He didn't care where it came from as long as he got his fix."

"You didn't know Miko, so don't pretend you wrote the book on his character analysis. I'm telling you right now, the man you just described was not my brother. He liked to play the hero, that much is true, and he truly thought he was doing good work. He was doing the jobs that others couldn't to keep his country safe. I'm sure he was devastated when he found out I.D. had played him false."

"So devastated he kept putting people in his gun sights and collecting those paychecks?" she mocked. Holden understood she was not buying one red cent of his plea. "You're spinning your wheels. Your brother screwed up and you're screwing up by championing a lost cause."

"A man of my brother's character would never pull the trigger on himself unless he was forced to," Holden stated matter-of-factly, ignoring her mockery. "He just wouldn't. Someone forced his hand. Aren't you the least bit curious—no, *worried*—about who is actually calling the shots? I owe it to my brother to figure things out, but *you* owe it to our country. I know that means something to you. We can't protect

our nation from outside threats if we can't even identify what threats may reside right in our own house."

He was reaching her—he could see it in her eyes.
"I don't like your methods," she finally said, looking as if she'd rather eat rat guts than admit he may
have a point, but she wasn't stupid and that was a
point in her favor. "You shouldn't have lied. Good,
bad or indifferent, you should've taken your chances
with the truth."

"Maybe. But what's done is done and I'm not about
to apologize. Are you with me or are you going to
turn tail and run back to the chief to tattle on me?"

Her lips pressed together in a tight line. She
didn't like being called a tattler. "Fine," she snapped.
"You've got one week. If at the end of the week we
don't have anything substantial to go on, we're closing this case and I never want to hear about it again.
Am I clear?"

"Crystal." He breathed a sigh of relief. If Jane had
marched into Reed's office and told their superior that
Holden had misrepresented the facts, he could have
been fired. It was a gamble he'd begrudgingly been
willing to take. Having Jane on his side would make
things a lot easier by half. Well, the investigating
process would go more smoothly. Now he just had to
find a way to stop thinking of her in terms that had
nothing to do with the job. *Focus, man.* "Since we've
sorted that out, I want to stop by my brother's bar. He
spent the most time there. We might find evidence."

"We went over the place with a fine-tooth comb.
There's nothing there. Besides, everything's been

packed up and stored in evidence. The bar is nothing but an empty shell. Plus, it's been put up for sale to satisfy debts levied against your brother's estate."

"I know all that. But I want to go anyway. I feel as if we missed something. If I know my brother, he left information behind."

Jane crossed her arms. "This is a waste of time. If you'd like, we can go through the evidence collected, but I don't relish the idea of traipsing around an empty bar, especially when there's no heat and it's snowing outside."

"You can go where you choose, but I'm heading to the bar." He scooped up his notebook and stuffed it into his satchel. It was hard to get used to—carrying the equivalent of a man purse—but it served its purpose.

She scowled. "Fine. I suppose since this whole investigation is a wild-goose chase, what's one more stop?" She grabbed her coat and slipped it on. "Any other ridiculous stops we'll be making along the way? Perhaps you'd like to get a latte while we're at it?"

"A latte sounds like a great idea," he shot back with a smirk. "I knew you were good for something." The glare she sent his way only made him grin wider. He really shouldn't enjoy ruffling her feathers, but when it was so easy…he couldn't help but grab the low-hanging fruit.

As they drove to Miko's former bar, Holden realized he needed to smooth things over if he and Jane were going to work together. Fact was, as much as he hated it, he needed her help and he wasn't going to get it by constantly needling her. "Listen, I'm sorry about the latte joke. I have mad respect for your investigative skills. And if that didn't come across when we first started this relationship, I apologize. Believe it or not, I was considered the smooth-talking brother." When his joke fell flat, he sighed. "C'mon, is this what it's going to be like for the next week? Shouldn't we at least *try* to get along?"

"You're asking me to willingly tear apart my own investigation to satisfy some gut instinct that your brother wasn't the bad guy, and you expect me to be happy about it? You're questioning my skills as an investigator. Sorry if that doesn't make me feel all warm and fuzzy."

"I remember what made you feel warm and fuzzy," he said, mostly to himself, but he enjoyed the sudden flush in her cheeks, which told him she remembered, too.

She cut him a dark look. "Keep the jokes to yourself, Archangelo. I'm certainly not in the mood for your bullshit."

He chuckled. "What a ball buster. Your family must be so proud. Tell me, Fallon, when was your father aware he had *three* sons instead of two?"

"I hate to break it to you, but you suck at stand-up comedy. Perhaps an alternative career in sanitation would be more suited for your skill set."

"Ouch. Sanitation…that's brutal. Are you calling me a piece of shit or just implying I'm only good for cleaning it up?"

"Take your pick." She shrugged.

Damn, this was gonna be one long week.

Jane was fuming. If she were a cartoon character, heat waves would've been steaming from the top of her head. She hated how Holden had manipulated her into opening this case, when in fact there'd been no true reason to do so. Now if she went to Reed and admitted she'd fallen for Holden's bait, she'd end up looking like the weak-minded investigator who had no confidence in her skills. And now he was trying to joke? Even worse, bring up their sexual history? Who the hell did he think he was? She found nothing funny about the situation and she sure as hell didn't appreciate him throwing in an inappropriate sexual reference. If she thought she could get away with it, she might've unloaded a clip into his numbskull. "What do you hope to find at the bar?" she asked in a clipped tone. "And if you thought there was something at the bar, why didn't you look before now?"

"Because I wasn't thinking clearly after I heard the news about my brother. It's called grief."

Oh, good gravy. She had to let that pass or else she'd end up looking like a heartless bitch. "Don't you think if you had such a tight bond with your brother he would have told you he was in some kind of trouble?"

"Yes." He nodded but added, "Unless he thought doing so would put me in danger. A few months before he died, he'd been acting really strange. Evasive. Twitchy, even. If I hadn't known better, I would've said he was doing drugs, but my brother was against illegal substances. We'd both seen too many good soldiers get messed up by meth or heroin. My brother would never touch that shit."

"But if you were so close, why didn't you try to pin him down and get the answers?"

"I tried. By that point, my brother must've been in too deep and I couldn't reach him. At the time, I thought Miko was just going through a weird phase and maybe needed some space. It happens with twins—going your whole life attached to another human being, you sort of lose your own identity— so I figured it might be something like that. But it wasn't, and by the time I realized something bad was about to happen he was dead."

"And you have no idea what he could've been into?"

"No. His work with I.D. was classified, and honestly, I didn't think I needed to care. It wasn't until he started acting weird that I realized maybe I ought to poke my nose where it didn't belong."

"And what makes you think Miko didn't know what he was doing?"

He shrugged. "I don't know. Maybe he did, but he was trapped by circumstance. Sometimes when you're knee-deep in mud and you're sinking fast, your first and only thought is staying alive. Maybe that's what happened."

That was a lot of *maybe*. "You're going to need a lot more than flimsy theory to make any meaningful change to your brother's file. Unfortunately, brotherly love doesn't supersede the facts."

He bristled with mild insult. "Of course not. I would never expect it to, but when you have a man who has lived his life by a certain code of honor and prides himself on being someone you can respect, ignoring the clues to dig deeper is just lazy investigating."

Did he just call her lazy? The man had balls. "Do not *ever* call me lazy. Just because you're having a hard time accepting facts doesn't mean you get to throw my skills under the bus. I went above and beyond to find the answers. More was at stake than just your brother's life. High-ranking officials were killed, and I.D.'s rot caused the disintegration of an *entire* department. I'd say more than your brother's *honor* was destroyed."

"You're right," he conceded, but followed by saying, "but my brother's honor is all that I care about."

Jane knew he spoke with raw honesty. He'd do anything to prove his brother's innocence, which made her wonder—would he be willing to lie to save his brother's ass? She'd have to keep a close eye on him.

Holden might be just as dangerous as Miko in an entirely different way.

Chapter 5

Reed Harris shook hands with his unexpected visitor, curious as to why Ulysses Rocha, one of the owners of Tessara Pharmaceuticals, had requested an audience. Ulysses, who, also with extensive military experience, had turned to the private sector for more lucrative opportunities; and in spite of the negative press incurred by the situation involving Penelope Granger, another high-profile shareholder, Tessara Pharm was still turning a substantial profit.

"Forgive me, but what is this about?" he asked, getting straight to the point. Ulysses, a barrel-chested man with eyes as hard as flint, cracked a smile that looked entirely out of place on his face, making Reed wonder what the hell was truly going on. "It isn't every day that I receive requests for a meeting outside of certain circles."

"I can appreciate that. As you know, Tessara Pharm has suffered a number of unfortunate events lately, most notably with one of our major founders, Penelope Granger, aka Penny Winslow, who was found guilty of running I.D. as her own personal hit squad through her association with Tom Wyatt."

"Yes, I am aware," Reed said. "Corruption is an equal-opportunity contaminant."

"Yes, so it would seem. Tessara Pharm has suffered its fair share of bad press, and as such, we would be happy to leave all that sordid business in the past, as you can well imagine."

"Of course."

"So when we heard the case involving Miko Archangelo had been reopened, we were concerned how that might affect Tessara Pharm."

Ah…the true reason for the visit. "These things happen. New evidence cropped up and we're obligated to follow the trail wherever it may lead."

"New evidence?" At Reed's noncommittal nod, Ulysses frowned. "What possible new evidence could there be? Both Penny and Miko are dead and I.D. has been shut down."

"Let's put a pin in that question for a moment and draw attention to a question I have—how exactly do you have knowledge of a classified investigation? As far as I'm aware, Tessara Pharm is not on the executive payroll…or is it?"

A slow, cold smile spread across his face, as if

amused that Reed was questioning him. That alone was enough to get the man thrown out, but something stayed Reed's hand. Something wasn't right and it wasn't just that Ulysses was trying to pry information out of him.

The man cocked his head to the side. "Let's just say that people in high places have expressed an interest in seeing that the Archangelo case remains closed. People need to be able to move on, Chief Harris. Surely you understand that?"

Reed didn't like the man's tone. A shiver of warning played "Taps" on his spine. He clasped his hands carefully atop his desk and waited. Again that cold smile appeared.

"There is no conspiracy," Ulysses continued. "No big cover-up. Just businesspeople concerned that dredging up bad history will lead to a bad future for their bottom line. Shareholders are sensitive to fluctuations in their dividends. It's our job to make sure those dips and valleys aren't too sharp."

"And it's my job to make sure the security of our nation isn't at risk," Reed countered smoothly. "Frankly, I could give two shits about your shareholders' bottom line, and you have some balls to come in here and expect me to dance to your tune just because you *know* a few people. Well, newsflash…I know a few people, too."

"I see." Ulysses dropped the smile, which was fine by Reed; they both knew it was fake. "I guess it'll have to come down to who knows the better people."

He laughed. "I answer to the president. Who do

you answer to? A bunch of entitled rich people? I think I win."

Ulysses rose and adjusted his suit coat. "I'd hoped we could see eye to eye on this."

"I don't see how we could," Reed said with frank amusement. "We seem to be on opposite continents."

"So it would seem."

Ulysses showed himself to the door and walked out without further comment. It wasn't until Ulysses had left the building that Reed let out his held breath. Something foul was afoot. It would appear Holden was right; there was more to the story than met the eye. Was Miko simply a pawn in a bigger game? And if so, who was the true game master? The entire situation left a bad taste in his mouth, but he had no doubt if there was something to be found, Holden would find it.

Reed's only fear? Miko had already paid for his involvement with his life. Reed sure as hell didn't want his two best agents to pay the same price.

The Realtor, none too happy to be out in the blustery weather with two people who plainly weren't going to be buying, opened the front door of the bar and stamped his feet free of the snow clinging to his boots. "Two floors. The upstairs was the office area." He looked at his watch. "Do you know how long this is going to take?"

"You can wait in your car if you prefer," Holden suggested and the Realtor was only too happy to take him up on his suggestion.

After the man had disappeared, Holden and Jane clicked on their flashlights, illuminating the dim interior. The bar had been closed for almost six months, but the stale smell of beer remained. Holden had visited a few times right after Miko purchased it. It was supposed to be the thing that kept him busy after retirement, he recalled, the memory springing to mind…

"A bar?" Holden had exclaimed as Miko drove them to the location for the first time. "You bought a bar?"

"Yeah, sounded like a good idea at the time," Miko had said, grinning. "What could be better than being the proprietor of good times? I figure I might as well make a little money at the place where I most often frequent on my downtime, right?"

"Owning a bar is more than just free beer, Miko," Holden had said, frowning. "It's a huge responsibility."

"Stop being such a wet blanket. Things are good. I'm no longer punching a clock and I've landed a pretty sweet side gig, so I can afford to lose money on the bar for years before I start to sweat. And if it gets to be too much of a pain in the ass, I'll just unload it. So stop worrying."

Holden had glanced around the bar, grudgingly noting the whiskey-soaked charm of the place, and he'd realized his brother could make a killing if managed properly. But Miko was all about the good time, not the profit margin. He had thought then that even if Miko put minimal effort into the bar, it'd still turn a profit, which had been reassuring. Good location, clean but not too pristine, with a lived-in, comfortable feel. Like the bar in that show *Cheers*. Where everyone knew your name. He had looked to Miko, who had still been awaiting his opinion, and said with a smile, "Tell me about this side gig." Miko had just shaken his head and hooked his arm around Holden's shoulders.

"First, we celebrate. Life is good, my brother. Life is good."

As Miko's voice faded from Holden's memory, his eyes stung. "You okay?" Jane asked, peering at him. "You look as if you're going to cry."

"I'm fine," he said roughly, heading toward the staircase, then taking the steps two at a time. He detoured to the left and opened the door to Miko's private office with Jane on his heels. To her credit, she didn't pester him to share his feelings, and he was grateful. His grief over the death of his twin was something he kept close to his heart and covered with plenty of layers—he didn't have the luxury of breaking down. The hardwood floor creaked beneath their feet and echoed in the nearly empty room. Everything of value had been stripped from the walls and sold at auction. Only Miko's desk remained for staging purposes. A small, high window let in cold, milky light, but the gloom in the room seemed to seep into Holden's bones. A sense of danger clung to the shadows, and he pushed the disquieting sensation away so he could focus.

It seemed he wasn't the only one keying in on the

weirdness in the room. "The mind plays tricks on you when you know someone died violently in the space you're in," Jane said, rubbing at her arms and shivering inside her thick jacket. "But even still, this place is giving me the creeps. Can we get on with it before hypothermia hits?" She glanced around with irritation. "I don't even know what we're looking for."

"Anything."

"Well, thank you for that completely unhelpful direction." She gestured to the still room. "Nothing's here. Everything's been cleaned out, either to sell or to put into evidence."

She wasn't saying anything that Holden couldn't see for himself, but his gut told him that something was here. *Show me, Miko. If you're in this room, watching me stumble around in the dark...give me something to go on....*

He crossed to the desk and began opening the drawers, the old wood scraping against the rollers with a screech. A few pens rolled out along with a puff of dust and an assortment of discarded paper clips. He picked up one of the pens and shone the light on the lettering. Tessara Pharm. Not surprising, since it had been discovered Penelope Granger, aka Penny Winslow, was the one pulling the strings. He pocketed the pen and closed the drawer.

Jane caught the movement and moved toward him. "What's that and why are you putting it in your pocket?"

"Calm down. It's a pen."

"Why are you taking it?"

"Because I am."

She let it go, which was good. He didn't know why he had scooped up the pen, either. "Where's it from?" she asked.

"Tessara Pharm."

"Ugh. That place leaves a bad taste in my mouth. Big pharm companies are usually up to no good, in my opinion."

"Yeah, I hear you," he agreed, moving to the next drawer and opening it. Empty. He slid his hand along the edge of the bottom, looking for anything that his brother might've hidden, but nothing aside from wood met his fingers. Dropping to his knees, he flashed the light beneath the desk, checking for evidence of a false bottom, but he saw nothing out of the ordinary. He rose with sharp disappointment, feeling as if he were missing what was right in front of him.

He thought Jane sensed his disappointment, though for a long moment, she didn't say anything. "I understand—" she began, and he immediately cut her off.

"You don't understand, and don't patronize me with your attempt," he said brusquely, moving away from the desk and flashing the light into the corners of the room.

"I'm just trying to help," she muttered.

"Yeah, well, help by looking. There's something here. I can feel it."

"Great—another gut instinct. Does your gut give a clue as to where exactly we should be looking, because all I see is a sad empty room that's as cold as a storage locker."

Frustration built under his breastbone. "Hell, I don't know," he said, walking slowly over the floorboards to listen for minute changes. He walked into the small supply closet and flashed the light around. Nothing but empty shelves and dust. He stamped the floor, listening for a sound change. He explained when he caught Jane watching him with a question in her gaze. "When Miko and I were kids, we would hide things in the floorboards of our old house. We were always trying to hide alcohol or important stuff from our old man, who was a raging alcoholic. When he was sober, he was an okay dad, but when he drank…let's just say he made living hard." He didn't know if Miko had held on to the habit, but it was worth a shot.

"How often did your dad drink?" she asked.

"Only on the days that ended in *Y*."

"Sorry." She seemed to mean it. "So what'd you hide?"

"Anything we didn't want him to sell or break. Sometimes we hid money, too. Otherwise, our dad would drink it all away and we'd have nothing left for food."

"That's rough."

He shrugged. "Everyone's got a sob story, right?"

"Yeah, I suppose."

"How about yours? I can only go from what I know firsthand, but your dad seems like a piece of work. Couldn't have been easy growing up with The Major."

"Oh, is this sharing time?" She lifted her brow. When he hiked his shoulder, she shook her head, not ready to reciprocate. "Let's just focus on the task at hand, all right?"

"I'm curious.... How happy was your dad when you broke things off with me? He probably threw a ticker-tape parade."

"My dad doesn't like showy extravagances," she answered, flashing her light along the ceiling, looking anywhere but at Holden. "And he'd never do anything that gave anyone the impression you mattered in the overall scheme of things."

"What was his problem? As far as I know, I never pissed in his cornflakes."

"Are we doing this now?" she asked, annoyed. "It's in the past and we're here to do a job. Story hour will have to wait."

"Suit yourself." He shrugged and continued to slowly pan the floor. Why was he looking for answers to a mystery that didn't need solving? Who cares if some self-important asshole didn't think he was good enough for his daughter? "But here's the thing, you dropped me like a bad habit all because Daddy said so. Frankly, Fallon, I thought you had bigger balls than that."

She stopped and met his gaze. "My balls, or lack thereof, are none of your business. Can we please stick to the task at hand, or would you rather pull up a chair and start a counseling session? I should warn you, I'm all out of tissues."

"You're a piece of work. You did me a favor," he

muttered, unable to believe he'd opened his mouth in the first place. "Forget I mentioned it."

"Already have."

Damn, he was stupid ten times over for bringing up ancient history at the worst possible time. But sometimes his mouth just took over and he had to run to catch up. Sort of like the day he'd taken it upon himself to have a talk with The Major. Yeah, that'd ended in all sorts of bad. He supposed good intentions didn't mean crap in the Fallon household. Holden's first real, solid relationship had gone down in flames all because some crotchety five-starred major general had really messed up ideals and expectations for his only daughter.

Holden looked at Jane. "You know, I feel sorry for you." Jane regarded him with a wary expression, but he continued. "Yeah, I do, because you're constantly looking for Daddy's approval and you've obviously never seen the movie before. Well, I have, and I can tell you—it never ends the way you want it to. Your dad is an overbearing prick and he'll never give you what you're looking—no, begging—for, yet you'll sacrifice everything in your life for that one tiny nugget of approval from a man who ought to just love you for who you are. And it's sad, Fallon. Really sad."

She swallowed audibly and he knew he'd hit a nerve, but in true Fallon style, she didn't bend or show weakness. "Are you finished?" she asked in a husky tone that immediately made him feel like a toad. What the hell was wrong with him? He should've just left it alone. What did it matter what her issues with her dad were? They didn't affect him any longer. Jane was free to live under her father's thumb if she chose.

He waved her off. "Forget it. I don't know what's come over me. I'm sorry…that was out of line. I guess I'm just on edge."

"Sure." She accepted his apology with a stiff nod and walked away as they both continued to search the office.

After ten minutes, Holden rose with a muttered expletive. "You're right, nothing's here."

"I'll meet you downstairs," Jane said, heading for the door. Although she had a reputation for being a hard-nosed investigator, she was plainly happy to get out of the room. Seemed Jane wasn't immune to the heebie-jeebies.

Holden took one final look at his brother's office, trying not to picture him sprawled across his desk with the back of his head shot off. Nathan had said in his statement that moments prior to Miko eating that bullet, he had told Nathan to dig deeper into Tessara Pharm. Nathan Isaacs, one of Miko's best friends and fellow snipers formerly employed by the now-defunct I.D., had managed to peel back a layer of corruption within the covert government agency, but he'd nearly died in the process.

Holden caught up with Jane on the stairs. "I didn't see any mention of Tessara Pharm in your report aside from the brief notation about Winslow. Didn't you ask any questions regarding Miko's involvement with the pharm company?"

"What involvement? Winslow was the only connection to Tessara Pharm, and she's dead, which I noted in my report."

"The last thing my brother said to Nathan Isaacs was for him to look deeper into Tessara. Don't you think that warrants a look?"

"He said that before Isaacs took down Winslow. Trust me, that was the only connection. You don't get government contracts without being thoroughly vetted. Tessara is clean."

He didn't believe it. Miko wouldn't have said that if that were the case. "I'd like to poke around Tessara, but first I want to talk to Nathan again and see if he left anything out of his statement."

"Such as?" Jane asked, frowning. "Are you saying that Isaacs could've withheld evidence?"

"No. But maybe he forgot some details. It's not as if Nathan didn't get caught up in some hairy shit, too. Winslow almost won that fight. Nathan was in ICU for weeks recovering from a bullet wound to the gut, and that's no cakewalk."

"I read the file. Even bleeding out, he managed to take a beating from Winslow before killing her. Impressive," she admitted. "Nathan Isaacs is a bit of a badass."

Yeah, it was true. He wouldn't steal Nathan's thunder just because the sudden admirable light in Jane's eyes caused a spurt of jealousy from out of nowhere. So instead, he said, "He's a good man. One of the best."

Jane nodded, and it was apparent he'd caused the

wheels to start moving, which was a good thing. He'd rather have her working with him than against. "Fine, we can talk to Isaacs, but everything is going on the record. I don't want anyone using the excuse they won't talk unless they have anonymity."

"Sometimes you have to bend the rules, Fallon," he told her, giving her no such promise. When lives were at stake, sometimes regs went out the window. He'd do whatever it took to get the real answers, and that included twisting the rules into a pretzel.

"You're impossible to work with," she groused under her breath as they walked into the main room. The bar was off to the right, and a pool table stood, dejected and forgotten, on the left. Jane noticed the table and said, "I'm surprised they didn't immediately sell that at auction."

"Me, too," he said, frowning. Everything of value had been stripped from the bar, including Miko's collectible tap handles he'd purchased for a steal on eBay. Holden strode to the pool table and ran his palm over the familiar green felt. He and Miko had played many games on this table and wagered more money than they should've because they were both so damn competitive. A smile tugged at his mouth at the memory. "Miko was a terrible pool player but a great cheater. I wouldn't be surprised if he'd found a way to slant the table to his advantage. He didn't even deny the fact he didn't play fair. The sucker was always taking me for a couple hundred every time we played."

"So much for that honor you were talking about," she quipped drily, and Holden shook his head.

"No, it wasn't like that. He considered any *competition* fair game. Second place is first loser. C'mon, Fallon, you can't tell me you don't feel the same."

"True," she agreed grudgingly. "But I don't condone cheating of any kind. If you can't win on your own merits, you don't deserve to win."

He grunted a concession and bent down to inspect the ball return. "Maybe it's broken and they figured whoever bought the place could either throw it away or have it repaired." He felt along the track. The balls gleamed in the dim light, a reminder of better times. He pulled three quarters from his pocket and slid them into the coin return, pushing it in, but the coins slid back out, answering that question. "Yeah, it's broken," he said, reaching underneath to feel along the underside. The pads of his fingers found a tiny button and he stopped, motioning for Jane to bring the light. "I feel something…a button of some sort. I don't know much about pool tables, but I can't imagine why there'd be a button underneath the table." Jane came closer and bent to peer beneath the table with the light. "You see anything?"

"That's odd," she agreed. "Press it and see what happens."

"Famous last words," Holden quipped with a grin and she grimaced at his humor. But soon neither were laughing because suddenly a hidden door released and a taped manila envelope dropped to the floor. "What the… Miko, you crafty son of a bitch…"

"What the hell is that?" Jane asked, the cold forgotten and her eyes trained on the envelope. "Why would your brother hide something in the pool table?"

"Because no one would think to look there," he answered with pride for his brother's smarts. "Good one, bro."

"That's evidence," she said, moving to stop him before he ripped open the package. "We should give it to the forensics team and let them determine what's inside."

"Screw that. My brother put it there. I'm sure of it."

"How can you be so sure?"

"Because of the way it's taped. Miko always wrapped envelopes with three strips of tape with a crisscross at the back so he'd know if anyone else tried to read his mail and then reseal it."

"Weird…but okay. We should still give it to forensics."

"Whatever is in this envelope is not leaving my hot little hands." He tucked the envelope into the interior pocket of his jacket, and after one final sweep of the bar, he headed for the door, satisfied they'd found all that would be of use to them there. "Let's go before we turn into popsicles."

"You're seriously not going to turn that envelope over to the proper authorities?"

"Nope. As far as I'm concerned, the proper authorities haven't done a good enough job to earn my trust with this case. And that definitely includes you."

She glared, but he didn't care. "You make it really hard to like you," she finally said.

He grinned. "That's okay, honey. I ain't looking for

a dinner date. C'mon, let's go someplace secure and see what my brother kept squirreled away."

His hands were frozen, but his heart was lighter than it'd been in months. Finally, a break. Thank God for Miko's penchant for hiding things. It was oddly comforting to know that even though Miko had changed, some things had remained the same.

Chapter 6

Jane remained silent once they'd climbed into the car. She'd been absolutely certain she'd missed nothing in her investigation, but the second Holden had discovered that hidden manila envelope, everything she'd thought she'd known came into question. Was there more to this case than she'd originally thought? And if so, what did that mean? Who was involved? It hurt her head to think the corruption centered at I.D. was bigger than they could imagine. "How had you known to keep looking?" she asked, breaking the silence. "As far as I could tell, we were staring at an empty building. But you sensed there was something hidden. How?"

Holden shrugged, as if he really didn't know and his inability to put it into words made him uncomfortable. "I guess it's the twin thing. Miko and I shared a bond. And I just knew I was missing something. It's like an itch you can't scratch, except that it's at the back of your mind, nagging, whining in your ear." He stopped as if he hadn't liked the way his explanation had come out and finished with another shrug, saying, "I don't know. I just knew."

"Why would Miko hide something in the pool table?" she asked, mostly to herself. "I have to be honest, the discovery of that envelope opens up a whole other realm of questions that I'm not entirely comfortable with."

"I can imagine."

"Oh? Can you?" She didn't try to hide the bitterness in her voice. Her father was not going to be happy about this newest development. "Obviously he didn't want anyone to find it. And if he didn't tell you about it, something in that envelope must be important."

"My thoughts, too. Which is why we're not taking it back to the office," he said, surprising her. He cut her a short look just as she started to protest. "Listen, I don't know how far or how deep the corruption went with I.D., but I do know that my brother got caught up in something bad. So forgive me if I'm not too trusting right now."

"Even with your own team?"

"It's nothing personal, but I can't afford mistakes. My brother died. Yes, he may have pulled the trigger, but someone else was pulling the strings. You know what I mean?"

"That's one theory," she reminded him, not quite on board yet that Miko hadn't been pulling the wool over everyone's eyes, including his brother's. "The other theory is that Miko had plenty to hide because he was doing things he knew were wrong."

"Miko was the soldier, more so than I ever was. He believed in doing the right thing and standing up for the little guy who couldn't stand up for himself. He had integrity, grit, a singular sense of justice," Holden said, holding his ground, obviously determined to defend his brother to anyone and everyone. "And I refuse to believe that in one year's time he became the polar opposite of everything he ever held true."

"People change," she said, trying to soften the harsh truth. "And sometimes we don't even know what happened."

"I'm going to find who's pulling the strings. I don't care how long it takes or what it costs me. And when I find him or her...I want to put that person into the ground."

She suppressed a shudder at the menace in Holden's voice. A part of her wanted to remind him this was the reason he hadn't been allowed to investigate the case in the first place. Emotional attachments muddied a person's ability to think rationally. But there was another part of her, the part that admired his loyalty and tenacity, that couldn't deny the sharp pull of attraction. He was damn sexy when he was going all *Rambo* and *Rebel Without a Cause,* even if it was the most reckless attitude she'd ever witnessed. She swallowed and cleared her voice, not liking the way her thoughts were tumbling through her head. "And just where do you plan to take this evidence?"

"Back to my place."

"It's evidence and needs to be logged properly," she maintained stubbornly. "You're dangerously close to going rogue. Don't screw your career trying to avenge your brother."

"I'm not killing my career. I'm chasing leads. You already had a chance to dig deep into this case. You were content to look at the surface, and that's just not the case with me. When I'm done learning whatever I can from the contents of the envelope, I will log it properly. Until then, it's not leaving my side."

She could tell it was no use arguing with him on this point. She'd been around enough stubborn men to know when the smartest course of action was to back down and try a different tact. *Motto for the day: Fight smart.* "Fine. But I'm coming with you. I need to make sure the integrity of the case remains unsullied, even if you are using unorthodox methods. And that point is nonnegotiable."

Holden probably didn't like her terms, but he didn't shoot them down, either. Holden was a lot of things— stupid wasn't one of them. At least they had that in their favor.

Soon enough, they arrived at Holden's apartment, and Jane had to tamp down the mild flutters erupting in her belly at the memories surfacing. She could chastise herself all day for allowing her thoughts to wander, but she enjoyed the seductive allure that came with lingering over that brief time in her life. She couldn't lie—they'd enjoyed some good times. "Did it ever occur to you when you were apartment shopping to consider a place that didn't look like a prison from the outside?" she asked with a healthy dose of sarcasm, and he responded with a grunt. Such a Chatty Cathy, she wanted to grumble. Would it kill him to engage just a little? She followed him through the gated entrance and then up the long flight of stairs to his door. From the outside, the nondescript gray building was nothing to look at, and since everything was covered in snow, not a hint of foliage was visible, either. "Not much for ambiance," she said under her breath, to which Holden just kept walking.

"I'm not interested in making the place look inviting. The less traffic, the better."

"Such the people person," she said, walking into his spacious apartment. The first time she'd seen his place, her jaw had dropped to the floor. Never in a million years would she have imagined such an awesome bachelor pad tucked in this building. It was like something featured in *Architectural Digest,* with its high ceilings and polished bamboo flooring, and the decor was tastefully masculine without appearing to lack a woman's touch. Holden had knocked down the walls connected to three more apartments, which heightened the chic appearance and immediately told people that this wasn't your average apartment. And seeing it again, not just through the sliver of an open door like the other night when she'd visited him, was enough to fill her with awe all over again.

"God, I'd forgotten how much I covet your apartment," she blurted.

The tiniest quirk of a smile was his only response as he tossed his keys into a small ceramic bowl by the door. He went straight to the gleaming kitchen and grabbed a bottled water from the stainless steel refrigerator and tossed another to her. "Sorry, but it's a package deal. Can't have the apartment without me," he said with a shrug. "And you've already kicked me to the curb."

Why'd he have to constantly bring up their past? It was getting old. She turned to face him. "Can you stop being a whiny baby for two minutes? I can't believe how petulant you sound."

"You're right," he said, grinning. "Can't seem to help myself when you're around. Low-hanging fruit and all that."

"Well, try," she told him and opened the water bottle. "Here's something I've always wondered…how did you manage to convince the owner to give you three apartments so you could make these changes?"

"I own the building. As long as I got the right permits, the city let me do whatever I want."

"You own the building?"

"Yeah? Didn't I mention that before?"

"No."

He chuckled as if it were no big deal and said, "Well, now you know. I own the building. It's the best way to control who your neighbors are."

Wasn't that the truth. If she'd been in charge of her apartment complex, she never would've allowed dogs.

Her immediate neighbor had a small, yappy purse dog that barked at all hours of the night. Before Jane had invested in earplugs, she'd wanted to commit a crime that PETA would've persecuted her for. She'd even gone so far as to measure the width of the trash chute and, yep, a small dog would totally fit through the opening. "I suppose so," she admitted with a shrug before slanting a curious gaze at him. "And *how* exactly did you afford this building?"

"Smart investments. I bought it years ago when housing values were still manageable. Cosmetically, it was in bad shape, but the bones were good, so I did the work myself, with some help from Miko when he could manage it. Once we were finished, I was judicious about who I rented to. All in all, it's worked out pretty well."

She whistled with appreciation. "I should say so. Holden, I never thought I'd say this about anything involving you, but I'm jealous."

"I don't blame you. Your apartment sucks."

Her cheeks heated and she wrinkled her nose at him. "Yeah, well, not everyone is independently wealthy, as you apparently are."

"Not wealthy, I just have an eye for good investments."

"I guess so. A bachelor pad like this probably bags plenty of chicks. I imagine the hardest part is getting them to leave."

"I suppose it could be, but I don't bring chicks here."

She tried not to let his admission floor her. Had

she been the only woman he'd brought here? She'd thought for sure he'd use this place to get plenty of tail. "Really? So all of this grand architecture and stylish decor is just for your benefit?"

"Pretty much. Your home should be your sanctuary. When I come home, I don't want other people crowding my space. You know what I mean? When I walk through my front door, I try to leave everything else behind. And if I started bringing chicks here, it would change the energy of the place. Plus, I don't like women knowing where I live. It gets messy."

"So why'd you bring me here?" She shouldn't have asked, but she had and there was no taking it back.

His gaze darkened. "Do you really want to know the answer to that?"

She swallowed. Maybe not. She nodded anyway. "Yeah."

"Because you were special. I know you don't believe me, but I don't go around telling women that I love them unless I mean it."

A strange, sizzling burn skidded across her chest, and she had to suck back the gasp from the unexpected pain. Why did he have to go throwing the *L* word around? It wasn't that she didn't believe him or she hadn't felt something in return, but she'd known that if she didn't end things, it would've ended messily later. "Well, I guess that's ancient history," she returned briskly, forcing a smile. "I think we both dodged a bullet. I don't think either one of us is cut out for the *until death do us part* thing. It would've been a nightmare in the end."

"I guess we'll never know." A shadow passed over his face and she suffered the knowledge that she'd hurt him, probably more so than she'd realized at the time. However, as evidenced by the way her dad had reacted to Holden's little sit-down-and-chat, she really had saved him years of misery. "And now the conversation just got too angsty," he announced, breaking the silence between them as he pulled the envelope from his satchel. "Let's put a pin in all that 'ancient history,' as you call it and see what's in this envelope," he suggested, redirecting. He had a point—they weren't here to gab like girlfriends; they were here to open that envelope. Jane took a long drink of water as Holden used his Leatherman pocket knife to slice open the envelope. He dumped the contents carefully onto his granite countertop.

"Wow, someone was saving for a rainy day," she observed as money, at least twenty thousand dollars, dropped to the counter along with several passports and driver's licenses. Jane grabbed the first passport closest to her. "This isn't your brother's name," she said, showing Holden the fake ID. "None of these are. Why would he need multiple aliases?"

He frowned. "I don't know." Holden pushed the cash out of the way and grabbed the IDs. "Three different identities, none of which I've ever heard of." He read the addresses. "Mexico, Switzerland, London. What were you into, Miko?" he muttered. "What the hell were you doing?"

Wasn't it painfully obvious? "Holden, he was getting ready to run because he knew he'd been caught.

For whatever reason, he decided to kill himself instead." Jane would have to be the bad guy. She tacked on, "I'm sorry," because she did feel the tiniest bit of regret that she'd been right all along. She wasn't an ogre. Holden had obviously loved his brother. "Give it some time," she suggested. "With some distance… you'll start to feel better."

Holden shook his head, that stubborn look returning to his expression. "No, my brother would never leave me behind. You can argue all you want, but I know he wouldn't. It's that twin thing I told you about earlier."

She smothered a sound of frustration. "How many more clues do you need that prove your brother was guilty?" she asked. "Look, I know how hard this must be. And honestly, I was kind of hoping we might find a different answer, but the facts seem pretty clear."

His dark chuckle made her groan. Holden braced himself on the counter, leaning toward her. "They're clear, are they? I'm sure they're *very* clear for you. We both know this investigation is not high on your priority list. I know how this looks for you. I'm not stupid. And I know I'm asking a lot for you to trust me, and sometimes we don't even like each other, but when I tell you there's more to this story, you're just going to have to believe me and help me get to the bottom of this."

"Why? Like you said, tearing apart my own investigation isn't high on my to-do list."

"Because your type A brain won't let the possibility that you screwed up pass you by. It'll eat at you until you find the answers, even if you don't like the answers you find."

He knew her pretty well. She'd like to say it was because working in the same office, rubbing shoulders—wanted or not—would do that if paired with an observant person, but Holden knew her in a way she wanted to forget because it hurt to remember. Of course, she couldn't let him know that. "Your point?" she shot back.

"My point is you know if you push past the obvious, you'll see what I see. There's more to this story than we've been told. And you want to get to the bottom of it."

"Yeah? Why?"

"Do I have to spell it out?"

"No," she allowed with a sigh, hating he had her figured out when he was constantly surprising her. "If it turns out you're right, cracking open the true case will look good for my résumé and help give you closure about your brother. I get it!" Jane glared, hating he was right. "I said I'd give you the week. My word is good. But we better find more than just an envelope full of cash and some fake IDs as your proof Miko wasn't a traitor."

"A week is all I'm asking for."

She was taking a big risk with Holden. It felt as if she were standing on the edge of a really big fall— and Holden was the one leading her straight to the cliff.

Chapter 7

Holden stared at the IDs Miko had stashed in the pool table. London, Switzerland, Mexico—all three places were common refuges for people who wanted to disappear. He lined the IDs in a row on the counter, letting his brain work through the tangle of questions. Next his focus moved to the cash. Twenty thousand was a lot of money, but it wasn't enough to live off of for long, which meant Miko likely had money stashed elsewhere. How to find the money was the question. He couldn't go through his usual channels; he had to go underground. He knew of a guy—through his friend Nathan Isaacs—but it wasn't a strong connection. And frankly, the guy had nearly got killed the last time he had helped out on a high-stakes mission. The memory of that mission was enough to make

Holden shake his head with a dark chuckle. Most people would freak out if they knew the kind of games the government played with everyday lives. Just ask Jake Isaacs, Nathan's younger brother, who was still recovering from a dose of MCX-209, an experimental drug that'd temporarily wiped out his memories. The drug should've been destroyed and all of the research on it thrown into an incinerator, but everything pertaining to MCX-209 was under the lock and key of the Defense Intelligence Agency—including the doctor who'd created the drug, Dr. Kat Odgers. But as much as Holden didn't want to involve another civilian, he didn't see another choice. He called up his friend Nathan and hoped for the best.

"Hey, Holden, everything okay?" Nathan said as soon as he answered. In spite of the three-hour time difference, Nathan didn't sound sleepy. Insomnia was something most vets came home with, and Nathan was no different. Miko and Nathan had been tight, serving in the same unit and later working for I.D. as snipers. They'd shared a bond, similar to what Holden and Miko had shared, and Holden trusted Nathan. "I heard about the decision to strip Miko of his honors. That's rough, man. Just know that Miko was not the sum of his medals but the integrity of his heart. Keep that close and it doesn't matter what the Powers That Be take from him."

Holden closed his eyes, riding out the sting. "Thanks, man. But that's not why I'm calling."

"No? What's up?"

"I have a real small window to prove that Miko didn't do the things he's been accused of."

"Really? How did you manage that?"

"Luck and being as stubborn as a mule. But listen, this is what I need your help with—do you still have contact information for that computer guy? You know the one that made the virus that disabled the Zephyr system at the compound?"

"James Cotton? Yeah, I have his digits. But Jaci will have a fit if she finds out we're dragging her friend back into danger. She stresses over all this 'spy stuff,' as she calls it."

Jaci and Nathan had certainly been through the ringer together during the I.D. investigation. Aside from Nathan almost dying, a thug had broken Jaci's finger in order to prove a point to Nathan. At the time, Jaci had been lucky only her finger had been broken—it could've been so much worse.

"I don't blame her. People die and sometimes there's no answers when they get involved with fringe government. All I can do is make my case. The guy will either say yes or he'll say no, right?"

"True enough. Chances are James will say yes because he lives for a challenge, and for all his smarts doesn't seem to have the good sense God gave a goose. Can you tell me what's going on?"

"I'm not sure what there is to tell, but I found three IDs and passports in a hidden location and I need to know if Miko was stashing money in other countries. The only way to find that out is to go through backdoor channels. I'm assuming your guy can do that, right?"

"James can do things that are so highly illegal I don't even know how he's still walking the streets."

Holden laughed. "Excellent. That's just the kind of guy I need."

"In all seriousness, do you really think you have some solid evidence that could save Miko's reputation?"

Holden heard the hope in Nathan's voice and he understood that yearning because he felt it, too. "I sure as hell hope so. It's weak, but it's all I have to go on. I just have this feeling that if I chase it down, I'll be able to find what I'm looking for."

"Is there anything I can do to help?"

"Not just yet. I don't want to drag you into this. You've been through enough."

"It's all in the past. Nothing but good things to look forward to now. You know, you might give Jake and his girl a call. They are up in Washington, too, doing that top-secret defense intelligence stuff. They might be able to open some doors for you that otherwise might stay closed. That is, if things with James don't work out."

"I appreciate it, man. How's Jake feeling?"

"He's not one hundred percent, but he's doing damn good considering what he went through. He still has gaps in his memory. He's getting better, though. He might even recover fully. Unfortunately, only time will tell."

"That drug was scary shit. I wish they would've

just dropped all the research into the ocean. Or down a deep, dark hole. That kind of stuff shouldn't be in anyone's hands. Not even our government's."

"Amen, brother."

Holden thanked Nathan and ended the call. A few moments later, his phone chirped with the contact information he needed. He logged the name into his phone and then called Cotton, aka Ghost.

"Yeah?" James answered. "Who's this?"

"Hey, James, not sure if you remember me, but my name's Holden Archangelo—"

"Yeah, I remember you. Your brother, Miko, used to run with Nathan Isaacs."

"You have a good memory."

"Comes with being a genius. I'm assuming this isn't a call to go get drinks or something. What do you need hacked?"

He appreciated the man's straightforward attack. Holden wasn't interested in chitchat either, so he got right to the point. "I need you to trace some money. My brother may have stashed cash in three different countries and I need to know why and how much."

"You're government grade, so why don't you do it yourself?" he asked, then added, "Unless you can't because you're doing this on the down low."

"Bingo. Think you can handle this?"

"Oh, I have no doubt I can handle it. The real question is, should I? The last time I had a play date with you cats, I nearly got my balls shot off and frankly, I'm fairly attached to that part of my anatomy."

"Fair enough. I can't guarantee your safety, and there's a chance my brother was hiding from seriously bad people. However, something tells me you can't help but hunger for a challenge."

"Nice pitch. So what I'm hearing is danger, high level of threat and virtually zero benefit for me aside from the street cred in my personal circles. I don't know, maybe I'm getting old, but that's not enough."

"You drive a hard bargain."

"Or maybe I just wised up."

"What's it going to take, then?"

"Well, my car got blown up the last go around and I'm still taking the bus."

"You want me to buy you a car?" Holden asked, incredulous at the guy's nerve.

"Seems only fair."

"The Isaacs brothers ought to be the ones buying you a car. That was their op that got your ride blown to bits."

"Yeah, well, Jaci is my best friend and that just seems wrong to demand that from her and her husband, and Jake, well, he's not quite right in the head, so how nice would it look if I was shaking down a guy with special needs?"

"Jake is hardly special needs. The guy could take you out with his bare hands and a piece of twine."

"MacGyver style, I get it. Still, doesn't seem right. Besides, they don't need my help—you do. And to be honest, I don't even know you, so why should I risk my neck for a stranger?"

Valid points. "All right. How about twenty grand? That ought to be enough scratch to buy you a car."

"Twenty Gs? Yeah, that'll work," he said, whistling. "I accept your offer. Wire the cash and then I'll contact you."

"Look at you, all eager and shit. No," he said, countering firmly. "Here's how it's going down. I will wire half of the cash now and half on delivery of the information. Got it?"

"I respect that. You have a deal."

Holden gave a minute shake of his head, silently laughing at the guy's tough-guy routine when he knew for a fact James Cotton was no marine. But hey, Holden respected his grab for some personal gain. People had to eat. "Expect the wire by the end of the day. And then I expect results within forty-eight hours. Got it?"

"Forty-eight hours? I'm not a magician."

"Well, if you want to be paid, you ought to start learning some new tricks."

"You government types are all the same—expecting the delivery of the moon and then demanding it within an impossible time frame."

"Hey, forty-eight was generous. My original offer was going to be twenty-four." At that he clicked off, smirking. From what he knew of James, the guy had an ego. With any luck, he'd beat that deadline with time to spare just so he could gloat. And that was fine by Holden. He wanted—no, he *needed*—answers now.

* * *

Jane sipped her wine and settled into the bathtub, giving in to a rare luxury. She never indulged in such a girlie thing, but her muscles ached and her brain was cluttered, and she was just ready to chill out for once.

Steam heated the room into a humid sauna. She didn't mind. She liked the heat. Living in Washington, she suffered through the horrid winters just so she could get to the humid summers. Maybe someday she'd move to Florida. No, scratch that—she didn't like alligators. Maybe Georgia or some other place in the South. She liked to fantasize about leaving D.C., but in truth, she knew she wasn't going anywhere. Her home was here, where she was firmly rooted. Her father and brothers would have a fit if she tried to move. She was the one who took care of the mundane details of their father's life, and neither of her brothers were going to take on that job. Nope. As her father liked to drill into his kids, everyone had a detail, a task, and only weaklings and pathetic losers shirked their responsibilities onto others. Like her mother.

Jane took a bigger sip of the wine, bordering on a gulp, and tried not to think of her mother, but sometimes, in spite of her best efforts, a memory or two squeaked by her defenses.

It'd been a sunny day in August when The Major had sat all three of his children on the sofa, requiring their undivided attention as he shared the intel of their mother abandoning them.

"It has come to my attention that your mother has gone AWOL from this family unit," he'd said gruffly, clasping both hands behind his back and pacing a short line before them. "This is both an unexpected and disappointing turn of events, but it's nothing we can't handle."

Faced with two stoic brothers who'd turned to stone the moment their father had shared the news, she'd had little choice but to keep a stiff upper lip, also. The Major didn't tolerate crybabies. Each of the Fallon children was expected to pick up the slack their defecting mother had created, and it didn't matter they were young and confused as to why their mother would suddenly abandon them. It was soldier on or get left behind.

Jane had taken on the house details—including cooking, shopping and paying the bills. Walker and Ian were in charge of everything related to the outside and repair work. They were a well-oiled machine.

Without a shred of emotion allowed.

Their mother had made contact once, but Jane had been too desperate for her father's love to accept her mom's attempt at reaching out. She winced at the memory....

"Janie," her mother had said. "I'm settled now. I know the boys would probably rather stay with their father but...perhaps you'd like to come and stay with me?"

"And why would I want to do that?" Jane had asked in a voice colder than any twelve-year-old should be able to muster. "You abandoned us all a year ago and now you want to act like you're a mother? Too little, too late."

"Janie!" her mother had admonished her in an anguished tone. "Why are you so cold to me? Let me explain...there are some things that a child simply can't understand."

"I understand that you left. What else is there?"

Her mother had skipped answering the question and tried a different tactic, almost desperately. "Sweetie...you're reaching an age when a girl needs her mother. Surely, you realize your father is ill equipped to handle the needs of a young girl."

She had realized that. The mere mention of bra shopping had been excruciating for them both. In the end, The Major had simply thrown a wad of cash in her direction and with reddened cheeks had instructed her to purchase whatever was necessary. Of course, Jane hadn't had a clue and ended up with a bra two sizes too small. It'd felt like wearing a corset. But she wasn't about to concede any weakness to the enemy, her mother. "Not necessary," she'd said. "I can care for myself."

"I could go to court and compel you to come stay with me," she'd said. "But I won't do that. If you don't want to be with me, I won't force you."

But a secret part of her had hoped her mother would do exactly that so she didn't have a choice in the matter. Surely, her father couldn't blame her if the court had stepped in. And she missed her mother. In her darkest, deepest, most shamefully weak part of herself...she wished her mother hadn't left. But that hadn't been her reality and she'd dealt with it. Her mother had tried a few more times, but Jane had finally stopped taking her calls and then, as expected, her mother had finally stopped phoning.

Jane swirled her wine. How would things have been different if her mother had stuck it out? Maybe if The Major hadn't been so rigid...well, that was like wishing the tide would stop licking the shore. As long as there was a moon, there would be a tide. Some things would never change.

Including her father.

Stop this melancholy over a past long gone, she chastised herself, banishing the memories. But apparently her brain was up to playing games because as soon as her thoughts cleared of family drama, she thought of Holden. The alcohol loosened her grip on what was appropriate, and she immediately mused on how perfect Holden's physique was and how, maybe, in an alternate universe, they could've stayed together.

She missed quiet evenings spent curled on his sofa, watching eighties movies and arguing over what constituted a cult classic. The memory of one particular night made her sigh.

"*The Breakfast Club* is vastly superior to *Top Gun,*" she'd protested, throwing popcorn at him when he'd refused to budge. "We're talking archetypal characters that completely capture the angst and uncertainty of being a teenager, all with a kickass soundtrack and the best dialogue ever written. There's no way a movie about the navy's cocky flybys is better."

Holden grinned as if he had the ace. "Anything with fighter jets in the movie automatically ratchets the score a few points, which, of course, buries your movie about a bunch of whiny teenagers bitching about spending an afternoon together."

"But don't you get it? It's an entire movie spent picking apart the daily lives of the American teen, showing in excruciating detail the pressures teens face in modern society."

Holden had rolled his eyes and faked a yawn, then added, "Fighter pilots. And a kick-ass soundtrack—not to mention—" he paused for effect "—Kelly McGillis. She's hot for an old lady."

"Really? You're such a man."

"Yes, I am," he had agreed with a shameless grin as he pulled her on top of him. She'd laughed and fallen against his chest, knocking popcorn everywhere. "You can concede defeat and I'll accept your surrender."

"Who says I'm surrendering?" She had looped her arms around his neck and pulled him close so their lips touched. After a long, deep kiss, she'd smiled against his mouth and said, "This feels like victory to me...."

"No fair using your womanly wiles. I have no defense against them."

"I know." She had laughed. "Now admit that my movie is better than yours."

"Never."

She'd nibbled his neck and nipped his ear, sweetening the deal. "Concede and I'll let you do whatever you want with me."

He had sucked in a sharp breath and rose up, wild excitement darkening his gaze. "Anything?"

"Anything," she'd promised in a sultry whisper.

"You win! I concede! *The Breakfast Club* rules." And then he'd hopped off and pulled her to her feet to scoop her up in his arms. "You, my dear, may find victory exhausting."

Holden had spent the rest of the night pleasuring Jane in ways that had to be illegal in some places, leaving her in a state of total sated lethargy that'd seeped into the following day at the office. The sizzling memory made it hard to focus on work and each time they invariably ran into each other, she hadn't been able to meet Holden's gaze without blushing and trying to hide the all-over body tingle that shivered over her skin. Oh, yeah, Holden had definitely won that round, even if he'd admitted defeat.

Jane's legs moved restlessly beneath the water, and she finished her wine with a quick swallow. What was she doing reminiscing about Holden? To what end? Total mortification, humiliation and endless mockery if he ever found out? Ugh. She rose from her bath and grabbed her towel. Enough tub time. She needed her head on straight if she was going to remain shoulder to shoulder with Archangelo. This girlie stuff was enough to give her the heebie-jeebies.

This ridiculous attraction to Holden could go right where she stored her feelings about her mother—tucked away in subzero.

Chapter 8

The following day, Reed called them both into his office first thing. The permanent frown marks etched into their boss's face seemed a bit deeper this morning, which meant he wasn't about to ask them if they were interested in purchasing Girl Scout cookies from his granddaughter. "Shut the door and take a seat," he directed, motioning to them both. "You know I'm not a fan of conspiracy theories, but something's not right about this case. Yesterday I got a visit from someone associated with Tessara Pharm with information that he shouldn't have had. *Classified* information. The whole conversation gave me a bad vibe, and frankly, pissed me off because the guy's attitude stank of arrogance."

"What kind of questions was he asking?" Jane

asked. "And how do you think he came by the information?"

"He was mostly asking about the investigation and why it had been reopened. The fact that he knew there was action on the case gave me a bad feeling. *No one* should know that you two are looking into new evidence. It seems Tessara Pharm has people with a long-armed reach."

"Nothing like finding out that classified information isn't as secure as you think," Jane said, concerned.

"Yeah, exactly. So what do you have so far?"

Holden shared a look with Jane, not entirely ready to share what they'd found, though it seemed he'd have to give Reed something. "We went back to my brother's bar and we found something that may have some significance, but it's too early to tell. We're in the process of chasing it down."

"Such as?" Reed gestured with impatience. "Don't make me drag it out of you. Just spit it out."

Jane jumped in, surprising Holden. "Sir, if I may, it's sensitive, and given the fact that information is being leaked to people outside of classified channels, Holden and I would rather keep our evidence close to the breast for the time being."

"All right." Reed grunted in understanding even if he didn't like it. "I'll give you that. I don't know how Ulysses Rocha came across the information that he did, but you're right in that our usual channels don't seem secure. Just answer me this—do you think there's something to your suspicion that Miko was involved in something bigger?"

Holden nodded gravely. "I do. I think the fact that Tessara Pharm is poking around in our investigation lends further credence to that belief."

Jane's nod betrayed none of her own misgivings. Holden owed her one. He knew that her word was solid. If she said she'd give him a week, a week he'd get and not a minute more or less. That was all he could ask for. "I think our next step should be to make a stop in at Tessara Pharm, don't you?"

"That's a long flight for a conversation," Reed groused. "What's wrong with the phone?"

"Gotta see the whites of their eyes, sir," Jane answered and Holden agreed. "Microexpressions, body language—those things you can't pick up on the phone."

"All right. I'll approve the expenditure, only because that Ulysses guy rubbed me wrong. But keep it short and sweet and don't go ruffling feathers. I don't want even more eyes on us during this investigation. This needs to be done by the numbers and without prejudice. Got it?"

Holden smiled. "Of course."

"Stow that shit-eating grin, Archangelo. Don't think for a second I don't regret letting you poke around in a closed case. I have a feeling this is going to earn more than just extra paperwork. I have a headache already."

Holden smothered his smile under an appropriately stern look of gratitude to his superior. "Yes, sir," he said, and followed Jane out of Harris's office and headed to their desks. Once in their respective seats, Jane booked plane reservations while he prepared to call Nathan. "Since we're going to be in California, we might as well hit up Nathan, too. I have some questions regarding the last time he saw my brother alive."

"You sure you want to do that?" Jane asked. "It's not a pretty story."

"I know. I've read your report. But Nathan might tell me a few things that weren't in the report."

Jane stiffened. "You mean you think he might've deliberately withheld information?"

"Calm down, G.I. Jane," he said drily. "Nathan and Miko were buds, that's all. They knew each other as friends, not just as peers. Maybe all we'll do is share a beer and swap stories. Or maybe he'll have something important to share." He gestured to the airline page on her computer, adding, "Oh, and make sure it's first class…I need the legroom."

Jane rolled her eyes and turned to her computer to book the reservations.

Determined to make good use of her time during the flight, Jane took out her notebook the moment they were buckled in and ascending. It was eight hours to California, and she didn't want to waste valuable time. "So let's go over what we know so far," she suggested, taking a second to appreciate the first-class accommodations. Holden was right—there *was* more legroom. "I figure it's a good idea to consolidate the facts before we land so we know exactly what we're doing and who we're going to be talking to when we get there."

A spark of appreciation lit up Holden's gaze, and she tried not to read more into it than the moment warranted. But even as he seemed to like her initiative, it seemed Holden wasn't about to discuss the case on the plane. "Your enthusiasm is admirable, but I don't feel comfortable talking about the case here. Too many ears."

Jane glanced around the first-class cabin. Although the odds were slim that anyone there might compromise their investigation, she sighed and tucked her notebook away because that 1 percent chance wouldn't let her insist. "I guess I could take a nap, then," she said, disappointed. She couldn't help but add, "For the record, I think you're being a little paranoid."

"Haven't you ever watched a spy movie? The person you overlook is always the one you should watch out for."

"I don't base my life around the flimsy plots of action movies."

"Flimsy? You've obviously never watched any of the Bourne movies. And this is coming from the same woman who once argued pretty convincingly about the merits of an eighties John Hughes movie?"

Her cheeks flushed at the casual reference of that night, and she shot him a quelling look. He dropped the jocularity to say, "I'm not discussing this case unless we're alone. Sorry, but the stakes are just too high for me to take the chance, no matter how slim the odds are that someone might be listening."

She supposed if one of her brothers' reputations was on the line, she wouldn't take any unnecessary risks, either. "I see your point," she conceded with an unhappy sigh. She could always take that nap. She ought to be tired because she hadn't slept well last night, but her eyes weren't about to close, not when she was wedged this close to Holden. She didn't trust what she might mumble in her sleep, given her recent private musings. Unsettled, she shifted away from Holden as much as the seat would allow. He caught the motion and called her on it. "Do you think I have cooties or something? I promise I do bathe regularly. I even brush my teeth on occasion." To illustrate, he flashed his pearly whites.

"It has nothing to do with you," she lied. "I just like my personal space. And I hate flying," she muttered, silencing him by adding tersely, "And don't try to lecture me that flying is safer than driving. I *know* the statistics. It's a mental thing, so just leave me be about it."

Holden seemed vastly amused by her admission, his grin widening. "You're afraid of flying?"

She bristled. "I didn't say I was *afraid*. I just said I don't like it. If God meant for us to fly, he would've given us wings."

Holden laughed. "Who knew that tough-as-nails Jane Fallon was afraid of a little modern technology?"

"I'm not afraid of modern technology," she insisted. "I love my smartphone. Just something about the idea of flying doesn't sit right in my head. I mean think about it…how are we even staying up in the air? No, don't answer. I know the physics. I'm simply saying fundamentally this giant cargo bus should not be flying around like a huge bumblebee in the sky."

"Just when I think I have you figured out—you go and say something that completely tips what I think I know on its head."

Holden thought he had her figured out? That would be the day. But she was a tiny bit flattered that he'd tried. "Don't get too comfortable, Archangelo. I'm a person you would never be able to figure out."

"When you say that, I hear a challenge. And I can't in good conscience let a challenge go without answering the siren call."

"Oh, is that so?" She tried not to find his smirk adorable, but it was doing weird things to her stomach. She bumped him with her shoulder like she would any ol' dude. "Talk about testosterone overload." Were all guys the same? Or maybe it was all guys in the military. Her brothers were the same way. And her father. "Let's put a pin in your curiosity about me and share something about Miko, maybe about growing up together."

Holden relaxed and a small smile formed on his lips, though she saw the ghost of grief hovering around the edges. "What do you want to know?"

"I don't know. What was he like as a kid? Was he like you?"

"People assume because we were twins we were

exact copies of one another, but really, we were nothing alike."

"How so?"

"For one, Miko was a better man than me."

That shocked her. "Why would you say that?"

"Because it's the truth. Miko was ruled by an intense need for justice. That's why he went into the military, whereas I went because I wanted someone to pay for my college. But Miko wanted to do something for the greater good. He took pride in the fact that he did what others couldn't. He was always one for the underdog."

"So how do you think he got involved with Tessara and Penny Winslow?" she asked, frowning against the information she knew from her investigation and the man Holden was championing. It almost seemed as if they were two different people. "It appears that Tessara got under his skin in a bad way."

He nodded, just as baffled. "That's the question that keeps me up at night. Everything I know about Miko doesn't jibe with the facts as they've been played out. He didn't care about money or material things, but that's exactly how that report paints him to be. A mercenary is all about the money, and that's the opposite of Miko. Yeah, he made good change with I.D.—no doubt about it—but it wasn't what he cared about. Others might be about the paycheck. However, for Miko, it was something different. I know he felt he was doing something for his country that no one else could." He sighed. "Somewhere along the way, things got tangled."

"Do you think at some point he realized he was in over his head?"

"Definitely. And Miko was never one to ask for help. He was always the one lending a hand. When it came to accepting help for himself, forget about it."

"Why?"

"I don't know. I could guess it probably had something to do with the way we were raised. Our dad was a bit of a prick—certainly not a contender for Father of the Year. Some of those lessons stuck with us like dog crap on our shoe. I guess Miko thought he would look weak if he admitted he was in over his head. Maybe he heard our dad's voice berating him for being pathetic."

She fought the urge to grasp Holden's hand in a show of solidarity. Instead, she folded her hands in her lap in a deliberate motion but confessed, "I know what it's like to live with an overbearing father." She was surprised the words fell from her mouth so easily. Nobody talked badly about The Major. He was highly respected, highly decorated—the kind of man that you wanted walking the line at Guantanamo Bay but not necessarily the man you wanted helping with your homework. "My dad used to say that sweat and tears were just weakness leaving the body. But while sweat was allowed, tears were not. It was a tough way to grow up."

"I'd heard stories about your father. When he was on active duty, he had the ability to make or break careers. Based on what I know of him, he doesn't seem the kind of man who read his kids bedtime stories."

She laughed derisively. "*Au contraire*. My father loved reading World War II historical documents to us. He said it was good for the mind to learn from the mistakes of the past. My father was a big fan of military strategy."

"Historical documents…sounds kind of dry. That would put me right to sleep."

"Oh, you weren't allowed to sleep. Are you kidding? If The Major saw you nodding off, you had to do twenty push-ups."

"Damn, that's rough." He cast her a sideways glance. "Let me guess, you fell asleep fairly often…."

She frowned. "Why? Because I'm a girl? Why would you say that?"

He chuckled at her defensiveness. "Calm down, she-cat. I was just saying you're in pretty good shape and have been since I've known you, so you must've been accustomed to doing push-ups fairly regularly."

She blushed. Why did she have to jump to the wrong conclusion? Had he just given her a compliment? Yep. And she'd overreacted. "Sorry. I'm a little sensitive about certain things. It's hard growing up the only girl surrounded by military men."

"What happened to your mom?"

"She left when I was 11. I guess she got tired of being a military wife."

"That's rough. Do you see her at all?"

She barked a disgusted laugh. "I don't tend to chase after people who leave me behind. It was her loss and her choice."

"True, but I could hazard a guess that your dad's

not an easy man to live with. You never had the chance to ask her why she left?"

Jane pinned him with a hard look. "I don't care why. She's a quitter, and I don't have time to figure out why she bailed. And frankly, I don't need her in my life. I'm a grown woman and past the point of needing a mother to guide me through life."

Holden dropped it, clearly sensing they were skirting a sensitive issue. Jane took a deep breath, hating she couldn't talk about her mother without getting snippy. Once, she'd seen a therapist to see if she could work out her issues. The first visit had ended badly when the therapist had suggested Jane reconnect with her mother as part of the healing process. Like that was going to happen. "Listen, I didn't mean to snap at you. I just get hot under the collar when people keep suggesting I talk to my mother. She's the one who left, not me. As far as I'm concerned, she made her bed, and she can lie in it all by her lonesome."

"So you don't know if she remarried?"

"Actually, I do know that she remarried. Not that I care. It's her life. She's welcome to it. How did we get stuck on the subject of my mother? I thought we were talking about Miko."

Holden spread his fingers in a conciliatory manner. "Just trying to get to know my partner. And so far I know that she does not like talking about her mother."

Jane smiled. "Very astute. Your investigative skills are top-notch. Now, back to Miko. You say that justice was an important theme in his life. Maybe Miko was working undercover, trying to get enough evidence to take down I.D."

"That would make more sense than my brother just shooting himself because of a guilty conscience. I can also see him taking his own life if he thought it would protect mine. Maybe someone threatened my life and Miko did what he had to do to protect me."

"But why would someone threaten your life? You haven't had anything to do with Tessara Pharm, right?"

"No, but someone might've known Miko well enough to know that he'd do anything for me. Pulling strings with that kind of leverage would've been easy."

Jane let the information sink in for a minute. In her mind, she saw two brothers, linked by blood and soul. She wished she had that kind of connection with another human being. Growing up, her brothers had been protective, but they'd been too consumed with following in The Major's footsteps, both in career and mindset, to truly let her into their circle. Somehow, as a woman, she'd always been made to feel second best when it came to the men in her family. Had her mother felt that way, too? "You're lucky to have someone who loved you that much," she murmured, the sentiment slipping out before she could stop it. She caught Holden's questioning gaze and she shook her head. *Leave it.* "Forget I said that. I'm just tired."

To his credit, Holden didn't pry, although she saw the questions behind his eyes, and when she decided she'd try for that nap after all, he let her. Her last thought before falling into a fitful sleep was that if she wasn't careful, she'd end up seeing Holden as more than just another uniform…and that wouldn't do at all.

Chapter 9

Holden and Jane arrived at Nathan and Jaci's place around 10:00 p.m., and though Holden was sore from sitting in a plane for eight hours and it was really 1:00 a.m. in D.C., he was happy to see Nathan again after so much time. Technically, Nathan had been Miko's buddy, but Holden also considered Nathan his friend. He caught Nathan in a manly hug and clapped him on the back in a solid greeting, "Hey, ugly! The last time I saw you, you were leading us into certain death. Good times. Everything good?"

Nathan grinned. "After surviving multiple attempts on my life, rescuing my brother from a government compound and pretty much kissing away any semblance of a normal life…yeah, life is pretty good." As his gaze flicked to Jane, he said, "And you must be the investigating agent, Jane Fallon. I'd like to say it's a pleasure, but the circumstances suck."

"No offense taken," Jane said. "I wish we were meeting socially rather than officially. You seem like a decent guy."

"Don't let my rugged good looks fool you—I'm as bad as they come," Nathan said with a completely straight face, but Holden wasn't so restrained, and guffawed. Nathan turned to punch Holden in the arm. "Hey! Stop ruining my street cred. I've got a reputation to uphold."

"I didn't know you had a flair for fiction," Holden said. "Maybe you missed your calling." He gestured to the house. "Are we going to freeze our asses off outside or go inside for a beer?"

"Depends. Are you housebroken?" Nathan asked. "The last time I invited you over for a beer, you pissed in my plant."

Holden looked to Jane, who wore a faintly bemused expression. "Nathan loves to tell that story, but he fails to share that we were both drunk off our asses that night, and how was I supposed to tell a giant potted plant from the latrine? It was years ago in another country, I might add."

"You peed in a plant?"

"He killed it, too," Nathan supplied with mock seriousness. "You know, Holden, you might consider drinking more water. Your piss was so concentrated it came out as a solid."

"Shut up," Holden said, and pushed the joker as he laughed.

"All right, come on in. Jaci thought you guys would be hungry, so she kept the spaghetti warm."

"Home-cooked meal," Holden said, grinning from ear to ear. "Now, that's some hospitality."

"You'd better wait until you taste the spaghetti before you start throwing out thank-yous," Nathan warned in a conspiratorial whisper. "Jaci is on this gluten-free kick. The noodles are a bit chewy."

"Can't be any worse than an MRE," Jane said, smiling.

"You would think, huh?" Nathan countered as they walked inside, but the moment they entered the living room, his smiled widened with pure love at the sight of Jaci. Holden felt a pang of envy for what his friend had. Jaci had changed Nathan—in a good way—and it was something to see in action. Holden loved the ladies, but the idea of being tied down permanently caused sweat to break out on his forehead.

His gaze swung to Jane, and his heartbeat kicked up a notch for no good reason. Sure, she was hot—he'd have to be blind to miss her perfectly sculpted body honed by hours of gym time—but Jane wasn't a good time…in any sense of the word. Before he and Jane had hooked up, he'd always preferred his women pliable and a little dumb. That had all changed after Jane. She made him realize that smart women were more exciting, more challenging and definitely sexier than the vapid types he'd been sharing time with. He'd quickly discovered that Jane was probably smarter than he was, and she'd kept him on his toes with her sharp mind. Even though there was no downtime with her and it was exhausting, Jane was freaking hot as hell and nothing would ever change that fact.

"Holden, it's so good to see you," Jaci said as he folded her into a hug. She was the prettiest redhead he'd ever seen. Nathan certainly had good taste. She pulled away and extended her hand to Jane with a welcoming smile. "And you must be Jane. I'm Jaci. Very nice to meet you."

"Likewise. You have a lovely home," Jane supplied with polite interest. "Thank you for agreeing to let us stay while we're in town. Your hospitality is much appreciated."

"I'd like to say she's not always this stiff, but I'd be lying. Jane lives and breathes by the regs," Holden teased, and enjoyed the flush of heat in Jane's cheeks. He liked ruffling her feathers, which was probably a bad idea, but it was strangely addicting to watch her loosen up. It made him remember what she was like in bed. He suffered a mental groan as he pushed the image out of his head. "I heard there's spaghetti?" He sniffed the air and rubbed his stomach. "Even in first class, the food isn't much to write home about."

"Oh! I'm so glad you're hungry," Jaci said, leading them to the kitchen. "You'll have to tell me what you think of this new recipe I'm trying. Did you know gluten is like poison to our systems? I'm learning all about what gluten does to the body, and it's fascinating."

"As long as it tastes good, I don't care what it's made from." He flashed a grin at Jane.

Everyone took a seat at the oak table while Jaci

bustled around getting plates ready. Within minutes, they were digging in. At first bite, Holden didn't notice anything different and tucked into a few more healthy bites, but after a few mouthfuls, he started to notice the texture and chewed more slowly. "Definitely filling," he said around a hot bite, giving a thumbs-up to Jaci, who beamed before slapping Nathan lightly on the shoulder.

"See? I told you, it's only you who notices the difference. If you'd stop being so picky, you'd forget all about the fact the noodles are made from squash."

Squash? Holden choked down the last bite. He hated squash. But like Jane said, if he could choke down an MRE, he could eat anything. Holden cleaned his plate and Jane did a serviceable job choking down her portion, too, but he could tell she wasn't loving it. Jane would never be so rude as to admit she didn't like it, and Holden had to give her props for being a good sport. He'd have to take her out for some fancy coffee drink tomorrow morning, his treat. All too soon, the conversation turned serious, but he supposed there was no getting around that because it was the whole reason they'd come to California.

"So tell me what's really going on," Nathan said, playing with the wrapper on his beer. "I know you're not here for social reasons."

"I told you I thought Miko was being pushed by someone else. Someone compelled him to end his life, and I aim to find out who."

Nathan lost his easy smile. Talking about Miko was hard for them all, but more so for Nathan because he had been there when Miko ate a bullet. "Look, more than anyone I want to believe Miko wasn't the sniper who took out Tom and all those innocent people, but I just don't see who else could be pulling the strings to make that happen. Penny is dead. She was the head of the monster—I.D.—and it's over."

"It's not over," Holden disagreed with an adamant shake of his head. "Think about it, Nathan. Was Miko the kind of man who killed innocent people? He was Captain America, for crying out loud."

"We didn't know they were innocent," Nathan said, trying to get Holden to understand. "We thought we were doing a service to our country. We had no idea that Penny was the one calling the shots and running I.D. as her own personal hit squad. It's not Miko's fault. We were both duped."

"What if Miko was working undercover to expose the true head of the beast?" Holden supplied, leaning forward. "Tell me if this sounds odd…. Ulysses Rocha, an executive at Tessara Pharm, came to my boss to inquire about the status of Miko's case mere days after Chief Harris had given us a soft okay to re-open it on a temporary basis. How the hell did Rocha even know the case had been reopened?"

"I don't know," Nathan admitted, looking troubled. "Did he say anything else?"

"Just that he was there to protect the shareholders' interests and suggested the case remain shut for the greater good."

"Only someone with something to hide would balk

at the case reopening, particularly if they thought they were in the clear."

Jaci, who'd unfortunately also been present at the time of Miko's death, spoke up. "Holden, even if you're right, what good will come of this? What if the beast you're so keen on exposing is bigger than you can possibly handle? Maybe Miko realized this and that's why he took his life."

"Maybe, but that's not who Miko was. He never backed down from a fight. Even when he should've."

"You didn't see him that day," Jaci said gently. "He couldn't hide the pain in his eyes. He was eaten with guilt. Whatever his role was, he'd reached the end of his rope and checked out."

"We found three passports, cash and IDs in a hidden location in his bar," Jane jumped in, surprising Holden. The firm set of her mouth and tilt of her chin suggested she believed Holden was right. Something shifted inside of him, aligning in a new position. He thanked her silently and Jane gave an imperceptible nod before continuing in a strong, clear voice, "We think there may be a bigger connection to Tessara than previously believed. Why else would a bigwig fly all the way to Washington for a sit-down with our chief if not to send home the message that people are watching?"

"That's a good point," Nathan allowed, a dark scowl forming on his brow. "Damn that place. They ought to burn it to the ground."

Knowing Nathan's animosity toward Tessara was

centered on his brother Jake's situation, Holden asked, "Jake getting better?"

"Yeah, he's about eighty percent right now. Kat seems to think he'll make a full recovery eventually, but it's hard watching him struggle with his memory. Personally, I question the decision to keep MCX-209 in cold storage when it should've been destroyed. That drug is a threat to everyone on this planet."

Holden agreed. At Jane's questioning look, Holden explained quickly, "Jake was given a dose of an experimental drug created in a Tessara lab called MCX-209. It was supposed to cure Alzheimer's, but instead it wipes out memories. In earlier trials of the drug, it pretty much reduced the test subject to a drooling mess, or worse, dead with their brains leaking from their ears." Jane grimaced and Holden continued. "Yeah, pretty nasty stuff. The worst part is Jake's girlfriend, Dr. Kat Odgers, actually created the drug and was the one forced by a rogue faction within a government branch to administer it to him. So, understandably, no one at this table has fond feelings toward Tessara."

The color drained from Jane's face. "Why wasn't it destroyed? A drug like that…it's too dangerous for anyone to have."

"Because it's quite possibly the most innovative weapon ever created to date, and of course, our government felt it necessary to control it."

"That doesn't fill me with confidence." She shuddered a little. "Sounds like something out of a movie—and not a feel-good movie."

"Agreed," Holden said. "Back to Miko… Listen, Nathan, Jaci, it's late and we're tired. Tomorrow we're going to drop by Tessara and poke around, but in the meantime, I want you guys to search your memories and see if there's anything else you can remember about that day. Miko was stashing money and IDs for a reason. We just have to find out what it was."

They nodded, although both didn't look happy about the idea of revisiting Miko's death, not that Holden blamed them. If he'd seen his brother kill himself, he might still be in a padded cell. "Thanks. I appreciate your help."

"Anything for Miko," Nathan said. "I don't care what they say—he was a good man."

Holden blinked back tears for his friend's solidarity. No more words were needed.

Time to put a pin in this night. Tomorrow would be here in a blink.

Chapter 10

They arrived at Tessara around noon and walked into the smart building with its gleaming glass and stately metal accents.

"Someone didn't spare any expense in the decor department," Jane said, whistling beneath her breath. "Pharmaceuticals must be big business."

"Yeah, apparently big enough to fund your own personal hit squad," Holden said, clearly referencing Penny Winslow. "Honestly, I don't understand why Tessara Pharm still has government contracts. I would think this place would be like poison in the eyes of the U.S. government, seeing as one of their top executives was as corrupt as they come."

"Well, when you have the world's best and brightest working for you, those little blemishes can be overlooked, apparently," Jane responded with dry amusement.

Holden grunted in agreement. "Get ready to be politely stonewalled," he said as an impeccably dressed woman in a pencil skirt and pristine white blouse walked toward them with a pleasant smile. Both he and Jane flashed their badges, and the woman extended a cool hand first to Holden and then Jane.

"Hello. My name is Selena Weston. Welcome to Tessara Pharmaceuticals."

"Thank you for agreeing to meet with us. My name is agent Holden Archangelo and this is my partner, Jane Fallon."

"We're always happy to help as we enjoy a good working relationship with many government agencies," Selena said, revealing a row of perfectly white teeth that looked almost fake and made Jane feel self-conscious about her own teeth. Hell, everything about the woman made Jane want to freshen up, even though she knew the feeling was ridiculous. Maybe if the woman didn't have the flawless skin of a baby or the impossible figure of a Barbie doll. "If you would just follow me…"

The woman spun on her heel, drawing Holden and Jane away from the main lobby and into a private conference room with plush carpeting and a large cherrywood table surrounded by Italian leather chairs. "Please help yourself to a beverage and snacks. Mr. Rocha will be with you momentarily."

The woman exited the conference room, closing the door softly behind her. When Holden's gaze didn't linger in the woman's direction, Jane suppressed a happy smile. "Not your type?" she asked casually, as if making conversation to kill time.

"What? Plastic girl? No. Not enough muscle, and definitely not enough substance. I like a girl who can best me in the gym or collapse trying."

That smile she'd been suppressing peeped through. Jane was ridiculously charmed by the fact he was plainly referencing her. "Good to know."

"Yeah? You gonna fix me up with someone?"

Her smile disappeared. "No," she answered with a tiny bit of a growl, and he chuckled at her knee-jerk reaction. Two can play that game. "I wouldn't want to subject any of my friends to you because I'd like to remain friends with them. Any matchmaking you'll have to manage on your own."

"Little kitty has her claws out," he said with a low, amused whistle. "I'd love to pursue this conversation later, perhaps over a glass of wine?"

"In your dreams, Archangelo." Time to switch the subject. "So we're meeting with Rocha? This should be interesting."

"What'll be more interesting is what Rocha will share."

"We both know nothing is the likely answer. And right now he's listening to our entire conversation, I'll wager."

"Of course. Why else bring us to a specific room and make us wait? Typical and a little cliché. Someone has been watching too many movies."

She smiled just as a door with an invisible seam

opened in the wall and Rocha stepped out, giving Jane a momentary fright. She frowned to cover her surprise and straightened her jacket. "Tessara Pharma's full of surprises, I see," she said in a cool tone. "I didn't realize secret doors and passageways were part of standard architecture for a pharmaceutical company."

Rocha smiled. "It's a unique building. Came with the standard government-issue listening devices, too."

Aah, he had *been listening.*

"Trying to get ahead of the pharmaceutical espionage? I didn't realize finding the next best allergy medication is so cutthroat," she said. Rocha only deepened his patronizing smile. Jane wanted to punch that smug look off his face, but Reed's stern admonition rang in her ears: *Keep things civil and don't ruffle feathers.* So she supposed it was time to play civil. "Thank you for meeting us. I can appreciate your busy schedule." She shot Holden a wry look.

Rocha took a seat in the big comfy leather chair at the head of the table and gestured, encouraging them to do the same. " To what do I owe this pleasant surprise? It isn't often we get agents asking questions around here. Most of the time all we see are more members of the geek squad. Very smart, but between them couldn't lift a fully loaded sandwich."

Holden and Jane both offered a small smile in deference to his attempt at humor, but Jane could tell from Holden's determined expression he was ready to jump in feetfirst, and that suited her just fine. "We know you came to Washington to discuss the Miko

Archangelo case. First, we'd like to know how you came by such classified information. Second, we would like to know why Tessara Pharm would possibly care about that particular investigation."

Rocha leaned back in his chair. "As you know, we handle and facilitate many government contracts. I feel safe in saying that we are the premier pharmaceutical lab, handling ninety percent of the government's clandestine chemical needs. The situation involving Penny Winslow and Miko Archangelo was a black eye to Tessara. Our stocks took a hit and our investors got nervous. We've worked hard to mitigate that unfortunate circumstance so, of course, we were less than thrilled when we heard the investigation had not been closed entirely. And frankly, it's our belief that it was an error in judgment to allow a distraught family member to reopen the case when it'd been satisfactorily investigated and closed."

"That doesn't answer the question of how you came across the information," Holden maintained stubbornly, ignoring the dig. "This is a classified investigation. You should not have access to any of that information."

But Rocha wasn't in the mood to satisfy their curiosity. Instead, he said, "Would you like a tour of the facility? We are proud of the work done here. Innovative, groundbreaking, brilliant work happens on these premises. Work far more involved than manufacturing the latest and greatest allergy medication." He smiled at Jane. "I would consider it a true pleasure to escort you around the grounds. The north side is quite scenic with the manmade lake."

"That won't be necessary. We're not here as tourists," Jane said, irritated at being treated like children who were easily distracted. "We'd like to see Penny Winslow's personnel file."

Rocha shook his head with a look of chagrin. "Not without a warrant. I hate to be a stickler for the rules, but even in death we strive to protect the privacy of our people."

Holden leaned across the table. "You know I don't need a warrant to see her personnel file because she's dead. I would consider your cooperation a point in your favor that Tessara has nothing to hide, and I'm sure that will be taken into consideration when it comes time to award new contracts." Holden drummed his finger on the table. "I can appreciate how embarrassed Tessara must've been with the whole Penny Winslow situation, but we may be dealing with a bigger threat, and your cooperation would be greatly appreciated."

"I see." Rocha steepled his fingers. "And if I let you see Penny's file, what do you think you'll find?"

"I'm not sure," Jane cut in. "But I think it's safe to say that Penny was a far more complex woman than any of you imagined. We'd also like to see all projects that she personally oversaw."

"I'm not sure Penny was actively involved in any projects," Rocha said. "The executive branch rarely had personal dealings with ongoing projects."

"Even so, something tells me Penny was very

hands-on. From what I know of her, she liked to stick her fingers in all sorts of pies," Holden said.

Rocha looked cornered but conceded with grace. "I'll have the files collected. Was there anything else I can help you with?"

Holden's eyes glittered. "Just one more thing— keep your nose out of our investigation," Holden instructed with false cheer. He looked more dangerous wearing a smile than holding a gun. "The next time you come poking around where you don't belong, you might find yourself out in the cold. Catch my drift?"

Rocha chuckled as if Holden's threat was faintly amusing, but he nodded. "Sure. And now if I may, a little advice from one former military man to another—careful where you step. You never know where the next mine might be." Rocha rose and bowed slightly. "Now, if you'll excuse me, I have work to attend. Selena will see to all of your needs."

The invisible door opened with a soft *snick* and Rocha disappeared behind it. Jane and Holden shared a look before she admitted, "I totally want to see where that door goes." Then she added with a wry twist of her mouth, "And damn him for having a cool secret door. I thought only castles had those."

Holden didn't share her amusement. He dropped the cold congeniality and a darkness filled his gaze. "That man knows more than he's telling."

Jane stopped joking around to agree. "Yes, but unless we find something to work with, he's not going to voluntarily spill what he knows."

Selena appeared, impossibly pretty and perfect,

and Jane almost quipped that the woman was probably made in a lab on the fourth floor. She kept her lip zipped, though, when Selena supplied the files they'd requested. "Mr. Rocha said you may take these copies with you. Is there anything else you require?" she asked politely, clasping her hands in front of her and waiting.

"We'll be in touch," Holden said, scooping up the files.

"We look forward to your next visit. Perhaps next time you can enjoy a walk around the lake. It's so pretty."

Selena led them out of the building and waited until they were in the car to disappear back inside Tessara Pharma. Jane turned to Holden. "That was weird, right?"

"Very."

"Tessara…they don't, like, create people, right? That's not even possible. Please tell me that's not possible."

"Who knows what they do in that building. All I know is that place houses something bad and it's up to us to figure out how it's all connected."

Jane nodded, but a pinch of tension followed. "People connected to Tessara end up dead. Let's not become part of the body count."

Holden put the car in Drive, and it wasn't until Tessara was in their rearview window that Jane could breathe again.

Chapter 11

When they returned to Nathan's house, they were in a lengthy discussion about the creepy factor of Selena the robo-babe when Nathan and Jaci walked into the living room to greet them. The worried tension in Jaci's expression immediately made Holden wary. Something was going down. "Everything okay?" he asked. "You look like you're about to be the bearer of bad news."

"Can we talk to you for a minute?" Jaci asked.

Nathan wore a different kind of tension, and when he reached for Jaci's hand in a show of support, Holden was momentarily envious of their devotion to one another. It must be amazing to have someone always watching your back, no matter what. Almost without thought, his gaze strayed to Jane and she seemed wary, watching the exchange with open speculation.

"Let's do this over a beer," Nathan said, going to the kitchen to grab a few cold ones. "There's no way to pretty up what has to be said, but it'll sure as hell go down a lot easier with a little alcohol."

"Sounds serious. Are you dying?" Holden quipped, a tingle of apprehension jangling his nerves. It wasn't like Nathan to beat around the bush, so he fully expected to find out quickly what all the fuss was about.

"Not dying. At least not yet, and I'd like to keep it that way."

"You and me both, brother." Holden swigged his beer, taking a moment to enjoy the crisp taste. "So out with it. What's up your tail?"

"It's not him. It's me," Jaci said, coming clean as she folded her arms across her chest. "I don't want to sound like a jerk, but I'm scared about this investigation into Miko's case and where it might lead. I don't want Nathan to get caught up in your search for the truth."

"I tried to tell her nothing's going to happen to me," Nathan said. "But she has the right to be concerned. Some hinky stuff has happened when Tessara is involved."

"Your concerns may be warranted," Jane said gravely. "I understand your anxiety. However, there's an equal chance we won't dig up anything and this investigation will end as it started—with Miko declared guilty of treason."

"Yeah, we get it," Holden grumbled, hating the

possibility. He understood where Jaci was coming from. She and Nathan had gone through hell the last time Tessara was involved, and if Tessara was truly involved again, who knew what lengths they'd go to protect their secrets?

Nathan spoke up, looking intensely uncomfortable. "Listen, I'm not asking you to give up, but Jaci has a good point. What if there's a bigger threat? Both my brother and I almost died the last time we went up against Tessara. Jaci doesn't want me to take that chance again."

"I get it, man. I do," Holden assured Nathan, because the guy looked like he was ready to vomit. It wasn't because Nathan was scared but because he thought he was taking the coward's way out and Holden knew it. The code of honor was ingrained in them all. "There's no judgment. This could be dangerous. I shouldn't have involved you. It's my fault."

"It's just that, look what happened to Jake," Jaci said, miserable. "He's never going to be the same. People who tangle with Tessara come out dead or damaged. And I don't want that to happen to either of us or *you*. Have you even thought of that? You might have a huge target on your back just for poking around."

Holden couldn't argue with Jaci's logic. It was true Tessara had a long reach.

Jane jumped in before he could. "We don't even know that Tessara is actually involved," she said gently, trying to calm Jaci's fears. "Penny Winslow is the only connection to Tessara at this point. We could be wrong and there is no big conspiracy…just a sad story of a man with a guilty conscience."

But Jaci shook her head. "As much as I want to believe that, my gut says something else. I have a bad feeling about this investigation. Let's just say, for argument's sake, that Holden is right. There's a possibility that the person actually pulling the strings is far more dangerous than Penny Winslow ever was. And if Nathan almost died going up against her—who was a lesser threat—what does that say for this newer threat? It scares me, Holden. Not just for me and Nathan, but for you, too."

"Miko was my closest friend," Nathan said. "He always had my back and he protected me when everything turned to shit. I know I owe him more than what I'm doing and that makes me want to punch myself in the face." Nathan folded Jaci into his arms, holding her tight before continuing. "But I have to think of Jaci's safety, too. We're planning on starting a family soon, and the threat hovering over our heads with you here…it's more than I can allow. I'm sorry, man."

"No apologies needed," Holden told Nathan, shaking his head, feeling for his friend's predicament. "I know you always had Miko's back and he wouldn't want you to put your life in danger over something he'd done."

Jaci's eyes sparkled with tears. "I'm sorry. I don't want to be harsh because you seem like a good guy, but I didn't know Miko and I barely know you. All I know is that I love this man right here and the thought of losing him for someone else's fight is something

I can't handle. That's not fair to either of us. I want a normal life, one that isn't punctuated by moments of sheer terror because someone is trying to kill us. And now that I've said that, I sound totally selfish, don't I?"

"No, you don't," Jane said. "You have every right to assert your feelings into this situation. If I were you, I would, too. There's potentially a lot at stake. And you've already been through enough. No one would fault you for wanting to step outside the ring for this fight."

"You sure?" Jaci asked, sniffing back tears. "I wish I was more badass, like you. Then maybe I wouldn't so scared."

Nathan pulled away with mock incredulousness. "What are you talking about? When we were holed up in the cabin and our safe house had been made, you beaned a guy with a frying pan. I'd say that's pretty badass. We might be dead if not for your quick thinking."

Jaci giggled in spite of the gravity of the conversation, and once again Holden was envious of their bond. Damn, he was turning into a weepy woman. Holden finished his beer and placed the empty bottle on the counter. "That does sound pretty badass to me."

"Oh, my God, you guys know how to soothe a woman's ego," Jaci said, smiling, then added with the tiniest amount of pride, "It was pretty awesome."

Nathan hugged her tightly. "Damn straight."

The tension broken, Jaci said, "When times are

different, you're totally welcome in our house, I promise. I'll even cook dinner and make a pie, but until then…you're going to have to take your spy stuff elsewhere, okay?"

"Can you recommend a good hotel?" Jane asked.

"That I can do," Jaci said, brightening. "Come with me."

While Jane and Jaci hunted down a suitable hotel, Nathan and Holden went to the garage to pound down another beer, taking advantage of the bro time. "You know I feel like shit turning you out like this," Nathan admitted.

"Don't worry about it. It's nothing to lose sleep over."

Nathan shook his head. "I want you to find the answers you're looking for, but I'm in a lose-lose situation. On one hand, I want there to be a bigger answer, something other than what we know to account for Miko's actions. But if that's the case, then that means a bigger threat is hanging over all of us. And I have to protect Jaci."

"Want to know a secret?" Holden asked, pausing for a second. "I envy what you have with Jaci."

"Yeah? You, the lone wolf?"

"Hey, as I recall, you were a card-carrying member of the lone-wolf club, too," Holden said with a smirk.

Nathan laughed. "So what's the deal with you and Fallon?"

"Deal? No deal. We're partners."

"Nothing else?"

"Naw. She's all business, and hooking up with her is the last thing I need right now. I mean, she's hot but comes with too much baggage."

"Baggage? I sense a story. You've already hooked up, haven't you?"

He grinned, unable to deny it, but his smile faded quickly enough. "Listen, don't say anything. We didn't part on good terms and it's hard enough working together without our past mucking things up."

"Hey, I understand. You got feelings for her?"

"Whoa! Where'd that come from?" Holden asked with nervous laughter. "Feelings? Sure, she's my partner and I'd take a bullet for her. That's what you're supposed to do for your partner. Do I want to pick out China patterns together? No." He rolled his eyes at the thought. "We'd end up shooting each other in the housewares aisle." He finished the conversation with "She's difficult," and left it at that.

"The best ones always are. Did I ever tell you how Jaci and I got back together?"

"No. Is it a long story? Because I bore easily," he quipped.

"Shut up and listen. It's a good story. You'll love it. And if you don't love it, too bad—you're listening anyway. Okay, so there was a hit out on her—"

"Ah, the way all good love stories start," Holden interrupted with a grin.

Nathan snickered, saying, "I know, right? Anyway, there's a hit on her life and I basically kidnap her moments before the hitter buries a bullet in her skull, just like he'd done her best friend seconds earlier."

"Jeez, Nathan, this is one helluva story. You might want to edit out the gore when you tell your future kids about how Mommy and Daddy met."

"Yeah, yeah, good advice. My point? She freaking hated me because I did some messed-up shit in a backward attempt at protecting her and, well, ultimately she was unable to resist my manly charms and the rest is history. The thing is, chemistry won't be denied, no matter what you try to do to squelch it and you, my friend, and your partner...you've got chemistry. I can see it coming off you in waves. Like pheromones and shit. That stuff's real, you know."

"Thank you, Love Doctor. I had no idea you were so versed in human biology. Chemistry or not, she's got issues that I don't think I can handle."

"Such as?"

"For starters? Her dad."

"Who's her dad?"

"Brace yourself—retired Major General Gregory Fallon."

Nathan whistled in recognition, then shook his head in commiseration. "Damn, that sucks. I heard that man keeps a box of other men's testicles as war prizes. Highly decorated and scary as hell...that's a tough break. I take it a meet with the pops didn't go so well?"

"You could say that. Anyway, there's no future between me and Fallon. I don't have time for that kind of drama."

"Yeah, I hear you. However," Nathan added with a shrug, "if I'd given up on Jaci the first time she punched me in the face, I would never have the love of my life right now."

Holden rolled his eyes, a moment of disquiet filling him. Should he have fought harder for Jane when they'd broken up? Maybe he'd run too quickly. Hell, maybe if he'd stood his ground, they might've found a way around that mountain of opposition known as The Major. Then again, maybe not. Maybe it would've ended the same way, only later and with more damage.

"Thanks for the pep talk—I think. I need to ask you something related to the case. You up to answering a few serious questions?"

"Sure, buddy. It's the least I can do after tossing you out on your ear."

"Did you happen to remember anything from that day, anything you didn't tell Jane when she interviewed you?"

Nathan's smile dimmed as he shook his head. "I've been racking my brain, trying to remember every detail. But everything I can remember I've already told Jane for her report."

"I appreciate you trying." Holden finished his beer. "We visited Tessara today. We have some reading material to go over."

"Should I even ask?" Nathan asked. "I can't believe they let you walk out with personnel files."

"Yeah, well, I can't tell if they're trying to cooperate or if they're trying to throw us off the scent. Either way, I'm interested in seeing what Penny Winslow had her fingers on."

"Knowing that sneaky bitch, she probably had her fingers on everything. She was not only greedy, but also consumed with her own ego. To this day, I'll never know what Tom saw in her."

"The heart is often blind," Holden said softly. "I'd say he paid for his error in judgment."

Nathan nodded. That was all that needed to be said about that. Tom Wyatt had been like a father figure to Nathan, and when he had been implicated in the illegal activities, it had damn near broken Nathan's heart. To make matters worse, Nathan had been in the room when a sniper took out Tom in his own den with a single bullet whizzing through the glass straight to the man's skull. A perfect hit. Tom was also on Miko's list of crimes.

Nathan settled a reassuring hand on Holden's shoulder. "Hey, try to remember that even if you're wrong and Miko is truly guilty of everything he's been accused of, he was still your brother and my friend. And we knew him as a good man. Nothing can take that from us."

Holden nodded, appreciating his friend's quiet wisdom. "Me and Jane better get to the hotel so we can start going over the Tessara files," he said, giving himself the chance to exit gracefully.

Nathan and Holden embraced like men—rough and hard—and then sprang apart with quick good-byes.

Once in the car, Jane looked to Holden. "You okay?

You two were in the garage for a while. I was starting to run out of things to talk about with Jaci. She's nice, but we don't really have a lot in common."

"Yeah I can imagine—the graphic designer and the hard-core marine. It's not as if you'd run in similar circles." Holden sighed as he rubbed his brow. "I don't blame Nathan. He did what he had to do. If I had someone I cared about and that person was threatened, I'd do the same."

"Growing up in a military family, it's hard to imagine living as a civilian. Weapons training, PT and hand-to-hand combat training has been part of my life since I was a kid. It must've been terrifying to go through what Jaci did with zero training."

"Yeah, but she held her own in the end from what Nathan told me. Same with Kat, Jake's wife. She was even more helpless. The woman had practically lived in the lab before Jake plucked her out and brought her to D.C. People grow when they have to, and I guess the strong will find a way to survive."

"Yeah, I guess so." There was something quiet and vulnerable about the way Jane said it that when she tucked a piece of hair behind her ear and turned her gaze out the window, he was struck by the knowledge that if someone were threatening Jane, he'd tear their spine out.

Nope, he didn't fault Nathan. He understood. He spotted the hotel Jaci recommended just off the highway. "We're here. Let's see if they have any vacancies."

* * *

They were able to immediately book two adjoining rooms. After ordering some Thai food for delivery, they tackled the personnel file. "Well, Holden, you are right about one thing—this woman was very hands-on. She's listed as the lead supervisor on a number of different projects." Jane pulled a highlighter from her purse and began marking the projects. "That seems a bit odd considering she was an executive, right?"

"Yes, but she was also one of the founders of Tessara. She had a biochemical engineering background."

"It says here she got her degree after serving her time in the military. I guess she was fairly brilliant," Jane said, a note of grudging respect entering her voice. "I mean, she was a total psychopath, of course. But you know what they say about geniuses—they're all a little crazy."

"That's a stereotype. I'm not crazy in the least," Holden joked, and Jane graced him with a sardonic smirk. He chuckled and balled up his napkin to toss it basketball-style in the wastebasket near the door. "She was crazy, that's for sure. So what are some of the projects?"

"Well, they all have names, which are likely code for whatever they were. So who's to say which is which or if they are connected to Miko?"

"At this point I think we have to grasp at any straw thrown our way."

Jane nodded. "Okay, so some of the project names

are Switchblade, Carousel, Serenade, Game Changer."
She looked up. "Any of those sounds familiar?"

Holden mulled over the information and then, pulling something from memory, said, "Game Changer…
that's what MCX-209 was nicknamed by that freak
responsible for what happened to Jake. That's how
they were presenting it on the black market."

"Are you saying that Jake's girlfriend was working for Penny Winslow?"

"Not directly, I'm sure. Kat would've answered
to her immediate supervisor, but that supervisor
would've answered to someone else higher up the
chain."

"Damn…the possibility that MCX-209 is involved
gives me hives. It's like finding out that time travel
is possible and a Terminator is coming to kill me.
Freaky stuff."

"Kat had been working on MCX-209 for a year
before all hell broke loose. I wonder if Penny was
keeping close tabs on her progress."

"If she had her fingers in this pie, chances are
the answer is yes. I mean, think about it, a drug that
can erase memory? She would've been unstoppable."
Jane shivered.

"True. It would've been a considerable asset in
her arsenal. But I don't know if MCX-209 had shown
any progress at that point. It would've been in its in-
fancy of testing."

Jane tapped the marker on the file. "But if Penny
had a background in biochemical engineering, she
would've been able to study Kat's notes, right?"

"Yeah?" He raised an eyebrow.

"Well, maybe she knew the drug was going to fail in its original inception but found a bigger, more nefarious purpose and thus kept Kat working on it under the guise of supporting her research."

"Sounds like something that woman would do. When we get back to Washington, we should hit up Kat and see what she remembers about that time at Tessara."

"Isn't she working for the Department of Defense now?"

He nodded. "Best way to control a threat is to control its funding."

"True. I'm surprised she agreed to work for the government after everything she'd been through."

"Yeah, me, too. But she's a scientist at her core and she was given an offer she couldn't pass up. I'm not going to judge her for doing what she felt was right for herself and Jake."

"No, of course not," she said, shuffling through the paperwork and stifling a yawn. "It's been a long day. Want to call it?"

Holden didn't appear happy with that idea, but his eyes were bloodshot, too. "Yeah, I guess so." He gathered the papers he'd been studying and tidied them into a pile. "We're a good team. Who knew, right?"

She caught his gaze and her cheeks heated for no good reason. One compliment from Holden and she goes all girlie on him? *Get a grip.* Jane smiled and nodded. "Seems that when we're not fighting one another, things get done."

"Yeah." He leaned back in his chair and popped his back. "I'm feeling not being able to work out for the past few days," he said, wincing as he stretched. "Working out keeps the kinks from permanently kinking."

She tried to keep her gaze on her paperwork, as her brain was currently objectifying his body like a rabid teen at a boy-band concert. All she had to do was think of how inappropriate it was to obsess on the rugged hills and valleys of every muscular portion of his body and she could smother this raging attraction, which seemed to be getting out of control with each passing second. Yep. Any second now she'd get things under control.

Any. Second.

Her gaze found his and what she saw there mirrored the hunger she felt curling in her belly. She breathed a distressed "Oh, no…" before he suddenly pulled her to him and planted a searing kiss on her upturned, nearly puckering lips.

And that was exactly how fires raged out of control—when you threw gasoline on them.

Chapter 12

Jane melted beneath Holden's touch, all resistance and good sense following in sequential order, leaving behind nothing but raging attraction and insane, career-killing lust. Every thwarted sexual impulse and smothered tingle of desire raged in her nerve endings, demanding more and then some. If she could think straight, she would remind Holden that morning afters were awkward, and even more so when the person you'd shagged was staring at you from across the debriefing room. But who could counter with reason when there was a tongue in your mouth, twisting your resolve into a tiny, minuscule pretzel?

"You have no idea how long I've wanted to do that. I've missed you, Jane," Holden said in a husky murmur against her lips. He grabbed her hand and pulled her from the chair, spinning her around so her backside was pressed firmly against his groin. "Feel that?" His hardened erection ground against her behind, stealing her breath. "That's what you do to me no matter how much I try to forget." His hand reached around to cup her through her jeans, and she squirmed as heat flooded her body at his possessive touch.

"This is probably a bad idea," she felt obligated to say, even as she bit her lip and held back a cry when he moved the heel of his hand against her. "This doesn't change anything if we do this. Coworkers only, right?"

"Of course," he said, nibbling her neck and sucking the flesh between his lips for a sharp bite. They walked slowly backward, and Holden gave her a hard push onto the bed. She gasped as he towered over her with that damnably sexy grin. She reached up and jerked him to her, obliterating that grin beneath the onslaught of her mouth. Their tongues tangled, fighting for dominance, leaving them both breathless and desperate to shuck their clothes. They wasted no time. Within seconds, the sound of ripping fabric and popping buttons filled the air. In a heartbeat, their naked bodies were sliding against one another in a gloriously dirty dance that left them both growling as they pushed one another to deeper, more complete absolution. Holden took care of the protection, impatiently sliding a condom onto his shaft before filling and stretching her with delicious intent. *Good God,* she thought dizzily, clinging to him. She'd missed this! She gasped as the head of his shaft punched that sweet spot with unerring accuracy, sending her into shuddering orbit as he did it again and again, demanding that she take every inch until she was no longer aware where he stopped and she began. An animalistic groan popped from her mouth when he stopped to flip her around to her belly. She arched her back with a hiss as he slid back inside her slick heat. She couldn't help herself, rocking and writhing against his shaft, taking her pleasure as surely as he was taking his own.

"Holden," she gasped his name like a prayer, begging for release, but he wasn't ready to give it to her. He was drawing it out, milking the moment for all it was worth, and she was thankful. They both knew this was a one-time deal, right? Might as well leave a mark to make it count. "Oh…Holden, please…"

"Not yet, sweet Janey," he said, squeezing her cheeks as he drove into her flesh, making her shake with each thrust. She groaned, then cried out in frustration when he withdrew again to roll her onto her backside. "What are you d—"

And then she sucked in a wild cry as his mouth descended between her folds, teasing that secret pleasure button, demanding her surrender without mercy. She couldn't run, couldn't hide from the pleasure that was building. And she didn't want to. She wanted it all. She wanted the pain, the sweetness, the delectable forbidden nature of everything they were doing together. At that moment, she wasn't the good girl, the perfect daughter who always made the decisions that would reflect well on her family. She was a wanton, sex-starved she-devil who wanted destruction and mayhem as much as she craved acceptance and praise. Dual natures clashed and she thrashed, gripping the bedsheet between her sweaty palms. When he lightly grazed his teeth across her hood and slipped his finger deep inside her, she shattered with a keening cry that surely the entire hotel heard, every muscle clenching in glorious unison, toes curling hard enough to start a cramp. Her breath left her lungs until they threatened to collapse. "H-Holden," she gasped, her head lolling to the side as her eyes glazed in postorgasmic bliss. "Holden..." It was all she could manage. But the blaze of hunger in his eyes told her this ride was just beginning. Before she could fully recover, Holden was inside her again; this time, he was going to push her harder than ever. It would be a miracle if she could walk by morning.

Sweat slicked their bodies as Holden worked himself back into Jane's hot core, gritting his teeth at the insane, delicious pressure ricocheting down his shaft and pooling in his balls. This was crazy, his brain bubbled with maniacal glee, but he was desperate to touch every inch of her honeyed skin. Maybe it was experiencing the tender bond between Nathan and Jaci that had ignited this fierce hunger inside him. Whatever the reason, he couldn't stop himself. Jane was toned, with feminine curves for a man to hold on to. Her hips flared in the most achingly perfect way, and he wanted to lose himself between her folds to devour her taste. It was a bad idea—all of this—but did that matter? Hell no! When he saw that dark look in her eyes, that split second of raw yearning peeking through the curtain of self-possessed reserve that she always maintained, he had lost it and stolen the moment. Maybe he'd live to regret it. Who cared? He was with her now and it was everything he remembered it to be.

He'd brought her to release once, but that wasn't enough. He wanted to make sure that when she closed her eyes at night, she thought of him and all the things he'd done to her. Maybe it was egotistical—okay, yeah, it was—but for some reason, he wanted to be the only man she remembered in her private thoughts. He wanted to dominate her fantasies until only he remained. What did that mean? He'd never cared before with his other lovers, but Jane had been a tough habit to quit cold turkey. In the past, he'd been happy to share and share alike. But not with Jane. The very idea of Jane being with someone else caused a growl to rumble from his chest, and he renewed his efforts to leave a brand on her soul.

"Holden, oh, Holden…" she breathed, clinging to him with her legs wrapped tightly around his torso as he drove into her without mercy. Her eyes were squeezed shut and he swept her mouth with his tongue, forcing her to remain in the here and now with him. She tensed and began to shake, and he knew the moment was here.

"Open your eyes, sweetheart," he instructed, needing to know that the moment she came, she'd know exactly who'd brought her to that sweet release. Her eyes popped open and she stared into his, gasping as she tumbled for the second time into a hard orgasm. Their connection felt cosmic as they locked eyes, and within the next breath, as she was crying out, he hurtled into his own release, losing himself for several blessed moments in sheer ecstasy. Holy…hell…he'd never…not like that. He collapsed beside her, both of them breathing hard and trying to recover from whatever it was that had just taken them on an epic ride. "That was…"

"Don't talk," she panted. "Shh."

And he agreed. Words weren't necessary. Their bodies had shared something he'd never experienced with anyone else. Something mind-blowing. Something…scary. Something like *chemistry*.

Everything had changed. He couldn't agree to go back to just being partners. He'd made the mistake the first time of letting her go without a fight. His ego had been bruised and a part of him had believed what The Major had said about him not being good enough for Jane. Who was he? And what did he have to offer Jane? But in this moment, he said, screw the haters. He'd been stupid and immature to walk away just so he could lick his wounds in private. Sure, he covered pretty well with his nonchalance, but it was forced. The real reason he worked out at the same time as Jane was because it was the only time he could possibly be around her without actually admitting he still needed and wanted her. Yeah, that ego was pretty strong.

He risked a glance at Jane, her eyes closed and lips parted as her chest rose and fell from their exertion. The sheer beauty of the woman struck him like a thunderbolt splitting the sky and crashing around him.

Yeah, things had changed, all right.

And something told him there was no putting that genie back in the bottle.

Faaantastic.

Jane was going to love this.

Chapter 13

The following morning, Jane rolled to her side and started to leave the bed when Holden stirred. She winced as muscles she'd never imagined were part of her body cried out in protest. It was a delicious pain, one that reminded her of everything they'd done last night, but in the same breath, the reminder made her want to hop the first rocket to another planet. What had they done? She wanted to cover her face with her hands and die. She popped from the bed and ran to the bathroom. *What were you thinking?* She stared hard at her reflection in the mirror, noting the wild bedhead and the stubble burn on her neck from Holden's lips. A delicate shudder rocked her frame as she sank into the memory with a heavy sigh. That man could do things that weren't natural.

Snap out of it. This kind of thinking wasn't productive. She straightened and stepped away from the sink to twist the shower knob to hot. The heat would burn away the evidence and soothe her sore muscles. Win-win. Jane stepped into the shower as the steam filled the room. She closed her eyes, the water pelting her head and running in rivulets down her body. Bracing herself against the wall with her forearms, she stood for a long moment simply enjoying the feel of the water running over her.

Suddenly, hands cupped her breasts and she yelped, immediately jabbing with her elbow and connecting with a hard chest as the person behind her grunted and pulled her to him. "Stand down, soldier," he murmured, and her knees threatened to melt into gooey piles of cartilage. Holden.

"What are you doing?" she asked, trying to stay focused, but Holden was teasing her nipples between his thumb and forefinger and rational thought was becoming difficult. "I thought we agreed it was a one-time thing. We can't be shagging each other like it's no big deal."

He kissed her neck and ignored her, reaching down to plunder her folds with his finger, reminding her of everything he'd done to her last night. She whimpered and sagged against him, giving him better access even as she cursed her own weakness. "This is a terrible—*aah*—idea!"

"The worst," he agreed, slowly working his finger inside her. "And yet...I think we should keep doing it. Over and over and over."

She shuddered as a sweet orgasm caught her by surprise, cresting over her in a gentle tide, nothing like what'd happened last night, and for that, she was grateful. She needed to be able to walk. A sigh rattled out of her mouth as she leaned against Holden, who was smiling as he withdrew his finger and popped it into his mouth. "Mmm…sweet like candy," he said, causing a blush to burn her cheeks. Had he just—? Oh, such a bad boy.

He turned her around to face him as the steam swirled around their bodies. His erection bobbed between them, but he seemed more content to stand there with her, damn the consequences and screw the good sense they were both ignoring. "I don't think I can 'hit it and quit it' when it comes to you." He drew her closer so their skin touched. The heat from his body made her want to climb into his skin and live there. He was like a human furnace, which would come in handy seeing as her toes were always cold. "I know it would be smarter if I did. But there's something about you that fills me with…hell, I don't even know what the word is. All I know is now that I've tasted you again, you're the only one I want, and I should've fought harder to keep you the first time around."

Jane thrilled at the dangerous words, though she knew they had no future. For one, her brothers and father would have a fit. Holden was too tainted by his brother's crime to be a suitable match. As far as her father was concerned, only five-star generals and Purple Heart recipients need apply for the role of significant other in Jane's life. As a rule, Jane had kept her dating exploits on the down low, and with good reason. Then Holden had gone against her express wishes and tried talking to her father as if he were a normal parent, and all hell had broken loose.

"What in the world are you thinking?" she'd asked in a harsh whisper as Holden had walked with purpose to her father's doorstep. "You have lost your mind! You don't know what you're doing and this is not going to end well. Stop this, Holden!"

"This is ridiculous. I'm sure you're overreacting. He's your father, not the pope."

"Please don't say that to him," she'd muttered, rubbing her right temple. "You don't know what you're getting into. This is not the way to meet my father for the first time."

"Yeah, well, I disagree. Time to stop sneaking around. Maybe we can go shoot a couple of rounds at the range."

"Do you realize he had the last guy I dated sent to the front lines in Afghanistan because he didn't like his haircut?"

"I've been to Afghanistan—no big deal," Holden had said with a negligent shrug that she'd found half adorable and half mad. "But just to be on the safe side, how's my hair?"

"High and tight. It's fine," she'd answered, swallowing her tongue when her father had appeared at the door. She'd forced a smile and said, "Hi, Dad. We were just in the neighborhood. If you're busy…"

"We? We who?" The Major had eyed Holden with

open suspicion and borderline dislike. "Is this the man you've been seeing on the QT?"

He knows, she'd thought. Damn those military connections. She'd wondered which old fart had ratted her out. No telling; her father's reach was pretty extensive and even crossed military branches. "Um…" Her words had dried up in her mouth and unfortunately Holden had taken the opportunity to insert himself.

"Yes, sir, I'm that guy. Pleasure to meet you. I've heard of your accomplishments. Pretty impressive."

Jane had wanted to groan. Her father was incapable of succumbing to flattery, and she'd known Holden's attempts at buttering him up would only end badly. Before she had been able to interject, her father had said, "Son, where I come from it's considered very bad form to attempt to date a man's only daughter without a proper introduction. How long has this been going on?"

"A few weeks," Holden had answered, looking to Jane when he'd realized this wasn't going as smoothly as he'd planned.

"I suppose you and I are overdue a chat." The Major had opened the door wider and motioned for Holden to come in. Jane had wanted to grab Holden and tell him to run for safety, but Holden had naively followed The Major before she could stop him. Just as she'd taken the first step, her father had said, "Jane, why don't you take a jog around the block? Your last PT report was a little weak in the running department."

"Dad? I'm not exactly dressed to go for a jog," she'd protested, but she'd been more keen on extracting Holden than anything else.

But her father never accepted excuses. "I know you keep some running shoes in the car because I taught you to."

She'd nodded, caught. "Yes, sir."

"By the time you circle back around I should be finished with my chat."

"Dad…"

"That'll be all, Jane."

And then she had been dismissed as he'd closed the door, effectively locking Holden inside and her out. "Crap," she'd muttered and returned to her car. She'd grabbed her tennis shoes and jerked them on. Whatever her father had been saying to Holden hadn't been "welcome to the family, son." She'd had a bad feeling it was going to be the opposite.

And she'd been right. Jane roused herself from that terrible memory and exhaled the tight breath caught in her chest. Why hadn't Holden just listened to her for once? Maybe if he hadn't been so cocksure of himself, they might've been able to figure out a plan together, but no, he'd been absolutely certain of his ability to charm The Major, and whatever he'd said to her dad had been the catalyst that ended their relationship.

"You're suddenly really quiet," Holden observed, drawing her back to the present. "Penny for your thoughts."

"They're not worth that much," she answered, deliberately giving him her back to tease him with the view as she reached for the shampoo. After a career in the military, modesty wasn't a luxury she remembered. "I think we've gotten all we can here in California. I'd like to get back to Washington as soon as possible so we can interview Jake and Kat. Is there anything else you need here in Cali?"

"Oh, that's how it's going to be?" he asked, a hint of amusement in his voice. She half turned and didn't pretend to not know what he was talking about.

"Yes. You and I both know that what we did was a mistake. There's no need to compound matters." Her gaze dipped to his erection and she swallowed before jerking back around to scrub her hair. "Don't get me wrong, I fully enjoyed myself, but we have to get back to business and wrap up this investigation. I have other cases waiting for me."

He reached past her and grabbed the shampoo. "First, what we did may have been a mistake, but I don't regret it. Second, you're crazy if you think I'm going to be able to forget how amazing we are together between the sheets and third, I can guarantee you're going to be thinking of us before we've even left the tarmac. Just admit it—we're good together. And we always were until your control-freak daddy got in the way. When you are going to stop letting him run your life?"

"Leave my dad out of this." She spun around, irritated. "Yes, we're good together. We're both in phenomenal shape, we have similar drives and our bodies fit together extraordinarily well, but that's not the point."

"It isn't?"

"No," she answered firmly, taking the shampoo from his hands and returning it to the ledge as he scrubbed. "The point is that you and I cannot be messing around like a couple of college coeds on spring break. We cannot do anything that will jeopardize the integrity of the case—both for my sake as the lead investigator and for your sake as you search for answers. We need to just forget it happened and move on. We did it once and we can't do it again." They switched places so Holden could rinse, and she clenched her fingers to keep from touching those rock-hard ridges of abdominal muscle that gave *washboard* a new definition. "Furthermore, we already have a deficit with you being all emotional about this case, and we certainly don't need to add to the already complicated situation." His lopsided grin appeared and she glared. "Are you listening at all?"

"To the words coming out of your mouth? No, not really. But in my defense, your boobs are definitely speaking my language." And with that, he pulled her to him, smothering her protests with a bone-searing kiss that left her with jelly on the inside. She whimpered as the fight left her temporarily. "There's my sexy girl," he murmured against her lips. When he had her quiet, he stared into her half-closed eyes and said, "I don't know why it took me so long to figure out that I should've told your father to go screw himself. As soon as we touch down in D.C., that's exactly what I'm going to do."

"You'll do no such thing," she said, glaring. "That's my father you're talking about."

"Yeah, and he's been running your life for long enough, don't you think?"

"He's not running my life," she shot back, indignant. "That's a helluva thing to say to someone you're hoping to have sex with again."

"I want more than sex," he said with a straight face. "I want you."

"Stop it," she told him, irritated that his admission caused her heart rate to hop, skip and jump like an Easter bunny on meth. "You're being ridiculous and I need you to focus. Remember the case? That's our priority—not whatever drama you're cooking up in your head right now. We had a past, a history, and it didn't work out. And not because of my dad, but because we're not suited in the big scheme of things, okay?"

"I call bullshit," he said. "You pushed me out of your life because Daddy told you to."

"You're one to talk. Whatever my dad said to you that day really must've hit a nerve because you couldn't get out fast enough."

He stiffened. "He was a real jerk."

"Yeah? Well, that's who he is and who he'll always be, and if you can't handle that, you can't handle being with me for the long haul. I realized that from the start, which is why I didn't pursue what we had. Got it? It had nothing to do with my dad."

Was that a lie? Well, they say the most convincing lies are grounded in truth. She hadn't wanted to rock the boat, not when things had started to level out with her dad and she'd finally found equal footing in her career. But she'd also known that Holden would never fit in with the exclusive boys' club of her brothers and father. So why push it? A tiny, pipsqueak of a voice whispered a stark truth that she'd struggled with ever since letting Holden go—she'd had real feelings for Holden. Not the kind that came and went, but the kind that reached down into her heart and tugged hard. Pushing him away had been a painful experience. Working alongside him as if he'd been merely a pleasant diversion had been even harder. Holden called her the ice queen because she had to shut down in order to function. Maybe she ought to tell him that. Or maybe she ought to stay the course because nothing had really changed. Her father and brothers, whom she loved and respected, would never accept Holden, and that was a fact, which meant, chemistry aside, their situation remained the same. "Why can't you just enjoy this one illicit moment and then let it go?" she asked, almost plaintively.

"Because I tried that before and it only made me miserable. Let's try it my way for once," he suggested, pulling her toward him even as she shook her head at the lusty haze slowly clouding his gaze. But he plainly wouldn't take no for an answer as he said, "If I'm spending my time fighting my attraction to you, I'll have that much less energy to focus on what we're supposed to be investigating. Make sense?"

In a hazy way, yes. She nodded slowly and his grin widened. "Good. Now, let me show you the art of the shower quickie…."

"But we don't have protection," she protested weakly, her tongue already sliding along her lower lip in anticipation. But Holden had thought ahead. He reached over her to the lip of the shower wall and grabbed the condom he'd stashed there. "You devil," she said with a reluctant smile. "What if I'd kicked you out of the shower?"

"Never crossed my mind," he said, shredding the packaging and slipping on the condom. His gaze darkened as he spun her around, pulling on her hips. "Brace yourself," he instructed; seconds later, he was buried inside her.

Oh, jeez. Quickie shower sex was one helluva good workout. And she loved a good workout.

Holden slipped his shirt over his head and slid his jeans on, his mind humming with thoughts that had nothing to do with the case and everything to do with the beautiful woman he couldn't take his eyes off. "When we broke up, was it so easy to forget about me?" he asked.

"I wouldn't exactly call what we were doing dating."

"Well, difference of opinion, I suppose. Humor me and answer the question," he said, tying his shoes and standing.

"Does it matter?"

"To me it does."

She heaved a short sigh, as if irritated that he seemed fixated on the past. "No, it wasn't easy, okay? It was pretty damn hard, but when you grow up like I did, you get used to hard."

"He doesn't have to rule your life anymore," he told her, gentling his voice. "All you have to do is stand up for yourself and what you want out of life."

"Holden, stop. You don't understand the relationship I have with my family. I'm not peppering you with judgment about your dedication to your brother, so don't give me crap about how I handle my relationship with my kin, okay?"

"My old man was a drunken prick most days and yours is a control-freak drill sergeant. I'd say we share some similarities in our upbringing. The one difference? I made the choice to put my life first. Somehow you got stuck playing second fiddle to every male in your family, and I think that's messed up because any father should be proud to have a daughter like you."

She startled at the unexpected compliment, but she held to her guns. "My dad needs me. When my mom left us, we all picked up the slack. It's what you do when your family is threatened—circle the wagons. You did it with your brother, right?"

"Yeah, I did," he admitted. "It's hard for me to watch you sacrifice your happiness on someone else's authority, though. Doesn't make sense."

"I'm not unhappy."

"Yeah, keep telling yourself that, Fallon," he said with a sad shake of his head. "But if this situation with my brother has taught me anything, it's that things can change in the blink of an eye and there aren't take-backs. You get one chance in this life, so don't throw it away."

"I know."

"Doesn't seem like it. You talk a good game. Your actions tell a different story. When are you going to choose your happiness over someone else's?"

She scowled. "Are we really having this conversation? We need to get back to the case."

"We will. Answer the question."

"If you don't drop it, I'll break your fingers," she said sweetly, tucking her gun into the back of her waistband and covering it with her shirt. "Let's get back to the point of this trip, which was not to rehash the past. Got it?"

"Fair enough. Still doesn't get you off the hook. This isn't finished yet."

She barked a short laugh at his statement. "Oh, is that so? We had some good times and now those good times have come to an end. Beautiful, simple and to the point."

"Yeah, sure." He pinned her with an intense look. "Kiss before we leave our little love nest?"

"Keep dreaming, Casanova. We have a plane to catch." And then she scooped up her carry-on and sauntered out of the room. Damn, that was harsh and yet so hot.

"Move your ass, Archangelo," she called over her shoulder. "Our plane leaves in an hour." He had no choice but to follow.

He took one last lingering look around the business hotel room, with its nondescript wallpaper and neutral carpet, but all he saw was the memory of him and Jane, defiling every discernible inch in wicked fashion. "Good times," he murmured with a sad exhale to be leaving it all behind. He closed the door. Jane was right. Time to get back to work.

Chapter 14

They were buckling into the car when Holden's cell rang. "It's James," he said, and answered the call. "Hold on, buddy. You're going on speaker." He clicked his smartphone and James's voice filled the car cab.

"Sleep is overrated, and I've found that when you're in a hyperaware state, your brain actually becomes more efficient."

"That's not actually accurate," Jane murmured, shooting Holden a quick look, but he compelled her to keep quiet as James rambled to his point.

"All right. You're not going to believe what I dug up about your boy, Miko…."

"Spit it out," Holden gritted his teeth. "We've got a plane to catch."

"Well, you might want to reschedule your flight because I've got some information that might interest you."

"Why can't you just tell me now?"

"Over the phone? Over an unsecure line? What? You think I was born yesterday? I don't think so. Meet me at Café Orange on Bluebell Street in twenty minutes."

Then the line went dead. Holden rolled his eyes. "Great. It's the Geek Supremacy. This guy is too much." He looked to Jane. "Can you reschedule our flight for tonight?"

"Sure. Let's hope this guy delivers, because he sounds like a fruit loop with an overinflated sense of importance."

"Oh, he's a genius. That about sums it up."

"Yes, it does."

Holden pocketed his phone while Jane brought up the GPS. Within fifteen minutes, they were walking into the small French café and heading straight for the twitchy man nursing what was likely his third espresso.

They slid into the seats across from James, and he startled at their appearance. "Hey, I didn't realize you'd actually make it in twenty minutes."

"Fifteen with five to spare. What do you have for us?" Jane said, cutting to the chase.

"Okay, here's the deal. I did what you asked and traced the money—that was child's play—and because you're friends with Nathan and Jaci, I decided to take it a step further, nose around and see what popped up. I hacked your brother's email account and found more interesting stuff than where he has money stashed. By the way, your brother had some serious cash flow to be tucking away the amounts he's got pocketed in Mexico."

"How much?" Holden asked.

"Brace yourself...one hundred Gs. Pow! That's a lot of margaritas," James said, cocking his fingers into guns with a grin, but Holden didn't find any of this funny. James slowly dropped his finger guns and refocused after a shaky drink of his espresso. "Okay, so anyway, yeah, he's got money in all those places, but Mexico had the biggest cash drop. But that's not the interesting part. He has a safety deposit box in Washington that I think you're going to want to open."

"What's in it?"

"I don't know, but he references it as his insurance policy, and something tells me he's not talking about MetLife."

Jane and Holden shared looks, then Holden prompted, "What else did you find?"

"He kept referencing a winery outside of Washington. Mean anything to you?"

"What?" Holden was confused. "My brother didn't like wine. He was more of a Jameson guy. Why would he be talking about a winery?"

"That's your job to figure out. The winery is owned by a Trevor Granger. The name is Butterfly Bend." James took a short breath and blew it out.

"And that's all I got. When can I get the wire for the second half of my fee?"

"You'll get it when I check out your story," Holden said, looking to Jane. "Granger…that name is familiar." He snapped his fingers in quick recognition. "That's right, Penny Winslow's maiden name was Granger. Do you believe in coincidences?"

"Not really," she answered. "Guess we're going back to Tessara?"

"Bet your ass we are." He stood and looked at James. "Thanks. I'll be in touch. Oh, and, James, get some sleep. You look like shit."

They left the café and booked it back to the car, his mind moving at the speed of light. Why did it always come back to Tessara? "I feel that place is at the epicenter of all bad things," he said darkly, and Jane nodded. "Why would my brother reference a winery unless there was something behind the curtain to keep watch on?"

"I'm curious as to what's in that security box. What do you think it could be?"

"I don't know, but I'm starting to lean toward the theory that my brother was on to something and he was trying—in true Miko fashion—to take whoever it was down by himself and got in over his head."

Jane nodded slowly and added, "I definitely think there's something going on, but I don't want to jump to conclusions."

"Of course not," he said, but his heart was beating like a wild thing in his chest at the possibilities.

"Should I call Rocha and let him know we're on our way?"

"Hell no. Let's surprise him and see what happens," Holden said with a short smile. "I'd love to show up with a warrant, but we don't have enough evidence for that...yet."

"By the numbers, Holden," she warned. "Don't go all cowboy on me. If Tessara is behind shady deals, we'll figure it out the legal way. Just be patient."

Holden wasn't in the habit of issuing promises—especially ones he didn't know if he could keep. He pressed his foot harder on the gas pedal and hurtled down the freeway toward Tessara Pharmaceuticals.

When they walked into the Tessara facility, Selena immediately appeared with a faint question marring her flawless skin, though her hands were clasped in front of her with complete serenity. Jane was pretty sure she wasn't human and was tempted to check for a pulse. "We're here to speak with Mr. Rocha."

"Mr. Rocha isn't here," Selena said with an apologetic smile. "He's a very busy man. Perhaps you could make an appointment?"

"Someone else has to be running this operation," Holden said. "Bring us that person."

Selena's smile faltered and she blinked as she processed the realization that they would plant their feet and wait until someone talked to them. "I see. Come with me," she instructed, turning to take them back into the conference room with the hidden door.

"Please help yourself to snacks and beverages. Everything is organic and fresh."

"Ironic given this is a pharmaceutical company, isn't it?" Jane said to Holden as Selena left the room, gracing them with a sugary sweet smile that oddly made Jane think of a shark. "That woman ain't right," she said once they were alone.

"Agreed. I get a definite serial killer vibe from that chick. I've never been so chilled by a pretty smile."

"You think she's pretty?" Jane asked diffidently, shooting for nonchalance. "I mean, not that I care, of course. Just curious."

"Um, I sense a trap," he said, and she snorted. "Hey, I've been well schooled in the belief that there are some questions you never answer because it's a zero-sum game. As in *no winner.*"

"Oh, good grief, Holden. It was just a silly question," she said, miffed that he was right. If he'd answered yes, he thought Selena was pretty, it would've eaten at her nerves, which in turn would've pissed her off for caring in the first place. If he'd said no, then she would've believed him a liar and definitely untrustworthy. "Fine. It was a trap." She scowled, then deliberately shook off the weird vibe. "Forget I said anything. It was dumb to even ask. I don't care who you find attractive."

Holden's gaze smoldered, taking her breath away, and if they weren't on official business, she had no doubt he would've shoved her up against the nearest wall to demonstrate just how attractive he found *her.* "Oh, crap. Don't look at me like that," she warned.

He chuckled. "Mind reading is part of your skill set?" he asked.

She shot him a cool look. "You don't have to read minds to know what'd just circulated through your brain. Get it together."

The lust slowly cleared from his stare and he shrugged in his jacket, adjusting himself with admirable efficiency just in time for Ulysses Rocha to walk in. "Agents. What a pleasant surprise," he said.

"Back so soon?" Jane asked pointedly. Ulysses smiled in apology.

"Selena tries to protect my schedule. She's a good assistant. However, the minute she told me my unexpected visitors were Agents Archangelo and Fallon, I made time. What can I do for you?"

"What relation is Penelope Granger, aka Penny Winslow, to Trevor Granger?" Jane got straight to the point.

Ulysses frowned. "A cousin, I believe, if memory serves. Why?"

Neither she nor Holden answered; instead, she pushed on to their next question. "Penny Winslow was involved in a number of projects here, most notably the Game Changer, which was the nickname for MCX-209."

"Yes," Ulysses confirmed with a shrug. "Penny liked to be involved in a number of high-profile projects. Unfortunately, ultimately, MCX-209 was a failure, as I'm sure you are already aware."

"I'm aware it failed as a cure for Alzheimer's," Holden said. "But something tells me Penny knew it would be because she was a brilliant scientist beneath that socialite veneer." Ulysses remained silent. "Nothing?"

"It wasn't my project. I have little working knowledge of the trials." Ulysses clasped his hands in front of him.

"Then perhaps we can speak with Dr. Odgers's direct supervisor?" Jane prompted.

"Tragically, her supervisor was killed in a freak accident. We were all very saddened by his death. Hector Olonzo was a valuable member of the Tessara family."

"He's dead?" she questioned, finding that way too convenient. Alarm bells clanged loudly in her head. "What kind of freak accident?"

"It was all very tragic. A mugging gone wrong. The man panicked and shot poor Hector as he was leaving his favorite restaurant on Laurel Avenue. Left him dead in the street. Fortunately, from what I understand, Hector, God rest his soul, didn't suffer. Died instantly."

And dead men tell no tales. She shared a look with Holden. "We'd like to take a look at the project files associated with MCX-209," Holden said.

"Again, sorry to disappoint, but due to the sensitive nature of the drug, the Defense Intelligence Department felt it prudent to remove all traces of the drug trials and research from the facility."

Jane nodded remembering something to that effect from Dr. Kat Odgers, Jake Isaac's wife. They could enlist her help to find the missing research. "Penny

Winslow's influence on any project, given the discovery that she was abusing her authority, is immediately suspect," he told Ulysses. "Were you aware of Penny's extracurricular activities outside of this lab?"

"I'm not sure what you're asking," he said calmly.

"I don't believe I need to spell it out," Holden said. "You're a smart man."

"I was unaware of Penny's involvement with I.D.," Ulysses answered, short and sweet and giving away nothing.

Jane glanced at Holden, signaling they were done. The secrets in this building could fill a space station. Whatever Ulysses was protecting, he wouldn't share without a court order to compel him.

"We'll be in touch," she said.

"Good luck in your investigation. As always, Tessara strives to be accommodating."

Did he mean that? Likely not. They were probably having a shredding party this very second, if they hadn't already.

After they left the building and headed to their car, Holden said, "Well, that wasn't entirely a bust. Do you think Hector was killed and it was framed as a tragic mishap?"

"My instincts say yes," Jane said, climbing into the car. She checked her watch. "We'd better hustle if we want to catch our rescheduled flight. I'm ready to put California in my rearview mirror."

Holden agreed. They'd learned everything they were going to learn in this place. Besides, more answers awaited them back in Washington when they hit up Kat Odgers for information on MCX-209.

Once on the plane, buckled in and ready for take-off, Holden asked Jane, "What do you think that winery has to do with all of this? Seemed kind of random."

She nodded. "Maybe we ought to pay a visit and see what shakes out?"

"Definitely. Put it on the list."

"What vibe are you getting from Rocha?" Jane asked.

"Not sure. He's definitely not happy that we're poking around, but I can't tell if it's because he's protecting his investments or because he truly has stuff to hide."

"Same. He hasn't been overtly helpful. Then again, he hasn't refused anything we've asked for, either. He could've made it more difficult to procure those personnel files, but he handed them over with minimal fuss."

"He's pretty tight-lipped about what he knew about Penny's exploits, though. Something tells me he's not quite as innocent as he wants us to think he is."

"Maybe."

A beat of silence followed before Holden said, "Watching you in action is pretty hot."

She sucked in a quick breath and shot him a warning look. "Stop that. We can't be talking like that once we get back to Washington."

"I know," he said, withdrawing with slightly ruffled feathers. Did she have to be so rigid all the time?

"I was just saying…I don't know, I read somewhere that women like to hear that stuff."

"Well, I'm not like most women."

Amen to that. It was one of the reasons he couldn't stop thinking about her. "Roger that," he said, deliberately closing his eyes. "I'm going to catch a few Zs. Some wildcat kept me up all night." He smiled to himself when he heard her gasp in embarrassed indignation. *That's right, babe. Good luck shelving that experience.* He'd liked knowing how to push her buttons before, but now? He knew all the *right* buttons to push to make her squirm—and that was information worth dying for.

Chapter 15

It was late by the time they flew into Washington, and, stubborn woman that she was, Jane insisted on driving home instead of crashing at his place. He tried not to be annoyed because he had no right to be, but when he woke the next morning he was less than refreshed. He'd reopened Pandora's Box and he wanted more. In the brief time they'd dated, he'd enjoyed going to sleep and waking up with Jane, which had been something of a change of pace for him because he never invited women to his apartment. Now he was missing the feel of her warm body next to his, and there was nothing he could do about it. She was determined to be bullheaded. A knock at his front door made him realize not only had he lost out on good REM, he'd overslept, too. He opened the front door and let Jane in with a mumbled good morning in between a big yawn.

"You look like hell," she observed, going to the coffeepot to pour herself a cup. "Still jet-lagged?"

If he looked jet-lagged, she was the exact opposite— she looked as fresh as a daisy. Of course, that rubbed him wrong, too. Why wasn't she suffering like he was? "I'm fine. There's nothing like having the whole bed to yourself."

She nodded. "Sometimes a California King just isn't big enough," she said with a bright smile. Damn, she was good at this game. "You better shower because we have an appointment at Butterfly Bend in an hour and it's at least a 45-minute drive from here."

He swore under his breath, then burned his tongue with hot coffee. "You couldn't have made an afternoon appointment? Jeez, Fallon, give a guy a chance to recover."

"No rest for the wicked, right?"

He had no response. Frankly, he didn't trust himself not to be rude. Maybe a shower would do him some good. Except when he stood under the spray he couldn't help but remember the last shower he shared with Jane, and suddenly it was hard to focus on anything aside from his raging erection. He pushed at his shaft, irritated. Nothing was gonna happen there. *Down, boy.* Think of baseball, grandmothers or the fact that Jane wasn't the least bit interested in picking up where they'd left off. Yeah, that ought to be a good-enough libido killer. He scrubbed down and got out of the shower. Taking little time to dress, he reappeared, hair wet but ready to work.

"You take a longer shower that most girls I know," Jane said, frowning. "What did you do in there, shave your legs?" She grabbed her keys and gestured. "Let's go. We're losing time."

"And you think you're driving?" he asked, incredulously. "If we're going to get there on time, I'd better drive."

Jane was such a stickler for the rules that she stuck religiously to the speed limit. He, on the other hand, treated each destination as a finish line. But Jane wasn't about to budge.

"I would like to arrive alive. How you even have a license is beyond me."

Holden had no choice but to follow. The only consolation was the nice view of Fallon's backside as they left his building. "So you really slept good last night?" he asked.

"Like a baby."

Like a baby, he mimicked in his head as he climbed into the car. Of course she had. Holden punched the address in the GPS and they were on their way. Jane's sensible Honda Accord was exactly the kind of car he'd imagined Jane would drive. It got good gas mileage, was luxurious to a point, but not overly so, and had a sensible price point. He chuckled at his own observation, which caused her to look at him sharply.

"What was that for?"

"Nothing. I was just thinking this car suits you."

She relaxed. "Yeah? It's a good car. *Consumer Re-*

ports lists it as one of the most reliable cars in its class."

"I bet it does." He smirked. "Let me guess…top speed is eighty miles per hour."

"Not that I would need to drive eighty for any reason—we're not on an autobahn. It does have a V6, you know. But why would I need to drive faster than the speed limit? Do you think I have a death wish?"

He barked a laugh. "Jane, live a little, why don't you? There's a whole world waiting for you when you decide to go crazy."

"You can keep crazy. I prefer stability and reliability."

He winced. "Are you a granny? And how is it that you work for the federal government with your low tolerance for risk?"

"Can we talk about something other than personal things? Let's talk about the case," she suggested almost desperately. "I was thinking last night when I couldn't fall asleep that there has to be a connection between Trevor and Penny other than being cousins. The fact that Miko referenced the winery tells me there's something there because why else would Miko mention something so obscure?"

"I thought you said you slept like a baby," he reminded her, latching on to the one thing that mattered to him at the moment. "Maybe you should've stayed with me like I suggested."

"Do you seriously have a one-track mind? Can we please stay on topic?"

He sighed, annoyed he was so easily pushed aside.

"Yeah, sure. I was just saying that, you know, it might have been nice.... Forget it."

"I told you we can't do what we did in California. You and I both know it's a huge mistake, and I'm not doing anything to jeopardize this case. I'm surprised you're fighting me on this. Why are you so hurt that I don't want a relationship with you?"

"Hurt? Who said I'm hurt?" he repeated, indignant. "You're right—we should just stick to the case."

"Thank you. Now you're making sense. All right, so here's the deal—I say we question this Trevor Granger and find out why Miko would've been aware of Trevor and Penny's relationship. And in the meantime, I wonder if we could get James to do some more poking around."

"Such as?"

"Such as taking a look around the Department of Defense and see if they are holding on to anything beyond our pay grade."

Holden whistled in appreciation. "I take it back. You do like to live dangerously. So you're saying we should set James on the trail that might lead to the Department of Defense's doorstep? Essentially hacking into a government mainframe? That might take more than twenty grand. Are you footing this bill?"

"He might be willing to do it just for fun. His type love the opportunity to hack into government mainframes. It's like a badge of honor," she said. "But I guess we can wait and see what we find out on our own before we tap that resource."

"It's worth keeping in our pocket for plan B,"

Holden said, eyeing her with deeper appreciation, not only for her sexy body, but also for her incredibly sexy brain. He angled himself toward her. "Listen, I know we said we wouldn't talk about personal stuff, but you have to admit there's still a spark between us."

"Obviously. That's not the point, though. Neither one of us is suited for a relationship with the other. Why complicate matters when there's no need?"

"Maybe I like complicated."

She made an exasperated noise. "That's the problem—I don't. It's just easier to keep things professional between us."

"Easy is boring. And you don't want boring. You're the kind of woman who needs a challenge or else you stagnate in your own rigid personality. My guess is before your dad made you dance to his tune, you were less buttoned-down."

"What makes you say that?"

"Because I've seen your wild side, and there's no way that sexy woman came out of nowhere. She's just been on lockdown for far too long."

Jane risked a small smile, but she smothered it quickly enough to drop a bomb on him. "Listen, I didn't want to do this, but the bottom line is this— you'll never be good enough in the eyes of my family. Even before this situation with Miko blew up, you had no cred with my dad. He has a certain standard, and you don't live up to it. I'm sorry. It's harsh, but those are the facts. I'm not going to spend my entire life defending you against my family or fighting with family over you."

Ouch. He felt as if she'd just delivered a round-house kick to his nuts. And what the hell? He wasn't good enough? How much more cred did he need? "Last time I checked I was a pretty good catch," he told her, his temper rising. "Highly decorated marine, level VI security clearance in the CIA and built like a Mack truck. I don't see the problem."

"I love your enthusiasm and confidence, but it has nothing to do with your qualifications *per se*. It has everything to do with the way my family perceives you."

"I'm confused. Are you saying it's not me, it's your family?"

"Sort of."

"Oh, good. For a second I thought you were throwing up imaginary obstacles." He rolled his eyes as his voice dripped with sarcasm. Unbelievable. He was considered a good catch by most standards. Except to the one person he wanted to impress, for some stupid reason. "Listen, just admit to me that you and I shared something pretty incredible, and I'll leave it at that."

"You'll drop it?"

"Sure," he lied. Drop it? He was going to gnaw on that sucker like a dog with a bone. But his ego demanded she tell the truth. "Just admit I rocked your world and we'll go back to being simply partners without benefits."

She drew a deep breath and blew it out in a long exhale. "Okay, Holden. We have chemistry. Real, visceral, unexplainable chemistry, and this weekend was a brutal reminder that we are desperately good

together. Is that what you want to hear? Well, I'll do
you a solid and go a step further. The reason I couldn't
sleep last night was because I was thinking of what
we did together and how I already missed the feeling
of you beside me. It that enough? Does that help? Because frankly, I think it makes it worse."

The tight band of tension cording his chest loosened and he could actually breathe again. As long
as she was fighting the same fight he was, there was
a chance. A chance at what, he wasn't sure, but he
wanted to find out. "Yeah, it'll do." He didn't even
try to smother the grin. "Now, tell me again why we
shouldn't be partners with benefits?"

"You're impossible," she growled, and shot him an
extremely irritated look. She switched on the radio
and effectively shut him out. "From now on, no more
talking."

What was his problem? Why did he care what her
family thought of him? Jane was baffled by Holden's
reaction, but even more so by the pinch she felt in her
conscience for hurting his feelings. They'd shared
a whirlwind of good times until it'd come grinding
to a halt, which had been the wake-up call she had
needed to put her head back on straight. The memory
of ending it popped into her mind as she drove, and
she lingered a little too long, because within seconds
she was back in that wretched moment.

"What do you mean, you're ending things?"
Holden had demanded to know, standing apart from
her, pissed as hell and more than a little hurt. "This

is crap and you know it. Everything was going fine until your dad got involved."

"And who got him involved?" she had shot back, still mad at him for thinking he knew how to handle the situation with her father better than her. "I told you to back off, but you refused and did whatever you thought was necessary and it blew up in our faces. Well, congrats—this is your reward!"

"You're punishing me for trying to talk to your dad for *us?*" he'd asked with open incredulity. "That's rich, Fallon. Totally rich. Remind me never to do you a solid ever again."

"Oh, don't try to delude yourself into thinking you did that for me. It was all about you. The charming Holden Archangelo thought he could bamboozle my father into liking him and it went sour. End of story."

"Believe what you want, but I did it for *you!* It's not natural for you to live under your father's thumb for the rest of your life. For crying out loud, Fallon, you're still balancing his damn checkbook!"

"There's nothing wrong with that," she'd said stubbornly, though she had tried to talk her father into hiring an accountant. The Major had shut her down pretty quickly, saying he couldn't trust strangers with his finances. Then when she'd tried to enlist the help of her brothers, The Major had shut her down on that score, too, saying Ian and Walker were too busy to handle an extra assignment. "If you were close to your father, Holden, you'd understand. My dad needs me and I enjoy being able to help."

"No, you crave that tiny pat on the head that he

doles out like a miser with his gold," Holden had returned, and her cheeks had burned with the insult because it was partly true. Even though she was overloaded with responsibilities, it gave her a small amount of pleasure knowing her father valued her help in this one way. He still managed to find fault each time, which always put a damper on the meager amount of satisfaction she received for the work. Holden must've peeked inside her brain because he'd then said, "See? Even you know it's true. When are you going to start living your life for you instead of everyone else? What about your brothers? Do they beg for your father's approval before they date someone?"

"No," she'd answered, her cheeks burning even hotter. "My dad doesn't seem to care who they date."

"Why? Because somehow they're perfect judges of character? And if that's so, why can't they trust your judgment?"

"Stop it!" She'd clapped her hands over her ears, unable to listen to another minute of Holden punching holes in her life. Everything he'd said rang with truth, but she hadn't been ready to burn down the house just because the roof leaked a little. "I don't tell you how to be with your family, so shut the hell up. I don't even know why you're so upset about my ending things. I thought you were the perennial bachelor? This should be a blessing. You ought to be thanking me for letting you off the hook. I mean, c'mon, Holden, what did you think? That we were going to run off and get married or something? We were just sleeping together. That's it. And now it's over."

Holden had held her stare, his mouth a tight line of frustrated anger, but there had been hurt in his eyes. It had been the secret pain he was trying to hide that had twisted her heart. She'd done that. She'd put that look in his eyes. And a part of her mourned her own actions, but if her father had taught her anything, it was how to make the hard choice with a stiff upper lip. *Thanks, Dad.*

"So you really didn't sleep well last night," Holden asked, breaking into her thoughts. She was so grateful to be out of her own head that she answered truthfully.

"Yeah, too many memories. Both good and bad," she admitted. "I feel as if I only got a few winks. Reminds me of when I was stationed in Iraq. That was a bloody awful time."

"Iraq is a dusty bowl of insurgent nightmares. I spent a tour there. Then I got shipped off to Afghanistan for another crap detail that nearly got my ass shot off."

She smiled in weary commiseration. "It feels like that. I swear I have sand in my eyes." He reached over and massaged the back of her neck, gently squeezing the muscles holding up her head, and she groaned. "That felt awesome," she said with a sigh, just for a moment enjoying the simple pleasure. Jane cast Holden a brief smile and he smiled back, igniting tiny bubbles in her stomach. She shook her head.

"You're a hard habit to break," she murmured, mostly to herself, but Holden heard and chuckled.

"Glad to hear it. Soothes my bruised ego a little."

Funny how the little sleep she'd managed with Holden had been wholly satisfying, yet the eight hours she had supposedly gotten last night made her feel as if she'd slept only two winks. She refused to believe it was anything more than wild, crazy attraction between two people who were turned on by the forbidden aspect of their relationship. What other option was there? Was she falling in love with Holden? Goodness gracious, she hoped not. She didn't need that complication. Maybe it wasn't love but simply the draw of a forbidden relationship. Maybe she was a bit of a bad girl. Maybe a latent naughtiness inside of her was spurring her to do things outside of her nature. That must be the answer, because ever since Holden had been thrown into her life, she'd been doing and saying things that were so far afield of what she would ever say or do she almost didn't recognize herself. The weird part? She kind of liked it. She liked this feeling of having no rules, or better yet, saying screw the rules and just going for it. Her grip tightened on the steering wheel. Yes, sometimes rule breaking was fun. Especially if it was with Holden. But right now they had a case to figure out. And she had a feeling they were only scratching the surface of something really bad.

Chapter 16

They pulled off the highway and found themselves on a long winding road that carved through the scenic mountainside cloaked in the bitter cold of winter. "It's a little creepy, yet beautiful at the same time," she observed. "I've never actually heard of a winery in Washington. Aren't most wineries in California?"

"Your guess is as good as mine. I'm not exactly a wine drinker. I prefer beer myself."

"Me, too."

Holden flashed her a grin as they pulled into the winery parking lot. "All right, let's see what this winery dude has to tell us," he said as they climbed from the car.

An imposing rock-and-brick building rose from the ground, the design both old world and modern at the same time. An affluent stamp marked the property; everywhere they looked the evidence of big money stared back. Rolling hills lined with rows upon rows of gnarled grape vines lashed to rigging to keep them upright went as far as the eye could see. Snow dotted the mountaintops above them. It was romantic and breathtakingly scenic. Too bad they weren't out sightseeing.

An older man with a sharp smile emerged from the house and quickly introduced himself. "You must be Agent Archangelo and Agent Fallon. Nice to meet you. My name is Trevor Granger. I own Butterfly Bend."

"Thank you for agreeing to see us on such short notice," Jane said.

"No problem. We're off season right now, so things slow to an acceptable pace around here. Now, if this meeting had happened in September, I would've had to tell you to take a number." He laughed at his own joke and Jane and Holden simply smiled politely as they followed him into the warmth of the building. Inside was just as lovely as the outside. Tastefully decorated with an understated wealth, it looked as if a set decorator had dressed it for a scene. "Can I get you some coffee or fresh scones?" he offered. A scone tempted Jane, but she declined, as did Holden. However, the man wouldn't take no for an answer. "Are you sure? Fresh from the oven. There is nothing better than a fresh scone with homemade cream. And don't even try to let anyone tell you the stuff in the can is just as good as cream whipped to a perfect peak. Lies, I tell you. It's the real deal or nothing."

"I agree, sir." Holden smiled. "Maybe I will take one of those scones."

Trevor snapped his fingers and a round dark-haired woman appeared from the kitchen carrying a tray. Her graying hair sprang from her head in unruly strands, and a warm smile wreathed her mouth as she offered the plate for his selection. "Maria is the best baker in all of Washington. I know this because she used to run her own bakery and I made her an offer she couldn't refuse. Now she bakes for me."

Jane looked to Maria, surprised. "You gave up your business to be the baker for Mr. Granger?"

Maria bobbed her head. "Oh, yes. Mr. Granger is very generous. And I love working here."

Trevor nodded at Maria's answer and then she scuttled off. "I always say treat your hired help well and you'll never be left with open positions," he shared with a patronizing smile. "Maria has been with us for two years now and it's because of her my waistline is getting a little bit thicker. I don't mind, though."

Holden groaned as he enjoyed his bite. "Whatever her salary is, she's worth it. This is the most amazing scone I've ever had in my life."

Jane startled when he pushed a scone at her. "No, thank you," she said in a low tone, annoyed that Holden was so easily distracted. Honestly, how did this man ever get anything done? She looked to Trevor. "Mr. Granger, you might wonder why we called this meeting today. We have some questions regarding your cousin, Penny Winslow, or as you knew her, Penelope Granger. Did you have anything to do with a company called Tessara?"

"Oh, yes. Penelope was helping me develop a new type of cork for my wine bottles. One of the problems that we have is cork disintegration over time. She was helping me create a coating that would go over the cork and prevent it from disintegrating without affecting the integrity of the wine."

"Why not just use plastic?" Jane suggested.

"My dear, one does not simply use plastic in the wine that has been selected as the Presidential Reserve. Plastic has chemicals that affect the wine's integrity. My reputation would be ruined if I dared to use a plastic cork."

"Oh," Jane said, not meaning to offend the man. "So was she successful?"

"Yes, she was. I received a shipment of the new corks last month. Unfortunately, Penelope is not here to celebrate with me. We were very close and her death took a toll on my health. I still get choked up when I let myself dwell. She was a tremendous woman and like a sister to me."

"I'm sorry for your loss," Jane murmured, but from what she had read, Penny Winslow was a sociopath. Her death was a blessing; however, this man had been her family, so Jane would try to be respectful. "It may grieve you to learn that Penny was involved in a number of illegal activities."

"I recall some of the more sordid newspaper headlines," Trevor said, his mouth pinching in a disgusted moue. "But I've come to realize the truth doesn't always make for the best headline. I choose not to believe such lies about my cousin. She was a generous woman who believed in volunteering and was involved in various humanitarian works. Surely you've read some of the many articles about her charitable giving? I'd hate to think that all my cousin Penny will be remembered for is the lies that were printed about her toward the end of her life."

"Penny was found guilty by the law—those were not lies," Holden said. "I'm sorry to be the bearer of bad news. I'm sure she was a different person with you."

Trevor jerked a short nod but kept his lips tight, which Jane had to respect. Sometimes it was hard to remember that even bad people were loved by someone.

"That's what brings us here today," Holden continued. "It seems Penny was involved with more than just good works."

"Such as capitalism," Jane murmured, unable to stop herself. Holden cast her a look, and she buttoned up. She knew that comments like that weren't exactly helpful. Thankfully, it didn't appear as if Trevor had caught her muttered dig.

"I don't want to tarnish the memory of your cousin, but the person she was to you isn't the person she was to everyone. Penny was abusing her position for personal gain. Again, I'm sorry to pour salt in the wound, but we need to know why my brother, Miko, would've mentioned your winery in covert notebooks that also involve your cousin Penny. Do you have any idea why he would have mentioned Butterfly Bend?"

Trevor shook his head with a faint frown. "I haven't a clue. I assure you, nothing illegal is happening on these premises. I have too much to lose to mess with anything that might cost me my livelihood. You don't get selected to create the Presidential Reserve without keeping your nose clean."

"What is the Presidential Reserve?" Jane asked. He'd mentioned it twice now, so it must be important.

"We were tasked to create an original blend specifically for the White House. Any event is served with a white and red of Butterfly Bend Presidential Reserve."

"Wow. That's quite a coup," Holden said, and Trevor nodded.

"See? I wouldn't risk everything I have for anyone, not even my beloved cousin."

"How does one earn the designation of the Presidential Reserve?" Holden asked.

"Cultivating the right connections along with creating award-winning wines is essential."

"And you obviously managed both criteria."

"For two years running now," Trevor said, puffing out his chest with pride. "In fact, we're shipping another batch of wine at the end of this month for a special presidential dinner. It's a small gathering, not the usual five hundred head count, just the executive branch."

"Nice," Holden said, holding a brief smile, but Jane could feel the frustration starting to roll off him that not even a delicious scone could divert. They were at another dead end. Trevor Granger didn't give off a criminal vibe, and they couldn't go after a guy simply because he had crappy relatives. "Thank you for your help. I think we've taken up enough of your time."

Trevor rose as they did, looking eager to please again. "I'm happy to be of service to the government in any way I can."

Yes, so keep those kickbacks flowing my way, Jane thought derisively as her smile remained fixed. "We'll be in touch if there's anything else we need."

Trevor saw them outside, then Jane and Holden put Butterfly Bend in their rearview mirror. "I really thought that was going to lead somewhere," Jane said once they hit the freeway. Holden's disappointment was tangible and squeezing out the air in the car. "Tomorrow we'll check out that safety deposit box," she said, trying to lift his spirits. "Something helpful is bound to be in that. I can feel it in my bones."

He graced her with a short smile to acknowledge her but otherwise remained silent the entire ride back to his place. But as they exited the car, Holden stopped her to ask, "How about dinner?" and she knew the smart thing to do would be to politely decline, but his vulnerable expression tugged at her in a way that, if she'd been thinking clearly, would've been a warning.

"Just dinner?"

"Sure."

"I don't believe you," she said bluntly.

"And would it be so bad if it turned out to be more than just dinner?"

She sighed. "Yes and no."

"Is it mostly yes or mostly no?"

"I think it's mostly freezing out here. Promise me it'll just be dinner and we'll talk about the case, and I'll stay."

With a look of resignation, he agreed. "Sure. A working dinner. Sounds great."

Oh, he's lying through his perfect teeth. He wants more and he'll try to get it, too. And yet... "All right. What's for dinner?"

"I have a few steaks in the fridge. How are you with a salad?"

She cast a derisive look his way as they entered the building. "I can make a salad that'll knock your socks off. Remember? Even my father, who is as persnickety as it comes, raves about my salads."

"Good." He smirked and started climbing the stairs, giving her an excellent view of his beautiful butt.

Yeah...this was so not a good idea.

Holden was trying not to let his disappointment color the evening, but it was there, beneath the surface, lurking like an unwelcome guest, sullying his enjoyment of a decent evening with Jane. By the time the wine came out, he was ready to talk.

"So how long are you going to pretend like everything is okay?" she asked as they walked to the living room and sat on the sofa together. It felt intimate as the fire crackled in the gas grate and filled the room with dancing light. Dinner had been fantastic. Between his grilling skills and Jane's epic salad-making talents, they'd made a dinner worth talking about. Jane tucked her feet beneath her and faced him as she sipped her wine. "I get it…I was hoping for more to go off, too."

He stared at his wine, wishing he'd grabbed a beer, but he took a measured sip anyway before answering. "The clock is ticking. I needed there to be more to go off. The end of the week is approaching fast. Going to California ate up valuable time."

"Chief Harris will give us more time if we can show him what we've got."

"What do we have? A bunch of uncomfortable co-incidences? A few plausible theories? Which translate to nothing that will stand up in court. I can't let this go, Jane. Why couldn't Miko have left behind less cryptic clues?" he asked with frustration.

"You miss him." It was a statement, not a question. Of course he missed him, but he sensed she knew that it went deeper than that. And she was right.

"Miko and I were always close. Goes with the twin territory. But I think because our old man was such a sorry excuse for a father we leaned on each other even more than most brothers would. We were each other's support system. We did everything together."

"From the limited information I know about twins, that sounds about right. What changed?"

"Miko changed. That last year he was standoffish and started pushing me away. He became surly and curt whenever I tried to find out what was wrong. By the time he died, we were barely speaking. Sometimes I wonder if that's why he did it—he didn't know how to reach out to me anymore."

"That must've been hard for you, not having your brother around like you used to."

"It was hell. I tried to blow it off, but it was there, sticking in my throat like a chicken bone, choking me to death. And there was nothing I could do about it. Miko was determined to keep me at arm's length. Now I kick myself for not pushing harder for answers."

"Before this investigation with you, I would've said he was reacting to a guilty conscience." She swirled her wine. "Now I think there might be some merit to the theory he was protecting you."

He thanked her with a smile. "Well, I sure hope so. Then again, I wish he would've just told me what was going on. I might've been able to help and maybe he'd still be here."

She nodded and sipped from her glass. They sat in easy, comfortable silence, and Holden wondered if he'd ever felt more at ease with a woman, much less one he'd slept with. He'd never been one for long-term attachments, but he liked the idea of attaching to Jane. Something about her turned his crank in all the right ways. Hell, even the way she stubbornly refused to be with him because of her father and brothers—that dogged loyalty—was sexy. "You close with your brothers?" he asked.

Jane took her time answering, as if she didn't

want to inadvertently say something that would reflect badly on her family. "Yeah, they're good guys. Sometimes I wish they'd stop mirroring our father and stop treating me like some fragile female who can't parallel park. Frankly, I pity the women they end up with. Impossible standards."

He chuckled at this rare bit of sharing. Must be the wine loosening her tongue. "So they've never brought home a special woman? Someone they were in a long-term relationship with?"

"No. I don't think either of them are interested in settling down. Sometimes I think my mom did a number on all of us. Fear of commitment seems a pretty common theme among the Fallon men."

"So that's why your dad never remarried?"

"I guess." A wry smile lifted her lips. "But what woman would put up with him? Aside from Claudine, of course. And even then…sometimes I wish she'd just whack him upside the head."

"Whoa…look at you, feeling your oats," Holden said, smiling. "And who is Claudine?"

"My dad's housekeeper and cook. She keeps him looking civilized. Heaven forbid he leave the house without his shirts perfectly pressed. Until Claudine came around, I was expected to handle that detail. To this day, I hate ironing," she revealed. "I send out my clothes to a dry cleaner. I'm not even sure I own an iron."

He laughed. "Feels good, huh? Breaking the rules?"

She shared his laughter. "Yeah. When I got my

first apartment, I ate straight from the peanut-butter jar, just stuck my finger in and took a dollop. My father would've had a heart attack if he'd seen me do that at home."

"My old man used to keep his fishing gear in the garage and never, under any circumstances, were we allowed to touch it. Well, he was drunk more often than he was sober and when the hell was he going to go fishing? So during the summer Miko and I would grab his gear and go down to the creek whenever he passed out. We'd catch a few fish, grill 'em up out in the woods, then come home with full bellies and the old man snoring off his bender, none the wiser. That is, until Miko broke the rod."

"Oh, damn. How'd you get out of that one?"

"We convinced the old man he'd broken it during one of his drunken rages. He couldn't ever remember what he did during those times, so he bought it. Saved our asses, I can tell you that."

Their shared laughter wove a tighter band of closeness around them, and it was hard not to feel it pulling them together. "This is nice," she said quietly. "I'm glad you invited me to dinner. You're not half-bad on the grill."

"And you're not half-bad with the greens."

"Not a bad team, I guess."

"Not bad at all."

Holden withheld the sigh building behind his chest. She was so beautiful. He could stare at her all night—and not in a creeper sort of way, but in an *I think I love you sort of way.* He couldn't tell her that yet.

That was a shortcut to losing all the good feelings between them. Wasn't that his dumb luck? *Find a good woman that you can't have. Good going, Archangelo.* Time to switch things up a bit before he sank too low into his own maudlin thoughts. "Tell me about growing up with The Major," he said. "I can imagine, but paint me a picture."

She groaned. "That's a boring picture and you've already painted a pretty accurate version."

"Humor me."

"Fine." She sighed, settling her empty glass on the coffee table. "Well, it was as you imagined. Very strict, very regimented and little room for dissent in the ranks. And I was always at the bottom of the chain of command."

"Is it because you were the youngest?"

"No. It was because I was a female."

"Your father is sexist?"

"Oh, in the worst way, and he doesn't even apologize for it. Men are smarter, more capable and more trustworthy—according to The Major."

"Ouch. But you're highly accomplished," he pointed out, really fighting the urge to tell Jane that her father was a card-carrying asshole.

"Yeah, and you'd think I'd get an *atta boy* now and then, but nope. I'm successful *because* of my father. He's flat-out told me the reason I've risen in the ranks is because of who my father is."

"That's total bullshit. I've seen your file."

She cocked a brow at him. "Oh? A little light reading?"

"If you've seen your file you know it's not light reading. You've got some serious cred behind your name, and it's not because of your father. You know, Jane, just because someone is serving up cow manure doesn't mean you have to take a bite."

A warm, vulnerable sweetness suffused her expression and he wondered if she knew just how fabulous she was. She was the total package: beauty, brawn and brains. Any guy would be lucky to call her his. And The Major was an idiot for not realizing what a treasure his daughter was. "You can be pretty charming when you put your mind to it," she said.

"I know," he grinned, placing his wineglass near hers and leaning toward her to steal a kiss. She stopped him with a gentle hand, her gaze searching his. "Let me kiss you," he said softly, but she shook her head in a small motion. "Why not?"

"You know why."

"Do you want me to kiss you?" he said, startling her with his abrupt change in tactic. She worried her bottom lip, almost in invitation, and when she slowly nodded, his smile deepened as he closed the distance between their lips. "Then let me."

Chapter 17

Jane allowed Holden to press her into the soft cushion as his mouth teased hers in a brutally devastating invasion that left her aching and wanting. The spiraling need drilling down to her groin flushed her system with hazy desire and she clung to Holden, needing to feel him against her. What was it about this man that sent her good sense running for cover? It wasn't that he was simply a good lover—she'd enjoyed plenty of men between the sheets—so what was it? Something about Holden called out to that distinctly feminine part of herself and caused it to go weak in the knees with butterfly wings in the belly. Talk about an occupational hazard.

"You are the most sensual woman I've ever met," he said against her lips, helping her out of her sweater and tossing it aside. He ran his fingers along the lacy cups of her bra and then nuzzled the valley of her breasts, inhaling her scent. "And your skin smells like cake and cookies." He sat up suddenly to ask, "Why is that, exactly?"

"Brown Sugar and Brownie body lotion," she answered with an embarrassed laugh. "I bought it on a whim."

"Well, it's amazing," he growled, moving to her neck. "As if you weren't delicious enough…."

She laughed with pure delight as he teased all the sensitive spots of her neck, sucking and biting until she was no longer laughing but panting and pulling at the buckle on his jeans. "So impatient," he chuckled as he leaned back to give her better access.

She pinned him with a sensual look as she made quick work of his jeans and shoved them down around his thighs. "If we're going to go balls to the wall with career-ending moves, we'd better make it worth our while."

"Hell yeah, baby," he agreed feverishly, sucking in a tight breath when her lips wrapped around the head of his erection. Jane thrilled at the way the backs of his knees trembled as she worked him with her mouth. His fingers threaded through her hair and pulled with delectable pressure. He guided her with his hands, his touch becoming urgent. "Oh, jeez, Janey…oh!" He tried to push her away, but she wasn't going to let him. She wanted him to know that she gave as good as she got and she expected his best. She wanted him to forget about Miko for tonight and just enjoy being in the company of a woman. His moan turned her on as much as his kisses. She rose and planted a kiss on his mouth before leading him to his bedroom. "Marry me, Jane Fallon," he said breathlessly as he tumbled to the bed, grinning like the devil as she straddled him. "You've just ruined me for other women."

"Too bad for you," she teased as she wiggled on top of him, taunting him with her body. "Now it's your turn. Whaddya got for me?"

His playful demeanor changed, and with a growl he rolled her onto her back so he towered over her. She knew that look and it thrilled her senseless. She felt stripped bare, as if he could see into her very soul, and although it was a foreign sensation, with Holden she wasn't afraid. "You shouldn't throw down gauntlets like that, sweet girl," he warned in a silky tone as he plucked at a puckered nipple with his lips. She shuddered and grinned. He was such a tease. "Now there will be no mercy."

"Bring it on," she dared, lifting her chin with a smile. "I can take whatever you can dish out."

One dark brow lifted as a slow, sexy smile formed on his lips, making her shiver in anticipation as he said, "Challenge accepted," right before sealing his mouth to hers in a mind-altering kiss.

As Holden moved between her legs, she clamped a hand over her eyes as she lost herself in pure pleasure and realized it was official—she was addicted to Holden Archangelo.

And just like all good addictions, he had the power to trash everything she'd worked so hard for in her life.

Holden awoke to the feel of Jane trying to stealthily climb from his bed. "Where are you going?" he asked groggily, rubbing his mouth and trying to focus his vision.

"Home."

The one-word answer made him roll his eyes. He was too tired to argue with her even though he thought she was being ridiculous. If she wanted to bail, sneaking out the door like a one-night stand, so be it. He wasn't going to stop her.

Yeah, that lasted about a minute. He jumped from the bed and followed her to the living room, where she was trying to collect her strewn clothing. "What are you doing, aside from being irritatingly stubborn?"

She straightened, and even in the moonlight he could see the flash in her eyes at his insult. "I never told you I would stay. I don't do that."

"Well, newsflash, I don't, either. Consider it an honor I want you to stay."

"Can you hear yourself? An honor? Get over yourself, Holden. Maybe it isn't about you. Ever think of that? I knew this was a mistake and I never should've let my emotions make the call." She pulled her sweater over her head and jerked on her jeans. "But trust me, it won't happen again. I'm not your partner with benefits. Got it?"

"Loud and clear, honey."

"Good. Then we won't have to ever revisit this conversation." She grabbed her purse, and seconds later she was gone.

Like a bullet exiting the chamber.

He swore under his breath and padded back to his bedroom, shutting the door and climbing back into bed. *Women—they were all crazy.*

Even ones who look stable.

Jane's fingers shook as she slipped her key into her front door. What was wrong with her? Had she no self-will? Holden was like a secret weapon, able to destroy a woman's defenses with one charming twist of his lips, and that wasn't even talking about once he had her on her back.

She walked into her living room and headed straight for her answering machine. Even though it was two in the morning, she couldn't ignore the blinking light of a waiting message. She yawned and pressed play. The nasally voice of a telemarketer followed and she quickly hit Delete. The second message started to play, but she heard nothing but dead air. She frowned and deleted. "No more messages" was the green light giving her permission to find her bed. She started to pull off her sweater and toss it into the laundry basket when something caught her eye. Just as she bent to investigate what turned out to be a coin on the carpet, the sharp tinkle of busting glass startled the drowsiness out of her and she dropped to the floor, her heart pounding. Broken glass littered the floor and cold, outside air seeped in from the small, bullet-shaped hole in her master bedroom window. Someone had been waiting for her. If she hadn't seen the penny on the floor, she'd be sporting metal in the back of her skull. She swallowed and closed her eyes, willing her heart rate to slow down. They might still be out there. She rolled away and slowly stood, her back hugging the wall as she grabbed her gun from the nightstand and crept to the window. She made a quick, peripheral scan and saw nothing but the usual cars parked in her neighborhood. She pulled her cell and quickly dialed Holden. He answered on the second ring. "Calling to apologize?"

"Someone just shot at me through my bedroom window," she whispered.

"Stay where you are," he said, all jocularity gone from his voice. "I'm coming."

"I'm capable of handling myself," she reminded him, and he groaned.

"Damn it, Janey, this isn't some macho attempt at treating you like a little lady who can't handle a crisis. This is about waiting for freaking backup so you don't end up getting killed."

She nodded, realizing he was right. Why else would she have called Holden, right? "Be careful," she said. "There could be more than one shooter out there."

"I'm calling it in. In the meantime, find a defensible spot and stay there."

"I will."

He clicked off and Jane tucked her phone into her pocket before going to her bedroom closet and shutting herself inside. She had a clear view of her bedroom door from the slats, and if anyone tried to follow up on that shot, she'd unload her clip in his or her face. That was a sniper shot, she realized, studying the damage with a critical eye. Chances were they knew they'd missed their mark, and snipers weren't usually the ones charging in for hand-to-hand combat. She double-checked her ammunition and waited, eyes adjusted to the darkness, waiting for anyone who didn't belong there to come busting through her bedroom door. *Go ahead, asshole. Make my day.*

Holden broke about four traffic laws as he nearly topped the speed barrier to get to Jane's. All the while, weaving in and out of traffic, he was on the phone to Reed.

"Someone shot at Jane," he said. "I'm on my way to her place now. Send backup. I don't know how many shooters there are or if they've compromised her house in any other way."

Even though Reed was in his sixties and had likely been fast asleep in dreamland, he snapped to action like a man half his age. "I'll send in a team. Don't worry—it's a team I trust."

"Thanks, Chief."

"Is Jane okay?" he asked.

"She's fine. But this takes it to a whole new level, wouldn't you say? Jane gets shot at after we start poking around in Miko's case?"

"Could be," Reed agreed. "We'll debrief later.

Right now, get to Jane. I want you both in a safe place for the rest of the night."

"I'll take her back to my place," he said. "It's constructed with reinforced steel and bulletproof glass. Ain't nothing getting through that place. I can guarantee it."

"Sounds good. I want a full report at 0800 hours."

Reed clicked off and Holden tossed his phone onto the passenger seat. Within ten minutes, he was at Jane's, and within another ten of his arrival, the cavalry arrived.

A quick but thorough perimeter sweep revealed the shooter had bailed, which didn't surprise Holden. It *did* fill him with impotent rage—he'd wanted to beat him or her to a bloody pulp. He texted Jane that he was coming to the front door, and she met him there. She hadn't changed from when she left his house, and though he had no doubt she could take care of herself, she still looked a bit shaken.

While the team collected forensics, Holden took Jane into the living room. "Tell me exactly what happened."

"There's not much to tell. I came home, I listened to messages and then I went to my bedroom to change for bed. I saw a penny on the floor and bent to retrieve it. That's when the bullet came through the window. Honestly, if the penny hadn't been there, I wouldn't be talking to you right now. That sniper was waiting for me."

Not much to go on. But then if a sniper had been hired to take Jane out, he or she wasn't going to leave tracks for anyone to follow. "Chief said you're to come home with me," he said, expecting and halting her protests with a firm shake of his head. "Your place is compromised and we don't have time to set up a safe house. No arguments—you're coming home with me."

She opened her mouth, then snapped it shut with an almost weary expression and nodded. "Fine. Whatever. I'm exhausted and I need sleep. Your couch is as good as any."

As if. If she wanted to pretend she was going to crash on the couch, so be it. But that wasn't going to happen. He wanted her right beside him. And that was nonnegotiable.

Chapter 18

Jane opened her eyes to the milky morning dawn and listened to Holden's steady breathing. Somehow she'd known she'd end up here, in his bed, but she'd tried to hold out only to cave when he'd simply steered her to the bedroom and started gently removing her clothing. And when he'd simply tucked her in and then climbed in beside her, pulling her to him and holding her tightly, her heart had melted a little. There'd been something so protective, so sweet, about the way he'd known what she had needed, even if she wasn't willing to admit it. She'd slept hard even though she'd only gotten four hours of shut-eye. Someone had tried to kill her. Someone had been lying in wait to end her life. A delicate shudder zinged through her. It'd been a long time since she'd seen active combat, and she'd forgotten how vulnerable it felt to have your life compromised at the drop of a hat.

"Why are you awake?" he asked in a voice husky with sleep. He nuzzled her neck and settled more firmly against her. "You should be sleeping."

"I can't sleep anymore. My mind is racing." At her answer, she sensed that he awoke more fully. She smiled as his breath tickled the back of her neck. "A penny saved my life. What are the odds of that?"

"Pretty damn spectacular. Talk about your lucky penny. I'd hold on to that one."

She nodded, chuckling. "Makes me think I ought to go play the slots or something to take advantage of this lucky streak."

"Now, there's an idea." Holden moved until he was covering her, settling his body along hers, pushing the hair from her eyes and meeting her gaze. "Listen, we're going to find the son of a bitch who tried to kill you, and then we're going to make them wish they'd never been born. Got it?"

She nodded, smiling up at him, loving the feel of his solid body pressing hers. She wrapped her arms around his torso. "I like it when you go all John Wayne," she teased.

"There's plenty more where that came from, missy, *whuha*," he drawled in a terrible John Wayne imitation, then bending to tease her neck in small, nipping kisses and tickling her until she squealed. "Now how about I show you how a real man wakes up his woman…."

And because he began doing things that made her

eyes roll up into her head with insane pleasure, she forgave him the term *his woman.* But a tiny part of her loved being his woman, even if only for this moment.

"I'm just saying," she teased. "I didn't know guys actually enjoyed foofy coffeehouse drinks." She laughed as they walked into the office, both carrying their respective drinks.

"There's nothing foofy about a chai tea latte," Holden insisted. "Besides, you can laugh all you like. You know you want a taste of my sweet, carefully brewed tea that has been perfectly infused with a splash of vanilla and plenty of fresh whipped cream."

Jane's peal of laughter lit up his soul and almost made him forget that someone had tried to kill her last night, but the reminder crashed into his reality seconds later when he saw a stern older man pacing inside the chief's office, obviously upset and demanding answers. Jane followed his gaze and suddenly her smile froze. "Guess who came to visit," he said, just as unhappy at seeing The Major again as Jane was to know the man was likely giving the chief a ration of shit over last night's event.

She set her cup on her desk and straightened. "Stay here, *please,*" she instructed firmly, halting him in midstep. He wanted to follow, but he sensed that would only make things worse for Jane. The Major looked the same as Holden remembered, and he certainly hadn't changed in his disposition, if his facial expression was anything to go on. He tried not to stare at the man through the glass panel of the

chief's office. He'd love to give Jane's father a piece
of his mind for being a jackass to his only daughter, but Jane wouldn't appreciate his interference. If
he learned anything from the last go-round, it was
that Jane prickled when it came to defending her father. He glanced down at himself and immediately
straightened his clothing and brushed at stray bits
of snow clinging to his suit. Jane had said that The
Major wouldn't accept him as a match for his daughter. What a crock of crap. Holden suspected no one
would be good enough for The Major's daughter, and
if the man weren't such a controlling jackass, that
might be an endearing thought by a concerned father. That was not where The Major's motivation was
grounded, though.

Everything inside Holden told him to follow her, to
not let her face her father alone. He sighed. He knew
he was reacting to some primal need to protect when
Jane was no weak-willed female. She could probably
break something of his without popping a sweat. He
grinned in spite of the odd train of his thoughts, but
when his gaze returned to Jane and The Major, his
smile faded. Whatever was going on in there did not
bode well.

He could feel it in his bones.

"My daughter will no longer be part of this investigation," The Major declared, ignoring Jane's gasp
of outrage that he should think he had the power to
snip careers and make life hell for anyone who dared

to naysay him. Maybe he did, but Jane didn't care. She wasn't allowing anyone to push her off this case.

"Stop it! You can't control what cases I investigate." She looked to the chief for backup.

"Let's just take a seat and breathe for a minute," Chief Harris suggested, his gaze remaining shrewd. When The Major didn't appear the least bit interested in taking a chill pill, the chief said, "I can appreciate your concern for your daughter given recent events, but Agent Fallon is a highly skilled investigator with combat training. She's more than capable of taking care of herself."

"My daughter was almost killed last night," The Major said in a hard tone. "This investigation is stirring up hornets' nests that don't need stirring."

Jane blinked. "Dad…do you know something? Do you know who's behind all this?"

The Major cast her a short glance with a curt, "No" before returning to the chief. "But I do know that whoever is pulling the strings is not going to stop until whoever is poking at things is compelled to quit. Last night was a warning."

She suppressed a shudder. "All the more reason why we can't stop now," she said, ignoring her dad's building rage at being denied obedience. "Listen, I thought we'd found all the answers to this case when I originally closed it. I was wrong, and I aim to close it properly this time. I will find whoever is behind this corruption and I will carve it out with a dull spoon if I have to."

"Someone is going to carve *you* up if you're not careful," her dad countered.

She took a page from Holden's playbook. "They'd have to catch me first. They caught me off guard is all. It happened once. It won't happen again. Besides, we have some new leads and we're closing in—I can feel it." Okay, so maybe that was a bit of an embellishment, but she sure as hell wasn't going to admit to her father they'd fallen flat on their faces with their last lead and they were going on fumes. Nope. She'd rather eat a toenail than admit that to him. She had to bring home a win, otherwise her father would never see her as anything more than a weak female who always needed protection and couldn't handle herself in a fight. She squared her shoulders and looked to the chief. "The attempt on my life only cements our theory that we are on to something. Someone is getting nervous."

"I have to agree," the chief said, then addressed The Major. "Agents Fallon and Archangelo are my two best investigators. If anyone can figure this out, it's them. Let's give them a chance."

The Major drew himself up. "Chief Harris, it seems to me this case is more suited to the FBI than the CIA. You're muddying jurisdictional lines, don't you think?"

"Not at all. Miko Archangelo's case landed in our jurisdiction due to the potential international threat to our country, as well as the military connection. This was, and still remains, a CIA case. We are well within our rights to hold on to this case."

Displeased, The Major pinned the chief with a wintry glare. "Do you have children, Chief Harris?"

"Yes. A daughter."

The Major made a faintly aggrieved face. "Then you understand the limitations of the weaker sex. It's not their fault—blame genetics. Jane is a fine agent, suitable for desk tasks, but for dangerous missions I would prefer you consider what you would do if it were your daughter facing certain death and then act accordingly."

Rage and despair at being humiliated in front her boss made something toxic burn at the back of Jane's throat, and she fought to keep it down. How could he embarrass her like that? To openly call her weak in front of her superior? Heat seared her cheeks as she tried to keep her composure. "Your input is neither appreciated nor warranted," she told her father, then she looked to the chief. "Excuse me, Chief Harris, but Holden and I have a new lead to chase down. Dad, I'm sure you can see yourself out."

Jane didn't wait for his reaction because she didn't care what else he had to say on the matter. She bolted from the office, jerked her jacket from her desk, scooped up her cooling coffee and barked to Holden, "Let's go."

Holden, a smart man, quickly followed.

Once they were inside the car, she allowed everything to fall out in a stream of angry, hurt and dizzying barrage of words. "How dare he do that to me! I've spent my entire life feeling as if I need to apologize for being the wrong gender and I've always had

to go out of my way to be more than just a weak female, but it doesn't matter what I do. That's all he'll
ever see me as! Would he do that to Walker or Ian?
Hell no. Of course not, because they're men and they
can take care of themselves. Of all the self-righteous,
misguided, sexist bullshit my father has ever spouted
from his mouth—this takes the ever-lovin' cake!"

"I'm going to take a guess things didn't go well in
there?" Holden rested his arm on the steering wheel
as he regarded her with faint concern. "Mind if you
clue me in so I can be righteously indignant with
you?"

She cast him an impatient look. "I'm not in the
mood for jokes."

"I'm not joking," he insisted, saying, "I'm completely serious. If he's made you this upset, clearly
he's an idiot."

"Don't call my dad an idiot," she whipped back
with a warning. "He's still my dad and I love him,
even if he is a jerk."

"Oh, sorry. I'm new to the rules of this particular
game," he said with a small grin.

She sighed, bouncing her head softly on the head-
rest. "Why is he so…*The Major* at all times? Why
can't he just be my *dad*? And a *normal* dad at that?
You know, he's never given me a true compliment
that wasn't prefaced or followed by some kind of dig
because I'm a woman? Every accomplishment comes
with a caveat. It's as if he can't possibly acknowledge
my skills with honest appreciation because that might
challenge his long-held beliefs that women are infe-

rior." She closed her eyes and groaned. "Why couldn't I have been born a man?"

"That would make our relationship awkward," Holden said, and she giggled in spite of her anger. She opened her eyes and stared at Holden, wondering why she felt safe sharing such personal information with him. She needed to vent and she knew he would keep her confidence.

He drew a deep breath and said, "Listen, I'm not the most experienced advice giver when it comes to dealing with difficult dads. Me and Miko split from our dad as soon as possible and we never looked back. To be fair, I don't think our dad cared one way or the other. By the time we were seventeen, we were just two rivals living in his house and eating his food. Once he even accused Miko of coming on to his skank girlfriend. Like that would happen. If anything, she came on to Miko and it just about scarred him for life. It's probably the reason he wanted to join the military, because after that woman dropped her towel in front of him, Miko figured there was nothing left out there to shock him."

"She dropped her towel in front of him?"

"Yeah. Horrifying. Did I mention she was a meth addict? No meat on her bones, pocked skin and terrible teeth. Honestly, it could've turned a man against women in general if she'd tried to do more than just entice him with her less-than-stellar goods."

She shouldn't laugh, but damn, Holden had a way of tickling her funny bone when she least expected it. "You're something else, Archangelo," she said, appreciating him just a smidge more, even if her feelings for him were becoming more confused by the minute. "Thanks."

"Hey, that's what I'm here for. Well, that and giving mind-blowing orgasms, of course. That's the very definition of partner with benefits. Didn't you know that?"

She groaned. "I hate that term."

"Really? Okay, let's brainstorm, then. Personally, I like *secret lovah* because it sounds so taboo, but in a classy way, or how about *booty-call benefactor,* but honestly that seems like a mouthful—and not in a good way. Or there's always—"

"Good God, please stop," she begged, shaking her head. "There aren't even words. Can we just put this conversation on the back burner for now and focus on the case? I'd rather put my brain to work doing something productive, okay?"

"You got it." He turned the key in the ignition. Before he put the car in Drive, he put his hand over Jane's. "Listen, I don't care what your dad says—I wouldn't want anyone else on this case with me. I trust you, Fallon. And I'm not just saying that because of our...unique relationship. Okay?"

Tears welled anew in her eyes and she wondered how she'd never seen Holden's true integrity shining past the facade he wore every day. "Thank you," she said with stark gratitude. "I needed to hear that."

"I know you did." He put the car in Drive. "Time to work."

"Amen," she murmured, more than ready to put

her mind to work, although as they drove to the bank where Miko had his safety deposit box, she wondered how the hell her father had known so quickly that she'd been shot at. A disquieting thought raced through her mind. What if her father had known because he'd arranged it? The Major was known for getting things done. Maybe he thought if he scared her, she'd startle like a little bunny and scamper off for the shelter of the underbrush, cowering like a female is wont to do—in her father's eyes.

That's a pretty far-fetched theory, Fallon. Yeah... probably. Her gaze followed the street-side scenery as her mind zinged in all kinds of crazy directions. What the hell? How could she even think that? Obviously, she was sleep deprived because her father was a lot of things, but he wasn't a cold-blooded killer and he certainly wouldn't hurt his own daughter. But even if he didn't call for the hit, the fact that her father knew was enough to make her gut ache. "I want to know how my dad knew about the hit," she said out loud. Maybe Holden would have some additional insight.

He frowned. "Your guess is as good as mine." He seemed perplexed. "All I can say is that his connections are pretty deep. Maybe someone heard it over dispatch and recognized the address? I don't know." He paused a moment to peer at her. "You don't think..."

"No," she said quickly. Just the shameful thought was enough to make her want to cover her head and hide. "My father would never do anything so despicable."

"I have to agree with you. I just wanted to make sure you weren't worried about it. That kind of thing could mess with your head."

"Tell me about it," she grumbled. "This whole situation has me staring at shadows looking for clues."

"It's enough to make you go cross-eyed. I wonder if that's how Miko felt. He never knew who he could trust, and the people he could trust, he didn't want to get involved. He must've felt very isolated."

She nodded and tenderly rubbed his cheek with her knuckles. "Thank you for talking me down and listening to me rant. I don't usually lose control like that."

"Maybe you need to."

She cast him a speculative glance before chuckling. "Yeah. Maybe I do. Felt good."

"So what'd you say to your dad while you were in there?" he asked.

"I basically told him to stop treating me like a child. He completely embarrassed me in front of the chief. It's one thing to be treated a certain way around family, but not out in the real world where you're respected in your field. It would be the equivalent of me dressing down my father in front of his old military cronies. It would humiliate him, which is why I would never do that. However, when it comes to me, he doesn't think twice about throwing me under the bus, and I don't understand what I've ever done to deserve being treated like that."

"You haven't done anything. That's the point of being a sexist jerk. Sorry, but it's the facts. He doesn't see you as a capable person in your own right—just as a woman who either needs protecting or subjugating."

"God, you're right," she moaned, hating that her father was so wrong about everything having to do with the female gender.

"Kinda makes you wonder if he treated your mom that way. If so, I'd leave his ass, too. Sorry, I know that's a touchy subject."

She glared even though what he said made sense. She'd never suffer a man to treat her like that in a relationship, though why she allowed her father to do so was a perplexing psychological puzzle. "Well, maybe she left because of him, or maybe she left because she was weak…who knows? It doesn't change the fact he embarrassed the ever-loving hell out of me back there and I said a few things that, if I don't end up backing up with proof, are going to bite me in the ass."

"Such as?" Holden asked, worried.

Jane sighed. "Let's just hope this safety deposit box provides some answers. Another dead end would only prove my father right."

Holden nodded in understanding. So much was riding on this case. More so than some political intrigue. She needed to prove something to her father and Holden needed to clear his brother's name. This case was about family. Screw the intrigue. Plain and simple…this case was about family.

Chapter 19

Holden and Jane arrived at First National Bank and Trust and walked straight to the bank manager, flashing their credentials and causing the pencil-thin man to eye them warily. "Good morning, agents. What can I do for you today?"

"We're here to open a safety deposit box belonging to my brother, Miko Archangelo," Holden answered. After reading the man's badge, he added, "Any help you could give us, Mr. Olgivey, would be most appreciated."

"Do you have the key?"

Holden pulled the key from his pocket and handed it to the manager. "And where is Mr. Archangelo, if I may ask?"

"He's dead."

Mr. Olgivey nodded and gestured for them to follow. Holden and Jane exchanged looks. Well, that
went smoothly. Perhaps a little too smoothly? They
passed through the security gates to the private re-
ceiving room and waited as the bank manager opened
the box and placed it on the small table. "Your brother
was an interesting man. He told me that someday his
brother might come for his box. I suppose that day is
here," he said, surprising Holden. "If there's anything
else you require, I'll be waiting outside." Then the
man let himself out and closed the door behind him.

"That was strange," Jane observed. "What do you
think that was about?"

"Who knows? I'll worry about the bank manager
later. Right now I want to know what's inside this
thing."

Holden opened the metal box and removed several
papers, stacks of more cash and a thumb drive. He
stared at the scant items and frowned. "That's it?"
he exclaimed, disappointed and frustrated. "What
the hell kind of cat-and-mouse game was my brother
playing?"

Jane gathered up the paperwork and began sorting through it. "Property deeds. Seems your brother
owned some undeveloped land in California…."

He sighed. "Yeah, he talked about building a hunting cabin up in the mountains like Nathan's. I guess
he finally got around to purchasing the land but never
got the chance to put the rest of his plan into action.
Damn it," he said under his breath, fighting the urge
to punch the wall or break a chair. His gaze fell on

the thumb drive at the same time Jane's did. He met her questioning stare and shrugged. "Your guess is as good as mine. We'll need a computer to open it."

"What about all this cash?" Jane asked, pushing the stacks around and counting. "At least another twenty thousand is here. It seems your brother was stockpiling cash for some reason. Paranoid much?"

He cast a dark look her way. "Not so paranoid if our suspicions are correct."

Immediately contrite, she said, "I'm sorry, Holden. I didn't mean to be insensitive."

He waved away her apology, irritated at himself for being a touchy puss. "No worries. I'm just frustrated. Sorry for snapping at you."

"It's okay." Her gaze strayed to the cash, and he knew what she was thinking, so he decided to just meet it head-on.

"I'll run the cash through the system to make sure it's not stolen," he assured her. She visibly relaxed. "But my brother wasn't a thief. I can guarantee you that."

"Are you his sole heir?"

"Yeah."

"Seems if it comes back clean, you've come into a fair bit of cash if you count the money still locked away in those foreign accounts."

He shrugged. Money didn't mean any more to him than it'd meant to Miko. He tucked the thumb drive into his pocket and returned the deed and the money to the box. "I'd rather have my brother back." And that was the damn truth. Money didn't mean anything if it came at such a high cost. "Let's go."

Holden was slipping into a black mood, and he couldn't seem to stop himself. He was tired of dead ends and cryptic clues that sent him running in the opposite direction. Was this what it had been like for Miko, trying to stay one step ahead of whoever was after him? Things would've been different if Miko had trusted him enough to just level with him. Maybe he'd still be alive. Or maybe they'd both be dead. Who knew?

Jane touched his arm. "I have a feeling there's something on this thumb drive that's going to be worth our while. Nobody keeps junk in their safety deposit box."

"Maybe."

"No maybe about it," she disagreed firmly, not letting him lose hope. "Listen, I know we've hit a brick wall a time or two, but we must be getting close if people are starting to shoot at us, right?"

A small smile found him. "Yeah, I guess so."

"Okay, then. No more pity parties. We got this. Let's head back to the office, fire up this thumb drive and see what was so important that Miko had to hide it in a bank box."

Holden nodded, thankful for Jane's cool head when he got stuck in his own loop of despair. She was a good partner. Hell, she was a good person. "You know, I really underestimated you before," he admitted. "I mean, I didn't try to see beyond the surface, and I'm sorry. I wish I had sooner. I couldn't have done this without you." She blushed prettily and he was gripped by the urge to plant a kiss on her pouty, sensual-without-even-trying lips. He held back. Now was not the time. But later, he promised himself. "How about dinner tonight? Let me take you out to a nice restaurant. Like a date."

Her smile faded. She tucked a chunk of hair behind her ear, her gaze clearing with no-nonsense seriousness, and he knew whatever ground he'd gained he'd just lost. "I'm not sure we should. Already things have gotten muddied, and please don't take this the wrong way because you've been there for me when I needed someone, but everything in our lives is such a mess that I don't think we need to add to it, okay?"

"Jane, when are you going to admit you want to be with me? It'd save us both a lot of energy if you'd stop fighting what you feel."

Her blush deepened and she scowled. "Can we focus on the case, please? I don't want to get into it right now. My dad is going to want to talk to me after I blew up at him in the chief's office and I don't want to have to explain you, too."

Ah…so he was going to remain her dirty little secret. Ordinarily, that wouldn't bother him because he rarely stuck around long enough to care. But with Jane, he cared.

He cared a lot.

They continued the rest of the drive in silence. Back at the office, they immediately headed to Holden's computer to open the thumb drive. Encrypted password protection stonewalled them. "You've got to be kidding me," he muttered, sliding his hand through his hair and wanting to scream. "C'mon, Miko. Cut me some slack, will ya?"

"We can give it to IT," Jane said. "They can probably jail break it."

"I don't trust anyone with this thumb drive. For all I know, my brother died protecting whatever is on it." He leaned back in his chair, thinking hard. All lines pointed in one direction. He swore under his breath and knew he didn't have a choice. "James Cotton."

Jane nodded and lifted her shoulder. "Well, at least you've got some more disposable cash to offer the little tech mercenary."

"True enough."

"All right, so we'll table that for later tonight. In the meantime, we'll visit Dr. Odgers at the Department of Defense. We need to talk with her anyway."

He nodded, knowing Jane was right. Besides, what could he do but wait and see what James's asking price would be for cracking into the thumb drive? Not much. Better to be active than sit on his ass doing nothing. He tucked the drive in his pocket and gestured as he swung his jacket back onto his shoulders. "Saddle up. Let's go talk to Kat."

Jane had heard a few things about Dr. Odgers, but she'd never actually met the supposedly brilliant scientist. Honestly, Jane found the idea of meeting with a genius intimidating, even though she wasn't dumb by any means.

When they arrived, they were cleared by security and then escorted through several more levels of clearance before they reached the state-of-the-art lab where Dr. Odgers worked.

Impeccably clean glass doors opened with a whisper at their arrival, and they passed through to find a willowy woman with her hair tucked into a messy bun wearing a lab coat and talking to an assistant. "Dr. Odgers?" Jane ventured, and the woman startled, pushing her glasses farther up the bridge of her nose. She smiled uncertainly until she saw Holden. "Oh! I heard you were coming. I'm so glad to see you!" She went straight to him and shook his hand vigorously. "You know, I never really got the chance to properly thank you for all your help in rescuing Jake during that whole abysmal situation with MCX-209. Horrid. Absolutely horrid. I still have nightmares about it all."

"He's a good man. I was happy to be a part of that mission," Holden said with the solemn integrity that was as part of him as breath. Jane waited to be properly introduced, and Holden did so a heartbeat later. "Dr. Odgers—"

"Please call me Kat. Dr. Odgers is way too formal for what we went through together. Facing certain death has a way of making you realize that all that silly formality is just for show."

He acquiesced with a slight tip of his head and began again. "Kat, I would like you to meet CIA agent Jane Fallon."

"A pleasure," Kat said, pushing her glasses again and shaking Jane's hand just as vigorously as she had Holden's. "What's the occasion? Want a tour of the lab? It's mind-blowing what the government has in resources. I would've died and gone to heaven at Tessara if I'd had access to such state-of-the-art equipment."

"Wasn't Tessara well funded?"

"Oh, yes, but I was a lower-level scientist so it's not as if I got the corner office, if you know what I mean."

"I guess that all changed the minute you created the Game Changer," Jane said, and Kat's expression darkened into a scowl.

"Please don't call it that. MCX-209 was an embarrassing failure and only that psychopath, Miles Jogan, and his bimbo, Camille, called it that."

Miles and Camille, formerly of the Defense Intelligence Agency, currently serving time for a host of crimes against the nation—and human beings in general—had been the ringleaders behind the plot to weaponize and consequently sell MCX-209 to the highest bidder. But in the process, they'd made Kat test the drug on human subjects, most of whom had died, with the exception of Kat's husband, Jake.

"Not exactly," Jane corrected, taking Kat aback. "Did you know Penny Winslow was monitoring your progress on that particular drug way before you started administering your drug trials?"

"What are you talking about?"

Holden held up his hand and said, "Is there someplace we can talk in private? This is a sensitive topic and we're not sure who all is listening, if you catch my drift."

"Oh, great. More secret government spy stuff,"

Kat grumbled. She motioned for them to follow her into her office. Once they were safely closed inside, she dropped into a leather-backed chair and said, "All right, now start again. Penny Winslow was watching my experiments?"

"Yes. It appears she also dubbed MCX-209 the Game Changer, possibly before Miles Jogan did. In fact, it might've been Penny who christened the drug in the first place. Did you ever have any contact with her?"

Kat shook her head. "No. All my contact was with my supervisor—"

"Hector Olonzo," Jane supplied. As Kat nodded, Jane added, "He's dead."

Kat's stare widened and she gasped in shock. "What happened? Hector was so sweet. On Tuesdays he always brought me caramel cookies from the snack cart."

"He was killed in a mugging gone wrong, but I'll be honest, I don't think it was an accident," Holden admitted.

"What do you mean?"

Jane held the woman's gaze. "He means we think someone may have killed Hector to keep him quiet. He was a loose end that someone needed to snip."

Kat's hand flew to her throat as she realized what they were saying. "Do you mean…I'm a loose end, too?"

"Potentially," Holden said. "But not yet. You're the only one with knowledge of how MCX-209 works. But, honestly, we don't even know if that's what this is all about. My brother killed himself and left behind a lot of unanswered questions that all seem to circle back to Tessara in one form or another."

"I understand," Kat murmured with a nod. "But MCX-209 has been shut down. The whole reason I agreed to come to work here was so I could be assured that no one else would get their hands on the formula."

"So you would know if anyone was poking around?"

Kat nodded. "Heck yes. I'm the lead scientist here. I answer directly to Director Michelle Rainier, and she answers to the president. I made sure of it. I don't want anyone ever getting their hands on that horrid drug."

"How is Jake holding up?" Holden asked quietly.

At the mention of her husband and the one person still recovering from an injection of the drug, Kat brightened. "Oh, he's doing so well! I'd say almost recovered and still going strong. He has minor gaps in his memory, but it seems to correlate with his interest in whatever he's doing, such as not doing the dishes when I ask him."

Jane and Holden chuckled. "Glad to hear he's on the mend," Holden said. "He's a good man."

Kat grinned, eyes sparkling behind her glasses. "I think so, too."

Jane cleared her throat and brought the topic back into focus. "It seems Penny Winslow was actively involved in a few other projects—Switchblade, Carousel, Serenade. Any of those ring a bell?"

Kat pursed her lips as she searched her memory but ultimately shook her head. "No, I was pretty focused on my own project. I truly thought I was on to something big."

"It was big, all right—just not what you thought it was going to be for," Holden said. "Do you keep samples of MCX-209 here on the premises?"

"Yes, why?"

"Would you mind checking to see that everything is where it should be?" Holden asked. "MCX-209 and Tessara seem to be the only common denominators, and we're grasping at straws."

"Sure. I can't take you into the restricted area, but I can show you the live feed from the security line."

"You have a video camera trained on the samples?" Jane asked incredulously. "That must make for some really boring footage."

"Very. But it's a clean room and only certain people have enough clearance to even access that portion of the building." She logged onto her computer and quickly brought up the live feed. Several tubes of blue liquid were suspended in liquid nitrogen, frozen for safekeeping. "See? All good and accounted for. The feed is also time-stamped for additional security. If there's a single, tiny blip in the time feed, it'll alert security. And so far, it's been quiet."

Jane released a pent-up breath. "That's good to know. That drug—and the fact that it's real—freaks me out."

"Yeah, it's pretty scary in action, too," Kat said with a bleak expression. "Anyway, you don't have to worry about this particular baddie getting out there in the world."

Holden nodded. "I guess we've taken up enough of your time. Listen, watch your back. Until we figure out who's all behind this, don't trust anyone."

Kat smiled nervously. "Boy, and here I thought I was done with dodging people trying to kill me."

Holden crooked a charming grin and said, "For me, that's a typical Thursday."

Jane rolled her eyes and gave him a slight push toward the door. "Okay, Mr. Bond, let's go. We have to find a way to break into this thumb drive."

"Oh, I can do that for you," Kat offered with an unexpected smile, adding shyly, "I'm a bit of a technogeek in my spare time. I could've been a hacker in a different life."

Jane liked this odd scientist woman. For all her admitted geekiness, she had a warmth to her. Holden produced the thumb drive and handed it to Kat. "Good luck. Work your magic. It seems to be encrypted—"

"No offense, but I break encryptions when I can't sleep at night. Well, it's either that or memorize formulas. Depends on my mood," Kat said brightly, accepting the drive and pushing it into the USB port on her computer. "Let's see how ambitious this encryption is."

Jane glanced at Holden and saw his anxious expression. They needed a bit of hope today. Within a few minutes, Kat chortled with a happy squee of excitement like a little kid, her feet dancing on the floor as she motioned with a "Ta-da!" for them both to join her behind the desk. "No problem-o. This was easy-peasy. Whoever encrypted it wasn't really serious about keeping people out. Now, who does this belong to?"

"My brother, Miko. He kept it in a safety deposit box along with some cash," Holden answered, peering over Kat's shoulder. He looked to Kat and said, "Mind if I poke around?"

"Be my guest." She rolled out of the way to give Holden more room. "Do you know what you're looking for?"

"Not a clue." But Holden and Jane saw soon enough what was on that drive, and it took Jane's breath away. Holden doubled-clicked the file marked Insurance Policy, and suddenly everything came into focus. "Am I looking at what I think I'm looking at?"

"It looks like a hit list," Jane answered under her breath, shocked. "I recognize some of these names from restricted files. These are I.D. hits."

"That's a lot of names," Kat observed with a worried expression. "Why would he keep this?"

"He called it his insurance policy for a reason. Someone doesn't want this information going public. I suppose Penny Winslow would've been pretty threatened by the knowledge that this list exists."

Jane nodded, pointing. "Click on the file marked Key."

Holden double-clicked and another set of notes opened on the screen. "You're kidding me." He shook his head. "This isn't good."

Jane looked to Kat. "Are you sure no one's been working on MCX-209 without your permission?"

"I'm positive," Kat answered. "Why?"

"Because according to Miko's notes, someone authorized another trial of the drug."

"That's impossible." Kat shook her head. "I supervise all experiments in this lab. Nothing gets by without my knowledge."

Holden frowned. "Someone's planning something with that drug. Maybe Miko was on to whoever had put plans into motion."

"If so, why didn't he just tell you?" Jane asked, sagging at the enormity of the situation. "Maybe we could've helped."

"I ask myself that question a hundred times a day and I still don't have a suitable answer," Holden said, scrolling through the notes, searching for clues. "Every single day."

Kat, visibly shaken by the realization that her drug was still sought after by the wrong people, said, "Listen, I hate to cut this short, but I have to talk to my boss about this. If someone is circumventing our security, we have to find out how and why."

"Can you trust your boss?"

Kat nodded emphatically. "Yes. She's the one who helped take down Miles and Camille, and she shut down The Compound. She's going to want to know about this newest development."

"If you feel confident without a shadow of a doubt that you can trust her..." Jane let it trail. If it were her, she wouldn't trust anyone outside of this room, especially given the history of that drug. It was the scientist's call, though.

"I do," Kat said, looking devastated. "I can't believe this is happening again. I wish I'd never created that stupid drug."

"Well, think of it this way—you never would've met Jake if you hadn't," Holden said, trying to cheer her up even though the situation was pretty dire for everyone involved.

Jane suppressed the immediate flood of warmth at his show of kindness toward the scientist. He was such a good guy. Why couldn't she just forget about her family and let her heart decide?

"Hey, have you ever heard of a winery called Butterfly Bend?" Holden asked Kat, switching gears quickly.

"Um…yeah, I think that's the winery owned by Penny Winslow's cousin. He came by Tessara a few times. They were real close, I guess. Why?"

"I don't know. Miko mentioned Butterfly Bend in his notes and we visited the winery and talked with the owner. He seems like a nice guy. He said Tessara was working on creating a cork that didn't disintegrate with time and protected the integrity of the wine. Sound familiar?"

"Not really. Then again, I was hyperfocused on my own trials. I don't doubt that Tessara was doing exactly that for him as a favor to Penny. Like I said, he and Penny seemed really close. Almost like brother and sister."

Jane pocketed that information. From the expression on Holden's face, he seemed to find that nugget interesting, too, even if they didn't know how the pieces fit together. He pulled the thumb drive free from the USB port and tucked it back in his pocket. "Thanks for all your help, Kat," he said, moving away from the computer and heading for the door. "Remember what I said—don't trust anyone if you can help it. Keep your circle of trust tight, and just to be on the safe side, go ahead and clue Jake in on this newest development. Wouldn't hurt to have him keeping an eye on things."

"He's going to freak out when I tell him." Kat grimaced. "But I'm a terrible liar, so he'll find out sooner or later anyway."

Holden smiled and thanked Kat once more, then they were escorted from the building.

"Is it just me or does this plot get more and more convoluted by the second?" Jane asked, glancing at Holden wearily. "I can't make heads or tails of which direction we're supposed to be traveling anymore. Tessara, MCX-209, fake IDs, hit lists…where does it end?"

"It ends with us finding out what really happened to my brother and who tried to shoot you," Holden answered grimly, pulling everything back into focus. "All the pieces are there. We just need to put the puzzle together."

"If you say so." Jane felt a headache coming on. "I think I need a beer."

"Now you're talking my language." He grinned, and her heart did a funny flip-flop that was entirely too telling for her liking, but what could she do? It seemed useless to fight what was happening between them. She knew without a doubt she could put on a show of keeping him at a distance, though by the end of the night, there was nowhere she'd rather be than snuggled up tight against his side. What a lovely mess they'd created.

"Fine, but I'm buying," she said almost grumpily, and he laughed.

"Far be it from me to turn down such a charming offer. Now tell me you're going to throw me down and have your wicked way with me, too, and I'll be a happy man," he said with a wink. She groaned. *Lord help us both.*

She climbed into the car and barked, "Get in the car before I make you walk."

"I love a take-charge woman," he laughed, climbing in beside her. "Especially when you do that thing with your—"

"If you value your life, stop," she warned, fighting the blush in her cheeks. His laughter tickled her insides, but she refused to give in. She may know the score between them, but damn it, she didn't have to be happy about it.

Chapter 20

Kat Odgers hurried to her boss's office, her soft lab shoes making light squeaking noises as she went. She found Michelle on the phone, but immediately went in anyway, shut the door behind her and waited somewhat patiently for her boss to finish her conversation.

Michelle, noting Kat's agitation, ended the call and looked to Kat with a raised brow. "Everything okay?"

"No. Everything is not okay. In fact, everything is pretty messed up and I don't know what to think."

"Okay, calm down. Start at the beginning. What's wrong?"

"Someone is poking around MCX-209 and restarting the trials." At that, Michelle paused and leaned back in her chair. Kat immediately felt panicked. "What a minute...you already knew this? How is that possible? You promised me that I would be in charge of MCX-209."

"Have a seat, Kat," Michelle suggested, but Kat didn't want to sit. She wanted answers. Her hands began to shake. When Kat continued to stand, Michelle said, "You are in charge of the initial formula, but there have been some preliminary trials of the modified version of MCX-209 that you formulated to save Jake."

"What?" Kat nearly screeched, her heart thundering in her chest. "What are you saying? Someone is testing that formula without my involvement? You promised me that wouldn't happen!"

"And I firmly stood behind that promise, but some things are above my pay grade."

Kat blinked. "How is that possible? You answer to the president."

"Yes, I do, and it's my job to ensure that we are in control of one of the most dangerous drugs on the planet, and we can't be in control if we don't understand how it works."

"It works by erasing memory," Kat said, wiping at the tears gathering in her eyes. "My husband suffered the most unimaginable horror of losing who he was. You know that! And what about the people who died when Miles forced me to inject them with the first test formula? Their brains leaked from their ears! I'll never forget their faces and how they trusted me not to hurt them."

"That wasn't your fault," Michelle reminded her, but Kat didn't want her platitudes. "Kat, I need you to calm down and listen to me. I should've told you, but I didn't want to upset you, which, judging by your reaction, was a wise decision."

"It wasn't wise. It was deceptive," Kat said hotly. "This drug should've been destroyed completely. It has no acceptable application, and the fact you lied to me means you're no better than Miles Jogan, tricking me into working for the very people who were responsible for this horror in my life."

"You're overreacting," Michelle said, losing patience, but Kat didn't care. She felt betrayed and, worse, terrified that the nightmare was about to start all over again. "The clinical trials are limited and supervised. You have nothing to fear."

"You're wrong," Kat said flatly, wiping at her tears. "This is going to end badly. That drug is evil and it brings terrible things wherever it goes."

"Kat…please. You're a scientist. Let's be sensible. Now that you're aware of the situation, we'd like to include you in the trials. It goes without saying your expertise in this is invaluable."

"I need to think," Kat said, moving to the door. "I thought I could trust you—"

"You can," Michelle insisted with a subtle frown, as if distressed by the realization that Kat felt betrayed. "Listen, I understand your concerns. I'd be lying if I said I didn't share them, but this was taken out of my hands."

"What do you mean?" she asked. "No one is higher than the president."

"I can't elaborate more than I have. Trust me when I say MCX-209 will not fall into the wrong hands."

"Sorry, but obviously, it already has." Kat held up her hand, halting Michelle; she'd heard enough. "I…I have to talk to Jake. This is…horrible, horrible news."

Before Michelle could say anything else, Kat bolted. She needed air. She needed clarity. Most of all, she needed Jake. Jake would know what to do.

Michelle watched Kat leave her office and exhaled a troubled sigh. Truthfully, the drug and its potential ramifications scared the hell out of her—and well it should—but as she'd told Kat, the directive came to her from very high channels. She tapped her fingers lightly on her desk, worried by Kat's reaction. What had she expected? Kat had suffered grievously at the hands of the drug and she certainly wouldn't welcome the idea that someone was tinkering with the formula. As much as she didn't want to, Michelle had to make a phone call.

She dialed the number, heart in her throat. "Dr. Odgers has found out the formula is back in active research," she said, swallowing the lump in her throat. "And she's very unhappy."

"That's unfortunate. Can you persuade her to get on board?"

"Not likely. She has every reason to hate MCX-209 and its potential ramifications."

"You like her."

Michelle didn't bother lying. "I do. She's a brilliant scientist and a good person."

"The world has plenty of brilliant scientists. If you value this one in particular, find a way to persuade her to get on board. Otherwise, she's a liability." A beat followed before the person on the other end said, "And how exactly did Dr. Odgers find out about this newest development?"

"Two CIA agents are investigating Miko Archangelo's death. Somehow they connected the dots."

"Yes, I'm well aware of those two. They've been poking around Tessara. Up until now I didn't think they had anything of interest. Seems I was wrong."

"I did as you asked," Michelle said, curling her fingers around the phone. "I held up my end of the bargain."

"Yes, we are pleased with your cooperation. We will be in touch."

"My sister..."

"She's fine for now, but I suspect her health may decline if you aren't able to persuade Dr. Odgers to be more helpful."

Sweat gathered along Michelle's hairline. "How am I supposed to do that?"

"That's your problem. You're a smart woman. You'll figure something out."

The line went dead, and Michelle replaced the phone with cold, shaking fingers. She was living in a nightmare. How had this happened? Tessara was the epicenter for all evil. She swallowed and willed herself to stop shaking, to think. Her gaze swept her office, knowing that somewhere a bug was nestled, catching her every word, her every movement. Contact had been made four months ago, soon after she'd busted Miles Jogan and Camille Stephens, shutting down their horror show featuring MCX-209. If only Michelle had known that she'd merely poked the dragon. Miles and Camille hadn't been the ringleaders. No, whoever was really pulling the strings was far more powerful than she'd imagined. And worse, she had no clue who was in charge.

And they had her younger sister as leverage. Michelle, as tough as they came, former marine, was held hostage by fear, weakened by her love for her sister.

Hang tight, Hilary. Just stay alive.

A plan—reckless and razor's-edge dangerous—took root.

Kat couldn't stop pacing. It was something she did out of nervous habit because it helped her think, but tonight her brain was just too filled with chaotic ramblings and frightened gibberish to be calmed by any amount of pacing. "They're going to do something terrible with that drug—I can feel it," she told Jake, nearly hysterical. "And you should've seen Michelle…cold as ice. I've never seen her so distant and mean. I thought we were friends! But she's using me, just like Miles and Camille did. But this is far worse than what they did because I didn't like them. I liked Michelle. I believed in her. I believed in what I was doing for the greater good. What a sap

I still am, still trying to see the good in people when I know for a fact—having seen the worst—that people can be totally evil."

"Calm down," Jake said gently. "Let's think this through."

"Calm down? Haven't you heard a thing I've said? MCX-209 is back in active research. That means somewhere in that government facility, someone is putting their hands all over my research in the hopes of finding the magic concoction for that wretched drug."

"Did she say how long the research has been going on?"

Kat shook her head. "No. I didn't ask. But what does this mean? She promised me no one would go near that drug or the research without my permission or authorization, and that was a flat-out lie. She lied to you, too!"

"Something doesn't feel right," Jake said, furrowing his brow in thought, remaining chill even as Kat was freaking out. Of course, that was one of the many reasons she loved him, but, c'mon, certainly she shouldn't be the only one jumping up and down in a total meltdown, right? Jake met her gaze and she stopped pacing for a moment. "Michelle isn't the kind of woman who goes back on her word. I've known her for many years. Something else is going on behind the scenes."

"Like what?"

"I don't know," he admitted. "But I'll bet it has

something to do with Holden and Jane poking around."

Kat nodded. "That's feasible, though I couldn't for the life of me tell you how. I mean, they were asking a lot of questions at Tessara, and they found out my old supervisor, Hector, is dead. One thing I've learned since hanging out with you and your friends—there's no such thing as a coincidence, right?"

"Exactly," Jake agreed, adding, "which is why I asked Holden and Jane to come over tonight."

Kat blinked. "You did?"

"Yes. I have some questions of my own to ask them, and now that the situation seems to be becoming more and more unstable, it's better to control the environment we're in. We have to assume your lab has been compromised, possibly bugged." Kat gasped and he continued with a nod, "Yeah, more than likely. It's what I would've done if the situation were reversed and I needed information. At least here in our home, we know we can speak freely."

"Why's that?"

He crooked a short grin that made her remember why she'd fallen for him in the first place. "Because I have antibug devices planted all over our home. Instant interference. Haven't you ever wondered why our cells don't work in the house?"

"D'oh!" she gasped softly as the knowledge sank in. "I just figured we were in a bad reception spot." She giggled briefly before sobering. "Okay, so what do you hope to find out from Holden and Jane?"

"Not sure, but if we put our heads together we

might be able to pinpoint where the threat is originating."

Her eyes suddenly watered and her lower lip trembled. "I don't want to go on the run again," she said as she climbed into his lap. His arms curled around her and she took momentary comfort in the solid feel of his touch. "The last time this happened, I almost lost you. I don't want to face that again. I would never step foot in another lab again if it meant you and I could live a normal life."

He chuckled and pressed a kiss to her forehead. "What is normal? It's been so long I don't remember."

"Not funny," she grumbled, pinching him for making jokes about something so serious. "I mean it. I can't go through this again. It was awful the first time around. I certainly don't want a repeat performance."

"Neither do I. I've only just started remembering how to tie my own shoes."

She laughed through the sheen of tears, loving him all the more that he could still joke, but it stung that she'd been the cause of his suffering. "I love you, Jake Isaacs," Kat said, wiping her nose with the back of her hand. "Don't you dare get yourself killed or I'll never forgive you."

"I love you more, Kat Isaacs. And I am too attached to living to get myself killed. I promise."

A shudder traveled through her. "Don't make promises you can't keep."

"I don't."

His solemn answer, devoid of laughter this time, reached into her heart and squeezed hard. She knew he'd do anything to protect her—even throw himself in the line of danger if it meant saving her life.

And that was what scared her the most.

Chapter 21

Holden and Jane, both surprised to get the call from Jake, hustled over to his house and were ushered in immediately. Holden shook Jake's hand and smiled. "You look better than the last time I saw you. At least now you're not drooling," he teased.

"I wasn't drooling," Jake shot back with mock irritation but broke it with a grin. "You look good, too. How are you doing?"

"Could be better, for sure. Things aren't exactly copacetic, if you know what I mean."

"I do," Jake agreed with a serious nod.

Holden quickly introduced Jane, and then all three walked into the living room, where a nervous Kat waited, biting her nails and fidgeting. "Good to see you again, Kat."

She smiled slightly but remained quiet. Jake handled the talking once they were all seated. "All right, unfortunately I didn't invite you over for board games and pizza. We've got a serious situation brewing. I've been down this road before and it's not pretty."

"So I've heard," Jane said. "You're pretty lucky to be alive, from what Holden has said."

"I'm lucky my wife is brilliant. If it weren't for her, I would be dead. She's the one who perfected the formula. Otherwise, my life would've ended with my brains leaking from my ears."

"It's not perfected," Kat protested, breaking her nervous silence to bounce from her chair and start pacing. "That's just it. It's just as dangerous as it ever was. I should've flushed everything down the toilet when I had the chance, but I was seduced by the idea of running my own state-of-the-art lab. This is my penance for having too big of an ego. This is karma."

"Kat, stop," Jake said gently, pulling her to him and soothing her frantic movements with a soft touch. "This isn't your fault. You have a gift for science. Okay? Stop berating yourself for something out of your control. We're going to get this figured out."

"What's going on? Something tells me we're missing a piece of the puzzle," Holden said.

"A big piece," Kat answered grimly, glancing at Jake for strength. "After you left, I went to my boss, Michelle, to confront her about the security break. She already knew! In fact, she'd authorized the active research, saying higher channels had given the clearance to bypass my involvement. She said it was out of her hands, but the PTB would like me back on board."

"Higher channels? Higher than the president?" Jane asked, confused.

"I don't know," Kat answered, just as confused. "I've never known Michelle to act like this. She was just as adamant as I was that MCX-209 end up locked away forever, but now she's changed her tune. It gave me a terrible stomachache and I immediately had diarrhea. Sorry for the TMI. When I get nervous I overshare."

Jake smiled indulgently at his wife and Holden felt a pang of envy for how in tune Kat and Jake were with one another. He stole a glance at Jane, and when he saw her wistful expression, he knew a moment of happiness, which was absurd, but it was there just the same.

Jane broke the silence first. "Is there any chance Michelle is working with someone at Tessara? My first guess is Ulysses Rocha. He gives me a corrupt vibe."

Kat wrung her hands. "Before today I would've said absolutely not, but I don't know what to think now."

"First and foremost, we need to figure out what the connection is between Tessara and whoever wants the research reactivated on MCX-209. What would anyone have to gain by restarting the study?"

"At first blush, I'd say world domination," Kat answered. "I mean, this drug is dangerous for many reasons. And if someone in high places is pushing the research, that must mean they already have something in mind for its use."

"Which certainly can't be good," Jake interjected, and Holden nodded.

A knock at the door startled them all. Everyone except Kat pulled a weapon. Kat laughed nervously. "Wouldn't we all feel dumb if it was just a pizza guy? Delivering a pizza we haven't ordered?" she tacked on with an audible gulp. Jane and Holden flanked the doorway while Jake prepared to open the door. He peered through the peephole and then pulled away with a quizzical expression. "It's Michelle," he mouthed before slowly opening the door. "Michelle? It's pretty late…what are you doing here?"

"I know how this looks, but it's not safe for me to talk outside. Will you invite me in? And act natural. I have eyes on me."

Jake nodded and ushered her inside, but everyone held their weapons at the ready.

"What are you doing here?" Kat asked. "What's going on?"

Michelle, dressed in a trench coat, shivered, her gaze sharp. "You were right. Something is going on. I couldn't say anything at the office. In fact, I haven't been able to say anything for months, and honestly, I was trying to keep you out of it for as long as possible, but time has run out. Someone blackmailed me into granting authorization for the active research. They have my sister, Hilary, and they've threatened her life if I didn't cover their tracks while they worked on your preliminary formula for the Game Changer."

"I wish people would stop calling it that," Kat groused. "Who is threatening you?"

"I haven't been able to figure that out. I only have a number that I've been unable to trace. They have my office and house bugged and I've been unable to make a move without them knowing about it. Frankly, I don't even know if it was safe to come here, except I'm supposed to be talking you into joining the research team. Otherwise, Hilary would be dead right now. For all I know, she already is dead."

"They haven't given you proof of life?" Jake asked.

Michelle shook her head. "Not in weeks. I fear the worst."

"You should've told someone," Holden said.

"I know, but I was afraid. She's the only family I have left. She's my kid sister and barely out of college. I never imagined something like this would ever happen. I never saw myself in a position where I couldn't protect myself or the ones I love. They struck where it hurt, and they knew exactly what to do to get me to cooperate."

"Sounds like a move Penny would make. If I didn't already know the bitch was dead, I'd say this was her doing," Holden said

"So who's at the heart of all this, then?" Jane asked the question they were all wondering. "Someone higher up in the food chain, for sure."

"How high are we talking?" Holden asked. "This goes pretty far if they're able to get to Michelle's level of clearance."

"My thoughts exactly," Jake said. "What do we know so far?"

"Well, it seems Miko was trying to gather enough evidence to bring down someone big, but he was so paranoid he left only cryptic clues. We have a list of ID hits, some connection to Butterfly Bend winery, Tessara Pharm and a really rampant information leak at high levels." Holden rubbed his jaw. "Now we also have someone wanting research to resume on MCX-209 and using Michelle to get it done. All in all, we've got a whole lot of loose ends and no way to tie them together."

"Not necessarily," Jane disagreed slowly, and Holden could see her mind working. "We know Penny Winslow was tight with her cousin, the owner of Butterfly Bend, and that Butterfly Bend was chosen for the Presidential Reserve wine, and the wine is being shipped at the end of this month for an executive dinner. We also know Tessara helped create the chemical coating for the cork used by Butterfly Bend. What if—and this is a wild theory—someone is planning to use those wine corks to spike the Presidential Reserve with MCX-209? Butterfly Bend has already been vetted, so it would easily pass the sniff test, putting the most dangerous drug on the planet right at the president's table."

"Holy crap," Holden breathed, his gaze widening at the very idea. "That's brilliant."

"But why?" Kat asked.

"Because the best way to take out an enemy is a surprise attack," Jake answered, his mouth tightening to a firm line. "If this is true, we're all targets, because a plan of this magnitude would've taken lots of careful planning and zero tolerance for loose ends. And every single one of us in this room is a loose end."

"Not again," Kat wailed, flopping into a chair and gripping her stomach with a groan. "There goes my stomach. Oh! Excuse me…" She ran for the restroom, leaving the rest of the group wrestling with their own nerves.

"We're in deep trouble," Jane murmured, glancing at Holden. "No wonder no one wanted this investigation reopened. We're talking the highest level of treason if you're right."

"I know." Holden knew in his bones they'd stumbled on the right theory, the one that'd cost Miko his life. But how to prove it without losing their own heads? Where to start? How to begin? "Time to put our heads together. We need answers and we need them by first light or else we all better polish up our passports because life in the States will no longer be possible. They'll find us, and when they do, it'll be lights out."

"I'll start the coffee," Jake said. "It's going to be a long night."

Several hours into brainstorming leads, Jane stumbled across something they'd missed. "Do you remember when we went to Tessara, we were greeted by that ultraperfect Stepford wife of a secretary, Selena?" When Holden nodded and everyone else was paying attention, she continued, holding up the personnel files they'd taken from Tessara. "It seems Selena has a master's degree in biochemical science. Doesn't that seem a little bit of an overqualification for a secretary?"

Holden nodded slowly as Jane handed over the personnel file attached to Penny's. "Seems Penny personally recruited her from Stanford University two years ago. Why?"

"Good question," Jake said. "But if Penny had a hand in anything, it was usually for her own benefit. That woman was a sociopath. I don't trust anyone she would personally handpick as someone trustworthy."

"She gave me an odd vibe." Jane recalled the ultrachic woman with impeccable manners. "No one is that nice or perfectly put together."

"The question is, why is a highly trained scientist slumming it as a lowly gopher for a pharmaceutical company when she could've been in the lab?" Michelle mused. "Doesn't add up."

"Here's a thought…." Jane said. "Maybe it was a ruse to cover her tracks. No one is going to pay attention to a secretary. She's a ghost, moving in and out of people's offices without arousing suspicion. Honestly, it's the best cover, because everyone always overlooks the secretary."

Holden nodded. "And if Penny handpicked Selena, she had to have a reason. Let's dig into Selena's background and see what pops up." He grabbed Jake's computer and did a preliminary search but came up with nothing except benign Google entries. "Top of her class in Stanford, a member of Mensa and on the chess club."

Jake frowned. "What about family connections? Is there a possibility that Selena is related to Penny?"

"It doesn't say in her file," Jane answered, shaking her head. "But then it probably wouldn't if that was something they were trying to conceal. According to her file, Selena is twenty-six. I guess it's feasible for Selena to be Penny's daughter, but I would imagine something like that would eventually be known, right?"

"Penny used to serve in the military," Holden said. "That's how she met Tom and Ulysses. They served in the same unit. Do you think Penny had a kid overseas and left her behind when she returned stateside?"

"I shudder to think of that woman as a mother," Jake said grimly, then shook his head. "I don't know. Even if that theory is correct and Selena is related to Penny somehow and she's continuing her work...to what end?"

Jane shoved her hand through her hair, exasperated and exhausted. "I don't know," she admitted with a long exhale, and fell back against the sofa cushion. "Everything is starting to swim in my head. Maybe we're completely off base and spinning our wheels." She looked at Jake with sympathy. "How's Kat? She doing okay?"

"Yeah, she's just not accustomed to all this intrigue and danger. Does terrible things to her nerves. Can't blame her. This crap is getting old, even for me."

Holden nodded with a yawn. "You and me both, brother."

Michelle rubbed red-rimmed eyes and said, "I'm going to call it a night. I can't keep my eyes open any longer."

"Are you sure? Maybe you ought to stay here," Jake said, his voice hoarse from too much coffee and not enough sleep. "It's not safe at your place."

"Probably not, but I can't run out of fear. They've been controlling my life for too long and I'm done. Chances are my sister is already dead. You and I both know how this works. If they're going to try to take me out, they can do it on my turf, at the very least."

Jake nodded, though he didn't look happy about it. They all had military backgrounds and understood her need to stand her ground. "Keep your gun loaded and under your pillow."

"And sleep with one eye open," Holden tacked on. "With any luck we'll come out alive when this is all said and done."

"From your mouth to God's ear," Michelle said with a small smile before letting herself out.

"Kat's going to be upset that you let her go home," Holden said.

"Michelle has to do what she feels is right. I can only imagine the guilt and fear she's been living with," Jake said quietly. "You guys going to stay here tonight?"

"No, my place is pretty secure. Jane is staying with me." Jane, too tired to put up a fuss, merely nodded in agreement. That was Holden's cue to pack it in.

"We better call it a night, too. We'll contact you to-morrow if we find out anything more. What's Kat going to do?"

"I don't know. Call in sick, I imagine."

"Good idea. But watch your doors and windows. Bullets have been flying lately, if you know what I mean."

"I do." Jake accepted Holden's advice. "Keep your head down."

"Copy that." Holden collected Jane and they walked to the car, eyes trained in the darkness, ears on alert. Danger didn't always announce itself with a bang. Sometimes it sailed through on the wind.

Chapter 22

The following morning, Holden and Jane were gulping down fresh coffee after very little sleep and browsing the web when something on a news site snagged their attention. A woman's body had been found floating in the reflecting pool at the Lincoln Memorial.

Holden double-clicked the news report, and he swore under his breath. "The bastards killed her." Jane quickly scanned the short article.

"Michelle's sister?" Jane supposed, and Holden nodded. "The age seems right. If that's Michelle's sister, that means they're snipping loose threads right now. They must have what they've been after."

Seconds later, Holden's cell rang. It was Jake. "You see the news?" he asked.

"Yeah, just now. Was that Michelle's sister?"

"Yeah. She's devastated."

"Understandable. You know what this means…"

"Whatever plan they were setting in motion has begun," Jake answered. "And we still have nothing concrete to go on. We have no idea who's pulling the strings and no idea where to start."

"Not entirely true. We know something's up with Selena. I say we bring her in."

"We need more evidence," Jake disagreed. "If we pull the trigger prematurely, it'll end up blowing up in our faces."

"What, then?"

"Let's see what we can dig up on Selena first. Try to make those connections before we pull the alarm. You have anyone you can trust with this information?"

Holden thought of Chief Harris and nodded. "Yeah."

"Good. We're going to need all the backup we can muster. In the meantime, I'll start cultivating my own posse."

"Sounds good." They clicked off. Jane waited for Holden to share, which he did. "We're going to need James Cotton again."

She raised a brow. "To dig up dirt on Little Miss Perfect?"

"Yep."

"Sounds like a plan. What about Ulysses or Trevor?" she asked. "Maybe we ought to dig into their pasts, too."

"Couldn't hurt," Holden agreed, then, acting on impulse, he grabbed Jane and pulled her into a hard kiss. When they broke apart, they were both gasping for breath with pupils dilated.

"What was that for?"

"Because we're heading into some serious shit. I know at any moment either one of us could bite the big one, and I didn't want to take the risk of going into the hereafter without one last kiss from the most beautiful woman in the world."

Jane stared, her eyes welling with tears. "You're killing me," she said softly, her body melting against his. "And don't talk about dying. You're not going to die. And neither am I."

"Tomorrow is promised to no one," he reminded her gently without a hint of his usual smart-ass wise-cracking. He wanted to show her the raw side of what he was feeling, the stuff he couldn't quite put into words without fumbling like an idiot. "Jane, I know you have a lot of reasons why you and I don't work, but I can give you one reason why we do."

"Yeah?" The lilt of wary hope in her voice gave him courage. "What's that one reason?"

"This." He brushed his lips across hers in the sweetest, most tender kiss he'd ever given to another human being. In that single motion, he tried communicating that somehow she'd captured his heart in a way he didn't understand nor could truly verbalize, but he knew was true just as he knew the sun would rise every day. He was pretty damn sure he'd fallen in love with Jane Fallon and he wanted her to know, even if he couldn't say the words just yet.

She blinked back tears, and when she closed her eyes, moisture slid from the corners. "Why are you doing this?" she asked plaintively. "This isn't doing either of us any favors."

Disappointment crashed around him when she didn't seem to appreciate his grand gesture. He released her and tried not to let the bitterness of his letdown seep into his voice. "I just wanted to seize the moment," he said with a twist of his lips. "You know, in case."

She nodded but turned away from him, saying, "Well, let's focus on catching this SOB so we don't have to end up running for our lives, okay?"

Good plan. Following Jane's lead, he shoved his heartbreak under the proverbial rug and got on the horn with James Cotton.

Jane fought with her fluttering heart, hating that she was on the verge of a total meltdown after Holden's kiss. It'd felt like a goodbye kiss. As if he knew something she didn't, and she hated the very idea of Holden not being there across the conference table, giving her a hard time or trying to best her in the gym. She especially hated the idea of not being able to wake up each morning in his arms, but that was a separate problem she'd have to deal with later. Right now, they both needed their heads on straight if they were going to survive, which meant *stop freaking crying!* She surreptitiously wiped at her eyes and cleared her throat, determined to suck it up. They had very little time left on their clock, and no doubt the sniper was already loading his gun with bullets inscribed with their names. While Holden gave James instructions, she logged onto the computer and started looking for connections they might've missed last night. She cross-referenced Butterfly Bend winery to anyone else associated with Tessara aside from Penny Winslow, and when that came up empty, she started looking for ties to Selena and the cofounders of Tessara. The answer was there—she could feel it. And because it was so tantalizingly close, yet still just out of reach, she wanted to scream.

Within a few hours, James returned Holden's call. Holden put him on speaker so Jane could hear, too.

"You are not going to believe this, but…"

"Selena is Penny's daughter?" Holden answered. Jane half expected James to confirm, but when he didn't, her eyes widened in shock.

"Nope. I don't think pure evil can gestate," James quipped. "No, but she definitely has ties to Penny. Penny was her aunt."

"Aunt?" Holden repeated in surprise, mirroring Jane's expression. "How so?"

"Selena's the daughter of Trevor Granger. Trevor and Penny were half brother and sister, not cousins as they told everyone."

"You've got to be kidding me," Jane gasped. "How'd we miss that?"

"They weren't raised together and didn't let people

know they were actually siblings, preferring to tell everyone they were cousins."

"But why?"

"They were pretty close. Perhaps too close?" James guessed, grossing out both Holden and Jane.

"Are you saying…oh, God, that's disgusting," Holden said, grimacing. "So Selena is Trevor's daughter. Funny how he failed to mention his daughter worked at Tessara."

"Seems a little suspect on his part," Jane agreed. "But that alone is not a crime. We need more to go on."

"Well, today is your lucky day," James said with a cocky grin in his voice. "I have something you might find of use."

"Such as?" Holden asked.

"Selena's godmother is someone pretty important."

"Spit it out, Cotton," Holden said, losing patience. "We're in a bit of a time crunch."

"You take the fun out of everything. All right, all right, her godmother is none other than…the veep."

"The what?"

"You know, the veep…as in the vice president of the United States. Talk about connections."

Jane met Holden's astonished gaze, which she was sure matched her own. "Are you sure?" Jane asked before Holden could. "How did you find that out?"

"The internet is a wondrous place. It was fairly easy. Once I tracked down how Selena, Penny and Trevor connected, I just did background checks, verified birth records and whatnot and found the VP's name on the christening details kept at the church in the town where Selena was born. That's where I struck gold."

"You're a freaking genius." Holden grinned, but there was an edge of fear in his gaze and Jane knew where he was going with that. "So our connection to the higher power pulling the strings is the woman closest to the president."

"The one who stands to gain everything if something were to happen to the president," Jane finished. Holden nodded grimly. "Holy hell. We have to tell the chief."

"This is what Miko was trying to piece together," Holden said. "Thanks, James. You may have just saved the life of the president of the United States."

Holden and Jane barreled into Reed Harris's office but skidded to a stop when they saw who was having a conference with the chief.

"What's he doing here?" Jane asked in a low tone.

"Good question," Holden muttered. "The last time he was here, it was to poke around in our investigation. I doubt he's here to bring us a muffin basket."

"More's the pity. I'm starved," she quipped. "Let's welcome him to D.C., shall we?"

They walked into the chief's office and pinned Ulysses Rocha with twin looks of solid unwelcome. He had the grace to flush. "Morning, Chief," Holden said. "Mr. Rocha, Tessara must have some incredible frequent-flyer miles. To what do we owe this pleasure today?"

"I apologize for the way I handled myself the first time I came here. Unfortunately, I was operating under a different assumption, but I have information you might find of use to your investigation."

"Oh? Please share," Jane said with a smile that didn't reach her eyes.

"It's come to my attention that Selena may have misrepresented herself and misused company resources. I found this in an encrypted file." He handed a manila envelope to Holden. "Selena has been using Tessara to continue where Penny left off on many of her less-than-FDA-approved experiments. Mainly, Game Changer and Switchblade. As soon as I found out, I put a stop to it. We've only just recently begun to recover from the bad press Penny created, and I wasn't about to go another round with Selena."

"Where is she now?" Jane asked.

"I don't know," he admitted. "That's why I'm here. I'm sure with your resources you'll be able to find her a lot easier than I will. Of course, it goes without saying that when she finally surfaces, she's fired."

"She's more than fired...she's facing criminal and federal charges," Holden said. "Do you have any idea what she was planning?"

"Only that she was going to do something that would change the course of history. Naturally, I was concerned."

"Too bad you couldn't have been this concerned when we were first talking," Jane said with a wry twist of her lips. "A young woman might still be alive. Selena may have blood on her hands."

"Well, that's for you to work out. I've done my part," Ulysses said with a distasteful shudder. "I trust you can take it from here. I have a flight to catch."

Jane turned to the chief. "Are we just going to let him walk? Surely we've got him on obstruction, at the very least."

"We've got bigger problems. Let him go," Chief Harris said, waving them off and gesturing for the file. They closed the door behind Rocha as Reed said, "Let me take a look at what we've got here."

"Chief, we've got bigger problems indeed," Jane said. "We believe the vice president of the United States is plotting to use MCX-209 on the president and the executive branch at a special dinner slated for the end of this month."

"That's a very serious accusation," Chief Harris said, steepling his fingers. "You'd better know what you're talking about before you start saying that in mixed company."

"Selena's godmother is the VP. We think this plan has been in motion since way before Penny was killed and Selena just kept the plan in motion. We were sure there was something bigger at the top of the food chain pulling strings, and what bigger puppet master could there be than the VP?"

"And how would this be accomplished?" he asked.

"Through Selena's father's winery, Butterfly Bend. Tessara created a special coating for the cork that will be used to bottle the Presidential Reserve. My guess is they're planning to coat the cork with the MCX-209 so the wine is contaminated with the drug."

"Holy hell…" The chief looked green, but he snapped into action quickly. "If that's the case, we're in a heap of trouble, because that dinner is tonight."

"Are you sure?" Holden asked, frowning. "Trevor Granger told us it was at the end of the month."

"That was a security measure. The true date of the dinner is known only to a select few. We've got to get to that dinner and make sure no one drinks the wine."

Chapter 23

Teams flanked all exits of the executive dining room as the sounds of the dinner plating from the kitchen staff filled the air, along with the low hum of chatter. Michelle, Holden, Jane, Jake and Reed all headed up individual teams, covering all bases, while Kat waited for the all-clear. When the scene had been secured, the plan was for Kat to come in and verify if, in fact, MCX-209 was in play. Badges were flashed at the Secret Service, and they filed into the room to the surprised gasps of the dinner-party guests.

"Mr. President," Michelle said. "I apologize for the unorthodox appearance and for ruining your dinner, but we feel a threat to national security is in this room." She marched straight to the wine bottle directly in front of the president's plate.

The vice president, Gloria Burroughs, stood with an indignant expression, glowering at the intrusion. "What is the meaning of this? Explain yourself immediately," she demanded, looking to the Secret Service. "Remove these people. This is a private dinner and they are clearly misguided. There is no threat in this room. For heaven's sake, everyone in this room has been vetted."

The Secret Service shuffled, unsure of what to do. Michelle trained her gun on the vice president and the woman gasped, wilting against her chair. "Have you lost your mind? What are you doing?"

The president, a man with a shock of white hair and deep lines etched into his forehead, stared at Gloria with disappointment. He nodded to Michelle, who then brought Kat forward as Jake popped the cork on the wine, ran a swab over the bottom, then poured a droplet of a chemical solution on the swab. It turned green.

Kat announced, "This wine is contaminated with the experimental drug MCX-209. I would advise everyone to step away from the table so we can collect every bottle."

Gasps from around the room ensued, and Gloria paled as she stammered, "What is going on?"

"Don't bother to pretend innocence," Michelle said, as she put the VP in cuffs. "We've already informed the president of your connection to Butterfly Bend and your goddaughter, Selena. Gloria Burroughs, you are charged with treason against your country."

The president stood with a stern expression. "This breaks my heart, Gloria. I trusted you. How could you betray my trust like this? And what did you hope to gain?"

"Surely you can see I've been framed," Gloria said, clearly trying to appeal to the president's sense of fair play. "The evidence against me is purely circumstantial. I have many enemies—as do you. It wouldn't be a far stretch to frame me for this."

Michelle ignored the VP's protests and clicked the cuffs on the woman's wrists. "Where is Selena?" she asked, cinching the cuffs as tightly as they would go. Gloria winced, her eyes watered and her chin trembled. Hard to believe this was the mastermind. Right now she just looked like a scared old woman.

"Where is Selena?" she repeated.

Gloria, realizing the game was over, hung her head and whispered an address. Michelle handed the sobbing woman over to the Secret Service, and they hauled her away.

Michelle approached the president. "Thank you for taking a chance on our theory. We were pretty sure we had the answer, but there's always that one percent that can ruin everything."

"I'm so sorry to hear about your sister," he said, his voice kind. "Is there anything I can do for you? I'm in your debt. Your service and sacrifice to your country won't be forgotten."

Michelle blinked back tears. She hadn't had time yet to grieve—that would come later. She accepted the president's gratitude with stiff grace. "Thank you, sir. I haven't yet dealt with the pain of losing her, but I know it's there, waiting. I still can't believe she's gone."

"Anything you need, anything at all…don't hesitate," he told her, then turned to Holden and Jane, but most specifically to Holden. "Your brother was the one who first uncovered this plot?"

"Yes, sir."

"I owe him a great debt, as well. I understand he's no longer with us?"

"No, sir. He killed himself before he was able to uncover the true breadth and scope of the plot."

"I've seen his file. I don't care what the protocol is, I will not allow anyone to take his honor. He earned it and he will have it."

Holden blinked back tears. "Thank you, sir. That's all I ever wanted. Honor was everything to my brother."

"A good man. I'm sorry we lost him. If only he could've found his way to confiding in someone. It might've made the difference."

The president then turned to Chief Harris, his expression stern. "And what about Trevor Granger and his daughter, Selena?"

"A team will converge on the address Gloria gave us. Selena will be in custody soon," Chief Harris assured the president. "Right now, teams are processing the winery. Trevor Granger is cooperating fully. I doubt he had any knowledge of what his daughter was involved with. He seemed genuinely shocked at her duplicity."

"Our nation owes your team its gratitude."

Chief Harris accepted the praise with a stiff upper lip, but Michelle could tell he was grinning on the inside. Military men were all the same. So stoic.

Kat walked up to the president and said, "Sir, with your permission, I'd like to destroy MCX-209 for good. No more holding on to the formula or keeping a batch in the cooler. This is bound to happen again and again unless we completely destroy the drug and all traces of it."

The president nodded in understanding. "Seeing as I was almost a victim of this drug, I agree. It's too dangerous for anyone to have." He turned to Michelle. "Please see that this is done."

She inclined her head, and everyone in the room breathed more easily knowing MCX-209 was going to be nothing more than a bad memory from now on.

Jane and Holden, along with a team, converged on the property address Gloria had given up, but they found it empty.

"Damn it," Holden muttered under his breath after the property had been cleared. "She's a slippery one. Someone must've tipped her off."

Jane gestured for Holden, saying, "Come over here. I think we've got something."

As he joined her, Jane showed him a picture that floored him. It was of Miko and Selena. "Are you kidding me?" he asked, incredulous and feeling a little sick. "What the hell is this?"

"I think Miko and Selena were sleeping together,"

she said, biting her lip as she grimaced. "I mean, they look pretty cozy here."

Holden gripped the photo and stared at Miko holding Selena in his arms, grinning for the camera. Their body language told a story. A story that made Holden want to vomit.

"I don't understand," Holden said, looking to Jane for answers. "This doesn't make sense. Why was he with her?"

"Maybe she's the reason he killed himself. Maybe he found out he'd been sleeping with the enemy and had inadvertently given the wrong side valuable intel. For a man like your brother…I imagine that would be devastating."

"My brother wouldn't kill himself over a woman," he disagreed hotly, but something in that picture twisted in his gut. His brother was clearly enamored with the beautiful woman in his arms. Whether or not he'd known what she was capable of, Holden didn't know. He supposed he'd never know. Miko's secrets had died with him.

He crinkled the picture and let it drop from his fingers. "Let's go. Nothing's left for us here." Then he stalked from the house, needing some air.

"Holden, wait up," Jane called out after him, but he wasn't in the mood to chat. Everything he'd believed about his brother had been called into question because of that one picture. What about honor and integrity? It was easier for him to believe that Miko had died trying to do something honorable than the realization that he may have offed himself over a woman. No, he couldn't accept that. He just couldn't.

"Holden," Jane said. "We don't have the facts. Don't insert theories in the absence of facts, okay? For all we know, Miko had been using Selena to get information."

"He loved her." There was no sense in denying what he could see with his own eyes. "And he never once told me about her. I never knew. I was his twin brother. We never had secrets."

"But he wasn't a kid anymore. He was entitled to his own life, right?" she pointed out gently. "When I first started this investigation, I thought you were blinded by emotion in this case, but it turns out you were seeing clearly when the rest of us were blinded by prejudice. I saw a man who betrayed his country and I didn't care what his reasons were. You made me realize there was more to the story, and you helped save the president's life. Miko made mistakes because he was human, but I don't believe for a second he betrayed his country. Not for a second."

He met her gaze and saw truth reflecting back at him. Was he more upset that Miko had shut him out of his personal life or because his ego was bruised? Maybe it was best for him to leave Miko's personal life in the past. Maybe it was none of Holden's business.

"I'm so happy the president said what he did, because I'd planned to amend my report and request that Miko retain full honors in light of his contribution to our case. He doesn't deserve to be shamed. He gave his life, and that's the ultimate sacrifice."

Holden held back a wash of tears and jerked a nod. "Thank you," he managed to say before ducking out. He needed a moment.

A long moment.

Jane watched Holden go, and she thought about following. Something held her back, though. Holden was processing a lot about his brother, and she sensed he needed time to work it through.

The case was technically closed. A federal BOLO had been issued for Selena Weston, and it was only a matter of time before she was brought in. All that was left was to tie up loose ends and do the paperwork.

Which meant she no longer needed to stay with Holden. Time to go back to her place. She should be glad, but the knowledge filled her with sadness, as if she were losing something precious or leaving behind a loved one.

What had happened between them…it wasn't real, right? Extreme situations spiked temporary endorphins, simulating love and attraction. It would fade soon enough.

Right?

It hadn't the last time. Nothing about Holden seemed any less vivid in her heart than before. If anything, she was more conflicted than ever.

Just factor in the fact her father would never approve of Holden as a match and the ensuing World

War III that would follow, and that ought to put things in perspective.

But that empty feeling in the center of her chest remained, and no amount of logic and reason would dispel it. Holden was going to be a tough habit to break.

Jane withheld a deep sigh born of sadness and regret, but if there was one thing Fallons did well, it was soldier on.

So soldier on, girl.
Your heart will recover.
Eventually.

Chapter 24

Holden finished his second beer for the night, staring morosely at the gas flames from the fireplace as he picked at the paper encircling the bottle. So many questions and absolutely no chance of having them answered. Disgusted, he rose to get himself another beer when he stopped short. A woman melted from the shadows, a gun trained on his heart.

"Selena."

Ever the picture of perfection, the woman moved like a cat, soft on her feet and deadly focused. There was something sexy but frightening about her. Holden could see how Selena would've hooked Miko in a second.

"Archangelo boys…who knew they'd be the ruin of me."

A dark thrill chased through him, even though Selena had come to kill him. A slow, cold smile curved his lips.

"You're not going to win this. Your face is on every law enforcement agency's radar in every state, every town, every parish. Eventually, your luck will run out and they'll catch you."

"I know that."

"So why waste time with me?"

"Because I don't like loose ends."

And he was a loose end. "Is that what Miko was, too?"

A faint shadow passed over her features. "I loved him."

"I find that hard to believe."

Selena smiled coldly. "Is it hard to imagine he loved me, too?"

The idea made Holden ill. "I'm not much for fiction," he stated, watching her carefully. She'd come here for a reason, and it wasn't just to shoot him. "Why don't you stop playing around and tell me why you're here."

"You think I'm not here to kill you?"

"Not entirely."

"You're right. You have something I need."

His ears perked up. "Such as?"

"Miko had a thumb drive with sensitive information on it. I want it."

"And why would you need that?" he asked. "Want a little light reading while you're on the run?"

"I want to protect my father. Without that list, the

evidence against my father is circumstantial. Nothing is tying him to the wine. Penny was in charge of that deal. As far as the law is concerned, my father was an innocent victim, caught up in a deadly game he had no idea he was playing."

"But that's not the truth, is it? Your father knew exactly what was happening and was happy to cash in on the spoils."

She smiled. "Let's just say my father is a very smart man, but he'd never make it in prison. Too soft. And I'll do anything to protect him."

"What a good daughter. Too bad you take after Auntie Penny in the I-have-no-soul department."

Selena shrugged, then narrowed her gaze. "Where's the thumb drive?"

"Sorry, I can't give that to you. Guess you're going to have to shoot me, but you won't get it that way, either. It seems your plan is fundamentally flawed."

"Thanks for keeping it interesting," Selena said right before burying a bullet in his left leg.

He yelled and dropped to the floor.

"Now, about that thumb drive…" She walked to where he lay, pain spiking through his leg as blood poured from the wound, and smiled down at him, pointing the gun at his other leg. "Did you know you can riddle a body with bullets without actually killing a person? Hurts a lot, from what I hear. Auntie Penny was a very good teacher."

"You're not getting that drive," he gritted out. "You can fill me with holes and it won't matter. That list is going to save my brother's reputation. He was trying to take you down...only he didn't know it was you, did he?"

Selena walked to his kitchen and helped herself to a beer. "No, he didn't know at first. Miko...so damn noble. When he found out what Auntie Penny was having him do, it killed his sense of justice. It was actually hard to watch him self-destruct."

"Don't talk about my brother like you have the right."

"I have every right to talk about my lover. That's right, Holden...we were lovers. He was a beast in bed." She smiled coyly as she purred. "Is it true what they say about twins? That they're alike in all things? Are you a beast in bed, too?"

"Bitch, that's none of your business."

He and Selena whirled to find Jane, feet planted and gun pointed straight at Selena's chest. Without dropping her gaze from the woman, Jane said to Holden, "I can't leave you alone for two seconds and you have another woman up in your apartment. And to think I was coming to ask you to dinner."

"I've got her right where I want her," he groaned. "But feel free to take over. I'm a little busy bleeding out."

"Well, well, this is an exciting development. Jane Fallon, the agent with daddy issues. Come to play?"

"I wouldn't piss her off," Holden warned, blinking against the spots dancing before his eyes. Ah, crap... he was going to pass out from blood loss. Not very manly. "Could you hurry it up? I think I'm about to pass out."

"Tick tock," Selena murmured with a cold smile. "What are you going to do? Help him or shoot me? Can't do both."

The tiniest smile lifted the corner of Jane's mouth as she quipped, "Why not?" and she sent a bullet right through Selena's model-perfect shoulder, sending her crashing to the floor screaming. Selena struggled to rise to her feet, and Jane clocked her, knocking her out.

"Nice shooting, Tex." Holden winced as she helped him to the sofa. "Good God, this freaking hurts. Getting shot is no picnic."

"Surely this isn't your first bullet wound," she asked incredulously as she wound a kitchen towel around his leg and pulled it tight. "Afghanistan? Iraq? Chicago?"

"Sorry to disappoint you, but I tried to avoid getting shot," he answered, breaking out in a sweat. "So…you're saying you've taken a bullet?"

She laughed and pulled up her sleeve, showing off a small circular scar that punched in one side and went out the other. "A through and through in Uzbekistan. Hurt like a bitch, but I still managed to complete the mission and go out for drinks with my unit afterward."

He grinned as his vision dimmed. "You're such a badass, Jane Fallon. Will you freaking marry me?"

His vision began to smoke around the edges and he vaguely heard her answer as if shouted through a tunnel four miles long. "I just might have to in order to keep you out of trouble, Archangelo."

And then he blacked out completely, but he was pretty sure he was wearing a smile.

Jane couldn't believe how narrowly Holden had skated kissing the big one. The surgeon was able to patch him back up and, lo and behold, Jane matched his blood type and was able to donate to replace the blood he'd lost. The knowledge that her blood had played a part in saving him gave her warm tingles of happiness...well, that and putting a hole in that beautiful bitch, Selena. Yeah, that gave her really happy tingles.

Jane smoothed Holden's hair and watched him as he slept off the anesthesia. So much had changed in a very short amount of time. Her life would never be the same.

She'd lived her life trying to earn some modicum of respect from her father when, in fact, she didn't need anyone's approval. And that was exactly what she'd told her father. Once she'd realized she'd nearly lost the one man who'd never tried to make her feel less than the men around her, the one who thought she was damn awesome just the way she was, she'd found herself at her dad's house with a heart filled with purpose even if her hands were shaking.

"Dad, we need to talk," she'd said, moving past him when he'd started to bluster. "No, actually, you've done enough talking in your life—you're going to listen while I do the talking."

"What's come over you?" he'd asked gruffly.

"Reality, Dad. That's what's come over me. I'm

tired of paying for the sins of my mother. I'm my own person and I'm a pretty great person. Here's the thing, Dad...I've spent my life trying to earn a smidge of your approval and I've never really gotten it because all this time you've been punishing me for being a girl. Or maybe you're punishing me because I look so much like my mother. I don't know and I don't care. It's over. I just helped uncover a plot to wipe out the president and half of his executive board. That's right—me. The one you think can't wipe her ass without assistance."

"Watch your mouth. I didn't raise you to be disrespectful," he'd said sharply, but she wasn't about to be cowed into silence. Not this time.

"See, there you go again. You can't even give me a single word of praise after I just told you that I saved the freaking president of the United States. And you know what? I don't need your approval any longer. I love you, I really do, but I'm sick and tired of your bullshit. And another thing—it's time you either hire an accountant or do your checkbook yourself because I have a life to plan."

She had left him sputtering in his chair, and she didn't feel the least bit guilty. In fact, the smile curving her lips felt just about perfect.

Holden had helped her realize that it was more important to live by your own code than try to conform to someone else's. She wished she'd known Miko the man so she could see him as Holden did; she had a feeling she would've liked him.

She wasn't entirely sure if Holden had meant

what he said when he'd asked her to marry him, but she knew she was ready to take a chance at a relationship—a real relationship where they watched movies at night, had sleepy morning sex and stashed a toothbrush at each other's places. Yeah, the real deal, not partners with benefits. A smile found her. She liked the sound of that. No, actually…she loved the sound of that.

But you know what? She loved the sound of something else too…Jane Archangelo. It had a nice ring to it.

She leaned in and nuzzled Holden's neck, inhaling his scent and committing it to memory. Whispering against the shell of his ear, she said, "I don't know how you did it, but somewhere along the way, you made me fall in love with you. What do you think about that?"

Holden sighed softly in his sleep, and she brushed a kiss across his mouth. "I'll take that as confirmation that you are tickled pink." She grinned. "Now, hurry up and get better. I think we have a wedding to plan."

Epilogue

Holden and Jane stood at attention as Miko Archangelo was given the military funeral he deserved with full honors intact. The white-gloved marine officer presented Holden with the American flag, saying in a tone steeped in respect, "On behalf of the president of the United States, the United States Marine Corps and a grateful nation, please accept this flag as a symbol of our appreciation for your loved one's honorable and faithful service."

Blinking back tears, Holden accepted the flag and held it tightly. *This is for you, brother.* A life without his twin flashed before his eyes, and it was almost more than he could stand. True grief rolled over him for the first time since hearing the news that Miko was dead. But even as the grief hurt, the pain was cathartic. He could finally let Miko go. His brother's integrity had been salvaged and they'd managed to finish the work Miko had failed to complete. Selena Weston was rotting in federal prison along with her father, Trevor Granger, and Holden had the most beautiful woman in the world at his side. All in all, things couldn't have ended better. Oh, and as a happy side note, MCX-209 would never see light again. Every shred of documentation and sample had been incinerated, so at the very least anyone suffering from memory loss would do so by natural causes.

"You good?" Jane asked, looking to him with love in her eyes.

"I'm golden." He sniffed back manly tears. "It's a good day." And he meant it. A hawk screeched overhead and he chuckled.

Miko, wherever you are, I hope you're kicking back enjoying a cold one, buddy. You earned it.

* * * * *

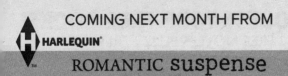

COMING NEXT MONTH FROM

ROMANTIC suspense

Available November 4, 2014

#1823 HER COLTON LAWMAN
The Coltons: Return to Wyoming
by Carla Cassidy

With his town under quarantine and an escaped killer on the loose, Sheriff Flint Colton must protect the one woman who can testify against the murderer. But getting close to Nina could just prove his undoing.

#1824 HIGH-STAKES BACHELOR
The Prescott Bachelors
by Cindy Dees

When stuntwoman Ana lands her first big role, she finds herself the target of an increasingly violent stalker. The movie's star, Jackson, insists she stay with him for her safety. Can she risk both her career and her heart?

#1825 TEXAS STAKEOUT
by Virna DePaul

An undercover stakeout becomes a mission to protect for U.S. marshal Dylan when the fugitive's widowed sister is targeted. Will he do his job and win the woman he's come to think of as his own?

#1826 DESIGNATED TARGET
To Protect and Serve
by Karen Anders

After rescuing the genius Dr. Skylar Baang, NCIS agent Fitzgerald must protect the beautiful scientist from betrayal by her own government—without falling too hard for her himself!

YOU CAN FIND MORE INFORMATION ON UPCOMING HARLEQUIN® TITLES, FREE EXCERPTS AND MORE AT WWW.HARLEQUIN.COM.

HRSCNM1014

REQUEST YOUR FREE BOOKS!
2 FREE NOVELS PLUS 2 FREE GIFTS!

H HARLEQUIN®

ROMANTIC suspense

Sparked by danger, fueled by passion

YES! Please send me 2 FREE Harlequin® Romantic Suspense novels and my 2 FREE gifts (gifts are worth about $10). After receiving them, if I don't wish to receive any more books, I can return the shipping statement marked "cancel." If I don't cancel, I will receive 4 brand-new novels every month and be billed just $4.74 per book in the U.S. or $5.24 per book in Canada. That's a savings of at least 14% off the cover price! It's quite a bargain! Shipping and handling is just 50¢ per book in the U.S. and 75¢ per book in Canada.* I understand that accepting the 2 free books and gifts places me under no obligation to buy anything. I can always return a shipment and cancel at any time. Even if I never buy another book, the two free books and gifts are mine to keep forever.

240/340 HDN F45N

Name _____ (PLEASE PRINT) _____

Address _____ Apt. #

City _____ State/Prov. _____ Zip/Postal Code

Signature (if under 18, a parent or guardian must sign)

Mail to the **Harlequin® Reader Service:**
IN U.S.A.: P.O. Box 1867, Buffalo, NY 14240-1867
IN CANADA: P.O. Box 609, Fort Erie, Ontario L2A 5X3

Want to try two free books from another line?
Call 1-800-873-8635 or visit www.ReaderService.com.

* Terms and prices subject to change without notice. Prices do not include applicable taxes. Sales tax applicable in N.Y. Canadian residents will be charged applicable taxes. Offer not valid in Quebec. This offer is limited to one order per household. Not valid for current subscribers to Harlequin Romantic Suspense books. All orders subject to credit approval. Credit or debit balances in a customer's account(s) may be offset by any other outstanding balance owed by or to the customer. Please allow 4 to 6 weeks for delivery. Offer available while quantities last.

Your Privacy—The Harlequin® Reader Service is committed to protecting your privacy. Our Privacy Policy is available online at www.ReaderService.com or upon request from the Harlequin Reader Service.

We make a portion of our mailing list available to reputable third parties that offer products we believe may interest you. If you prefer that we not exchange your name with third parties, or if you wish to clarify or modify your communication preferences, please visit us at www.ReaderService.com/consumerschoice or write to us at Harlequin Reader Service Preference Service, P.O. Box 9062, Buffalo, NY 14269. Include your complete name and address.

SPECIAL EXCERPT FROM

 HARLEQUIN®

ROMANTIC suspense

With his town under quarantine and an escaped killer on the loose, Sheriff Flint Colton must protect the one woman who can testify against the murderer, but getting close to Nina could just prove his undoing.

Read on for a sneak peek of

HER COLTON LAWMAN

by *New York Times* bestselling author
Carla Cassidy, coming November 2014 from Harlequin® Romantic Suspense.

Pink panties.

Hot pink panties.

Flint closed the door to his master bedroom and began to change out of his uniform.

He'd gone into the store on high alert, hovering near Nina and watching to make sure that nobody else got close to her.

What he hadn't realized was that shopping with a woman could be such an intimate experience. He'd been fine as she'd grabbed several T-shirts and sweatshirts, some jogging pants and a nightshirt.

His close presence next to her felt a little more intrusive as she shopped for toiletries. Peach-scented shampoo joined a bottle of peach and vanilla scented body cream. It was then that things began to get a little wonky in his head.

He imagined her slathering that lotion up and down her

shapely legs and rubbing it over her slender shoulders. He imagined the two of them showering together, the scent of peaches filling the steamy air as he washed the length of her glorious hair and then stroked a sponge all over her body.

He'd finally managed to snap himself back into professional mode when she'd headed to the intimates section. He was okay when she grabbed a white bra and threw it into the shopping basket. He even remained calm and cool when the bra was followed by a package of underpants.

It was when she tossed that single pair of hot pink panties in the cart that his head once again went a little wonky. Pink panties and peach lotion, those things had been all he'd been able to think about.

He sat on the edge of his bed to get every inappropriate vision and thought he'd had of Nina over the past couple of hours out of his head.

She was the witness to a vicious crime and a victim of arson. She was here to be in his protective custody, not to be an object of his sexual fantasies. Speaking of protective custody, he pulled himself off the bed, grabbed his gun and went in search of his houseguest.

Don't miss
HER COLTON LAWMAN
by *New York Times* bestselling author
Carla Cassidy, coming November 2014 from

⊞ HARLEQUIN®
ROMANTIC suspense

HARLEQUIN®

ROMANTIC suspense

Heart-racing romance, high-stakes suspense!

TEXAS STAKEOUT

by *New York Times* bestselling author

Virna DePaul

*A killer in waiting. A brother in hiding.
Could they be the same person?*

Dylan Rooney is out of his element. A U.S. marshal and city-wrangler at heart, he must adopt a new cover—and a new client—in the heart of Texas. The assignment: protect Rachel Kincaid...a widow with a young son who realizes her struggles are just beginning when her ranch hand is killed. Posing as the new ranch hand, Dylan quickly learns that catching a killer may not be so simple—especially when Rachel's fugitive brother is the prime suspect. And the woman he's vowed to protect is the same woman he's falling in love with.

Available **NOVEMBER 2014**
Wherever books and ebooks are sold.

HARLEQUIN®

ROMANTIC suspense

Heart-racing romance, high-stakes suspense!

HIGH-STAKES BACHELOR
by Cindy Dees

More than hearts are at stake for a legendary Hollywood family in Cindy Dees' brand new miniseries, The Prescott Bachelors!

Wannabe stuntwoman Ana Izzolo can't believe she lands a starring role in actor-producer Jackson Prescott's new film. A plain-Jane nobody and a megastar? Their on-screen chemistry is electric, burning up the celluloid...but offscreen, Ana is stalked by danger.

Like a true Hollywood hero, Jackson whisks her to his oceanfront mansion, practicing love scenes while keeping her safe. But when their real-life relationship starts mirroring the movie's leading couple, the confirmed bachelor fears he may fall for the doe-eyed ingenue. If the stalker doesn't get her first....

Available **NOVEMBER 2014**

Wherever books and ebooks are sold

www.Harlequin.com

HARLEQUIN®

ROMANTIC suspense

Heart-racing romance, high-stakes suspense!

DESIGNATED TARGET
by **Karen Anders**

A NCIS agent must protect a brainy scientist who criminals are after—for her mind.

NCIS special agent Vincent Fitzgerald's mission: to find missing naval scientist Dr. Skylar Baang. The brilliant American-Filipino beauty has been kidnapped for her brain and research on top secret projects. But even as Vin rescues her from a dangerous group, he knows they'll be back.

A long-ago promise has kept Skylar committed to her work—love is a distraction she's never allowed herself. Now in the protective custody of a complicated NCIS agent who surprises her at every turn, Skylar wants to stop thinking and start *feeling*. But as the thugs come after her, she'll need everything she is—and smart, sexy Vin—to stay alive.

Available **NOVEMBER 2014**
Wherever books and ebooks are sold.

HRS78961

HARLEQUIN®

A Romance FOR EVERY MOOD™

Love the Harlequin book you just read?

Your opinion matters.

Review this book on your favorite book site, review site, blog or your own social media properties and share your opinion with other readers!